Sandalwood Death

CHINESE LITERATURE TODAY BOOK SERIES

Sandalwood Death

A Novel

Mo Yan

Mo, Yan

Translated by Howard Goldblatt

UNIVERSITY OF OKLAHOMA PRESS : NORMAN

This book is published with the generous assistance of China's National Office for Teaching Chinese as a Foreign Language, Beijing Normal University's College of Chinese Language and Literature, the University of Oklahoma's College of Arts and Sciences, and *World Literature Today* magazine.

The translator gratefully acknowledges the John Simon Guggenheim Memorial Foundation for its generous support.

This translation is dedicated to the memory of Michael Henry Heim, master translator and dear friend.

Library of Congress Cataloging-in-Publication Data
Mo Yan, 1955–
[Tanxiang xing. English]
Sandalwood death = (Tanxiang xing): a novel / Mo Yan; translated by Howard Goldblatt.
   p.   cm.—(Chinese literature today book series ; v. 2)
ISBN 978-0-8061-4339-2 (pbk. : alk. paper)
1. China—History—Boxer Rebellion, 1899–1901—Fiction. 2. China—History—Qing dynasty, 1644–1912—Fiction. I. Goldblatt, Howard, 1939– II. Title. III. Title: Tanxiang xing.
PL2886.O1684T3613 2013
895.1'352—dc23

                                        2012028823

Sandalwood Death: A Novel is Volume 2 in the Chinese Literature Today Book Series.

The paper in this book meets the guidelines for permanence and durability of the Committee on Production Guidelines for Book Longevity of the Council on Library Resources, Inc. ∞

First published in Chinese in 2001 as *Tanxiang xing.* English edition copyright © 2013 by the University of Oklahoma Press, Norman, Publishing Division of the University. Manufactured in the U.S.A.

1 2 3 4 5 6 7 8 9 10

"The finest play ever staged cannot compete with the spectacle of a public slicing"

Zhao Jia

Contents

Book Three: *Tail of the Leopard*

Translator's Note

The challenges for the translator of Mo Yan's powerful historical novel begin with the title, *Tanxiang xing*, whose literal meaning is "sandalwood punishment" or, in an alternate reading, "sandalwood torture." For a work so utterly reliant on sound, rhythm, and tone, I felt that neither of those served the novel's purpose. At one point, the executioner draws out the name of the punishment he has devised (fictional, by the way) for ultimate effect: "Tan—xiang—xing!" Since the word "sandalwood" already used up the three original syllables, I needed to find a short word to replicate the Chinese as closely as possible. Thus: "Sandal—wood—death!"

Beyond that, as the novelist makes clear in his "Author's Note," language befitting the character and status of the narrators in Parts One and Three helps give the work its special quality of sound. Adjusting the register for the various characters, from an illiterate, vulgar butcher to a top graduate of the Qing Imperial Examination, without devolving to American street lingo or becoming overly Victorian, has been an added challenge. Finally, there are the rhymes. Chinese rhymes far more easily than English, and Chinese opera has always employed rhyme in nearly every line, whatever the length. I have exhausted my storehouse of rhyming words in translating the many arias, keeping as close to the meaning as possible or necessary.

As with all languages, some words, some terms, simply do not translate. They can be defined, described, and deconstructed, but they steadfastly resist translation. Many words and terms from a host of languages have found their way into English and settled in comfortably. Most of those from Chinese, it seems, date from foreign imperialists' and missionaries' unfortunately misread or misheard Chinese-isms: "coolie," "gung ho," "rickshaw" (actually, that comes via Japanese), "godown," "kungfu," and so on. I think it is time to update and increase the meager list, and to that end, I have left a handful of terms untranslated; a glossary appears at the end of the book. Only one is given in a form that differs slightly from standard Pinyin: that is "dieh," commonly used for one's father in northern China. The Pinyin would be "die"!

This is a long, very "Chinese" novel, both part of and unique to Mo Yan's impressive fictional oeuvre. There are places that are difficult to read (imagine how difficult they were to translate), but their broader significance and their stark beauty are integral to the work.

I have been the beneficiary of much encouragement in this engrossing project. My gratitude to the John Simon Guggenheim Foundation for its generous support, and to Ed, Mike, Jonathan, and David for writing for me. Jonathan Stalling has been in my corner from the beginning, as have representatives of the University of Oklahoma Press, for whose new and important series this is the inaugural work of fiction. Thanks to Jane Lyle for her meticulous editing. Finally, my thanks to the author for making clear some of the more opaque passages and for leaving me on my own for others. And, of course, to Sylvia, my best reader, sharpest critic, and, from time to time, biggest fan.

HOWARD GOLDBLATT

BOOK ONE

Head of the Phoenix

CHAPTER ONE

Meiniang's Lewd Talk

The sun rose, a bright red ball (the eastern sky a flaming pall), from Qingdao a German contingent looms. (Red hair, green eyes.) To build a rail line they defiled our ancestral tombs. (The people are up in arms!) My dieh led the resistance against the invaders, who responded with cannon booms. (A deafening noise.) Enemies met, anger boiled red in their eyes. Swords chopped, axes hewed, spears jabbed. The bloody battle lasted all day, leaving corpses and deathly fumes. (I was scared witless!) In the end, my dieh was taken to South Prison, where my gongdieh's sandalwood death sealed his doom. (My dieh, who gave me life!)

—Maoqiang Sandalwood Death. *A mournful aria*

1

That morning, my gongdieh, Zhao Jia, could never, even in his wildest dreams, have imagined that in seven days he would die at my hands, his death more momentous than that of a loyal old dog. And never could I have imagined that I, a mere woman, would take knife in hand and with it kill my own husband's father. Even harder to believe was that this old man, who had seemingly fallen from the sky half a year earlier, was an executioner, someone who could kill without blinking. In his red-tasseled skullcap and long robe, topped by a short jacket with buttons down the front, he paced the courtyard, counting the beads on his Buddhist rosary like a retired yuanwailang, or, better yet, I think, a laotaiye, with a houseful of sons and grandsons. But he was neither a laotaiye nor a yuanwailang—he was the preeminent executioner in the Board of Punishments, a magician with the knife, a peerless decapitator, a man capable of inflicting the cruelest punishments, including some of his own design, a true creative genius. During his four decades in the Board of Punishments, he had—to hear him say it—lopped off more heads than the yearly output of Gaomi County watermelons.

My thoughts kept me awake that night, as I tossed and turned on the brick kang, like flipping fried bread. My dieh, Sun Bing, had been arrested and locked up by County Magistrate Qian, that pitiless son of a bitch. Even if he were the worst person in the world, he would still be my dieh, and my mind was in such turmoil I could not sleep, forestalling any possibility of rest. I heard large mongrels grunting in their cages and fat pigs barking in their pens—pig noises had become dog sounds, and dog barks had turned into pig songs. Even in the short time they had left to live, they were tuning up for an opera. If a dog grunts, it is still a dog, and when a pig barks, it remains a pig. And a dieh is still a dieh, even if he does not act like one. *Grunt grunt, arf arf.* The noise drove me crazy. They knew they would be dead soon. So would my dieh. But animals are smarter than humans, for they detected the smell of blood that spread from our yard, and could see the ghosts of pigs and dogs that prowled in the moon-light. They knew that daybreak, soon after the red rays of sun appeared, would mark the hour that they went to meet Yama, the King of Hell. And so they set up a yowl—the plaintive call of impending death. And you, Dieh, what was it like in your death cell? Did you grunt? Bark? Or did you sing Maoqiang? I heard jailers say that condemned prisoners could scoop up fleas by the handfuls in their cells and that the bedbugs were as big as broad beans. You had lived a steady, conservative life, Dieh, so how could a rock one day fall from the sky and knock you straight into a death cell? Oh, Dieh . . .

The knife goes in white and comes out red! No one is better at butchering dogs and slaughtering pigs than my husband, Zhao Xiaojia, whose fame has spread throughout Gaomi County. He is tall and he is big, nearly bald, and beardless. During the day he walks in a fog, and at night he lies in bed like a gnarled log. Since the day I married him, he has badgered me with his mother's tale of a tiger's whisker. One day some roguish creature goaded him into pes-tering me to obtain one of those curly golden tiger whiskers that, when held in the mouth, confer the ability to see a person's true form. The moron, more like a rotting fish bladder than a man, badgered me all one night, until I had no choice but to give in. Well, the moron curled up on the kang and, as he snored and ground his teeth, began to talk in his sleep: "Dieh Dieh Dieh, see see see, scratch the eggs, flip the noodle . . ." He drove me crazy. When I nudged him with my foot, he curled up even tighter and rolled over, smacking his lips as if he'd just enjoyed a tasty treat. Then the talk started again, and the snoring and the grinding of teeth. To hell with him! Let the dullard sleep!

I sat up, leaned against the cold wall, and looked out the window, to see watery moonlight spread across the ground. The eyes of the penned dogs glistened like green lanterns—one pair, another, a third . . . a whole stream of them. Lonely autumn insects set up a desolate racket. A night watchman clomped down the cobblestone street in oiled boots with wooden soles, clapper beats mixed with the clangs of a gong—it was already the third watch. The third, late-night, watch in a city where everyone slept, everyone but me and the pigs and the dogs and, I'm sure, my dieh.

Kip kip kip, a rat was gnawing on the wooden chest. It scampered off when I threw a whiskbroom at it. Then I heard the faint sound of beans rolling across a table in my gongdieh's room. I later discovered that the old wretch was counting human heads, one bean for each detached head. Even at night the old degenerate dreamed of heads he had chopped off, that old reprobate . . . I see him raise the devil's-head sword and bring it down on the nape of my dieh's neck; the head rolls down the street, chased by a pack of kids who kick it along until it rolls into our yard after hopping up the gate steps in an attempt to escape. It then circles the yard, chased by a hungry dog. Experience has told Dieh's head that when the dog gets too close—which it does several times—the queue in back lashes it in its eye, producing yelps of pain as it runs in circles. Now free of the dog, the head starts rolling again and, like a large tadpole, swims along, its queue trailing on the surface, a tadpole's tail . . .

The clapper and gong sounding the fourth watch startled me out of my nightmare. I was damp with cold sweat, and many hearts—not just one—thudded against my chest. My gongdieh was still counting beans, and now I knew how the old wretch was able to intimidate people: his body emitted breaths of shuddering cold that could be felt at great distances. In only six months he had turned his room, with its southern exposure, into an icy tomb—so gloomy the cat dared not enter, not even to catch mice. I was reluctant to step inside, since it made me break out in gooseflesh. But Xiaojia went in whenever he could and, like a snotty three-year-old, stuck close to his storytelling dieh. He hated to leave that room, even to come to my bed during the hottest days of the year, in effect switching the roles of parent and spouse. In order to keep unsold meat from going bad, he actually hung it from the rafters in his dieh's room. Did that make him smart? Or stupid? On those rare occasions when my gongdieh went out, even snarling dogs ran off as he passed, whining piteously from the safety of corners. Tall tales about the old man were rampant: people said that if he laid a hand on a cypress tree, it shuddered and began to shed its leaves. I was thinking about my dieh, Sun Bing. Dieh, you pulled off something grand this time, like An Lushan screwing the Imperial Concubine Yang Guifei, or Cheng Yaojin stealing gifts belonging to the Sui Emperor and suffering grievously for it. I had thoughts of Qian Ding, our magistrate, who had claimed success at the Imperial Examination, a grade five official, almost a prefect, what's known as a County Magistrate; but to me, this gandieh, my so-called benefactor, was a double-dealing monkey monster. The adage goes, "If you won't do it for the monk, then do it for the Buddha; if not for the fish, then for the water." You turned your back on the three years I shared your bed. How many pots of my heated millet spirits did you drink during those three years, how many bowls of my fatty dog meat did you eat, and how many of my Maoqiang arias swirled in your head? Hot millet spirits, fatty dog meat, and me lying beside you. Magistrate, I waited on you with more care than any emperor has known. Magistrate, I presented you with a body silkier than the finest Suzhou satin and sweeter than Cantonese sugar melon, all for your dissolute pleasure; now, after all the pampering and the voyages into an erotic fairyland, why will you not let my dieh go free? Why did you team up with those German devils to seize him and burn down our village? Had I known you were such an unfeeling, unrighteous bastard, I'd have poured my millet spirits into the latrine, fed my fatty dog meat to the pigs, and sung my arias to a brick wall. And as for my body, I'd have given that to a dog . . .

2

With one last frenetic banging of the watchman's clappers, dawn broke. I climbed down off the kang, dressed in new clothes, and fetched water to wash up, then applied powder and rouge to my face and oiled my hair. After taking a well-cooked dog's leg out of the pot, I wrapped it in a lotus leaf and put it in my basket, then walked out the door and down the cobblestone road as the moon settled in the west. I was headed to the yamen prison, where I'd gone every day since my dieh's arrest. They would not let me see him. Damn you, Qian Ding; in the past, if I went three days without bringing you some dog meat, you sent that little bastard Chunsheng to my door. Now you are hiding from me; you have even posted guards. Musketeers and archers who once bowed and scraped when I arrived now glare at me with looks of supercilious arrogance. You even let four German soldiers threaten me with bayonets when I approached the gate with my basket. Their faces told me they meant business. Qian Ding, oh, Qian Ding, you turncoat, your illicit relations with foreigners have made me angry enough to take my grievance to the capital and accuse you of eating my dog meat without paying and of forcing yourself upon a married woman. Qian Ding, I will do what I must in the name of justice, and I will strip that tiger skin from your body to reveal what a heartless, no-good scoundrel you are.

Reluctantly I left the yamen, and as I walked away, I heard those little bastards having a good laugh at my expense. Little Tiger, you ungrateful dog, have you forgotten how you and your damnable father got down on your knees and kowtowed to me? If I hadn't spoken up for you, do you think a common little sandal peddler could have enjoyed the lucrative benefits of a yamen guard? And you, Little Shun, a common beggar who sought warmth from a cook stand in the dead of winter, if I hadn't put in a good word for you, do you think you would now be one of his select archers? I let Military Inspector Li Jinbao kiss me and feel my bottom and District Jailer Su Lantong feel my bottom and kiss me, all for you two. How dare you make fun of me! Dogs think they are better than humans; well, you dog bastards, if a curing rack fell over, I would not be tempted by the meat, nor pay for spirits even if I were falling-down drunk. I will be back on my feet one day, and when I am, I will make sure that each of you gets what is coming to him.

I put the wicked yamen behind me and walked home along the same cobblestone street. Dieh, you old fool, as you moved from your forties into your fifties, instead of leading a Maoqiang troupe down city streets and country roads to sing of emperors, kings, generals, and ministers, or playing the roles of worthy scholars and beautiful maidens, toying with star-crossed lovers, earning a lot or a little, dining on spoiled cat and rotting dog, drinking strong spirits and rice wine, and when your belly was full, spending time with no-account friends, scaling cold walls to sleep in someone's warm bed, enjoying your pleasures, big and small, and living as if in a fairyland, you decided to strut around saying whatever popped into your head: things a highwayman would not say found voice with you, and things no bandit would dare try were for you a challenge. You offended yayi and you provoked the County Magistrate. Even when your backside was beaten till it bled, you refused to bow your head and admit defeat. You challenged a foe and lost your beard, like a plucked rooster or a fine horse without a tail. When you could no longer sing opera, you opened a teashop, a move that promised a peaceful life. But you had to let your wife go off by herself and court disaster. A man laid his hands on her body, and that should have been the end of it; but you could not swallow your anger, as an ordinary citizen would have done. As they say, a loss suffered is a benefit delayed, and patience is a virtue. You succumbed to your anger and clubbed a German engineer to the ground, bringing a monstrous calamity down on your head. Even the Emperor fears the Germans, but not you. So, thanks to you, the village was bathed in blood, with twenty-seven dead, including your young son and daughter, even their mother, your second wife. But you were not finished, for you ran to Southwest Shandong to join the Boxers of Righteous Harmony, then returned to set up a spirit altar and raise the flag of rebellion. A thousand rebels armed with crude firearms, swords, and spears sabotaged the foreigners' rail line with arson and murder. You called yourself a hero. Yet in the end, a town was destroyed, civilians lay dead, and you wound up in a jail cell, beaten black and blue . . . my poor benighted dieh, with what did you coat your heart? What possessed you? A fox spirit? Maybe a weasel phantom stole your soul. So what if the Germans wanted to build a railroad that ruined the feng shui of Northeast Gaomi Township and blocked our waterways? The feng shui and waterways are not ours alone, so why did you have to lead the rebellion? This is what it has come to: the bird in front gets the buckshot; the king of thieves is first to fall. As the adage has it, "When the beans are fried, everyone eats; but if the pot is broken, you suffer the consequences alone." What you did this time, Dieh, sent shock waves all the way to the Imperial Court and outraged the Great Powers. People say that Shandong Governor Yuan Shikai himself was carried into the county yamen in his eight-man palanquin last night, and that the Jiaozhou Plenipotentiary rode his foreign charger in through the yamen gate, a blue-steel Mauser bolt-action rifle slung over his back. The archer Sun Huzi—Bearded Sun—who stood guard at the gate, tried to stop him, for which he was rewarded with a taste of the foreign devil's whip. He slunk out of the way, but not before a gash the width of his finger had opened up on his fleshy ear. This time, Dieh, the odds are stacked against you, and that gourd-like head of yours will soon hang at the yamen entrance for all to see. Even if Qian Ding, Eminence Qian, were of a mind to free you as a favor to me, Governor Yuan Shikai would not permit it. And if he wanted to free you, Plenipotentiary von Ketteler would not allow it. Your fate is no longer in your hands, Dieh.

With the red sun before me, and my mind a jumble of thoughts, I trotted down the cobblestone road, heading east, enveloped in aromatic waves from the dog's leg in my basket. Puddles of bloody water dotted the roadway, and in my trance-like state I saw Dieh's head rolling down the street, singing an aria on the way. For him, Maoqiang opera was the bait to attract a wife. He turned a minor musical form that had never quite caught on into a major one. His voice, soft and pliable, like watermelon pulp, captivated scores of Northeast Gaomi Township beauties, including my late niang, who married him solely on the strength of his voice. One of the township's true beauties, she even turned down a marriage proposal on behalf of Provincial Licentiate Du, preferring to follow my impoverished dieh, the opera singer, wherever he went . . . Licentiate Du's hired hand, Deaf Zhou, was walking my way with a load of water, bent over by the weight, his red neck stretched forward as far as it would go. His white hair was a fright, his face dotted with crystalline beads of sweat. He was panting from the exertion, taking big, hurried strides, splashing water over the sides of his buckets that formed liquid beads on the road stones. All of a sudden, Dieh, I saw your head in Deaf Zhou's bucket, where the water had turned into blood that filled my nostrils with its hot, rank odor, the sort of smell that bursts from the split bellies of the dogs and pigs my husband, Zhao Xiaojia, butchers. Not just rank, but a foul stench. Of course, Deaf Zhou had no way of knowing that seven days later, when he went to the site of my dieh's execution to listen to a Maoqiang aria, a bullet from a German devil's Mauser would rip open his belly and release guts that slithered out like an eel.

When we passed on the street, he strained to look up and greeted me with an ugly smirk. Even a wooden-headed deaf man is audacious enough to smirk at me, Dieh, which can only mean there is no way you can escape death this time, not even if His Imperial Majesty—forget about the likes of Qian Ding—were to come to stop it. I am discouraged, of course I am, but unwilling to give up. "You hit the tree whether there are dates or not; you treat a dead horse as if it were alive." If I had to guess, I would say that at that moment Magistrate Qian was with Governor Yuan, who had come to the yamen from Jinan, and Clemens von Ketteler, who had ridden over from Qingdao, all lying on an opium bed in the guest house to enjoy a pipeful, so I decided to wait till Yuan and the foreigner left before taking my dog's leg into the yamen. If they would let me see the Magistrate, I was sure I could get him to listen to me, for at that moment he would not be Magistrate Qian, but Creepy Eminence Qian, who keeps circling me. What frightens me, Dieh, is that they will transport you to the capital in a prison van. We can deal with them so long as they carry out the sentence here in the county. We'll find a beggar to take your place, what they call stealing beams and changing pillars, to manage a bit of trickery. You were so mean to my niang, I should not be trying to save your skin; once you are dead and buried, you can never hurt another woman. But you are my dieh. Without heaven there can be no earth, without an egg there can be no chicken, without feelings there can be no opera, and without you there could be no me. Tattered clothes can be replaced, but I have only one dieh. The Temple of the Matriarch is up ahead, and I rush to prostrate myself at the Buddha's feet. When you are sick, any doctor will do. I will beg the Matriarch to display her powers and extract you from the jaws of death.

The Temple of the Matriarch was eerily dark, too murky to see a thing, but I heard bats flying around, their wings flapping against the rafters—oh, maybe they were swallows, not bats, yes, that's what they were, swallows. Slowly my eyes adapted to the darkness, and I saw a dozen beggars lying on the floor in front of the Matriarch. My head reeled from the stink of urine, farts, and spoiled food; I nearly retched. Revered Matriarch of Sons and Grandsons, how you must suffer, forced to live with these wild tomcats. Like snakes emerging from their hibernation, they stretched their stiff bodies and got lazily to their feet, one after the other. Zhu Ba—Zhu the Eighth—the white-haired, red-eyed beggar chief, made a face and fired a gob of spit my way.

"Bad omen, bad omen, truly bad omen!" he shouted. "This rabbit's a female!"

His motley pack followed his lead and spat at me, then shouted in unison: "Bad omen, bad omen, truly bad omen! This rabbit's a female!"

A red-bottomed monkey was on my shoulder like a bolt of lightning, frightening two and a half of my three souls right out of my body, and by the time I gathered my wits, the little bastard had reached into my basket and stolen my dog's leg. It scampered over to an incense table and in a flash was perched on the Matriarch's shoulder. All that movement produced jangles from the chain around its neck, while its tail swept up clouds of dust that made me sneeze— *ah-choo*! The damned, stinking monkey, as much human as beast, perched on the Matriarch's shoulder and bared its teeth as it gnawed noisily on the dog's leg, making a mess of the Matriarch's face with its greasy paws. But she bore it meekly, without complaint, merciful and benevolent. If the Matriarch was powerless to control a monkey, how could she possibly save my dieh's life?

Dieh, oh, Dieh, your bluster knew no bounds, like a weasel on a camel, the biggest mate it could find. You have forged such a monstrous calamity that even the Old Buddha, Empress Dowager Cixi, knows your name, and Kaiser Wilhelm himself has been told what you have done. For an ordinary, worthless opera singer who haunted city streets and country roads to put food in his belly, you now know that your life did not pass through the world unnoticed. The opera lyric says: "Better to live three days and go out in a blaze of glory than to live a thousand years as a timid soul." You sang on the stage for most of your life, Dieh, acting out other people's stories. This time you were determined to insert yourself into the drama; you acted and acted, until you yourself became the drama.

The beggars surrounded me. Some held out rotting arms oozing with pus; others exposed their ulcerated midriffs. Catcalls and jeers rose from their ranks, a cacophony of bizarre sounds, some loud, some soft: songs, calls to the dead, wolf bays, donkey brays, every sound imaginable, all tangled, like feathers on a chicken.

"Help me, Dog-Meat Xishi, please, Sister Zhao, be charitable. Hand over a couple of coppers now, and you'll find two silver dollars on your way home . . . if you refuse, I won't worry, for in this life you'll be sorry . . ."

All the time they were filling the temple with their horrid noise, those dogshit bastards pinched me on the thigh or squeezed my bottom or manhandled my breasts . . . groping here and fondling there, whatever they could do to have their way with me. I tried to get away, but they grabbed my arms and held me around the waist, so I threw myself at Zhu Ba. "Zhu Ba," I said, "Zhu Ba, let this be between you and me." Well, he picked up a willow switch and poked me in the back of the knee, dropping me to the floor. With a smirk, he said:

"When a fat pig comes to your door, you'd be a fool not to kill and eat it. Boys," he said, "Magistrate Qian might feast on the meat, but you can have a taste of the soup."

The beggars piled onto me and pulled my pants down. Out of desperation, I said, "Zhu Ba, you dog-shit bastard, a true burglar does not wait for a fire. You may not care, but my dieh was imprisoned by Qian Ding, and now has a date with the executioner." He rolled his pus-filled eyes.

"Who is your dieh?" he asked.

"Zhu Ba," I said, "your eyes are open, yet you pretend to be asleep. How could you not know who he is, when all of China knows? He is Sun Bing, from Northeast Gaomi Township, the Sun Bing who sings Maoqiang opera, the Sun Bing who pried up railroad tracks, the Sun Bing who led the fight between local residents and the German devils!" Zhu Ba rose up, cupped his hands in front of his chest, and said:

"Do not take offense, Elder Sister; I did not know. We were aware that Qian Ding was your gandieh, but not that Sun Bing was your real dieh. Qian Ding is a no-good bastard; your dieh is a hero who courageously stood up to the foreign devils, pitting sword against sword and gun against gun. How we envy him. If there is anything you need from us, do not hesitate to ask. On your knees, boys, and kowtow to the fair lady as an act of contrition."

As one, the gang of beggars knelt down and kowtowed to me, banging their heads on the floor, which marked their foreheads with dust.

"Great blessings for Elder Sister, great blessings!" they shouted in unison.

Even the monkey crouching on the Matriarch's shoulder tossed away the dog's leg and bounded headlong to the floor, where, in imitation of the men, it kowtowed to me in its own strange way, to my delight.

"Boys," Zhu Ba announced, "tomorrow we deliver several dog's legs to the fair lady."

"That is not necessary," I said.

"Your generosity is appreciated," said Zhu Ba, "but these boys can catch a dog faster than they can pluck a flea out of their pants."

The beggars laughed, some revealing yellow teeth and others toothless gums, and I was struck by the feeling that these were decent men who lived simple yet interesting lives. Sunlight burst in through the temple entrance, its red, warm rays lighting up the smiles on the beggars' faces. My nose began to ache; hot tears filled my eyes.

"Elder Sister, do you want us to break him out of jail?"

"No," I said, "that you cannot do. My dieh is no run-of-the-mill case, and the prison gate is guarded not only by yamen soldiers, but by armed Germans as well."

"Hou Xiaoqi," Zhu Ba said, "go check things out. Report back with anything you hear."

"Understood!" Hou replied as he picked up a bronze gong that was lying in front of the Matriarch. Then he strapped on a sack and whistled. "Come along with your papa, my boy." The monkey leaped onto his shoulder, and Hou Xiaoqi walked out of the temple banging his gong and singing, the monkey riding on his shoulders. I looked up at the Matriarch, whose body exuded ancient airs, and whose face, like a silver plate, was beaded with sweat. She was making her presence known; she was telling me something! Use your power, Matriarch, to protect my dieh!

3

I returned home full of hope. Xiaojia was already up and was out in the yard sharpening his knife. He smiled at me, a warm, friendly greeting. I returned the smile, equally warm and friendly. After he tested the point of the knife on his finger and found it still not sharp enough, he went back to work—*zzzp zzzp*. He was wearing only a singlet; the exposed skin showed off his taut muscles, like cloves of garlic, a powerful man with a patch of black chest hair. I walked inside, where my gongdieh was sitting in a sandalwood armchair made unique by a dragon inlaid with gold filaments; he'd had it sent over from the capital. He was resting, eyes closed, and softly muttering as he fingered the sandalwood beads of his rosary, and I could not tell whether he was reciting a Buddhist sutra or mouthing curses. The room had a gloomy feel, with faint streams of sunlight filtering in through the latticed window. One of those sunbeams, bright like gold or silver, lit up his gaunt face: sunken eyes, a high nose bridge, and a tightly shut mouth that sliced above his chin like a knife. No hairs decorated his short upper lip or his long chin. No wonder there was talk that he was a eunuch who had escaped from the Imperial Court. His hair had thinned out so much he could make a queue only by adding black thread. His eyes slitted open, sending icy rays my way. "You're up, Gongdieh," I said. He nodded without interrupting the fingering of his beads.

A routine had developed over the months for me to groom his queue with an ox-horn comb, a task ordinarily performed by a maidservant, which we did not have. That was not something daughters-in-law were expected to do, and if word had gotten out, rumors of an incestuous relationship would have swirled. But something the old man knew put me at his mercy, and if he wanted me to comb his hair, I did so. In fact, it was I who had started the routine. One morning soon after his arrival, as he struggled with a comb with missing teeth, his son, my husband, went up to do it for him.

"Dieh," he said as he worked, "I have sparse hair, and as a boy I once heard Niang say that most of it had fallen out from scabies. Is that why yours is so sparse?"

My idiot husband's clumsy hands forced a grimace onto the old man's face. He was lucky enough to have a son willing to comb his hair, though his head was being scraped like a debristled hog. I had just returned from Magistrate Qian's and was in a decent mood, so to make them happy, I said, "Here, let me do that." By adding black threads to the scant few strands of hair, I gave him a nice thick queue, and when I was finished, I handed him a mirror. He pulled the thing around front—half hair, half threads—and the gloomy look in his eyes gave way to glistening tears. It was a rare event, to say the least. Xiaojia dabbed at his father's eyes.

"Are you crying, Dieh?" he asked.

The old man shook his head.

"The Empress Dowager had a eunuch whose only task was to comb Her hair," he said, "but She never used him. That responsibility She handed to Her favorite eunuch, Li Lianying." I had no idea why he was telling us this, but Xiaojia, who was besotted by anything having to do with Peking, begged him to say more. Ignoring his son, the old man handed me a silver certificate.

"Go into town and have some nice clothes made, Daughter-in-law. That's the least I can do considering how you've looked after me these past few days."

The next morning, Xiaojia woke me out of a sound sleep. "What are you doing?" I snapped.

"Get up," he said with uncharacteristic boldness. "My dieh is waiting for you to comb his hair."

This unexpected news made me very uncomfortable. The door to goodness is easy to open, they say, and hard to close. What did he expect of me? You are not the Empress Dowager, old wretch, and I am not Li Lianying. For the favor of having those few scraggly strands of washed-out, smelly dog hair combed out one time, you can thank eight generations of your pious ancestors. But like a cat that's had a taste of fish, an old bachelor who's had a taste of the good life, you can't get enough. Did you really think that a five-ounce silver certificate was all you needed to buy my favors? Hah! Ponder for a moment who you are and who I am. I climbed down off the kang, boiling mad and of a mind to say exactly what I thought and teach him a lesson. But before I could open my mouth, the old wretch looked up and, as if talking to himself, said to the wall:

"I wonder who combs the County Magistrate's hair for him."

I shuddered. The old wretch was not human, I felt, but an invisible, all-knowing ghost. How else would he know that I combed Magistrate Qian's hair? Having said what he wanted to say, he turned back around, sat up in his chair, and fixed his gloomy eyes on me. My anger suddenly gone, I meekly walked around and began combing his dog hair. And as I was doing that, I unconsciously thought about my gandieh's nice black hair—sleek, glossy, fragrant. And when I grabbed hold of a queue that resembled nothing so much as a shedding donkey's tail, my thoughts drifted to my gandieh's heavy, fleshy queue, which seemed capable of moving all by itself. He could brush my body with that queue, from the top of my head down to my heels, gentle claws that burrowed into my heart and squeezed waves of seduction out of every pore.

I had no choice but to work the comb. It was time to drink the bitter brew of my own creation. Whenever I combed my gandieh's hair, he began touching me, and before I had a chance to finish, our bodies were intertwined. I found it hard to believe that this old wretch was unmoved by my ministrations, and I was waiting for him to start climbing the pole. Old wretch, if you even try, I'll make sure you can't climb down once you're up there. Yes, when that happens, you'll start doing my bidding, and I'll be damned if I'll ever comb your hair again! Rumors swirled that the old wretch was in possession of a hundred thousand in silver certificates; sooner or later, he would have to bring it out for me to see. So I looked forward to the day when he would try to make the climb; but that day had yet to come. Still, I was not prepared to believe that there is a cat anywhere that does not like fish. Old wretch, we'll see how long you can hold out. I loosened his queue and ran my comb through those soft, scraggly hairs. I was especially gentle that day, though it was a struggle not to vomit as my fingers touched the base of his ears and I pressed my breasts against the nape of his neck. "My dieh has been arrested," I said, "and thrown in jail. With all the time you spent in the capital, and the reputation you enjoyed there, you can get him out." He made no sound in response. He sat like a deaf mute, so with a gentle squeeze of his shoulder I repeated myself. Still no response. As the sun's rays drifted by, they made the brass buttons on his brown silk Mandarin jacket shine, and then moved on to his hands, with which he unhurriedly fingered his sandalwood Buddhist beads. Pale and soft, those delicate hands seemed not to belong to someone of his sex and age. You could put a knife to my throat, and I still could not believe that they wielded an executioner's sword. At least that is what I thought at the time; now I wasn't so sure. I pressed myself even harder against him and said coyly, "Gongdieh, my dieh did something bad, but you, after all you've seen and done in the capital, you can do or say something to help him." I squeezed his bony shoulder a second time and rested my full breasts on the nape of his neck as my lips formed a series of provocative sounds.

When I used tricks like that on Qian Ding, Eminence Ding went limp and was ready to do whatever I asked. But the balding old wretch in front of me now was like an egg that could never be cooked; I could bounce my soft, supple breasts up and down in front of him or send enough seductive waves his way to submerge Gold Mountain Temple without getting a rise out of him. But then he abruptly stopped fingering the beads; I thought I saw those small, meaty hands begin to shake, and I was ecstatic. Have I finally gotten to you, you old wretch? A toad can hold up a bedpost only so long. I don't believe you can keep those silver certificates hidden forever, and I don't believe you will use my relationship with the County Magistrate to force me to comb your dog hair. Dieh, help me think of something. So I kept up the seductive act behind him, until, that is, I heard a contemptuous laugh, like the chilling hoot of an owl emerging from a graveyard deep in a dark woods on a moonless night. I froze. It felt as if ice ran through my veins, and all my thoughts and wishes flew off to I don't know where. The old wretch, was he even human? Could a human being produce a laugh like that? No, he was not human; he was a demon. And so he must not be my gongdieh. In more than a dozen years with Xiaojia, I had never heard him say he had a dieh who lived in the capital. And he was not alone: our neighbors, too, who had seen much of the world and knew a thing or two, had never mentioned him. He could be a lot of things, but not my gongdieh. He and my husband looked nothing alike. Old baldy, you must be a beast in human form. Others might fear demons and spirits, but not the people in this family. I'll have Xiaojia butcher the black dog out in the pen and keep its blood in a basin. Then, when you're not looking, I'll dump it over your bald pate to reveal your true form.

4

A light rain fell on Tomb-Sweeping Day; dirty gray clouds rolled lazily low in the sky as I walked out of town through South Gate, along with colorfully dressed young men and women. I was carrying an umbrella decorated with a copy of the painting *Xu Xian Encounters a White Snake at West Lake*, and I had oiled my hair and pinned it with a butterfly clip. I had lightly powdered my face and dabbed rouge on each cheek, had added a beauty mark at a spot between my eyebrows, and had painted my lips red. I was wearing a cerise jacket over green slacks, both of imported fabric. However terrible foreigners might be, their fabrics are first-rate. On my feet I wore full-sized cloth shoes

whose green silk tops were embroidered with yellow Mandarin ducks floating amid pink lotus flowers. You people laugh at me because of my unbound
feet, don't you? Well, I'll give you something to look at. I stole a glance at the
quicksilver mirror, and there I saw a radiant, amorous beauty. That was someone even I could love, to say nothing of all those young men. Of course I was
griefstricken over my dieh's situation, but my gandieh once said that the deeper
the sadness, the more important it was to put on a happy face and not give the
impression of being a slave to your emotions. All right all right all right, take a
look. Today this old madam is going to see how she stacks up against Gaomi's
city girls. I don't care if it's the daughter of the provincial licentiate or the apple
of the Hanlin scholar's eye, they cannot compete with one of my big toes. Big
feet are the only things holding me back. When my niang died so young, there
was no one at home to bind my feet, and it hurts me even to hear feet mentioned. But my gandieh says he loves big, natural feet, loves the natural feel of
them, and whenever he is on top of me, he has me pummel his bare bottom
with my heels.

"Big feet are best!" he shouts when I do that. "Big feet are best! Golden
ingots, better than bound feet, those goat hooves . . ."

Back then, even though my dieh was playing with magical powers and had
erected a spirit altar in Northeast Gaomi as part of his plan to engage the Germans in mortal combat, and even though his activities drove my gandieh to
distraction, and even though he was depressed over the deaths of twenty-seven
citizens, peace reigned in the town. The bloody events that had occurred in
Northeast Township had had no effect on the big city. My gandieh, Eminence
Qian, had built a swing set out of China fir on the grounds of the military
academy outside South Gate, attracting boys and girls from all over town. The
girls dressed in their finest; the boys combed and oiled their queues until they
shone. Shrieks of joy and whoops of laughter filled the sky and were joined by
the shouts of peddlers:

Candied——crabapples——!

Melon seeds——peanuts——!

After folding my umbrella, I made my way into the crowd and looked around.
My eyes fell first on the young mistress of the Qi family, who was attended by
a pair of maidservants. Renowned as someone who wrote especially well—
verse and prose—she was splendidly dressed and resplendently jeweled. Too
bad she had a long, horse-like face, pale as a salt flat, on which lay two anemic
grassy clumps—her eyebrows. I also saw the daughter of Hanlin Scholar Ji,
who was attended by four maidservants; she was reputed to be peerless in the
art of embroidery and was a talented musician, proficient in instruments from
the zither to the lute and balloon guitar. Sadly, she had a small nose and under-

sized ears that combined to make her look like a little bitch with tiny, toad-like eyes. The whores who walked out of Rouge Alley, on the other hand, laughed and wiggled like chimps and had a lively good time. After taking in everything around me, I held my head up proudly and threw out my chest, drawing approving stares from all the young scamps, who looked me over admiringly. Their mouths hung open like dark caves; slobber wetted their chins. I smiled and struck a pose. My dear boys, my little darlings, go home and enjoy your erotic dreams. Take a long look—this is my good deed for the day. Well, they stood there besotted for a while, and when they finally regained their senses, they let out a roar that made the ground tremble. Then came the lusty shouts:

"Dog-Meat Xishi, the best in Gaomi!"

"Look look look at that peach-blossom face and willow waist. The graceful neck of a mantis and the shapely legs of a white crane!"

"The top part is to die for; the bottom part will petrify you! Only Eminence Qian, with his strange obsession, can appreciate the big feet of a living fairy!"

Watch your tongues, boys. What you say by the roadside is heard in the grass. If someone reports you, you'll be whisked inside the yamen to have your backsides turned to mush by forty swats of the paddle.

Go on, little monkeys, say what you want. I'm in no mood today to take offense. Who cares what you imps think as long as His Eminence likes what he sees? I'm here for the swings, not to listen to your silly talk. I know you'd just love to lap up my pee.

At the moment no one was using the swings, their thick, wet ropes swaying in the drizzle, waiting for me. I tossed away my umbrella, which was caught by a little monkey that ran up as I jumped forward, like a carp leaping out of the water. I grabbed the ropes, jumped a second time, and landed on the swing seat with both feet. Now you children will see the advantage of having big feet. "Hey, boys and girls," I shouted, "open your eyes and take a lesson on the art of swinging. Coal looks clean compared to the face of the fat, clumsy girl who sat on the swing before me. A millstone is tiny compared to her backside, and water chestnuts are bigger than her feet. What was someone like that doing on a swing set? How mortifying! She looked like a lizard. What is a swing set, after all? It's a moving stage for an actor to display her skills and show off her face; she's a sampan riding the waves, she's the wind of desire, the surge of seduction, the rage of passion, the epitome of lust. This is a chance for a woman to act the siren. Why do you think my gandieh chose this spot to build a swing set? Because of his devotion to the people? Hah! You think too highly of yourselves. I'll tell you why. He built it for me, as my Qingming gift. Go ask him if you don't believe me. I took dog meat to him last night, and after our frolic in bed, he put his arms around me and said, 'Tomorrow is Qingming, my pet, my precious, and I have built you a swing set on the Southern Academy parade ground. I know you once played the sword-and-horse role, so go out there and put your feet to work. You might not make a splash for all of Shandong, but for my sake make one for all of Gaomi County. Let those commoners know that Qian's little pet is special, another Hua Mulan! Let them know that big feet are better than bound ones, and that Qian will change prevailing customs by prohibiting the practice of binding women's feet.'

"I said, 'Gandieh, you have been so sad about what happened to my dieh. You are taking a risk by protecting him. And when you are unhappy, I am in no mood for entertainments.' Well, he kissed my foot and said with an emotional sigh:

"'Meiniang, my dearest, I want to use Qingming to sweep all gloomy, inauspicious signs out of the county. The dead cannot be brought back to life, but the living have a right to a little gaiety. No one sympathizes with a grumbler, who winds up being the butt of jokes. But if you square your shoulders and get tough, tougher than everyone else, ready to take them on, you'll have them where you want them. Writers will put you in their books; playwrights will write plays about you. So climb onto those swings and show them what you're made of. Ten years from now, the repertoire of that Maoqiang opera of yours might well include a play called *Sun Meiniang Raises Eyebrows on a Swing!*'

"'I may not be able to do much, Gandieh,' I said as I lifted his beard with my feet, 'but I will not cause you embarrassment when I am on the swing.'"

Holding the ropes with both hands, I squatted down, bent my legs, and stood on the balls of my feet; then, sticking my rear end out and leaning forward, I threw out my chest, raised my head, and, with my midriff as a fulcrum, began to swing. I pulled the ropes back toward me and, feet on the seat, again threw out my chest and raised my head, pushing with my legs, bent at the knees. The metal rings cried out with urgency as my swing gained momentum, higher, faster, steeper, harder, deeper; the taut ropes sang like the wind; the rings made a fearful noise. I was transported to a fairyland; I felt like a bird soaring aloft, my arms transformed into wings, feathers sprouting on my chest. At the summit, the swing and my body hung in the air together, while tides of ocean waves surged through my heart—swelling high, then falling low, one wave hard upon another, foam gathering in the air. Big fish chasing little fish, little fish chasing shrimp. Waa waa waa waa . . . higher higher higher, not yet high enough, just a little higher, a little more . . . my body laid out horizontally, my face bumped into the soft yellow belly of a curious swallow; I felt as if I were lying on a cushiony pad woven of wind and rain, and when I reached the highest possible point, I bit a flower off the tip of the highest branch of the oldest and tallest apricot tree around. Shouts erupted on the ground below. I was carefree, I was relaxed and at ease, I had achieved the Tao, I was an immortal . . . and then, a breach in the dam, the waters retreated, waves returning to sea, taking foam with them; big fish tugged on little fish, little fish dragged shrimps, la la la la, all in retreat. I reached bottom, and then flew up again. My head pitched back between the twin ropes as they grew taut again and trembled in my hands, and I was nearly parallel to the ground. I could see fresh soil where purple sprouts of new grass were beginning to poke through. The apricot blossom was still between my teeth, its subtle fragrance filling my nostrils.

All the while I was having a frisky good time on the swing, my earthbound audience, especially all those sons and grandsons, those little hooligans, were as frenzied as I was. They ooh-ed on my way up and aah-ed on my way back down. "Ooh, there she goes! Aah, here she comes!" My clothes fluttered in the wind, carrying fine drops of rain—damp and cloyingly sweet, like wet cowhide—which filled my heart to overflowing. Sure, my dieh had gotten into a terrible fix, but a married daughter is like water splashed on the ground—it cannot be taken back. You will have to look out for yourself, Dieh, and I will do the same from here on out. I have a kind and simple husband at home, a man who can keep out the wind and the rain for me, and a powerful, affectionate, and entertaining lover outside the home. There is strong drink when I feel like it, meat when I want it, and no one can stop me from crying or laughing or flirting or causing a scene. That is the definition of happiness. It is the happiness that my devout, sutra-chanting, long-suffering niang made possible for me; it is the happiness that fate had in store for me. I thank the heavens for that. I thank the Emperor and Empress for that. I thank His Eminence Magistrate Qian for that. I thank my dull and peculiar husband, Xiaojia, for that. And I thank Magistrate Qian's supernatural "club" for that. It is a rare treasure seldom found in heaven or on earth; it is the medicine that cures my ills.

5

A popular adage has it that "When the moon is full, the decline begins; when the river is high, water flows away. When someone is too happy, bad things happen; and when dogs feel good, they fight over shit." While I was the center of attention on the swing, a mob from Northeast Gaomi Township, armed with shovels, pickaxes, pitchforks, carrying poles, wooden spears, and rakes, and led by my dieh, Sun Bing, was surrounding a railroad shed that housed German rail workers, killing many of the invaders' lackeys, and taking three German soldiers hostage. After stripping the soldiers naked and tying them to scholar trees, they sprayed their faces with urine. Then they burned the wooden construction signs, dug up the tracks and dumped them into the river, and carried the railroad ties home to build pigsties. They also burned the shed to the ground.

At the height of my arc, above the public wall, I could see the warren of houses in town; I also saw the cobblestone street in front of the yamen and rows of tiled buildings in my gandieh's official compound. I saw his four-man palanquin being carried out through the ceremonial gate, led by a black-clad yayi in a red cap who banged a gong to clear the way. He was followed by two rows of yayi dressed the same way, carrying tall poles with banners of his official insignia, sunshades, and fans. Two sword-bearing guards walked directly ahead of the chair, holding the shafts with one hand. The procession behind the chair included the secretaries of the six bureaus and personal servants. Three long and one short clangs of the gong were followed by impressive shouts; the palanquin barriers moved with swift, nimble steps, as if their legs had springs. The chair rose and fell rhythmically, like a boat tossed on ocean swells.

My gaze carried beyond the town, to the northeast, where the German-built rail line was crawling our way from Qingdao like an elongated insect with a crushed head, trying to squirm forward. A swarm of men on fields bursting with early spring green sprouts waved multicolored banners, heading for the railroad tracks. At the time, I did not know that my dieh was leading the rebellion; if I had, I would not have been so self-indulgent on the swing set. I watched as black smoke billowed from spots along the tracks, like dark trees on the move. Thudding sounds came on the wind.

My gandieh's procession drew ever nearer to the city's South Gate. The sound of the gong grew crisper by the minute, the shouted commands clearer. Banners hung low in the drizzle, like bloody dog pelts. I saw beads of sweat on the carriers' faces and heard their labored breathing. People lined the street, heads bowed, afraid to make a sound or a false move. Even the notoriously vicious dog that belonged to Provincial Scholar Lu knew better than to bark. Anyone could see that my gandieh was a more intimidating presence than Mt. Tai, since even animals shied away from him. The buildup of heat in my heart was like a stove warming a decanter of wine. My dearest, thoughts of you have entered the marrow of my bones; you are steeping in a decanter of wine. I stood tall on the swing seat to give him an unobstructed view of my figure when he looked through the parted curtain.

From my perch I could see the black-haired mob—a ground-hugging cloud of humanity—though at that distance they all—man or woman, young or old—looked alike. I have to admit that the waving banners dazzled my eyes.

You were all yelling and shouting—truth is, I couldn't hear any of you, but I'd have been surprised if you weren't shouting. My dieh was an opera singer, a second-generation Maoqiang Patriarch. Maoqiang had emerged from the masses as a minor form of popular drama, and prospered thanks to my dieh: it traveled north to Laizhou, south to Jiaozhou, west to Qingzhou, and east to Dengzhou. In all, it gained popularity in eighteen counties. When Sun Bing sang, women wept. He was always ready to shout something, so how could he not shout with such a martial following? This was too good a scene to miss. I pushed harder to get a better look. The nitwits on the ground, who assumed that I was merely putting on a show, were dancing joyously, all of them, dizzy with the thought that I was doing it for them. I was wearing only a thin garment that day, yet I was sweating—my gandieh liked to say that my sweat smelled of rose petals—and I knew that those two little darlings on my chest were in full view. With my bottom sticking out in back and my breasts jutting out in front, I gave those lecherous little devils an eyeful. Cool breezes found their way under my clothes and made little eddies in my armpits. There was a mixture of sounds—of wind and rain, of peach blossoms opening and drooping heavily with rainwater. Shouts from the yayi, the urgent cries of the metal rings, the hawking of peddlers, and the lowing of calves formed a chorus. It had turned into a lively Qingming Festival, a flourishing third day of the third month. White-haired old women burned spirit money in an ancient cemetery in the southwest corner; dust devils curled the smoke straight up, little white arboreal columns that merged with the stand of dark trees. My gandieh's procession finally passed through South Gate and immediately caught the attention of the gawking crowd below. "His Eminence the County Magistrate is coming!" someone shouted. As the procession made a full turn around the parade ground, the yayi perked up, throwing out their chests and sucking in their guts, eyes staring straight ahead. Gandieh, I see your feathered cap through the gaps in your bamboo curtain, and I see your square, ruddy face. You have a long beard, so straight and wiry-stiff it will not float if immersed in water. That beard is what binds our hearts together, the red silk thread cast down by the man in the moon. If not for your and my father's beards, where would you have found such a sweet melon as me?

Once the yayi had paraded their prestige, which, in truth, came from you, they set the palanquin down at the edge of the parade ground. Flowers bloomed in profusion on peach trees bordering the ground, producing a fine pink mist in the drizzle. A yayi with a sword on his hip parted the curtain to let you emerge from the palanquin. You straightened your feathered hat, shook the wide sleeves of your official robe, clasped your hands, brought them up to your chest, and bowed to us all.

"Local elders," he said in a booming voice, "citizens, a joyous holiday to you!"

That was just an act. I thought back to when you and I were frolicking in the Western Parlor, and could barely keep from laughing out loud. But when I thought of all you had suffered this spring, I was on the verge of tears. I stopped swinging and, steadying myself with the ropes, stood still on the seat. My lips were pursed, my eyes moist, my heart assailed by waves of emotion—bitter, acrid, sour, and sweet—as I watched my gandieh put on a show for the monkeys.

"In this county we have long promoted the planting of trees," he said, "especially peach trees——"

His lackey from the Southern Society, Junior Officer Li, cried out:

"His Eminence sets an example for us all; he is first in all things. On this drizzly Qingming day, he has come to plant a peach tree to bring blessings to the common people . . ."

My gandieh greeted this interruption with a stern look at Li, then continued:

"Citizens, go back to your homes and plant peach trees, in front and in back, and on the borders of your fields. Citizens, as the poet reminds us, 'Spend less time meddling in others' affairs and idling in the marketplace, and more on reading good books and planting trees.' In fewer than ten years, Gaomi County will enjoy wonderful days. The poem also says, 'Thousands of trees with peach-red flowers, the people sing and dance, celebrating world peace.'"

After intoning the lines of poetry, he picked up a shovel and began to dig. Just as his shovel hit a buried rock and sent sparks flying, Chunsheng, who hardly ever left his side, rolled up to him like a dirt clod and fell frantically to one reverent knee.

"Laoye," he said breathlessly, "it's bad, really bad."

"Bad?" my gandieh demanded. "What's bad?"

"The unruly citizens of Northeast Township are in revolt!"

Without a word, my gandieh dropped the shovel, shook his sleeves, and climbed back into his palanquin. The bearers picked it up and ran with it on their shoulders, followed by a contingent of yayi, who stumbled along like a pack of homeless curs.

Gripped by ineffable dejection, I watched the procession head away from me. Gandieh, you have ruined a perfectly good holiday. Listlessly I alighted from my perch and walked into the clamorous crowd, where I was manhandled by little imps as I tried to decide whether to lose myself in the grove of peach trees and all those flowers or go home and prepare some dog meat. Before I could make up my mind, Xiaojia, my dullard husband, strode vigorously up to me, his face beet red, eyes wide, lips trembling.

"My, my dieh," he stammered, "my dieh is back . . ."

Strange, strange, how very strange: a gongdieh has dropped into our laps. I thought your dieh was long dead. Hasn't it been more than twenty years since you heard from him?

Xiaojia was sweating profusely. "He, he's back," he stammered. "He's really back."

6

Together with Xiaojia I sped toward home, and was soon gasping for breath. "How could a dieh just show up out of nowhere?" I asked. "He's probably looking for a handout." But I wanted to see what sort of goblin had just entered my life. If he was all right, well and good. But if he had a mind to upset me, or tried anything funny, I would break his legs and deliver him to the yamen, where, guilty or not, he'd get two hundred strokes with a paddle, leaving his backside bloody and covered with his own filth. Then we'd see if he dared pass himself off as somebody's dieh. Xiaojia stopped everyone we met along the way to say enigmatically:

"My dieh is back."

And when it was obvious that they could make no sense of what he was talking about, he raised his voice:

"I have a dieh!"

Before we'd reached home, I spotted a horse-drawn carriage outside our front gate and a swarm of curious neighbors, including top-knotted youngsters who were threading their way in and out of the crowd. The horse was a young, dark red, overfed stallion. The accumulated dirt and grime on the vehicle gave ample evidence of the distance it had traveled. I received the strangest looks when the people spotted me, their eyes flashing like graveyard will-o'-the-wisps. Aunty Wu, who owned a general store, greeted me with a false display of good wishes:

"Congratulations!" she said. "'Fortunate people live a life of ease; the wretched among us spend their life on their knees,' as the adage has it. The god of wealth favors the rich, that's for sure. You were already the envy of others, and now heaven has sent you a super-rich gongdieh. Good Mrs. Zhao, a nice big porker has landed at your door, while your stable is crowded with horses and mules. You are blessed, truly blessed!"

I glared at the woman, with her piss pot of a mouth, and said, "Aunty Wu, does that mouth of yours ever stop spouting gibberish? If your family is short a dieh, you can have this one. I certainly don't cherish him."

"Do you mean it?" she said, with a false laugh.

"Yes, and anyone who doesn't take me up on it is the product of a horse-humping donkey!"

Angered by the argument, Xiaojia put a stop to it:

"I'll screw the life out of any woman who tries to take my dieh away!"

Aunty Wu's flat face turned bright red. Known in the neighborhood as an inveterate gossip and rumormonger, she knew all about my dealings with Magistrate Qian, and was so full of sour jealousy that her teeth itched. After being humiliated by me and cursed by Xiaojia until her bunghole itched, she stormed off in a huff, muttering to herself. I walked up the stone steps and turned back to the crowd. "Come on in, good neighbors, for a really good look. If you don't want to, then get your dung beetle asses out of here and stop being so damned nosy!" Soundly embarrassed, they left. I knew they spoke of me in glowing terms to my face and gnashed their teeth, cursing me, behind my back. They'd have liked nothing better than to see me singing in the street to fill my belly. Appealing to their better instincts and treating them with courtesy was a waste of time.

Once inside the yard, I commented loudly, "I wonder which heavenly spirit has dropped into our world? Let's see, maybe I can broaden my mind." This was no time to be genteel. I needed to give him a firm warning, whether he was a real gongdieh or not, to let him know who he was dealing with and to keep him from trying to lord it over me in the future. A gaunt old man with a scrawny queue was bent over carefully dusting a purple sandalwood armchair with gold inlay and a silk pad. The wood was so highly polished and dust-free I could have seen my reflection in it. He straightened up slowly when he heard my blustery entrance, turned, and sized me up coolly. Mother dear! His sunken, furtive eyes were colder than the steel of Xiaojia's butcher knife. My husband stumbled across the yard and, with a foolish laugh, said ingratiatingly:

"This is my wife, Dieh. Niang made the match for me."

Without even looking at me, the old wretch emitted a throaty, indecipherable noise.

Just then, the carriage driver, who had eaten a big meal and washed it down at Wang Sheng's restaurant across the way, walked into the yard to say goodbye. The old wretch handed him a silver certificate and gestured politely to show his gratitude.

"Have a safe trip, driver," he said in fine-sounding cadence.

Well, the old wretch spoke the standard Peking dialect! Like Magistrate Qian. When the driver saw the amount printed on the bill, his scrunched-up little face blossomed like a flower. He bowed deeply, not once but three times, and repeated rapidly:

"Thank you, sir, thank you, sir, thank you, sir . . ."

So, old wretch, you have an interesting background! None but a rich man hands out money that freely, and those bulges inside your jacket must hide wads more. Certificates worth a thousand ounces? Maybe even ten thousand! All right, then. Anyone with breasts can be my niang, and anyone with money can be my dieh. I got down on my hands and knees to kowtow with a good, loud banging of my head.

"Your obedient daughter-in-law respectfully welcomes the father of her husband!" I intoned in a stage voice.

Xiaojia could not follow my lead fast enough. He banged his head on the ground but said nothing, for he was too busy chortling.

The old wretch, thrown off balance by my excessive show of courtesy, reached out—I was struck dumb by the sight of his hands; what strange hands they were—as if he wanted to help me to my feet. But he did not; nor did he assist his son. He just said:

"No need for that. After all, we're family."

Stung by the snub, I stood up, and so did Xiaojia. The old wretch reached under his jacket, which made my heart race in wild anticipation of being rewarded with a handful of silver certificates. It seemed to take him forever to find what he was looking for, but he finally produced a small jade-green object, which he held out to me.

"I don't have much to give you on this, our first meeting," he said. "So take this little bauble."

As I accepted the gift, I parroted his earlier comment: "There's no need to give me anything. After all, we're family." It felt heavy in my hand, but supple and smooth, and it was so green I couldn't help but like it. In all the years I'd slept with Magistrate Qian, I'd received much cultural nurturing, until I no longer considered myself to be a vulgar person, so I knew at once that this was no common gift, but I had no idea what it was.

Xiaojia clicked his tongue and gazed mournfully at his father, who merely smiled.

"Head down!" he commanded.

Xiaojia complied without a whimper. The old wretch hung a glistening silver pendant on a red string around his son's neck. Xiaojia showed it off to me, but when I saw that it was a longevity talisman, I couldn't help but curl my lip. Why, the old wretch treats his son like an infant on his hundredth day.

Sometime later, I showed my first-meeting gift to my gandieh, who recognized it as an archery thumb guard, one carved from the finest jade. More valuable than gold, such a prized object was something that only members of the Imperial family and the nobility could afford. With his left hand on my breast, he held the thumb guard in his right and said admiringly, "This is wonderful, truly wonderful." When I told him he could have it, he replied, "No, this is yours. 'A superior man does not take someone's prized object.'" "But why would a woman consider an archery thumb guard a prized object?" I said. In an uncharacteristically prudish tone, he waved me off. "Do you want it or don't you?" I asked him. "If you don't, I'll smash it to pieces." "Aiya, my little treasure," he blurted out, "don't you dare. I'll take it, I'll take it!" He slipped it over his thumb and held it out, so engrossed in looking at it that he forgot the important business of fondling my breast. But later, he draped a red string with a jade bodhisattva around my neck. I took an immediate liking to that, a woman's gift. I tugged on his beard. "Thank you, my fine gandieh." He laid me down and started riding me like a horse. "Meiniang," he gasped, "Meiniang, I'm going to find out everything I can about this gongdieh of yours . . ."

7

With his gloomy, grim laughter as a backdrop, dizzying whiffs of sandalwood abruptly emerged from my gongdieh's armchair, and the prayer beads in his hand and made my heart flutter. He was unmoved by my dieh's plight, and my flirtatious moves were wasted on him. He stood up on shaky legs and tossed away the prayer beads that virtually never left his hand, star-like flashes of light bursting from his eyes, a sign that something had either pleased him or struck fear in his heart. Those demonic small hands of his reached out to me as he muttered something under his breath, a look of deep anxiety in his eyes. The ferocity of his gaze was gone, completely gone.

"Wash my hands," he pleaded, "I need to wash my hands . . ."

I ladled cold water from the vat into our brass basin and watched as he thrust his hands into it. A hissing sound escaped from between his lips, but he gave no hint of what that meant. His hands were as red as hot cinders, his delicate fingers curling inward like the feet of a young red-legged rooster. I was struck by the image of fingers of molten metal, underscored by the sizzle of the water in the basin, which had begun to bubble and steam. I had never seen anything like it, and did not expect to ever see it again. Immersing his feverish hands in cold water obviously brought soothing comfort to him, since he seemed to sag and go limp all over; his eyes were slitted, and every intake of air whistled through his teeth. The way he held his breath each time was the sign of an opium addiction, the sort of otherworldly languor that only an old donkey like him could manage. It all seemed quite sinister, and unexpected. He was, it was now clear, the embodiment of an evil spirit, a worrisome old degenerate.

Once his self-indulgence had run its course, he took his red hands out of the water and returned to his chair without drying them off. Now, however, instead of shutting his eyes, he kept them wide open and fixed on his hands to watch drops of water slide down his fingers to the ground. He was relaxed almost to the point of lethargy, physically spent but luxuriantly content . . . like my gandieh when he climbs off my body . . .

That was before I knew that he was a renowned executioner, and when all I could think about were the silver certificates tucked into his clothes. "Gongdieh, I said in as solicitous a tone as I could manage, "it seems I've made you comfortable. Well, I expect my dieh's life to end either tonight or tomorrow morning, and given our family connection, won't you help me think of something? Mull that over while I go inside and prepare a bowl of congee with forbidden rice and pig's blood."

I felt empty inside as I washed rice at the well. When I looked up, I saw the flying eaves of the towering City God Temple, where pigeons were cooing and crowding together, and I wondered what they found so interesting. The crisp clack of horse hooves resounded on the cobblestone road beyond the gate. Some German devils were riding by, their tall, rounded, feathered hats visible above the wall. The sight made my heart pound, since I was sure that my dieh was what was on their minds. Xiaojia, who by then had sharpened his butcher knife and readied the necessary tools, picked up a hooked Chinese ash pole and went into the sty, where he selected a black pig and quickly hooked it under the chin. Squeals tore from its mouth, and the bristles on its neck stood straight as it struggled to back up, its hind legs and rump flat on the ground, blood seeming to seep from its eyes. It was no match for Xiaojia, who hunkered down and pulled so hard that his feet sank at least three inches into the dirt, like a pair of hoes, as he backed up, one powerful step at a time, pulling the pig along like a plow, its feet digging furrows in the sty. In less time than it takes to tell, Xiaojia had pulled the pig up to the killing rack. Then, gripping the hooked pole in one hand and the pig's tail in the other, he straightened up and, with a loud grunt, lifted a creature weighing two hundred jin up onto the rack, so disorienting it that it forgot to struggle—but not to squeal. Now that all four legs were sticking straight up, Xiaojia removed the hook from the pig's chin and tossed it to the side, picking his razor-sharp butcher knife out of the blood trough in the same motion. Then—slurp—with the sort of casual indifference of slicing bean curd, he plunged his knife high in the pig's chest. A second push and it was buried deep inside the animal, bringing an end to the squeals, which were replaced by moans that lasted only a moment. Now all that remained were the twitches—legs, skin, even the bristles. Xiaojia pulled the knife out and turned the pig over to let its blood spill into the trough below. Great quantities of bright, hot blood the color of red silk pulsed into the waiting trough.

The stench of fresh blood hung over the half acre of our courtyard, which was big enough to accommodate dog pens and pigsties, Chinese roses and peonies, plus a rack for curing meat, vats to hold fermented drink, and an open-air cook pit. The odor attracted blood-drinking bluebottle flies that danced in the air, a testament to their keen sense of smell.

Two yayi, attired in soft red leather caps, black livery secured around the middle with dark cloth sashes, and soft-soled boots with ridges down the middle, swords in scabbards on their hips, opened the gate. I knew they were constables, fast yayi from the yamen who tracked down criminals, but I did not know their names. Feeling a lack of self-assurance, since my dieh was in their jail, I smiled. Normally I would not have deigned to look their way, not at contemptuous toadying jackasses who were a scourge of the people. They returned my courtesy with nods and tiny smiles squeezed out of their fiendish faces. But only for a second. One of them reached under his tunic and pulled out a black bamboo tally, which he waved in the air and intoned somberly:

"We bring orders from His Eminence the County Magistrate to escort Zhao Jia to the yamen for questioning."

Xiaojia came running up, bent humbly at the waist, still gripping his bloody butcher knife, and, with a bow, asked:

"What is it, Your Honors?"

With frosty looks, the yayi asked:

"Are you Zhao Jia?"

"I am Xiaojia; Zhao Jia is my dieh."

"Where is your dieh?" one of the puffed-up yayi demanded.

"In the house."

"Inform him that he is to accompany us to the yamen."

I had taken all I was about to take from this pair of nasty dogs.

"My gongdieh never goes anywhere," I said angrily. "What offense has he committed?"

My display of temper was not lost on them.

"Mistress of the Zhao home, we merely follow orders," they said, looking for sympathy. "And we are only messengers. If he is guilty of an offense, we do not know what it is."

"One moment, good sirs. Are you inviting my dieh to the yamen for a social visit?" Xiaojia asked, his curiosity bubbling over.

"How should we know?" the yayi said with a shake of his head and an enigmatic grin. "Maybe he'll be treated to some nice dog meat and millet spirits."

Of course I knew exactly what kind of dog filth and cow crap had come out of the little mutt's yap: a not so subtle hint at what went on between Magistrate Qian and me. Xiaojia? How could a blubber-head like him have any idea what this was all about? He was only too happy to run inside.

I followed him in.

Qian Ding, you fucking dog, what are you up to? You arrest my dieh, but hide from me. Then early this morning, two of your lackeys show up to take my gongdieh away. The plot certainly thickens. First my own dieh, then my husband's dieh, and now my gandieh, three diehs coming together in the Great Hall. I've sung the aria "Three Judges at Court," but this is the first time I've heard of "Three Diehs at Court." I doubt that you can stand being away from me for the rest of your life, damn you, and the next time I see you, I'm going to find out what you have in your bag of tricks.

Xiaojia wiped his oily, sweaty face with his sleeve and said excitedly:

"Good news, Dieh! The County Magistrate has invited you to the yamen for some millet spirits and dog meat!"

My gongdieh remained seated in his chair, his bloodless little hands resting squarely on the arms. He made not a sound, and I could not tell whether he was resting calmly or putting on a show.

"Say something, Dieh. The yayi are out in the yard waiting for you." Xiaojia's nerves were beginning to show. "Will you take me with you, Dieh? Seeing the Great Hall would be a real treat. All those times my wife went, she never once agreed to take me along . . ."

I jumped in to put a stop to what the buffoon was saying:

"Don't listen to him, Gongdieh. Why would they invite you for a social visit? I'm sure they plan to detain you. Have you committed a crime?"

My gongdieh lazily opened his eyes and sighed.

"If I have," he said, "it is what was expected of me. As they say, 'Confront soldiers with generals and dam water with earth.' There is nothing to get excited about. Go invite them in."

Xiaojia turned and shouted out the door:

"Did you hear that? My dieh wants you to come in."

With a hint of a smile, my gongdieh said:

"Good boy; that's the right tone for people like that."

So Xiaojia went outside and said to the yayi:

"Are you aware of the fact that my wife and Magistrate Qian enjoy a close relationship?"

"You foolish boy," his dieh said, shaking his head in exasperation before fixing his gaze on me.

I watched as the smirking yayi pushed Xiaojia to the side, hands on the hilts of their swords, resolute and ruthless in their determination as they rushed into the room where we were talking.

My gongdieh opened his eyes a crack, barely wide enough for two chilling rays to escape and smother the two men with contempt. Then he turned his gaze to the wall and ignored the intruders.

After a quick exchange of looks that seemed to bespeak their embarrassment, one of them said officiously, "Are you Zhao Jia?"

He appeared to be asleep.

"My dieh is getting on in years and doesn't hear so well," Xiaojia said breathlessly. "Ask him again, but louder."

So the fellow tried again:

"Zhao Jia," he said more forcefully, "we are here by order of the County Magistrate to have you visit him in the yamen."

"You go back and tell your Eminence Qian," he replied unhurriedly, without looking at them, "that Zhao Jia has weak legs and aching feet and cannot answer the summons."

That prompted another quick exchange of looks, followed by an audible snigger from one of the men. But he turned serious and, with a display of biting sarcasm, said:

"Maybe His Eminence ought to send his palanquin for you."

"I think that would be best."

This was met with an outburst of laughter.

"All right, fine," they said. "You wait here for His Eminence to come in his palanquin."

They turned and walked out, still laughing, and by the time they were in the yard, their laughter was uncontrollable.

Xiaojia followed them into the yard and said proudly:

"My dieh is really something, don't you think? Everyone else is afraid of you, but not him."

One look at Xiaojia set them off laughing again, this time so hard that they weaved their way out the gate. I could hear them out on the street. I knew why they were laughing, and so did my gongdieh.

But not Xiaojia, who came back inside and asked, clearly puzzled:

"Why were they laughing, Dieh? Did they drink a crazy old woman's piss? Baldy Huang once told me that if you drink a crazy old woman's piss, you can laugh yourself crazy. That must be what they did. The question is, which crazy old woman's piss did they drink?"

The wretch replied, but for my benefit, not his son's:

"Son," he said, "a man must not underestimate himself. That is something your dieh learned late in life. Even if the Gaomi County Magistrate is a member of the Tiger group, someone who passed the Imperial Examination with distinction, what is he but a grade five County Magistrate whose hat bears the crystal symbol of office in front and a one-eyed peacock feather in back? Even though his wife is the maternal granddaughter of Zeng Guofan, a dead prefect is no match for a live rat. Your dieh has never held official rank, but the number of red-capped heads he has lopped off could fill two large wicker baskets. So, for that matter, could the heads of nobles and aristocrats!"

Xiaojia stood there with a foolish grin on his face, his teeth showing, likely not understanding what his father had just said. But I did, every word of it. I'd learned a great deal in my years with Magistrate Qian, and my gongdieh's brief monologue nearly froze my heart and raised gooseflesh on my arms. I'm sure my face must have been ghostly white. Rumors about my gongdieh had been swirling around town for months and had naturally reached my ears. Having somehow found a cache of hidden courage, I asked:

"Is that really what you did, Gongdieh?"

He fixed his hawk-like gaze on me and said, one slow word at a time, as if spitting out steel pellets, "Every—trade—has—its—master, its zhuangyuan! Know who said that?"

"It's a well-known popular adage."

"No," he said. "One person said that to me. Know who it was?"

I shook my head.

He got up out of his chair, prayer beads in his hands—once more the stifling aroma of sandalwood spread through the room. His gaunt face had a somber, golden glow. Arrogantly, reverently, gratefully, he said:

"The Empress Dowager Cixi Herself!"

CHAPTER TWO

Zhao Jia's Ravings

The adage has it: By the Northern Dipper one is born, by the Southern Dipper a person dies; people follow the Kingly Way, wind blows where the grass lies. People's hearts are iron, laws the crucible, and even the hardest stone under the hammer dies. (How true!) I served the Qing Court as its preeminent executioner, an enviable reputation in the Board of Punishments. (You can check with your own eyes!) A new minister was appointed each year, like a musical reprise. My appointment alone was secure, for I performed a great service by killing the nation's enemies. (A beheading is like chopping greens; a flaying differs little from peeling an onion.) Cotton cannot contain fire; the dead cannot be buried in frozen ground. I poke a hole in the window paper to speak the truth and admonish, prick up your ears if you seek to be wise.

—*Maoqiang* Sandalwood Death. *A galloping aria*

1

My dear dissolute daughter-in-law, why do you glare like that? Do you not worry that your eyes will pop out of your head? Yes, that is my profession. From my seventeenth year, when I dissevered the body of a thieving clerk at the silver repository, to my sixtieth year, when I administered the lingering death to the would-be assassin of His Excellency Yuan Shikai, I earned my living at that calling for forty-four years. You still glare. Well, I have witnessed many glares in my life, some far more insistent than yours, the likes of which no one in all of Shandong Province, let alone you people, has ever seen. You need not even see them in person. Merely describing them could make you soil yourself out of fear.

In the tenth year of the Xianfeng Emperor, a eunuch called Little Insect audaciously pilfered His Majesty's Seven Star fowling piece from the Imperial Armory, where he worked, and sold it. A tribute gift from the Russian Tsarina to the Emperor, it was no ordinary hunting rifle. It had a golden barrel, a silver trigger, and a sandalwood stock in which were inlaid seven diamonds, each the size of a peanut. It fired silver bullets that could bring down a phoenix from the sky and a unicorn on land. No fowling piece like it had graced the world since Pangu divided heaven from earth. The larcenous Little Insect, believing that the sickly Emperor was rapidly losing his faculties, impudently removed the piece from the armory and sold it for the reported price of three thousand silver ingots, which his father used to buy a tract of farmland. The poor delusional youngster forgot one basic principle: Anyone who becomes Emperor is, by definition, a dragon, a Son of Heaven. Has there even been a dragon, a Son of Heaven, who was not endowed with peerless wisdom? One who could not foretell everything under the sun? Emperor Xianfeng, a man of extraordinary mystical skills, could see and identify the tip of an animal's autumn hair with dragon eyes that appeared normal during the day, but emitted such powerful rays of light when night fell that he needed no lamp to put brush to paper or to read a book. It was said that the Emperor planned a hunting expedition beyond the Great Wall and called for his Seven Star fowling piece. A panicky Little Insect made up bizarre explanations for why that was not possible: first an old fox with white fur had stolen it, then it was a magical hawk that had flown off with it. Emperor Xianfeng's dragon mien turned red with anger, and He handed down an Imperial Edict, ordering that Little Insect be turned over to the Office of Palace Justice, which was responsible for disciplining eunuchs. The standard employment of interrogation tactics secured a confession from the miscreant, so angering His Majesty that golden flashes shot from His eyes. He jumped to His feet in the Hall of Golden Chimes and roared:

"Little Insect, We shit upon eight generations of your ancestors! Like the rat that licks the cat's anus, you are an audacious fool. How dare you practice your thieving ways in Our home! If We do not make an example of you, We do not deserve to be Emperor!"

With that, Emperor Xianfeng decided that Little Insect would be subjected to a special punishment as a warning to all, and He called upon the Office of Palace Justice to read him a list, not unlike a menu for an Imperial meal. Officials presented all the punishments used in the past for the Emperor's selection: flogging, crushing, suffocating, quartering, dismemberment, and more. After hearing them out, the Emperor shook His head and said, "Ordinary, too common. Like stale, spoiled leftovers. No," He said, "you must seek advice from the experts in the Board of Punishments to provide an appropriate punishment." On the very night that His Excellency, President of the Board of Punishments Wang, received the Imperial Edict, he went looking for Grandma Yu.

Who was Grandma Yu? you ask. My mentor, that's who. A man, of course. So why do I call him Grandma? Listen, and I will tell you. It is a reference peculiar to our profession. Four executioners are listed in the Board of Punishments register. The oldest, most senior, and most accomplished among them is Grandma. Next in line, ranked by seniority and skills, are First Aunt, Second Aunt, and Young Aunt. During the busy months, when there is more work than they can handle, outside helpers are taken on, and they are called nephews. I started out as a nephew and gradually worked my way up to Grandma. Easy? No, by no means. I served the Board of Punishments as Grandma for thirty years. Presidents and Vice Presidents came and went, but only I remained as tall and sturdy as Mt. Tai. People may despise our profession, but once someone joins its ranks, he looks down on all people, in the same way that you look down on pigs and dogs.

To continue, His Excellency, Board President Wang, summoned Grandma Yu and me, your father, to his official document room. I, barely twenty that year, had been elevated from Second Aunt to First Aunt, an unprecedented promotion and a display of great Imperial favor.

"Xiaojiazi," Grandma Yu said to me, "your shifu did not ascend to First Aunt until he was over forty, while you, young scamp that you are, have reached the plateau of First Aunt at the age of twenty. Like sorghum in the sixth month, you have shot upward."

But that is talk for another time.

"His Imperial Majesty has issued an edict to the Board of Punishments to provide a special, even unique, punishment for a eunuch who stole a fowling piece," Board President Wang said. "You are the experts, so give this your full attention. We do not want to disappoint His Imperial Majesty or show this Board in a bad light."

A sound like a moan emerged from Grandma Yu's mouth.

"Excellency," he said after a moment, "your humble servant opines that His Imperial Majesty loathes Little Insect because he has eyes but does not see. We must therefore carry out the Emperor's will."

"How true," Board President Wang said. "What do you have in mind? Tell me quick."

"There is a punishment," Grandma Yu said, "known as Yama's Hoop, named after the doorway to the King of Hell's realm. Another name for it is Two Dragons Sport with Pearls. I wonder if it might be appropriate."

"Tell me about it."

So Grandma Yu described Yama's Hoop in detail, and when he was finished, His Excellency beamed in delight.

"Go make preparations," he said, "while I seek permission from His Imperial Majesty."

To which Grandma Yu replied, "The construction of Yama's Hoop is a burdensome task. The iron hoop alone is a unique challenge. It can be neither very hard nor too soft. Only the finest wrought iron, repeatedly fired and hammered, will do, and there is no blacksmith anywhere in the capital who is up to the task. Will His Excellency approve a delay of several days, giving me and my apprentice time to make it ourselves? We of course have no adequate tools or facilities and must somehow make do. Will His Excellency favor us with a bit of silver to purchase what we need?"

Wang sneered.

"Don't you receive enough income by selling cured human flesh for medicinal purposes?"

Grandma Yu fell to his knees, and naturally I, your father, followed.

"Nothing escapes His Excellency's eyes," Grandma Yu said. "But constructing Yama's Hoop serves the public good . . ."

"Get up," Wang said. "I'll see that you are given two hundred ounces of silver, one hundred for each—master and apprentice—but you must spare no effort in the service of perfection. I will tolerate no shoddy work. Throughout history, from dynasty to dynasty, generation upon generation, the discipline and punishment of eunuchs has been the responsibility of the Office of Palace Justice. For the Emperor to deliver this case to the Board of Punishments is unprecedented, a manifestation of the trust and high regard His Imperial Majesty has in us. We could ask no higher honor! It is incumbent upon you to take great care in this enterprise. If it is performed well enough to please the Emperor, our future is bright. If not, if His Imperial Majesty is displeased, our Board will be in for bad times, and that will provide a moment for your dog heads to find a new place to perch."

Grandma Yu and I accepted this glorious task with trepidation, though we were delighted to receive the silver, which we took to Smithy Lane south of the Temple of National Protection in search of a shop capable of fabricating a hoop to our specifications. Once that was done, we went to Mule Avenue, where we bought several untanned cowhides and hired someone to turn them into leather straps to affix to the iron hoop. In all, we spent a grand total of four ounces of silver, with a hundred ninety-six ounces left over, twenty ounces of which we used to buy a gold bracelet for Board President Wang's concubine, whom he had installed in Jingling Lane. From the remaining one hundred seventy-six ounces, we gave six each to Second Aunt and Third Aunt. We kept the rest, a hundred for Grandma and seventy for me, your father. I brought that back to our hometown and bought this house, marrying your mother while I was at it. If the eunuch Little Insect had not stolen the Emperor's fowling piece, I would never have had enough to buy a house or get married. And without a wife, you would not have been born. And if I had missed out on the opportunity to have a son, there would never be a daughter-in-law in this house. Now you understand why I feel it is important to tell you about the Little Insect affair. There are root causes for everything that happens. The theft of a fowling piece by Little Insect is the root cause of your existence.

Excellency Wang, who was on pins and needles the day before the punishment was to be carried out, ordered that a prisoner awaiting decapitation be taken from the condemned cell and brought to his audience hall as a subject on whom we were to practice our technique. We did as we were told, affixing the iron hoop over the poor man's head.

"Laoye!" the man screamed. "Laoye, I did not commit the unforgivable act of retracting my confession, I did not. Why are you doing this to me?"

"All for the sake of the Emperor," Excellency Wang declared. "Begin!"

From start to finish, the punishment lasted no longer than it takes to smoke a pipeful of tobacco. The man's head split open, and he died as his brains spilled out.

"That was impressive," Wang declared, "but he died too quickly. His Imperial Majesty went to the trouble of allowing us to choose a method of execution that will inflict maximum suffering on Little Insect. A death of utter anguish will serve as a trenchant warning to all palace eunuchs. So what do we get from you? You placed the hoop on the man's head, tightened it, and poof, it was over. Strangling a rabbit takes more time than that. Is that the best you can manage? I demand that you slow the process down, make it last at least two hours. It must be more enjoyable than a stage play. You know that the palace supports troupes that employ thousands of actors who have performed every play in existence. I expect Little Insect's body to be drained of fluids and for you two to work up a mighty sweat in the process. That is the only way this Board and the punishment you call Yama's Hoop can gain the reputation they deserve."

Excellency Wang then ordered that a second condemned prisoner be brought over for us to practice on. The head of this particular man was the size of a willow basket, almost too big for the hoop, which we struggled to affix to his head, inept like coopers, greatly displeasing His Excellency.

"That little toy is what I get for two hundred ounces of silver?"

Sweat oozed from my pores at his comment. But Grandma Yu appeared not to let it bother him, although he later told me he was quaking from fear. Our performance this time was a distinct improvement, as we drew it out for a full two hours, inflicting untold anguish on the pitiful man with the big head before he died. That earned a smile from His Excellency. With an eye on the two corpses laid out in the center of the audience hall, he said:

"Go ahead, get everything ready. Replace the bloodstained leather straps, clean the hoop, and add a coat of varnish. Be sure to clean the garments you plan to wear, so His Majesty and His court followers will see that the executioners attached to the Board of Punishments are a refined lot. There may be many ways of putting it, but in simplest terms, only success matters. You will not fail! If there is the slightest flaw in your performance, casting the Board in a poor light, you will experience Yama's Hoop from a more personal angle."

We rose at second cockcrow the next morning and set to making our preparations. Our minds were filled with the gravity of performing a palace execution, making sleep impossible. Even Grandma Yu, who had weathered many storms, tossed and turned all night, getting out of bed every hour or so to take the urinal down from the windowsill and empty his bladder, then sitting down to smoke. Second and Third Aunts busied themselves lighting the stove and preparing breakfast, while I concentrated on subjecting Yama's Hoop to a meticulous inspection. After convincing myself that it was in flawless condition, I handed it to Grandma Yu for one final inspection. He rubbed his hand over every inch of the device, nodded his approval, and wrapped it in a three-foot length of red silk before reverently laying it on the Patriarch's altar. The Patriarch of our profession is Gao Tao, a sagely eminence from the period of the Three Kings and Five Emperors, who nearly succeeded the legendary Yu on the Imperial Throne. Many of the punishments in use and the penal codes honored today originated with him. My shifu told me that our Patriarch needed no knife to dispatch a victim—by staring at the victim's neck and slowly rolling his eyes, he could make the man's head fall to the ground on its own. Ancestor Gao Tao had phoenix eyes, brows like reclining silkworms, a face the color of a jujube, eyes as bright as stars, and three handsome tufts of whiskers on his chin. He bore an uncanny resemblance to the warrior Guan Gong of the Three Kingdoms period. "The truth is," Grandma Yu said, "Guan Gong was a reincarnation of Gao Tao."

Following a hurried breakfast, we rinsed our mouths, cleaned our teeth, and washed our faces. Second and Third Aunts helped us into our new court attire and placed red felt caps on our heads.

"Shifu, Elder Apprentice, you look like bridegrooms," Third Aunt complimented us.

Grandma Yu gave him a stern look, showing his displeasure with the comment. One of the conventions of our profession is a proscription against silly or foolish words before or during an execution. Any violation of that taboo can summon the ghosts of wronged victims or evil spirits. You often see little spinning dust devils in the marketplace. What do you think they are? They are caused not by wind, but by the spirits of those who were put to death unjustly.

Grandma Yu took a bundle of prized sandalwood incense from a willow case, gently extracted three sticks, lit them from the flickering candle on the Patriarch's altar, and inserted them into the incense burner. He went down on his knees, followed hastily by his three assistants. Grandma began muttering softly:

"Patriarch, Patriarch, today we will carry out our task in the palace, with enormous consequences. Your offspring ask for your protection and guidance in the proper performance of our duties, and for that we kowtow to you."

Grandma Yu banged his head loudly against the brick floor. We did the same. Our Patriarch's face glowed red in the candlelight. Altogether we each kowtowed nine times before standing up, starting with Grandma Yu, and stepping back three paces. Second Aunt went outside to fetch a celadon bowl; Third Aunt went outside and returned with a white rooster with a black comb. Second Aunt placed the bowl in front of the Patriarch's altar and stepped aside, going down on his knees. Third Aunt knelt directly in front of the altar and held the rooster by the neck with one hand and by the feet with the other, stretching it out horizontal. Second Aunt then took a dagger out of the bowl and neatly sliced the rooster's neck. For a moment no blood appeared—our hearts nearly stopped, for killing a rooster and drawing no blood augured a botched execution. But then the blood—so red it was almost black—spurted from the wound and into the bowl. Blood surges through the veins of roosters with white feathers and black combs, and killing one before an execution is for us an essential ritual. Once all the blood had drained out of the rooster, the two aunts placed the bowl on the altar, kowtowed again, and backed away, bent at the waist. Grandma Yu and I stepped forward, fell to our knees, and kowtowed three times. Then I followed his lead by sticking the first two fingers of my left hand into the bowl and painting my face with the rooster's blood, like an actor applying stage paint. The warm blood made the tips of my fingers tingle. There was enough to paint both our faces, and a bit left over to turn all four hands red. Now our faces, mine and Grandma Yu's, were the same color as the face of the Patriarch. Why had we used rooster blood? To unite us with the Patriarch, but also to notify those spirits of the wrongly executed and evil spirits that we were descendants of Master Gao Tao, and that when we put someone to death, we were gods, not humans. We were the law of the land. With our hands and faces painted red, Grandma Yu and I sat peacefully on stools to await the official summons from the Imperial Palace.

As the red sun wheeled into the sky, crows in scholar trees set up a racket of caws. A woman was keening in the Imperial Dungeon. Condemned to die for killing her husband, she keened like that every day—for heaven, for earth, and for her children. By now she had descended into madness. Your dieh, I, being young, soon began to fidget and could not sit still. I stole a glance at Grandma Yu, who sat straight and unmoving as an iron bell, and I followed his lead by holding my breath to calm myself. The blood-paint had dried and become stiff, turning our faces into something resembling sugarcoated berries, and I strained to experience the feeling of armor covering my skin. Little by little my thoughts blurred, and a hazy picture formed in my mind of me following Grandma Yu down a deep, dark trench, walking on and on without ever reaching the end.

The Office of Palace Justice Director, Eminence Cao, led us up to a pair of small, blue-curtained palanquins and gestured for us to climb in. This sudden and unexpected indulgence nearly unnerved me, for I had never ridden in a palanquin before. I glanced at Grandma Yu, who, to my surprise, stood without moving, open-mouthed, as if he were about to cry or sneeze. A eunuch with a double chin standing beside the palanquins said in a throaty voice:

"What's the matter, chairs too small for you?"

Still, neither Grandma Yu nor I was willing to climb in. Our eyes were fixed on Eminence Cao, who said:

"These are not intended as a show of respect, but to keep you from attracting too much attention. What are you waiting for? Get in! It is true, you cannot put a dog's head on a golden platter."

The four bearers, all unwhiskered eunuchs, stood in front of the chairs, their hands tucked into their sleeves, looks of disdain on their faces. That actually emboldened me. Stinking castrati, fuck you and your mothers. Thanks to your Little Insect, I am going to ride on the shoulders of you two-legged beasts today. I stepped up to a chair, pulled the curtain aside, and climbed in. Grandma Yu did the same.

Our transports left the ground and began the bumpy ride to the Imperial Palace. I heard the hoarse grumbling of one of the eunuchs:

"This executioner is heavy, dead weight, probably from drinking all that human blood!"

These men, who normally carried the Empress or one of the Imperial Consorts, had never imagined that they would one day carry an executioner, not in their worst nightmare. That made me so proud that I began to rock back and forth to make the trip harder on those stinking castrati. But before we'd even left the Board of Punishments compound, Young Aunt shouted from behind:

"Grandma, Grandma, you forgot Yama's Hoop!"

An explosion went off in my head; I saw stars; sweat seeped from my pores and rained to the ground as I tumbled out of the chair and took the red-wrapped Yama's Hoop from Young Aunt. I cannot describe what I felt at that moment. Grandma Yu had also gotten out of his chair, I saw, his face similarly beaded with sweat, his legs quaking. If not for Young Aunt's quick thinking, we would have been in very hot water that day.

"Your mother be fucked!" Eminence Cao cursed. "Can an official misplace his official seal? Does a tailor lose his scissors?"

I was all set to enjoy the privilege of riding in a palanquin, but this turn of events soured my mood. I crawled back in and sat quietly, making no more trouble for the eunuchs.

I don't know how long we had been riding when my chair abruptly landed with a thud and I emerged, confused and disoriented, nearly blinded by my resplendent surroundings. Holding on to Yama's Hoop, my back bent slightly, I followed Grandma Yu, who was being led into the palace by a eunuch, down one winding corridor after another, until we emerged into a large courtyard in which a line of men with no whiskers on their faces and dressed in tan clothing with black skullcaps were kneeling in the dirt. Little Insect, the fowling piece thief, was already bound to a post. He was a good-looking youngster with delicate features, so daintily demure he could easily have passed for a girl, especially his beautiful eyes—double-fold lids, long lashes, and moist pupils that looked like grapes. What a shame! I had to sigh over such a fine specimen, a good-looking boy brought into the palace only to be castrated and made to serve as a eunuch. What kind of parents could do that to their own son?

A temporary viewing stand had been erected in front of the post on which Little Insect was bound. A row of carved sandalwood chairs had been placed on the viewing stand, the central one larger than the others. That particular chair had a yellow cushion embroidered with a golden dragon. His Imperial Majesty's Dragon Seat, no doubt. Already present were Excellency Wang, the President of the Board of Punishments; his deputy, Eminence Tie; and, standing in front of them, a host of other officials, all in caps inlaid with jade or coral, officials from the various boards and bureaus. None of them dared even cough. This was, after all, the Imperial Palace, with an atmosphere that set it apart from all other places: silent, hushed, so quiet I could hear my own heartbeat. Only the sparrows nesting beneath the glazed roof tiles did not know enough to keep silent, as they chirped insistently. Suddenly, without warning, a white-haired, red-faced old eunuch on the platform sang out smoothly, letting each syllable hang in the air:

"His Majesty the Emperor!"

The lines of red caps sank to the ground, the only sound the swish of their wide sleeves; and faster than it takes to tell, officials from the Six Boards, palace women, and eunuchs were all kneeling in the dirt. I was about to fall to my knees when something stomped on my foot. I looked up and was pinned by the blazing glare in Grandma Yu's eyes as he stood beside the post, head up, motionless as a stone carving. That jogged my memory: for generations, one of the conventions associated with our profession has been that an executioner whose face is smeared with chicken blood is no longer a person, but has become the sacred and somber symbol of the Law. We are not required to kneel, not even in the presence of the Emperor. And so, following Grandma's lead, I threw out my chest, sucked in my gut, and stood as motionless as a stone carving. I tell you, son, such unprecedented glory had never before been bequeathed to a third person here in Gaomi County, or in all of Shandong, or for that matter in any of the territory belonging to the Great Qing Empire.

At that moment, the toots and whistles of pipes and flutes drew near; behind the languishing musical notes, His Majesty's procession appeared between two high walls. A pair of tan-clad eunuchs led the way, carrying incense burners in the shape of auspicious creatures, from whose mouths emerged clouds of dark green smoke, so fragrant that it penetrated my brain, sharpening my senses one moment and dulling them the next. On the heels of the two eunuchs came the Imperial Musicians, followed by two columns of eunuchs carrying flags, banners, umbrellas, and fans, all in reds and yellows. Next came the Imperial Bodyguard, armed with golden battleaxes, brass spears, and silver lances, marching ahead of a bright yellow palanquin carried on the shoulders of two powerful eunuchs; in it sat the Manchu Emperor, protected from the sun's rays by an oversized peacock fan held by a pair of palace women. That was followed by dozens of resplendently attired women of great beauty, the Imperial Harem, of course, all riding in palanquins and forming a florid array of colors. A long tail constituted the end of the procession. Grandma Yu told me later that since all of this was taking place within the palace grounds, the Imperial Procession was greatly simplified. If it had occurred outside, it would have been so long that the head would have passed long before the tail appeared. The Emperor's palanquin alone would have been carried by sixty-four men.

The eunuchs were so well trained that everything was quickly in place. His Majesty and His consorts were seated in the viewing stand. Emperor Xianfeng, in yellow robes and a golden crown, sat no more than ten feet from me. I stared with rapt attention, taking in all the royal features. He had a gaunt face around a nose with a high bridge. His left eye was a bit bigger than the right. A large mouth, white teeth. A neatly divided moustache adorned his upper lip, a goatee his chin. His cheeks were dotted with white pockmarks. Bothered by a persistent cough, he made liberal use of a glittering spittoon held for him by a serving girl. He was sandwiched between a dozen or more palace ladies, creating the image of a phoenix with spread wings. Their towering coiffures were adorned with brightly colored red flowers, from which silk tassels dangled, the sort of decoration you see on stage actresses. Every one of the palace ladies was a striking beauty; their bodies emitted bewitching perfumes. The woman to the Emperor's immediate right, powdered and rouged, had the appearance of a celestial maiden come down to earth. Know who she was? You'll shudder when I tell you. The one we now call Cixi, the Empress Dowager.

Taking advantage of the Emperor's turn to use his spittoon, the imposing old eunuch lightly swished his horsetail whisk as if it were a flyswatter, a sign for the ministers and officials, as well as the dark-haired lines of eunuchs and palace ladies, to shout at the top of their lungs:

"Long live Our Imperial Majesty! May He live forever and ever!"

That is when I discovered that, far from keeping their heads down so as not to look up, they were all sneaking peeks at the viewing stand. Between coughs, the Emperor declared:

"Worthy ministers, you may rise."

To which they responded with a kowtow and a shout in unison:

"Praise His Majesty's generosity!"

Another kowtow, a flicking of wide sleeves, and they rose to their feet, before, bent at the waist, retreating to the periphery. The President of the Board of Punishments, Excellency Wang, emerged from the cluster of officials, flicked his sleeves, and fell to his knees to kowtow once more.

"Your loyal servant Wang Rui, President of the Board of Punishments, in compliance with the Imperial Edict, has ordered the fabrication of Yama's Hoop and has selected two eminently qualified executioners to bring their equipment into the Palace to carry out the execution. May it please His Majesty."

"Yes, We know. You may rise."

Excellency Wang kowtowed yet again, thanked the Emperor for His favor, and retreated to one side. The Emperor said something, but it was so garbled I couldn't make out what it was. Obviously, in the throes of consumption, He was short of breath. The old eunuch made another announcement, drawing out each syllable like an operatic aria:

"His Majesty decrees that President of the Board of Punishments Wang present Yama's Hoop for his inspection————"

Wang scurried over to where I stood and snatched the red silk bundle in which Yama's Hoop was wrapped out of my hand. He returned to the viewing stand, holding the bundle gently in both hands, as if it were a steaming-hot pot. There he went down on his knees and raised his hands above his head, offering up Yama's Hoop. The old eunuch walked up, bent down, and took the proffered bundle, which he carried up to the Emperor, laid it gently on a table, and slowly unwrapped the red silk until the object itself was in full view. It glistened in all its terrifying grandeur. It had not cost much to make, but I had put considerable effort into it. When first produced, it was an ugly black thing, but

I'd rubbed and scoured it for three days to make it shine. I'd earned every one of those seventy ounces of silver.

His Majesty reached out with one sallow hand and tapped the object tentatively with the long, yellowed nail of His index finger. Whether it felt too hot or too cold was impossible to gauge, but the golden finger jerked backward almost immediately, and I heard the aging ruler mumble something. Knowing what that something was, the old eunuch stepped up, retrieved the object, and carried it down the line to let the members of the Imperial Harem have a look at it. They each followed the Emperor's lead by touching it tentatively with index fingers shaped like jade bamboo shoots. Some put on a show of terror, quickly turning their heads away; others simply stared at the thing with no discernible expression. When he had finished, the old eunuch returned the object to Excellency Wang, who was still on his knees; accepting it with deference, he stood up and, walking backward, bent at the waist, returned to where I was standing and handed it to me.

Up on the reviewing stand, the old eunuch bent to whisper something in the Emperor's ear. I saw His Majesty nod. The old eunuch stepped up to the front of the reviewing stand and announced in a singsong cadence:

"His Majesty decrees: Carry out the punishment of the monstrous offender Little Insect—"

That elicited a howl from the pole-bound Little Insect:

"Your Majesty," he wailed, "Your Majesty, be merciful and spare the life of this dog of a slave . . . your slave will never again . . ."

The Emperor's bodyguard snapped to attention. Little Insect, his face waxen, his lips bloodless, and his eyes blinking fiercely, stopped shouting as he wet himself. Turning to us, he whispered:

"Laoye, Shaoye, do your job quickly, and when I'm down in the bowels of Hell, I will be forever grateful for your kindness . . ."

Listening to him rant was the furthest thing from our minds. It would have taken more courage than we possessed to listen to him. We could have made things easy on him by looping a rope around his neck and strangling him, but that would have been the beginning of our downfall. Even if the Emperor had granted us forgiveness, Board President Wang would not have been so charitable. We hurriedly unwrapped the instrument of torture. Grandma Yu and I held it between us—it seemed considerably heftier after passing through the hands of the Emperor and His harem—each holding one of the leather straps, and carried out our rehearsed routine: first we displayed it to the Emperor and His harem, then to Board President Wang and the other officials, and lastly to the gathering of eunuchs and palace ladies, like actors. The Head of the Office of Palace Justice, Eunuch Chen, and Board President Wang exchanged glances before calling out in unison:

"Let the execution begin!"

It was as if the heavens had eyes—the gleaming iron hoop might as well have been made for Little Insect's head. With hardly any effort, it fit perfectly. His fetching eyes peered out from two holes in the device. Once it was in place, Grandma Yu and I, your dieh, took two steps backward and gripped the leather straps firmly. Little Insect was still muttering:

"Laoye . . . Shaoye . . . make it quick . . ."

At a time like that, who cared what he wanted? I glanced at Grandma Yu; he returned the glance. I knew what to do, and I was ready. We nodded, and I saw the beginning of a smile on Grandma Yu's lips, the old master's customary expression when he was working, for he was an urbane executioner. That smile was my signal to begin, so I flexed my muscles and pulled at half strength, and then quickly let up—anyone not of our profession could not detect the alternating tightening and loosening, and saw only that the leather straps were pulled taut . . . But Little Insect released a tortured cry, shrill and forceful, one that would have put the howl of a wolf in the zoological garden to shame. Knowing that this was a sound the Emperor and His women loved to hear, we kept it up, subtly tightening and loosening—no longer involved in putting a man to death, we had become conductors producing exquisite music.

That day, as it turned out, was the Autumn Equinox: the sky was blue, and the sun shone down bright, causing the red walls and glazed tiles on the roofs around us to shimmer in the light, like little reflecting mirrors. All of a sudden a terrible smell filled the air, and I knew at once that the little bastard had shit his pants. I sneaked a look at the viewing stand, where the Emperor sat staring at the scene, His face a rich golden color. Some of His consorts were ashen-faced; others looked on with the black holes of their mouths in full view. The ministers and other officials stood ramrod straight, their arms at their sides, barely able to breathe. Eunuchs and serving girls were banging their heads on the ground as if they were crushing cloves of garlic; the weakest among them had already fainted. I looked over at Grandma Yu and knew he shared my view that the results so far were about what we had expected. The time had come; Little Insect had suffered enough, and we knew that we must not let his stink reach the nostrils of the Emperor and His women. By then, some of the consorts were already covering their mouths with silk hankies. Their sense of smell was keener than the Emperor's, who had abused His nose with snuff until it barely functioned. We needed to put an end to this quickly. If a wayward breeze rose up and carried the stink of Little Insect's shit into the Emperor's nose, and His Majesty was looking to place the blame somewhere, we would get more than we bargained for. Little Insect's innards had probably turned to mush by now anyway, and that stench, which went straight to the brain, was decidedly non-human. It took all my willpower to keep from running to one side to throw up—needless to say, that was out of the question. If Grandma Yu and I had been unable to keep from retching, the impulse would have quickly spread to the viewing stand, with disaster the inevitable result. The sacrifice of our lives—Grandma Yu's and mine—would have been inconsequential, as would the stripping of Board President Wang's official standing. All that mattered was the health and well being of His Imperial Majesty. That thought had already entered my mind. Grandma Yu's, too. It was time for the performance to come to an end. So, on a secret signal, we pulled the straps with all our might, squeezing the iron hoop tighter. Little by little, poor Little Insect's head began to look like a narrow-waisted bottle gourd. The last drop of his sweat had long since left his body, and what came out of him now was a glistening, sticky, foul-smelling grease, reeking nearly as badly as the rancid crotch odor. His howls at this point used up what little of his strength remained and made my flesh crawl, despite my familiarity with killing. No one, not even someone made of iron or steel, could bear up under Yama's Hoop. Why, not even Sun Wukong, the all but indestructible magic monkey who was tempered for forty-nine days in the Jade Emperor's hexagram crucible without capitulating, could endure the pressure of the iron hoop placed on his head by the monk Tripitaka.

The real genius of Yama's Hoop manifested itself in the victim's eyes. As Grandma Yu and I slowly leaned back, the tremors of Little Insect's body traveled through the leather straps and affected our arms. What a pity, those lovely eyes, so expressive, capable of capturing the souls of pretty maidens, slowly began to bulge in the holes of Yama's Hoop. Black, white, streaks of red. Bigger and bigger, like eggs emerging from the backsides of mother hens, little by little, until . . . *pop*. Then another—*pop*—and Little Insect's eyes were hanging by threads on the edge of Yama's Hoop. That, of course, is what Grandma Yu and I had hoped would happen. We followed our planned course of action, at a snail's pace, increasing pressure bit by bit, like inserting a carrot up a bunghole, to narrow the gourd's waist. And when the fateful moment was at hand, we pulled the straps with one final jerk, producing a crunch. Finally, after all that time, Grandma Yu and I released loud sighs. At some point during the process, rivulets of sweat had soaked our backs, while streaks of dried chicken blood had run onto our necks; to the unfocused eye, that made us appear to be bleeding. I knew how I looked by what I saw on Grandma Yu's face.

Little Insect was still alive, but no longer conscious and clearly on the verge of death. Brain matter and blood seeped out through the cracks in his skull. I heard the sound of women vomiting up on the viewing stand, and saw that an elderly, red-capped man had crumpled to the ground, his cap rolling off in the dirt. The moment had arrived:

"The sentence has been carried out!" we shouted in unison. "May it please Your Excellency!"

Board President Wang looked at us over the sleeve covering the lower half of his face, then turned to the viewing stand, assumed a respectful rigid stance, raised his hand, and, with a flicking of his sleeve, knelt in the dirt.

"The sentence has been carried out!" he announced. "May it please Your Majesty!"

Following a prolonged fit of coughing, His Imperial Majesty announced to the assemblage:

"You all saw that, yes? Let him be an example to you!"

His Majesty's voice was not loud, but each word was clear as a bell to the people on and below the viewing stand. While His words were intended for the ears of the eunuchs and palace girls, every leader of the Six Boards, every member of the royal family, and all the ranking officials fell to their knees as if their legs had been snapped. Amid the thumping of heads on the ground, shouts of "Long live His Imperial Majesty, may He live forever!" "This unworthy official deserves a cruel death!" and "Undying gratitude to the Imperial Dragon!" vied in the air like chicken clucks and duck quacks, and that told me, your dieh, and Grandma Yu everything we needed to know about these so-called men of power.

His Majesty stood up. The old eunuch intoned:

"Return to the Palace!"

The Emperor was carried away.

Followed by His royal consorts.

And the palace eunuchs.

Only a clutch of snot-worthy officials and Little Insect, who had died like a tiger, remained.

My legs were so rubbery I could barely stand, and golden stars danced before my eyes. If Grandma Yu had not reached out to hold me up, I would have crumpled to the ground next to Little Insect's corpse before the royal procession had left the site.

2

How dare you glare at me like that!

I've nearly talked myself out, and by now you should understand why I had the nerve to rage against those yayi. If an insignificant County Magistrate, an official about as important as a sesame seed, thinks he can summon me by sending a pair of lackeys to my house, he has too high an opinion of himself. In the presence of the Xianfeng Emperor and the consort who would one day become the Empress Dowager, I, your dieh, had done something that would make your knees buckle before I'd reached my twentieth birthday. When it was all over, word came from the palace that His Imperial Majesty, He with the mouth of gold and speech of jade, had said:

"The executioners from the Board of Punishments performed their task well—methodical, cadenced, and measured. We were treated to a fine performance!"

Justice Board President Wang was granted the title of Junior Guardian to the Crown Prince and was promoted in the official hierarchy. To show his appreciation for this happy turn of events, he presented each of us with two pieces of red silk. Now go ask that Qian fellow if he has ever laid eyes on the Xianfeng Emperor. The answer will be no. Why, he has never even been in the presence of the current occupant of the Dragon Throne, the Guangxu Emperor. How about the Empress Dowager, has he ever seen Her face? Again, no. Not even Her back. And that is why I, your dieh, am not afraid to assume superior airs with him.

I believe that Qian Ding, the Gaomi County Magistrate, will personally come with an invitation, not because he wants to, but at the behest of Governor Yuan. His Excellency and I have met on several occasions. I once did a job for him and did it well, so well, in fact, that he rewarded me with a box of Tianjin's Eighteenth Street Crullers. I know you think that since I have barely stepped out of the house in all the months I have been back, I am little more than a rotting log. Well, for your information, I am being clever by acting dumb. There is a mirror inside me that lets me see the world for exactly what it is. My dear daughter-in-law, do you believe that I do not know what you have been up to? My son is an idiot, so I cannot blame you for sneaking around the way you have been doing. You are a woman, a young woman, and there is nothing wrong with being hot-blooded in ways that involve men. I know that your dieh nearly turned the world upside down and that he is now rotting in prison. The Germans demanded his arrest by name, and not a soul in this county, or for that matter all of Shandong, would dare set him free. He will not escape death. Excellency Yuan Shikai is ruthless. To him, killing a man is no different than squashing a bedbug. He is a man so favored by the foreigners that even the Empress Dowager must rely upon him to get things done. The way I see it, your dieh's life is a pawn in Excellency Yuan's plans. He wants to show not only the Germans, but the people of Gaomi County and all of Shandong the benefits of being law-abiding citizens and the cost of murder, arson, and banditry. The

Imperial Court has given the Germans permission to build their railroad, and that has nothing to do with your dieh. He is like a carpenter locked in stocks of his own creation, a victim of his own actions. You cannot save him, and neither can that Qian fellow of yours. Son, the time has come for you and me to act. It was my wish to, as they say, wash my hands in the golden basin, to keep a low profile and end my days in my country home. But the powers that be have decreed otherwise. This morning, these hands of mine began to itch and grow hot, and I now know that my work is not yet finished. It is heaven's will, from which there is no escape. As for you, daughter-in-law, you accomplish nothing by weeping or venting your loathing. I was the recipient of the Empress Dowager's magnanimity, and will do nothing to displease or dishonor the Court. If I do not kill your dieh, someone else will, and he will be better off in my hands than at the mercy of a butcher, what we call a three-legged cat. There is a popular adage that goes, "If you're kin, you're family." I will do everything in my power to ensure that his is a spectacular death, one that will go down in history. Son, I am going to help you make a name for yourself that will open the eyes of your neighbors. They find us beneath them, do they not? Well and good, we will show them that what is known as "execution" is an art, one that a good man will not do and anyone who is not a good man cannot do. Executioner is an occupation that represents the heart and soul of the Imperial Court. When the calling flourishes, the Imperial Court prospers. But when it languishes, the Imperial Court nears its fated end.

Son, I am using the time before Eminence Qian's palanquin arrives to fill you in on family affairs. I was afraid that if I did not say this to you today, there might not be another chance.

———

3

———

Your grandfather contracted cholera when I, your dieh, was ten years old. The sickness took hold in the morning, and by noon he was dead. Every family in Gaomi County lost someone to the disease that year, and no house was spared the sound of wailing. People were too busy burying their own to give thought to their neighbors' troubles. Your grandmother and I—I know this sounds terrible—dragged your grandfather like a dead dog over to the nearest potter's field and buried him in a makeshift grave. We had no sooner turned to head back home than a pack of wild dogs ran over and dug him up out of the ground. I picked up a piece of broken brick and went after those dogs with carnage on my mind. But they just glared at me through bloodshot eyes, baring their fangs and baying. They feasted on the dead until their whiskers were slick with grease, their bodies sleek and powerful. Fierce as a pack of little tigers, they were a fearful enemy. Your grandmother pulled me away.

"Your grandfather isn't the only one, boy," she said, "so let them go ahead and eat."

Knowing that I had no chance to ward off those crazed dogs, I backed off and watched as they tore the clothes off your grandfather and sank their fangs into his body. They went first to the internal organs and finished by gnawing at his bones.

Five years later, typhoid fever came to Gaomi County and carried off your grandmother, who, like her husband, fell ill in the morning and was dead by noon. But this time I dragged the corpse over to a haystack and cremated it. Now I was on my own, all alone. All day long I roamed the land with a stick in one hand and a wooden ladle in the other, begging for food. At night I slept anywhere I could, staying warm in a haystack or by the lingering heat from a stove frame. Back then, there were lots of young beggars like me, and that made survival especially hard. On some days I knocked on hundreds of doors without getting even the scrapings of a sweet potato for my effort. I was on the verge of starvation when I recalled something your grandmother had told me about a cousin who lived and worked in a yamen in the capital. Life was so good for him, he often sent gifts of silver back home. I decided on the spot what to do. Off to the capital.

I survived the trip by begging or doing occasional odd jobs for people. And so it went, breaking up the journey by staying in a place long enough to earn a little travel money, my progress slow but steady—hungry one day, full the next—until I reached my destination. Joining a bunch of liquor traders, I entered Peking through Chongwen Gate. I vaguely recalled your grandmother's telling me that her cousin worked at the Board of Punishments; by asking along the way, I made it to the Six Boards District, where I walked up to one of the two hard-looking soldier-types who guarded the Board of Punishments gate and was sent flying by the back of his sword. A setback, to be sure, but not nearly enough for me to abandon my plan, not after traveling all that distance. All I could do was hang around the Board, pacing back and forth until my luck changed. The street was fronted by restaurants with fancy entrances, places with names like "Where Immortals Gather" and "The Inn of Sages," all bustling with hungry customers whose carriages and other conveyances interrupted the flow of traffic. The air was heavy with the smells of cooked meat, fish, and poultry. The street was also home to nameless food stands where stuffed buns, wheat cakes, flatbreads, bean curd, and other treats were sold . . . who could have guessed that there could be so many good things to eat in Peking? No wonder people flocked to the city. I've been a survivor all my life, and have enviable judgment. I do not let opportunities pass me by. I did odd jobs for the restaurants, working for leftovers, and since Peking was so big, begging was easier than here in Gaomi. Rich diners would order a table filled with meat or fish or poultry, take a few bites, and leave the rest, which made it possible for me to keep my belly full without spending anything. Then, after filling up with someone's leftovers, I'd find a quiet spot out of the elements and sleep. In the warmth of the sun's rays, I heard my skeleton creak and pop as it grew bigger and stronger. By my second year in Peking, I was a head taller than when I'd arrived. I was like a thirsty rice shoot after a spring rain.

But then, just when I had settled into a carefree life with plenty of food, a gang of beggars attacked me and beat me half to death. The leader, a scary-looking one-eyed man with a knife scar on his cheek, fixed his good eye on me and said:

"You little bastard, what rock did you crawl out from under? Who said you could fill your belly with food in my territory? If I ever see you around here again, I'll break your dog legs and gouge out your dog eyes!"

Sometime in the middle of the night, I crawled out of a foul-smelling ditch and curled up beside a wall, hurting all over, shivering, and hungry. I thought I was going to die. But then, through a haze, I saw your grandmother standing in front of me.

"Don't let this get you down, son," she said. "You are about to enjoy a stroke of good luck."

My eyes snapped open—there was nothing there but the autumn wind making the tips of tree branches moan, nothing but the last chirps of some half-dead crickets in the rotting weeds, that and a sky full of winking stars. But when I closed my eyes again, your grandmother was still there, telling me that my luck was about to change. I opened my eyes, and she was gone. Early the next morning, the sun rose round and red in the eastern sky, making the dew on dead grass shimmer beautifully. A flock of crows flew by, trailing caws behind them on their way to the south side of the city, for what reason I could not say. I would later learn the reason. I was so hungry I could barely stand, and I contemplated going over to beg for something to eat from one of the food stands. What held me back was the fear that I would run into that one-eyed beggar dragon. But then I spotted a piece of cabbage in a little pile of charcoal. I ran over, grabbed it, and carried it back to my spot beside the wall, where I took big crunching bites, just as mounted soldiers in gray uniforms with red borders and hats with red tassels emerged from the Board of Punishments and broke into a trot down the street, newly smoothed over with yellow earth. They had swords on their hips and whips in their hands. Every human who got in their way tasted the whips, as did the dogs. The street was swept clean of obstacles in no time. A few moments later, a prison van rolled out through the gate, pulled by a scrawny mule whose protruding backbone was as sharp as a knife and whose legs looked like spindles. I could not make out the features of the shaggy-haired prisoner standing in the caged wagon, whose ungreased axles creaked as it rolled along, swaying from side to side. The way ahead was led by the horsemen, who had ridden up and back earlier and were followed by a dozen or so men blowing horns, making a noise that could have been mistaken for weeping cattle. A clutch of officials on horseback came next, all in fancy court attire. In the middle was a rotund man with a thin moustache that looked as if it were pasted on. Another ten or fifteen mounted soldiers brought up the rear. Two men in black, with sashes around their waists and red caps on their heads, walked alongside the prison van, each holding a broadsword. They appeared to have ruddy complexions—at the time, I was not aware that they had smeared rooster blood on their faces. They had a spring in their steps, but their footfalls made no noise. I could not take my eyes off them. Fascinated by their impressive bearing, I wondered if I would ever get a chance to learn how to walk that way, like a big black cat. All of a sudden, I heard your grandmother say from behind me:

"That's your uncle, son."

I spun around. There was nothing behind me but the same old gray wall, not a trace of your grandmother. But I knew that her spirit had spoken to me. So I shouted out, "Uncle!" at the same time that someone behind me—or so I thought—shoved me up close to the prison van.

I had no idea what I was doing, but the procession—officials, cavalrymen, everyone—froze. A horse reared up with a loud whinny and threw its rider. I ran up to the swordsmen in black and called out, "Uncle, at last I've found you!" All the bitterness and sorrow I'd experienced over the years came pouring out in a cascade of tears. The two men in black were dumbstruck, their mouths hanging open as they exchanged surprised looks, as if to say:

"Are you that beggar's uncle?"

But before they could gather their wits, soldiers came riding up from front and back, shouting and brandishing their swords until I was hemmed in. I felt a cold shadow settle above my head and immediately felt an enormous hand close around my neck. Whoever it was lifted me off the ground, and I thought he was going to break my neck. With my arms and legs flailing in the air, I kept shouting "Uncle! Uncle!" Until whoever it was flung me to the ground, where, with a splat, I crushed a frog in the road. Worst of all, my face landed in a pile of still-warm horse manure.

A fat, dark-faced man on an enormous roan charger behind the prison van wore a robe with a white leopard embroidered on the chest and a plumed hat studded with crystalline blue gems. One look told me that he was a high official. The soldier got down on one knee and, in a resounding voice, announced:

"Excellency, it is a little beggar."

Two of the soldiers dragged me up in front of the official, where one of them jerked my head back by my hair to give the man on horseback a good look at me. He barely glanced at me. With a heavy sigh, he cursed:

"The little prick has a death wish! Toss him off the road!"

"Sir!" the soldiers barked in unison as they picked me up by my arms, dragged me to the side of the road, and flung me into the air with a "Fuck off!"

Accompanied by their curse, I landed headfirst in the thick mud of the ditch.

Climbing out of that ditch was no easy feat, especially because I couldn't see a thing. By groping my way along, I got my hands on some weeds, with which I managed to clean the muck from my face, just in time to see that the execution procession was heading south, raising clouds of dust on the road. My mind was a blank as I sat there staring at the horses and their riders. But then your grandmother's voice sounded in my ear:

"Go watch them, son; he is your uncle."

I looked around, trying to find your grandmother, but all I saw was the dirt road, some steaming horse manure, and a bunch of sparrows, their heads cocked, their beady black eyes searching for undigested food in the manure. There was no sign of your grandmother. "Niang!" I felt so bad I started to cry, my wails stretching out longer than the ditch I was sitting in. Oh, how I missed your grandmother, and how she disappointed me. You told me to go up to my uncle, Niang, but which one was he? They picked your son up like a dead cat or a rotting dog and flung him into a filthy roadside ditch. I'm lucky I wasn't killed. You must have seen what happened. If your spirit has the power, Niang, light up my path ahead so I can find my way out of this sea of bitterness. If it does not, then please do not talk to me anymore, and stop interfering in my life. Let me live or die, with my little pecker pointing to heaven, on my own. But she ignored my plea. The sound of her aged voice kept swirling inside my head, over and over:

"Go watch them, son; he is your uncle . . . he is your uncle . . ."

So I ran like a maniac to catch up with the procession. One of the benefits of running fast was that your grandmother's voice was stilled. But as soon as I slowed down, that maddening, nagging voice found its way back into my ears. Running like a madman was the only way I could escape the mutterings of her floating spirit, even if it meant getting flung into another foul ditch by soldiers in their red-tasseled straw hats. I fell in behind the procession as it passed through Xuanwu Gate and headed down the narrow, bumpy road on its way to the execution ground by the open-air market. It was my first time on this infamous road. By now there are layers of my footprints on it. The scenery outside the wall had a more desolate feel than inside. Dark green vegetable plots separating the squat houses on both sides of the road were planted with cabbages, turnips, and beans on trellises, the leaves now withered, the vines all jumbled. People working plots had little or no interest in the raucous procession passing in front of them. A few cast stony glances behind them, but most went on about their business without looking up.

As the procession neared its destination, the twisting road opened out onto a broad execution ground in which a pack of bored observers were milling around a raised platform. There were several beggars, including the one-eyed dragon who had beaten me. This was obviously his territory. The mounted soldiers spurred their horses on to form a line. The pair of magnificent executioners opened the cage and pulled the prisoner out. His legs must have been broken by the way they dragged him along the ground. The useless limbs reminded me of wilted onions. They carried him up onto the execution platform, where he crumpled to the floor as soon as they let go. He was all flesh and no bones. The onlookers began to make noise, shouting their disapproval of the condemned man's poor showing. "Coward!" "Softy!" "Get up!" "Sing a line of opera!" The shouts seemed to have an effect on the man, who began to stir, a little bit at a time, flesh and bones, with painful slowness, but enough to earn him a round of applause and shouts of encouragement. He pushed himself up onto his knees as best he could. The crowd demanded more:

"Good man, show some bravado! Say something. How about 'Take off my head and leave a bowl-sized scar!' or 'I'll be back in twenty years, better than ever!'"

The man's mouth twisted as he cried out tearfully:

"Heaven is my witness, I am innocent!"

The spectators gazed at the man in stunned silence. The two executioners were impassive, as always. And then your grandmother's spirit spoke to me from behind.

"Shout, son, be a good boy and shout. Call to them. He's your uncle!"

There was a sense of urgency in her voice, as the pitch rose and grew increasingly shrill. Cold, shuddering blasts of air hit the nape of my neck. If I hadn't shouted, she'd have throttled me. There was no way out, so, risking retaliation from one of the fierce sword-wielding soldiers, I cried out in a choked voice:

"Uncle—"

Every eye in the crowd was on me in an instant—the official witnesses, the soldiers, the beggars, though I've forgotten what the looks in those eyes were like. But not those of the prisoner; I'll never forget the look in his eyes. His blood-encrusted head jerked upward as he opened his bloodshot eyes and looked straight at me; I fell backward as if I'd been struck by red-tipped arrows. The next thing I heard was the voice of the dark, fat official in charge:

"It's time—"

Trumpets blared, and the soldiers pursed their lips to make mournful sounds as one of the executioners grabbed the prisoner's queue and pulled his head forward to expose the scruff of his neck for the other man, who raised his sword, turned slightly to the right, then handsomely to the left, and—*swish*—the glinting blade arced downward, truncating a scream of tragic innocence. The man in front was already holding aloft the severed head. He and the other man now stood shoulder to shoulder, faced the witnessing official, and shouted in unison:

"May it please Your Excellency, the sentence has been carried out!"

The dark, fat official, who was still sitting astride his horse, waved his hand in the direction of the severed head, as if seeing off an old friend, then reined his horse around and clip-clopped away from the execution ground. Whoops of excitement burst from the crowd of onlookers, as the beggars boldly rushed up to the stand to await the moment when they could climb up and strip the man's clothing off. Blood was still pumping from the corpse, which had pitched forward and was resting on the stump of its neck, conjuring up the image of an overturned liquor vat.

That was the moment everything became clear. The official witness to the execution was not my uncle, nor were the executioners or any of the soldiers. My uncle was the man whose head had just been lopped off.

That night I went looking for a willow tree with a low-hanging branch, and when I found it, I took the sash from around my waist, made a noose, tossed it over the branch, and stuck my head in. Dieh was dead, and so was Niang; and now my uncle, the only family member I had left, had just been beheaded. There wasn't another soul in this world I could turn to. Ending my life now was the only answer. But at the very moment I was about to rub noses with King Yama of the Underworld, a huge hand grabbed me by the seat of my pants.

It was the man who had just beheaded my uncle.

He took me to a restaurant called The Casserole, where he ordered a plate of bean curd and fish heads. While I was eating—just me—he sat watching me. He didn't even touch the tea the waiter had brought him. When I finished with a loud belch, he said:

"I was your uncle's good friend, and if you are willing, you can be my apprentice."

The impressive image he'd created earlier that day reappeared: standing tall and unmoving, then quickly turning slightly to the right, his right arm circling the air like a crescent moon, and *swish*—my uncle's head was raised high in the air, accompanied by his scream of innocence . . . your grandmother's voice sounded again in my ear, but now it was uncommonly gentle, and the sense of gratitude she felt was clear and sustaining.

"My dear son," she said, "get down on your knees and kowtow to your shifu."

I did that, and with tears in my eyes, though if you want to know the truth, my uncle's death meant nothing to me. I was concerned only about myself. The cause of those hot tears was the realization that my daydream was about to come true. I wanted nothing more than to become a man who could lop off someone's head without blinking. Those two men's carriage and icy demeanor lit up my dreams.

Son, your dieh's shifu was the man I've mentioned to you hundreds of times—Grandma Yu. He later told me that he had been sworn brothers with my jailer uncle, who had committed a capital crime, and that it had been his good fortune to die by his hand. *Swish*, faster than the wind. Grandma said that when his sword severed my uncle's head, he heard it say:

"That is my nephew, Elder Brother. Watch over him for me!"

CHAPTER THREE

Xiaojia's Foolish Talk

My name is Zhao, Zhao Xiaojia. I get up early with a laugh, ha-ha.
(Damned fool, aha!) In my dream last night, I saw a white tiger at our
house. Wearing a red jacket, tail standing up in the air. (Ha-ha-ha.) Big
tail big tail big tail. White Tiger sat across from me, mouth open, white
fangs, a great big maw. Big white fangs big white fangs big white fangs.
(Ha-ha-ha.) Do you plan to eat me, White Tiger? There are more fat
pigs and fat sheep than I can eat, White Tiger said, so why eat you raw?
If you're not going to eat me, why have you come to the house of my Pa?
Zhao Xiaojia, White Tiger said, listen to me. I hear you are obsessed with
a desire for tiger's whiskers. So I've brought some for you to pluck from my
jaw. (Ha-ha-ha, a damned fool, aha!)

—*Maoqiang* Sandalwood Death. *A child's aria*

1

Meow, meow, I learned how to sound like a cat before I could talk. My niang
said that the longest whisker on a tiger is precious, and that anyone who owns
one can carry it on his body and see a person's true form. All living humans,
she said, are reincarnations of animals. If a person gets one of those precious
whiskers, what he sees is not people. On the street, in alleyways, in taverns,
in a public bath, what he sees are oxen, horses, dogs, cats, and the like. *Meow,
meow.* There was once a man, Niang said, who traveled east of the Shanhai Pass,
where he killed a tiger to get one of those precious whiskers. He was afraid of
losing it, so he wrapped it in three outer and three inner layers, then sewed it
into the lining of his padded jacket. When he returned home, his mother asked
him, "Did you make your fortune during all those years you were away up
north, son?" "My fortune? No," he said proudly, "but I did lay my hands on a
rare treasure." He reached inside his jacket, tore open the lining, and removed
the bundle, which he unwrapped to show her the whisker. But when he looked
up, she'd vanished, her place taken by a nearsighted old dog. The poor man

was so frightened by this that he ran outside and collided with an old horse carrying a hoe over its shoulder. The horse was puffing on a pipe and snorting streams of smoke from its flared nostrils. The man nearly died of fright at this encounter, and was about to run away when he heard the horse call out his childhood name: "Aren't you Xiaobao? Don't you even recognize your own dieh, you little bastard?" The whisker, that's what made all this happen. He quickly rewrapped it and put it away. Now he could see that his dieh was not an old horse and his niang was not an old dog.

Getting one of those whiskers has long been a dream of mine. *Meow, meow.* I make this clear to everyone I know and ask people I meet if they can tell me where I can get one. Someone once said that the forests of the great Northeast are the best place. I was burning to go see, and would have if it hadn't meant leaving my wife. A precious tiger's whisker, just think how wonderful that would be! Well, I'd just put up a meat rack on the street when a huge boar in a long robe under a short jacket, wearing a black silk skullcap and carrying a thrush in a birdcage, sauntered up. "Two catties of pork, Xiaojia," it said. "Give me a good weigh, and make it streaky pork." There was no question that it was a boar standing in front of me, but the voice was that of Li Shizhai, Elder Li, the father of Graduate Li, a learned local scholar respected by all. If he didn't get the respect he thought he deserved, he intoned in a loud voice, "A base man cannot be taught!" Who could have guessed that he'd actually be a boar? Even he didn't know. No one but I knew. But if I told him, I'd get a taste of his drag-onhead cane, for sure. The boar hadn't even left when a white swan sashayed up carrying a bamboo basket on its wing. When it was right in front of me, it gave me a dirty look and said in a voice dripping with spite, "Xiaojia, you heartless fiend. I found a fingernail when I bit into the dog meat jelly you sold me yesterday. Are you selling human flesh and calling it dog meat?" It turned to the boar. "Did you hear what happened? Two nights ago, the Zheng family's child bride was beaten to death. Her battered body was a mass of bruises!" Now that the swan had spewed its garbage, it turned back to me and said, "Give me two catties of dog meat jerky. We'll try something different." "Who do you think you are, you stinking bitch? A big-assed swan is what you are. I ought to turn you into swan jelly. That'd shut that mouth of yours once and for all."

—If I'd owned a tiger's whisker, think how wonderful that would have been! But I didn't.

Uncle He was having a drink in the tavern that rainy afternoon—he was an ugly man with a pointed mouth, an ape-like chin, and shifty eyes, a damned gorilla if I ever saw one—when I told him about the tiger's whisker. "You're a man of the world, Uncle He," I said, "so this is something you must know about. And you must know where to get one." "Xiaojia," he said with a chuckle, "you idiot. What's your wife up to while you're here selling meat?" "My wife is delivering dog meat to Eminence Qian, her gandieh." "I'd say she's delivering the human kind," Uncle He said. "She's a nice morsel, tender and tasty." "Stop trying to be funny, Uncle; we sell pork and dog meat, that's all. Who ever heard of selling the human kind? Besides, Eminence Qian isn't a tiger, so why would he want to feast on my wife's flesh? If he did, he'd have finished her off by now. But she's still here, in the flesh." With a strange laugh, Uncle He said, "Eminence Qian is not a White Tiger, he's a Green Dragon, the Taoist guardian. It's your wife who's the White Tiger." "Now you're really not making sense, Uncle He. Without one of those tiger's whiskers, how could you see the true form of Eminence Qian *or* my wife?" "Pour me another drink, idiot," Uncle He said, "and I'll tell you where you can get a tiger's whisker." I filled his glass to the brim.

"You know," he said, "that they're real treasures, worth a great quantity of silver." "I'm not interested in selling them," I said. "I want one for myself. Just think, I could walk down the street with my tiger's whisker and meet up with all kinds of animals wearing clothes and talking just like you and me. Wouldn't that be terrific?" "Are you serious about getting a tiger's whisker?" Uncle He asked. "Yes," I said, "very serious. I dream about it." "Well, then, give me a plate of chopped dog meat, and I'll tell you." "If you'll tell me where to get a tiger's whisker, Uncle He, you can have the whole dog, and I won't charge you anything." I cut off a dog's leg and handed it to him. Then I stood there, gaping expectantly. He leisurely sipped what was in his glass and sampled the dog meat. "Idiot," he said with slow deliberation, "do you really want a tiger's whisker?" "Uncle He, I've given you spirits to drink and dog to eat, so if you won't tell me now, you've been playing tricks on me, and I'll go home and tell my wife what you've done. You can fool me easily enough, but she's a different story. All she has to do is curl her lip, and you'll find yourself in the county yamen getting your ass whipped." Now that I'd brought my wife into the discussion, he said, with a note of urgency, "Xiaojia, my good little nephew, if I tell you, you must promise never to tell anybody who you heard it from, especially your wife. If you do, any tiger's whisker you get your hands on will lose its power." "All right, I promise, I won't tell a soul, and that includes my wife. If I do, I hope her belly starts to hurt." "I'll be damned, Xiaojia, what the hell kind of oath is that? What does a pain in your wife's belly have to do with anything?" "Are you joking? Any time her belly starts to hurt, my heart aches and I end up bawling like a baby." "All right, then," Uncle He said, "I'll tell you." He took a look out on the street to make sure that no one was listening. Rain was sheeting off of eaves, a curtain of white. I pressed him to tell me. "We must be very careful," he said. "If somebody hears us, you'll never get your treasure." He leaned over and put his burning lips up to my ear. "Your wife goes to see His Eminence every day," he whispered. "His bed is covered by a tiger skin, and what are the chances of *not* finding a tiger's whisker on a complete pelt? Now, pay attention. Have your wife pluck a curly golden whisker for you. Those, my friend, are the real treasures. None of the others are any good."

When my wife returned home from delivering the dog meat, the night sky was inky black. "Why are you so late?" With a smile, she said, "Use your head, you poor fool. I had to wait till His Eminence ate every bite. And don't forget, it's raining, so it gets dark early. Why haven't you lit the lamp?" "I'm not doing needlework, and I'm not reading, so why waste the oil?" "My dear Xiaojia, you're all about getting by, aren't you? A little bit of oil won't make the difference between rich and poor. And we're certainly not poor. My gandieh told me that from this year on, we're exempt from paying taxes. Go ahead, light the lamp." So I lit the bean-oil lamp, and she adjusted the wick with one of her hairpins, flooding the room with bright, holiday-like light. I saw that her face was red and her eyes were moist, the way she looked when she was drinking. "Have you been drinking?" "Greedy cats have pointy noses," she said. "My gandieh was afraid I'd be cold on the way home, so he gave me what little was left in his flask. It was pouring out there, as if the River of Heaven had been diverted to earth. Now turn around; I'm going to change into dry clothes." "Why? What you need is to climb into a nice warm bed." "Now, that's a good idea," she said with a giggle. "Who'd dare call our Xiaojia a fool? No, he's brilliant!" With that she began undressing, throwing one item of clothing after another into a wooden tub, until she stood there, milky white, like a luscious eel just out of the water. She arched her back and hopped up onto the heated bed, then arched it again and slipped under the covers. I stripped and climbed in beside her. But she rolled herself up in the bedding. "Don't bother me, my young fool; I've been running around so much today I can barely keep my bones attached to my body." "I won't bother you," I said, "but you have to promise something. I want you to get me a tiger's whisker." Again she giggled. "Where, my little fool, am I going to find you a tiger's whisker?" "Somebody said you could get one. I want a curly one with a golden-yellow tip." Her face turned bright red. "What son of a bitch told you that? I'll flay his dog hide right off him! Give me the name of the bastard who put you up to this!" "You'll have to kill me first. I've sworn on your belly not to tell. If I say who it was, your belly is going to hurt." She just shook her head. "You poor fool, your niang was teasing you. Use your head. Things like that don't happen in this world." "Other people can tease me, but not my niang. I want a tiger's whisker; I've wanted one all my life, so help me get one, I beg you." "Where am I going to do that?" She was getting angry. "And a curly one, at that. You're not a fool, you're a big fool!" "The person told me that Eminence Qian uses a tiger pelt as a bedspread, and where there's a tiger pelt, there must be tiger's whiskers." "Xiaojia," she said with a heavy sigh, "Xiaojia, what do you expect me to say to that?" "Help me get one. I'm begging you. If you won't do it, then I won't let you deliver any more dog meat. Someone said you really deliver the human kind." "Who said that?" she demanded, gnashing her teeth. "All you need to know is that somebody said it." "All right, Xiaojia, if I get you what you want, will you leave me alone?" I just grinned.

My wife was as good as her word—she brought me a tiger's whisker the next night. It had a golden-yellow tip. "Don't let it fly away," she said as she handed it to me. Then she doubled over laughing. My heart beat wildly as I clutched my whisker. A treasure I'd longed for most of my life, how could it have come so easily? Well, I examined it closely. It was just as Uncle He had described, curly with a golden-yellow tip. I held it between my fingers till my wrist tingled. It felt heavy in my hand. I looked up and said to my wife, "Let's see what you really are." She curled her lip. "Sure," she said with a smile, "take a good look and tell me if I'm a phoenix or a peacock." "Uncle He says you're a white tiger." Her face colored. "So it was that lousy maggot who told you," she cursed. "I'm going to have my gandieh drag him over to the yamen tomorrow and see that he gets two hundred whacks with the paddle. He'll know what it feels like to have his ass turned into fried bamboo shoots and meat!"

Still clutching the tiger's whisker in the lighted room, I stared at her. My heart was racing, my wrist shaking. Now, with heaven's help, I was going to see my wife's true form! She was an animal, but which one? A pig? A dog? A rabbit? A goat? A fox? A hedgehog? I didn't care what she was, as long as it wasn't a snake. I've been afraid of snakes since I was a little boy, and I'm more afraid of them now than ever before. If I so much as step on a rope, I jump three feet in the air. My niang said that snakes usually turn into women, and that most beautiful women are transformed snakes. Sooner or later, one of those snake-women will suck dry the brain of any man who sleeps with her, she told me. Don't let me down, heaven. I don't care what my wife is, even a toad or a gecko, just so it isn't a snake. And if she is, well, I'll pick up my butcher's tools and run off with my tail between my legs. So with all those wild thoughts scrambling the landscape in my head, I sized up my wife, who turned the lamp up as high as it would go, until the wick was as red as a pomegranate and really lit up the room. Her hair was so black it was almost blue, as if oiled. Her shiny forehead was as bright as the belly of a porcelain vase. Her brows arched and curved like a pair of willow leaves. Her nose was so white it was nearly transparent, as if carved from a tender lotus root. Her limpid eyes looked like grapes floating in egg white. Her mouth, which was a little too big for her face, curled upward at the corners, like water chestnuts, the lips naturally red. I could have looked till my eyes ached and not known what she was before she was a woman.

She curled her lips into a sneer and said with palpable sarcasm, "Well? Tell me, what am I?"

Bewildered, I shook my head. "I don't know, you're just you. How can this treasure lose its effectiveness when it's in my hand?"

She reached out and tapped me on the forehead with one finger. "You're possessed," she said. "You've let a whisker take control of your life. Your niang told you a story one time, and you elevated it into your life's work, like treating a stick as a needle. Are you ready to finally give it up now?"

I shook my head again. "You're wrong. My niang wouldn't lie to me. The rest of the world might, but not her."

"Then why doesn't it let you see what I am? I don't need a tiger's whisker to show me what you are—you're a pig, a big, stupid pig."

I knew this was her way to make me feel bad. She couldn't possibly see my true form without a tiger's whisker. But why wasn't I able to see hers, either, even *with* one? Why wasn't my little treasure working? Oh, no! Uncle He had said that if I mentioned his name, the thing wouldn't work. And that's what I'd just done without realizing it. I was crushed. How stupid could I have been, ruining something I'd worked so hard to get? I stood there with the whisker in my hand, in a daze. Hot tears streamed from my eyes.

My wife sighed when she saw me crying. "You fool, when will you grow up?" She sat up, snatched the whisker out of my hand, and, with a single puff, blew it out of sight. "My treasure—!" I shrieked tearfully. She wrapped her arms around my neck and tried to calm me down. "There, now, don't be foolish. Here, let me hold you, and we can get some sleep." But I fought my way out of her grip. "My tiger's whisker! It's mine!" Frantically, I groped all over the bed trying to find it. Oh, how I hated her at that moment. "I want my tiger's whisker! You owe me!" I went over and picked up the lamp to help me look for my treasure, cursing and crying the whole time. She just sat there watching me, shaking her head one minute and sighing the next. "Stop looking," she said at last. "It's right here." I was thrilled. "Where? Where is it?" With her thumb and index finger, she held the curly tiger's whisker with its golden-yellow tip and laid it across my palm. "Do a better job of holding on to it this time," she said. "If you lose it again, don't blame me." I curled my fingers tightly around it. It might not do what I wanted it to do, but it was still a treasure. But why wouldn't it work for me? I needed to try again. So once again, I stared into my wife's face. If it works this time, I was thinking, if she turns out to be a snake, then so be it. But once again she was just my wife, nothing more.

"Hear me out, my foolish husband. My niang told me the same story yours told you. She said the whisker doesn't work all the time, only at critical moments. Otherwise, it would be nothing but trouble. How would you live if all you ever saw were animals? So listen to me and put that thing in a safe place, where you can retrieve it at a critical moment. It'll work then."

"Honest? You're not lying, are you?"

She nodded. "Why would I want to lie to my beloved husband?"

I believed her. After scaring up a piece of red cloth, I wrapped up my treasure, tied it tight with string, and hid it in a crack in the wall.

2

My dieh is a force unto himself. He sent Magistrate Qian's two yayi back to the yamen empty-handed. You might not know what the Magistrate is capable of, Dieh, but I do. When Xiaokui from the Dongguan oil mill spat at his palanquin as it passed by, a pair of yayi dragged him off in chains. Two weeks later, his father sold two acres of land to pay someone to stand as guarantor to get his son back. But by then one of Xiaokui's legs was shorter than the other, and he not only walked with a limp, but the toes of one foot dragged along the ground. They started calling him the foreigner, because the lines he scraped in the dirt looked like foreign writing. After that, any time he heard the name "Magistrate Qian," he foamed at the mouth and fainted. Xiaokui knew what Magistrate Qian was capable of. Not only doesn't he dare spit at the palanquin when it passes by anymore, but the minute he sees it, he wraps his arms around his head, turns tail, and hobbles off. What you've done today, Dieh, is a lot worse than spitting at his palanquin. I may be a fool in other things, but where Magistrate Qian is concerned, I'm as smart as I need to be. Even though my wife is the Magistrate's little pet, he is strictly impartial. How could he let you get away with what you've done when he went and arrested that disappointing gongdieh of mine?

On the other hand, I could see that my dieh was no pushover. He was hard as nails, not soft as bean curd, a man who'd done and seen plenty in the nation's capital, where he'd lopped off a truckload—maybe a shipload—of heads; a power struggle between him and Magistrate Qian would be like a fight between a dragon and a tiger, and I could not say who would come out ahead. Now, at this critical moment, I was suddenly reminded of my tiger's whisker. Truth is, that treasure was never far from my mind. According to my wife, it was my amulet, which could turn bad luck into good as long as I kept it with me. So I jumped onto the bed, reached over to the wall, and retrieved my red bundle, which I frantically unwrapped to make sure the curly, golden-tipped tiger's whisker was still there. It was. As my little treasure lay in my hand, I felt it move, little flicks, sort of like a hornet's stinger, against my palm.

A huge white snake, as big around as a water bucket, stood in front of the bed and thrust its head toward me, a purple forked tongue darting in and out between its red lips. "Xiaojia." It was my wife's voice! "What do you think you're doing?" Heaven help me, how could you do this to me? You know I'm afraid of snakes, and so you made sure that's what my wife is. Someone I've frolicked in bed with for the last ten years without knowing she was a snake. My own wife, a reincarnated white snake. Of course, *The Legend of the White Snake*, now I get it. Back when she was on the stage, she played the part of the white snake, and I'm the scholar she married, Xu Xian. But why hasn't she sucked out my brains? Because she isn't all snake. She has a snake's head, but arms and legs, too, and breasts. And there's hair on her head. Still, well and truly frightened, I flung the whisker away like a piece of hot charcoal and broke out in a full-body sweat.

My wife stood there sneering at me. Since I'd just had a glimpse of her true form, seeing her now as my wife was both strange and unsettling. That big, fleshy snake living inside her could break through the flimsy skin covering and take its true form any time it wanted. Maybe she already knew that I'd seen her true form, which would have explained the strange, forced smile on her lips. "Well, did you see it?" she asked. "What am I behind this human façade?" Cold rays of light shot from her eyes, eyes once beautiful but now ugly and malignant, the eyes of a snake.

A foolish grin was the best I could manage to mask my terror. My lips had stopped doing my bidding; my skin tingled. She must have released a cloud of noxious airs onto my face. "No, I didn't," I stammered, "I saw nothing."

"Liar," she said with a sneer, "I'm sure you saw something." A chilling, foul odor emerging from her mouth—snake's breath—hit me square in the face.

"Tell me the truth, what am I beneath all this?" She smiled in a peculiar way, and light glinted off the shiny, scaly things on her face. I could not tell the truth, not without harm to myself, and I was suddenly no longer the fool I'd always been. "Really, I didn't see a thing." "You can't fool me, Xiaojia, you're a terrible liar. Your face is red, and you're sweating. So, come on, tell me. Am I a fox? Or maybe a weasel. Or how about a white eel?" White eels are members of the snake family, real close members. She was trying to trick me. But I was not about to be fooled. The only way I'd let my tongue betray me was if she came out and admitted that in reality she was a white snake. The surest way to have her take on her true form was to tell her I'd seen that she was a reincarnated white snake. She'd open that bloody mouth wide and swallow me up. No, she knew I always carried a knife, and if I wound up inside her, I'd slice her open. That would be the end of her. So instead, she'd open a hole in my head with her tongue, which was harder than a woodpecker's beak, and suck out my brains. Then she'd suck the marrow from my bones, followed by my blood, reducing me to a pile of hollow bones wrapped in human skin. You cannot pry the words out of me, not even in your dreams. My niang used to say to me, "Pretend you know nothing, and the spirits will have no control over you." "Honest, I saw nothing." This time she reacted by laughing and changing form. Laughing made her look more human and less snake-like. Pretty much all human. She began crawling out of the room, her body soft and pliable, saying on her way out, "Take that treasure of yours and see what animal your dieh is after spending forty-four years killing people. This is just a guess, but I'll say eight or nine chances out of ten, he's a poisonous snake." More talk of snakes! I knew she was like the fleeing bandit who yells "Stop, thief!" and I was not about to be fooled by that.

I put my treasure back in its hiding place in the wall, beginning to wish I'd never gotten it in the first place. The less you know, the better, most of the time. Knowledge only gets you into trouble. Knowing a person's true form is especially dangerous, because that's something you cannot get past. Now that I'd seen what my wife really was, that was the end of it for me. If I'd been ignorant of her snake background, nothing could have stopped me from wrapping my arms around her in bed. Think I'd dare do that now? That was reason enough not to want to know what my dieh was. I was already pretty much a loner, and now that my wife was a snake, my dieh was all I had.

So I hid my treasure and went into the living room, where I got the shock of my life. Heaven help me, there on my dieh's sandalwood chair sat an emaciated panther! It turned to look at me out of the corner of its eye. I'd seen that look before, and it didn't take a genius to know that it was in fact my dieh in an earlier form. It opened its mouth, making its whiskers twitch. "Son," it said, "so now you know. Your dieh was the preeminent executioner at the Great Qing Court, the recipient of accolades from the Empress Dowager Herself. It is a calling that must stay in the family."

My heart skipped a beat. Heaven help me, what was *that* all about? In the story my niang told me about the tiger's whisker, she said that after the man hid the whisker he'd gone up north to get, he could only see people as people—his dieh was not a horse and his niang was not a dog. I'd tucked my whisker back into a crack in the wall, so why was I now seeing my dieh as a panther? My eyes must have been deceiving me. Maybe the effects of that thing lingered on my hand. I was already having trouble accepting the fact that my wife was a white snake, and now that I'd discovered that my dieh was a panther, well, for me the road ahead was a dead end. In a state of panic, I ran into the yard, where I scooped up a pail of water and frantically washed my hands and rinsed out my eyes. Then I buried my head in the water. One weird occurrence after another that day had swelled my head, and I was hoping that a cold-water bath would bring it down to size.

I returned to the living room, only to find the panther still sitting in my dieh's sandalwood armchair. There was a look of disdain in those eyes, disappointment that I hadn't made much of myself. A red-tasseled skullcap was perched atop its large, furry head; two hairy ears were pricked straight up in a state of vigilance. Dozens of long, wiry whiskers fanned out from the sides of its wide mouth. After licking its chops and the tip of its nose with a spiky, slurpy tongue, it yawned with red grandeur. It was wearing a tea-colored short jacket over a long robe, from whose wide sleeves fleshy, clawed paws emerged. It was such a strange, comical scene, I didn't know whether to laugh or to cry. At the moment, those claws were deftly manipulating a string of sandalwood prayer beads.

Niang once told me that a tiger manipulates Buddhist prayer beads to give the impression of goodness. She never said anything about a panther.

I backed up slowly, barely able to keep from turning and running. My wife was a snake, my dieh a panther. This house was no place for me. I'd be in real trouble if either one of them reverted back to its original form. Even if what we'd meant to each other kept them from eating me, I don't think I could stand the crushing anxiety of doubt. I forced a smile, hoping that would keep him from getting suspicious. It was my only hope. That panther was showing its age, but its hind legs, folded into a crouch in the armchair, looked to have plenty of spring left—leaping a good five or six feet would be no problem. Sure, its teeth had worn down over the years, but those steely fangs would have no trouble crushing my throat. And let's say I had the leg strength to get away from the panther; there'd still be the white snake. According to my niang, a snake that has gained spirit status is half a dragon and can move like the wind, faster than a racehorse. She said she'd actually seen a snake as thick as her arm and as long as a carrying pole chase down a fawn in the wild. The young deer had run and bounded through the grass, fast as an arrow off the bow. The snake? With the front half of its body raised off the ground, it parted the grass with a *whoosh*. In the end, it swallowed the fawn whole. My wife was as big around as a water bucket and had reached heights of Taoist cultivation way beyond that of the snake that ate the fawn. I could run faster than a jackrabbit and still not escape something that could soar with the clouds and mist.

"Where are you going, Xiaojia?" A gloom-laden voice sounded behind me. I turned to look. The panther had risen up out of the sandalwood chair, its forelegs pressing down on the armrests, its hind legs now touching the brick floor. I was caught in a withering glare. Heaven help me, the old-timer was ready to pounce, and could easily make it out into the yard in one leap! Don't panic, I told myself to boost my courage; calm down. Heh-heh, I feigned a laugh. "I'm going to take care of that pig, Dieh. Pork must be sold when it's fresh. It's heavier on the scale and it looks better." The panther smirked. "It's time for you to take up a new calling, son," the panther said. "It too involves 'killing,' but pig-killing is one of the three debased occupations, while man-killing has been elevated to one of the nine chosen occupations." I kept backing up. "You're right, Dieh. From today on, I'll stop killing pigs and learn from you how to kill a man . . ." At that moment the white snake raised its head, a head covered with glistening, scary coin-sized scales all the way down its white neck. "Cluck cluck cluck cluck" . . . a strand of laughter sounding more like a laying hen sputtered from her mouth. "Xiaojia," she said, "did you see it? What animal was your dieh? A wolf? A tiger? A poisonous snake?" I watched her scaly white neck rise up as the red jacket and green pants she was wearing slid off her body like a multihued snakeskin. Her red-tinged black tongue was within striking distance of my eyes. Niang! I lost it then, jumping backward in terror, and— bang! I heard what sounded like a thunderclap and saw stars—Niang! I passed out, foaming at the mouth. My wife later said I'd suffered an epilepsy attack. Nonsense! How can someone who's not an epileptic suffer one of those? What happened is that in my panicky jump I hit my head on a doorjamb nail. The pain knocked me out.

A woman was calling me from far, far off: "Xiaojia . . . Xiaojia . . ." I couldn't tell whether it was my niang or my wife. I had a splitting headache, and when I tried to open my eyes, I couldn't—my lids were stuck shut by something gummy. There was a perfumed smell in the air, and then the smell of crushed grass, and finally the heavy, rank odor of boiled pig entrails. The calls kept coming: "Xiaojia, Xiaojia . . ." Then something cool and refreshing pelted me in the face, and my mind was abruptly as clear as a bell.

The first thing I saw when I opened my eyes was a rainbow of dancing colors. Then I saw brilliant flashes of light, followed by a big, pasty face that nearly touched mine. It belonged to my wife. "Xiaojia," I heard her say, "you scared me half to death." She was tugging me with a hand that felt sweaty, and finally managed, very clumsily, to pull me up off the floor. I shook my head. "Where am I?" "Where are you? You're home, you poor fool." Home. Feeling a sense of agony, I frowned, as everything that had just happened came back in a flash. "As heaven is my witness, I don't want that tiger's whisker, I don't! I'm going to throw it into the fire." She smirked and put her mouth up close to my ear. "You big fool," she said, "did you really think that's a tiger's whisker? It's one of my hairs." I shook my head. It hurt, it hurt like crazy. "No, that can't be. You don't have hair like that. But even if you did, how do you explain the fact that when I held it in my hand, I could see your true form? And I saw my dieh's true form even when I wasn't holding it." "Tell me, then," she said, her curiosity piqued, "what was I?" As I looked into that fair, fresh face, then down at her arms and legs, before glancing over at my dieh, who was slumped in his armchair, everything suddenly cleared up. I must have been dreaming. My wife as a snake, my dieh as a panther, it was all a dream. She laughed a strange little laugh. "Who knows, maybe I am a snake. Yes, that's exactly what I am, a snake!" Her face lengthened, and her eyes turned green. "If I'm a snake," she added venomously, "I'll wriggle my way into your belly!" Her face grew longer and longer, her eyes a deeper and deeper green, and scales reappeared on her neck. I covered my eyes with my hands and screamed: "No, you're not, you're not a snake, you're human!"

3

The gate to our compound flew open.

There stood the two yayi my father had sent packing, except that now they were gray wolves in human clothing. Hands resting on their swords, they stood one on each side of the door. Scared out of my wits, I shut my eyes in hopes that this would rescue me from my dream. When I reopened my eyes, I saw that they now had yayi faces, but the backs of their hands were coated with fur, and their fingers ended in sharp claws. I was struck by the sad realization that my wife's hair was more powerful than any tiger's whisker could ever be. The whisker worked its magic only when you held it in your hand, but all my wife's hair had to do was touch your hand to hold you in its supernatural power, and then it made no difference whether you kept it or threw it away, whether you were aware of its existence or not.

After the wolf-yayi took their positions by the sides of the gate, a four-man palanquin was set down on the cobblestone street in front of the gate. The bearers—a quartet of donkeys, with big, floppy ears hidden under stovepipe caps, but with easily identifiable faces—rested their glistening front hooves on the chair shafts, slobber oozing from their mouths as their breath came in snorts. By all appearances, they had run the whole way, their hoof-encased boots covered with a thick layer of dust. The legal secretary, Diao, whom everyone called Diao Laoye—he was a pointy-faced hedgehog—grabbed a corner of the chair curtain with his pink paw and pulled it open. I knew it was Magistrate Qian's official palanquin, the one Xiaokui had spat at to bring the wrath of its owner down on his head, and I knew that the person about to step out was Gaomi County's Magistrate, His Eminence Qian Ding, my wife's gandieh. Logically, that made him my gandieh as well. But when I told my wife that I'd like to go along to pay my respects to him, she flatly refused. Fairness requires me to admit that Magistrate Qian had generously exempted us from paying taxes over the years, saving us a lot of silver. But he really shouldn't have broken Xiaokui's leg just because he spat at his palanquin. Xiaokui was a friend of mine, after all, even though he'd said to me, "You really are a fool, Xiaojia. Magistrate Qian has given you a cuckold's green hat, so why don't you wear it?" Well, I went home and said to my wife, "Dear wife, Xiaokui said that Magistrate Qian has given me a green hat. What's it look like? Why won't you show me?" "You idiot," she cursed, "Xiaokui is a bad person, and I don't want you spending time with him. If you do, I won't sleep with you anymore." Before three days had passed, some yayi had broken Xiaokui's leg. Breaking somebody's leg just because he spits at you makes you a very cruel man, Magistrate Qian. So now here you are, and I want to see just what you used to be.

I watched as a white tiger head, as big as a willow basket, emerged from the palanquin. Heaven help me, Magistrate Qian was a white tiger in human form! No wonder my niang said that the Emperor is a reincarnated dragon and that high officials are reincarnated tigers. A blue official's cap sat atop the tiger's head, while its body was sheathed in a red official's robe with a pair of strange-looking white birds—neither chickens nor ducks—embroidered on the chest. Bigger than my dieh, a skinny panther, this was a very fat tiger. It was doughy white, my dieh coal black. The tiger stepped down and lumbered in through our gate, taking slow, measured steps. The hedgehog dashed ahead of it into the courtyard and announced, "His Eminence the County Magistrate has arrived!"

The tiger and I were face to face. It snarled, and I shut my eyes in fear. "You must be Zhao Xiaojia."

Bent like a shrimp, I replied, "Yes, yes, I am Zhao Xiaojia."

While I was bent over like that, he hid the bulk of his original form, leaving only the tip of his tail showing beneath his robe and dragging it along the muddy ground. I had a very private thought: Tiger, there's pig's blood and dog shit in our compound mud, so pretty soon flies will be landing on your tail. My thought still hung in the air when flies resting on the wall swarmed over, buzzing and raising a din as they landed not just on the Magistrate's tail, but on his cap, his sleeves, and his collar. "Xiaojia," the Magistrate said amiably, "go inside and announce that the County Magistrate has come calling."

I said, "The Magistrate can go on in. But my dieh might bite."

The legal secretary reverted to human form and said angrily, "Are you really so reckless as to disobey the County Magistrate? Go inside and tell your dieh to come out here!"

His Eminence raised his hand to stop his secretary and, bending slightly at the waist, stepped inside. I rushed in after him, wanting to see what would happen when tiger and panther met. I hoped they would be enemies at first sight—growling, their hackles raised, green lights shooting from their eyes, white fangs bared. The white tiger glares at the panther; the panther glares right back. The white tiger circles the panther; the panther does the same. No backing down. My niang told me that wild beasts display their aggressive power to potential enemies by snarling, glaring, and showing their fangs, trying to drive them away without a fight. If one shows a hint of vulnerability by pricking up its ears or wagging its tail or lowering its eyes, the other one will snap at it a time or two, and the battle is won. But if neither is willing to back down, a savage fight is inevitable. No fight, how much fun is that? A good fight, now that's worth waiting for. And that's what I was doing—waiting, no, hoping, for a tiger-panther fight to the death between my dieh and Magistrate Qian. They circle one another, faster and faster, more and more aggressively, alternating black and white trails of smoke, moving from the living room out to the yard, and from there to the street beyond, round and round and round, until I am dizzy just watching them, spinning like a top. At one point the two merge, with black encircling white, like an egg, and white encircling black, like a twisted rope. They spin from the east end of the compound to the west, and from the south to the north. One minute they are up on the roof, the next down deep in the well. A sudden shriek—mountains echoing, oceans roaring, rabbits mating—until finally the settling—heaven and earth—arrives. I see a white tiger and a black panther, separated by no more than a couple of yards, sitting on their haunches as they lick the wounds on their shoulders. My mind was awhirl from watching the tiger-panther battle, and I was wild with joy, trembling from fear, and damp with sweat, all at the same time. Nothing had been resolved—no winner and no loser. While they were locked in battle, tooth and claw, I was wishing that I could help my panther dieh somehow, but I never found an opening.

Magistrate Qian glowered at my dieh, a contemptuous smirk on his face. Dieh wore a contemptuous smirk as he glowered at Magistrate Qian. In his eyes, this County Magistrate, who had ordered his lackeys to beat Xiaokui nearly to death, was beneath contempt. Dieh was panther-savage, mule-stubborn, ox-bold. The looks in the combatants' eyes were like crossed swords, embodying clangs that produced sparks, some of which blistered my face. They held their intense gazes, neither willing to turn away, and by then my heart was in my throat, on the verge of leaping out of my body and turning into a jackrabbit, its tail sticking up as it bounded away, out of the yard and onto the street, to be chased by dogs all the way to the southern foothills to graze on fresh grass. What kind of grass? Butter grass. Eats a lot, hits the spot, too much and it grows a pot. When it returns, in my chest it's a knot. Their muscles were taut, claws unsheathed from the folds of their paws. They could pounce at any minute and be at each other's throat. At that critical moment, my wife walked in, bringing her feminine perfume into the room. Her smile was a rose in bloom, petals arching outward, opening wide. Her hips shifted from side to side like braiding a rope. Her original form glimmered for a brief moment, but was quickly hidden beneath fair, tender, fragrant, sweet skin. She knelt down dramatically and, in a voice dripping with honey yet sour as vinegar, said, "Sun Meiniang, a woman of the people, bows down before His Eminence the County Magistrate!"

That bow took the steam out of Magistrate Qian. He looked away and coughed, sounding like a billy goat with a cold: ahek ahek ahek ahek, ahek ahek ahek ahek. It was obviously contrived. I might have been a bit of an idiot, but I was not fooled. He sneaked a glance at my wife, willing neither to look her in the eye nor to look for long. That look was a grasshopper, bouncing all over the place, until it finally smacked into the wall. His face twitched, a pitiful sight, whether from shyness or fear I could not say. "No need for that," he said; "please get up."

My wife stood up. "I understand that His Eminence has locked up my dieh, for which he was handsomely rewarded by the foreigners. I have prepared some good strong drink and dog meat to offer His Eminence my congratulations!"

After a hollow laugh and a pregnant pause, Magistrate Qian replied, "As an official in the service of the throne, I must carry out my duties."

As she exploded in lascivious laughter, my wife reached up and audaciously tugged on the Magistrate's black beard, then twisted his thick queue—how come my niang never gave me one of those?—and marched him over behind the sandalwood chair, where she grabbed my dieh's queue and said, "You two, one is my gandieh, the other my gongdieh. My gandieh has arrested my real dieh and wants my gongdieh to put him to death. So, Gandieh, Gongdieh, my real dieh's fate is in your hands."

She had barely gotten this crazed talk out of her mouth before she ran over to the wall and had an attack of the dry heaves. The sight nearly broke my heart, so I walked up to shyly thump her on the back. "Have they driven you crazy?" I wondered aloud. She straightened up and, with tears in her eyes, growled, "You fool, where do you get off asking me that? At this moment I am carrying the next generation's evil bastard for your family!"

My wife's barbs were directed at me, but her eyes were on Magistrate Qian. My dieh was staring at the wall, probably looking for the fat gecko that often appeared there. Magistrate Qian's rear end began to shift uncomfortably, like a boy trying to keep from soiling himself. His forehead was beaded with sweat. Diao Laoye stepped up and, with a bow to his superior, said, "Eminence, business first. His Excellency Yuan Shikai is waiting at Court for your response."

Magistrate Qian mopped his brow with the sleeve of his robe and tidied his beard, which my wife had ruffled. He coughed, sounding more like a goat than a man, and then composed himself, clasped his hands in front of his chest, and, with obvious reluctance, bowed to my dieh. "Unless I am mistaken, you must be the renowned Grandma, Zhao Jia."

My dieh, sandalwood prayer beads in hand, stood up and replied smugly, "I am your public servant Zhao Jia, and since I am holding a string of prayer beads that were a gift from the Empress Dowager Herself, you'll forgive me for not kneeling before a local official."

Once the words were out, he lifted the sandalwood beads, which looked to be weightier than a chain of steel, over his head, as if waiting for something to happen.

Magistrate Qian took a step backward, brought his legs together, and straightened his wide sleeves. Then, with a swish of those sleeves, he fell to his knees and banged his head on the floor. "I, Magistrate of Gaomi County, Qian Ding," he called out, his voice cracking, "wish Her Royal Highness, our Empress Dowager, a long, long life!"

The ritual of respect completed, Magistrate Qian scrambled to his feet and said, "This humble official would never presume to trouble the revered Grandma on his own. I come on behalf of the Governor of Shandong, Excellency Yuan Shikai, who requests an audience."

Dieh's reaction to the invitation was to finger his beads, ignoring the request, and gaze at the gecko on the wall. "Honorable Magistrate," he said, "the sandalwood chair upon which I have been sitting was a gift from His Imperial Majesty the Emperor, and the custom is to treat any object from His Royal Personage as if it were the Emperor Himself."

Magistrate Qian's face turned the color of the darkest sandalwood. Flames of anger seemed to burn in his chest, but he managed to keep them from bursting forth. I thought my dieh had gone a bit overboard by forcing the Magistrate to kneel, an act that could be seen as turning the world upside down, reversing the order of official and subject. But to do it twice? I think you're flirting with danger, Dieh. Niang said it best: The Emperor is a mighty force, but a distant one. A County Magistrate is a low-ranking official, but local. It would not be hard for him to find an excuse to make our lives difficult. Magistrate Qian is not someone you want to provoke, Dieh. I told you how he broke my friend Xiaokui's leg just because he spat at the Magistrate's palanquin.

Magistrate Qian rolled his eyes. "When did the Emperor sit in this chair?" he asked frostily.

"On the eighteenth day of the twelfth month in the Ji-Hai year of 1899 at the Imperial Residence in the Hall of Benevolence and Longevity. When the Empress Dowager heard Grand Steward Li's report on how I had carried out my duties, She favored me with a private audience. It was then that She presented me with this string of Buddhist prayer beads, telling me that when I laid down my executioner's sword, I ought to become a Buddha. She then had me seek a reward from the Emperor Himself. His Imperial Majesty stood up and said, "We have nothing at hand to give you, and if you are not bothered by a bulky object, you may take this chair with you.""

A smirk appeared on the County Magistrate's gloomy face. "I am a man of little learning and few talents. Yet however ignorant and ill-informed I may be, I have read a classic or two, ancient and modern, domestic and foreign, and in none have I ever read that an emperor would willingly surrender the chair in which he is sitting to anyone—especially not to an executioner. I submit, Grandma Zhao, that this tale is a bit far-fetched, even for you, and that you display unwarranted audacity. Why not go further and maintain that His Imperial Majesty rewarded you with three hundred years of property belonging to the Great Qing Empire, including its rivers and mountains? You wielded a sword for the Board of Punishments for many years, from which we must conclude that you are familiar with most, if not all, national laws. And so, I ask you, how should your fabrication of an Imperial Edict, your bogus assertion that you have come into possession of Imperial furniture, be dealt with under the law, given that you have created a rumor that touches upon the persons of the Empress Dowager and His Imperial Majesty? The slicing death? Or perhaps being cleaved in two at the waist. Shall your entire clan be exterminated?"

Oh, Dieh, how could you make such wild claims first thing in the morning? Now look what you've done—we're doomed. I was so frightened, my soul flew out of my body, but not before I fell to my knees to beg for forgiveness. "My dieh has offended you, Your Eminence," I said to Magistrate Qian, "and he is fully deserving of being chopped to pieces that are then tossed to the dogs. But she and I are blameless, and I beg you to be lenient. Please do not exterminate our clan, for if you did, who would bring you dog meat and spirits from now on? On top of that, my wife has now informed me that she is carrying a child, and if there is no way to avoid extermination, you must wait until after the child is born."

Diao Laoye rebuffed me: "Use your head, Zhao Xiaojia. Exterminating a clan means precisely that, not letting a single member off the hook. Do you really think they would let a son off just so you could have an heir?"

My dieh walked up and kicked me. "What are you up to, you no-account son? You are the perfect son so long as there is no trouble. But in a crisis, this is what you turn into!" Then he spun around to face Magistrate Qian. "Since the County Magistrate seems to believe that I am spreading a rumor to dupe him, why not ask the Empress Dowager and His Imperial Majesty in the capital? If you are afraid that is too great a distance to travel, we can go to the yamen to see what Excellency Yuan has to say. He ought to recognize this particular chair."

My father's brief monologue sounded as soft as silk, but a barb was hidden inside it. A stunned and frightened Magistrate Qian shut his eyes and sighed. Then, opening his eyes again, he said, "No need for that. I am a man of inadequate knowledge and deserve Grandma Zhao's ridicule." He cupped his hands in front of him in a gesture of respect, after which he once again lowered his wide sleeves, assumed a look of distress, and fell to his knees with a swish of those sleeves, facing the chair. When his head hit the floor this time, the sound resonated throughout the room. "I, Gaomi County Magistrate Qian Ding," he said as loud as a curse, "wish His Imperial Majesty a long life, a very, very long life!"

My dieh's hands quaked as he fingered his prayer beads. An irrepressible look of triumph shone in his eyes.

Now that he was back on his feet, the Magistrate said, "Grandma Zhao, may I ask if there are other Imperial treasures in your possession? I have been on my knees once and then twice, so I can surely do it yet again."

With a smile, Dieh said, "Your Eminence, that is not my fault. The custom has been dictated by the Imperial Court."

"Well, then, since there is no more, will Grandma Zhao accompany me to the yamen, where Governor Yuan and Plenipotentiary von Ketteler await?"

"May it please the Magistrate to have his men pick up this chair? I would like for Governor Yuan to determine its authenticity."

Magistrate Qian hesitated for a moment. "Very well," he said with a wave of his hand. "Come take this!"

The two wolf-yayi picked up the Dragon Chair and followed my father and Magistrate Qian, who walked side by side out our gate. My wife stayed behind to vomit in the yard, crying between her stomach upheavals, "Dear Father, you must live on, for your daughter is carrying your grandchild!"

I watched as Magistrate Qian's face went from red to white, proof of his discomfort, while the look of arrogance and self-satisfaction on my dieh's face was, if anything, more apparent than ever. The two of them vied to let the other mount the palanquin first, like officials of equal rank or best friends. In the end, they both chose not to climb aboard, while the yayi tried to squeeze the Dragon Chair inside. When they failed, they hung it upside down from the shaft. My dieh leaned into the palanquin to set his prayer beads inside, and then leaned back out, as the curtain fell to keep the sacred object from view. Now that his soft white hands were empty, he looked contentedly at Magistrate Qian. With a leering smile, the Magistrate raised his hand and—*whack*—spun my father's head around with a slap that sounded like the squashing of a toad. Caught unawares, my dieh stumbled, trying hard not to fall, but the moment he steadied himself, a second slap, more savage than the first, sent him thudding to the ground, where he sat only semi-conscious, his eyes glazed over. He leaned forward and spat out a mouthful of blood and, it appeared, a tooth or two. "Forward!" Magistrate Qian commanded.

The carriers picked up the palanquin and trotted off, leaving the two yayi behind to pick my dieh up by his arms and drag him along like a dead dog. Magistrate Qian walked on, head high, chest out, the epitome of power and prestige, like a rooster that has just climbed off a hen's back. The head-up posture did not serve him well, as he nearly fell when his foot bumped into a brick in the middle of the road, and would have had it not been for the quick action of Diao Laoye. Not so fortunate was the Magistrate's hat, which fell to the ground in the flurry of activity. He reached down, scooped it up, and put it back on his head—cockeyed, as it turned out. He straightened it, then continued walking behind the palanquin, followed by Diao Laoye; the yayi brought up the rear with my dieh in tow, his legs dragging along the ground. A bunch of impudent neighborhood children fell in behind my dieh, bringing the total number in the procession to a dozen or more traveling along the bumpy road on their way to the county yamen.

Tears spurted from my eyes. Oh, how I wished I had thrown myself at Magistrate Qian for what he'd done. No wonder Dieh said I was the perfect son so long as there was no trouble, but in a crisis, I turned into a no-account son. I should have broken the man's leg with a club; I should have cut open his belly with a knife . . . Well, I picked up my butcher knife and ran out of the yard, intent on chasing down Magistrate Qian's palanquin. But my curiosity got the better of me, and I followed a trail of houseflies to the spot where the puddle Dieh had made lay in the sun. Yes, there they were, two of his teeth, both molars. I moved them around with the tip of my knife, feelings of sadness bringing fresh tears to my eyes. After I got to my feet, I turned toward their retreating backs, spat mightily in their direction, and cursed at the top of my lungs, Fuck you—followed, in a barely audible voice, by: Qian Ding.

CHAPTER FOUR

Qian Ding's Bitter Words

The Gaomi Magistrate, drunk in the Western Parlor, his mind on the lovely Sun Meiniang. (A drunken body, not a drunken heart!) Eyes limpid as ripples on an autumn lake, red lips, ivory teeth, a maiden young. Dog meat and strong drink stir my emotions, an affecting aria from the opera Maoqiang. *No general can pass up a beautiful woman, the adage goes, a hero prostrates himself before feminine charms. You and I are like fish in water, cavorting together. We shy not from carrying on in the yamen court (outraging our ancestors). Alas, a shame that a dream that seems so right soon gives way to what is wrong. Fighting has broken out in Northeast Township, led by Sun Bing, once an opera singer with a beard so long. I think back to early days in Gaomi County, when he spouted nonsense in a song. When a red tally was tossed, he was detained at my command and sent in chains to be flogged. At a competition over beards, he was weak, I was strong. That day I first saw Sun Meiniang, like the Tang Consort reborn. The daughter of Sun Bing means that he and I to a single family must belong. The cruel German devils want to punish him with savagery at the hands of the executioner, Zhao Jia, gongdieh of the fair Meiniang . . .*

—Maoqiang *Sandalwood Death.* Drunken ramblings

1

Please sit, dear wife. I cannot ask you to bother with the lowly chore of preparing food and drink. I have told you so a thousand times, and yet you treat my words as wind passing by your ear. So please sit, dear wife; tonight you and I shall drink to our hearts' content, till we are both pleasurably tipsy, and then retire to my sleeping quarters. Do not fear the prospect of inebriation or how the spirits will loosen your tongue. Though it be true that we are in the depths of this compound, where secrets are safe, even in a teahouse or wine shop surrounded by a gathered crowd I would say what is in my heart, for I could not rest until I had my say. Dear wife, you are descended from a towering official of the Great Qing, born into a family of affluence, maternal granddaughter of Zeng Guofan, who came to the rescue of the dynasty, expending energy under the most difficult of circumstances, sparing no effort as a true loyalist amid a desperate state of affairs, to become a mainstay of the nation. The Great Qing would not exist today but for the Zeng family. A toast, dear wife, to us. Do not assume that I am drunk, for I am not. Oh, if only I were! While drink may have an effect on my body, my soul remains beyond its power. I will not mislead you, dear wife, nor could I if I tried, for this once-great dynasty is nearing its fated end. The Empress Dowager holds the reins of power; the Emperor is but a puppet. The rooster broods the eggs; the hen heralds the dawn—yin and yang are reversed, black and white all mixed up, with villains holding sway and black arts running wild. It would be a monstrous absurdity if the death knell of such a royal house were not struck. Let me have my say, dear wife, for I shall burst if I do not. Great Qing Court, you magnificent edifice on the verge of toppling, do so quickly and let your demise come swiftly. Why must you hang on between life and death, neither yin nor yang? Do not try to stop me, dear wife, and do not take my glass from me. Let me drink to my heart's content and speak my piece! Revered Empress Dowager and He Who Has Received His Mandate from Heaven, as beneficiaries of a nation's respect, how could You show no regard for Your exalted position and make a grand show of allowing an audience with an executioner? An executioner—the dregs of society, a man at the bottom of the heap! We who serve in official positions rise before dawn and do not eat until it is dark, performing our duties with diligence, and even a glimpse of the Dragon countenance is an event of earth-shaking rarity. Yet a bottom-feeding denizen spurned by dogs and pigs has been accorded the dignity of a grand and solemn audience, at which Her Royal Highness presented him with a fine ring of prayer beads and His Imperial Majesty favored him with the very chair occupied by His noble person, treatment that barely fell short of granting high rank and hereditary title. Dear wife, your esteemed grandfather, Zeng Guofan, devised strategies that ensured victory in his command of the nation's armed forces in campaigns all across the land, winning glory in battle after battle, and yet His Imperial Majesty did not favor him with the chair in which He sat, did He? Your grandfather's younger brother, Zeng Guoquan, charged enemy lines under heavy fire, engaging in bloody battles, narrowly escaping death time and again. But Her Royal Highness did not present him with a ring of prayer beads, did She? No, they chose to make gifts of a Dragon Chair and a ring of prayer beads to a bottom-feeding denizen spurned by dogs and pigs. And that overweening swine, a beneficiary of the Emperor and Dowager's munificence, forced me to perform the reverential ritual of three bows and nine kowtows before the exalted chair and prayer beads—in other words, before him. If that can be tolerated, is there anything that cannot? Subjecting a successful candidate of the metropolitan examination, a grade five official, however modest his standing, to such humiliating treatment goes beyond indignation. And please do not insult me with the adage "A lack of forbearance in small matters upsets great plans," for recent events make a mockery of so-called "great plans." On the street, rumors are flying that the Eight-Power Allied Forces have reached the outskirts of the city and that Her Highness the Empress Dowager and His Majesty the Emperor are about to abandon the capital and flee to the west. The Great Qing Empire, many believe, will fall at any moment. At a time like this, of what use is forbearance? I forbear nothing! No, it is revenge I seek. Dear wife, when that swine placed the Dragon Chair and the prayer beads into my palanquin, I delivered two well-placed slaps across his cadaverous dog face, satisfyingly resounding blows with such force that the swine looked down and spat out two bloody dog teeth. The stinging sensation on my hand persists even now. Ah, how good it felt! Fill my cup again, please, dear wife.

Those slaps swept away every shred of the swine's sense of esteem and made him slink away like a mangy dog with its tail between its legs. But I could tell that deep down he did not admit defeat, no, not for a minute, as I saw in his eyes, set deep in sockets so dark that no trace of white emerged, only rays of emerald-green light like will-o'-the-wisps. And yet that swine was no craven pushover. As we stood outside the yamen gate, I asked: "How did that feel, Grandma Zhao?" Do you know what he said? The swine actually giggled and said to me, "Those were fine slaps, Your Eminence, and one day I shall return the favor." "Well," I said, "that day will never come. I may one day swallow gold, hang myself, take poison, or cut my throat, but my demise will not come at your hands." "My only fear," he said, "is that when the time comes, Your Eminence will not be in a position to control his own fate." He then added, "There are precedents for that."

Yes, dear wife, you are right. I soiled my hand by using it on him. A County Magistrate, a representative of the Imperial Court, should not lower himself to vie with so lowly an antagonist. What is he, after all? A pig? No, a pig has more grace than he. A dog? No, a dog is nobler. But what was I to do? Excellency Yuan ordered me to extend the invitation, and once a grand official of that elevated status had spoken, I had no choice but to send messengers, who failed, necessitating my personal attention to it. One would be a fool not to see that in the eyes of Excellency Yuan, the Gaomi County Magistrate is of less worth than a common executioner.

Before we went into the hall, I took the hand of that swine—it was as hot as cinders and as soft as dough, a hand unlike any other—with the idea to lead him inside with feigned affection, making him uncomfortable but unable to say so. But the swine gently pulled his hand from mine and fixed his eyes on me with an enigmatic look. Sinister thoughts, impossible to interpret, were running through his head. He climbed back into my palanquin, where he draped the prayer beads around his neck and emerged with the Dragon Chair over his head, legs up. I was amazed to see that this skeletal dog of a man actually had the strength to carry such a heavy wooden chair. The swine then entered the hall, swaying from side to side under the heft of his protective talisman. Feeling incredibly awkward, I followed him inside, where I saw Excellency Yuan sitting shoulder to shoulder with the Jiao'ao Plenipotentiary, von Ketteler, looking rather bewildered. The foreign bastard was winking and making strange faces.

The swine, still holding the chair over his head, knelt in the middle of the hall and announced crisply, "Your humble servant Zhao Jia, a former executioner who was granted retirement from the Board of Punishments by Her Royal Highness and permitted to return home, is here in response to Your Excellency's summons."

Excellency Yuan nearly jumped to his feet and trotted across the hall to where that swine knelt, his protruding paunch leading the way, and reached out to relieve him of the weighty chair. Seeing that it was too heavy for His Excellency to manage by himself, I rushed over to help him take it from the swine and then carefully turn it right side up and set it down in the middle of the hall. As for Excellency Yuan, he shook his wide sleeves, removed his cap with both hands, and fell to his knees. After touching his head to the floor, he intoned: "Shandong Governor Yuan Shikai humbly wishes His Imperial Majesty and Her Royal Highness a long and prosperous life!" I stood mutely off to one side as if struck by a thunderbolt for a moment before being abruptly awakened to the knowledge that my lack of action was a monumental affront to the august Son of Heaven. I could not fall to my knees fast enough, as I again performed the three bows and nine kowtows to that swine and his chair and prayer beads. The cold brick flooring raised blisters on my forehead. As I was banging my head on the floor to the Imperial chair, that foreign bastard whispered something to his interpreter and wore a contemptuous smirk on his long, skinny, goat-like face. Oh, Great Qing Empire, what you excel in is trampling your own officials underfoot and pandering to the foreigners. That bastard von Ketteler and I have clashed many times, so I am confident that he would never speak kindly of me to Excellency Yuan. There may be nothing I can do about those bastards, but no matter what you say, it was I who made it possible for them to take Sun Bing into custody.

That swine remained on his knees, even when Excellency Yuan reached down to help him to his feet, and I steeled myself for the worst. The moment for that swine to get his revenge over those two slaps had arrived. As I feared, he took the prayer beads from around his neck, held them out with two hands, and said, "Your humble servant asks His Excellency to be his arbiter."

With a derisive snort and a quick glance at me, Excellency Yuan said, "State your case."

"His Eminence Qian has accused me of gross fabrication and spreading a rumor."

"What did he accuse you of fabricating, and what rumor are you supposed to have spread?"

"He said that the Dragon Chair and prayer beads are common items among the populace, and he has accused me of using deception to burnish my name."

Excellency Yuan glared at me. "He is just ignorant and ill-informed!" he said.

"Excellency," I defended myself, "your humble servant believes that propriety does not extend to the lower classes and that punishments do not accrue to the elite. How could the exalted Imperial Majesty and Royal Highness grant an audience to an executioner and reward him with gifts of inestimable value? That is why your humble servant was suspicious."

Excellency Yuan replied, "You are a man of shallow learning who has swallowed the lessons of antiquity without digesting them. In conforming to the times in their desire to make the country prosper, His Imperial Majesty and Her Royal Highness have dedicated Themselves to loving the common people as Their own children, to understanding and sympathizing with those at the bottom, in the same way that the sun shines down on all creation. Tall trees and minuscule blades of grass alike receive nourishment. You are narrow-minded and petty, adhering blindly to convention, an ignorant man too easily surprised."

Then that swine said, "His Eminence Qian also slapped me so hard I lost two teeth."

Excellency Yuan pounded the table and sputtered angrily, "Grandma Zhao has served three emperors in his role of punishing miscreants for the Board of Punishments Bureau of Detentions. He has made great contributions in meting out punishments with such skill and loyalty that even the Emperor and the Empress Dowager have commended and rewarded him, and yet you, a mere County Magistrate, had the audacity to knock out two of his teeth. Do His Imperial Majesty and Her Royal Highness mean nothing to you?"

I was paralyzed with fear, as if struck by lightning, until I was covered with perspiration that soaked my clothes. My legs were so weak they could not hold me up. I fell to my knees and began banging my head on the floor. "This humble, small-minded subordinate, who cannot see what is under his nose, has offended Grandma and sinned against the Son of Heaven," I said. "I deserve ten thousand deaths and throw myself upon His Excellency's mercy!"

Excellency Yuan was silent for a moment before he said, "By physically abusing an ordinary citizen, you have proven that the Imperial Court means nothing to you, and you deserve to be severely punished. However, you aided the Plenipotentiary in capturing the bandit chieftain Sun Bing alive, a notable achievement, and I shall let that erase your crime."

I banged my head again on the floor and said, "Eternal thanks to Your Excellency!"

"There is a popular adage that goes, 'Do not hit someone in the face or reveal another's shortcomings,'" he continued. "You struck him in the face without provocation and dislodged two teeth. If I were to simply absolve you of that, Grandma Zhao might well object. So here is what we shall do: You kowtow twice to Grandma Zhao and give him twenty ounces of silver to replace his missing teeth."

Now you know, dear wife, the extent of the humiliation to which I was subjected today. But when I stand beneath low eaves, how can I not lower my head? So I steeled myself and once again fell to my knees, though it caused me excruciating pain to do so, and, as I saw red, gave that swine two kowtows.

The swine grinned as he accepted my obeisance and had the unmitigated gall to say, "Your Eminence, this humble servant is one of society's poorest, lacking even rice for the next meal, so I look forward to receiving those twenty ounces of silver very soon."

That got a big laugh out of Excellency Yuan. Yuan Shikai, Excellency Yuan, you son of a bitch, how dare you humiliate one of your subordinates by siding with a common executioner in front of a foreigner! I was an impressively successful double candidate at the metropolitan examination and am a respected representative of the Imperial government. I ask you, Excellency Yuan, by humiliating a man of letters, have you not inflicted emotional pain upon all who serve? On the surface it looks as if you and he together have humiliated only the insignificant Magistrate of Gaomi County, whereas in fact you have brought dishonor to the Great Qing Court. A sallow-faced interpreter repeated everything that was said in the hall to the Plenipotentiary, a man who can kill without blinking, and whose laughter drowned out even that of Excellency Yuan. Dear wife, they treated your husband like a trained chimp. Utter abasement and degradation! Let me drink, dear wife, until I am drunk and as good as dead. Excellency Yuan, has the reality that "you can kill a gentleman but you must not humiliate him" escaped you? Do not worry, dear wife, I have no desire to kill myself. Sooner or later I will sacrifice myself in the cause of the Great Qing enterprise, but now is not the time.

That swine, having received the tacit approval of Excellency Yuan, sat proudly in his sandalwood chair, while I stood off to one side, like a common yayi. An overwhelming sense of indignation filled my heart, and heated blood rushed to my head. My ears were buzzing, my hands seemed to swell, and it was all I could do to keep from throttling that swine. But knowing what a coward I am, that was not to be. Instead, I tucked in my head, raised my shoulders, and managed a forced smile. I am a shameful, debased, contemptible, disgraced clown, dear wife, the most pathologically restrained person anywhere. Do you hear me, dear wife?

Excellency Yuan asked that swine, "Has it really been almost a year since we parted at Tianjin, Grandma?"

"Eight months, Excellency," the swine replied.

"Do you know why we invited you here?" Excellency Yuan asked him.

"No, Excellency, your humble servant does not," the swine replied.

"Do you know why Her Royal Highness requested an audience?" Excellency Yuan asked.

"Your humble servant heard from Grand Steward Li that Excellency Yuan spoke highly of your humble servant to Her Royal Highness Herself."

"You and I are tied together by fate," Excellency Yuan said.

"Your humble servant will remember Your Excellency's benevolence to the end of his days," the swine said as he got out of his chair to kowtow to Excellency Yuan; he then sat down again.

Excellency Yuan said, "I have asked you here today to perform another task for me—and, of course, for the Imperial Court."

"What task does Your Excellency wish your humble servant to perform?" the swine asked.

The great man laughed. "You are a damned executioner. What do you think it could be?"

The swine replied, "Your humble servant must be honest with Your Excellency. Ever since the executions at Tianjin, an infirmity of the wrist has made holding a knife impossible."

Excellency Yuan merely sneered. "If you can lift the Dragon Chair, a mere knife cannot present a problem. I can only hope that, in the wake of an audience with Her Royal Highness, you have not actually become a Buddha."

Well, that swine slid out of his chair and knelt on both knees. "Excellency," he said, "nothing could be further from the truth. Your humble servant is a pig, a dog, someone who will never become a Buddha."

Excellency Yuan sneered again. "If even you were to become a Buddha, then the same could not be denied to a stinking turtle!"

"Your Excellency speaks the truth," the swine said.

"Have you heard news of Sun Bing's rebellion?" Excellency Yuan asked.

The swine replied, "Since your humble servant's return to his native home, that is where I have stayed. I know nothing of events in the outside world."

Excellency Yuan said to him, "You are aware that Sun Bing is your married son's qinjia, I assume."

The swine said, "Your humble servant plied his trade in the capital for decades without returning home. The marriage of my son was arranged by my departed wife."

"Sun Bing has allied himself with the Boxer bandits," Excellency Yuan said, "inciting rebellion among the people and creating an international incident that has caused unimaginable grief to His Imperial Majesty and Her Royal Highness. In accordance with the Qing legal code, accountability for a crime of this magnitude must extend to the culprit's extended family, wouldn't you say?"

The swine replied, "Your humble servant merely carries out punishments and has no knowledge of the law."

Excellency Yuan said, "According to the law, you count as a member of his extended family."

The swine replied, "Your humble servant returned home barely six months ago, and would not recognize Sun Bing if he saw him."

Excellency Yuan said, "The people's hearts are iron, the law is a furnace. Since last year's rebellious disturbance by the Boxers, their anti-religion movement and murderous attacks on foreigners have led to an international incident, a calamity of monstrous proportions. As we speak, Peking is ringed by the Great Powers, and the capital is in imminent peril. Sun Bing has been apprehended, but surviving members of his clique are prepared to stir up the countryside again. The people of Shandong are known for their quick tempers, especially those in Gaomi County. With the nation in extreme peril, caught up in the chaos of war, only the most severe punishments can strike fear into the hearts of the unruly. I have asked you here today both to recall our days of friendship and to ask you to devise a means of execution for Sun Bing that will have the power to terrorize and serve as a warning to his unruly adherents."

I looked over at that swine and saw telltale flashes in his eyes light up his cadaverous face, like steel fresh from the furnace. His strange little hands, which were resting on his knees, began to twitch like tiny animals, and I knew that was not because the swine was frightened, for I do not believe there is anything in this world that can intimidate a man who has taken the lives of a thousand human beings. I knew that excitement was the cause of the twitching hands, no different from that of a wolf when it sees its prey. A sinister glow filled his eyes, but humble, submissive words emerged from his mouth. The swine may be a coarse, uncultured executioner, but his knowledge of Qing officialdom is bewilderingly extensive. He succeeds in things by keeping his inadequacies hidden, seizing his prey by feigning to let go, and pretending to be dull-witted. "Excellency," he said as he bowed his head, "your humble servant is a man of little refinement who carries out only those punishments deemed appropriate by his superiors."

Excellency Yuan had a big laugh over that, and when he was finished, he said with a kindly smile, "Grandma Zhao, you are unwilling to devise anything particularly brutal since he is your qinjia. Am I right in that?"

The swine truly is a demonic creature, for he detected the vicious undertone in Excellency Yuan's mocking comment and the fiendish expression masked by the smile. He jumped out of the Dragon Chair, fell to his knees, and said, "Your humble servant has said that he has returned home to live out his days and would not dare to usurp the prerogatives of the local tradesmen . . ."

"So that is what has been bothering you," His Excellency said. "The abler one is, the more he ought to do."

Well, that swine said, "Since His Excellency extends such magnanimity, your humble servant will display his inadequacies."

"Tell me, then," His Excellency said, "down through the ages, from dynasty to dynasty, what forms of punishment have been used, official and popular. Speak slowly, one at a time, so the interpreter can pass them on to the foreigner."

The swine said, "Your humble servant heard his shifu say that among the punishments permitted by the current regime, none exceeds the slicing death in terms of brutality."

"That is your specialty," His Excellency said. "It is the one you used on Qian Xiongfei in Tianjin. It is a worthy punishment, but death comes a bit too quickly, I think."

His Excellency then turned and nodded meaningfully to me. Dear wife, few men are as crafty as Excellency Yuan, and no one is better informed. He clearly knew that Qian Xiongfei and I were related. Yes, he stared at me with a squinting smile, a smile that would have been welcome were it not for the light that shone from his eyes—like the sting of a scorpion or the bite of a hornet—and then, as if he had just been reminded, he said, "Gaomi Magistrate, they say that Qian Xiongfei, the man who tried to assassinate me, was your cousin. Is that true?" Dear wife, I felt as if I had been struck by lightning. Cold sweat oozed from my pores as I fell to my knees and banged my head on the floor as if I were crushing cloves of garlic. I tell you, dear wife, your husband's head has been badly abused today! Backed into a corner, I was reminded of a rustic adage that goes, "Whether one lives or dies is already written somewhere," and if I simply admitted the relationship, I would not have to suffer the consequences of trying to cover something up. So I said, "May it please Your Excellency, Qian Xiongfei was your humble servant's third brother, but because my uncle had no heir, he raised him as his son." His Excellency nodded and said, "A dragon has nine sons, each different from the others. I have read the letters you wrote to him, and they are worthy of a successful double candidate at the metropolitan examination. As the descendant of an illustrious family, you write eloquently, with fine calligraphy and an elevated tone. But you have not seen the letter he wrote to you, one in which he severed relations with you and poured out a stream of invective against you. Gaomi County, you are an honest man, and an intelligent one, and it has always been my belief that honesty equals intelligence. Gaomi County, though there are no wings on your cap, it is on the verge of soaring into the sky. Get up!" I tell you, dear wife, this has been an extraordinary day, with danger lurking at every turn. Pour the spirits, dear wife. It would be unreasonable for you to refuse me. I shall get drunk before I take my rest.

Dear wife, we know that my third brother suffered the slicing death in Tianjin, but were surprised to learn that his executioner was that swine Zhao Jia. How true the adage that "Old foes are fated to meet." Yuan Shikai is a man of wisdom and wide experience, with honey on his lips and murder in his heart, and my misfortune will be certain now that I have fallen into his hands. Drink up, dear wife, take advantage of the good days, for the arrival of bad times is ensured. Man has but one life, grass sees but one spring. I am prepared for anything.

That swine cast a furtive look at me, his gaze sweeping across my neck, probably searching out the junctures to determine the best spot for the sword to enter.

Excellency Yuan left me standing there and turned to Zhao Jia. "Besides the slicing death, can you think of any other splendid forms of punishment?"

The swine said, "Other than the slicing death, the cruelest form of punishment approved by the current regime, Your Excellency, is cleaving at the waist."

Excellency Yuan asked him, "Have you ever performed that?"

"Once," the swine said.

"Describe it for the benefit of the Plenipotentiary," Excellency Yuan said.

"Your Excellency," the swine said, "in the seventh year of the Xianfeng reign, your humble servant was a seventeen-year-old 'nephew' in the Board of Punishments Bureau of Detentions, serving his shifu, assisting the Grandma at executions and attentively studying his every move and action. The person to be killed by waist cleaving that day was a clerk at the Imperial Treasury, a big man with a mouth so large he could fit his entire fist in it. These clerks, Your Excellency, were master thieves, specializing in silver. Each time they entered the Treasury, they were required to strip naked. The same was true, of course, when they left. But that did not stop them from stealing silver. Can you guess, Excellency, where they hid the silver they stole from the Treasury? They hid it in their grain passages." The sallow-faced interpreter asked, "What do you mean by a grain passage?" Excellency Yuan glared at the man. "The anus! Keep it short." The swine said, "Yes, Excellency, I shall." Throughout the history of the Qing, each year has seen a lessening of the silver in the Treasury, for which many innocent superintendents have died. The idea that clerks might be the culprits somehow never occurred to anyone. Every trade has its rules and customs, just as every family has its way of doing things. Even though the clerks received meager wages, they lived in lavish surroundings, dressed their womenfolk in finery, and displayed ostentatious wealth, all thanks to their grain passages. Now, one can say that such passages are tender spots sensitive to even a stray grain of sand. But those men had no trouble inserting a fifty-ounce silver ingot into them. At home, it turned out, they enlarged the openings to their rectums with sandalwood clubs soaked in sesame oil for years until the wood had turned red and was unbelievably slippery. They came in three sizes: small, medium, and large, and their use proceeded along those lines. The training went on day and night, until the passage was unnaturally wide and all was in readiness to steal silver from the Treasury. But that was a bad day for one of them. The clerk with the big mouth had stuffed three ingots up his grain passage, but while he was being searched on his way out, he grimaced and had trouble walking, as if he were carrying a bowl of water on his head or holding back an urgent bowel movement. The superintendent, suddenly suspicious, kicked him in the buttocks, which by itself was of no consequence. But the man relaxed just long enough for one of the ingots to slide out of his anus. The momentarily dumbstruck superintendent kicked him again and again, and out came the other two ingots. "You son of a bitch!" the superintendent cursed. "What you shoved up your ass is worth more than I make in three years!" The source of the clerks' riches was a secret no longer. Now when they leave the

Treasury, they are required to bend over and have their rectums reamed for hidden treasure. When the report reached Emperor Xianfeng's ears, He was livid and angrily ordered that all the Treasury clerks be put to death and their property be confiscated. If that weren't enough, He told Grandma Yu to devise a new means of execution, which was to jam red-hot pokers up their grain passages. All but the big-mouthed man, who was to be cleaved in half in public, a warning to the masses.

A sea of faces filled the marketplace on the day of the execution, for this was something new and exciting for people who had had their fill of beheadings. The chief witness to this solemn event was Excellency Xu, Vice President of the Board of Punishments. Also in attendance was Chief Justice Sang of the Supreme Court. The assigned team of executioners was up half the night in preparation. Grandma Yu personally sharpened the broadax, while First Aunt and Second Aunt—Third Aunt had recently died—prepared the wooden block, the ropes, and the other things they would need. I had always assumed that a sword was used for this punishment, but Grandma Yu told me that as far back as the founding of our calling, it was always a broadax. But before we set out, Grandma Yu told me to take a broadsword along in case anything went wrong.

They dragged the condemned man out, obviously drunk from the alcohol they'd poured down his throat. Red-eyed and foaming at the mouth, he thrashed around like a mad ox. He was as strong as an ox, almost too much for Second and Third Aunts, and every show of strength drew approving roars from the crowd, which further emboldened him. Finally they were able to tie him down on the wooden block, with First Aunt holding down his head and Second Aunt his legs. He fought us at every turn, flailing his arms, kicking with both feet, and twisting his body in all directions, like a snake, even arching his back like an inchworm. The chief witness found the display so disturbing that he gave the order before the team had the man completely subdued. So Grandma raised the ax high over his head and brought it down with all his might, creating a streak of white and a gust of wind. While the ax was still over Grandma's head, absolute silence settled over the crowd; but when he buried it in the man's body, a mighty roar erupted. I heard a slurping sound and watched as a tower of red shot into the air. The two aunts' faces were drenched in blood. To Grandma's discredit, one chop had not severed the man cleanly in half. At the last second he had twisted his body, and the ax had only cut through half his midsection. His inhuman shrieks drowned out the crowd noise as his guts slurped over the sides and covered the wooden block. Grandma wanted to make a second chop, but he had swung so hard the first time he'd buried the blade in the wood under the man's body. When he tried to pull it free, the handle was too slimy with the man's gore for him to get a grip. Jeers arose from the crowd;

the victim's arms and legs flailed wildly, and his horrifying screams rocked the area. The situation had turned ugly, and I knew instinctively what to do. Without waiting for Grandma to give the order, I stepped up, raised the broadsword over my head, and—teeth clenched, eyes shut—completed what Grandma had left undone. The one-time Treasury clerk was now severed in two. That had given Grandma enough time to gather his wits. He turned and announced to the chief witness, "The execution has been carried out. May it please Your Excellency!" The officials sat there in shock, their faces drained of blood. First and Second Aunts released their grip and, confused and bewildered, stood up. The lower half of the victim's body was twitching, noticeably if not violently. The top half was a different story altogether. Excellency, you did not see it with your own eyes, and may not believe what I am about to tell you. Even people who saw it thought that their eyes were deceiving them, or wondered if it was all just a bad dream. The man must have been the reincarnation of a dragonfly, which can fly even without the lower half of its body. By pressing down with his elbows, he pushed his truncated body into an upright position and started bouncing up and down, his blood and guts soaking and getting tangled in our feet. The man's face was the color of gold foil that shone in our eyes. His large mouth was like a sampan tossed on the waves, from which gushed incomprehensible, blood-soaked howls. Strangest of all was his queue, which curled up behind him like a scorpion's tail, then fell back limply, over and over. The crowd was stilled, some with their eyes boldly open, others with their eyes timidly shut. A number of them were retching loudly. The ranking officials were by then galloping away on their horses, leaving the four of us standing there like wooden statues, eyes glued to the half clerk as he performed his remarkable feats. He kept it up for as long as it takes to smoke a bowlful of tobacco, before reluctantly pitching forward, gurgling noises emerging from his mouth; if you closed your eyes and listened, it sounded like a suckling infant.

3

The swine went quiet after finishing his graphic description of the execution. Strings of slobber hung from his mouth, and his eyes rolled around in their sockets as he looked up at Excellency Yuan and the Plenipotentiary. The ghastly image of the dissevered Treasury clerk floated in front of my eyes, and I could almost hear the man's screams. But Excellency Yuan obviously liked what he'd heard. He sat there squinting, not saying a word while the interpreter finished jabbering into the ear of von Ketteler, who cocked his head and looked first at Yuan and then at Zhao. His jerky movements and the look on his face reminded me of a hawk perched on a rock.

Excellency Yuan finally spoke up. "As I see it, Plenipotentiary, that is how we ought to do it."

The interpreter translated Excellency Yuan's comment in a soft voice. Von Ketteler said something in that devilish language of his, which the interpreter translated: "The Plenipotentiary wants to know how long the condemned can live after he's cut in half."

With a slight upward tilt of his chin, Excellency Yuan signaled the swine to answer.

"About as long as it takes to smoke a bowlful of tobacco," he said, "but it is hard to say. Some die on the spot, like lopping off the branch of a tree."

Von Ketteler said something to the interpreter, who translated: "The Plenipotentiary does not approve. He says death might come too fast and will not serve as a proper warning to people with evil thoughts in their heads. He would like you to find a uniquely cruel method that will inflict the maximum amount of suffering and draw it out as long as possible. The Plenipotentiary would like to see an execution where the subject holds on for at least five days. Ideally, the man would still be alive on August twentieth, the day the section of railroad between Qingdao and Gaomi is completed."

Excellency Yuan said, "Think hard, is there any punishment that fits the bill?"

The swine shook his head. "He'd die if you hung him up for five days and did nothing else to him."

Von Ketteler said something to the interpreter. "The Plenipotentiary says that China is backward in everything but punishment techniques. This is one area in which the Chinese are world-beaters. Inflicting unbearable pain on someone before killing him is a uniquely Chinese art and is at the core of its governing philosophy."

"Horse shit," I heard Excellency Yuan mutter under his breath. But he quickly smothered that with a loud, impatient command to the swine: "Think hard," he said, before he turned to von Ketteler and said, "Esteemed Plenipotentiary, if such a punishment exists in your country, I would be happy if you taught him. It would take less effort to learn that than how to build a railroad."

The interpreter did his job, after which I saw von Ketteler scrunch up his forehead as he pondered a response. With his head down, the swine was trying to come up with something.

Then, abruptly, he excitedly jabbered something to the interpreter.

"The esteemed Plenipotentiary says that there is a punishment in Europe that guarantees prolonged suffering before death. The condemned is nailed to an upright cross and left there."

But then, just as abruptly, the swine's eyes lit up, and he blurted out excitedly, "Excellency, your humble servant has an idea. Years ago I heard my shifu say that during the Yongzheng reign, his master's master put to death a man who had emptied his bowels in the Imperial Mausoleum by means of what he called the sandalwood death."

"What does it consist of?" His Excellency asked.

The swine said, "My master described it to me only in vague terms, but the gist of it is that a pointed sandalwood stake is inserted into the subject's grain passage and forced up all the way to the nape of his neck and out. Then he is bound to a tree."

With a satisfied sneer, His Excellency said, "Great minds think alike. How long before the man died?"

"Three days, I think," the swine said, "or maybe four."

Excellency Yuan told the interpreter to immediately inform von Ketteler, who reacted almost rapturously. He stammered in stilted Chinese, "Good, the sandalwood death, that's it!"

His Excellency said, "Since Plenipotentiary von Ketteler approves, that is what we shall do. Sun Bing will suffer the sandalwood death, but you must make sure that he lives five days. Today is the thirteenth of August. Tomorrow you make your preparations, and the day after that, the fifteenth, the punishment will be carried out."

The swine fell to his knees. "Excellency, your humble servant is getting on in age and is not as spry as he once was. He will require an assistant for an execution of this magnitude."

His Excellency turned to me. "Have an assistant chosen from among the executioners at Gaomi's South Prison."

The swine objected: "Excellency," he said, "I would rather that the county not be involved."

Excellency Yuan laughed. "Are you afraid they will steal your thunder on this?"

The swine merely said, "I ask that Your Excellency grant me permission to have my son serve as an assistant."

"What does your son do?" Excellency Yuan asked.

"He butchers pigs and dogs," the swine replied.

Again His Excellency laughed. "He sounds qualified. All right, then, in battle one relies on his brothers; in a fight, only father and son will do. Permission granted." The swine remained kneeling on the floor.

"What else do you have to say?" Excellency Yuan asked.

"Excellency," the swine said, "carrying out the sandalwood death will require a thick post with a crossbar on top of a high wooden platform, with an access plank on one side."

"Make a drawing and give it to the County Magistrate for construction," Yuan said.

The swine said, "I will also require two stakes made of the finest sandalwood and shaved down like spikes. Your humble servant will personally do the work."

"The County Magistrate will see to that," Excellency Yuan said.

Then the swine said, "I will also require two hundred jin of refined sesame oil."

Excellency Yuan laughed. "Are you planning to fry Sun Bing to go with fine spirits?"

"Excellency," the swine said, "after the stakes are properly carved, they must steep in sesame oil all day and all night if they are to slip through the body without soaking up blood."

"Have Gaomi County take care of everything," Yuan said. "Is there anything else? Now is the time to give me the complete list."

The swine said, "I will also require ten strips of leather, a wooden hammer, a rooster with white feathers, two red felt caps, two pairs of high-top boots, two sets of black clothing, two red satin sashes, two bull's-ear daggers, plus a hundred jin of white rice, a hundred jin of wheat flour, a hundred chicken eggs, twenty jin each of pork and beef, half a jin of top-quality ginseng, a medicinal pot, three hundred jin of kindling, two buckets, a water vat, and two woks, one large and one small."

"What do you need ginseng for?" Excellency Yuan asked.

The swine said, "Hear me out, Excellency. The subject's stomach will not be affected by the insertion of the stake, but there will be a significant loss of blood, and keeping him alive will require a daily infusion of ginseng. That is the only way your humble servant can ensure that the subject will last five days."

Excellency Yuan said, "Can you guarantee that he will not die for at least five days with the infusion of ginseng?"

"Your humble servant guarantees it," the swine replied emphatically.

Excellency Yuan said, "Gaomi County, go make a list and have it filled without delay!"

The swine would still not rise.

"Rise," Excellency Yuan said.

But the swine kept knocking his head on the floor.

"That's enough," Excellency Yuan said. "I don't want you to break that dog head of yours. Now listen carefully. If you satisfactorily carry out this assignment, I will reward you, father and son, with one hundred ounces of silver each. But if something goes wrong, I will have you both speared with sandalwood stakes and hung on posts until you are desiccated corpses!"

With one last resounding kowtow, the swine said, "Thank you, Excellency."

"Gaomi County," Excellency Yuan said to me, "the same goes for you!"

I said, "Your humble servant will spare no effort."

Yuan stood up and, together with von Ketteler, started out of the hall. But he had taken only a few steps when he turned back, as if he'd forgotten something. "Gaomi County," he said nonchalantly, "I hear you have brought Liu Peicun's son here from Sichuan and given him an official position. Is that true?"

"Yes, Your Excellency," I replied frankly. "Liu Peicun was from Fushun County in Sichuan Province, where I was once posted. When his widow and family returned to Fushun with his coffin, I paid my respects as someone who was born in the same year as he and made a gift to the family of ten ounces of silver. Not long after that, his grieving widow passed away, but not before turning her son, Liu Pu, over to my care. When I saw how intelligent and conscientious he was, I gave him a job in the county yamen."

"Gaomi County, you are a straightforward man of integrity," His Excellency said somewhat enigmatically, "not someone who curries favor with the powerful, a man with a big heart. But you show a lack of judgment."

I laid my head against the floor and said, "Thank you, Excellency, for your instruction."

"Zhao Jia," Excellency Yuan said, "you are the sworn enemy of Liu Pu for killing his father!"

The swine's clever response was, "I was carrying out Her Royal Highness's decree."

4

Dear wife, why aren't you pouring? Pour! Fill them up! Let's drink. You are so pale. Are you crying? Don't cry, dear wife, I've already decided what to do. I'll make sure those hundred ounces of silver never reach that swine and that von Ketteler's plot falls through. And I will stop Yuan Shikai from getting his wish. Yuan saw to it that my brother, my own flesh and blood, was sliced to shreds. Cruel! Barbaric! Savage! Yuan Shikai has honey on his lips but murder in his heart. A dagger is hidden in his smile, and I know that he will not lightly spare me. Once he has disposed of Sun Bing, he will come for your husband. Since death is inevitable, one way or the other, dear wife, why not do it right! In times like this, only the dead are men; the living are dogs. Dear wife, you and I have been husband and wife for more than ten years, and even though we have been denied a child, we treat each other with respect in domestic harmony. I want you to leave for Hunan tomorrow morning. Your transportation has already been arranged. There you will find ten acres of paddy land, a five-room house, and savings of three hundred ounces of silver, enough for you for the rest of your life if you live frugally. After you have left, there will be nothing for me to worry about. Please, dear wife, do not cry. It breaks my heart. We are living in chaotic times, hell on earth for officials and commoners alike. It is better to be a dog in peace than a human being in times of chaos. Dear wife, when you are back home in Hunan, adopt one of Second Brother's sons. He will take care of you in your old age and see to your funeral. I have written a letter to that effect, and they will not object. When a bird is about to die, its cry is sorrowful; when a man is about to die, there is kindness in his words. Do not talk like that, dear wife, for if you were to die, who would burn incense and spirit money for me? You must leave, for if you were to remain here, my willpower would suffer.

Dear wife, I have a confession to make to you. I have wanted to own up to this for a long time, but you probably already know. For the last three years, I have carried on a liaison with Meiniang, Sun Bing's daughter and the daughter-in-law of Zhao Jia. She is now pregnant with my child. Dear wife, in light of more than a decade of marriage, I ask that if the child is a boy, you will find a way to have him brought to Hunan with you. If it is a girl, let that be the end of it. Consider this my last will and testament, dear wife, and an expression of Qian Ding's enduring gratitude.

BOOK TWO

Belly of the Pig

CHAPTER FIVE

Battle of the Beards

1

Qian Ding, newly appointed Magistrate of Gaomi County, had a spectacular beard that cascaded from his chin down across his chest. At his first official audience, this beard served to warn the wily clerks in the six boards and three ranks of devilishly crafty yayi against insubordination. His predecessor, a man with protruding lips and the chin of an ape, from which had sprouted a few dozen ratty whiskers, had bought his position. The man had been ignorant and incompetent, his only skill the accumulation of riches. He'd sat in the audience hall pulling his ears and scratching his cheeks like a macaque monkey. His wretched appearance and shameless immorality had created a psychological benchmark for his successor, Qian Ding. The gathered petty officials witnessed something fresh and appealing in the dignified demeanor of the new County Magistrate, and Qian Ding was struck by the light of amicability in the eyes of the men arrayed in front of him.

Qian had passed the Imperial Examination with distinction, achieving one of the highest rankings, in 1883, the eighth year of the Qing Guangxu Emperor's reign, sharing honors with Liu Guangdi, one of the renowned Six Gentlemen of the Wuxu Reform Movement. Liu was the thirty-seventh successful candidate of the Second Rank, Qian the thirty-eighth. After passing the examination, he spent two years in the capital in a minor government office, then bribed his way into a provincial assignment. He had served as Magistrate before, first in Guangdong's Dianbai County, and then in Sichuan's Fushun County, the latter being the birthplace of Liu Guangdi. Both Dianbai and Fushun were remote, inaccessible locales with barren mountains and untamed rivers; the people led such impoverished, wretched lives that even had he aspired to be a corrupt official, there was no grease to skim. And so, for his third posting, he came to Gaomi, where access was convenient and riches abounded. While it was a lateral appointment, in his eyes it was a promotion. A man of spirited aspirations and robust vitality, he had a radiantly ruddy face, eyebrows like sleeping silkworms, and a gaze that had the quality of lacquer; every strand in his beard was as thick as horsehair and long enough to touch the desktop behind which he sat. An impressive beard represented half of what it took to gain credibility among the governed. His colleagues were fond of teasing him: "Elder Brother Qian," they would say, "if the Old Buddha Herself were to lay eyes on you, at the very least you would be posted as a Circuit Magistrate." Unfortunately, there had been no opportunity to display his dignified demeanor in the Imperial presence, and as he sat at his mirror combing out his beard, he could only sigh and lament, "What a shame that this face, with its dignified appearance, and this fine, ethereal beard are ill regarded at Court!"

On the long journey from Sichuan to take up his new post in Shandong, he had stopped at a small temple on the Yellow River in Shaanxi to draw a divination lot, and was rewarded with great good tidings. The inscribed poem read: "Should the bream reach the western Yangtze, thunder will rend the sky." This tally swept away the deep-seated depression that had accompanied his career failures, and instilled in him confidence and high hopes. Upon his arrival in the county, despite being fatigued and covered with dust after a long journey, not to mention suffering from symptoms of a minor cold, he set right to work. After receiving the symbols of office from his predecessor, he summoned his subordinates to the audience hall, where he spoke to them for the first time. Splendid words flowing from a cheerful frame of mind gushed from his mouth. His predecessor had been a simple-minded dolt who could not string three simple sentences together. He, on the other hand, had a full-throated, richly seductive voice that at this moment was enhanced by a slightly nasal tone caused by the cold. The looks in the eyes of the listeners arrayed below him signaled success. When his speech was finished, he stroked his impressive beard with his thumb and forefinger and announced an end to the formal audience. His gaze then swept across the faces of the gathered functionaries, each of whom felt that the honorable Magistrate was looking only at him. The enigmatic look in those eyes seemed to include equal parts warning and encouragement. He then stood, turned, and walked out of the hall, a neat, orderly departure, like a breath of fresh air.

Soon afterward, at a banquet for local worthies, his handsome demeanor and impressive beard were once again the focus of attention for all who were present. The nasal obstruction had cleared up, and Gaomi County's local specialty, aged millet spirits, and fatty dog meat—the spirits relaxed his muscles and joints and enhanced the flow of blood, while the fatty dog meat improved his looks—made his face glow with conspicuous health and lent increased elegance to his beard. He offered a toast in a cadenced voice, announcing to his elite guests that he was determined to use his office to enrich the lives of the local population. His speech was interrupted frequently by thunderous applause and shouts of approval, and when he had finished, the ovation lasted until the incense sticks had burned halfway down. He then raised his glass to all the skullcaps and goatees at the table. The men's legs trembled when they stood; their hands shook and their lips quaked as they emptied their glasses. The Magistrate then called their attention to one of the dishes—a head of cabbage a vivid emerald green that gave no sign of being cooked. None of the guests dared touch the spectacular dish with his chopsticks for fear of making a fool of himself. "Worthy gentlemen," the Magistrate said, "not only is this cabbage fully cooked, it has been stuffed with more than a dozen rare delicacies." He touched the seemingly unblemished head gently with his chopsticks, and it opened like a flower bud, to reveal a rich, pulpy interior and fill the room with an aroma of great refinement. Most of the honored guests—unsophisticated locals and voracious meat and fish eaters—were ignorant of the more poetic forms of cuisine. But urged on by their illustrious host, they reached out, snagged cabbage leaves with their chopsticks, and put them into their mouths. Approving headshakes and words of praise followed. Elder Xiong, Magistrate Qian's revenue clerk, who had joined him at the table, wasted no time in introducing the Magistrate's wife, Gaomi County's First Lady, to the honored guests: she was the maternal granddaughter of Zeng Guofan—given the posthumous title and name of Lord Wenzheng. She had personally prepared the dish, Emerald Cabbage, the recipe having been passed down by her grandfather, who had created it with his master chef when he served in the capital as Vice President of the Board of Rites. Together they had tried several variants before reaching the perfection they were enjoying today. It embodied the wisdom of a generation of renowned officials. The revered Lord Wenzheng, who had mastered both the pen and the sword, had also been a chef par excellence, second to none. Xiong's introduction was greeted with even greater applause; tears spilling from the eyes of aging worthies sluiced down through the wrinkles in their cheeks. Snivel hung from the strands of their feeble goatees.

After all around the table had emptied three glasses, the local worthies approached the Magistrate, one at a time, to toast his arrival and sing his praises, each in his own way. And while their comments differed in style if not in elegance, the one constant was a mention of the revered one's beard. One intoned, "Our esteemed Magistrate is a reincarnation of Guan Yu, a rebirth of Wu Zixu." Another pronounced that Zhuge Liang had returned in the person of the esteemed Magistrate; the Deva King had descended from heaven. Now, while Qian Ding could tolerate a great deal, this group of toadies was more than he could endure. He could not, of course, refuse to be toasted and was obliged to empty his glass each time, and the more he drank, the further he moved away from his official airs. He chatted energetically, he talked and laughed merrily, he shuffled and gestured, his head was turned by the effusive praise, and he began to display his unrestrained nature as he moved steadily closer to the people.

That day he drank himself into a stupor; his worthy guests, too, lay passed out around the table. It was a banquet that rocked Gaomi County to its core and became a popular topic of conversation far and wide. The Emerald Cabbage gained almost mythical qualities on the people's tongues. People said that it was a mysterious viand that could not be separated until Magistrate Qian touched it with his chopsticks, at which time it opened like a white lily, with dozens of petals, each tipped with a glistening pearl.

Word quickly spread that the new Magistrate was the grandson-in-law of Lord Wenzheng. Endowed with an imposing presence, he sported a beard worthy of Guan Yu himself. Not only was the Magistrate the epitome of dignity, but his name had appeared high on the list of successful candidates at the Imperial Examination, and he thus joined the circle of Imperial attendants. Brimming with talent, he was a master of eloquence. With an unmatched capacity for spirits, even drunk he retained his poise, like a jade tree standing tall before a wind or a mountain withstanding a spring deluge. Then there was the Magistrate's wife, descendant of an illustrious family, a woman of matchless beauty and incomparable virtue. Their arrival in Gaomi County promised immense blessings for the people.

2

Northeast Gaomi Township was home to the leader of the local Maoqiang troupe, Sun Bing, a man who was also endowed with a splendid beard. Maoqiang, otherwise known as Cat Opera, is an operatic genre created and developed in Northeast Gaomi Township. The arias are exquisite, the staging unique, the ambience magical; in short, it is the ideal portrayal of life in the township. Sun Bing was both a reformer and an inheritor of the Maoqiang tradition, a man who enjoyed high prestige among his peers. As a performer of the old-man role, playing respected old men, he was never in need of a stage beard, since none could match the natural appeal of his own. As luck would have it, upon the birth of his grandson, the township's richest man, Master Liu, hosted a celebration banquet, to which Sun Bing was invited. Also in attendance was a yamen clerk by the name of Li Wu, who sat at the head of a table in a pompous demonstration of his stature, and proceeded to sing the praises of the County Magistrate, from his eloquence to his every action, from his interests to his favorite activities. But the climactic note was sounded in his tribute to the Magistrate's impressive beard.

Now, even though Li Wu was on leave from his post, on this occasion he was dressed in full formal attire, minus only his baton of authority. Gesticulating dramatically and blustering nonstop, he so intimidated the other guests, all decent, simple men, that they could only gape in stupefaction, the meal in front of them forgotten. With ears pricked, they listened wide-eyed to the man's voluble outbursts as he slung slobber into the air. Sun Bing, a man of the world, had been to many places and seen many things, and had Li Wu not been present, Sun would have been the center of attention. But Li *was* present, and since everyone knew that he was in attendance to the County Magistrate, Sun was ignored. He could only drink alone to drown his melancholy, casting disdainful looks and snorts of derision in the direction of the despicable lackey. No one noticed, and in the eyes of Li Wu, Sun might as well not have been at the table at all, so intent was he on elaborately extolling the virtues of the Magistrate's beard.

"Among ordinary mortals, no more than a thousand strands make up the finest beard. But can you guess how many strands His Eminence's superb specimen contains? Ha ha, I see you are stumped. I am not surprised. Last month I accompanied His Eminence on a tour to observe the people's mood, and engaged him in a conversation. 'Young Li,' he said to me, 'how many strands do you think are in this official's beard?' 'I dare not presume to guess, Your Eminence,' I replied. 'I am not surprised,' he remarked. 'Well, I shall tell you. This official's beard is comprised of nine thousand nine hundred and ninety-nine strands! One short of ten thousand! The First Lady performed the calculation.' How, I asked, was the calculation of such a beard accomplished? 'The First Lady is as finely meticulous as a human hair and endowed with surpassing intelligence. By counting one hundred strands at a time and tying them off with a silk thread, she accomplished the feat. She could not possibly be wrong.' 'Your Eminence,' I said, 'if you grew but one more strand, you would have the ultimate round number.' To which he replied, 'That, young Li, shows your lack of understanding. In the affairs of the world, perfection is a taboo. Take the moon, for instance. Once it is a perfect circle, the erosion begins. Or fruit on a tree. The moment it is perfectly ripe, it falls to the ground. A degree of deficiency is vital for all things if they are to last. There is no more auspicious number than nine thousand nine hundred and ninety-nine. Ten thousand is detrimental for the people and for those who govern them. This, my young Li, is a paradox you must work hard to grasp.' That comment by His Eminence is an arcane truth of boundless import, yet one that I have yet to unlock. He then said to me, 'Young Li, the number of strands in this official's beard is known to only three people alive. One is you, I am another, and the third is my wife. You must not breathe a word of it to anyone, for if it were to be revealed, it not only would be a harbinger of bad tidings, but might well spawn a great calamity.'"

Li Wu picked up his glass, drank from it, and then picked at dishes with his chopsticks, clicking his tongue in a display of criticism over the crude array of food. Finally he picked up a bean sprout, which he chewed noisily with his front teeth, like a mouse that lazily grinds its teeth after eating its fill. Master Liu's son, the father of the new grandson, rushed up with a plate of steaming pig's-head meat and placed it in front of Li Wu before wiping his sweaty brow with the back of his greasy hand. "We have treated you shamelessly, Uncle Li," he said. "We are peasants, untrained in the preparation of fine cuisine. Won't you do us the honor of sampling this?"

Li Wu spat out the bean sprout, which had been stuck between his front teeth, and banged his chopsticks down on the table. Clearly unhappy, he forced himself to speak with laudable forbearance: "Elder nephew Liu," he said, "your concern is misplaced. Do you really think I am here because of the food? If it were a meal I desired, I could visit any establishment in town and, without a word, be served fine sea cucumbers and abalone, camel's hoof and bear's paw, monkey brains and bird's nest soup, one dish after another. Eating one while sampling another with an eye to the third, that, my boy, is a banquet worthy of the name. And what has your family provided? Some half-cooked bean sprouts, a plate of rotting, pestilential pig's head, and a decanter of sour millet spirits neither hot nor cold enough. Is this what you call a celebration banquet? It is more like a meal to get rid of stinking actors. No, I have deigned to attend for two reasons: first as a favor to your father, to prop up your family, and second to mix with the local gentry. I am kept so busy that flames shoot out of my ass, and finding this little bit of time has not been easy."

The elder son of the Liu family could only nod and bow in response to Li Wu's rebuke, and make a quick, desperate exit when Li paused to cough.

"Master Liu, you are a learned, cultivated man," Li Wu said. "How could you have raised such an empty-headed turtle?"

None of the embarrassed guests dared make a sound. But Sun Bing, infuriated by what he had witnessed, pulled the plate of pig's head over in front of him. "Since the eminent Li Wu is used to eating delicacies from land and sea, placing this pig's head in front of him is clearly meant to sicken him. For those of us who survive on a diet of chaff and coarse greens, this nicely greases our innards and helps us shit!"

That said, without so much as a glance around the table, he began stuffing greasy, dripping chunks of meat into his mouth, one after the other. "Um, good," he mumbled, "really good, fucking delicious!"

Li Wu glowered at Sun Bing, who did not so much as look up. Gaining no satisfaction from his angry glare, Li blinked and turned his gaze on the others around the table. With a curl of his lip, he shook his head in the sort of contempt typical of those in high position, the common display of a gentleman in the presence of petty men. The guests, fearful of causing trouble, held out their glasses in a show of respect for Li, who, like a man who dismounts from his mule on a downward slope, emptied his glass, wiped his mouth on his sleeve, and, picking up the thread of conversation lost in the remonstrance of the elder Liu son, said:

"Worthy gentlemen, I revealed the secret of the Lord Magistrate's beard to you only because we are all friends. As the adage goes, 'While we are not related, we come from the same place.' Now that you have been let in on the secret, you must keep it inside and let it rot there. Under no circumstances is what I said to leave this room, for if it were to find its way to the ear of His Eminence, my rice bowl would be unalterably smashed. These are things known only to the Magistrate, to the First Lady, and to me. Kindly take heed!"

Clasping his fists together at his chest, Li Wu bowed to each of the guests in turn; they returned the gesture. "You needn't worry. It is a rare honor for a place like ours to have in its midst a superior man like Elder Li Wu! Our residents, one and all, wait with bated breath to benefit from their association with you. With that in mind, by speaking out of turn, we would be doing injury to ourselves."

"It is precisely because we are one big family that I am willing to speak my mind." Li Wu took another drink and then lowered his voice to speak conspiratorially: "His Eminence frequently summons me to his official document room as a conversation partner. We sit across from one another, like brothers, drinking millet spirits, eating dog meat, and chatting about everything under the sun, past and present. Our Magistrate is a man of erudition, familiar with the affairs of the world, and never happier than when he is engaged in such conversations, with a supply of meat and spirits at hand. These talks frequently continue late into the night, so unnerving the Magistrate's wife that she sends a maidservant to rap on the window and call out, 'Master, the Mistress says it is getting late; time to take your rest.' He invariably replies, 'Meixiang, go back and tell the Mistress not to wait up for me, that our young Li and I have yet to finish our chat.' I am not in favor with the Mistress, and that is the cause. A few days ago, on my way to the rear hall on an assignment, I met up with her, and as she blocked my way, she said, 'Aren't you something, Little Li, keeping the Magistrate up half the night talking about who knows what, to the point that he has even begun to neglect me. You little wretch, do you or do you not deserve a beating?' Shaken to the core, I stammered, 'I do, I do!'"

"Elder Brother Li," Collegian Ma Da interrupted, "none of us here has ever laid eyes on the First Lady, though there is talk that her face is cratered with pockmarks . . ."

"Rubbish! Utter nonsense. Anyone who says that deserves to wind up in the layer of Hell for wayward tongues!" Li Wu was red in the face from anger. "I ask you, Collegian Ma Da, what is that head of yours filled with, soy milk or rice congee? You have been taught in the 'Zhao Qian Sun Li Zhou Wu Zheng Wang' of the *Hundred Family Surnames* and 'Heaven is black and Earth is yellow, the universe is in chaos,' from the *Book of Changes*, so why do you not use your head and consider the august lady's lineage! Born into a great family, she was a pearl in the hand of a doting father, raised by a nanny and waited on by a household of maidservants. Her quarters are kept in such immaculate condition that a slice of sticky-rice cake dropped to the floor can be retrieved without a speck of dust. How, I ask you, could anyone emerge from such an environment scarred by the unspeakable affliction of smallpox? The only way she would have marks on her face is if you, Collegian Ma, were to scratch it with your fingernails!"

No amount of discipline could have kept the gathered elites from bursting into sidesplitting laughter, and no amount of self-control could have kept Collegian Ma's face from turning bright red. "Yes, of course," he said, both to defend and to mock himself. "How could a fairy among mortals possibly have pockmarks? What an ugly, hateful rumor that is!"

Li Wu cast a sideways glance at the nearly empty plate of meat in front of Sun Bing and swallowed a mouthful of saliva. "That His Eminence Qian and I, his subordinate, have a close and cordial relationship goes without saying. He once said to me, 'Little Li, there is a natural affinity between us. I cannot tell you why, but it seems to me that you and I are of one heart and mind, adjacent lungs, entwined intestines, and overlapping stomachs."

Sun Bing nearly spat out the food in his mouth along with his derisive snort, and only by stretching out his neck was he able to swallow it down. "What that means to me," he said, "is that when Magistrate Qian has eaten his fill, you are no longer hungry."

"Sun Bing!" Li Wu bellowed. "What is that supposed to mean? Aren't you an actor who plays emperors and kings, ministers and princes, scholars and beauties, praising the virtues of loyalty, piety, benevolence, and righteousness resounding across the heavens, day in and day out? Then how can you be ignorant of what it means to live in civilized society? You have taken for your sole enjoyment the only meat dish on the table, to which the grease on your lips bears testimony. And yet you have the audacity to slander others, you filthy maggot!"

"Now that you have grown tired of your sea cucumber, bird's nest, camel's hoof, and bear's paw," Sun Bing said with a laugh, "how can you drool over a plate of pork?"

"You are trying to measure the stature of a great man with the yardstick of a petty one! I object not for myself, but for my fellow guests."

Again Sun Bing laughed. "They have filled their bellies by licking your hot ass, so what need do they have for meat?"

Stung by Sun's comment, the guests cursed him all at the same time. Unaffected by their anger, he finished what was left of the meat on the plate, then picked up a steamed bun and used it to sop up the gravy. That done, he belched, lit his pipe, and enjoyed a relaxing smoke.

Li Wu shook his head and sighed. "Born of parents, but raised without them, you should be sent into the city by Magistrate Qian to be given fifty lashes!"

"I say we let it go, brother Li Wu," Collegian Ma Da chimed in. "The ancients have taught us that idle talk is our drink and free chats our meat. Tell us more about Magistrate Qian and the goings-on in the yamen. That will be a sumptuous feast."

"I've lost interest," Li Wu replied. "What I can say is, the people of Gaomi County are blessed to have Eminence Qian as their wise and caring Magistrate. Given the depth of his talents, how can we residents of such a trifling little county expect to keep him with us? The day will come when our illustrious official will move up and away from us, if for no other reason than the supernatural beard that adorns his chin. He will attain no less an appointment than Provincial Governor, and when the opportunity presents itself, he, like his esteemed father-in-law, Lord Wenzheng, will become a renowned official for whom the sky is the limit, a pillar of the nation a real possibility."

"When Eminence Qian rises to fame, Li Wu will move up along with him," Collegian Ma remarked. "That is what is meant by 'When the moon is bright, a bald man shines, and when the water rises, the ferryboat floats highest.' Brother Li Wu, a toast from your humble servant. What worries me is that once your career is in ascent, I can imagine how difficult it will be to see you!"

After draining his glass, Li Wu said, "Truth is, for a subordinate, all the fine language in the world can be refined down to a single word: loyalty. If your superior smiles your way, that is no reason to turn up your nose at others, and if he gives you a swift kick, there is no need to bemoan your fate. That does not hold true, however, for men like Magistrate Qian and Lord Wenzheng, who are either heavenly constellations come down to earth or mighty dragons who have returned to the land of mortals, and live in a different universe than us common folk. What, I ask, is Lord Wenzheng? He is a giant python come back to be among us. People have said that he suffered from ringworm, and that when he climbed out of bed each morning, his servants could fill a ladle with the flakes of pale skin on the sheet. But Magistrate Qian took me aside and told me that what they found was snake molt. And what, I ask you, is Magistrate Qian? I'll tell you, but you must keep it to yourselves. Once, after he and I had talked late into the night, we were so tired we climbed onto the kang in the Western Parlor, curled up, and went to sleep. All of a sudden, I felt something heavy on top of me—I was dreaming that a tiger had its claws in me. I awoke with a fright, and guess what I saw: one of the Magistrate's legs was draped across my body . . ."

The men around the table held their breath as their faces paled; their eyes were glued to Li Wu's mouth, into which he emptied yet another glass. "That is when I grasped the truth that the Magistrate's beard is so lush that, in reality, it is the beard of a tiger."

Sun Bing knocked the ashes from his pipe on a table leg, then puffed up his cheeks and blew the tar out of the stem. After tucking his pipe away, he grasped his beard with both hands and, with an exaggerated and strikingly artistic stage gesture, flung it to one side. Assuming the articulated cadence of an operatic old man, he intoned:

"Little Li Wu, go back and tell your master for me that the beard on his chin cannot compare with the hair around my prick!"

3

Bright and early the next morning, before all the fatty pork he'd eaten had moved beyond his stomach, Sun Bing was yanked out of bed by four yamen bailiffs and thrown naked to the floor. His bed partner, Little Peach, an actress who took leading lady dan roles, curled up in a corner, wearing only a red belly warmer, and shuddered from fear. In the chaos that followed, the attackers smashed a chamber pot with a misplaced kick, filling the air with the pungent smell of urine and raising welts all over Sun's body.

"Worthy brothers," he shouted, "let's talk this out, what do you say?"

Two of the men picked him up off the floor, twisting his arms behind him, while a third lit a lamp in a wall recess. Sun Bing saw Li Wu's smirking face in the golden light.

"Li Wu," he said, "there is no bad blood between us, never has been, so why are you doing this to me?"

Li Wu stepped up, slapped Sun, and then spat in his face.

"You stinking actor," he said contemptuously, "you're right, there is no bad blood between you and me. But there is great enmity between you and Magistrate Qian. As his subordinate, I have no choice but to take you into custody, for which I ask your forbearance."

"What enmity is there between Magistrate Qian and me?"

Li Wu smirked. "Dear brother, you really do have a short memory. Last night you said that the beard on his chin cannot compare with the hair around your prick, if I'm not mistaken."

Sun Bing rolled his eyes. "That is malicious slander, Li Wu. When did I say something like that? I'd have to be crazy or stupid to utter something as idiotic as that, and I am neither."

"You may not be crazy or stupid, but greasy pork muddled your mind."

"Dry shit does not stick to one's body!"

"Any man worthy of the name stands behind his words and deeds!" Li Wu insisted. "Now, do you want to get dressed, or shall we take you along naked? If you dress, make it snappy. We don't have time to argue with a stinking actor, for Magistrate Qian is waiting at the yamen to get a look at the hair around your prick!"

<hr>

4

<hr>

The bailiffs dragged and pushed Sun Bing into a hall in the county yamen. He was in a bit of a daze, and his body ached and burned from the beatings he'd suffered over the last three days in a jail cell, where he had played host to legions of bedbugs and fleas. During those three days, he had been taken out of his cell and blindfolded six times by guards, who proceeded to beat him with leather whips and clubs until he was banging into walls like a blind donkey. During those three days, he was given one cup of foul water and a single bowl of spoiled rice. Now, at the end of those three days, he was famished and parched, he ached all over, and most of his blood had been sucked dry by the fleas and bedbugs, whose bodies glistened on the walls like buckwheat soaked in oil. He felt that he was on his last legs, that he would not be able to survive three more days. He regretted his impetuous comment, no matter how pleased he'd been with it at the time. He also wished he hadn't taken the plate of pork all for himself. Now would be a good time to reach up and punish his trouble-making mouth with several vicious slaps. But no sooner had he raised his arm than he saw stars. Sore and stiff, that arm felt like a piece of cold steel. It fell back to his side, a heavy weight, and hung from his shoulder like a yoke.

On that overcast day, the yamen hall was illuminated by a dozen or more thick candles made of mutton tallow, the odor spreading through the hall from the flickering flames. It was a rancid smell that fogged his mind and made him nauseous; something hard seemed to bounce off the walls of his stomach and churn up a vile liquid that rose into his throat and spewed onto the floor. More than ashamed, he experienced remorse. After wiping the muck from his lips and beard, he was about to apologize for vomiting when, suddenly, a resonant, even, practiced "WOO—WAY" emerged from the dark recesses on both sides of the hall, a scary sound that made him jump. What was he supposed to do now? The answer to that question came in the form of bailiffs' feet buried in the backs of his knees that forced him to kneel on the hard, unforgiving floor as the official made his way into the hall.

Kneeling was actually more comfortable than standing, and the expulsion of the foul contents of his stomach had cleared his mind. Now, he realized, was not the time to whine or display any weakness: any man worthy of the name accepts the consequences of his actions. Even a beheading leaves only a bowl-sized scar. Under the circumstances, the Magistrate would not be in the mood for leniency, so it would do no good to pretend otherwise. He knew he was going to die, so he might as well go out in style; in another twenty years or so, that could find its way into a libretto and keep his good name alive for generations to come. This thought set the blood racing through his veins and his temples throbbing. His dry, thirsty mouth, his empty, hungry stomach, and his bruised, aching body all seemed to bother him less. His eyes watered, bringing the eyeballs to life. His mind was back in working order, as reminders of all the solemn roles he had played and the fervent arias he had sung surged into his head: *I clench my teeth and bear up under abuse, for this cursed official I have no use.* Inspired by these heroic sentiments, he threw out his chest and raised his head in the mysterious, forbidding surroundings, as the yayi, secure in the power of the office, kept up the din of "WOO—WAY."

What was the first thing he saw after raising his head off his chest? There, seated stiffly beneath a board inscribed with the words "justice" and "honor," seated properly amid the aura of brilliant candlelight, seated correctly behind a heavy carved blood-red table, impressive with a ruddy face and long beard, sober and dignified as an idol, was the County Magistrate himself. One look told Sun Bing that he was under the powerful official's watchful eye, and he had to admit, however grudgingly, that the man had a formidable presence. Li Wu had not painted a false portrait. Most impressive was the beard that tapered down across the man's chest, each strand as fine as the silken thread of a horse's tail. Struck by a sense of shame and inferiority, he experienced a spontaneous affinity for the Magistrate, akin to being reunited with a long-lost brother. *Brothers come together in a Magistrate's hall, a scene of nostalgia brings tears to all.*

The Magistrate pounded his gavel, the crisp sound reverberating through the hall. Sun Bing tensed, caught unprepared by the sound, and as he looked into the stately visage of the Magistrate, he awoke, as from a dream, to the reality that this was not a staged performance, that the Magistrate was not an old-man actor, and that at this moment, he was not playing a stage role.

"You there, on your knees, tell us your name!"

"Your humble servant is Sun Bing."

"Home of record?"

"Northeast Township."

"Age?"

"Forty-five."

"Occupation?"

"Opera troupe leader."

"Do you know why you have been brought here?"

"I had too much to drink and was betrayed by my tongue, casting aspersions on His Eminence."

"Just what were those aspersions?"

"I dare not repeat them."

"No harm will come to you for repeating them now."

"I dare not."

"I order you to do so."

"I said that the beard on the County Magistrate's chin cannot compare with the hair around my prick."

The comment was met with giggles all around. Sun Bing glanced at the Magistrate, who appeared to have found the comment humorous, but only for a moment, as a stern look replaced the evanescent smile.

"Reckless Sun Bing!" His Eminence thundered, pounding his gavel a second time. "What prompted you to subject this official to humiliation?"

"I deserve death . . . I had heard that the Magistrate had grown a fine beard, news that I did not want to hear, so I said something foolish."

"Is it your desire to compare beards?"

"Your servant is unskilled and lacks talent. But I have always thought that my beard is second to none. When I perform the role of Guan Gong in *The Single Sword Meeting*, I do not need to wear a false beard."

The Great River flows east, wave upon wave, from the west floats a little boat, oh so brave. After leaving nine-tiered Dragon Phoenix Tower, we explore the depths of Dragon Lake and Tiger Cave.

"Stand up. Let me see your beard."

Sun Bing stood up and rocked from side to side, as if riding waves on a sampan.

Pendants and banners flutter looking east to Wu, a tiger loose in a flock of sheep, a fear of Cao not true . . .

"That is indeed a fine beard, but not necessarily finer than mine."

"Your servant does not yield."

"How do you propose to compare beards?"

"Water would be my choice."

"Go on."

"Your servant's beard does not float when placed in water, but goes straight to the bottom."

"Can that be?" The Magistrate stroked his beard and paused for a moment. "What do you propose should you lose?"

"If your servant loses, then his beard will be the hair around the Magistrate's prick."

This time the yayi exploded in laughter. The Magistrate slammed his gavel on the table. "Reckless Sun Bing!" he bellowed, "how dare you say such things here!"

"I deserve death."

"Sun Bing, directing vile epithets toward an official in his hall deserves severe punishment, but in light of your penchant for straight talk and a willingness to accept the consequences of your speech, I shall show mercy and approve the competition. If you win, all your crimes will be expunged. But if you lose, I shall order you to personally pull out every strand of your beard and never grow another. Do you agree?"

"Your servant agrees."

"The audience is concluded!" The Magistrate stood up and, like a bright, airy breeze, disappeared behind the screen.

5

The battle of the beards was to take place in the spacious courtyard between the yamen's main and secondary gates. Wanting not to make it too grand an affair, Magistrate Qian invited fewer than twenty of the county's most renowned members of the local gentry as spectators and witnesses. But word of the battle between His Eminence and Sun Bing spread like wildfire, and by that morning, crowds of commoners had already gathered at the yamen gate, eager to get in on the fun. The earliest arrivals, always awestruck by the power and prestige of the yamen, kept their distance from the site, but as more and more people came, pushes and shoves moved the crowd closer to the gate. Crowds sometimes fall beyond the law. Commoners, who on most days would not dare even to look up as they passed by the yamen gate, now elbowed the gate guards out of the way and spilled into the yard as if a dam had burst. A mass of humanity quickly filled the spacious yard, while even more people arrived to take their place beyond the gate. Adventurous and unruly youngsters went so far as to climb trees and sit on the perimeter wall.

Invited members of the local gentry were seated on catalpa wood benches arranged in a polygonal circle, looking as if they were carrying the weight of the world on their shoulders. They were joined by the Judicial Secretary, the Revenue Clerk, and scribes from the Six Boards. Arrayed in a circle behind them were yayi whose job it was to keep the gawkers from surging forward. Smack in the middle of the circle stood two large tubs of clear water. The principals had not yet arrived. Sweaty, oily faces gave evidence of growing anxiety. Young children, like slippery loaches, were wreaking havoc in the crowd with their erratic movements, pressing against the phalanx of yayi and throwing them off balance, like cornstalks bent before a raging flood. Most of the time these men were a ferocious, threatening lot, but on this day they seemed well disposed to the local residents. This strange and unique contest would actually create an unprecedented cordial relationship between the people and those who governed them. Then one of the benches was overturned by the crush of people, sending its occupant, a tall member of the gentry, jumping to safety. He stood there, water pipe in hand, staring cross-eyed at the crowd, his head cocked to the side like a puzzled rooster. Then a fat man with a long white beard fell to the ground, where he began crawling like a rooting pig, managing to get back on his feet only with considerable effort. As he brushed mud off of his silk gown, he filled the air with hoarse curses until his face puffed up like a red mass of dough right out of the oven. One of the yayi was shoved down onto a bench so hard that he injured his ribcage. He screamed like a stuck pig until his fellow yayi rescued him from his misery. The individual in charge of the yayi, Liu Pu, a young man with a gaunt face and dark skin, stood on one of the benches and, in a lilting Sichuan accent, made a friendly announcement:

"Please don't push and shove, fellow townsmen. Lives are at stake."

Midway through the morning, the stars of the show made their entrance. Magistrate Qian strode grandly down the steps of the Great Hall and entered the yard through the secondary gate. Bright sunlight lit up his face as he greeted the spectators with a wave of his hand. Smiling broadly, he displayed a mouth full of spotless white teeth. The crowd was moved, but not so that anyone would notice. They did not jump for joy, they did not they shed a tear, and they did not cheer. They were simply overwhelmed by the Magistrate's presence. They had, of course, heard that he was a handsome man, but few of them had actually laid eyes on him. On this day he was dressed casually, not in his official robes. Since he was hatless, his broad forehead was freshly shaved, the shiny green of a crab shell; his scalp was slicked down with oil, leading to a long, thick braid that fell down the rise in his buttocks and was secured at the end by a jade ornament from which hung a tiny silver bell that tinkled crisply with each move. The venerable official wore a loose white silk robe and thick-soled green cloth shoes with ribs down the middle; his ankles were tied off with silk garters. The trousers under his robe were so baggy that his midsection looked like a giant floating jellyfish. The highlight of his appearance, of course, was the beard that fell from his chin. Ah, but that was no ordinary beard; it was, rather, a strip of black satin lying atop the man's chest. So bright it was, so shiny, so glossy, and so sleek. The bright shiny glossy sleek beard hanging in front of the Magistrate's snow-white chest had a comforting, cheery effect on all who saw it. A woman in the crowd was so taken by the sight of the venerable Magistrate, elegant and graceful, like a jade tree standing before a breeze, that her heart melted, as she seemed to float above the ground, her eyes filling with tears. On a drizzly night only months before, she had been captivated by the easy manner of Magistrate Qian, but on that occasion he had been dressed in his official attire and was properly stern, altogether different from the casual look he affected now. If one were to say that the Magistrate existed on an unattainable plane in his official robes, then one must admit that in everyday attire, he was quite approachable. The young woman was none other than Sun Meiniang.

Meiniang threaded her way forward, her unblinking eyes glued to His Eminence, whose every gesture and every look intoxicated her heart and possessed her soul. She cared not if she stepped on someone's foot, was not bothered if she bumped into people's shoulders; the angry shouts that followed her fell on deaf ears. Some in the crowd recognized her as the daughter of one of the principals in today's battle of the beards, the actor Sun Bing, and immediately assumed that she had come to fret over her father's fate. They generously made space for her to squeeze her way up to the front row behind the ringed field of combat. At last her knee bumped into a hard wooden bench, and she peered between the heads of some yayi. Her heart had already taken flight and landed on His Eminence's breast, like a pet bird, there to make its nest and raise its young in bone-penetrating warmth.

The radiant sunlight filled the Magistrate's eyes with incandescent passion. With hands clasped in front of his chest, he bowed to the assembled members of the local gentry, then turned and did the same to the ordinary residents. Saying not a word, he caressed the crowd with a bewitching smile. Sun Meiniang sensed his gaze brushing her face and stopped for a moment—she felt numb all over. All the fluids in her body—tears, mucus, sweat, blood, marrow—flowed out like quicksilver. She now felt as weightless as a spotless white feather, floating in the air, like a dream, like a breeze.

At that moment, two yayi emerged from the fearful lockup east of the yard, leading the way for the tall, once-robust Sun Bing, looking stern and resolute. His face seemed puffier than usual, and there were purple bruises on his neck. But none of that detracted from his spirited demeanor, however forced it might have been. Sun immediately earned the crowd's respect when he walked up and stood shoulder to shoulder with the County Magistrate. In neither his attire nor the apparent state of his health could he hold a candle to the venerable Magistrate, but his beard was in a class by itself. It looked to be fuller than his opponent's, but somewhat disheveled and not as glossy. That aside, it was a remarkable specimen of facial hair.

"That is a dignified appearance," a thin member of the local gentry said confidentially to his fat companion. "He looks exultant. There is nothing ordinary about the man."

"Not so fast," the fat man said scornfully. "What is he but a Maoqiang actor!"

The Judicial Secretary, who was to preside over the competition, rose from the bench on which he was sitting, cleared his opium-scarred throat, and announced:

"Honored gentry, county elders, today's competition is being held in response to a defamatory comment uttered by the unruly citizen Sun Bing against the venerable County Magistrate. For his felonious transgression, Sun Bing deserves to be punished to the fullest extent of the law, but since this constitutes his first offense, the Magistrate has chosen to dispose of the case with compassion. In order to disprove once and for all his defamatory comment, the Magistrate has accepted the miscreant's challenge to hold a battle of the beards. If Sun emerges the victor, the Magistrate agrees to drop all charges. But if the Magistrate wins the competition, Sun Bing must personally pull out every strand of his beard and never grow another. Is this your understanding, Sun Bing?"

"It is," Sun Bing said, his head held high. "I am grateful for the Magistrate's magnanimity!"

The Judicial Secretary then turned to the Magistrate for confirmation, which came in the form of a barely noticeable nod.

"Let the competition begin!" the Secretary announced grandly.

Without further ado, Sun Bing tore off his shirt to reveal lash marks across his shoulders. After curling his queue on top of his head, he tightened his trouser sash, struck a martial pose—legs apart, arms spread—took a deep breath, and concentrated all his strength in his chin. Like magic, his beard began to vibrate, just long enough for each strand to stretch out as straight and rigid as wire. Then, finally, he lifted his chin, keeping his back straight, as he lowered his body and slowly began to immerse his beard in the water.

This elicited no discernible reaction from Magistrate Qian, who stood off to the side with a smile and gently waved the paper fan in his hand as he watched Sun Bing concentrate his strength in his beard. The onlookers, won over by the Magistrate's graceful bearing, viewed Sun Bing's performance as artificial and repulsive, on a par with the common scoundrels who spin spears and twirl clubs to draw attention to the fake nostrums they sell. As soon as Sun began immersing his beard in the vat of water, Magistrate Qian snapped his fan shut and tucked it into his wide sleeve. Then, with a slight shift of his body, he took his beard in both hands, moved it away from his chest, and shook it, displaying boundless elegance and grace, and nearly inducing a mortal swoon in Sun Mei-niang in the process. He lifted his chin, keeping his back straight, as he lowered his body and slowly began to immerse his beard in the water.

People stood on tiptoe and craned their necks to see how the beards were faring in the water. But no matter how widely they opened their eyes, most were able to see only the Magistrate's composed, smiling countenance and Sun Bing's taut, purple face. Not even those a bit closer to the action had a view of how the beards were faring in the water. The sun was too bright, the brown wooden vats too dark.

The Judicial Secretary and Licentiate Shan, who were to judge the contest, walked back and forth between the two vats, comparing and contrasting, their faces brimming with delight. As a gesture to convince the crowd and forestall any objection, the Secretary called out:

"Those of you who want to see for yourself, come closer!"

Sun Meiniang all but leaped over the benches and strode purposefully up to the Magistrate, lowering her head to the level of the tip of his thick queue, where the inward curve of his spine and the fair lobes of his ear were displayed before her eyes. Her lips burned; a greedy desire gnawed at her heart like a little insect. She yearned to bend down and cover the Magistrate's body with kisses from her pliant lips, but she lacked the courage. A sensation more profound than pain rose up in her heart and sent a scant few teardrops onto the Magistrate's potent, handsome, well-proportioned neck. She detected a subtle fragrance emanating from the vat, in which she saw every strand of the Magistrate's beard perfectly vertical in the water, like the root system of a well-tended plant. She hated the idea of leaving the spot beside his vat, but the Judicial Secretary and Licentiate Shan nudged her over to Sun Bing's vat. There she saw that her father's beard had also gone straight to the bottom, also like a plant's root system. But the Secretary pointed to the few white whiskers floating on the surface.

"Do you see what I see, madam?" he said. "Tell everyone exactly what you see. What we say does not count, but what you say does. Go ahead, tell them who has won and who has lost."

Sun Meiniang faltered. She looked into her dieh's red face and bloodshot eyes, and in them she saw the ardent hope he placed in her. But then she turned and saw the expressive eyes of the Magistrate, and she felt as if her mouth were sealed by a sticky substance. In the end, thanks to the prodding of the Judicial Secretary and Licentiate Shan, she broke down and sobbed:

"His Eminence has won and my dieh has lost . . ."

Two heads shot up from their respective vats, bringing with them beards dripping with water. They shook them, sending drops spraying in all directions. Their eyes met. Sun Bing, breathing hard, was dumbfounded; His Eminence was smiling, calm and composed.

"Is there anything else you care to say, Sun Bing?" the Magistrate asked with a smile.

Sun's lips were twitching. He said nothing.

"In accordance with our agreement, Sun Bing, you are obligated to pluck out your beard!

Sun Bing, I say, Sun Bing, you haven't forgotten, have you? Does your word mean nothing?"

Sun grabbed his beard with both hands, looked up at the sky, and sighed. "All right, I shall pluck out these annoying threads!" With a violent tug, he jerked out a skein of whiskers and flung them to the ground; drops of blood fell from his chin. He grabbed another skein and was about to pull them out as well, when Sun Meiniang fell to her knees before the Magistrate. Her face, lovely as a peach blossom, could soften any heart. With tears in her eyes, she looked up and pleaded in a delicate voice:

"Your Eminence, I beg you to pardon my dieh."

The Magistrate squinted, a look of amazement on his face, tinged with gladness and, even more obviously, emotion. His lips fluttered. It hardly seemed as if he spoke at all:

"It's you . . ."

"Stand up, daughter." Tears spurted from Sun Bing's eyes. "I do not want you begging from anyone," he said softly.

Magistrate Qian, momentarily taken aback by this exchange, burst out laughing, and when he had finished, he said:

"Do you think I really wanted Sun Bing to pluck out that beard of his? Even though he came in second best in today's competition, a beard like his is rarely seen anywhere in the world. I would feel a sense of loss if he were to pluck it out. The goal of this competition was, first, to stamp out his arrogance, and, second, to supply this august assemblage with a bit of entertainment. Sun Bing, I forgive you your transgressions and spare you your beard. Now, go home and sing your operas!"

Sun Bing fell to his knees and kowtowed.

The commoners in attendance sighed with deep emotion.

The local gentry drenched the Magistrate in flattering words.

Sun Meiniang remained kneeling, looking into the face of the venerable Magistrate Qian with rapt concentration.

"Daughter of the Sun family, you have proven your impartiality, and though you are a woman, you have the pluck of a man, a rarity in this world." Magistrate Qian turned to his revenue clerk and said, "Reward her with an ounce of silver!"

CHAPTER SIX

Competing Feet

1

A clear and very bright moon hung high in the sky, looking like a naked beauty. The third-watch gong had just sounded, and the county town lay in stillness. Smells of nature—plants and trees and insects and fish—were carried on the summer-night breeze to cover heaven and earth like fine gauze decorated with pearl ornaments. The naked moon shone down on Sun Meiniang as she strolled alone in her courtyard. She too was naked; she and the moon enhanced each other's beauty. Moonbeams flowed like water in which she swam like a large silvery fish. This was a fully bloomed flower, a piece of ripe fruit, a youthful, vigorous, and graceful body. From head to toe, with the exception of her feet—which were large and unbound—she was flawless. Her skin was glossy, the only blemish a scar on her head that was hidden by her lush hair.

That scar was the result of a bite from a donkey before she had taken her first step as an infant. Unaware that her mother lay dead on the kang from swallowing opium, she had crawled up on her mother's neatly dressed body, like climbing a resplendent mountain range. She was hungry, searching for the nipple, but in vain. She cried, and in the process she fell to the floor, where she cried even louder. No one came. So she crawled out the door, attracted by the smell of milk. No sooner had she reached the yard than she saw a young donkey drinking its mother's milk. The ill-tempered adult had been tied to a tree by her owner, and when the little girl crawled up to feed alongside, or in place of, her baby, the donkey bit down on the girl's head, gave her a shake, and flung her away, where she was immediately stained by her own blood. This time her terrified wails reached a neighbor woman, who picked her up and covered the wound with powdered lime to stop the bleeding. The injury was so severe that most people believed she would not survive. Even her normally buoyant father was sure she would die, but she hung on tenaciously. For the first fourteen years of her life, she was a scrawny, frail girl with a conspicuous scar on the back of her skull. She tagged along behind her dieh as he made the opera circuit, taking the stage in a variety of parts: little girls, little demons, even kittens. But in

115

her fifteenth year, like a desiccated wheat sprout nourished by a spring rain, she grew like a weed, and at the age of sixteen, her hair grew lush and black, the way dense new shoots burst forth from a willow tree whose canopy has been lopped off. The scar disappeared beneath all that hair. At seventeen, she fleshed out, and people discovered that she was a girl. Prior to this, because of her unbound feet and sparse hair, most of the performers in the troupe had assumed that she was a nearly bald little boy. At eighteen, she had become the prettiest maiden in Northeast Gaomi Township.

"If not for her big feet," people lamented, "the girl could become the Imperial Consort!"

It was this damning flaw—big, unbound feet—that caused her to be considered unmarriageable at the age of twenty, and was why, with no other prospects, Sun Meiniang, still lovely as a flower, was forced by harsh circumstances to marry Zhao Xiaojia, a butcher who lived and worked on the east side of town. When Meiniang moved in, Xiaojia's bound-footed mother was still alive. She hated the sight of her daughter-in-law's big feet, and tried to get her son to trim them down to size with his boning knife. When he refused, she decided to do it herself. Having lived up till then among a performing troupe, Meiniang knew all the acrobatic moves for the opera stage, and she had never been schooled in the traditional feminine imperatives of "three obediences"—first to father, then to husband, and finally to son—and the "four virtues" of fidelity, physical charm, propriety, and fine needlework. She was, not surprisingly, an untamed young woman who, now that she was married, found it suffocating to keep her temper in check and hold back her sobs. So when her mother-in-law came at her on her tiny feet, knife in hand, Meiniang's pent-up anger burst to the surface. She leaped up and let loose a flying kick, a perfect demonstration of the "virtues" of unbound feet and testimony to her training and hard work in the troupe. Not particularly steady to begin with, her bound-footed mother-in-law was knocked to the floor. Meiniang rushed up, straddled her like Wu Song on the back of a tiger, and beat her with her fists until the poor woman could only scream piteously and soil herself, front and back. In the wake of this beating, the distraught old woman's abdomen became dangerously distended, which soon led to her death. It was, for Sun Meiniang, a liberation, for she stepped up as head of the household. She converted a room with a southern exposure, facing the street, into a little public house that featured warm millet spirits and stewed dog meat for the general public. Burdened with a dullard of a husband, she relied upon her beauty to ensure a thriving business. All the local dandies entertained thoughts of finding their way into her favor, but none succeeded. Sun Meiniang was known by three nicknames: Big-Footed Fairy,

Half-Way Beauty, and Dog-Meat Xishi, a play on the name of a legendary beauty.

2

Even ten days after the battle of the beards, the people's excitement over Magistrate Qian's striking appearance and broad-minded approach to governing had not abated, and they now looked forward with eager anticipation to the festive day on which they would meet his wife. Custom dictated that on the eighteenth day of the fourth month, the doors of the three halls, access to which was severely restricted, even to leading yamen officials, the rest of the year, were thrown open for women and children for the day. The wife of the County Magistrate would rise early in the morning and, in her finest attire, sit beneath the eaves of the Third Hall in the company of her husband, smiling broadly as she received members of the local populace. A gesture of goodwill toward the people, it also served as a grand display of the adage "A revered husband deserves an honored wife."

Many of the county's ordinary residents had been witness to His Eminence's elegant bearing, and details of his wife's background and education had early on filled local women's ears. Anticipation leading to this special day had reached a fever pitch. What they yearned to know was, what sort of woman was a worthy spouse to a virtually celestial County Magistrate? Comments and opinions swirled above streets and byways like willow catkins: some said that the Magistrate's wife was a woman of unrivaled beauty, capable of toppling a city with a smile; others said that the face of the Magistrate's wife was scarred by pockmarks, that she was a demon in disguise. These two diametrically opposed views ignited avid curiosity among local women. Younger women were natural proponents of the view that the County Magistrate's wife must be favored with the beauty of fresh flowers and fine jade. Slightly older, more experienced women doubted that this romantic view was sustainable in the world in which they lived, and were more inclined to accept the folk adage that says "A desirable man is burdened with an undesirable wife, while an ugly man marries a lovely maiden." They cited as proof of this view the so-called "flower and moon" beauty of the former Magistrate's wife, he of the wretched features. But younger women, especially the unmarried maidens, were firm in their desire to believe that the wife of the new Magistrate must be the sort of beauty who had fallen to earth from heaven.

Sun Meiniang looked forward to this day more fervently than any other woman in the county. She had already seen the County Magistrate on two occasions, the first on a drizzly night in early spring. While she was trying to hit a cat that had run off with a fish, the missile struck the Magistrate's palanquin by mistake. Inviting him into her establishment, she noted his elegant appearance and demeanor in the candlelight, and was taken by his poise and easy manner, almost as if he had stepped out of a New Year's painting. His conversational skills were extraordinary, his attitude one of pure affability, and even when he discussed serious matters, a unique sense of intimacy and gentility was ever-present. Any comparison of that man with her hog-butchering husband . . . well, there *was* no comparison. If truth be known, at that moment there was no room anywhere in her heart or mind to accommodate the image of Xiaojia. She walked as if floating on air, her heart raced, and her cheeks burned. She masked her confusion with excessively polite conversation and frenetic industry in order to keep busy, but in the process she knocked over a wineglass with her sleeve and overturned a bench with her knee. All that time, with everyone's eyes on him, the Magistrate maintained the airs of his office, but she could tell, either from his coughs, which did not seem natural, or from the limpid expression in his eyes, that tender feelings lay beneath His Eminence's tough exterior. The second time she saw him was at the battle of the beards. On that occasion, as the person chosen to validate the outcome, she was close enough not only to drink in His Eminence's features with her eyes, but to smell the exquisite fragrance emanating from his body. Her lips were so close to his thick, glossy queue and his powerful neck, so very close . . . she seemed to recall that her tears fell on his neck: Ah, Your Eminence, how I hope that my tears really did fall on your neck . . . To acknowledge her impartiality, His Eminence rewarded her with an ounce of silver. But when she went to claim her reward, the goateed revenue clerk looked at her askance, with a strange gleam in his eye, resting on her feet for a very long time, which abruptly brought her back to earth. She guessed, from the look in his eyes, what he was about to say, and her heart cried out in silent agony: Oh, heaven, oh, earth, oh, Dieh, oh, Niang, my feet have spelled my doom! If only I had let my mother-in-law pare my feet with that boning knife when I had the chance, no matter how great the pain. If having small feet cost ten years of my life for each, I would gladly die twenty years before my time. Those thoughts produced a loathing for her dieh. Dieh, you not only caused the death of my niang, but might as well have caused mine as well; you cared only for your own romantic escapades and had no thoughts for your daughter; you raised your daughter like a son and refused to bind her feet . . . even if your beard had been superior to that of His Eminence, I would still have declared him the winner. Though, in fact, yours is inferior to his.

Sun Meiniang returned home with the County Magistrate's gift of silver, her passion rising whenever she recalled the look of tenderness in his eyes; but icicles formed on her heart when she conjured up the censorious look in the eyes of the revenue clerk. As the day to see the Magistrate's wife drew near, women flocked to the shops to buy cosmetics and fussed over new clothes, like maidens preparing for their wedding. But Sun Meiniang still had not made up her mind to go. Although she had seen His Eminence on but two occasions, at which he had not bestowed upon her any sweet words or honeyed phrases, she stubbornly clung to the belief that they had feelings for one another and that one day they would be together like a pair of mandarin ducks with their necks entwined. When women on the street engaged in debate over what the Magistrate's wife, whom they would soon see in person, looked like, her cheeks burned as if they were talking about a member of her family. Truth be told, she could not say whether she wished His Eminence's wife to be angelically lovely or demonically hideous. If she had the face of an angel, would that not be the end of her dream? But if she had the features of a demon, would His Eminence not be an object of pity? So she looked forward to the arrival of the special day, yet was simultaneously apprehensive of it. The day would surely come anyway, however, whether its inevitability filled her with hope or with apprehension.

She awoke amid a chorus of cockcrows. Somehow she had survived till dawn. Having no interest in making breakfast, she was even less inclined to dress up. Time and again she went outside, only to walk right back into the house, catching the eye even of Xiaojia, her gnarled log of a hog-butcher husband.

"What's wrong with you, wife," he asked, "the way you're going in and out of the house? Do you have itchy soles? I can scratch them for you with a chunk of bottle gourd."

Itchy soles? I've got a bloated belly, and I have to walk to keep from going crazy! That is what she thought of her husband's good intentions. A pomegranate tree beside the well was so red with flowers that it seemed to be on fire; she plucked one of the flowers and said a silent prayer: If the petals come out even, I'll go to the yamen to see the First Lady, but if they come out odd, I won't go, and I'll give up my dream of ever being with him.

And so she began: one petal, two petals, three . . . nineteen. An odd number. A chill settled over her heart; her mood plummeted to the depths. No, that didn't count. My prayer lacked devotion, so it doesn't count. She plucked another flower from the tree, bigger and fuller than the first one. This time she held it in both hands, closed her eyes, and mouthed a new prayer: Gods in the heavens, Immortals on earth, give me a sign . . . She began with the petals in a mood of extreme solemnity: one petal, two petals, three . . . twenty-seven.

Again, an odd number. She tore up what was left of the flower and flung it to the ground. Her head hung disconsolately on her chest. Xiaojia walked up.

"Do you want to wear a flower, my wife?" he asked in a cautious, fawning tone. "Here, let me pick one for you."

"Get away from me!" she thundered before spinning around and storming into the house, where she lay down on the kang, covered her face with the comforter, and sobbed.

Crying helped a little. She got up, washed her face, and combed her hair. Then she took a pair of half-sewn shoe soles out of her dresser, sat cross-legged on the kang, and began to sew to keep her restlessness under control and avoid having to listen to the animated chatter of the women out on the street. Her husband, foolish as ever, followed her into the house.

"They're all going to see the Magistrate's wife. Aren't you going?"

That threw her back into a state of turmoil.

"People say they're going to pass out sweets. Take me along so I can grab some."

With an exasperated sigh, she said to him, as if speaking to a child, "Are you still a little boy, Xiaojia? This is an event for women only. Why in the world would you want to go, a hulking man like you? Aren't you afraid the yayi would drive you off with their clubs?"

"But I want to grab some sweets."

"Go out and buy some if you want them so badly."

"They don't taste as good as the ones you grab."

The lively chatter of the women on the street rolled into the house like a fireball and singed her painfully. She jabbed her awl into the shoe sole; it snapped in two. She threw the sole, with the embedded awl, down onto the kang, and threw herself down on it right after. Upset and confused, she pounded the bed mat with her fists.

"Is your belly bloated again?" Xiaojia asked timidly.

Grinding her teeth, she shouted:

"I'll go! I'll go see what that dignified wife of his is like!"

She jumped down off the kang and drove all thoughts of the recent flower petal fiasco out of her mind, acting as if there had never been any hesitation where the matter of meeting the Magistrate's wife at the yamen was concerned. Once again she filled the basin and washed her face, then sat down at her mirror to put on makeup. The face looking back at her, powdered and rouged, had slightly puffy eyes, but remained as lovely as ever. Reaching into her wardrobe, she took out the new clothes she had hung in preparation for the visit, and dressed in front of her husband, who was aroused at the sight of her naked breasts. "Be a good boy, Xiaojia," she said, as if he were a child, "and wait for me at home. I'll grab some sweets for you."

Dressed in a red jacket atop green trousers beneath a floor-length green skirt, Meiniang looked like a cockscomb flower transplanted onto the street. Warm southern breezes carried the fresh fragrance of ripe yellow wheat on that resplendent sunlit day. It was the season for women in love, teased by those warm spring breezes. Burning with impatience, Meiniang wished that she could transport herself to the yamen in a single step, but the full-length skirt kept her from walking briskly. A restive heart agonized over the slow pace and was tormented by the distance that lay before her. So she scooped up the train of her skirt, lengthened her stride, and quickly overtook all the bound-footed women, who proceeded in mincing steps, hips undulating from side to side.

"What's the hurry, Mistress Zhao?"

"Where's the fire, Mistress Zhao?"

She ignored the women's queries, intent on making a beeline from Dai Family Lane all the way to the yamen's secondary gate. Half of the flower-laden branches of a pear tree at the home of Dai Banqing spread over the wall above the street. A subtle sweet aroma, the buzzing of bees, the twittering of swallows. She reached up and plucked one of the flowers and tucked it behind her ear, the barely perceptible noise drawing a string of barks from the always alert Dai family dog. With one final brush of nonexistent dust from her clothing, she let the hem of her skirt drop to the ground and entered the compound. The gate guard nodded, she responded with a smile, and before she knew it, she found herself in front of the entrance to the Third Hall courtyard, her body moistened by a thin coat of perspiration. Attending the gate was a young, fierce-looking yayi whose accent marked him as an out-of-towner, the one she'd seen at the battle of the beards. She knew that he was one of the Magistrate's trusted aides. He nodded, and once again she responded with a smile. The courtyard was filled with women, children running freely in their midst. Meiniang pushed her way into the crowd, slipping sideways up to the front, where she had an unobstructed view of a long table in the passageway beneath the Third Hall eaves. Two chairs behind the table were occupied—the one on the left by Eminence Qian, the one on the right by his wife. In her phoenix coronet and ceremonial dress, she sat with her back perfectly straight. Her red dress shone like a rosy cloud under the sun's bright rays, while her face was covered by a gauzy pink veil, which allowed for a blurred view of the shape, but none of the features. The sight had an immediate calming effect on Meiniang, for now she knew that what she had feared more than anything else was that the Magistrate's wife had a face like moonbeams and flowers. Her unwillingness to show her face in public must mean that she was, in fact, unattractive.

Instinctively, Meiniang threw out her chest, as hope was rekindled in her heart, just as she detected the heavy aroma of lilacs. She looked around and spotted a pair of mature lilac trees, one on each side of the courtyard, in full bloom. She also spotted a row of swallow nests beneath the Third Hall eaves, busily attended by adult birds flying in and out, accompanied by the chirps of fledglings inside. Legend had it that swallows never built their nests in government yamens, choosing instead the homes of good and decent farmers. But there they were, flocks of them, all tending their nests, which could only be a wonderful omen, good fortune brought to them by His Eminence, with his immense talent and strong moral character, but, needless to say, not by his veiled wife. Meiniang's gaze drifted over from her face to his, and their eyes met. To her it felt as if his eyes held the promise of adoration, and tender feelings welled up in her heart. Your Eminence, oh, Your Eminence, how could someone who is nearly an immortal take as his wife a woman who must cover her face so as not to be seen? Do pockmarks scar her face? Does she have scabby eyelids, a flat nose, a mouth full of blackened teeth? I grieve for you, Your Eminence . . . Meiniang's thoughts were a wild jumble, but then she heard a tiny cough, and that sound from his wife dispelled the intensity in the Magistrate's eyes. He turned and had a whispered conversation with her. A maidservant, her hair combed into tufts above her ears, walked up with a basket filled with dates and peanuts, which she tossed to the crowd by the fistful. Chaos erupted as the children fought over the scattered delicacies. Meiniang watched as the First Lady casually adjusted her skirts, revealing a pair of tiny, pointed golden lotuses. A gasp of admiration rose from the crowd behind her. The woman had exquisite feet, and Meiniang felt ashamed to show her face. Granted, Meiniang's skirt covered her feet, but she could not help feeling that the woman knew that her feet were big and ugly. And there was more—she knew about Meiniang's infatuation with her husband. Revealing her golden lotuses had been a conscious act, intended to humiliate her, to go on the offensive. Meiniang did not want to look, was unwilling to look at the woman's bound feet, but she could not help herself. They had pointed, slightly upturned tips like water chestnuts. And what beautiful little shoes, green satin embroidered with red flowers. The First Lady's feet were magical weapons that subdued Meiniang, the girl from the Sun family, as she felt a pair of mocking rays pass through the pink gauze and land unerringly on her face. No, not her face—they passed through the veil and her skirt to land on her big feet. Meiniang was sure she saw a haughty smile on the lips of the Magistrate's wife, and she knew she had been beaten, roundly defeated. She had the face of a goddess, but the feet of a serving girl. Her thoughts in total disarray, she began backing up. Was that mocking laughter behind her? And then it dawned on her that she had set herself apart from the others, putting on a performance in front of the Magistrate and the First Lady. Her humiliation now complete, she backed up in earnest, feet moving all over the place, ultimately stepping on the hem of her skirt and ripping it just before she fell backward in the dirt.

In the days to come, she recalled that when she fell to the ground, the Magistrate jumped to his feet on the other side of the table, with what she confidently believed was affection and concern in his eyes, the sort of look one expects only from someone near and dear. She also knew with the same degree of confidence that she saw the Magistrate's wife angrily kick him in the calf with one of her tiny feet just as he was about to leap over the table and come to her aid. Momentarily dazed, the Magistrate slowly settled back down in his seat. Interestingly, despite his wife's movements under the table, she remained poised and proper, as if nothing were amiss.

Meiniang picked herself up off the ground, her sorry plight accentuated by the humiliating laughter behind her. She scooped up her skirt and, without pausing to hide the big feet that had been shamefully exposed to the Magistrate and his wife when she fell backward, pushed her way back into the crowd. She kept herself from crying only by biting down on her lip, although tears had begun spilling from her eyes. Finally, she was as far away from the front as she could get, only to hear giggles and praise for the wife's tiny feet from the women she had just left behind. She knew instinctively that the woman was showing off those bound feet without giving the impression of doing so. How true the adage that "One beauty mark can negate a hundred moles"! Her perfectly bound feet more than compensated for a face that needed to be veiled. As she was leaving the site, Meiniang turned for one last look at His Eminence, and once more there was a bit of magic when their eyes met. His, it seemed, was a mournful look, as if to console or perhaps show his sympathy. With a sweep of the arm to cover her face with her sleeve, she ran out through the Third Hall gate into Dai Family Lane and wailed at the top of her lungs.

Meiniang returned home utterly distraught, only to have Xiaojia cling to her in search of the sweets. She shoved him away and went into the house, where she flung herself down on the kang and wept piteously. Xiaojia, who had followed her inside, stood beside the kang and cried along with her. She rolled over, sat up, grabbed the whiskbroom, and began lashing her feet. Frightened out of his wits, he stayed her hand. Then, looking up into his ugly, stupid face, she said, "Xiaojia, get a knife and cut my feet down to size."

3

The First Lady's tiny feet were like a bucket of ice water that cleared Meiniang's head, for a few days at least. But after encountering the Magistrate three
times, especially that one time when he had looked at her with infinite concern
and emotion, the scenes of their encounters waged a staunch resistance against
those tiny feet. In the end, their image grew increasingly murky, while the look
of tenderness in the Magistrate's eyes and his elegant features gained increasing clarity. Magistrate Qian filled the void in her mind. If she stared at a tree,
it flickered and swayed until it was transformed into Magistrate Qian. If she
spotted a dog's tail, it shook and wagged until it was turned into Magistrate
Qian's thick queue. If she was stoking a fire in the stove, the flames danced and
cavorted until Magistrate Qian's smiling face appeared before her. She bumped
into walls when she was out walking. She cut her fingers when she was chopping meat and felt no pain. She burned a whole pot of dog meat without notic-
ing the smell. Whatever she laid eyes on became Magistrate Qian or some part
of him. When she closed her eyes, she felt Magistrate Qian come and lie down
beside her. She could feel his rough beard prickle her soft, dainty skin. She
dreamed of Magistrate Qian touching that skin every night, and her nocturnal
screams frequently sent her husband rolling off the bed. She developed a sickly
pallor and lost weight at a perilous rate; but her eyes shone and were continu-
ously moist. For some strange reason, she suffered from hoarseness, releasing
the sort of guttural, husky laughter that is unique to women in whom passion
burns hot. She knew she had a severe case of lovesickness, and was aware of
how frightful an affliction it could be. The only way a lovesick woman can
survive is to share a bed with the man over whom she obsesses. Absent that,
her veins will dry up, she will be consumptive, and once she begins spitting
up blood, she will wither away and die. Meiniang had reached the point where
home could no longer contain her. Things that had once interested or pleased
her, like earning money or admiring a flower garden, now seemed insipid and
meaningless. Fine spirits lay flavorless on her tongue; lovely flowers turned
ghostly white in her eyes. Carrying a bamboo basket that held a dog's leg, she
passed in front of the county yamen three times a day, hoping for an accidental
meeting with the Magistrate, and if that was not to be, she would be content to
spot the green woolen curtain of his palanquin. But Magistrate Qian was like a
giant turtle hiding in deep water, leaving no trace of his existence. Her hoarse,
wanton laughter as she passed by the yamen gate so enticed the gate guards
that they rubbed their ears and scratched their cheeks in anxious delight. Oh,
how she would have liked to shout deep into the compound, purging her heart

of pent-up lustful thoughts, loud enough for Magistrate Qian to hear. But she could only mutter under her breath:

"My dear . . . my darling . . . thoughts of you are killing me . . . be merciful . . . take pity on me . . . *The County Magistrate is an immortal peach, the embodiment of manly might! I fall in love with an image that after three lifetimes still burns bright. I long to make it mine, but the best fruit is at an unreachable height, behind a leaf and out of sight. Your willing slave looks up to see your face, she thinks of you day and night. But her love you do not requite. I salivate hungrily as I shake the tree with all my might, and if the peach will not fall, the tree . . .*"

In her heart, that monologue, sizzling with passion, quickly evolved into a Maoqiang aria of infatuation, which, as she intoned it over and over, brought a glow to her face and a salacious twinkle to her eyes, leaving the impression of a moth performing a fervent dance around a flame. Her actions threw a grievous fright into the gate guards and yayi, through whose minds raced fantasies of ravishing the woman, although thoughts of the trouble that would bring down on them brought their lust under control. Flames of desire engulfed her; an ocean of passion threatened to submerge her. But that all ended when she spat up blood.

The act of spitting up blood opened a seam in the confusion that gripped her mind. He is a dignified County Magistrate, a representative of the Royal Court. What are you? The daughter of an actor, the wife of a butcher, a woman with big feet. He lives on high, you exist in the dirt; he is a unicorn, you are a feral dog. This one-sided burning lovesickness is doomed to lead nowhere. You could exhaust yourself mind and body over him, and he would not so much as notice. But if somehow he did, he would react with a disdainful smirk, one devoid of feeling for you. You can torment yourself until there is no more breath in your body, and people will conclude that you got exactly what you deserved—no sympathy, and certainly no understanding. People will not merely laugh at you, they will hurl insults. They will mock you for thinking too highly of yourself and for your inability to think straight. They will fling abuse at you for your fanciful thoughts, for acting like a monkey trying to scoop the moon out of the lake, for drawing water with a bamboo basket, for being the warty toad that wants to feast on a swan. Wake up, Sun Meiniang, and know your place in the scheme of things. Put Magistrate Qian out of your mind. For all its beauty, you cannot take the moon to bed with you. For all his wondrous ways, he belongs to heaven. Forcing herself to purge all thoughts of Magistrate Qian, over whom she had now spat up blood, she dug her fingernails into her thighs, pricked her fingers with a needle, and thumped her head with her fists, but his spirit clung to her. It followed her like a shadow, unshakable by either wind or rain, impervious to knives and flames. Holding her head in her hands, she wept out of despair.

"Defiler of my heart," she cursed softly, "set me free . . . I beg you to let me go, for I have changed and will bother you no more. Is it your wish to see me dead?"

In order to forget Magistrate Qian, she led her doltish husband to the marital bed. But Xiaojia was no Magistrate Qian, as ginseng is not Chinese rhubarb. He was not a cure for what ailed Meiniang. Sex with her husband only increased the urgency of her longing for Magistrate Qian; it was like spraying oil on a raging fire. When she went to the well, the skeletal reflection in the water nearly made her pass out; something brackish and saccharine sweet stopped up her throat. Heaven help me, is this how it ends? Is this how death will claim me, my quest unresolved? No, I mustn't die; I need to keep going.

In an attempt to revitalize herself, she took her basket, in which she had placed a dog's leg and two strings of cash, through the town's winding streets and alleys to Celestial Lane in the Nanguan District, where she banged on the door of Aunty Lü, the local sorceress. She placed the fragrant dog's leg and greasy strings of cash on the altar to the Celestial Fox—Aunty Lü's nostrils twitched at the smell of the meat; her dull eyes lit up at the sight of the money. She stilled her labored breathing by lighting a stemmed datura flower and greedily sucking in its smoke.

"Good Sister," she said at last, "you are terribly ill."

Sun Meiniang fell to her knees and sobbed.

"Please, Aunty, save me . . ."

"Tell me about it, my child." As she breathed in more of the datura smoke, she took a long look at Sun Meiniang and pronounced, "You can fool your parents, but not your healer. Tell me about it."

"I cannot, it is too hard . . ."

"You can fool the healer, but not the spirits . . ."

"I have fallen in love with someone, Aunty . . . and that love is destroying me."

With a crafty laugh, Aunty Lü asked:

"With a face like yours, Good Sister, can you not have anyone you desire?"

"You do not know who he is, Aunty."

"Who could he be? The Spirit Master of the Nine Caves? Or perhaps the Arhat of the West."

"No, Aunty, he is neither of those. It is County Magistrate Qian."

Radiant light shot from Aunty Lü's eyes. As she held her curiosity and deep interest in check, she asked Meiniang:

"What is it you wish to do, Good Sister? Are you hoping that I will work some magic to help you achieve your aim?"

"No, no . . ." Tears spilled from her eyes as she struggled to say: "Heaven and earth are separate realms, so that is not possible . . ."

"Good Sister, you are a novice in the affairs of men and women. If you are willing to pay your respects to the Celestial Fox, the man will take the bait even if he has a heart of stone."

"Aunty . . ." Meiniang buried her face in her hands; hot tears oozed from between her fingers. "Work your magic," she sobbed, "to help me forget him . . ."

"Why do you want to do that, Good Sister? Since he is the one you desire, why don't we make something good happen? Can there be anything in the world more perfect than the love between a man and a woman? Clear your mind of those foolish thoughts, Good Sister!"

"Could something good really . . . happen?"

"If you are sincere."

"I am!"

"Kneel."

4

Following Aunty Lü's instructions, Meiniang ran into a field carrying a spotless white silk scarf. After a lifetime of an unreasonable fear of snakes, on this day snakes were precisely what she was looking for. Aunty Lü had told her to kneel before an altar, close her eyes, and offer up a prayer to the Fox Spirit. Aunty Lü then intoned a chant that quickly brought the Fox Spirit into her body. At that moment, her voice turned shrill and tinny, like that of a little girl. The Fox Spirit commanded Meiniang to go into the field, where she was to find a pair of mating snakes and tie them together with the silk scarf. Once the coupling was over, the snakes would separate, leaving a spot of blood on the white silk. "Take this silk scarf," the Fox Spirit said, "to the one you love and wave it in front of him. He will then be yours, since his soul will forever after reside in you. The only way to then keep him from wanting you is to kill him with a knife."

So Meiniang, bamboo staff in hand, went to a weedy area far from the county town; there she chose a marshy spot where water plants grew in profusion. Curious birds noisily circled the sky overhead. Butterflies kept a respectable distance from her as they flitted to and fro. With her heart mimicking the dance of those butterflies, her feet sank into the spongy ground, nearly making her fall as she beat the bushes with her staff, scaring hordes of grasshoppers, katydids, hedgehogs, and jackrabbits . . . but no snakes. Snakes—what she sought and what she feared. Harboring those contradictory feelings, she continued pounding the bushes. Suddenly there was a raspy hiss, and a big brown snake wriggled out from the bushes to confront her with a hideous look, its forked tongue flicking in and out. Its eyes were hooded and gloomy, but there was a grin on its triangular face. An explosion went off in Meiniang's head, and everything went black. For a brief moment she was blinded, but she heard a meandering scream tear from her mouth just before she sat down hard on the grassy ground. By the time she had come to, the snake was long gone. Her sweat-soaked shirt felt clammy; her heart was pounding wildly, as if someone were hurling rocks inside her chest. Her lips parted, and she spat out a mouthful of blood.

What a fool I was, she chided herself, to put any faith in the sorceress's false words. And why do I keep thinking of Qian Ding? He is, after all, only a man, someone who eats and drinks and then eliminates it all, just like everyone else. Even if he climbed onto my body and squirmed in and out, it would be a sexual encounter and nothing more. What distinguishes him from Xiaojia, anyway? Get a grip on yourself, Meiniang! The rebuke, in a somber voice, seemed to come from high above, so she looked up into the clear blue and cloudless sky, where passing birds were calling out happily. Her mood was a mirror of the blue sky—clear and bright. She sighed, as if waking from a bad dream, then stood up, brushed off some blades of grass that had stuck to her dress, straightened her hair, and started walking home.

But as she passed the marshy spot, her gay mood underwent a change, for she spotted a pair of white egrets standing in the shallow water of a tiny pool whose surface shone like a mirror. Neither of them moved, as if they had been standing in the same spot for a millennium. The female was resting her head on the back of the male, whose head was turned so he could look into her eyes. They were lovers for whom no speech was needed to draw full enjoyment from mutual intimacy. Suddenly, all that changed, owing perhaps to Meiniang's unexpected arrival on the scene, or maybe they had been waiting for her to show up, and it was now time to put on a special show. They thrust out their long necks, spread their wings to reveal black feathers hidden beneath the white, and in loud voices, as if shedding their hearts' blood, welcomed her into their midst. The passionate greeting completed, they entwined their long, snake-like necks. She could hardly believe that any neck could be that soft and supple, with his and hers forming a long braid of deep emotion. Over and over they coiled and uncoiled, a seemingly endless process, one that could have gone on forever, never to end. But then they separated and began to preen one another's feathers, tenderly yet with amazing speed. Their affection was manifest in the caresses, one feather at a time, and each feather from head to tail. The display of love between the two birds moved Meiniang to tears. Prostrating herself on the damp ground, she let her hot tears merge with the grass as her heart beat a rhythm on the muddy earth. With emotions flooding her soul, she muttered:

"Heavenly beings, transform me into an egret, then do the same with Master Qian . . . with humans there are high and low, noble and base. But all birds are equal. I beg you, heavenly beings, let my neck entwine with his until we form a red rope. Let me cover his body with kisses, every inch and every pore. What I long for is his kisses covering my body. Oh, that I could swallow him whole, and be swallowed whole by him. Heavenly beings, let our necks entwine for all time, let us fan our feathers like a peacock's tail . . . I can imagine no greater pleasure, nor any more profound gift . . ."

Her feverish face wilted the grass beneath it; her fingers dug so deeply into the mud that she was pulling up roots.

Then she stood up and walked toward the birds as if in a stupor, a radiant smile creasing her mud-and-grass-covered face. She held out her white silk scarf, which billowed slightly in a breeze. Her thoughts took flight.

"Birds," she murmured, "birds, give me a drop of your blood. One drop, no more, and make my dream come true. I am you, birds, and you are him. Letting him know what is in my heart is knowing what is in your hearts, so let our hearts beat as one. All I ask, birds, is some of your happiness, just a little. I am not greedy; a tiny bit will do. Won't you take pity on me, birds, a woman whose heart has been seared by love?"

The egrets abruptly spread their wings and took off together, four strange, rail-thin legs breaking the mirrored surface of the pond in what some might have seen as awkward and others as nimble steps that left tiny ripples in their wake. Faster and faster they ran, their strength increasing, each step producing a sound like crackling glaze and sending modest sprays of water into the air. Once their legs were as straight as they would ever be, they fanned out their feathered wings, lifted their tails, and were airborne. Flying. At first they skimmed the surface, and then began to settle, reaching a spot opposite the pond, where now they were nothing but white blurs . . . Her legs had sunk into the loose mud, as if she had been standing there for a millennium . . . deeper and deeper, until the mud was up to her thighs and she felt her heated buttocks sitting on the cool mud . . .

Xiaojia rushed up and pulled her out of the mud.

For a very long time Meiniang was deathly ill, but even after the sickness passed, her longing for Magistrate Qian hung on. Aunty Lü slipped her a packet of yellow powder and said sympathetically:

"Child, having taken pity on you, the Fox Fairy has asked me to give you this love-lost powder. Take it."

With her eyes fixed on the powder, she asked:

"Aunty Lü, what is it?"

"I'll tell you after you take it. That is the only way it will be effective."

So she dumped the powder into a bowl, added water and stirred it, and then, holding her nose, swallowed the foul-smelling stuff.

"Tell me, child," Aunty Lü said, "do you really want to know what it is?"

"Yes, I do."

"I'll tell you, then," she said. "Your aunty is too soft-hearted to see a vivacious young beauty like you come to grief, so I have conjured up my ultimate power. The Fox Spirit disapproves of my decision, but you are too far gone for it to save you. What I have come up with is a secret passed down from my ancestors, one that can be applied only to daughters-in-law, never to daughters. I will hold nothing back from you. What you just drank was distilled from the feces of your beloved. It was absolutely genuine, and very costly, not a cheap imitation. It was not easy to get my hands on it, I can assure you. I paid Magistrate Qian's chef, Hu Si, three strings of cash to fetch it from the master's privy. After baking it on a clay tile, I ground it into powder, then added croton seed and Chinese rhubarb to create a powerful medicine that can relieve internal heat. Believe me, I did not prepare this lightly. You see, the Fox Spirit told me that this method can shorten the practitioner's life. But I felt so sorry for you that I was willing to give up a couple of years of my life. Child, there is one lesson you must take from ingesting this nostrum, and that is that the excretions from even a great man like Magistrate Qian are foul and smelly . . ."

Before Aunty Lü had finished her monologue, Sun Meiniang bent over and vomited, and kept vomiting till all that came up was green bile.

With this difficult episode behind her, clarity slowly returned to Meiniang's mind, which had been mired in lard. While her longing for Magistrate Qian lingered on, it was no longer an obsession. The wounds to her heart were still painful, but scabs had formed. Her appetite returned: salt now tasted like salt, and sugar was sweet again. And her body was on the mend. This baptism of love, which had rocked her to her soul, had taken a toll on her seductiveness and replaced it with innocence and purity. But sleep remained evasive, especially on moonlit nights.

5

The moonbeams were like sands of gold and silvery powder. Xiaojia was sprawled on the kang, fast asleep and filling the room with thunderous snores. She walked into the yard, where moonbeams washed over her naked body. Lingering feelings of dejection diminished the sensation, as the source of her illness lost no time in producing fresh new sprouts. Qian Ding, ah, Qian Ding! Magistrate Qian, my star-crossed lover, when will you realize that somewhere there is a woman who cannot sleep because of you? When will it dawn on you that there exists a body as ripe as a juicy peach just waiting for you to enjoy it? Bright moon, you are a woman's divinity, her best friend. The heavenly matchmaker of legend, is that not you? If it is, then what is keeping you from delivering a message for me? If it is not, then which constellation is in charge of love between a man and a woman? Or which earthbound deity? Just then a white night bird flew out from the moon and perched on a parasol tree in a corner of the yard. Her heart began to race. Oh, moon, you are, after all, the heavenly matchmaker. Though you have no eyes, there is nothing on earth that escapes your vision. Though you have no ears, you can hear whispers in the darkest rooms. You have sent down this feathered messenger after hearing my prayer. What kind is it, this great bird? Its pristine white feathers sparkle in your moonbeams; its eyes are like gold, white inlaid with yellow. It has perched on the highest and finest branch of the tree and is gazing down at me with the loveliest, most intimate look in its eyes. Bird, oh, bird, magical bird, you with a beak carved from white jade, use it to deliver my yearnings—hotter than a raging fire, more persistent than autumn rain, and more thriving than wild grass—to the man I love. If only he knew what was in my heart, I would willingly climb a mountain of knives or leap into a sea of fire. Tell him I would be happy to be a door threshold on which to scrape his feet, and that I would be content to be the horse on which he rode, whipping it to make it run fast. Tell him I have eaten his feces . . . Eminence, dear Eminence, my brother my heart my life . . . Bird, oh, bird, don't waste another second, fly away, for I am afraid my yearnings and feelings may be too much for you to carry. They are like the flowers on that tree, soaked with my blood and my tears to give off my fragrance. Each flower represents one of my intimate utterances, and there are thousands of those on that one tree. My darling . . . Sun Meiniang, her face awash in tears, fell to her knees beneath the parasol tree and gazed at the bird perched at the top. Her lips trembled as a jumble of indecipherable words poured from between those red lips and the white teeth behind them. Her sincerity was so moving that the bird cried out as it spread its wings and disappeared without a trace in the moonlight, like ice melting in water or rays of light overwhelmed by bright flames.

A pounding at the gate startled her out of her crippling infatuation. She ran back into the house and dressed quickly, then, with no shoes on her big feet, ran across the muddy ground to the gate, where, with her hand held over her pounding heart, she asked in a shaky voice:

"Who is it?"

She hoped, nearly prayed, for a miracle, that the person on the other side of the gate was the beneficiary of her impassioned sincerity, the one the gods had linked to her by a red thread. He had come to her in the moonlight. It was all she could do to keep from falling to her knees and praying for her dream to come true. But the person outside the gate called her name softly:

"Meiniang, open the gate."

"Who are you?"

"It's your dieh."

"Dieh? What are you doing here at this late hour?"

"Don't ask, daughter, your dieh is in trouble. Open the gate!"

After hurriedly sliding back the bolt, she opened the squeaky gate for Northeast Gaomi Township's famous actor, Sun Bing—who fell heavily to the ground.

Moonlight revealed patches of blood on her dieh's face. His beard, which had been the loser in a contest not long before, but had not been torn out completely, was now reduced to a few scraggly strands curled up on his bloody chin.

"What happened?" she asked in alarm.

She ran inside and woke up Xiaojia to help her dieh over to the kang, where she pried open his mouth with a chopstick and poured in half a bowlful of water. He came to, and the first thing he did was reach up to feel his chin. He burst into tears, like a little boy who has been bullied. Blood continued to ooze from his injured chin, staining the few remaining hairs, which she removed with a pair of scissors before daubing on a handful of white flour. His face had undergone a transformation; he now resembled a very strange creature.

"Who did this to you?" Meiniang demanded.

Green sparks seemed to shoot out of his tear-filled eyes. His cheek muscles tensed; his teeth ground against each other.

"It was him, it had to be him. He was the one who pulled out my beard. He won the contest, why couldn't he let it go at that? He pardoned me in front of everyone, said I didn't have to do it, but then he carried out his revenge in secret. Why? He's more vicious than a viper, a marauding blight on humanity!"

At that moment, her lovesickness was suddenly cured, and as she pondered her dazed and confused thoughts over the past several months, she felt both shame and remorse. It was almost as if she had conspired with Qian Ding to rip out her own father's beard. Magistrate Qian, she said to herself, you are a mean and sinister man, someone to whom justice means nothing. What made me think that you were a tolerant, loving people's Magistrate, instead of a cruel and ruthless thug? So what if I hovered between human and ghost because of you? That was my fault for demeaning myself. But what gave you the right to treat my father with such cruelty after he publicly acknowledged his defeat? When you pardoned him in front of everyone, I was so moved that I got down on my knees and let you tear my heart to shreds. That gesture earned for you a reputation of magnanimity, while all the time you planned to seek revenge in secret. How could I have let myself become besotted by a beast in human form, a true scoundrel? Do you have any idea what sort of life I have lived over the past few months? It was a simple question that produced both sadness and anger in her. Qian Ding, I will one day erase your dog life for tearing out my father's beard.

6

After picking out two nice fatty dog's legs, she cleaned and tossed them into a pot of soup stock, where they boiled noisily. She added spices to enhance the flavor of the meat, and tended to the fire herself, making it as strong as possible at first and then letting the meat stew over a low flame. People out on the street could smell it cooking, and big-eared Lü Seven, a regular customer, banged on the door when the aroma drifted his way. "Hey, Big-Footed Fairy," he shouted, "what wind cleared the air this time? You're cooking dog's legs again, so put me down for one."

"I'll put you down for one of your damned mother's legs!" she cursed loudly and banged the side of the pot with a spoon. In the space of a single night, she had recaptured Dog-Meat Xishi's nature—easy to laugh and quick to curse—and had regained her looks. Where the enchanting gentility that had characterized the days of all encompassing yearning for Qian Ding had gone, no one knew, but it was gone. After polishing off a bowl of pig's-blood gruel and a plate of chopped-up dog entrails, she brushed her teeth with salt, rinsed her mouth, combed her hair, and washed her face, then applied powder and dabbed on some rouge before changing out of her old clothes and taking a good look at herself in the mirror. She touched up her hair with wet fingers and placed a red velvet flower over one ear. Her eyes were moist and bright, her appearance one of grace and elegance. Even she was so taken by her own beauty that tender feelings made a reappearance. An assassin in the making? Hardly. More like a sexual provocateur. She nearly crumbled under the weight of her tender feelings, and hastily turned the mirror around so she could grind her teeth and let the hatred reignite inside her. In order to reinforce her confidence and keep her will from dissolving, she went inside to take another look at her father's chin. The flour she'd spread on it had formed clumps and was giving off a sour, unpleasant odor that had drawn flies to it. Presenting an appearance that both nauseated and pained her, he awoke with a shout when she lightly poked his chin with a piece of kindling; obviously in pain, he gazed at her with a vacant look in his puffy eyes.

"I want to ask you, Dieh," she said coldly. "What were you doing in town at that hour?"

"I went to a whorehouse," he admitted frankly.

"Pfft!" she uttered in a mocking tone. "Maybe some whore picked your beard clean to make herself a flyswatter."

"No, we're all on good terms. They would never do that to me," he insisted. "When I came out of the whorehouse, I was walking down the lane behind the county yamen when a masked man jumped out of the darkness, knocked me to the ground, and yanked out my beard, hair by hair!"

"One man could do all that?"

"He knew his martial arts. Besides, I was pretty drunk."

"How do you know it was him?"

"He had a black bag hanging from his chin," he said confidently. "Nobody but a man with a fine beard would take such care of it."

"All right, then, I'll avenge you," she said. "You may be a scoundrel, but you are my dieh!"

"How do you plan to avenge me?"

"I'll kill him!"

"No, you can't do that. That is beyond your ability. If you can yank out a handful of his beard, that will be vengeance enough for me."

"All right, that's what I'll do."

"But that is impossible too," he said, shaking his head. "With his powerful legs, he can jump three feet in the air, which is how I know he is a practiced fighter."

"Don't you know the adage 'When virtue rises one foot, vice rises ten'?"

"I'll wait here for good news," he said sarcastically. "Except there is another adage that bothers me, and that is 'Throw a meaty bun at a dog and it'll never come back.'"

"You just wait."

"Your dieh may be good for little, but I am still your dieh, and I'd rather you didn't go. I've had a good long sleep, and that's given me a chance to think some things through. Losing my beard like that is fit punishment for my misdeeds, and I cannot hold anyone else to blame. I'm going to head back, but no more singing opera for me. I've spent my whole life doing that, and it has turned me into an undesirable character. There is a line in opera that goes, 'Cast off your old self and be a new man.' Well, in my case let's change it to 'Lose your beard and be a new man.'"

"I'm not doing this for you alone."

She went into the kitchen and scooped the cooked dog's legs out of the pot with tongs, drained the liquid, and covered them with a layer of fragrant pepper salt. Then she wrapped them in dry lotus leaves and put them in her basket. From Xiaojia's tool kit she removed a paring knife and tested the point on her fingernail. Satisfied that it was sharp enough, she slipped it into the bottom of her basket.

"What do you need a knife for?" her puzzled husband asked her.

"To kill someone!"

"Who?"

"You!"

He rubbed his neck and snickered.

7

At the entrance to the county yamen, Sun Meiniang gave one of her silver bracelets to Xiaotun, who was standing guard at the gate with his fowling piece, and pinched him playfully on the thigh.

"My good brother," she said softly, "won't you let me in?"

"Let you in to do what?" Xiaotun was so pleased by the attention that his eyes had narrowed to slits. With his chin he motioned to the big drum that stood to the side of the gate. "You're supposed to beat that drum if you want to lodge a complaint."

"What sort of complaint could someone like me have that was serious enough to beat that drum?" Her sweet-smelling cheek nearly touched Xiaotun's ear. "Your Magistrate sent a message that he wanted me to bring him some dog meat."

With a series of exaggerated sniffs, Xiaotun said:

"That does smell good, really good! Who'd have imagined that Magistrate Qian liked this stuff?"

"I've never known one of you vulgar males who didn't like this stuff."

"Good sister, after you've seen to it that the Magistrate has eaten his fill, you can bring me the bones to gnaw on . . ."

She pretended to spit in his face.

"You naughty boy, do you really think I'd forget you? So tell me, where will I find the Magistrate at this hour?"

"At this hour . . ." Xiaotun looked up to see where the sun was in the sky. "I expect he'll be in the document room attending to business. Over there."

After being let in, she followed the path that took her through the garden where the beard competition had been held, past the secondary gate, and into the official compound, with its six offices; she walked down the eastern passageway, skirting the main building, where he held court, drawing curious looks from everyone she met and responding with a sweet smile that let their imaginations run wild and set their souls on fire. Yayi drooling at the sight of her swaying hips exchanged hungry looks and knowing nods of the head. Dog meat, that's right, taking him some dog meat, turns out it's the Magistrate's favorite. She is quite the sleek, plump bitch . . . pleased with themselves, the yayi smiled lasciviously.

Her heart began to race, her mouth was dry, and her knees went weak when she stepped into the Second Hall compound. The young clerk leading the way stopped and pointed with his pursed lips to the document room. She turned to thank him, but he had already left her side and returned to his courtyard. As she stood in front of the high carved and latticed door, she took a deep breath to settle the turmoil in her heart. Blasts of the heavy fragrance of lilac emerging from the Budgetary Office area behind the Second Hall made her restless. She touched up the curls at her ears, straightened the red velvet flower tucked behind one of them, then ran her hand down over her jacket, from the slanted collar to the hem. When she gently opened the door, a green curtain embroidered with two silver egrets blocked her way, and in that instant the blood seemed to race uncontrollably through her body, as the image of the intimate pair of white egrets she'd seen kissing on the pond leaped into her head. She had to bite her lip to keep from crying out, and was mystified by her inability to tell whether the turmoil she was experiencing was caused by love or by hate, by resentment or by injustice. What she did know was that her chest felt as if it might explode. With difficulty, she took several steps backward and rested her head against the coolness of the wall.

By clenching her teeth, in time she was able to calm the rough seas inside. She returned to the door, where she heard the faint rustle of pages in a book being turned and the clink of a lid as it was placed on a teacup. When that was followed by a light cough, her throat clamped shut and she could hardly breathe. It was his cough, a cough by the man of her dreams, but also the cough of a bitter enemy, the man who had yanked out every hair of her father's beard, a man with a benevolent exterior but a cruel nature. She was reminded of the humiliation stemming from her unrequited love and of Aunty Lü's advice, plus the filthy remedy she had consumed. You thug, now I know why I have come. I fooled myself into believing that I wanted to avenge my father, but in fact, the sickness is in my bones and cannot be cured, not in this life. I have come for release, though I know he could never give a passing glance to the big-footed wife of a butcher. If I throw myself at him, he will only push me away. For me there is no hope and no salvation, so I will let you watch me die, or maybe I will watch you die and then follow you by my own hand.

In order to find the courage to break through the curtain before her, she had to intensify her hatred. But that sense was like nothing so much as willow catkins lifted into the air by a spring breeze—rootless and insubstantial, powerless to keep from being blown out of existence by even the slightest breath of air. The bouquet of lilac dulled her mind and unsettled her heart, just as a faint whistle rose from the other side of the curtain, like the melodious twitter of a bird. The idea that an eminent personage such as the County Magistrate was capable of whistling like a frivolous young man caught her by surprise. A cool breezed seemed to caress her, raising gooseflesh and opening a seam in her mind. Heavenly Laoye, if I don't do something fast, my courage will desert me altogether. She needed an immediate change of plans. Reaching into her basket, she took out the knife, intending to rush into the room and stab him in the heart before turning the knife on herself. Their blood would flow together. Steeling herself, she tore open the curtain, took one step, and was in the document room; the egrets on the embroidered curtain fell back into place to cut the two of them off from the outside world.

The document room's broad writing desk, the writing implements atop it, the scrolls of calligraphy hanging on the walls, a flower rack in the corner, the flower pots on it, and the flowers and plants in them were illuminated by sunlight streaming in through the latticed window; it all slowly entered her consciousness once the intense emotions had peaked and were beginning to retreat. When she'd first parted the curtain, the only thing that had entered the curtain of her vision was the Magistrate. Casually dressed in a baggy robe, he was leaning back in an armchair with his white-stockinged feet on the table. Startled by her entrance, he took his feet down, a look of astonishment frozen on his face. He sat up, laid down the book he was reading, and stared at her.

"You . . ."

Then two pairs of eyes were riveted to each other, as if linked by red threads that quickly became entangled. An invisible rope seemed to bind her tightly, and she hadn't an ounce of strength to struggle against it. The basket over her arm and the knife in her hand clattered to the brick floor. Light glinted off the knife. She did not see it; neither did he. The cooked dog's legs gave off a mouth-watering aroma. She did not smell it; neither did he. Hot tears gurgled from her eyes and wetted her face as well as the front of her jacket. She'd put on a lotus-colored satin top whose sleeves, collar, and hem were all embroidered with pea-green floral piping. The high collar enhanced her long, delicate, fair neck. Her haughty breasts cried out from under her jacket, and her slightly reddened face looked like a dew-covered pink lotus—fragile, tender, timid, abashed. Magistrate Qian was profoundly moved. This beautiful woman, who seemed to have fallen out of the sky, was like a lover who had returned after a long absence.

He stood up and walked around the table, oblivious to the bruising bump on his leg when he skirted the corner of the desk. He could not take his eyes off hers. She filled his heart, leaving room for nothing else, like a butterfly-to-be imprisoned by the thin skin of its cocoon. His eyes were moist, his breathing labored. He stretched out his arms, opening up to her, stopping just before they met. Their eyes never wavered, despite the tears filling them. Their strength was gathering, the heat was rising, until finally they were in each other's arms, though who had made the first move would always remain a mystery. They were quickly entwined, like a pair of snakes, investing all their strength in the embrace. They stopped breathing at the same moment; their joints cracked noisily. Lips drew closer and were frozen together. Their eyes closed in the midst of a frenzy of activity by hot lips and searching tongues. Rivers roiled, seas churned; you swallow me, I devour you, lips began to melt from the heat . . . afterward, flowing water formed a channel, ripe melons fell from the vine, and no power on earth could stand in their way. There in broad daylight, amid the solemnity of a document room, absent an ivory bed and a conjugal quilt, he and she shed their cocoons and emerged with natural beauty as they achieved immortality.

CHAPTER SEVEN

Elegy

1

On the Chinese lunar calendar, March 2, 1900, was the second day of the second month in the twenty-sixth year of the Great Qing Guangxu Emperor. According to legend, that date is when the hibernating dragon lifts its head. After that day, spring sunlight begins to raise the temperature on the ground, and it is nearly time to take the oxen out into the fields to begin the plowing. For the citizens of Northeast Gaomi Township's Masang Town, who themselves had emerged from a sort of winter hibernation, it was time to crowd into the marketplace, whether or not they had business there. Those with no money to spend strolled around the area taking in the sights and watching a bit of street opera; those lucky enough to have money enjoyed buns fresh from the oven, passed the time in teashops, or enjoyed glasses of sorghum spirits. It was a bright, sunny day that year, with a slight breeze from the north, a typical early spring day when the chill of winter gives way to the warmth of spring. Fashion-conscious young women changed out of their bulky winter clothes into unlined jackets that showed off their curves.

Early in the morning, the proprietor of the Sun Family Teashop, Sun Bing, climbed up one side of the steep riverbank with his carrying pole and down the other to the Masang River, where he stepped onto the wooden pier to fill his buckets with fresh, clean water for the day's business. He saw that the last of the river ice had melted overnight, replaced by ripples on the surface of the blue-green water, from which a chilled vapor rose into the air.

The year before had seen its problems—an arid spring and a soggy autumn—but since the area had been spared hailstorms and locusts, it could not be considered an especially bad year. As evidence of his solicitude for the people's well being, Magistrate Qian had reported a flood to his superiors, which had led to a fifty percent reduction in taxes for all of Northeast Gaomi Township—making their lives even better than in years with good harvests. To show their gratitude, the residents contributed to the purchase of a people's umbrella and chose Sun Bing to present this token of respect to the Magistrate. He did everything possible to decline the request, so the people simply dumped the umbrella in his teashop.

Left with no choice, Sun Bing carried the people's umbrella to the county yamen to present it to the Magistrate. It would be his first time back since losing his beard, and as he walked down the street, though he was not sure if what he felt was shame or anger or sadness, a painful chin, hot ears, and sweaty palms were proof of something. When he met people he knew, his cheeks reddened before a word of greeting was exchanged, for no matter what they said, he detected a mocking tone and a note of derision. Worst of all, he could find no valid excuse to react with anger.

After entering the yamen compound, he was led by a yayi to the official reception hall, where he deposited the umbrella and turned to leave, just as the sound of Magistrate Qian's booming laughter was carried in on the air. Qian walked in wearing a short jacket over his long gown, a red tasseled cap on his head and a white fan in his hand. He looked and acted every bit the part of an impressive County Magistrate. He strode forward, hand outstretched, and said cordially:

"Ah, Sun Bing, a competition has formed a true bond between us."

The gamut of emotions—sweet, sour, bitter, hot, and salty—crowded Sun Bing's feelings as he gazed at the beautiful beard adorning Qian Ding's chin and thought back to the beard he had once sported, only to be replaced by an ugly, mangy-looking pitted chin. He had prepared a biting comment, but was able only to sputter, "Your humble servant has been deputized by the people of Northeast Township to present Your Eminence with this umbrella . . ." He opened the red umbrella to display the signatures of the official's subjects and held it up for him to see.

"My, my," Qian Ding uttered, clearly touched by the gesture. "How can I, a man with few talents and no virtue, accept such a grand honor? I am unworthy, truly unworthy . . ."

Qian Ding's expression of humility had a relaxing effect on Sun Bing, who straightened up and said, "If Your Honor has no further instructions, your humble servant will take his leave."

"As a representative of the good people who have honored me with this umbrella, you cannot simply leave. Chunsheng!" he shouted.

Chunsheng rushed in and bowed. "What can I do for Your Eminence?"

"Have the kitchen prepare a grand banquet," Qian Ding commanded, "and while you're at it, have my correspondence secretary deliver invitations to the banquet to senior members of the local gentry."

It was indeed a grand banquet, at which the Magistrate personally poured spirits for his guests, who took turns proposing toasts and, in the process, getting Sun Bing roaring drunk, too drunk to stand. The grudge he had carried in his heart and an indescribable sense of awkwardness vanished without a trace. So when he was lugged outside, he burst into song, a line from a Maoqiang opera:

In Peach Blossom Palace a king alone is hidden, as thoughts of the fair maiden Zhao come to him unbidden . . .

Over the year just passed, residents of Northeast Gaomi Township had felt good about things in general; but it had not been a year without troubling concerns, and foremost among them was that teams of German civil engineers had begun laying track for a rail line from Qingdao to Jinan, which would run through Gaomi Township. News of the impending construction had been in the wind for years, but had not been taken seriously. Not, that is, until the year before, when the rail bed had reached their borders. This, they all felt, was serious. All one had to do was stand on the Masang River levee to see that the rail bed had already come out of the southeast and lay across the flat open country like a turf dragon. The Germans had erected a construction shed and material storehouse to the rear of Masang Town, in the vicinity of the new rail bed, which looked from a distance like a pair of enormous ships.

After returning with his buckets of water, Sun Bing put down his carrying pole and told his newly hired helper, a youngster called Stone, to boil the water while he went out front to clean off the tables, chairs, and benches, wash the teapots and cups, and open the door to the street. That done, he sat behind the counter and enjoyed a smoke as he waited for customers.

2

The forcible loss of Sun Bing's beard had introduced profound changes in his life.

He lay in bed that morning staring up at the rope hanging from the rafters, waiting to hear whether or not his daughter had been successful in her intended assassination. He was ready at a moment's notice to take his own life, for he knew that however the attempt turned out, he was not likely to avoid implication, which would mean imprisonment—again. He knew the horrors of the county lockup from his earlier experience, and would kill himself before going back there.

He stayed in bed the whole day, awake most of the time and sleeping the rest, or lying somewhere between the two, and at those times the image of that thug seemed to fall out of the moonlit sky straight into his head. Big and tall, he had powerful legs and moved like a black cat, quick and nimble. Sun Bing had been walking down the narrow cobblestone lane that ran from Ten Fragrances Tower to the Cao Family Inn; the stones beneath his feet turned a watery bright in the moonlight, as he dragged a long shadow behind him. His legs were rubbery, his head foggy, thanks to his drinking and whoring at Ten Fragrances Tower, so when the man in black suddenly appeared in front of him, he thought he was seeing things. But the man's chilling laughter quickly cleared his head. He instinctively dug out the few coins he had in his pocket and tossed them to the ground in front of him. As the coins clinked on the stone-paved road, he slurred the words "Friend, my name is Sun Bing; I'm a poor Mao-qiang actor from Northeast Gaomi Township. I just spent all my money on a bit of debauchery, but come see me where I live someday, and I'll sing a whole play for you." The man in black did not even look at the coins on the ground. Instead, he pressed closer and closer, so close that Sun Bing felt a chill emanating from the man's body. He was clear-headed enough to realize that he was face to face, not with a run-of-the-mill mugger who wanted money, but with someone intent on harming him. His mind spun like a carousel as he scrolled through his potential enemies and backed up slowly, all the way to a corner formed by a pair of walls, out of the moonlight. The man in black, however, remained in the light, silvery rays reflecting off his body. Though his face was masked, the outlines of his face were discernible, and the loose black sack that hung from his chin down past his chest flashed into Sun Bing's field of vision, a sight that opened up a crack in his mind to let in the light of understanding; the image of the County Magistrate seemed to emerge from the cocoon of black clothing. A sense of terror was abruptly replaced by loathing and contempt. "So, it's His Eminence," he said disdainfully. More chilling laughter was the response of the man in black as he took hold of the loose sack and shook it, as if to confirm the accuracy of Sun Bing's conjecture. "So tell me, Your Eminence," Sun Bing said, "what do you want from me?" He clenched his fists in readiness to engage the County Magistrate, who was disguised as a man of the night. But before a punch was thrown, his chin felt as if the skin had been ripped off, and he saw that the man was holding a handful of his beard. With a screech, Sun Bing rushed at his attacker. Half a lifetime of singing opera had taught him how to execute a somersault and perform tumbling acts, and although these were only play-acting martial moves, in a fight with a scholar they were more than adequate. Sun Bing's anger stoked his fighting spirit as he moved into the moonlight to accost the man in black. But before his first punch landed, Sun Bing was lying flat on his back, his head reverberating from thudding against the stones in the lane; he lost consciousness from the excruciating pain, and when he came to, the man in black was standing over him, his foot planted on Sun Bing's chest. He had trouble breathing. "Your Eminence," he said with difficulty, "didn't you already pardon me? Then why . . ." More chilling laughter, but not a word in response. He reached down and grabbed Sun's beard, yanked hard, and pulled most of it out of his chin. Sun Bing screamed in agony. The man in black tossed the beard away, picked up a stone, and stuffed it into Sun's mouth. Then, with amazing skill and strength, he jerked out the remaining whiskers. By the time Sun Bing struggled to his feet, the man in black was gone, and if not for the searing pain in his chin and the back of his head, he'd have thought it had all been a dream. But there was also the stone that filled his mouth, which he removed with his fingers and immediately burst into tears. He looked down on the ground, and there, in the moonlight, he saw the remnants of his beard on the cobblestones, like clumps of water grass, still twitching sadly.

Just before nightfall, his son-in-law walked in buoyantly, tossed him a chunk of flatbread, and walked out, still buoyant. His daughter did not return until it was time to light the lamps. In the glow of red candlelight, she appeared to be wild with joy, not at all like a woman who had just killed someone, not even like a woman who had tried but failed to kill someone. She was acting like a woman who had just returned from a wedding banquet. Before he could open his mouth to say anything, she said sternly:

"Dieh, you could not have been more wrong if you had tried. Magistrate Qian is a scholar whose hands are as soft as cotton batting. How could someone like that be a masked thug? If you ask me, you let those whores of yours pour horse piss down your throat, and you went half blind and half mad. I can't think of any other reason why you would say something so crazy. Think about it: if His Eminence wanted your beard removed, do you really think that he, a high official, would do it himself? Besides, if he wanted your beard gone, he could have made you do it yourself after the contest, couldn't he? Why go to the trouble of pardoning you? Not only that, but with what you said about him, he could have had you killed on the spot or put you in the local lockup and left you there to die, like so many before you. But instead he challenged you to a contest. Dieh, you have already left your forties and entered your fifties, so you ought to act your age instead of whoring around and womanizing. The way I see it, the old man in the sky sent someone down to remove that beard of yours as a warning, and if you don't wise up, the next time it will be your head."

His daughter's rapid-fire rebuke made Sun Bing break out in a sweat, and he gazed at her, feeling that something was amiss, however serious she might look. The absurdity of it all had him thinking that most of what she'd said sounded nothing like his daughter. She'd become a different person in the space of a single day.

"Meiniang," he said with a sneer, "what magic has that Qian fellow performed on you?"

"Is that the sort of thing a father says to his daughter?" she replied angrily. "Magistrate Qian is an upright gentleman who would not look cross-eyed at me." She took a silver ingot out of her pocket and tossed it onto the bed. "He said about you, 'He's a damned actor acting like a turtle awaiting an Imperial Edict.' No proper man acts like that. He is giving you fifty taels of silver to disband the opera troupe and go into business for yourself."

Burning with indignation, Sun Bing was tempted to throw the silver back to show what a Northeast Gaomi Township man was made of. Instead, once he picked up the ingot, its cold heft made it impossible to let go.

"Daughter," he said, "this ingot isn't lead wrapped in tinfoil, is it?"

"What are you talking about, Dieh?" Meiniang's anger was palpable. "Don't think I don't know how you treated Niang. The way you cheated, it's no wonder she died an angry woman. Then you let our black donkey nearly bite me to death! For that alone I'll hate you for the rest of my life. But I'm stuck with you. No matter how much I resent you, you're still my dieh. If there's only one person in the world who wishes you well, that person will be me. Please, Dieh, take Magistrate Qian's advice and do what's right. If you can find the right woman, marry her and live a peaceful life for as long as you have." And so Sun Bing returned to Northeast Gaomi Township with the silver ingot, a trip characterized by nearly uncontrollable rage one minute and unbearable shame the next. When he met people on the road, he covered his mouth with his sleeve to keep them from seeing his blood-streaked chin. Not long before he arrived home, he stopped alongside the Masang River to take a look at his reflection; looking back at him was a truly ugly face, striped with wrinkles, frosty gray temples, all in all the face of a doddering old man. With a sigh, he scooped up some water to wash his face, no matter how much it hurt, before heading home.

Sun Bing disbanded the opera troupe. Since he'd already had an intimate relationship with Little Peach, an orphan who sang the female leads, he went ahead and married her. They seemed well suited to one another, despite the substantial difference in age. With the silver given by Magistrate Qian, they bought a compound that faced the street, made some modifications, and opened the Sun Family Teashop. In the spring, Little Peach delivered twins, a boy and a girl, which made him deliriously happy. Magistrate Qian sent a congratulatory gift, a pair of silver necklaces, each weighing an ounce. The news spread like a thunderclap through Northeast Gaomi Township. Congratulations arrived from so many township residents that a banquet consisting of forty tables was necessary as an expression of appreciation. In their private conversations, people began referring to Magistrate Qian as Sun Bing's semi-son-in-law and to Sun Meiniang as a semi-Magistrate. When this talk reached Sun Bing's ears, he was, of course, mortified, but as time passed, apathy set in. Now that he had a smooth chin, like a wild horse shorn of its mane and tail, he had lost the air of intimidation and was no longer so easy to anger. A nearly permanent scowl was replaced by a gentle, mellow look. Life was good for the new Sun Bing. His face had regained its color, he was at peace with the world, and he had become a country squire.

3

At mid-morning, customers filled the teashop. Sun Bing, who was wearing only a thin jacket with a towel draped over his shoulder, was sweating as he went from table to table with a long-nosed brass teapot to fill people's glasses. As a one-time singer of old men's roles in opera, he had a sonorous voice with a tragic air, a talent he put to use in his business, shouting out orders as he worked, rhythmical and cadenced. He moved quickly and poured with great accuracy, his hands and feet in perfect harmony with a distinct tempo. His ears seemed always to echo with the enchanting sounds of Maoqiang drumbeats, the strumming of a Maoqiang zither, a lute, and flutes: *Lin Chong Flees at Night. Xu Ce Runs to the City Wall. Three Kingdoms Operas: The Wind and Wave Pavilion, Wang Han Borrows Money at Year's End, Chang Mao Cries over His Cat* . . . As he made his rounds with the teapot, those operas drove out thoughts of his past and concerns for the future, keeping him focused on the joy that his work brought him. A kettle whistled in the yard out back. He ran out to replenish his teapot with boiling water. There his helper, Stone, stood by the fire, ashes in his hair and soot on his face, which made his teeth look snowy white. He reacted to the appearance of the shopkeeper by redoubling his efforts with the bellows beneath a four-burner stove on top of which sat four brass teapots. The fire blazed and crackled as drops of boiling water splashed onto the flames and turned to white, fragrant steam. Little Peach was holding a toddler in each arm, on her way to the Masang Market to take in the sights. The children's laughing faces were like bright, shiny flowers.

"Bao'er, Yun'er, say hello to Dieh-dieh," she said to them.

Together they slurred a greeting. Sun Bing set down his teapot, wiped his hands on his sleeves, and picked them up, one in each arm; and as he affectionately touched their tender little faces with his scarred chin, he breathed in their delightful milk smell. They giggled from the tickly feeling, which all but melted his heart, like soft candy, the sweetness reaching a peak before turning slightly sour. Now he moved more quickly and nimbly in the shop; his voice had more of a ring than ever as he responded to his customers. He was all smiles, and even the dullest among them could tell that he was a happy man.

Managing to steal a minute out of the busy morning, he leaned against the counter, lit his pipe, and breathed in deeply. Looking out through the double door, he watched his wife and children mingle with the crowd as they headed to the market.

A rich man with big ears was sitting at the window table. His family name was Zhang, and while he had both a formal name—Haogu—and a style name—Nianzu—everyone called him Second Master. For a man in his early fifties, he had a healthy, ruddy complexion. Perched atop his rounded head was a black satin skullcap into which a rectangular piece of green jade had been sewn. Second Master was Northeast Gaomi Township's preeminent scholar, a man who had purchased an appointment to the Imperial College. Having traveled south to the Yangtze Valley and north beyond the Great Wall, he told of spending a night with Sai Jinhua, the notorious courtesan of Peking. No one who started a conversation with him ever found him unworthy of bringing it to an end. A regular at the Sun Family Teashop, he monopolized every conversation for as long as he sat there. Picking up his glazed porcelain teacup, he removed the lid with three fingers and made the leaves on top swirl a bit before blowing on the surface and taking a sip.

"Proprietor," he called out after smacking his lips, "why is this tea so bland? It has hardly any taste."

After hurriedly knocking the ashes out of his pipe, Sun Bing trotted over and, with a bit of bowing and scraping, said:

"Second Master, it's the same tea you always drink—the best Dragon Well."

Second Master took a second sip.

"No, it still lacks taste."

"Why don't I make some in a gourd?" Sun Bing said, anxious to please.

"Scorch it ever so slightly."

Sun ran back behind the counter, where he stuck a silver needle into an opium pill and held it over a bean-oil lantern that burned all day long, turning it round and round. A peculiar odor spread throughout the shop.

After drinking half a cup of the strong, opium-infused tea, Second Master was clearly invigorated. His gaze swept the faces of the other customers like a pair of lively fish, and Sun Bing knew that he was about to launch into one of his voluble monologues. Gaunt, sallow-faced Young Master Wu Da opened his mouth to reveal teeth stained black by tea and tobacco.

"Second Master," he said, "any news of the railway?"

Second Master put down his teacup, puckered his upper lip, emitted an audible snort, and, having formed a response, declaimed:

"Of course there is. I have told you people about our family friend Jiang Runhua of the Wandong District, the lead editorial writer for the *Globe*, who has installed two teletypes to receive the latest news from Japan and the West. Well, yesterday he received an urgent message that the Old Buddha Cixi received Kaiser Wilhelm's special envoy in the Longevity Hall of the Summer Palace to discuss the construction of the rail line between Qingdao and Jinan."

Young Master Wu clapped his hands.

"Second Master," he said, "don't tell me, let me guess."

"Go ahead, guess," Second Master said. "If you're right, yours truly will pay for everyone's tea."

"Second Master is a forthright man who is unafraid to show his emotions," Young Master Wu said. "No wonder the people all love him. Here is my guess: Our mass petition worked. They are going to alter the planned route."

"Glory be! Great news!" muttered an old man with a white beard. "The Old Buddha is wise, truly wise."

But Second Master shook his head and said with a sigh:

"Sorry, gentlemen, but today you will have to pay for your own tea."

"They're not going to change it?" Young Master Wu said, his hackles rising. "Our mass petition was a waste of time, is that it?"

"Your mass petition was probably used by some official as toilet paper," Second Master said resentfully. "Just who do you think you are? The Old Buddha said, 'We can alter the course of the Yellow River, but not the course of the Jiaozhou-Jinan rail line.'"

Dejection settled over the room, punctuated by long sighs. County Scholar Qu, he with the facial blemish, said:

"Well, then, did the German Kaiser send his envoy to pay restitution for the destruction of our burial grounds?"

"Scholar Qu has finally touched upon something," Second Master said animatedly. "When the special envoy was led into the Old Buddha's presence, he prostrated himself three times and kowtowed nine before handing up an account book printed on vellum that could last millennia. 'The Great Kaiser,' the envoy said, 'will under no circumstances do anything to bring harm to the people of Northeast Gaomi Township. We will pay a hundred ounces of silver for every acre of land utilized and two hundred for every gravesite disturbed. A steamship with a load of silver ingots has already been dispatched.'"

The news was met with a moment of stunned silence, then greeted with an uproar.

"Damned liar! They took an acre and a quarter of my land, and gave me eight ounces."

"They destroyed two of my ancestors' gravesites, and gave me twelve."

"Silver? Where is it? I don't see any silver."

"What are you all bawling about?" Second Master demanded unhappily as he banged his fist on the table. "All your complaints don't make a damned bit of difference! Silver? I'll tell you where it went. It was skimmed away by those crooked interpreters, traitors, and compradors, that's where!"

"He's right," Young Master Wu agreed. "You all know Xiaoqiu, who sells oil fritters in Front Village, don't you? Well, he worked as an attendant for a man who interpreted for a German engineer for three months, and wound up with half a sack of silver dollars that he picked up off the floor during their nightly card games. As long as you're involved with the railroad—you can be a bloody tortoise or a bastard turtle—you'll strike it rich. Let me put it differently: 'When the train whistle blows, gold in thousands flows.'"

"Second Master," Scholar Qu said tentatively, "does the Old Buddha know any of this?"

"Why ask me?" He wore a scowl. "I'll just have to go ask someone else."

His comment was met with forced smiles all around, before the men returned to their tea, slurping loudly.

An awkward silence settled over the room. Second Master cast a furtive look out the door to make sure that no one was outside listening.

"And that's not the worst of it," he said softly. "Interested in hearing more?"

Every eye turned to Second Master's mouth, waiting expectantly.

After looking around the room, he said with a sense of heightened mystery:

"A good friend of the family, Wang Peiran, works as an assistant to one of the Jiaozhou yamen officials. He tells me that many strange incidents have occurred over the past few days, including men who have woken up in the morning to find that their queues have been cut off!"

Looks of incomprehension decorated all the faces around him. No one dared utter a word. Ears pricked, they waited for him to continue.

"The immediate effect has been light-headedness and a general weakness that spreads to their limbs. They then fall into a trance that nearly destroys their ability to speak. They have become blithering idiots, impervious to medical intervention, because they do not suffer from a physical malady."

"I hope this won't usher in a second Taiping Rebellion," Young Master Wu said. "I've heard old people recall the time in the Xianfeng reign when the Taipings came north, how they first cut off queues, and then heads."

"No, nothing like that," Second Master said. "This time it's German missionaries casting their secret spells, or so I heard."

Scholar Qu had his doubts.

"What could they expect to accomplish by cutting off queues?" he asked.

"Don't be such a naïve pedant," Second Master replied, clearly annoyed. "Do you really think that's what they are after, a bunch of queues? What they want is our souls! Why else would those particular symptoms appear in men who lost their queues? It's a clear sign of losing their souls."

"I still don't quite understand, Second Master," Scholar Qu said. "What good can it do the Germans to take all those souls?"

Second Master smirked in response.

"I think I know the answer," Young Master Wu said. "It's tied to the construction of the railway, isn't it?"

"Our young Wu is nobody's fool," Second Master said. Then he lowered his voice and added in a mysterious tone, "What I am going to tell you now must remain here with us. The Germans bury men's queues beneath the railroad tracks, one for each railroad tie. Every one of those queues represents a soul, and each soul represents a hale and hearty man. Here is something to think about: The trains are manufactured out of pig iron and weigh a ton. They neither drink nor eat, so how can they move across the land? And not just move, but move at an unthinkably high speed. What powers them? Think that over."

The mind-numbing thought produced an eerie silence. The whistle of a teakettle out back pierced the men's eardrums. Disaster loomed; they all felt it. Chills ran down their necks, touched, it seemed, by an invisible pair of scissors.

As anxiety over the safety of their queues gripped the men, the young clerk from the town dispensary, Qiusheng, scurried into the teashop as if flames were nipping at his heels.

"Proprietor Sun," he said breathlessly, "bad news . . . my shopkeeper sent me to tell you . . . German engineers . . . making improper advances to your wife . . . shopkeeper says you have to hurry or something terrible could happen . . ."

The news stunned Sun Bing, who dropped the teakettle in his hand and sprayed hot water and steam all around him. But shock quickly turned to anger and a pulsing of hot blood through his veins. The patrons looked on as his scarred chin began to twitch and the peaceful, benign look on his face took wing and flew away, supplanted by a fiendish grimace. Using his right hand for leverage, he leaped over the counter and grabbed the date-wood club resting against the door before running out into the street.

The excited teashop customers were all abuzz; still reeling from the frightful news about pigtails, they had now been given a second dose of bad news, with Germans taking advantage of a Chinese woman, effectively transforming terror into anger. A storehouse of resentment had been building among local residents ever since the Germans had begun construction of the Jiaozhou-Jinan line, resentment that had spilled over into loathing. Courage that had long been hidden within the residents of Northeast Gaomi Township burst to the surface, and a sense of righteous indignation took hold in people's hearts, erasing all concerns over their own physical safety. Sun Bing's patrons fell in behind him, shouting loudly on the road to the marketplace.

4

The wind whistled past Sun Bing's ears as he ran down the narrow street, the blood in his veins surging to his head, causing his eardrums to throb and hum and his eyes to glaze over. People along the way might as well have been made of paper the way they rocked back and forth as bursts of air emanating from his frantic passage hit them in waves. Distorted faces brushed past his shoulders. He saw a tight circle of people in the square in front of the Jishengtang Pharmacy and the Li Jin General Store. He could not see what they were looking at, but he heard his wife's screams and curses and the bawling of his twins, Bao'er and Yun'er, coming from inside the circle. He roared like a lion, raised his club over his head, and leaped into the fray, the crowd parting to make room. What he saw was a pair of long-legged German engineers, their heads looking like wooden clappers, one in front and one in back, with their hands all over his wife. She was fighting off their grasp, but could not keep their hands away from top and bottom at the same time. The Germans' soft pink hands, covered with fine hair, were all over her, like octopus tentacles; their green eyes seemed lit up with will-o'-the-wisps. Several Chinese lackeys stood off to the side clapping and shouting encouragement. Sun's twins were rolling and crawling on the ground and sending up a heart-rending howl. Roaring like a wounded animal, Sun charged the man who was bent over fondling his wife's crotch with both hands, his back to Sun, and brought the club—so heavy it felt like iron or steel—down on the back of his head, as if carried by a dark red burst of wind. A sickening crunch announced the meeting of the silver-gray, glossy, elongated head and the date-wood club, which vibrated in his hands. The German's body jerked upward in a strange arc before going limp; his hands were still inside Little Peach's pants as he fell over, taking her with him, and pinning her to the ground. Sun Bing saw a rivulet of blood flowing from the engineer's head a brief moment before he smelled it. The next thing he saw was the almost demonic look on the face of the other German, who had been fondling his wife's breasts, no longer the silly grin that had borne witness to the fun he was having. Sun tried to raise his club a second time to repeat the scene on the foreign devil who was fondling his wife, but his arms suddenly seemed paralyzed, and the club fell harmlessly to the ground. The fatal blow had used up all his strength. Yet out of the corner of his eye, he saw aligned behind him a small forest of raised weapons: carrying poles, hoes, shovels, brooms, but mainly fists. A deafening battle cry pounded his eardrums. Railway workers and the Chinese lackeys who had been looking on grabbed hold of the terrified engineer and carried him out of the way, stumbling past the angry mob and leaving the clubbed German at the mercy of the crowd.

After standing there nearly dumbstruck for a few moments, Sun Bing bent down and, with what little strength he could muster, pulled the still-twitching German engineer off of his wife. The man's hands seemed to have taken root in her pants; his blood was smeared all over her back. Sun Bing was sickened and felt like throwing up. The urge to vomit was stronger even than the desire to help his wife up off the ground. She managed to get to her feet on her own. Her hair was a mass of tangles, her gaunt face disfigured with smears of mud, tears, and blood. She looked ugly and scary. With a burst of sobs, she threw herself into his arms. And all he wanted to do was vomit. He was too weak to even hold her. Abruptly, she broke free and rushed to her children, who were still on the ground, still bawling. He stood there staring down at the German engineer, whose body was still wracked by spasms.

<hr />

5

<hr />

Faced with the German's corpse, which lay coiled like a dead snake, Sun Bing vaguely sensed that something terrible lay in his immediate future. And yet a voice inside rose to his defense, presenting him with the rationale for his action: Those men were molesting my wife, this one with his hands inside her pants. And look what they did to my children. I hit him; what else was I to do? Would you stand by and watch while somebody did that to your wife? And I never meant to kill him. Who knew he'd have such a soft skull? Imbued with a sense of righteous behavior, he claimed a just and reasonable defense. My fellow villagers saw it all; they are my witnesses. So are the railroad workers. You can even ask the other German engineer, who will back me up if he has a conscience. It was their fault for molesting my wife and abusing my children. I reacted instinctively with understandable anger. I wouldn't have hit him otherwise. And yet Sun Bing's sense of reason and justice did nothing to make his legs less rubbery or his mouth less dry or foul tasting. Foreboding filled his mind and would not go away, no matter how hard he tried; it incapacitated his ability to entertain complex thoughts. Large numbers of the spectators were slipping quietly away; roadside peddlers scampered to pack up and leave: the risks of hanging around even a minute longer were too great. Shops on both sides of the broad avenue shut their doors—for inventory, the signs said—in the middle of the day. The gray avenue was suddenly broader and emptier than it had been, clearing the way for a strong wind to send dead leaves and scraps of paper tumbling and swirling in from the north. A small pack of dirty mutts that had taken refuge in one of the lanes set up a chorus of barks.

A blurry image of his family performing a drama at center stage in front of a large audience took shape in his head. Probing rays beheld them from cracks in shop doors, from neighborhood windows, and from many dark, gloomy places. His wife stood there shivering in the cold wind, holding both children in her arms and looking pitifully up at her husband, silently pleading for his forgiveness and understanding. Both children buried their faces in the folds of her jacket, like terror-stricken fledglings so worried about their heads that they left their backsides exposed. He felt as if his heart had been gouged out of his body. His suffering was immeasurable. His eyes burned, his nose ached, and a sense of impending tragedy was born. He kicked the twitching German's foot. "You can goddamn stop playing dead!" he cursed and then looked up at the converging gazes and said loudly, "You all saw what happened here today. If the authorities come to investigate, please, whoever you are, tell them what you saw; do that for me, please." With his hands clasped in front, he made a turn around the square. "I am the one who killed him," he said. "I will take full responsibility and not implicate any of you, I promise you that!"

As he swept his children up in his arms, he told his wife to hold on to his jacket for the slow walk home. A blast of cold air sent chills up his spine; his sweat-soaked shirt scraped against his skin like armor.

6

Bright and early the next morning, he opened the shop and began the day as always by wiping down the tables and chairs. His helper, Stone, was out back pumping the bellows with all his might to keep the water boiling. Four brass teapots steam-whistled on the stove. But even after the sun came up over the eastern horizon, not a single customer had stepped inside. The street in front was cold, cheerless, and deserted. Gusts of chilled wind blew leaves past his door. His wife held tight to the twins' hands and stuck to him wherever he went, flashes of sheer terror emanating from her eyes. He patted each of the children on the head and said with a light-hearted laugh:

"Go back inside, there's nothing to be afraid of. It was all their doing, taking advantage of a good and decent woman. They're the ones who deserve to lose their heads."

He knew he was saying that to calm himself as well, since the hand holding the cleaning rag was shaking. Eventually, he managed to get his wife to go out back, so he could sit alone in the shop, tap a beat on a table, and sing a Mao-qiang aria:

She is home and far away, who will watch over her, I cannot say. What will happen to me, good or ill, and will she survive to live another day? Ha! Fear squeezes sweat from my feverish body, let this all end well, I pray . . .

The song ended, the dam burst, and a lifetime of opera tunes poured out of him. The more he sang, the sadder he became, and the more despondent. Two lines of tears snaked down his cheeks and onto his naked chin.

The residents of Masang Township all quietly listened to Sun Bing's songs that day.

And so he sang, all that day, till sunset, when the blood-red rays of a dying sun shone down on the willow trees lining the river, where flocks of sparrows perched in the airy canopy of the highest tree to announce the day's end, as if sending him a sign. He closed up the shop and sat at the window, club in hand, after ripping off the paper covering so he could see everything that was happening outside. Stone brought him a bowl of cooked dry millet. The first bite stuck in his throat, and he erupted in a series of hacking coughs that sent kernels of millet shooting out of his nose like buckshot.

"Youngster," he said to Stone, "I am in big trouble. Sooner or later the Germans will be here to exact revenge, so get out of here while you can."

"I'm not going anywhere, Shifu," Stone said as he brought a slingshot out from under his shirt. "I won't let you fight them alone. I'm a crack shot with one of these."

He let the boy have his way, in part because he was so hoarse he could barely talk. The pain in his chest was nearly unbearable, the same sensation he experienced when his voice cracked as he was training to sing opera. And still, though his hands trembled, now joined by his feet, he hummed arias to himself.

The clack of hooves on the cobblestone street sounded to the west soon after a crescent moon had ascended into the sky. He jumped to his feet, gripped the club tightly in his feverish hand, and readied himself for a fight. In the weak starlight, he saw the outline of a big, black mule running his way with an awkward gait. The rider, all in black, wore a mask.

The rider slid neatly off the mule in front of the teashop and knocked at the door.

Gripping his club even tighter, he held his breath and hid behind the door.

The pounding was not loud, but it was persistent.

"Who is it?" he asked hoarsely.

"It's me!"

He recognized his daughter's voice immediately. The door opened, and in rushed Meiniang, all in black.

"Don't say a word, Dieh," she said. "You have to get out of here."

"Why?" For some reason, this made him angry. "They're the ones who took liberties with a good and decent woman—"

She cut him off.

"It doesn't get any worse than this, Dieh. The Germans have already sent a telegram to Peking and Jinan. Yuan Shikai has ordered Magistrate Qian to arrest you. The constables are on their way, and will be here soon."

"Is there no justice, no fairness anywhere—"

She was in no mood to let him defend his actions.

"How can you jabber about things like that when the flames are singeing your eyebrows? If you want to get out of this alive, you must go into hiding. If not, then wait here, for they won't be long."

"What happens to my family if I run away?"

"They're almost here," she said, cocking her ear. The sound of horses was faint for the moment, but getting louder. "Are you leaving or are you staying? It's up to you." She turned and ran out the door, but immediately stuck her head back in and said, "If you go, tell Little Peach to fake madness."

He watched as his daughter nimbly jumped into the saddle and leaned forward until she looked like she was part of the mule she was riding. With a snort, the animal took off running, its flanks flashing for a moment before it disappeared in the surrounding darkness. The sound of its hooves sped east.

He shut the door, turned, and saw Little Peach standing in the room, her hair already down around her shoulders, soot smeared over her face. A torn blouse revealed her fair bosom. She came up to him and, in a voice that brooked no nonsense, said:

"Do as Meiniang said: leave, and leave now!"

An agonizing emotion welled up inside him as he looked into his wife's eyes, which flashed in the dark room, and in the midst of that seminal moment, he realized that this woman, so gentle and fragile in appearance, was blessed with great courage and a quick mind. He wrapped his arms around her, but she pushed him away.

"There's no time; you must go. Don't worry about us."

So he ran out of the shop and headed down the street he knew so well from fetching water, then ran up the Masang River bank and hid behind a large willow tree, where he could look down at the peaceful village below, the gray street, and his house. He could hear Bao'er and Yun'er—they were crying—and that nearly broke his heart. The new moon, hanging low in the western sky, was especially beautiful; the vast canopy of sky was dotted with stars that twinkled like diamonds. Every house in town was dark, and yet he knew that the occupants were not asleep, but were silently and expectantly listening for any activity outside, almost as if darkness was their best protection against bad tidings. The clack of horse hooves neared; dogs began to bark. A dark, tight formation of horses approached—how many it was impossible to say—and reddish sparks flew as the staccato beat of horseshoes on cobblestones announced their arrival.

The posse rode up and, after some confused jockeying, stopped in front of the shop. He witnessed the blurred silhouette of constables appearing to dismount from the blurred outlines of their horses, a spurt of boisterous wrangling seemingly intended to alert people to their purpose in coming. That accomplished, they lit torches they'd brought with them. The burst of light illuminated the street and nearby houses, as well as the willows on the riverbank, where he cowered behind the tree, from whose branches a flock of startled birds flew off. With a backward glance at the river behind him, he readied himself to jump in to save his skin, if necessary. But the constables took no note of the sudden bird migration, and gave no thought to searching the riverbank.

Now he could see clearly enough to count the horses—altogether nine piebald animals, a few black and white, some of the others red and brown, and all local horses: unattractive, neither plump nor robust-looking, with ragged manes and well-used saddles and fittings. Two did not even have saddles, their riders forced to make do with gunnysacks thrown over their backs. In the flickering light of the torches, the horses' heads looked big and clumsy, but their eyes were bright and clear. After shining the light of their torches on the signboard over the door, the constables calmly knocked at the door.

No response from inside.

They attacked the door.

From his vantage point, he had a vague suspicion that the constables had no intention of arresting him. They would not have dawdled like that if they had, and they would have knocked more aggressively. No, they would have scaled the wall to get inside if they'd had to, something many of them were good at. Agreeable feelings toward the constables washed over him. He did not have to be told that Magistrate Qian was in the background, and behind him, his own daughter, Meiniang.

The door eventually gave way to the assault on it, and the torch-bearing constables swaggered into the shop. Almost immediately, he heard his wife's feigned wails of insanity and crazed laughter, accompanied by the bawling of his terrified children.

The constables put up with the racket as long as they could before reemerging with their torches, some jabbering something he couldn't hear, others yawning. After a brief discussion in front of the shop and some shouted commands, they mounted up and rode off. As soon as the hoofbeats and torchlight disappeared, peace and quiet returned to the town. He was about to come out of hiding when lights flared up in town, all at once, as if on command. Everything stopped for a moment, and then dozens of lanterns appeared on the street, forming a luminous, fast-moving line that snaked its way toward him. Hot tears slipped out of his eyes.

7

Relying on the guidance of an experienced old man, he hid during the daylight hours over the days that followed and slipped back into town at night, when the streets were quiet and deserted. He spent his days in the woods on the opposite bank of the Masang River, where there were a dozen or so cottages the villagers used to cure tobacco. That was where he slept during the days, crossing the river to return home late at night. He headed back to his cottages first thing the next morning with a bundle of flatbreads and a gourd filled with water.

Many of the willow trees near the cottages were home to nesting magpies. He would lie on the kang, eating and sleeping, sleeping and eating. At first he could not screw up the courage to step outside, but gradually he grew less guarded and slipped out to look up at the squawking magpies in their nests. He and a tall, well-built young shepherd struck up a friendship. He shared his flatbreads with Mudu, the simple, honest young man, and even told him who he was—Sun Bing, the man who had killed the railroad engineer.

On the seventh day of the second lunar month, five days after killing the German, he finished off several of the flatbreads and a bowlful of water in the afternoon and was lying on the kang listening to the magpies and to the tattoos of a woodpecker attacking a tree. As he slipped into that twilight zone between sleep and wakefulness, the sharp crack of gunfire snapped him out of his stupor. He had never before heard the sound of a breech-loading rifle, which was nothing like that of a local hunting rifle. He knew immediately that this was bad. Jumping off the kang and picking up his club, he flattened himself against the wall behind the door to await the arrival of his enemies. More gunfire. It came from the opposite bank. Unable to sit still in the cottage, he slipped out the door, bent at the waist, and scrambled over a series of crumbling walls to move in among the willow trees. A cacophony of shrill sounds erupted in town: his wife was crying, his children were bawling, horses whinnied, mules brayed, and dogs barked, all at the same time. But he could not see a thing. Then an idea struck him. Slipping his club into his belt, he began climbing the tallest tree he saw. When the magpies spotted the invader, they launched an attack, but he drove them off with his club, once, twice, over and over, until they retreated. He stood on a limb next to a large nest and, holding on to keep from falling, looked down at the far side of the river. Now he could see what was happening, all of it.

At least fifty foreign horses were arrayed in front of his teashop, all ridden by foreign soldiers in bright, fancy uniforms with round, feathered caps, and firing bayonet-fitted blue-steel automatic rifles at the shop door and windows. Puffs of white smoke, like daisy blossoms, floated out of the muzzles and hung in the air for a long moment. Sunlight danced off the brass buttons on the soldiers' tunics and the bayonets attached to the barrels of their guns, blinding bright. A squad of Imperial troops wearing red-tasseled summer straw hats and tunics with white circles in the center, front and back, was arrayed behind them. Suddenly dazed, he dropped the club, which fell to the ground, banging into one limb after another on its way down. Lucky for him he was holding on to a branch, or he'd have followed the club down.

Panic took hold. He knew that this was the calamity he had dreaded. But he held on to a thread of hope that his wife's acting skills, honed over the years, especially her convincing acts of madness, would work on the German soldiers the way they had on His Eminence Magistrate Qian's constables, that they would make a fuss until they were sure he was not there and then leave. At that moment he promised himself that if they somehow escaped with their lives, he would pack up and move his family away, far away.

Nothing could have been worse than what happened next. He watched as two of the soldiers dragged his wife, kicking and screaming, down to the river, while a third soldier, bigger and taller than the others, followed with the children, dragging each of them by one leg, as if they were ducks or chickens, and deposited them on the riverbank. Stone broke free from the soldier who was restraining him by biting him on the arm. But then he saw Stone's small, dark figure back down off the riverbank, down and down, until he bumped into the rifle of a soldier behind him. The glinting blade of the bayonet ran him through. It looked like he screamed, but there was no sound as he rolled like a little black ball down the bank. From his vantage point up in the tree, Sun Bing was blinded by the sight of all that blood.

The German soldiers backed up against the riverbank, where some of them got down on one knee and others remained standing as they aimed at the townspeople. Their aim was unerring—one victim fell for each shot fired. The street and yards were littered with corpses, either face down or on their backs. Then the Imperial troops ran over and put a torch to his shop. First came the black smoke, rising into the sky, followed by golden yellow flames that crackled like firecrackers. The wind rose up and blew the smoke and fire in all directions, even carrying thick, choking clouds of smoke and the smell of fire up to his hiding place.

Then came something even worse. He looked on as the German soldiers began shoving and pulling his wife back and forth, slowly ripping off her clothes as they did so, until she was stark naked. He bit down on the branch he was holding and hit it so hard with his head that it broke the skin. While his heart flew to the opposite bank like a fireball, his body remained bound to a tree; he couldn't move. They lifted up his wife's fair body, swung her back and forth, and then let go, her momentum carrying her into the Masang River like a big white fish. Sprays of white transparent water splashed into the air without a sound and fell silently back. Finally, the soldiers speared his children and flung them into the river, too. His eyes filled with blood, nightmarishly, and his heart was on fire, yet he was frozen in place. He struggled with all his might, but in the end he could only roar, freeing his body from its paralysis; bending forward, he managed to topple over, snapping several branches as he fell before landing on the spongy ground at the base of the willow tree.

CHAPTER EIGHT

Divine Altar

1

He opened his eyes and was nearly blinded by sunlight streaming in through the branches of the willow trees. The horrific sight he'd witnessed from his perch flashed through his mind, and the constricting pain in his heart leveled him. At that moment the sound of drums pounded against his eardrums, like the drumbeats preceding the first act of a Maoqiang opera, followed by the doleful sounds of a suona, a horn, and then finally the circular, repetitive performance of a cat zither. These sounds, which had been a steady accompaniment for more than half of his lifetime, blunted the stabbing pain in his heart, like shearing off a mountain peak or filling in a ravine and turning it into a boundless plateau. The calls of magpies followed the rhythms of his heart as they flew in dramatic fashion, forming a blue cloud in the air above. A woodpecker attacked a tree—incessantly, tirelessly—echoing the urgent sounds around him. Willow catkins floating on breezy gusts of wind resembled the handsome beard he'd once worn. *With a date-wood club in my, my, my hand and a glinting dagger tucked in my waistband~~I take a step and release a wail~~take two steps as anger blazes like a fire fanned~~I, I, I race down a meandering path, this journey too great a demand.* A song of grief and indignation thundered inside him as he struggled to his feet, bracing himself against the tree trunk, his head wobbly, his feet stomping the ground. ——Bong bong bong bong bong bong——kebong kebong kebong——bong! Alas! *I, Sun Bing, gaze northward to my home, where flames send black smoke into the air. My wife murdered, she, she, she is buried in the bellies of fish, and my children so fair~~cruel, how cruel, so cruel! A little boy and a little girl consigned to the Devil's lair~~Those loathsome foreign devils with their green eyes and white hair, vipers' hearts, bereft of conscience, slaughtered the innocent, destroyed my home, and killed my family, I am alone, I, I, I~~cruel, how cruel, so cruel!~~more than I can bear!* He picked up the club that had brought such a calamity down on his head and staggered out of the woods. *I, I, I am like a wild goose separated from its flock, like a tiger out in the open, a dragon caught in the shallows . . .* He struck out with his club, pointing east and striking west, pointing south and hitting north, shattering bark. Willows wept. *You German devils! You, you, you cruelly murdered my wife and butchered my children~~this is a blood debt that will be avenged———Bong bong bong bong bong—Clang cuh-lang clang Only revenge makes me a man.* He staggered into the Masang River, swinging his club as he went, wading in till the water nearly reached his chest. The ice was breaking up, now that it was the second month, yet the water was still bone-chilling cold. But he was unmindful of the cold, as fires of vengeful loathing burned in his breast. Walking along the riverbed was difficult; the water hindered his progress like a line of foreign soldiers holding him back. He pressed forward, kept moving, striking the surface of the water with his club, pow pow pow pow pow pow! Splash, splash, water everywhere—like a tiger loose in a flock of sheep—water hit him in the face, a watery blur, a sheet of white, a sheet of blood-red. *Charging into the dragon's den, the tiger's lair, looses a murderous river of blood, I, I, I am that judge from Hell, the messenger of death.* He clawed and crawled his way up to the bank, where he fell to his knees and rubbed his hands across traces of blood that had yet to dry *My beloved children, I see that you have been sent down to the Devil's lair, and for my pain there is no gauge~~My head swims, my eyes glaze over, my world is spinning, my, my, my towering rage.* His hands were stained with blood and mud. His house was still burning, releasing waves of heat and filling the sky with hot cinders. The cloyingly sweet taste of bile was caught in his throat. He leaned over and spat out a mouthful of blood.

The bloodbath had blotted out the lives of twenty-seven citizens of Masang Township. People carried their dead to the embankment, where they lined up to await the arrival of the County Magistrate. Under the direction of Second Master Zhang, young men went into the river to retrieve the bodies of Little Peach and her twin children, Bao'er and Yun'er, which the currents had taken five li downriver. They were laid out beside the other victims. Her upper body was covered by a tattered coat, leaving her horribly pale, stiff legs exposed. Sun Bing thought back to her opera roles as chaste women, in her pheasant hat, a sword at her hip, and embroidered shoes with red velvet flowers on the tips. She swirled and twirled her broad sleeves as she sang and danced, face like a peach and waist as thin as a willow branch. She sang like an oriole, exuding charm with her alluring looks. *My wife, how do I accept that the blush of spring has been shattered by a hailstone chime, and worse, how do I endure the blade of wind and sword of rime, my, my, my tears of blood fall in a steady stream . . . I see the red moon sink in the west, where a silver crescent once hung high in the sky~~the shepherd's sad song, an old crow sings in the nighttime~~bong bong goes the gong, the palanquin shafts tremble, here comes the Gaomi County Magistrate to the scene of the crime . . .*

Sun Bing watched as Magistrate Qian stepped out of his palanquin, bent at the waist. His back, which had always been as stiff and straight as a board, was strangely hunched; his normally smiling face twitched horribly. The beard, once lush and full as a stallion's tail, looked more like the scraggly appendage of a donkey. And his eyes, usually bright and keen, were now clouded and dull. His hands clenched into fists one minute and slapped his forehead the next. A squad of bodyguards, swords at the ready, followed cautiously. Whether they were protecting him or keeping watch on him was unclear. One by one, he examined the corpses laid out on the embankment under the quiet, watchful gaze of surviving family members. As his eyes swept the line of solemn villagers, crystalline beads of sweat soaked his hair. His agitated pacing ended. He wiped his perspiring face with his sleeve and said:

"Village elders and worthy citizens, you must exercise restraint . . ."

"Laoye, we want you to plead our case . . ." Wails of grief rose from the villagers, who knelt at his feet.

"Fellow villagers, please rise. This tragic incident has struck your bereaved official like a knife to the heart. But we cannot bring the dead back to life, so please prepare coffins for your loved ones. The quicker they are buried, the earlier they will find peace . . ."

"Are you telling us they died for nothing? Are you saying the foreign devils should be free to tyrannize us?"

"Fellow villagers, I share your sorrow," said the tearful County Magistrate. "Your fathers and mothers are my parents, your sons and daughters my children. Now I must ask you, village elders and worthy citizens, to settle your mood and not take matters into your own hands. Tomorrow I will travel to the capital to seek an audience with His Excellency the Provincial Governor. I will see that you get the justice you deserve."

"We are going to carry our dead into the provincial capital!"

"No, you cannot do that, you mustn't!" It was a worrying possibility. "Please trust me to vigorously argue your case. I am prepared to sacrifice my feathered official's cap for you."

In the midst of bitter wailing on all sides, Sun Bing watched as Magistrate Qian walked up, awkwardly avoiding the villagers, and sputtered:

"Sun Bing, please come with me."

The music swirling around inside Sun Bing suddenly reached a fever pitch, as if the earth were opening up and mountains crumbling, a frenzied soaring. His brows arched upward, his tiger-eyes rounded, as he raised his club. *You sanctimonious dog of an official, shedding crocodile tears, empty promises to plead the villagers' case, when all along your plan is to take credit for making an arrest in haste. You speak not for the people you serve, but are a willing conspirator with the murderers we faced. My, my, my wife and children are dead, my hopes all turned to ashes, for which my vengeance they will taste. That would not change even for His Imperial Majesty the*

Emperor, let alone a mere Magistrate. I, I, I rub my hands and clench my fists, eager to crush the head of an official by corruption debased. He aimed his club at Magistrate Qian's head. *I care, care, care not, for a lopped-off head means only a bowl-sized scar. You are an accomplice to the ferocious tiger who deserves only death.* Magistrate Qian nimbly leaped out of the way, and Sun Bing's club merely stirred up the air. The bodyguards, seeing the danger facing their Magistrate, drew their swords and rushed Sun Bing, but they were no match for a man unafraid of death; he rent the air with a shout and leaped up like a crazed beast, as fiery sparks flew from his eyes. A roar of intimidation rose from the crowd as they advanced in anger. Sun Bing swung his club, now his weapon, and connected with a fat yayi who could not get out of the way fast enough; he tumbled head over heels down the riverbank. Magistrate Qian looked into the sky and sighed.

"Hear me out," he breathed, "I have given this much thought, as the Son of Heaven is my witness. Countrymen, this event is tied up with foreign affairs, and you must not act rashly. Sun Bing, I must let you go today, but mark my word, you may be able to make it past the first of the month, as they say, but you will not make it past the fifteenth. You are on your own, so take care."

Under the protection of his yayi, Magistrate Qian slipped back into his palanquin, which was hoisted up by his bearers, who beat a hasty retreat and were swallowed up by the dark of night.

The residents of Masang Township passed a sleepless night, with the rising and falling of wails from women and the sounds of coffin-making continuing till daybreak.

As the day began, with neighbors helping out, the dead were placed into coffins, which were lined up on the ground and sealed with nails.

Then, after the dead were buried, the survivors, whose senses were dulled, as if they had awakened from a terrible nightmare, gathered at the levee and gazed out at the railroad shed erected in one of their fields. Tracks had already been laid up to Liuting, the easternmost village of Northeast Gaomi Township, no more than six li from Masang. Their ancestral graves would soon be overrun, their flood-relief channel filled in, and their thousand-year feng shui destroyed. Rumors flew that their souls would be taken by having their queues cut off and laid beneath railroad ties; everyone's head was imperiled. The so-called mother and father officials were running dogs of the foreigners, and bitter times lay ahead for the people. Sun Bing's hair turned white overnight; the few scraggly whiskers on his chin were like dead, brittle grass. He bounced around the village, dragging his club behind him, like a feverish old opera character. People felt sorry for him, assuming he was not in his right mind, so they were surprised to hear him speak with clarity and wisdom:

"Fellow villagers, I, Sun Bing, caused this devastation when I killed that German engineer, and you have suffered, for which *I, I, I feel much anguish. I, I, I am terrified of what might happen.* So tie me up and deliver me to Qian Ding and ask him to explain the situation to the Germans. He can tell them that if they alter the path of the railroad, Sun Bing will die with no regrets."

The people lifted Sun Bing up and bombarded him with a chorus of voices:

Sun Bing, oh, Sun Bing, you are brave, upright, and bold, a man whom officials, foreign and local, must behold. Masang Township has suffered over what you did, but we knew that someday this story would be told. Better now than later, for once those foreign devils complete their railroad, all talk of peace will grow old. They say that when the fire-dragon passes, the ground trembles, and that will surely bring down our homes. We've heard that the Righteous Harmony Boxers have fought the foreign devils in Caozhou. So, Sun Bing, take what you need and flee for your life. Go to Caozhou and bring back those Boxers to eradicate the foreign devils, the common people's lives to enfold.

They took up a collection for Sun Bing and sent him on his way that very night. With tears in his eyes, he chanted:

Fellow villagers, hometown water tastes fresher, hometown sentiments are more pure. I, Sun Bing, shall not forget your generosity, and will not return without the aid you seek, that is for sure.

The villagers chanted in return:

Your voyage will be long and arduous, so take great care. You must keep a clear head and be prepared for anything, foul or fair. We will await your return with great anticipation, for then the heavenly soldiers will our rescue declare.

2

One afternoon twenty days later, Sun Bing swaggered back into Masang Township in a full-length white robe under silver armor, six silver command flags sticking up over his back. His face, beneath a silver helmet with a fist-sized red tassel, was stained bright red, and his brows were drawn in the shape of an inverted spear; he wore boots with thick soles and carried his date-wood club. He was followed into town by a pair of fearsome generals—one walked with a quick, nimble step, wore a tiger-skin apron around his waist, and had a golden hoop around his head. He carried a magic cudgel and uttered shrill cries as he bounced and jumped down the street, all in all a fine replica of Sun Wukong, the magic monkey of legend. The second general, sporting a huge paunch, wore a loose monk's robe and a square Buddhist hat. The manure rake he dragged behind him was a dead giveaway—he was Marshal Zhu Wuneng, or Zhu Bajie, the legendary Pigsy.

The threesome first appeared on the levee, sunlit apparitions breaking through a patch of dark clouds. With glistening armor, they presented a strange sight, three heavenly soldiers who had, it seemed, dropped out of the cloud-filled sky. The first person to see the figures, Young Master Wu, failed to recognize Sun Bing, so when Sun smiled at him, he did not know what to make of the man, and was terrified. He watched them enter the shop in the west where stuffed buns were made and sold; they did not reemerge.

As night fell, the villagers, as was their custom, took their coarse porcelain bowls out into the streets to eat their rice porridge. Young Master Wu ran from the east end of the village to the west, spreading the news that a trio of demonic figures had shown up. Most of the time, people discounted anything young Wu said, since his mind was more than a little muddled and he tended to spread wild stories. They were unsure whether they should believe him now, or treat it as a snack to go with their evening meal. But then, from the west end of the village, the clang of a gong rang out, and they saw the clerk Sixi emerge spiritedly from the shop wearing a black cat-skin cap, his face painted like a leopard cat, the tail of the cap swinging back and forth behind his neck. He sang out loudly as he banged his gong:

This Sun Bing, no ordinary man, in Caozhou learned from the Righteous Harmony band. He returned with two immortals, Sun Wukong and Zhu Bajie, to uproot railroad tracks, kill the traitors, and drive out the foreign devils, till peace is at hand. Nights for Boxer training at the bridgehead, where old and young, men and women, come to watch and learn as best they can. When the magic is mastered, no bullet, no knife can harm them, it prolongs their lifespan. With the magic absorbed, all men are brothers, and all eat for free. With the magic absorbed, the Emperor grants amnesty to each and every clan. When that is done, men attain high rank, their wives and children honorary titles, and all receive food stores and land.

"Aha," Young Master Wu exclaimed in happy astonishment, "so that *was* Sun Bing! No wonder he looked familiar, and no wonder he smiled at me." After the evening meal, a bonfire was lit at the bridgehead to light up the night sky, attracting all able-bodied villagers, their excitement tempered by curiosity. They were there to see Sun Bing display his boxing skills.

A burner with three sticks of glowing incense had been placed between a pair of candlesticks on an octagonal table standing near the bonfire. Two thick red tallow candles flickered and burned brightly, producing a distinct air of mystery. The bonfire crackled and turned the river surface into a sheet of quicksilver. The shop door was shut tight. People were on edge.

"Sun Bing," someone shouted, "you have been gone only a few short days. Do you think we do not know you? What good is served by acting so mysteriously? Come out and display your divine boxing skills for us."

Sixi squeezed through the shop door and said softly:

"Not so loud. They are inside drinking the ashes of a magic charm."

Then, with shocking abruptness, the door flew open, like the mouth of a rapacious beast. Silenced by the sight, the people waited wide-eyed for the appearance of Sun Bing and the two immortals he had brought back with him with the anticipation normally displayed for the arrival on the opera stage of a famous singer. But Sun Bing did not emerge. Silence, complete silence. Fast-flowing water crashed noisily into the bridge pilings; bonfire flames crackled like red silk snapping in the wind. The crowd was growing impatient when the silence was broken—no, shattered. The thundering, high-pitched voice of a Maoqiang old-man actor tore through the night air, a slight hoarseness enhancing its appeal:

I left my native place to avenge an evil deed. The individual words were as clipped as joints of green bamboo, climbing one by one into the clouds above, then settling slowly to earth, where they somersaulted back into the sky, higher than before, until they were out of sight. Sixi's gong rang out wildly, abandoning all rhythm. Finally, Sun Bing emerged from the shop. He looked the same as when he'd first appeared in the village: white robe and silver helmet, painted face and extended eyebrows, thick-soled boots and a date-wood club. Sun Wukong and Zhu Bajie followed close on his heels. Sun Bing took a turn around the bonfire, running so fast his feet seemed not to touch the ground, building upon the normal gait of the old-man role by adding the acrobatic moves of the sword-and-horse role, and highlighted by short, fast-moving steps that seemed as natural as drifting clouds and flowing water. He began to kick and twist, to tumble and turn somersaults, then ended his exhibition by striking a heroic pose and singing:

I acquired divine boxing skills in Caozhou, aided by immortals of every school, all to ensure that the foreign devils do not survive. Before I left, the Patriarch said to erect a divine altar in Gaomi after I arrive. Here I am to teach divine skills and demonstrate the martial arts, until the people have gained the will to move even Mt. Tai. Immortal brothers Sun Wukong and Zhu Bajie have been sent down from the celestial kingdom, bequeathed by the Tao that remains alive.

By the time Sun Bing had finished his aria, the people's faith in him had vanished. Divine boxing skills indeed! This was nothing more than his old stage show! With his hands cupped at his chest as a sign of respect, Sun Bing said:

"Fellow villagers, I traveled to Caozhou to study at the feet of the Patriarch of the Righteous Harmony Boxers. The revered elder had heard that the German devils who were laying track in Northeast Gaomi Township against the people's wishes were on a murderous rampage, and the fires of loathing burned in his breast. At first the revered elder vowed to lead a divine army to crush the foreigners, but so many military affairs demanded his attention that he could not tear himself away. Instead he passed on to me his secrets of divine boxing and told me to return and erect a divine altar, then to teach divine boxing skills that would succeed in driving the foreign devils out of our land. My companions, Elder Brothers Wukong and Bajie, have been sent to aid me in my mission. Their bodies are impervious to all manner of weapons, a divine art that they will teach you. But first I will demonstrate the skills I have learned, in order, as the adage goes, to cast a brick to attract jade."

Sun Bing laid down his club, took some sheets of yellow mounting paper from a bundle Sun Wukong was carrying, and lit them from a candle. The paper curled as it burned in his hand and rose into the air, where it merged with the swirling currents above the bonfire. When all the paper had been burned, he knelt in front of the incense stand and performed three solemn kowtows. Back on his feet, he reached into his own bundle and removed a tally, which he laid in a large black bowl and set on fire. Then he unhooked a gourd from his waistband and poured its watery contents into the black bowl, stirring the muddy ash with an unused red chopstick. After placing the bowl on the incense stand, he knelt a second time and performed three more kowtows. This time, however, he remained on his knees as he picked up the bowl with both hands and drank down the contents. Having drunk the tally, he kowtowed three more times before closing his eyes and beginning to chant. An occasional word seemed discernible in his incantation, but to the untrained ear it was speaking in tongues, ranging from high to low, the notes lingering in the air like unbroken threads in a piece of beautiful embroidery and affecting those who heard it like a soporific, replete with yawns and drooping eyes. That somnolent air was abruptly shattered by a piercing shout, as he began to foam at the mouth and his body was wracked by spastic jerks, just before he keeled over backward. The crowd reacted with fear and shock, but before they could rush to his aid, Sun Wukong and Zhu Bajie stopped them.

Slowly the crowd settled down and fixed their eyes on Sun Bing as he flopped up and down, like a fish on dry land, until his stalwart body began to levitate, light as a feather, attaining a height of three feet or more before settling firmly back to earth. Well acquainted with Sun Bing, the locals knew him as an outdoor opera actor, a man who was breathless after a couple of somersaults on stage. Seeing him perform so expertly now left them speechless and secretly amazed. In the blazing flames of the bonfire, they saw strange lights in Sun Bing's eyes and a vivid expression sweep across his red face, one that struck everyone who saw it as intimate and unfamiliar at the same time. Normally they knew what to expect when he spoke, but this time they heard things they could not believe were coming from his mouth. An unfamiliar modulation rang with majestic power and proclaimed a noble, stern, indomitable spirit:

"I am the heroic general of the Great Song Dynasty, Yue Fei, known as Pengju, a resident of Tangyin in Henan Province."

The people's hearts seemed suddenly and precariously suspended, like red apples hanging heavily from supple branches, swaying in a breeze before snapping off and falling with a metallic thud to the ground.

"It's the great General Yue!"

"It's the spirit of the martyred Yue Fei!"

Someone in the crowd fell to his knees; others followed, until no one was left standing. Sun Bing, now the transformed spirit of General Yue Fei, circled the area with flying kicks, light and nimble on his feet, all with remarkable poise and skill. As his body rose and fell, the commanding flags behind his back fluttered in the wind. Waves of light glinted off the scales of his silver armor. At this moment, Sun Bing was no longer a man, he was a mythical dragon among men. After the dance, he clutched his date-wood club and whirled it like a silver spear, stabbing left and parrying right, thrusting upward, thwarting below, like a strange python, a coiled snake. The people were dazzled as they watched him—he had won their hearts. One by one, they fell to their knees and kowtowed. Now that his club display had ended, he raised his golden voice:

The hateful twelve edicts have doomed the nation, the three armies howl in protest, as waves on the Yellow River in rage implore. Alas, the aged suffer. Alas, the Imperial carriage does not return to the palace. When will dust from barbarian hordes be swept from the northern shore? My fury at treacherous court officials will not easily be appeased. To whom can I vent the grief and indignation in my heart? I look to heaven, sword in hand, and roar.

I am Yue Fei, Yue Pengju. I have descended onto the divine altar and taken possession of the body of Sun Bing by Imperial Demand. I shall transmit my martial skills to you who will engage the foreign devils in a life-or-death struggle. Wukong, heed my command.

The general who had taken on the appearance of Wukong took a step forward and knelt on one knee.

"Your servant is here!" he replied in a childish voice.

"I command you to demonstrate for this crowd the eighteen stages of cudgel fighting."

"As you command!"

Sun Wukong adjusted the apron around his waist, raised one hand, and brushed it across his face. When the hand fell away, it was as if a mask had been put in place. It was now a lively, vigorous face, like that of a monkey—nose twitching, eyes winking. The crowd nearly laughed at this strange simian behavior, but dared not. After demonstrating the range of facial expressions, he uttered a peculiar cry, grabbed his cudgel with both hands, and executed a perfect somersault. The crowd roared its approval. He responded to the acclamation with a more impressively spirited performance: flinging his cudgel high into the air, he sprang up after it, made two complete flips, and landed solidly on his feet, where he steadily, silently, confidently reached up and caught the falling cudgel before it hit the ground. Every move, every maneuver, was accomplished with perfection, and the crowd reacted with frenzied applause; the Monkey King performed his cudgel artistry in the light of the bonfire: he became a coiled dragon, his cudgel a swimming dragon. Jab, strike, brush, sweep, pound, press, block, draw, mix, poke, every move done with precision, each maneuver a sight to behold. The cudgel whistled like the wind as it flew through the air. The demonstration came to an end when he flung it to the ground, where it stood on end like a stake. He leaped into the air, landed with one foot on the top of the cudgel, and assumed the golden rooster stance, shading his eyes with his hand, like a monkey gazing into the distance. The finale: a backward leap sent him back to the ground, where he landed solidly, brought his hands together in front of his chest, and bowed to his audience. Neither breathing hard nor sweating, he was perfectly poised, entirely natural, an extraordinary individual. The crowd applauded and shouted:

"Bravo!"

General Yue Fei issued a second command:

"Bajie, heed my command—"

The general who had taken on the appearance of Zhu Bajie waddled forward.

"Your servant is here!" he replied in a muffled voice.

"I order you to demonstrate for this crowd the eighteen models of manure rake skills."

"As you command!"

Dragging his manure rake up in front of the crowd, Zhu Bajie greeted them with a foolish laugh—*ke ke ke*—the way a simple-minded farmer would approach a pile of manure to be raked. There was no mistaking his weapon: it was an ordinary manure rake, the sort that all families owned and all farmers knew how to use. Dragging it behind him, he circled the crowd with a silly grin, did it again, and then a third time. The crowd laughed, but they were getting annoyed, as they wondered whether walking around them with a silly grin was all this general was capable of doing. After the third revolution, he threw away his rake, got down on his hands and knees, and crawled on the ground, making pig noises—*oink oink*—like an old sow rooting for food. The crowd could hold back no longer. An explosion of laughter greeted this sight, but stopped abruptly when the people glanced at General Yue, who stood ramrod straight and immobile as a statue. Maybe, the people wondered, maybe this third general is leading up to some unique skills.

Sure enough, once he'd finished his rooting old sow act, his hands and feet began to speed up, until he was crawling along faster than any pig could possibly run, oinking the whole time. He crawled and he crawled, and then he rolled on the ground, rolled and rolled, quickly becoming a black whirlwind that spun him into a standing position. How, his puzzled audience wondered, had his manure rake wound up back in his hand? His movements seemed clumsy and awkward, but any expert could have told them that clumsy, awkward movements sometimes hide beauty in motion. Every move, every maneuver, was just as it should have been, and the crowd showed their appreciation with a generous round of applause.

General Yue said:

"Revered villagers, be heedful. The Jade Emperor has commanded me to take control of the divine altar in order to form and train a homeborn army to make war against the foreign devils. They are the reincarnation of Jin soldiers; you will be the disseminators of the way of Yue Fei. The foreign enemy is in possession of powerful rifles and cannons, and of sharp bayonets. How will you ward off their assaults unless you master the martial arts? The Heavenly Emperor has sent me to pass on the secrets of the divine fists, whose mastery will make you impervious to their knives and bullets, unaffected by water or fire, immune to death. Are you willing to do as your general asks?"

"We await your instructions, great general!" the crowd roared.

"Sun, Zhu, heed my command!" General Yue said.

"Your servant awaits his orders!" one said.

"Your servant awaits his orders!" the other said.

The General commanded:

"Demonstrate the Golden Bell Shield technique of divine boxing to the assembled crowd."

"As commanded!" Sun and Zhu replied in unison.

General Yue Fei personally turned two paper tallies into ashes and told Wukong and Bajie to swallow the solution. Then he recited a secret incantation, this time clearly enunciating every word, as if wanting the crowd to commit it to memory:

"Golden Bell Shield, iron shirt, both parts of Righteous Harmony fist. Righteous Harmony fist holds up the sky, ingesting tallies as an iron immortal in the celestial mist. An iron immortal sits on an iron lotus terrace. Iron head, iron waist, iron stockade, all fortified against enemy weapons . . ."

The incantation ended, the General sprayed a mouthful of water over Wukong. Then he sprayed another mouthful over Bajie.

"It is done!" he said. "Now perform!"

Sun Wukong concentrated his strength and pointed to his head; Zhu Bajie twirled his manure rake, took aim at Sun Wukong's head, and swung. Wukong straightened his neck—his head was unmarked.

Zhu Bajie concentrated his strength in his paunch. Sun Wukong twirled his cudgel over his head, took aim at Bajie's paunch, and swung with such force that he recoiled backward when he hit his target. Bajie massaged his belly and laughed—*ke ke ke*.

General Yue said:

"If there are those among you who do not believe, come forward to see for yourselves."

A young hothead by the name of Yu Jin, who had once felled an ox with a single punch, leaped into the ring, picked up a brick, and flung it at Wukong's head. The brick disintegrated, but Wukong's head suffered no injury. So then Yu Jin asked Sixi to fetch a cleaver from his shop.

"General," he said, "may I?"

General Yue smiled but said nothing.

Zhu Bajie nodded his approval.

Yu Jin raised the cleaver and swung it with all his might at Bajie's paunch. There was a loud clang, as if he'd struck iron. Bajie's belly sported a new white mark; the blade of the cleaver was ruined.

There were no more disbelievers in that crowd, all of whom asked to be taught the magical boxing skills.

General Yue said:

"The most wonderful aspect of divine boxing is speed. You may lack the strength to tie up a chicken, but if you are pure of heart, the spirit will come. When you drink the ashes of an amulet, that spirit will attach itself to your body, and whichever divine host you desire will be yours. If you ask for Huang Tianba, Huang Tianba will be there; if it is Lü Dongbin you prefer, he will come. And when that divine host attaches himself to your body, you will be a master with unimaginable power. Drink down another tally, and you will have a body that can ward off all weapons and attacks, be impervious to water and fire. The virtues of Righteous Harmony fists are legion. In battle you crush the enemy, and off the battlefield it keeps you safe and healthy."

"We accept General Yue as our leader!" the crowd erupted as one.

3

On a misty, drizzly morning ten days later—during the 1900 Qingming Festival—Sun Bing issued an order for the army whose training had just ended to launch an attack on the shed that served as the German engineers' construction headquarters.

For ten uninterrupted days, day and night, before a divine altar erected at the bridgehead, he and his guardians, Sun Wukong and Zhu Bajie, had spared no effort in drawing magic tallies and chanting incantations to propagate the physical art of warding off bayonets and bullets.

Every able-bodied young man in the township was a member of the divine army; they worshipped at the divine altar and practiced divine boxing skills. Even young men from surrounding villages came carrying their own provisions to join the army. The young shepherd from the south bank of the Masang River, Mudu, and the hothead Yu Jin became Sun Bing's staunchest disciples. Mudu took the role of Zhang Bao, who preceded Yue Fei's horse; Yu Jin took the role of Wang Heng, who followed it. During the training, each man chose the heroic figure, celestial or mundane, ancient or modern, whom he most revered as his possessing spirit. Yue Yun, Niu Gao, Yang Zaixing, Zhang Fei, Zhao Yun, Ma Chao, Huang Zhong, Li Kui, Wu Song, Lu Zhishen, Tuxing Sun, Lei Zhenzi, Jiang Taigong, Yang Jian, Cheng Yaojin, Qin Shubao, Yuchi Jingde, Yang Qilang, Huyan Qing, Meng Liang, Jiao Zan . . . in a word, characters from opera, heroes in books, and strange figures of legend emerged from their caves and came down from the mountains to attach themselves to the bodies of Masang Township men in order to display their magic powers. Sun Bing, the great loyalist general and leader of the resistance against Jin, Yue Fei, gathered all those heroes and paladins, the epitome of loyalty and righteousness, whose martial skills were second to none, and in the short span of ten days trained a cadre of indestructible warriors who hungered to fight the German devils to the death.

General Yue's prestige was at its zenith—his every call drew a response from his followers in an army that numbered eight hundred. He recruited local women to dye red cloth for use in making turbans and sashes for the warriors under his command. He personally designed a fiery red battle flag embroidered with the seven stars of the Big Dipper. His eight hundred men were divided into eight contingents, each further divided into ten squads. Contingent commanders and squad leaders were appointed. Squad leaders reported to the contingent commanders, who took orders from the two guardians, Sun Wukong and Zhu Bajie, who in turn obeyed the commands of Yue Fei.

As the sun rose on a hazy Qingming morning, General Yue and his two guardians set up an incense stand and planted the General's flag at the bridgehead. Red turbans and sashes had been distributed the night before. When the cock crowed the third time, the order to muster at the bridgehead was given. Women in all the homes had risen before dawn to prepare food. What exactly? General Yue ordered: *Today before the fight, warriors must eat their fill, white flour cakes and red preserved eggs will hunger pangs still.* To improve the taste of the food, he told the women of each family to prepare yellow onions in broad-bean sauce. The women, who loved hearing General Yue speak, did as he asked. General Yue said that anyone who did not do as he was told was asking for trouble. What sort of trouble? On the battlefield, their amulets would lose their power, and a bullet does not have eyes. General Yue also told his warriors that they must abstain from relations with a woman that night so their bodies could ward off enemy bullets. Everyone took General Yue's words to heart—their lives depended on it.

When the early birds had exhausted their songs, all the many heroic warriors, in twos and threes, mustered at the bridgehead, as if on their way to market. General Yue was disappointed in the sloppy way they answered the call, but upon further consideration, he decided not to punish them, as he might have done. Ten days earlier, after all, they had been farmers, used to being carefree and undisciplined, and joining him now, during a holiday season between crops, spoke well of them. In fact, some of the more committed individuals had actually shown up before him.

General Yue looked up into the misty sky. Though he could not see the sun, he figured it must be mid-morning. He had wanted to surprise the Germans in their beds, but it was too late for that. The plan to attack, however, would not be affected, given the difficulty in bringing together so many people at one time. The good news was that enthusiasm was running high. The men were talking and laughing, unlike the days soon after the massacre, when so many families had lost loved ones. After conferring with his two guardians, General Yue decided to start without delay by performing rites before the altar and the flags.

Sixi, the youngster in the cat-skin cap, who had been assigned to transmit General Yue's orders, raised a ferocious beat on his gong to quiet the noisy gathering of warriors. The General jumped onto a bench and issued his orders:

"Find your contingents and squads, then line up to pay your respects at the divine altar."

Following a brief commotion, they managed to fall in line, all sporting red turbans and red sashes. Some of them—descendants of men trained in martial arts, families in possession of weapons of war—carried spears; others held cleavers, and still others had shown up with tiger-tail whips. Far more men had arrived with ordinary tools: shovels, pitchforks, double-sided hooks, and manure rakes. But there is strength in numbers, and seven or eight hundred men made a force to be reckoned with. General Yue's excitement was palpable, for he knew that only by being fired in a furnace does iron become steel, and only by the baptism of battle does a group of men become a fighting force. Transforming a bunch of farmers into the assemblage before him in a mere ten days was nothing short of miraculous. Having no experience in the business of organizing and deploying forces, he had relied on instructions passed quietly to him by Zhu Bajie, who had put in time as a soldier at a small military center in Tianjin, where he had received training in modern drilling, and had even had the privilege of seeing the famous Yuan Shikai, who was overseeing training at the center.

"Pay respects at the altar!" General Yue ordered. "And to the flags!"

The so-called divine altar was in reality an octagonal table with an incense burner. A pair of flags on fresh, unstripped willow branches had been planted in the ground behind the table, one white, the other red. The red flag was the altar banner, with the seven stars of the Big Dipper embroidered in white. The white flag was the commander's banner, with a large "Yue" embroidered in red. The needlework was the contribution of two nimble-fingered unmarried daughters of tailor Du. Married women were not permitted to do this work, since the hands of married women are considered dirty and would break the spell.

A drizzle began to fall while they were paying their respects to the flags; there was no wind. Both flags hung limply. A flag that did not wave spoiled an otherwise perfect scene, but that could not be helped. On the other hand, the red turbans were resplendent against the overcast sky and in the light drizzle. The red wetness filled General Yue's eyes and raised his excitement to a fever pitch.

In his role as the young hero Ai Hu in the novel *The Seven Heroes and Five Gallants*, Sixi raised an ear-splitting din on his gong; he had been banging it so hard over a period of days that he had nearly destroyed the brass instrument and had broken the skin on the hand that was holding it, which was now wrapped in white cloth. The urgent beat of the gong focused the men's minds and bodies on the task before them. A solemn, reverential mood settled heavily over the assemblage; a mystical aura grew in intensity. Sun Wukong and Zhu Bajie lifted a lamb with its legs bound onto the octagonal table. The animal struggled, raising its head up off the table, and rolled its eyes as it pierced the air with a fearful bleat, a cry that wound its way around the men's hearts and aroused sympathy for the animal. But sympathy was an emotion that had no place at that moment.

War entails sacrifice. Before taking on the foreign devils, it was important to first sacrifice a lamb in anticipation of auspicious results. Sun Wukong pressed the lamb hard onto the table and stretched out its neck; Zhu Bajie picked up a hay-chopping knife and gripped the handle with both hands after spitting in them. He then took two steps backward, raised the knife over his head, and, with a shout, chopped the lamb's head off. Sun Wukong held the severed head up to show everyone as a fountain of blood spewed from the animal's truncated neck.

General Yue, a grave look frozen on his face, caught some of the blood in his hands and splashed it onto the limp flags, then got down on his knees and kowtowed. His men fell to their knees. After the General was back on his feet, he splashed the remaining blood over the heads of the people; there were far too many people and too little blood to reach more than a few of those nearest to him, who were thrilled to have been so honored. As he released the blood in his hands, the General chanted something, a request to all the spirits, since, as he had made clear to all, there would not be enough time to invite each and every spirit to attach itself to one of the men's bodies. And so General Yue assumed the task of inviting all the spirits. "If you are pure of heart, the spirits will come," he had said. Now he told them to call up their individual spirits in their minds and to enter a semi-hypnotic state. After the passage of some time, the General intoned loudly:

"Spirits of Heaven, spirits of the Earth, I respectfully invite you patriarchs to make your presence known. First, the Tang monk Tripitaka and Zhu Bajie; second, Sandy the Monk and Monkey Sun Wukong; third, Liu Bei and Zhuge Liang; fourth, Guan Gong and Zhao Zilong; fifth, Ji Dian, the Buddha; sixth, Li Kui, the Black Whirlwind; seventh, Shi Qian and Yang Xiangwu; eighth, Wu Song and Luo Cheng; ninth, Bianque, curer of maladies; and tenth, I invite the Heavenly King Natha and his three sons—Jinzha, Muzha, and Nazha—to lead a hundred thousand celestial soldiers down to earth to help exterminate the foreign army, for when that is done, the world will be at peace. I beseech the Jade Emperor to urgently give the command——"

The response was immediate, as a rush of extraordinary power infused the body of every man there; blood vessels dilated, energy levels rose, muscles grew taut—they were bursting with strength. A chorus of shouts rent the sky as they leaped and jumped, like big, predatory cats; they frothed at the mouth and glared in anger, flexing arms and kicking legs, every one of them assuming a superhuman pose.

General Yue issued his command:

"We march!"

The General, club in hand, set out on his horse. Sun Wukong, with the red altar flag, Zhu Bajie, with the white commander's flag, and the little hero, Ai Hu, the gong beater, were hard on his heels. The spirited army marched behind them shouting out a cadence.

Masang Township had been built on the bank of the river; its southern boundary was the great Masang River levee, while a seemingly endless plain marked its northern end. A semicircular defensive wall, with a western, an eastern, and a northern gate, had been built to keep roving bandits at bay. The wall, as tall as an average man, was fronted by a moat with a drawbridge.

General Yue, at the head of his army, passed through the northern gate, followed by a contingent of thrill-seeking children. Armed with tree branches, dry sorghum stalks, and sunflower stems, they had painted their faces with ashes or red coloring. Taking their cue from the adults, they raised shouts in immature voices and swaggered in high spirits as they marched along. Old folks had taken positions on the wall to burn incense and pray for a battlefield victory.

General Yue picked up the pace when they reached the outskirts of town. Ai Hu's urgent gong beats increased the speed of marching. The railroad shed was not far from town; in fact, it was visible as soon as the army passed through the gate. A light drizzle created patches of mist over the fields. Winter wheat had already turned green; the smell of mud was in the air. Flowers on the sowthistle facing the sun in ditches and furrows looked like specks of gold. Roadside wild apricots were in full bloom, turning the trees a snowy white. A pair of turtledoves, startled by the marching column, flew out of the underbrush; cuckoos made a racket in a distant grove.

The Qingdao-to-Gaomi portion of the Jiaozhou-Jinan line was basically completed; the tracks lay cold and detached in the open field, like a dragon whose head was visible but whose tail extended out of view. Men were already out working on the tracks, pounding spikes into the ground and creating a symphony of metallic rhythms. Milky white smoke streamed into the sky from the railroad shed, and even at that distance—several li—General Yue detected the aroma of meat cooking.

When he was about one li from the railroad shed, General Yue turned to look at his troops. A disciplined army when it set out from town had devolved into a ragtag assemblage of men with mud-caked shoes, stomping along like wayward bears. The General had Sun Wukong and Zhu Bajie slow down and told Ai Hu to stop beating the gong. Once the main body of troops had caught up, he issued his orders:

"Clean the mud from your feet, my sons, and get ready to attack!"

They did as he commanded, but gobs of mud wound up in other men's faces, which led to unpleasant grumblings. Some of the men shook their feet so hard that their shoes flew off with the mud. Seeing that the time was ripe, General Yue announced loudly:

"Iron head, iron waist, iron stockade, impervious to bullets. Valiant warriors, charge the enemy, tear up the tracks, kill the foreign soldiers, and bring peace for generations to come!"

After exhorting his troops, General Yue raised his club and, with a war whoop, bravely led the charge, with Sun Wukong and Zhu Bajie right behind him, holding high the war flags. Ai Hu fell face first into the mud and lost his shoes to the gooey mess. But he scrambled to his feet and took off running barefoot. Shouts emerged from the throats of the rest of the army as they launched their attack on the railroad shed like a swarm of bees.

The men working on the tracks thought it was an opera troupe heading their way, not realizing that the masses were rebelling until the invaders were nearly upon them. They threw down their tools and fled for their lives.

Guarding the work under way was a squad of German marines, a mere dozen men. The earsplitting shouts interrupted their breakfast, and bad news greeted the squad leader when he stepped outside to see what was happening. He rushed back inside and ordered his men to grab their rifles. By the time General Yue and his men were ten or fifteen meters from the shed, the armed Germans were already outside with their rifles.

General Yue saw puffs of white smoke emerge from several of the German rifles and heard the crack of gunfire. Someone screamed behind him, but he had the time neither to turn back to look nor to think. He envisioned himself as a piece of driftwood propelled by surging waves as he virtually flew into the German devils' shed, in the center of which stood a large table with a pot of stewed pork and some shiny silverware. The meaty smell filled his nostrils. The top half of a German marine had made it under the table; his long legs had not. Zhu Bajie's rake quickly made its mark on the man's legs, producing a long and loud shriek. The words sounded like gibberish, but the meaning was clear—he was crying out for his mother and father. General Yue ran out of the shed to lead the pursuit of the fleeing German marines. Most were headed for the sub-grade of the tracks, trying to escape the mob of shouting men behind them.

One of the marines was running in the opposite direction. General Yue and Ai Hu went after him. The man did not seem to be running all-out, and the distance between them shrank rapidly. General Yue watched in fascination as the man stumbled along stiff-legged, as if he had sticks for legs. It was almost comical. Then, without warning, the German dove into a ditch, out of which a puff of green smoke rose almost immediately. An instant later, Ai Hu, who was running ahead of the General, jerked upward before tumbling headlong to the ground. At first he thought the youngster had gotten his legs tangled up, but only until he saw fresh blood seeping from a hole in his forehead. Ai Hu, he knew for certain, had been hit by a bullet from the German's gun, and he was grief-stricken. He charged the enemy marine, swinging his club over his head, and was nearly brought down by a bullet that whizzed past his ear. But in no time he was upon the German, who came out to meet him, a bayonet attached to his rifle. One swing of his club knocked the rifle out of the man's hands; with a fearful shout, he turned and ran down the ditch, with General Yue hot on his heels. The German's high-topped boots slurped in the mud with every step, as if he were dragging mud buckets behind him. General Yue swung his club again, this time connecting with the nape of the man's neck. A strange bleat burst from the man's lips, whose body released a muttony odor, and the General's immediate thought was that the man's mother might have been a ewe.

The German tripped and fell, burying his face in the mud, and he no sooner realized what had happened than General Yue's club had flattened his tall helmet. The General was about to keep clubbing him when he saw that the man's blue eyes were like those of the lamb they'd sacrificed earlier—sad eyes, blinking pitifully, and the General's wrist failed him. This time the club hit the German marine not on the head but on the shoulder.

CHAPTER NINE

Masterpiece

Razor-tipped knife in hand, Zhao Jia stood in the center of the parade ground, a bowlegged young apprentice at his side, facing a tall pine post to which the failed assassin of Yuan Shikai was bound, awaiting execution by the slicing death of five hundred cuts. Arrayed behind him were dozens of high-ranking officers of the New Army, seated on fine horses, while behind the execution post, five thousand foot soldiers stood in tight formation, looking from a distance like a forest, and up close like marionettes. Dry early winter winds swept powdery alkaline dirt into the soldiers' faces. All those gazes made Zhao Jia, who had carried out hundreds of executions, slightly nervous, and somewhat self-conscious. By force of will he suppressed these feelings, which could only have a negative impact on his work, and focused on the condemned man before him, refusing to look at either the mounted officers or the formation of soldiers.

Something his shifu, Grandma Yu, had told him was on his mind: A model executioner does not see a living being as he prepares to carry out his task. Before him is nothing but strips of muscle and flesh, discrete internal organs, and a skeleton. After forty years in the trade, Zhao Jia had attained that degree of perfection. But for some reason, on this day he was on edge. After plying his trade for decades, during which he had ended the lives of nearly a thousand people, before him now was the finest specimen of the male body he had ever seen: a proud nose and capacious mouth, slanting eyebrows and starry eyes, his naked body a scene of perfection, with chiseled chest muscles and a flat, taut abdomen, all covered with glossy bronze skin. What truly caught his attention, however, was the ubiquitous taunting smile on the face of the young man, who was returning Zhao Jia's scrutiny. A sense of shame engulfed Zhao in much the same way that a misbehaving child cannot bear to look his father in the eye.

Three steel cannons stood on the edge of the parade ground, busily attended by a squad of a dozen soldiers. Three rapid explosions startled Zhao Jia and made his ears ring. For a moment that was all he could hear. The acrid smell of gunpowder nearly choked him. The condemned man nodded in the direction of the cannons, as if in praise of the artillerymen's skill. Zhao Jia, who was badly shaken, saw flames spew from the mouths of the cannons, followed immediately by another series of explosions. He watched as the bright, golden-hued shell casings flew behind the big guns, so hot they seared the patches of grass they landed on, marked by puffs of white smoke. Then three more explosions, after which the artillerymen stepped behind their guns and stood at attention, a sign that the fusillade was over, although the echoes hung in the air.

"Present—arms!" came a shouted command.

Five thousand soldiers raised Steyr rifles over their heads, forming a forest of long guns, a vast expanse of glossy blue steel to the rear of the execution post. Zhao Jia stared tongue-tied at this demonstration of military might. He had observed many martial drills by the Imperial Guard during his years in the capital, but nothing he had seen could compare with what he was witnessing today. The effect on him was apprehension and a powerful sense of unease. His self-confidence was shaken, his self-possessed demeanor, which had never wavered on the capital's marketplace execution ground, now gone.

The foot soldiers and mounted officials remained at respectful attention for the arrival of their commander, which was heralded by the blare of trumpets and a clash of cymbals. A palanquin, covered in dark green wool and carried by eight bearers, emerged from a path through a grove of white poplars like a multi-decked ship riding the waves, crossed the parade ground, and settled gently earthward in front of the execution post. A young recruit ran up with a stepping stool, which he placed on the ground before reaching up to pull back the curtain. Out stepped a hulking figure, a red-capped official with big ears, a square face, and a prominent moustache. Zhao Jia recognized him immediately, an acquaintance from twenty-three years earlier, when he was still the young scion of an official family; now he was Commander of the New Army, His Excellency Yuan Shikai, who, in a break from the usual protocol, had summoned him from the capital to Tianjin to carry out the execution.

Dressed in full uniform under a fox fur cape, he cut an impressive figure. With a wave to the military complement assembled on the parade ground, he sat in a chair draped with a tiger skin. The commanding officer of the mounted troops shouted:

"Parade rest—!"

The soldiers shouldered their rifles on command, sending a deafening shock wave across the field. A young officer with a ruddy complexion and yellowed teeth, a sheet of paper in his hand, bent low to whisper something in Excellency Yuan's ear. With a frown, Yuan turned his head away, as if to avoid the young officer's bad breath. But "yellow teeth" would not let the distance between his mouth and Yuan's ear increase. Zhao Jia could not have known, and never would learn, that the dark, gaunt young man with the yellow teeth would one day be known throughout the land as the Imperial Restorationist General Zhang Xun. Zhao Jia actually felt sorry for Yuan Shikai, being subjected to the stench from Zhang Xun's mouth. Once Zhang had finished what he had to say, Yuan Shikai nodded and straightened up in his chair, while Zhang Xun stood on a bench and read what was on the paper in a voice loud enough for all to hear:

"The condemned, twenty-eight-year-old Qian Xiongfei, known also as Pengju, is from the city of Yiyang in Hunan Province. In the twenty-first year of the Guangxu reign, Qian took up studies at a military school in Japan, where he cut off his queue and joined an outlaw gang of conspirators. Upon his return to China, he joined forces with the Kang Youwei–Liang Qichao rebel clique. Under instructions from Kang and Liang, he assumed the role of a loyalist and infiltrated the Imperial Guard, where he operated as a planted agent for the rebels. When the Wuxu rebels were executed in the capital, like the fox that mourns the death of the hare, the frenzied Qian made an attempt on the life of our commander on the eleventh day of the tenth month. Heaven interceded to spare the life of Excellency Yuan. The criminal Qian was thwarted from carrying out this sinister and unpardonable act. In accordance with the laws of the Great Qing Empire, anyone found guilty of an assassination attempt on a representative of the Court is to suffer the slicing death of five hundred cuts. The sentence, approved by the Board of Punishments, will be carried out by an executioner brought from the capital to Tianjin . . ."

Zhao Jia felt the eyes of the assembled witnesses on him. Sending an executioner from the capital to the provinces was unprecedented, not just during the Qing Dynasty, but throughout the country's history. The enormity of his responsibility put him in a state approaching alarm.

Now that the death warrant had been read, Yuan Shikai removed his fox fur cape and stood up, his eyes sweeping the formation of five thousand soldiers before he began to speak. Blessed with powerful lungs, he began, his words ringing out with great sonority:

"Men, I have been a military commander for many years and love my troops as if you were my own sons. If a mosquito bites you, my heart aches. This you already know. The idea that Qian Xiongfei, whom I had regarded with such favor, could one day turn his deadly rage on his own commander was alien to me. This act came as not only a horrible shock, but an even greater disappointment."

"Men," Qian Xiongfei shouted from the execution post to which he was bound, "the treacherous Yuan Shikai has betrayed friends and allies in order to seek Imperial favor, crimes for which death is too good for him. Do not be taken in by his fine-sounding words!"

Zhang Xun, who saw Yuan Shikai's face redden, ran up to the execution post and punched Qian Xiongfei in the face.

"Keep your fucking mouth shut and die with a little class!"

Qian spat a mouthful of bloody saliva in Zhang Xun's face.

With a wave of his hand, Yuan Shikai stopped Zhang Xun, who was about to hit Qian a second time.

"Qian Xiongfei, you were a wizard with a gun and smarter than most people. That was why I gave you a pair of gold-handled pistols and granted you special responsibilities as a trusted confidant. My benevolence not only went unappreciated, but actually led you to make an attempt on my life. If that can be tolerated, what then cannot? Even though I nearly died at your hands, I grieve over the loss of your talent and cannot bear the thought of your punishment. But the law can show no favoritism, and military law is unimpeachable. I am powerless to save you from it."

"If you're going to kill me, do it, but spare me the sermon!"

"Now that things have reached this point, I can only take a lesson from Marquis Zhuge Liang, who 'wept as he beheaded Ma Su.'"

"Excellency Yuan, drop the act!"

Yuan Shikai shook his head and sighed.

"Since you insist on being stubborn and stupid, there is nothing I can do for you."

"I am prepared to die, and have been for some time. Do what you must, Excellency Yuan!"

"For you I have done everything humanity and duty call for. Tell me of your last wishes, and I shall see that they are carried out."

"Excellency Yuan, though Qian Ding, the Gaomi County Magistrate, is my brother, I disavowed our kinship long ago. I ask that he not be implicated in my activities."

"You may rest easy on that score."

"I thank Your Excellency for that," Qian said, "but that you would send someone to remove the bullets from my guns to ensure my defeat when victory was within reach was unimaginable. Pity, what a pity!"

"No one removed your bullets," Yuan said with a laugh. "It was heaven's intervention."

"If heaven decided to spare the life of Yuan Shikai," he said with a sigh, "then you win, Excellency."

Yuan Shikai cleared his throat and declared:

"Men, your commander's heart is breaking over the need to subject Qian Xiongfei to the slicing death, for he was once an officer with a bright future. I had great expectations for him, but he cast his lot with those rebelling against the Throne and committed a heinous, unpardonable act. It is not I who am putting him to death, nor the Throne. No, this is an act of suicide. I would have been willing to grant him a simple execution, keeping his body intact, but the national penal code is involved, and I dare not bend the law for one of my own. In my desire to allow him a dignified death, I made a point of asking the Board of Punishments to send us its finest executioner. Qian Xiongfei, that is my final gift to you, and I hope you calmly accept your punishment as an example for the soldiers of our New Army. Listen to me, men. You have been brought here to witness this execution in order, as the adage goes, to scare the monkeys by killing the chicken. It is my hope that you will take away with you a lesson learned on the body of Qian Xiongfei, one of fealty and good faith, caution and prudence, fidelity to the Throne and obedience to your superiors. If you act in accordance with my guidance, I can guarantee you a bright future."

Led by their commanding officers, the soldiers shouted in unison:

"Absolute fidelity to the Throne, devoted service to His Excellency!"

Yuan Shikai returned to his seat and nodded imperceptibly to his aide, Zhang Xun, who grasped his meaning at once.

"Let the execution begin!" he shouted.

Zhao Jia stepped up in front of Qian Xiongfei, where his apprentice handed him a knife of the highest quality, one made specifically for this purpose.

"My friend," he said under his breath, "I ask your pardon."

Despite his attempt to face death without flinching, Qian Xiongfei could not keep his pale lips from quivering, and his irrepressible terror was exactly what Zhao Jia needed to recoup his pride of profession. In that instant, his heart turned as hard as steel and he was as calm as still water. He no longer saw a living human being in front of him. Bound to the execution post was nothing more than blood, flesh, tendons, and bones, assembled in a pattern determined by heavenly forces. Without warning, he drove his fist into Qian Xiongfei's chest directly above the heart. Qian's eyes rolled up into his head, and before the effect of that blow had worn off, with a quick circular motion of the hand holding the knife, Zhao snipped a circle of flesh the size of a bronze coin off of the other side of Qian's chest. He had neatly excised one of Qian's nipples, leaving a wound that looked like a blind man's eye.

In accordance with an unwritten practice of the profession, Zhao Jia held the nipple on the tip of his blade in full view of His Excellency Yuan and the officers behind him. Then he displayed the fleshy coin to the five thousand foot soldiers in front of him, as his apprentice announced:

"The first cut!"

The detached nipple seemed to him to jiggle. He heard the rapid, nervous breathing of the officers behind him and a forced little cough from Excellency Yuan. He did not have to look to picture the bloodless faces of the mounted officers. He knew also that their hearts, including Yuan Shikai's, were pounding at that moment. And that thought instilled in him pleasant feelings of gratification. In recent years, many important men had fallen into the hands of Board of Punishments executioners, and he had grown used to seeing pitiful exhibitions on the execution ground by high-ranking officials who had swaggered through life when they were in power. Not one in a hundred was worthy of the manly Qian Xiongfei, who could suppress his feelings of terror while undergoing cruel torture to the point that they were virtually imperceptible. At that moment, at least, Zhao felt a sense of supremacy. I am not me; I am the agent of the Emperor and the Empress Dowager, the embodiment of the laws of the Great Qing Dynasty!

Sunlight flashed on his blade as, with a flick of his wrist, the piece of human flesh flew from the tip of the knife high into the air, like a pellet, before settling heavily on the head of a swarthy soldier, like a glob of bird shit. The man screeched, as if a brick had landed on his head; he wobbled uncertainly.

Based on an age-old executioner's custom, the first piece of the victim is a sacrifice to heaven.

Fresh blood oozed from the hole in Qian's chest like a string of bright red pearls. Some dripped to the ground; some snaked down from the edges of the wound to stain his muscular chest.

The second cut, taken from the left side, was as deftly and neatly accomplished as the first. The remaining nipple was cut away. Qian's chest was now decorated by matching holes the size of bronze coins. Less blood flowed this time. The blow to his chest had made his heart contract, and that had abated the flow of blood throughout his body, a technique that had evolved out of the experience of generations of executioners in the Bureau of Detentions, perfection based on trial and error.

Qian maintained the noble expression of fearlessness he had worn before the first cut, but a series of moans so soft that only Zhao Jia could hear them emerged, seemingly from his ears, not his mouth. Zhao forced himself to look away from Qian's face. He was used to hearing wretched shrieks of pain from condemned prisoners as they were being sliced, howls that did nothing to disturb his unfaltering composure. But not hearing a sound from the valiant Qian Xiongfei, who clenched his teeth to keep from crying out, actually rattled him, as if something terrible were about to happen. Forcibly controlling his emotions, he raised the fleshy coin on the tip of his knife, as he knew he must do, displaying it first to His Excellency, then to the officers, and last to the ashen-faced soldiers, who stood before him like clay statues. His apprentice announced:

"The second cut!"

Zhao Jia had figured out that the legal and psychological foundation for the ritual of displaying fleshy parts sliced from the prisoner's body to the officials in charge of the execution and to the observers was built on three principles: First, it was a display of the harsh rule of law and the unflinching dedication to it by the executioner. Second, it served to instill the fear of retribution in the minds of witnesses, who could be counted on to turn away from evil thoughts and criminal behavior. That was why the Imperial Court had staged public executions and encouraged attendance by the populace throughout the nation's dynastic history. Third, it satisfied people's bloodlust. The finest play ever staged cannot compete with the spectacle of a public slicing, and for this more than any other reason, executioners in the capital were contemptuous of actors, who were so highly favored in royal circles.

As he held up the second piece of Qian's flesh for all to see, Zhao was reminded of scenes from his youth, when he was learning the trade from his shifu. In order to perfect the fine art of the slicing death, executioners for the Bureau of Detentions worked closely with a butcher shop just outside Chong-wen Gate. During the off-season, the shifu took his students to the shop to practice their skills; there they helped turn the meat from countless pigs into filling for dumplings, and in the process developed a dexterity of hand and eye as accurate as a scale. If the call was for a pound of meat, a single cut would produce exactly sixteen ounces. When Grandma Yu was the keeper of the Bureau of Detentions official seal, the execution team opened a butcher shop on Walking Stick Lane in the Xisi, or West Fourth, District, where they slaughtered animals in back and sold the meat up front, enjoying a brisk business until one day someone revealed their identities. People not only stopped coming to buy their meat, they obsessively avoided the area, fearing they might be taken off the street and butchered.

He recalled that his shifu kept a secret book with brittle, yellowing pages and crude drawings, with coded writing. According to Grandma Yu, the book, *Secrets of a Penal Office*, had been passed down by a Ming Dynasty grandma; it comprised lists of punishments, their concrete applications, matters to take into consideration, and copious illustrations. In a word, it was a classic text for executioners. Shifu pointed out to him and his fellow apprentices an illustration and accompanying text that described in detail the particulars of the slicing death, of which there were three levels. The first level required 3,357 cuts. For the second level it was 2,896, and for the third, 1,585. Regardless of how many cuts there were to be, he recalled hearing Shifu say, the final cut was the one that ended the prisoner's life. So when the cutting began, the spacing between cuts must be precisely designed to fit the sex and physique of the condemned individual. If the prisoner died before the required number of cuts had been reached or was still alive after, the executioner had not done his job well. His shifu said that the minimum standard for the slicing death was the proportional size of the flesh removed—when placed on a scale, there should be only minimal differences. To that end, during an execution, the man with the knife must have his emotions under complete control. His mind must be clear and focused, his hand ruthless and resolute; he must simultaneously be like a maiden practicing embroidery and a butcher slaughtering a mule. The slightest hesitancy or indecision, even a spur-of-the-moment thought, would affect the hand in unwanted ways. This, the pinnacle of achievement, was exceedingly difficult to attain. The musculature of a human being varies from spot to spot in density and coherence. Knowing where to insert the knife, and with how much pressure, requires a skill that, over time, had become second nature. Gifted executioners, such as Elder Gao Tao and Elder Zhang Tang, sliced not with a knife and not with their hands, but with their minds and their eyes. Among the thousands of slicing deaths carried out down through the ages, none, it seems, had achieved perfection and been worthy of the term "masterpiece." In virtually every case, what was accomplished was merely the dissection of a living human being. That appeared to explain why fewer cuts were required for slicing deaths in recent years. In the current dynasty, five hundred was the apex. And yet, precious few executions lasted nearly that long. Board of Punishments executioners, in respectful devotion to the sacred nature of this ancient profession, performed their duties in accordance with established practices handed down over time. But at the provincial, prefectural, sub-prefectural, and county levels, dragons and fish were all jumbled together—the good mixed with the bad—and most practitioners were hacks and local riffraff who did shoddy work and exerted minimal effort. If on a prisoner sentenced to five hundred cuts they made it to two or three hundred, that was considered a success. Most of the time, they chopped the victim into several chunks and quickly put him out of his misery.

Zhao Jia flung the second piece of meat cut from Qian's body to the ground. To an executioner, the second piece of the victim is a sacrifice to the earth.

When Zhao was displaying the piece of meat on the tip of his knife for all to see, he was, he felt, the central figure, while the tip of his knife and the flesh stuck on it were the center of that center. The eyes of everyone in attendance, from the supremely prideful Excellency Yuan down to the most junior soldier in the formation, followed the progress of his knife, or, more accurately, the progress of Qian's flesh impaled on that knife. When Qian's flesh flew into the air, the observers' eyes followed its ascent; when Qian's flesh was flung to the ground, the observers' eyes followed its descent. According to his shifu, in slicing deaths of old, every piece of flesh cut from the victim was laid out on a specially prepared surface, so that when the execution was completed, the official observer, along with members of the victim's family, could come forward to count. One piece too many or too few was a serious transgression. According to his master, one slapdash executioner of the Song Dynasty made one too many cuts, and the complaint by the victim's family cost him his life. Public executioner has always been a precarious profession, since a poor performance can itself be a death sentence. Consider: you must remove pieces of roughly the same size, the last cut must be the fatal one, and you must keep track of every cut you make. Three thousand three hundred and fifty-seven cuts require a full day, and there were times, by order of the sentencing authority, when the process was stretched out to three or as many as five days, making the work that much harder. A staunchly dedicated executioner invariably collapsed from fatigue at the end of a slicing death. As time went on, executioners heeded the travails of their predecessors by flinging away the excised flesh rather than laying it out for others to count. Old execution grounds were known for the wild dogs, crows, and vultures that prowled the area; slicing deaths provided feast days for these visitors.

He dipped a clean chamois into a basin of salty water and wiped the blood from Qian's chest. The knife holes now resembled the fresh scars of severed tree branches. Then he made his third cut on Qian's chest. Also about the size of a bronze coin, it was made in the shape of a fish scale. This fresh wound abutted the edge of one of the earlier wounds but retained its distinct shape. His shifu had said that this had a name of its own—the fish-scale cut, for that is exactly what it resembled. The flesh exposed by the third cut was a ghostly white, from which only a few drops of blood poked out, the sign of a good beginning; that augured well for the entire process, to his immense satisfaction. Shifu had said that a successful slicing death was marked by a modest flow of blood. He had told him that the blow to the heart before the first cut constricted the victim's major arteries. Most of the blood was then concentrated in his abdomen and calves. Only then can you make a series of cuts, like slicing a cucumber, without killing the victim. Absent this technique, blood will flow unchecked, creating a terrible stench and staining the body, which has a powerful effect on the observers and destroys the symmetry of the cuts—a real mess. To be sure, a lifetime of experience had equipped these men with a talent to deal with any unanticipated situation. They were not easily flustered or caught unprepared. For instance, if a heavy flow of blood made cutting difficult or impossible, the immediate recourse was to empty a bucket of cold water on the victim. The shock would constrict his arteries. If that did not work, a bucket of vinegar would. According to the *Compendium of Materia Medica*, vinegar is an astringent whose properties work to stanch the flow of blood. If that too failed, removing a piece of flesh from each calf served as a bloodletting. This last technique, however, normally led to an early death from a loss of blood. But Qian's arteries appeared to be well constricted. Zhao Jia could relax, for indications were that today's affair had a good chance of success, and the bucket of aged Shanxi vinegar on the ground near the post would not be needed. In the unwritten code of the profession, the shop that supplied a bucket of vinegar received no payment for it and was required to give the executioner a "vinegar reclaim fee" if it was not used. The vinegar had to be donated by the merchant, not sold, and a fee for its non-use was an extravagantly unreasonable demand. And yet the Qing Dynasty placed greater value on ancestral precedents than on the law. However outmoded or irrational a practice, so long as there was a historical precedent, it could not and must not be abandoned. To the contrary, it gained increased inviolability over time. In Qing tradition, a criminal who was about to be executed enjoyed the privilege of sampling food and drink at any establishment passed on his way to the execution ground, free of charge. And the executioner enjoyed the privilege of receiving a free bucket of vinegar as well as a fee for not using it. By rights, the vinegar should have been returned to the shop that supplied it, but it was sold to a pharmacy instead, for now that it had soaked up the blood airs of the executed criminal, it was no longer ordinary vinegar, but a cure-all for the sick and dying, and had acquired the name "blessed vinegar." Naturally, the pharmacy paid for this bucket of "blessed vinegar," and since executioners were given no fees for the tasks they performed, they were forced to rely upon such earnings to make a living. He flung the third piece of flesh into the air, a sacrifice to the ghosts and gods. His apprentice announced:

"The third cut!"

Having flung away the third piece, Zhao went immediately to the fourth cut. Qian's flesh was crisp, easy to cut, a quality he found only in criminals who were in excellent physical shape. Slicing up a criminal as fat as a pig or as skinny as a monkey was exhausting work. But beyond exhaustion, a messy job was inevitable. An apt comparison would be a fine chef forced to work with substandard ingredients. Even the most skillful preparation cannot produce an outstanding banquet without the finest ingredients. Or for a carpenter who lacks the right material for his task, even uncanny workmanship is inadequate to produce high-grade furniture. Shifu told him that during the Daoguang reign he was assigned the task of dispatching a woman who had conspired with her lover to murder her husband. The woman was as blubbery as a sack of starchy noodles, so loose that her flesh quivered whenever the knife touched her. The stuff he cut off her body was like frothy snot, and not even the dogs would eat it. And she shrieked like a banshee, howling and wailing that so upset him, a work of art was out of the question. He said there had been good specimens of her sex, women whose skin and flesh had the texture of congealed fat that cut with ease and precision. It was like cutting through autumn water. The knife moved on its own, without the slightest deviation. He said he had dispatched just such an ideal woman during the Xianfeng reign. She had been condemned, it was said, as a prostitute who had murdered one of her clients for money. According to Shifu, she was a woman of surpassing beauty, the sort of gentle, demure woman who draws people to her at first sight. No one would have believed that she could actually commit murder. He said that the greatest degree of compassion an executioner can bestow upon his victim is to do his job well. If you respect or love her, then it is your duty to see that she becomes a model for execution. If you truly respect her, then you must fearlessly make her body the canvas on which you display the highest standards of your artistry. It is no different from a renowned actor performing onstage. Shifu said that so many Peking citizens thronged to watch the beautiful prostitute suffer the slicing death that more than twenty people were crushed or trampled to death on the marketplace execution ground. He said that in the presence of such a beautiful body, it would have been a sin, a crime, not to put all he had into the task before him, heart and soul. More to the point, if he had made a mess of things, an angry crowd might have torn him to pieces, for Peking crowds at executions were harder to please than any other. He did a fine job that day, with the cooperation of the woman herself. Seen from one angle, it was, from start to finish, a stage performance, acted out by the executioner and his victim. Such performances were spoiled if the criminal overdid the screaming part; but a total lack of sounds was just as bad. The ideal was just the right number of rhythmic wails, producing sham expressions of sympathy among the observers while satisfying their evil aestheticism. Shifu said that he had gained an insight into people only after thousands of individuals had died at his hands over a stretch of decades: All people, he said, are two-faced beasts. One of those faces displays the virtues of humanity, justice, and morality, representing the three cardinal guides and five constant virtues. The other is the face of bloodsucking thieves and whores. The appetite for evil is stimulated in anyone who willingly watches the spectacle of a beautiful woman being dismembered one cut at a time, whether that person be a man of honor, a virtuous wife, or a chaste maiden. Subjecting a beautiful woman to the slicing death is mankind's most exquisitely cruel exhibition. The people who flock to such exhibitions, Shifu said, are far more malicious than those of us who wield the knife. He said he spent many sleepless nights reliving every detail of that day's execution, like a chess master replaying each move in a brilliant match that has forged his reputation. That night he mentally dismembered her body, then pictured it all coming back together. Her tearful yet melodic moans and shrieks swirled around his ears from start to finish in an unbroken stream. And the captivating odor that emerged from her body as it was being ravaged by his knife filled his nostrils. An ill wind struck the nape of his neck, a swoosh created by the beating wings of impatient, rapacious birds of prey. His infatuated recollections paused briefly at that juncture, like a pose struck by an actor on the operatic stage. At this point, little skin or flesh remained on her body, but her face was unmarked, and it was time for the coup de grace. His heart lurched as he sliced off a piece of her heart. It was deep red, the color of a fresh date; he held it on the tip of his knife like a precious gem as he looked into her ashen oval face, moved by the sight. He heard a sigh emerge from somewhere deep down in her chest. Sparks—not many, just a few—seemed to glimmer in her eyes, from which two large teardrops slipped down her face. He saw her lips move with difficulty and heard her say, soft as a mosquito's buzz: "not . . . guilty . . ." The light went out of her eyes; the flame of life was extinguished. Her head, which had rocked back and forth throughout the ordeal, slumped forward, covered by a curtain of hair so black it looked as if it had just been taken out of a dyeing vat.

Zhao Jia's fiftieth cut completed the paring of Qian's chest muscles. The first tenth of his work was now behind him. After his apprentice handed him a new knife, he took two deep breaths in order to normalize his breathing. Qian's ribs were exposed, as he could see, connected by thin membranes. The man's heart was pumping like a jackrabbit wrapped in gauze. He felt good about his progress so far. The flow of blood had been stanched, and the fiftieth cut had removed the chest muscles, just as he had planned. The sole blemish so far was that the valiant man bound to the post had not made a sound, had not yelled in pain. This flaw had turned what should have been a spirited drama into a mime performance that lacked appeal. In the eyes of these people, he was thinking, I am a butcher, a meat merchant. He deeply admired this Qian fellow, who, except for a few barely perceptible moans during the first two cuts, had not made a sound. He looked into the man's face, and what he saw were: hair standing up straight, eyes wide and round, the dark pupils nearly blue, the whites now red, nostrils flaring, teeth grinding, and taut cheek muscles bulging like a pair of mice. The ferocity of that face secretly astounded him. Soreness crept into the hand holding the knife. If the victim was a man, tradition demanded that once the chest muscles had been pared away, next to be taken from the body were his genitals. For this, three cuts were permitted, and the size of the excised portions need not complement other portions. Decades of experience had shown his shifu that what male subjects feared most was not the loss of skin or tendons, but the treasured object between their legs. Not because it was especially painful—it wasn't—but because it gave rise to a psychological dread and a sense of shame. Most men would choose to lose their head over losing their maleness. According to the shifu, once you have removed even the bravest man's genitals, you have taken the fight out of him, the same effect as cutting the mane of a warhorse or the plume of a proud rooster. Zhao Jia turned away from the solemn and tragic face that was putting him on edge and sized up his flaccid organ. It was shriveled pathetically, like a silkworm tucked into its cocoon. I'm truly sorry, young friend, he muttered to himself as he picked it out of its nest with his left hand and, in one lightning-fast motion, sliced it off at its base. His apprentice announced:

"The fifty-first cut!"

He flung the once-treasured object away, and a skinny, mangy dog that had come out of nowhere snatched it up and darted in amid the military formation, where it began to yelp as soldiers kicked it. A forlorn howl of despair tore from the mouth of Qian, who until then had endured the torture by clenching his teeth. Zhao Jia had expected that, and yet it shocked him. He was not aware that he was blinking lightning-fast, but his hands were burning and swelling, as if red-hot needles were pricking his fingers. It was a discomfort he could not possibly describe. Qian's howl—neither human nor beastly—had a horrifying quality that both unnerved and sent shivers through the ranks of the Right Militant Guard, who were witnessing the execution. Logic demanded that His Excellency ought to have been moved by the sound, but Zhao Jia had no time to turn back and scrutinize the reaction of Yuan and the high-ranking officials around him. He heard snorts of terror from the horses, which were loudly champing the bits in their mouths and agitating the bells hanging from their necks; he saw how the tight leggings arrayed behind the execution post seemed to be straining to break free. Qian's body squirmed in concert with his repeated howls, while his heart, which could be seen behind exposed ribs, was thumping loudly enough to hear and so violently that Zhao Jia actually worried it might leap out of his chest. If that happened, the execution, a slicing death that had been days in the planning, would end in abject failure. Not only would it be a loss of face for the Board of Punishments, but it would make even His Excellency Yuan look bad. That was the last thing Zhao wanted, but it was made more possible by Qian's head, which began to rock backward and forward and from side to side, producing loud thumps against the post. His eyes were blood-streaked, his features twisted beyond recognition, a look that would forever haunt the dreams of anyone seeing that face. Zhao Jia had never seen anything like it, nor, he knew, had his shifu. His hands were tingly and so uncomfortably swollen he could barely hold the knife. He glanced up at his apprentice, whose face was the color of clay and whose mouth hung wide open. For him to take over and finish the job was out of the question. So he forced himself to bend down and dig out one of Qian's testicles, which had shrunk into his body. One swift cut detached it. The fifty-second cut, he coached his apprentice, who stood there transfixed until he was able to announce, barely able to keep from sobbing:

"The . . . fifty-second . . . cut . . ."

He tossed the sac to the ground, where it lay in the dirt looking hideous. For the first time in all his years in the profession, he experienced something unique, for him, at least: disgust.

"Fucking . . . bastard!" In an earthshaking display of loathing, Qian Xiongfei somehow found the strength to curse: "Yuan Shikai, Yuan Shikai, you turncoat, I may not be able to kill you in this life, but I will return as a ghost to take your life!"

Zhao Jia, afraid to turn his head, could only imagine the look on Excellency Yuan's face at that moment. Desperate to finish the job, he bent down again, dug out the second testicle, and cut it off. But as he was straightening up, Qian Xiongfei leaned over and bit him on the head. Since he was wearing a cap, the bite did not inflict serious damage, but it did break the skin, even through the cloth cap. Well after the incident, Zhao shuddered when he considered the possibility that Qian could have bitten him on the neck and chewed his way into his throat; or if he had bitten him on the ear, he'd have lost that organ for sure. Experiencing a strange pain on his scalp, he jerked his head upward and connected with Qian's chin. He heard the frightful crunch of Qian's teeth as they bit through his tongue, which sent blood spurting from his mouth. But that did not keep him from hurling epithets, now less intelligible, though by no means incoherent, and still directed at Yuan Shikai. The fifty-third cut. As Zhao Jia threw down the thing in his hand, he saw flashes of light in front of his eyes, he felt light-headed, and his stomach lurched. He clenched his teeth to keep whatever it was down, telling himself that he mustn't vomit, not now; for if he did, the power of intimidation enjoyed by Board of Punishments executioners would die in his hands.

"Cut out his tongue!"

Yuan Shikai's voice thundered behind him in all its fury. Instinctively, he turned to look. Yuan's face was livid as he smacked his knee with his fist and forcefully repeated his command:

"Cut out his tongue!"

Zhao Jia wanted to tell him that this was not the way of his ancestors, but the look of rage, born of mortification, on His Excellency's face made him swallow his words. What good would it have done to say anything, when even the Empress Dowager respected almost anything that Excellency Yuan said? So he turned his attention to Qian's tongue.

Qian's damaged tongue had turned his face into too bloody a mess to make Zhao's knife effective. Cutting out the tongue of a crazed condemned individual was a bit like trying to pull the teeth of a tiger. But Zhao was not foolhardy enough to ignore Yuan's command. Without wasting time, he thought back to his shifu's teachings and what experience he had gained from them, but nothing helpful came to mind. Qian was still shouting invectives. Excellency Yuan repeated his command yet again:

"I said, cut out his tongue!"

At that critical moment, the spirit of the profession's founder saved the day with an inspiration. After placing the knife between his teeth, he picked a bucket of water up off the ground and emptied it into Qian's face, bringing an immediate halt to his curses. Then he wrapped his hands around Qian's throat and squeezed with all his might. Qian's face turned the color of pig's liver as his purple tongue emerged from between his teeth. Squeezing the man's throat with one hand, Zhao reached up with the other, took the knife from between his teeth, and sliced off the tongue. This spur-of-the-moment change to the ritual brought a roar from the formation of soldiers, like a wave crashing over a sandbar.

Zhao displayed Qian's defiant tongue in the palm of his hand, feeling it twitch like a dying frog. "The fifty-fourth cut," he murmured weakly before throwing Qian's tongue onto the ground in front of Excellency Yuan.

"The fifty . . . fourth cut . . ." his apprentice announced.

Qian Xiongfei's face had turned the color of gold. Blood gurgled from his lips. A mixture of blood and water slid down his body. He was still cursing, even without a tongue. But now there was no way to tell what he was saying and whom he was cursing.

Zhao Jia's hands were burning up and seemed in danger of being reduced to ashes. He was on the verge of collapse. Professional pride, however, kept him focused on the job at hand. Yuan's disruptive order to cut out the man's tongue had freed him to put his victim out of his misery without delay, but a sense of responsibility and personal ethics would not let him do that. As he saw it, not inflicting the requisite number of cuts was more than a blasphemy against the laws of the Great Qing Dynasty; it was an act of disrespect toward the good man tied to the post before him. Under no circumstances could he allow Qian to die before the five-hundredth cut. If he did, he would give credence to the view that Board of Punishments executioners were little more than common butchers.

Zhao Jia wiped the bloody water from Qian Xiongfei's skin with a chamois dipped in saltwater; then, while rinsing it in a bucket of clean water, he cooled his overheated hands and dried them. Qian's tongue-less mouth was still vigorously opening and closing, but the sounds coming out of it were growing weak. Zhao knew he needed to speed up the process, remove smaller pieces of flesh, and avoid spots with heavy concentrations of blood vessels. It had become necessary to make a practical adjustment in the cutting scheme he'd begun with. Rather than call into question the skills of a Board of Punishments executioner, this change was a direct result of Yuan's disruptive command. In a move that went unnoticed by the witnesses, he jabbed the tip of his knife into his own thigh to produce a sharp pain that drove away his sluggishness and at the same time took his mind off his burning hands. With renewed energy, he stopped worrying about Yuan Shikai and the ranking officials behind him and gave no more thought to the five thousand soldiers arrayed in front. His knife began swirling like the wind, removing pieces of Qian's flesh that rained down like hailstones or a swarm of beetles. The next two hundred cuts removed all the flesh and muscles from Qian's thighs, followed by fifty cuts to do the same to his upper arms. Fifty cuts in the abdomen preceded seventy-five on each side of his buttocks. By that time, Qian's life was hanging by a thread, though light still burned in his eyes. Bloody foam oozed from his mouth, while his viscera, now bereft of constraint by muscles and skin, strained to exit his body. That was particularly true of his intestines, which were writhing like a nest of vipers beneath a thin membrane cover. Zhao Jia straightened up and exhaled. He was sweating profusely; his crotch had gotten sticky, from either blood or sweat, it was hard to tell which. He was paying for his desire to honor the life of Qian Xiongfei and uphold the prestige of the Board of Punishments executioners with his own blood and sweat.

Six cuts remained. With the knowledge that success was within his grasp, Zhao Jia could bring an end to the performance at a more comfortable pace. With the four hundred ninety-fifth cut, he sliced off Qian's left ear. It had felt like a chunk of ice in his hand. Then came the right ear, and when he threw it to the ground, the formerly emaciated dog whose full belly now scraped the ground ambled up to sniff the latest offering before turning and walking off in a show of contempt, leaving behind a foul-smelling discharge from beneath its tail. Qian's ears lay untouched and unwanted in the dirt, like a matching pair of gray seashells. Zhao Jia was reminded of something his shifu had told him. When he was carrying out the slicing death on that exquisite prostitute on the marketplace execution ground, he had sliced off her delicate left ear, from which a pearl-studded gold earring dangled. The ear had held a powerful attraction for him; forbidden, however, from taking anything away from the execution ground, he had no choice but to reluctantly throw it to the ground. A mob of transfixed observers broke through the cordon of guards and swarmed to the spot like a tidal wave; their crazed, terrifying behavior drove away the birds of prey and wild animals prowling the execution site, all in pursuit of the detached ear. It may have been the gold earring they were after, but the shifu, knowing that this interruption could ruin everything, sprang into action by immediately slicing off the prostitute's other ear and flinging it as far as he could. His quick action saved the day by diverting the onrushing crowd. His reputation as a man of superior intelligence was well earned.

Qian Xiongfei now presented a ghastly sight. Zhao readied himself for the four hundred ninety-seventh cut. By tradition, he had two options. He could cut out the condemned man's eyes or cut off his lips. Since Qian's lips were already such an awful mess, to do more seemed a shame, so he decided to cut out his eyes. Zhao knew that Qian was going to die with an unresolved grievance, but in the end, what did that matter? Young brother, he muttered to himself, you have no voice in this decision, but by removing your eyes, I will let you become a ghost that is content with its lot. The heart cannot grieve over what the eyes cannot see. This will cause you less suffering down in the bowels of Hell. No suffering in either this world or the next.

Qian closed his eyes just as Zhao held his knife up to them, catching him by surprise. This cooperation brought Zhao feelings of immense gratitude, since removing the organs of sight was an unpleasant task, even for someone who killed for a living. Taking advantage of the opportunity granted him, he inserted the tip of his knife into a socket and, with an almost imperceptible flick of his wrist, out popped a clearly defined eyeball. "The four hundred ninety-seventh cut," he said weakly.

"The four hundred ninety-seventh cut . . ." His apprentice's announcement was barely audible.

But when Zhao held his knife up to the right eye, it opened unexpectedly; at the same time, Qian released the last howl of his life. Even Zhao shuddered at the sound, and dozens of soldiers fell to the ground like bricks in a collapsing wall. Zhao had no choice but to apply his knife to Qian Xiongfei's remaining eye, which was blazing. What emerged from that eye was not so much a ray of light as a red-hot gas. Zhao Jia's hand was burning as he fought to hold on to the slippery handle. Young brother, he said prayerfully, close your eye. But this time Qian would not cooperate, and Zhao knew he mustn't delay, not even for a moment. He forced himself to act, slipping the tip of his knife into the right eye, and as he circled the socket, he heard a barely audible hissing sound. Yuan Shikai could not hear it; the ranking officials standing in front of their horses, looks of utter terror on their faces, perhaps like foxes grieving over the death of the hare, could not hear it; and the five thousand soldiers who had been reduced to wooden statues with bowed heads could not hear it. What they all heard was the flaming, toxic howl that exploded out of the ruined mouth of Qian Xiong-fei, a sound that had the power to drive an ordinary man insane. But it had no effect on Zhao Jia. What had affected him, nearly rocked him to his soul, was the hissing sound the tip of his knife made as it circled the eye socket. For a brief moment, he went blind and deaf as the hiss entered his body, encircled his viscera, and took root in the marrow of his bones. It would not leave easily, not then and not later. "The four hundred ninety-eighth cut," he said.

His apprentice lay passed out in the dirt.

Dozens more soldiers fell headlong to the ground.

Qian's eyes lay brightly on the ground, sending gloomy, deathly blue-white rays through the mud that all but covered them, as if staring at something. Zhao Jia knew exactly what they were staring at—it was Yuan Shikai—and the thought that crowded his mind was: would Yuan recall the gaze from those two eyes in his memories of that day?

Zhao Jia was beyond exhaustion. Not long before this, he had beheaded the Six Gentlemen of the failed Hundred Days Reform movement, an event that had caused a national, even an international, sensation. In appreciation of the great Liu Guangdi's talents in front of his apprentices, he had sharpened the sword named "Generalissimo," which had become rusty and saw-toothed, until it could cut a hair that fell on it in half. The other five gentlemen owed their swift, painless deaths to their association with Liu Guangdi. When he lopped off their heads with Generalissimo, it was lightning quick, and he was sure that all they felt when their heads were separated from their bodies was a momentary breath of cool air on their necks. Owing to the speed of decapitation, some of the headless bodies flopped forward, and others jerked upward. The faces all had the appearance of being alive, and he believed that long after the heads were rolling in the dirt, clear thoughts continued to swirl inside. After the Six Gentlemen had been dispatched, talk of miracles created by a Board of Punishments executioner swept through the capital. All sorts of fanciful tales relating to the six executions passed from mouth to ear. One story, for instance, related how the headless body of Tan Sitong, of Hunan's Liuyang County, ran up to Excellency Gang Yi, the official in charge of the executions, and slapped him across the face. In another, as it rolled along the ground, the head of Liu Guangdi, known also as Liu Peicun, intoned a poem in such a loud voice that thousands of witnesses heard it. Even an event of this magnitude had failed to tire Grandma Zhao, and yet on this day, in the city of Tianjin, the responsibility of carrying out the slicing death on an insignificant captain of a mounted bodyguard unit had so enervated the preeminent executioner of the land that he could barely stand. Even stranger was the fact that he could not keep his hands from feeling as if they were burning up.

The nose fell at the four hundred ninety-ninth cut. By then, nothing emerged from Qian's mouth but bloody froth—no more sounds. His head, once supported by a strong, rigid neck, now hung limply to his chest.

The final cut—the coup de grace—entered Qian's heart, from which black blood the color and consistency of melted malt sugar slid down the knife blade. The strong smell of that blood once again made Zhao nauseous. He cut out a piece of the heart with the tip of his knife and, with his head slumped, announced to his feet:

"May it please Your Excellency, the five hundredth cut."

CHAPTER TEN

A Promise Kept

1

Peking experienced a heavy snowfall on the eighth night of the twelfth month in the twenty-second year of the Guangxu reign, 1896. Residents awoke early to a blanket of silvery white. As temple bells rang out across the city, the chief executioner assigned to the Board of Punishments Bureau of Detentions, Zhao Jia, got out of bed, dressed in casual clothes, and, after summoning his new apprentice, left for a temple to fill the bowl tucked under his arm with gruel. After leaving the chilled atmosphere of Board of Punishments Avenue, they met up with a fast-moving crowd of beggars and the city's poor. It was a good day for beggars and the city's poor, as attested by the joyful looks on faces turned a range of colors from the biting cold. Snow crunched beneath their feet. Limbs and branches on roadside scholar trees were a collage of silvery white and jade green, as if clusters of white flowers were abloom. The sun broke its way through a dense layer of gray clouds, creating a captivating contrast of white and red. The two men merged with a stream of humanity heading northwest along Xidan Boulevard, where most of Peking's temples were located, and where great pots of charity gruel sent steam skyward from makeshift tents. As they neared the Xisi gateway, whose history was written in blood, flocks of crows and gray cranes were startled into flight out of the jumble of trees behind the Western Ten Storehouses.

He and his alert, quick-witted apprentice lined up at the Guangji Temple to receive their bowls of charity gruel from an enormous pot that had been set up in the temple yard. The blazing pine kindling under the pot dispersed heated air in all directions, which created a psychological dilemma for the beggars in their tattered clothes, who craved the tempting warmth but could not bring themselves to give up their precious spots in the food line. Heat waves formed a mist high above the steaming pot, creating an invisible shield like one of those legendary carriage canopies. A pair of disheveled, dirty-faced monks stood at the pot, bent at the waist, stirring the gruel with gigantic metal spades. The scraping sound of the spades on the bottom of the pot set his teeth on edge. People in line stomped their nearly frostbitten feet on the snowy ground, quickly turning it into a dirty, icy mess. At last the smell of cooked gruel began to spread. In the cold, clean air, the unimaginably rich aroma of food had a stimulating effect on men whose stomachs were rumbling. The light in the eyes of the derelicts was impossible to miss. Several little beggars, their heads tucked down into their shoulders, ran up front and stuck their heads over the edge of the bubbling pot, like little monkeys, to breathe in deeply before running back to their places in line. The foot stomping increased in frequency as the men's bodies began to sway visibly.

Zhao Jia, who was wearing dog-skin socks under felt boots, did not feel the cold. He neither stomped his feet nor, of course, swayed from side to side. He had not gone without food; for him, lining up for charity gruel had nothing to do with hunger. It was a ritual passed down by earlier generations of executioners. According to the explanation given by his shifu, lining up for a bowl of charity gruel on the eighth day of the twelfth lunar month gave executioners the opportunity to demonstrate to the Buddha that this profession merely provided a livelihood, like begging, and was not undertaken by men who were somehow born to kill other men. Lining up for charity gruel was an acknowledgment of their low standing in society. For executioners in the Bureau of Detentions, meat-stuffed buns were available every day, but this bowl of gruel was a once-a-year affair.

Zhao Jia considered himself to be the most dignified individual in the long line of men. But there, just beyond several beggars with their swaying heads and panting mouths ahead of him, was a man standing as tall and unmoving as Mt. Tai. He was wearing a black robe and a felt hat and carried a blue bundle under one arm. He had the typical look of a low- or mid-level official in what was known as a "plain water yamen," one with limited funds and few opportunities to enrich oneself. He would change into his official attire, which was in the bundle under his arm, once he was inside the yamen. But no matter how hard up a Peking official might be, he could always get something from officials from the provinces on their annual treks to the capital on official business. At the very least, he was in line for "ice and coal fees." But if he was so incorruptible that he refused even that sort of "iron rice bowl" subsistence, his government salary surely made a range of baked goods affordable, so there was no need to line up with beggars and the city poor for a handout of charity gruel at a local temple. He wondered what the man looked like, but was well aware that the capital attracted people of exceptional hidden abilities, that even the crudest inn could be home to a man of special talents, and that a customer at a won-ton stand could easily be a heroic figure. A true man does not reveal his identity; if he does, he's not a true man. The Tongzhi Emperor, having tired of his imperial harem, ran off to Hanjiatan to cavort with prostitutes, and when he lost his taste for delicacies from the Imperial kitchen, he went to Tianqiao for bowls of soybean milk. How, then, could Zhao Jia be sure what lay behind the man's purpose in lining up for charity gruel? He could not, so there was no need to go up to take a look. Instinctively the men in line edged forward as the aroma of gruel intensified, pressing the line tighter and tighter, which shortened the distance between Zhao Jia and the man up front. By leaning to the side, he had a view of his profile. But no more than that, since the man kept his eyes straight ahead. All Zhao could see was his somewhat unruly queue and a shirt collar made shiny by unwashed hair. Chilblains dotted the lobes and rims of his fleshy ears, some already oozing pus. Finally the anticipated moment arrived: it was time to hand out the gruel. Slowly the line began to move forward. Curtained carriages drawn by horses and mules and residents of the city with baskets to deliver gruel to friends and families made their way together to the oversized pot from both sides of the line. The alluring aroma grew stronger with each step closer to the pot, and Zhao Jia heard stomachs growling all around. Holding their bowls in hands that were black as coal, the men crouched down by the side of the road or stood against a wall to slurp the contents. The two monks were now leaning over the pot, dipping large, long-handled metal scoops into the gruel and impatiently pouring the contents into one bowl after another; inevitably some dripped to the ground from the scoop or the sides of the bowls, and was immediately lapped up by mangy dogs whose hunger was stronger than the pain from the kicks they received. Now it was the man up front's turn. Zhao Jia watched as he took a small bowl from under his robe and held it out to the monks, who gave him a curious look. Each of the bowls held out by the others in line seemed larger than the one before, and some could rightly be called basins. He, on the other hand, could cover the lid of his porcelain bowl with one hand. The monks used extraordinary care when they poured gruel into his bowl, filling it to the brim almost as soon as they tipped the scoop, which held several times the amount of the bowl. With his bundle still tucked under his arm, the man gripped his bowl in both hands and politely bowed his thanks before walking, head down, to the side of the road, where he lifted the hem of his robe, sat down, and quietly began to eat. The moment he turned around, Zhao Jia spotted his high nose, large mouth, and sickly pallor, and he knew who the imposing man was—the director of one of the Board of Punishments' many bureaus—though he did not know his name. He reacted by sighing inwardly at the man's plight. To be the head of a Bureau in one of the Six Boards meant that he had passed the Imperial Civil Service Examination, yet here he was, so poor he had to beg a bowl of gruel in a charity tent. It was the height of absurdity. From decades of experience in official yamens, Zhao

Jia was well acquainted with the means by which various officials fattened their purses and the vagaries of promotion. This fellow, who was crouching in the snow by the side of the road eating a bowl of charity gruel, was either hopelessly incompetent or a man of rare virtue.

After Zhao and his apprentice received their gruel, they too crouched by the side of the road, and as Zhao ate, his eyes remained on the man who had caught his attention. He was grasping his delicate ceramic bowl tightly in both hands, obviously for the warmth it afforded. The beggars and city poor all around raised a din as they slurped their gruel. He alone ate without making a sound, and when he was finished, he covered his bowl and his face with one of his wide sleeves. Zhao could not say for certain why he did that, but it was worth a guess. And he was right. When the man lowered his sleeve, Zhao could see that the little bowl had been licked clean. The man stood up, put the bowl back inside his robe, and headed southeast at a quick pace.

So Zhao Jia and his apprentice followed the man; that is to say, they too set out for the Board of Punishments. The man took long strides, his head tilting forward at each step, like a galloping horse, and Zhao and his apprentice had to trot just to keep up. Later, when he thought back to the occasion, he could not say what had motivated him to follow the man, who, as it turned out, slipped and fell as he was turning into a narrow lane near a hot-pot restaurant; his arms and legs were splayed on the ground, and his blue bundle went flying. Zhao's initial reaction had been to rush over and help him up, but thoughts of the trouble that might cause held him back; so he stopped and watched to see what would happen. The man was having a hard time getting up, and once he was on his feet, he managed only a few steps before falling again, and this time Zhao could see that he was rather badly hurt. So, handing his bowl to his apprentice, he rushed over and helped the man, whose face was beaded with sweat, to his feet.

"Are you hurt, sir?" Zhao asked.

Without replying, the man took a few steps, supporting himself with his hand on Zhao Jia's shoulder, his face twisted in pain.

"It looks to me, sir, that you are badly hurt."

"Who are you?" the man asked with obvious suspicion.

"I work in the Board of Punishments, sir."

"The Board of Punishments?" the man said. "If that's true, how come I don't know you?"

"You don't know me, sir, but I know who you are," Zhao said. "Tell me what you would like me to do."

The man took a few more tentative steps, but his body gave out and he plopped down on the snowy ground. "My legs won't carry me," he said. "Find some transportation to take me home."

2

Zhao Jia flagged down a donkey-drawn coal cart and accompanied the injured official to a broken-down little temple outside Xizhi Gate, where a tall, lanky young man was practicing kungfu in the yard. Despite the cold, he was wearing only a thin singlet; his pale face was beaded with sweat. As soon as Zhao Jia helped the official into the yard, the young man ran up. "Father," he shouted, and burst into tears. Icy winds whistled through the flimsy paper covering the windows in the unheated temple, where cracks in the walls were stuffed with cotton wadding. A woman sitting on the chilled kang was shivering as she spooled thread. She looked like an old granny, with a sickly pallor and gray hair. Zhao Jia and the young man helped the official over to the kang, where, after a respectful bow, he turned to leave.

"My name is Liu Guangdi," the man said. "I passed the Imperial Examination in 1883, the twenty-second year of the Guangxu reign, and have been the director of a Board of Punishments Bureau for several years," the man said in a genial tone. "This is my wife, and he is my son. I must ask Grandma to excuse the humble place we call home."

"You know who I am," Zhao said, embarrassment showing on his face.

"Truth is," Liu Guangdi said, "our jobs are essentially the same. We both work for the nation and serve the Emperor. But you are more important than I." He sighed. "Dismissing several Bureau directors would have no effect on the Board of Punishments. But without Grandma Zhao, it would no longer be the Board of Punishments. Among all the thousands of national laws and statutes, none is more important than those upheld by your knife."

Zhao fell to his knees and, with moist eyes, said:

"Excellency Liu, your words have moved me deeply. In the eyes of most observers, people in my line of work are lower than pigs, worse than dogs, while you, Excellency, esteem our work."

"Get up, Old Zhao, please get up," Liu said. "I won't keep you any longer. One of these days we'll sit down over something strong to drink." He turned to his son, the gaunt young man. "Pu'er, see Grandma Zhao out."

"I cannot let your honorable son . . ." Zhao was clearly flustered.

The young man smiled and made a polite gesture with his hands. Zhao Jia would not easily forget his fine manners and humility.

3

On the first day of the New Year, 1897, Liu Guangdi strode into the eastern side room of the executioners' quarters, dressed in official attire and carrying an oilpaper bundle. The men were drinking and playing finger-guessing games to welcome in the New Year, and the sight of a senior official walking in unannounced threw them into a panic. Zhao Jia jumped down off the kang barefoot and knelt on the floor.

"Best wishes for the New Year, Excellency!"

The other executioners followed his lead:

"Best wishes for the New Year, Excellency!" they cried out from their knees.

"Get up," Liu said, "all of you, get up. The floor is cold. Get back up on the kang."

The men stood up but, hands at their sides, did not dare to move.

"I am on duty, so I figured I'd spend the day with you men." He opened his bundle, which was filled with cured meat, then took out a bottle of spirits from under his robe. "My wife prepared this meat herself; the spirits were a gift from a friend. See what you think."

"We would not dare to think of sharing a meal with Your Excellency," Zhao said.

"It's New Year's, so we can dispense with the formalities," Liu replied.

"We truly dare not," Zhao insisted.

"What has gotten into you, Old Zhao?" Liu said as he took off his hat and official robe. "We all work in the same yamen, so let's act like it."

The other men looked at Zhao Jia.

"Since Your Excellency does us this honor, it is better to accept humbly than to courteously decline," Zhao said. "After you, sir."

Liu Guangdi removed his shoes and sat on the communal kang with his legs folded. "You've got this nice and hot," he said.

The men received the compliment with a foolish grin. "You don't expect me to lift each one of you up here, do you?" he said.

"Go on, get up," Zhao said. "We mustn't offend Excellency Liu."

So the execution team climbed back onto the kang, where they made themselves as small as possible. Zhao Jia picked up a glass, filled it from the bottle, then knelt on the kang and held it out with both hands.

"On behalf of my fellows, Your Excellency, I wish you wealth and promotions."

Liu Guangdi accepted the glass and drained it.

"Fine stuff," he said as he licked his lips. "Now join me, all of you."

Zhao Jia drank a glass and felt his heart bubble over with warmth.

Liu Guangdi raised his glass.

"Old Zhao," he said, "I am in your debt for helping me get home that time. Come on, men, fill your glasses and accept my toast!"

They drained their glasses with great emotion. With tears in his eyes, Zhao Jia said:

"Excellency, not since Pangu split heaven and earth and the ancient emperors ruled the earth has a senior official actually joined a group of executioners to celebrate New Year's with a bottle. Let us raise our glasses to His Excellency, everyone!"

The executioners knelt in place, raised their glasses, and toasted Liu, who clinked glasses with each of them and, as his eyes brightened, said:

"I can see that you are all men of indomitable spirit. It takes courage to engage in your profession. And nothing celebrates courage like fine spirits. So drink up!"

The men grew increasingly spirited as the level of the alcohol in the bottle dropped. No longer so tense or concerned about where they placed their arms and legs, they took turns toasting Liu, their constraints disappearing as fast as the spirits and the meat. Liu Guangdi, who had abandoned his official airs, picked up a pig's foot and attacked it with such vigor that his cheeks shone from the grease.

By the time the meat and spirits were gone, they were all fairly drunk. Zhao Jia was beaming; Liu Guangdi had tears in his eyes. First Aunt was sputtering nonsense; Second Aunt was snoring with his eyes open. Third Aunt's tongue was so thick that no one could understand a word he said.

Liu got down off the kang. "Wonderful," he said, "this was just wonderful!"

Zhao helped Liu into his boots, and the young nephews helped him back into his official robe and hat. With the executioners in tow, Liu stumbled his way into the room where the tools of the trade were kept. His eyes fell on the sword whose handle proclaimed it "Generalissimo."

"Grandma Zhao," he blurted out, "how many red-capped heads has this sword separated from their bodies?"

"I never counted."

Liu tested the rusty blade with his finger.

"It's not very sharp," he said.

"Nothing dulls a blade like human blood, Excellency. We have to hone it before we use it."

With a laugh, Liu said:

"By now you and I are old friends, Grandma Zhao. If I fall into your hands one day, I hope this blade is at its sharpest."

"Excellency . . ." It was an awkward moment. "You are an upright, incorruptible official, a noble man of great integrity . . ."

"An upright, incorruptible man deserves to die like anyone else. The slicing death repays nobility and integrity!" Liu sighed before going on. "Let's say it's a deal, Grandma Zhao."

"Excellency . . ."

Liu Guangdi left the room weaving from side to side, watched by the executioners with tears in their eyes.

4

As a dozen horns blared their mournful music, the celebrated Six Gentlemen of the Wuxu Reform Movement were lifted down off a dilapidated prison van by a dozen uniformed guards and up onto the elevated execution platform, over which a thick red felt mat had been laid. A fresh layer of dirt had been spread on the ground around the platform. Zhao Jia, the principal "grandma" of the Board of Punishments, was somewhat comforted by the sight of these preparations. He and his apprentice followed the Six Gentlemen onto the platform. The mournful music was persistent and increasingly shrill. The musicians' foreheads were sweaty; their cheeks had ballooned out. Zhao Jia took a good look at the six distinguished men lined up on the platform, and saw a range of expressions. Tan Sitong's chin was raised as he looked skyward, a solemn, tragic look on his dark, gaunt face. The face of the young man, Lin Xu, who was next in line, was ghostly white; his thin, bloodless lips quivered. Heavy-set Yang Shenxiu had cocked his square head to one side; drool oozed from his twisted mouth. The delicate features of Kang Guangren were distorted by incessant twitches as he kept wiping tears and snot with his sleeve. Yang Rui, short in stature but full of energy, kept sweeping the area around the platform with his dark eyes, as if hoping to find an old friend amid the spectators. Liu Guangdi, the tallest among them, wore a solemn expression; eyes downcast, he was making a guttural sound.

It was approaching noon. The shadow cast by a fir pole behind the platform was slowly forming a straight line with the pole. It was a brilliant autumn day, with radiant sunshine and a deep blue sky. Sunlight reflecting off the platform mat, the red capes of the official witnesses, the red flags, banners, and umbrella canopies of the honor guard, the officials' red caps, the red tassels on the soldiers' helmets, and the red hilt of Generalissimo sent fiery rays of light in all directions. Flocks of doves flew in circles above the execution ground, round and round, filling the air with the whisper of flapping wings and their shrill cries. Throngs of spectators kept a hundred paces away by soldiers craned their necks and stared wide-eyed at the platform, waiting anxiously for the moment to arrive that would excite, sadden, or terrify them.

Zhao Jia was waiting too, waiting impatiently for the supervising official to give the order, so he could do his job and leave the premises. Facing the deeply affecting looks on the six men made him ill at ease. Even though he had smeared his face with chicken blood, which served as a mask of sorts, his nerves were still on edge, and he was actually somewhat self-conscious, as if standing in front of a gaping crowd without his pants. Never before in his long career had he been so unsettled or lost his sense of detachment. In the past, so long as he was wearing red and had chicken blood smeared on his face, his heart was as cold as a black stone at the bottom of a deep lake. He had the vague feeling that while he was putting someone to death, his soul was hibernating in the fissures of the coldest, deepest stone, and that a killing machine bereft of heat and emotion performed the deeds. And so, when the job was over, he could wash his hands and face and be free of any feeling that he had just killed someone. It was all a haze, a sort of half sleep. But on this day he felt as if the hardened mask of chicken blood had been peeled away, like the outer layer of a wall soaked by a rainsquall. His soul squirmed in the fissures of the stone, and a host of emotions—pity, terror, agitation, and more—seeped out like tiny rivulets. When an expert executioner stood on the platform to carry out his somber task, he was expected to show no emotion. If, however, indifference was considered an emotion of sorts, then it was the only one permitted; all others could serve only to ruin a reputation. He did not have the nerve to look at the Six Gentlemen, especially the one-time Board of Punishments Bureau director with whom he had established a unique and genuine friendship—Liu Guangdi. If he were to look into the man's eyes, in which burned unalloyed rage, his palms would be wet with cold sweat for the first time ever. So he looked up at the doves circling above him. All those flapping wings made him dizzy. The chief official witness—Vice Minister of the Left, His Excellency Gang Yi—squinted up into the sky from his seat at the base of the platform before casting a sideways glance at the Six Gentlemen.

"It's time," he said in a shaky voice. "Criminals, on your knees to give thanks for the blessings of the Emperor."

Like a man who had received absolution, Zhao Jia turned to his apprentice and took from him the unwieldy sword reserved for the decapitation of fourth-ranked officials and higher—Generalissimo. Out of respect for Excellency Liu, he had spent the whole night honing the blade to hair-splitting perfection. After drying his hands with his sleeves, he held his right arm across his chest so that the sword was pointing straight up.

Some of the Six Gentlemen wept; others sighed.

With appropriate decorum, Zhao Jia said:

"Please, gentlemen, take your places."

Tan Sitong cried out:

"I have the intention to kill thieves, but lack the strength to change the course of events. It is a worthy death, and I have no regrets!"

His last words spoken, he had a coughing fit that turned his face the color of gold paper; his eyes were bloodshot. He then fell to his knees, placed his hands on the platform, and stretched out his neck. His loosened queue spilled across his neck down to the platform.

Lin, Yang, Yang, and Kang knelt beside Tan in utter dejection. Lin Xu sobbed like a mistreated little girl. Kang Guangren wailed loudly and smacked his palms on the platform. Yang Shenxiu also rested his hands on the platform, his eyes darting from one side to the other, but giving no hint as to what he was looking for. Liu Guangdi stood alone, his head held high, refusing to kneel. As he stared at Liu's tattered boots, Zhao Jia said timidly:

"Your Excellency, please take your place."

Glaring wide-eyed at the seated Gang Yi, Liu demanded hoarsely:

"Why are we being killed with no trial?"

Lacking the nerve to look at Liu, Gang Yi turned his fat, swarthy face to the side.

"Why are we being killed with no trial?" Liu Guangdi repeated. "Is this a nation bereft of laws?"

"My orders are to supervise the execution, that is all I know. I beg Peicun's indulgence on this . . ." Gang Yi's distress was palpable.

Yang Rui, who was kneeling alongside Liu Guangdi, tugged at his clothing.

"Peicun," he said, "at this point, what is there to say? Kneel with us. It is what is expected."

"Great Qing Dynasty!" Liu shouted, drawing the words out as he straightened his clothes, bent his knees, and knelt on the platform. A functionary standing behind the chief witness announced in a loud voice:

"Give thanks for the blessings of Her Royal Highness!"

Of the Six Gentlemen, only Lin, Yang, Yang, and Kang numbly performed the rite of kowtows to her. Tan Sitong and Liu Guangdi held their necks straight and refused to kowtow.

Then the functionary announced loudly:

"Criminals, give thanks for the blessings of His Imperial Majesty!"

After this announcement, all six men kowtowed. Tan Sitong banged his head on the platform as if he were crushing cloves of garlic, interspersed with shouts:

"Your Majesty, Your Majesty, I have failed you, Your Majesty!"

The thuds from Liu Guangdi's kowtows were loud and insistent; tears lined both sides of his gaunt face.

In a voice that betrayed his discomfort, Gang Yi gave the command:

"Carry out the sentence!"

Zhao Jia bowed deeply to the Six Gentlemen.

"I will send Your Excellencies to your glory," he said softly.

He braced himself to drive out all personal thoughts and concentrate his strength and spirit into the wrist of his right arm. In his mind, the execution sword and his body had already merged. He took one step forward, reached down with his left hand, and grabbed the tip of Liu Guangdi's queue. With it he pulled Liu's head toward him to expose the taut skin of his neck. Thanks to years of experience, he immediately spotted the precise spot where the sword would enter the neck. He lowered Liu's head slightly as he turned to the right before he would swing back and bring down the sword in one motion, when a desperate howl emerged from the throng of spectators:

"Father—"

A tall, lanky, and badly disheveled young man stumbled forward at the very moment Zhao Jia was about to slice the sword through Liu's neck. He aborted the move. His wrist felt the power of the bloodthirsty Generalissimo in that sudden stop. The young man staggering up to the platform was Liu Pu, Guangdi's son, whom he had met that time in the little temple outside Xizhi Gate. A surge of compassion that had been suppressed for many years by weighty professional considerations flowed past his heart. Bewildered soldiers, armed with red-tasseled spears, recovered from their shock and rushed up in confusion. A badly shaken Gang Yi jumped to his feet and cried out shrilly, "Grab him." Palace guards behind him drew their swords and converged on the young man, but before they could use their weapons, Liu Pu fell to his knees and was kowtowing to Gang Yi. That stopped the guards, who gaped vacantly at the handsome young man, whose ashen face was wet with tears and snot.

"Be merciful, Your Excellency," he pleaded with Gang Yi. "Let me take my father's place . . ."

Liu Guangdi looked up and, choked with sobs, managed to say:

"Pu, my son, don't be foolish . . ."

Liu Pu crawled forward on his knees and gazed up at his father, his words muffled by sobs:

"Father, let me die in your place . . ."

"My dear son . . ." Liu Guangdi sighed. His face was haggard, his features twisted in his agony. "I want no extravagant funeral, and you are to take no bereavement gifts from anyone. Do not send my body back to my hometown, but bury it somewhere nearby. Once that is done, I want you and your mother to leave Peking and return to Sichuan. I want my descendants to receive an education, but I want no sons or grandsons to sit for an official examination. I entrust all this to you. Now, leave, and don't make me waver in my resolve." With that he closed his eyes, stretched out his neck, and said to Zhao Jia, "Old Zhao, do it now. For the sake of our friendship, make it a good job."

Zhao's eyes burned. He was nearly in tears.

"I promise, Your Excellency."

Liu Pu howled from below the platform and crawled on his knees up to Gang Yi.

"Excellency . . . Excellency . . . let me take my father's place . . ."

Gang Yi covered his face with his wide sleeve.

"Take him away!"

Soldiers rushed up and dragged the hysterical, sobbing Liu Pu away.

"Carry out the sentence!" Gang Yi commanded.

Zhao Jia grabbed Liu Guangdi's queue for the second time. "An offense against Your Excellency," he said softly as he made a rapid half circle, and Liu Guangdi's detached head was in his hand. It felt extraordinarily heavy, the heaviest he'd ever held. Both hands—the one holding the sword and the one dangling Liu's head—ached and felt swollen. Holding the head high over his own, he announced loudly to the Chief Witness:

"May it please Your Excellency, the sentence has been carried out!"

Gang Yi merely glanced at the platform before quickly averting his eyes.

Zhao Jiu followed custom by displaying the severed head to the observers. Some shouted their macabre appreciation; some wept openly. Liu Pu lay on the ground unconscious. Zhao Jia saw that the eyes in Liu's head were open, the eyebrows raised. A grinding sound emerged from between chattering teeth; he was convinced that Liu's brain was still functioning and that the eyes saw him. His left arm, in which he held the severed head, was getting sore and numb. Liu's queue was like a slippery eel struggling to break free from the sweaty, blood-streaked hand holding it. There were tears in the great man's eyes, which dimmed slowly, like cinders dying out from splashes of water. When Zhao Jia laid the head down, he noticed that it wore a peaceful look, and that made him feel better. "Excellency Liu," he muttered under his breath, "as promised, I made a good job of it. You did not suffer, and I did no disservice to our friendship." He now turned to the others and, with the help of his apprentice, dispatched Tan, Lin, Yang, Yang, and Kang with the same practiced skill. Thus, with consummate skill, he demonstrated his respect for the Six Gentlemen.

The capital was abuzz with talk of the spectacular execution, with most of the discussion centering on two aspects: one was the exceptional skill of the executioner, Zhao Jia; the other was the disparity in how the six men faced their deaths. People said that after Liu Guangdi's head was severed, it wept copious tears and called out to the Emperor, and when Tan Sitong's head left his neck, it proudly intoned a seven-syllable quatrain . . .

This new folklore, which contained particles of truth, burnished Zhao Jia's reputation and elevated this ancient yet lowly profession far enough up the social ladder for people to take approving notice of it. It also insinuated its way into the Palace, like a gentle breeze, where it reached the ears of Cixi, the Empress Dowager. It would soon pave the way for great glory to find its way to Zhao Jia.

CHAPTER ELEVEN

Golden Pistols

1

In the early morning hours, high-ranking officers from the Tianjin branch of the Right Imperial Guard led a delegation that included a military band and a cavalry unit to the little pier on the northern bank of the Hai River to welcome the return of the Vice Minister of War and Judicial Commissioner of Zhili, Yuan Shikai, from Peking, where he had presented longevity gifts to the Empress Dowager Cixi upon Her resumption of the Regency.

Among the members of the delegation were the Deputy Chief of the Military Affairs General Staff, Xu Shichang, who would later serve as President of the Republic of China; Deputy Adjutant of the Office of Military Affairs and future President of the Republic of China, Feng Guozhang; Zhang Xun, future Changjiang Patrolling Inspector and so-called "Pigtail General," who would later attempt to restore the abdicated Emperor Pu Yi; Duan Zhigui, Commander of the Second Infantry Battalion and future Chief of the Republic of China General Staff; Commander of the Third Artillery Battalion and future Premier of the Republic of China, Duan Qirui; Xu Bangjie, Commander of the Third Infantry Battalion and future General Director of the Republic of China Presidential Palace; Deputy Commander of the Third Infantry Battalion and future Premier of the Republic of China, Wang Shizhen . . . all relatively young, enterprising military officers whose ambitions were not, at the time, excessive. None could possibly have imagined that within a matter of decades, the fate of China would rest in the hands of this cadre of men.

Also part of the delegation was the most promising member of the Right Imperial Guard in terms of moral character and knowledge, the captain of Yuan Shikai's mounted guard, Qian Xiongfei. Qian was among the first delegation of students sent to study in Japan, where he graduated from a military academy. He was tall and trim and had bushy eyebrows, big eyes, and white, even teeth. A man of enviable self-discipline, he neither smoked nor drank nor gambled nor whored around. Always vigilant and a wizard with a gun, he was highly prized by Yuan Shikai himself. He rode up that day on a snow-white stallion, the creases in his uniform as sharp as knives, his riding boots shined to a high gloss, a pair of gold-handled pistols holstered on his leather belt. A contingent of sixty warhorses fanned out behind him like a swallowtail, with elite young military guards in the saddles, each armed with German thirteen-shot repeater rifles. Extremely fit, they kept their eyes focused straight ahead, and though there was a bit of a scripted look about the detachment, they managed to inspire awe in anyone who laid eyes on them.

It was nearly noon, and there was still no sight of the steamboat carrying Excellency Yuan. No fishing boats were visible anywhere on the Hai River, whose broad vista was broken only by flocks of seagulls that occasionally dipped down just above the waves. Since it was late autumn, the trees were bare, all but the oaks and maples, on which a smattering of vivid red or golden yellow leaves remained, bringing a bit of color to both banks of the river, a bright spot in an otherwise bleak panorama. Gloomy patches of cloud cover hung above the river, over which damp winds blew in from the northeast, carrying the rank, salty smell of the Bohai Sea. The horses were getting restless, swishing their tails, kicking out their rear hooves, and snorting. Qian Xiongfei's mount kept turning its head back to nip at its rider's knee. When Qian stole a look at the senior officers around him, he saw how their faces had darkened as the cold, damp late autumn winds bored through their uniforms and chilled them to the bone. Drops of snivel hung from the tip of Xu Shichang's nose; Zhang Xun was yawning, which made his eyes water; and Duan Qirui was rocking back and forth in the saddle, looking perilously close to toppling off his horse. The term "sorry sight" perfectly described the delegation. Qian, who held his fellow officials in contempt, was ashamed to be counted among them. He was no less weary than they, but he, at least, valued his responsibility to maintain the proper military bearing. The best way to pass the time in the midst of the boredom of waiting was to let his thoughts roam wherever they desired. To the observer, his gaze was focused on the wide river before him, but what played out before his eyes were episodes from his past.

2

Little Xizi, Little Xizi! That sound, so touchingly intimate, buzzed in his ears, near one moment and far the next, like a game of hide-and-seek. Youthful visions of playing tag with his older brother danced in front of his eyes. As they chased one another through the fields of their village, the image of his brother slowly expanded, growing taller and wider, while he hopped and jumped, grabbing at the shiny queue flying just out of reach. Even when he touched it with his finger, it nimbly flicked away, like a black dragon's tail. Anxious and frustrated, he stomped his foot and burst into tears; his brother stopped and spun around. And in that brief moment, a youngster without a single whisker on his chin was transformed into a court official with an impressive beard. The next recollection that crowded into his head was of the quarrel he'd had with his brother before leaving for Japan. His brother had been opposed to his abandoning his studies for the Imperial Civil Service Examination. He had responded by saying that the examination produced an army of walking corpses, so angering his brother that he pounded his fist on the table, spilling most of the tea in their cups. "How dare you be so arrogant!" scolded his brother, his impressive beard quivering as anger undermined his stately bearing. But only for a moment, as that wrath was replaced by a desolate sense of self-mockery. "If that is so," his brother had said, "then generations of sages and heroes have been nothing but walking corpses. That includes Wen Tianxiang, whom you revere, and even the great Tang poet Lu You. Zeng Guofan, Li Hongzhang, and Zhang Zhidong, officials in the present dynasty, are all walking corpses. Poor ignorant specimens like your brother are zombies that cannot even walk." "That is not what I meant, Elder Brother." "Then what did you mean?" "I meant that if China is going to move forward, the Imperial Civil Service Examination must be discarded and replaced by modern schools, and the ossified eight-part essay must give way to forms of scientific education. Fresh water must flow into this filthy, stagnant lake. China has to change, or she will surely perish. And the tactics required to effect the needed changes must be borrowed from the barbarians. I have made up my mind to go, so do not try to stop me, Elder Brother." His brother could only sigh. "A man's aspirations are unique to him, and no amount of coercion can change that. But I, your ignorant Elder Brother, believe that only by being tempered in the examination hall can one lay claim to dignity and prestige. All others are imposters who may achieve high office, but will never earn the respect of others." "Brother," he had replied, "troubled times demand a martial spirit—a civil ethos is reserved for days of peace and tranquility. Our family has had the good fortune of boasting one metropolitan scholar: you. We do not need more. So let me go take up studies in the martial realm." His brother sighed again. "Metropolitan Scholar," he said, "an empty label and nothing more. You carry a bundle of clothes to work in an unimportant yamen with little chance to benefit monetarily and are reduced to eating half a duck's egg mixed into plain rice . . ." "If that is so, then why does my own brother want me to follow the same dead-end path?" With a dry laugh, his brother said, "The deep-rooted notion of a walking corpse . . ."

The winds were getting stronger; the river was beset by gray waves. He was reminded of his return trip on the *Pusan Maru* and thought back to Kang You-wei's letter of introduction to gain him an audience with Yuan Shikai . . .

3

The town of Small Station in autumn; golden tassels on rice paddies as far as the eye could see gave off an intoxicating fragrance. Before his audience with Excellency Yuan in Shanxi, he had already quietly surveyed the area around Small Station for two days, secretly taking note of everything with the eye of a trained observer. He noted, for instance, that the soldiers of the New Army who took the parade ground every day carried themselves with military bearing, were armed with modern weapons, marched with precision, and made a fine impression, everything that the corrupt, inept old army was not. To know what a general is like, one need only look at his troops, and he held Excellency Yuan in the highest regard before he'd even met him.

Yuan's official quarters, which were only a couple of arrow shots from camp, were protected by four swarthy guards the size of small pagodas who stood at the arched gateway. They wore leather boots, leggings, and leather cartridge belts, and carried German breech-loading rifles whose barrels were the blue color of swallows' wings. He handed Kang Youwei's introduction letter to the gatekeeper, who took it inside.

It was mealtime for Excellency Yuan, who was waited on by two beautiful attendants.

"I humbly offer my respects to Your Excellency!" He did not kneel and did not bow with his hands folded in front; instead, he stood straight and snapped off a Japanese-style salute.

He saw Yuan's face undergo a subtle change, from a look of displeasure to a cold, sweeping examination with his eyes, and finally to an expression of admiration. With the briefest of nods, Excellency Yuan said, "A chair."

He knew immediately that he had made a good first impression and that his plan had worked perfectly.

One of the attendants struggled to bring over a chair that was obviously too heavy for her. With the sound of her girlish panting in his ears and the smell of orchids emanating from her neck in his nostrils, he held his rigid stance and said, "I dare not sit in Your Excellency's presence."

"Stand, then," Yuan said.

He studied His Excellency's square face: big eyes, bushy eyebrows, wide mouth, and large ears, the very definition of eminence. Yuan, who had not shed the sounds of his rural home—thick and mellow, like aged spirits—went back to his meal, seemingly having forgotten his visitor, who stood there, rigid, unmoving as a poplar. His Excellency was in his nightgown and slippers; his queue hung loose. Breakfast that morning consisted of braised pig's feet, a roast duck, a bowl of stewed lamb, a plate of braised mandarin fish, hardboiled eggs, and a basket of fluffy white steamed buns. Yuan enjoyed a healthy appetite and a love of food. He ate with rapt attention, as if he were alone. One of the attendants was responsible for peeling the eggs, the other for deboning the fish. He ate four eggs, gnawed on the feet of two pigs, finished off all the crispy skin of the duck, ate a dozen slices of lamb and half a fish, plus two steamed buns, washing it all down with three cups of wine. His meal finished, he rinsed his mouth with tea and wiped his hands on a napkin. Then he leaned back in his chair, belched, and shut his eyes while picking his teeth, as if he were alone in the room.

Knowing that all great men have their peculiarities, including the unique ways in which they observe and appraise talent, Qian Xiongfei assumed that the rude demonstration was how this one chose to evaluate his visitor. By then he had been standing at attention for more than an hour, but his legs remained steady, his eyes and ears clear and unaffected by the wait. By maintaining his military bearing, he had demonstrated that he was a model of military deportment and was exceptionally fit.

Excellency Yuan sat with his eyes closed, with one attractive attendant massaging his legs, the other rubbing his back. As loud snores rose from his throat, the attendants stole a glance at Qian Xiongfei and rewarded him with friendly smiles. Finally the snores stopped and His Excellency opened his eyes, fixing Qian with a penetrating stare that revealed no sign of having just awakened from a nap.

"Kang Youwei says you have acquired considerable learning and that your military skills are second to none," he said abruptly. "Is that true?"

"Excellency Kang's praise embarrasses and unnerves me."

"I do not care if you have acquired real learning or worthless pedantry. I want to know what you studied in Japan."

"The infantry drill manual, marksmanship, field logistics, tactics, armaments, fortifications, topography . . ."

"Can you shoot?" Yuan Shikai cut him off as he sat up in his chair.

"I am an expert in all infantry weapons, especially small arms, and with both hands. I may not be able to hit a tree at a hundred paces, but at fifty I never miss my target."

"Anyone who boasts to me is in for a rude awakening," Yuan Shikai said in a chilling voice. "I will not tolerate a man who overstates his abilities!"

"I will be happy to give Your Excellency a demonstration."

"Excellent!" Yuan said with a hearty clap of his hands. "We have an adage in my hometown: 'You can tell a mule from a horse by taking it out for a ride.' Enter!" A young guard ran in to do Yuan's bidding. "Prepare pistols, ammunition, and some targets."

A rattan chair and a tea table were set up under a parasol on the firing range. Yuan removed a pair of pistols with gold-inlaid handles from an exquisite satin-covered box.

"These were given to me by a German friend," Yuan said. "They have never been fired."

"Please take the first shot, Your Excellency."

The guard loaded his pistols and handed them to Yuan, who said with a smile:

"I've heard people say that for a true soldier, his weapon is his woman, and he will not permit another man to touch it. Do you believe that?"

"As Your Excellency says, many soldiers treat their weapons as if they were their women." But then, with no apprehension, he added, "But I am of the opinion that anyone who treats his weapon as his woman scorns and considers his weapon to be a slave. I believe that a true soldier ought to treat his weapon as his mother."

"Treating one's weapon as his woman is absurd enough; treating it as one's mother is preposterous," Yuan said in a voice dripping with mockery. "You say that a soldier who treats his weapon as his woman scorns his weapon. Don't you think that treating it as your mother is scornful of her? You can change weapons any time you want. How about your mother? A weapon is used to kill. How about your mother? Or better put, can your mother aid you in killing someone?" Under this withering interrogation, cracks formed in the foundation of his composure.

"Once you young officers receive a bit of Japanese or Western education, you develop an exaggerated sense of your abilities or worth, and when you open your mouths, all that comes out is wild talk and nonsense." Yuan nonchalantly fired a round into the ground in front of them; the smell of gunpowder suffused the air around them. Then he raised the other pistol and fired into the air, sending a bullet whistling into the clouds. He lowered the gold-handled pistol and said, with a cold edge to his voice, "The truth is, a weapon is just a weapon. It is not one's woman, and it is assuredly not one's mother."

He stood, head bowed, and responded, "I gratefully accept Your Excellency's instruction and will alter my viewpoint. As you say, sir, a weapon is just a weapon. It is not one's woman, and it is assuredly not one's mother."

"There is no need for you to climb high using my pole. While I do not agree with your comparison of a weapon to a mother, there is something to be said for comparing it to a woman. Here is a woman, a gift from me." Yuan Shikai tossed him one of the pistols, which he grabbed as if catching a live parrot. Yuan Shikai tossed him the second pistol. "Another woman for you. That makes two sisters." This one, too, he grabbed as if catching another parrot. And now, with the gold-handled pistols in his hands, it seemed as if all his veins and arteries had expanded. It had pained him to see Yuan Shikai fire those two shots so offhandedly; to him that was like schoolgirls being manhandled by a coarse, boorish man. But there was nothing he could do about that. He gripped the pistols, feeling them tremble in his hands and hearing them moan softly. Even stronger was the feeling that they had immediately given themselves to him. Deep down, he had already abandoned his shocking metaphor of a weapon as one's mother, so why not treat them as beautiful women? The end result of the debate over weapon metaphors was a realization that Yuan Shikai was not only a military genius, but a man of considerable leaning.

"Show me what you can do," Yuan Shikai said.

After blowing on the mouths of both barrels, he tested their heft for a few seconds. They sparkled in the sunlight, as fine a pair of pistols as he had ever seen. He took a couple of steps forward and, seemingly without taking careful aim, fired a total of six shots from the two weapons in less than thirty seconds. The guard ran up to the target and brought it back for Yuan's inspection. Six bullets had hit the bull's-eye in the shape of a peach blossom. Applause broke out from the men around Yuan Shikai.

"Nice shooting!" His Excellency said approvingly, a genuine smile on his face for the first time during the audience. "Now, what would you like?"

"I'd like to own these," he replied unflinchingly.

Taken by surprise, Yuan Shikai stared at him for a long moment before bursting into laughter.

"Go ahead," he said. "You can be their husband!"

4

As he recalled those moments, he reached down and stroked the handles of the two pistols on his belt. They had been chilled by gusts of cold wind. "Don't be frightened, my friends," he said encouragingly as he warmed them with his hand. Then he pleaded: "Help me, my friends. When I have done what I came to do, I will be shot dead, but the tale of the gold-handled pistols will live on for generations." They were, he could feel, beginning to warm up. "Yes," he said to his pistols, "we must be patient as we await the man's return. A year from today will be the first anniversary." The mounted contingent behind him was getting increasingly restless—they were freezing cold and hungry, horses and riders. With cool detachment, he surveyed the two ranks of senior officers. They presented an amazingly ugly sight, all seemingly on the verge of falling off their horses, which nervously nipped at one another. There was no calming the mounts behind him, with one agitated wave coming hard upon the other. Heaven is on my side, he was thinking. Weariness has claimed everyone here, dulling their senses. I could not ask for a better time to act.

At last he, and only he, heard the faint toot of a steamship upriver. Instinctively, as his nerves grew taut, he tightened his grip on the handles of his pistols, but only for a brief moment. "Excellency Yuan has returned!" he called out in feigned excitement to the troops behind him and the ranking officers lined up on either side. Bestirred by the shout, the officers blew their noses or dried their weepy eyes or cleared their throats, each man eager to greet Excellency Yuan in a manner befitting his station.

The undersized glossy black steamship appeared around the bend in the river, puffing black clouds from its smokestack, each accompanying breath louder than the one before, until they were thudding against people's eardrums. The ship's bow cleaved through the water, arcing whitecaps to each side, while a wake sent ripples from the stern all the way to the riverbank. "Mounted troops," he commanded, "double file!" With trained precision, the soldiers spurred their mounts into two files, spaced at roughly ten paces, all facing the river. The soldiers sat perfectly straight in their saddles, rifles off their shoulders and held at present arms, muzzles pointing skyward.

The military band struck up a tune of welcome.

The ship slowed down and edged sideways up to the wharf.

With his hands on the grips, he felt the pistols quake, like trapped fledglings—no, like a pair of women. Don't be afraid, my friends, you mustn't be afraid.

When the ship nestled up to the pier, it released a long whistle as sailors at the bow and the stern tossed over mooring lines, which were secured to bollards. At that moment, the ship's engine shut down, and a party of subordinates emerged from the cabin to form lines on both sides of the hatch, from which Excellency Yuan's nicely rounded head peeked out.

Again the pistols began to quake in his hands.

5

A couple of weeks earlier, when news of the execution of the Six Gentlemen in Peking had reached the small camp, he was in his barracks room oiling the gold-handled pistols. His orderly rushed in and reported:

"Sir, Excellency Yuan is on his way to see you!"

He hastened to put his weapons away, but Yuan Shikai walked in before he could manage. He jumped to his feet, holding out his oily hands. His heart raced as he saw the four hulking guards walk in behind His Excellency, their hands resting on the grips of their side arms. The ferocious looks in their eyes were a sign that they would not hesitate to use them. Despite his status as Commander of the Mounted Guard Detachment, he had no authority over Yuan's four personal bodyguards, who were all from the commander's hometown. He snapped to attention.

"Your humble servant did not know Your Excellency was coming," he reported. "I beg forgiveness for my unpardonable slight!"

Yuan Shikai glanced at the weapons parts scattered on the table and said in a jocular tone:

"What are you're doing, Detachment Commander Qian?"

"Your humble servant is cleaning his weapons."

"I think not," Yuan Shikai said with a barely concealed snicker. "You should have said that you are bathing your women."

Reminded of his comment regarding weapons and women, he smiled awkwardly.

"What can you tell me about your association with Tan Sitong?"

"Your humble servant met him once at Kang Youwei's home."

"Only once?"

"Your humble servant would not dare lie to Your Excellency."

"What is your opinion of the man?"

"Your Excellency, your humble servant believes," he said with conviction, "that Tan Sitong is a courageous and upright man. If he were your friend, he'd tell you when you were wrong, but he could also be your mortal enemy."

"Just what does that mean?"

"Tan Sitong is a dragon among men. He would unhesitatingly die for a friend, and would not be a secret enemy. To kill him would ensure an envious reputation; to die at his hands would be a worthy death."

"I appreciate your candor," Yuan Shikai said with a sigh. "Too bad Tan Sitong was not someone I could use. Are you aware that he was beheaded in the capital's marketplace?"

"Your humble servant knows that."

"How does that make you feel?"

"It breaks my heart."

"Bring them in." With a wave of his hand, two of Yuan's attendants carried in a large black lacquer food hamper with gold-inlaid borders. "I've had them prepare two separate meals for you," Yuan said. "The choice is yours."

The attendants opened the large hamper, in which were two smaller ones. They laid them out on the table.

"Go ahead," Yuan said with a grin.

He opened the first box, which held a red floral porcelain bowl filled with six large braised meatballs.

He opened the second box, which held only a single bone with a tiny bit of meat.

He looked up at Yuan, who was smiling at him.

He looked down and thought for a moment before reaching in and picking up the bone.

Yuan Shikai nodded appreciatively as he walked up and patted him on the shoulder.

"Smart, very smart. The Empress Dowager Herself presented this bone to me. There is little meat left on it, but what there is has a wonderful flavor. Try it."

<hr>

6

<hr>

With fires of rage blazing in his heart, he gripped the pistols with trembling hands and watched as Yuan Shikai negotiated the shaky gangplank with the help of his bodyguards. Strains of the welcome melody floated in the air as the senior officers fell to their knees to greet the great man. He, on the other hand, remained seated on his horse. Yuan Shikai acknowledged the greeting with a mere wave of his hand. An easy, magnanimous smile adorned his ample face as he swept the prostrated welcoming delegation with his eyes, resting in the end on the sole mounted figure. At that moment it was abundantly clear that Yuan Shikai knew, and that was part of his plan. He wanted Yuan Shikai to know who it was who killed him. He nudged his horse forward and drew one of his pistols; it took only a second for the horse's muzzle to bump up against Yuan's chest.

"Excellency Yuan," he shouted, "this is to avenge the deaths of the Six Gentlemen!"

He took aim with his right hand and pulled the trigger, expecting to hear an explosion, smell gunpowder, and see the man's head shatter, just as it had so many times in his mind's eye. But not this time.

He drew the second pistol with his left hand, aimed, and pulled the trigger, once again expecting to hear an explosion, smell gunpowder, and see the man's head shatter, just as it had so many times in his mind's eye. But not this time, either.

Members of the official delegation looked on in amazement. If it had been any other than his gold-handled pistols, he would have had ample time to put bullets into every one of those future presidents and premiers, necessitating a complete rewriting of China's recent history. But at that critical moment, his gold-handled pistols had betrayed him. Raising them to his eyes for a quick examination, he angrily flung them into the river.

"You whores!" he shouted.

Yuan Shikai's bodyguards stormed up and dragged him down from his horse. The prostrated officers clambered to their feet, ran up, and began clawing and tearing at his body.

Yuan Shikai, unfazed, merely walked up, lightly kicked him in his face, which the guards had pressed down into the dirt, and said:

"What a shame, a true shame!"

"Excellency Yuan," he said in an anguished voice, "you were right, a weapon is not one's mother."

With a smile, Yuan replied:

"Nor is it a woman."

CHAPTER TWELVE

Crevice

1

The day after the massacre in Masang Township, the County Magistrate sat in his document room composing a telegram to the Prefect of Laizhou, Cao Gui, the Circuit Attendant of Laiqing, Tan Rong, and the Governor of Shandong Province, Yuan Shikai, to report that the Germans had perpetrated grave crimes in Gaomi County. The tragic scene from the night before kept reappearing in front of his eyes; the wails and curses of the citizenry swirled endlessly in his ears. His brush moved across the paper like a whirlwind, as rage swelled unchecked in his breast, solemn umbrage guiding each passionate stroke. His aging legal secretary entered as if walking on eggshells and handed the Magistrate a newly received telegram. Sent by Governor Yuan Shikai to Laizhou Prefecture and forwarded to Gaomi County, it contained the Governor's demand that the Magistrate take Sun Bing into custody and bring him to justice without delay. The Magistrate was also told to come up with five thousand taels of silver as restitution to the Germans for their losses. Finally, he was ordered to prepare compensation for the German engineer whose head had been injured in the incident, personally deliver it to the Qingdao church-run hospital, and ensure that no more such incidents arose.

The Magistrate jumped to his feet, pounded the table with his fist, and cursed, "The bastard!" Whether the curse was directed at Yuan Shikai or the German engineer was unclear, but he saw his assistant's goatee quiver and noticed a phosphorescent glimmer in the man's tiny eyes. He had never been fond of this secretary, but he relied heavily on him, for he was skilled at preparing indictments and appeals, was experienced and astute, knew all the ins and outs of official circles, and just happened to be the brother of the legal secretary at the Prefect's yamen. If the County Magistrate wanted to ensure that the document he had written would not be sent back by the Prefect, the secretary was indispensable.

"Have them prepare my horse," he said.

"May I ask where you are going?"

"To Laizhou Prefecture."

"May I ask the purpose of the trip?"

"I want to see Excellency Cao and demand justice for the people of Gaomi County!"

With no attempt to maintain decorum, the secretary reached down, picked up the document, and scanned it quickly.

"Is this telegram intended for the eyes of Excellency Yuan?"

"Yes, and I'd like you to put a final touch to it."

"Eminence, my eyesight and hearing are beginning to fail me. My mind is not as sharp as it once was, and at this rate I am afraid I will do you a disservice. I beg you to release me from my duties so I can return to my native home to live in retirement." With an awkward little laugh, he reached into his sleeve and extracted a letter, which he laid on the table. "My letter of resignation."

The Magistrate merely glanced at the letter and, with a sarcastic laugh, said:

"It seems the monkeys are abandoning the tree even before it falls."

Rather than lose his temper, the secretary laughed politely.

"Tying two people together does not make them husband and wife," the Magistrate said. "Since you desire to leave, trying to stop you would be meaningless. Do as you please."

"I thank you for your generosity."

"After I return from Laizhou, I shall see you off with a banquet."

"I thank you for your kindness."

"You may go," the Magistrate said with a wave of his hand.

The secretary made it only to the door before turning to say:

"Eminence, I am only an advisor, but if you want my opinion, you must not go to Laizhou and you must not send this telegram."

"And why is that?"

"I humbly submit, Your Eminence, that you are in the service of your superiors, not the people. A conscience has no place in the life of an official. You must choose one over the other."

With a snide grin, the Magistrate replied:

"Well spoken and very incisive. If you have anything else to say, now is the time."

"Arresting Sun Bing and quickly bringing him to justice is Your Eminence's only path to survival." The secretary's eyes flashed as he went on, "But I know you cannot do it."

"And so you are leaving," the Magistrate said, "not to return home to live in retirement, but to steer clear of trouble."

"Your Eminence is very perceptive," the secretary remarked. "In truth, if you could abandon your personal feelings for Sun Bing's daughter, capturing him would be as easy as turning over your hand. And if you did not want to do so yourself, I, your humble servant, would gladly render his services."

"Do not trouble yourself!" the Magistrate said coldly. "You may leave."

Grasping his hands in a salute, the secretary said:

"Very well, then, farewell, Your Eminence. I wish you well."

"Take care of yourself, Yamen Secretary," the Magistrate said before shouting out the door: "Chunsheng, ready my horse!"

2

At high noon the County Magistrate, in full official regalia, rode his young stallion out of town through the north gate, accompanied by his trusted personal attendant Chunsheng and his messenger, Liu Pu. Chunsheng, astride a powerful black mule, and Liu Pu, on his black mare, fell in close behind the County Magistrate's white horse. After being stabled through a long winter, the animals were energized by the broad expanse of fields and the scent of spring in the air. They kicked their hind legs in frisky abandon and whinnied excitedly. Liu Pu's mare nipped at the rump of the Magistrate's horse, which bolted forward. The rough road surface had begun to thaw and was now coated with a layer of black, gummy mud that made for tough going. The Magistrate leaned forward in the saddle and held tightly to the horse's untidy mane.

After heading northeast for an hour, they crossed the fast-flowing Masang River and entered the broad expanse of Northeast Township. Gentle golden early afternoon rays of sunlight fell on dry, withered grass and on the downy green sprouts just now breaking through the surface. Startled jackrabbits and foxes leaped and bounded out of the path of the horses' hooves. As they rode along, the travelers could see the raised roadbed of the Jiaozhou–Jinan rail line and the railroad workers laying track. Steel rails snaking across the landscape, a sight that sullied the vista of open fields under a towering blue sky, destroyed the Magistrate's cheerful mood. Disturbed by scenes from the recent bloody massacre at Masang Township that flashed through his mind, he was having trouble breathing, so he dug in the heels of his boots to speed up the pace. His horse reacted to the pain in its sides by breaking into a gallop, causing its rider to bounce around in the saddle, which seemed to lessen his melancholy.

The riders did not enter Pingdu County until the sun was low in the western sky. In a little village called Qianqiu, they stopped at the home of a wealthy family to feed the horses and rest up. Their host, a white-haired old county-level scholar, displayed his respect for his superior, the County Magistrate, by offering tobacco and tea and ordering a welcoming banquet that included braised wild rabbit and carrots, stewed cabbage with bean curd, and, from his own cask, rice wine. The old scholar's obsequious and generous welcome restored the Magistrate's sense of well being. A nobility of spirit swelled in his breast; his veins felt the rush of hot blood. The old scholar invited them to spend the night in his house, but the Magistrate was determined to get back on the road. With tears in his eyes, the old scholar took the Magistrate's hand and said:

"Eminence Qian, an upright official who unstintingly pleads on behalf of his people is as rare as phoenix feathers and unicorn horns. The residents of Gaomi County are truly blessed."

"Elderly squire," the County Magistrate replied emotionally, "as an official whose livelihood is in the hands of the Imperial Court, I am entrusted with service to the masses and am obliged to spare no effort in carrying out my duties."

He mounted his horse as a blood-red sunset spread in the west. After bidding farewell to the elderly scholar, who saw him to the edge of the village, he whipped the flank of his white charger, which reared up, a mighty steed, and shot forward with a burst of power, like an arrow leaving the bow. Though the Magistrate did not turn to cast a backward glance, a host of phrases from classic poems of parting rose up in his mind: the setting sun, a dazzling sunset, wilderness, ancient roads, a withered tree, winter ravens . . . all encapsulating a sense of solemn tragedy, yet filling his heart with boldness.

As they left the village behind, they rode out onto a landscape that was bleaker and more extensive than anywhere in Northeast Gaomi Township, with few signs of humanity on the low-lying land. The animals raced proudly, heads high, on a gray serpentine path that was mostly hidden in dry waist-high grass that brushed noisily against the riders' legs. As the evening deepened, a new moon sent its silvery beams through the purple canopy of a starry sky. The Magistrate looked heavenward, where he saw the outline of the Big Dipper, the glittering Milky Way, and a shooting star ripping open the darkening curtain. Damp, heavy air chilled the riders as the night wore on. The horses' gait slackened, from a gallop to a canter, then to a trot, and finally to a lazy walk. When the Magistrate used his whip, the horse reared its head and ran a few yards before slowing again, weary and sluggish. The Magistrate's agitation was waning; his feverish body was beginning to cool down. Moisture-laden air on that windless night attacked exposed skin like razor blades, so he hung his whip on the pommel, buried his hands in his wide sleeves, and draped the reins over his wrist before hunkering down and letting the horse go where it wanted. In the surrounding wilderness, the animals' snorts and the sound of dry grass brushing against the men's pants were almost deafening. The occasional muted bark of a dog in a distant village deepened the cryptic sense of mystery and struck the Magistrate's nerves like pangs of sorrow. He had been in such a hurry to leave, he'd forgotten to put on the fox fur vest his father-in-law had given him. That had been one of the more solemn moments in his life, for the item, a relic by any standard, had been given to his father-in-law's father-in-law, the great Zeng Guofan, by the Empress Dowager Herself. Although time, the elements, and insects had eaten away at the fur, wearing it imparted an indescribable sense of warmth. Thoughts of his missing fox fur vest took the Magistrate back in time, to recollections of the life he'd lived.

Recalling the poverty of his youth and the hardships of endless studies, he was reminded of the joys of passing the Imperial Civil Service Examination and the marriage alliance formed between him and Zeng Guofan's maternal granddaughter, for which he received the good wishes of his fellow candidates, including those of his classmate Liu Guangdi, known then as Liu Peicun. Even at that age, Liu was a fine calligrapher, his writing as bold and sturdy as he himself. Having also mastered the art of poetry in its many forms, he inscribed a pair of scrolls for the wedding: "Strings of pearls, girdles of jade" on one, "Talented scholar and beautiful girl" on the other. At the time, a bright road of unlimited potential seemed to open up before him. But as they say, "Better a live rat than a dead prefect." He spent six years in the Board of Public Works, mired in such debilitating poverty that he had no choice but to take advantage of his wife's family connections to secure an assignment in the provinces, where he moved around for several years before landing on the relatively fertile ground of Gaomi County. Soon after his arrival, he vowed to put his talents in the service of notable achievements, which would ensure his slow climb up the official ladder. But he soon learned that Gaomi, a place coveted by foreigners, was a fancy title but a poor launching site for official promotion. Managing to survive in office until his term ended was the best he could hope for. Sigh! The last days of the Imperial House were approaching; the death knell for sage men had sounded; the earthly doings of base men resounded like thunder. He could only follow the currents and try to maintain his integrity . . .

The Magistrate was startled out of his reveries by a series of frantic equine snorts, and when he looked, he saw four emerald-green eyes glimmering in the bushes close ahead. "Wolves!" he shouted as he dug his stiff legs into the horse's sides and pulled back on the reins. With a whinny that shattered the silence, the horse reared up and threw its rider out of the saddle.

It all happened so fast that Chunsheng and Liu Pu, who had been riding close behind the Magistrate, their teeth chattering from the freezing cold, were dumbstruck. They remained in a sort of daze until they saw two wolves moving to run down the Magistrate's white stallion, and their dulled brains began to work again. Shouting to their horses, they drew their swords, awkwardly, and drove off the predators, sending them scurrying into the underbrush, where they vanished from view.

"Laoye!" both Chunsheng and Liu Pu shouted as they jumped off their horses and half ran, half stumbled over to the County Magistrate. "Laoye!"

The Magistrate was hanging upside down, his foot caught in the stirrup. Spooked by Chunsheng and Liu Pu's shouts, the stallion bolted and began dragging the shrieking Magistrate after him; had it not been for the dry grass, the hard ground would have turned his head into a bloody gourd. The more experienced Liu Pu told Chunsheng to stop yelling and, like him, call out to the horse gently: "Good horse, be good, white horse, don't be afraid . . ." Aided by the bright starlight, they cautiously approached the animal, and when he was near enough, Liu Pu rushed up and threw his arms around its neck. Chunsheng seemed to have fallen into a trance. "Idiot!" Liu Pu shouted, "get over here and free the Magistrate's foot!"

Chunsheng tried, but made a mess of his rescue effort, causing the Magistrate even worse discomfort. "Can't you do anything right?" Liu Pu complained. "Come up here and keep the horse from moving."

Liu Pu managed to free the stiff leg from the stirrup and then wrapped his arms around the Magistrate's waist to right him. His leg buckled the minute it touched the ground, wrenching a painful scream from him as he sat down hard on the ground.

Feeling numb all over, the Magistrate could not get his body to do his bidding. His head and foot throbbed unbearably; he was nearly bursting with indignation, but did not know how to vent it.

"Are you all right, Laoye?" Chunsheng and Liu Pu asked tentatively as they bent down close to him.

The men's faces were blurred; the Magistrate could only sigh.

"It's damned hard trying to be an upright official," he said.

"Someone up there is always watching, Laoye," Liu Pu said. "Your good deeds are not going unnoticed by the old man in the sky."

"The old man in the sky will see to it that Laoye receives the promotions and riches he deserves," Chunsheng added.

"Is there really an old man in the sky?" the Magistrate wondered aloud. "I guess the fact that my horse did not pull me to my death proves something. Don't you agree? Now, take a look at my leg and see if it's broken."

Liu Pu untied the band around the Magistrate's leg, reached up inside, and felt around.

"You can breathe easy, Laoye," he said, "it's not broken."

"Are you sure?"

"My father taught me the basics of therapeutic massage and bone-setting when I was a boy."

"Who'd have thought that Peicun could be a bone expert, too?" the Magistrate said with a sigh. "While we were riding a while ago, I was recalling the days when your father and I passed the examination. We were filled with such youthful energy and high spirits, eager to shoulder heavy responsibilities and help the country be strong and prosperous. But now . . ." Momentarily overcome with emotion, he said, "I guess there must be someone up there, since my leg is not broken. Help me to my feet, men."

The two aides picked him up by his arms and supported him as he tried to walk. But his legs failed him—they had a mind of their own, or no mind at all—and produced stabbing pains that shot from the soles of his feet all the way up to the top of his head.

"Gather some dry grass, men, and light a fire to warm us. I can't ride a horse like this."

The Magistrate sat on the ground rubbing his hands and watching Chunsheng and Liu Pu gather grass by the side of the path. Up and down their bodies moved, a bit of a blur in the starlight, like large creatures building a nest on the ground. The sound of their labored breathing and the snapping of broken stalks of grass were heavy in the surrounding darkness; the Milky Way shimmered in a shower of shooting stars that lit up the faces—dark and purple from the cold—of his trusted aides and the overgrown gray wilderness behind them. Those faces gave him an indication of what he must look like: in the cold air, weariness had erased the self-assured looks they had started out with. He was suddenly reminded of his hat, the official symbol of his position and status.

"Chunsheng," he called out anxiously, "forget that for now. I've lost my hat."

"Wait till we get a fire going," Chunsheng replied. "We'll need the light to find it."

With this simple statement, Chunsheng not only had disobeyed an order but, for the first time, had actually offered an opinion of his own, which the Magistrate found quite touching. On that dark night out in the wilds, all standards and norms were subject to modification.

They piled up layers of grass until they had a small stack. The Magistrate reached out to feel the grass, which was damp with dew.

"Chunsheng, did you bring something to start a fire?"

"Damn!" Chunsheng replied. "I forgot."

"I have what we need in my pack," Liu Pu volunteered.

The Magistrate breathed a sigh of relief.

"You think of everything, Liu Pu. Start a fire, I'm freezing."

The young man took a steel, a flint, and a tinder from his backpack, crouched down beside the pile of grass, and began striking steel and flint together. Weak polygonal sparks flew from his hands onto the grass, making faint sizzles as they landed. He blew on the tinder with each spark, and as it slowly turned red, a tiny popping sound produced the first actual flames. The County Magistrate's mood lightened considerably, the flames temporarily driving away the physical aches and pains and the mental anguish. Liu Pu touched the tinder to the grass, which reluctantly caught fire, the weak flames barely able to stay burning. So he picked up a handful of grass and twirled it in the air to make the fire burn stronger and brighter, until it was a blazing torch, which he then touched to the stack. White smoke began to rise skyward, filling the air with an acrid fragrance and the County Magistrate's heart with emotion. The smoke was soon so thick that a man could almost reach out and grab a handful; and then, seemingly without warning, golden flames licked through the darkness with a roar. The smoke thinned out as dazzling bursts of light turned a swath of wilderness into daytime. The three animals snorted, swished their tails, and edged closer to the warmth of the fire. What looked like smiles adorned their long faces; their eyes shone like crystal, and their heads seemed unnaturally large. The County Magistrate spotted his hat nestling in the grass like a black hen hatching an egg. He had Chunsheng retrieve the hat, which was mud-spotted and grass-stained. The crystal ornament that represented his rank hung to one side, and one of the pheasant feathers, which had the same significance, had snapped in two. All inauspicious signs, he was thinking. But so what, damn it! How lucky would I have been if I'd been dragged to my death a moment ago? So he put on his hat, not to reclaim his dignity, but to help ward off the cold. The bonfire quickly heated up his chest, but his back felt like a slab of cold steel. As it warmed up, his nearly frozen skin turned prickly and painful. He scooted backward, and the heat moved with him, so he stood up and turned his back to the fire; but that no sooner warmed up than the front had cooled off. He turned back to face the fire. And so it went, front and back, over and over, until his body could once more move freely, although his leg still hurt. Knowing that he had not sustained a serious injury helped his mood, so he turned his attention to the three animals, which, as he saw by the light of the fire, were hungrily grazing, the bits in their mouths making crisp metallic sounds. The white horse's tail seemed made of silvery threads as it swished back and forth. The flames got shorter as the crackle of dried grass being consumed was less frequent and not nearly as loud. The flames moved outward in all directions, much as water seeks lower ground, and spread with great speed. The wind began to pick up. Furry things were visible in the light from the fire, jumping and leaping—rabbits or foxes, probably. Birds flew into the dark sky with shrill cries, skylarks or turtledoves. The fire directly in front of the three men slowly died out, leaving only scattered red cinders. The wildfire, on the other hand, was rapidly gaining in intensity. The Magistrate, excited by the sight, his eyes lighting up, called out happily:

"This is something we might see once in a lifetime, if that! Chunsheng, Liu Pu, this alone was worth the trip."

They climbed back on their horses and set out once more for Laizhou. By then the wildfire had spread far into the distance, like an illuminated riptide. The redolence of fire suffused the cold night air.

3

The County Magistrate and his traveling companions arrived at the Laizhou outskirts as dawn was breaking. The city gate was shut tight, the drawbridge was raised, and no gate guards were at their posts. The trees and groundcover were blanketed with frost as roosters crowed in a new day. Frost even decorated Chunsheng and Liu Pu's eyebrows, in contrast to the soot that covered their faces. One glance made it clear to the Magistrate what his face must look like, and he hoped that look—frosty white beard and hair and a road-dusted face—would not disappear before he met the prefectural officials, for that would impress his superiors. In the past, he recalled, there had been a stone bridge leading to the city gate. But that had been replaced by a pine drawbridge, an emergency measure to defend against a surge in attacks across the city moat by Righteous Harmony Boxers. The Magistrate disagreed with the policy, refusing to believe that farmers would rise up in rebellion unless they were starving.

The city gate swung open as the sun rose red above the horizon, and the drawbridge made a creaky descent. After reporting their purpose in entering the city, they crossed the moat, the shod hooves of their mounts clattering on cobblestone streets that were deserted except for a few early-rising residents who were fetching water at a well, as mist rose off the frosted wooden frame. The red rays of the sun fell on the travelers' skin, creating a painful itch, which was partially eased by the comforting sound of metal bucket handles scraping against the hooks of carrying poles. People shouldering those poles watched the passage of the visitors with surprise.

A cook pot had been set up outside a small diner specializing in tripe on a narrow street fronting the prefectural yamen. A fair-skinned woman was stirring something with a long-handled ladle. Steam rose from the boiling liquid, suffusing the air around it with the fragrance of viscera and coriander. When the three travelers dismounted, the Magistrate's legs could barely support him; Chunsheng and Liu Pu also had trouble standing, although they managed to help the Magistrate over to a bench beside the pot. Unhappily, his broad backside was too much for the narrow seat, and he wound up on the ground, his arms and legs pointing skyward. His official hat, which seemed unwilling to stay put, rolled off into a muddy ditch. Chunsheng and Liu Pu rushed to his aid, looking sheepish over failing to properly attend to their superior, whose back and queue showed the effects of landing on dirty ground. Taking a fall early in the morning and losing his official hat in the process were bad omens. Frustrated and angry, he felt like lashing out at his attendants, but a glance at the downcast looks on their faces sent the words back down his throat.

Chunsheng and Liu helped the Magistrate up, steadying themselves on legs that were still bowed from the long ride. The woman hurriedly laid down her ladle and ran over to retrieve the Magistrate's miserable-looking hat, cleaning it off as best she could with the lapel of her jacket before handing it to him.

"My apologies, Laoye," she said as she handed over the hat.

She had a clear voice, filled with such fervor that the Magistrate felt warm all over. As he took the hat from her and put it on, he spotted a pea-sized mole at the corner of her mouth. Meanwhile, Liu Pu did his best to clean the Magistrate's queue, which was as filthy as a cow's excrement-coated tail, with the wrapping cloth from his bundle. With fire in his eyes, Chunsheng railed at the woman:

"Are you blind?" he said. You should have had a chair ready for Laoye as soon as you saw him ride up!"

The Magistrate immediately silenced his rude companion and instead thanked the woman, who blushed as she ran inside to fetch a greasy chair and set it down behind the Magistrate.

The minute he sat down, every muscle in his body ached, and the appendage suspended between his legs was as cold and hard as ice. The skin on his groin felt like it was on fire. But deep down, he was moved by his own selfless behavior of riding through the night, buffeted by the wind and dampened by frost, all in the name of justice for the common people. A nobility of purpose swept over him like the aroma of the tripe cooking in the pot and spread out on the early morning air. His body was like an enormous frozen turnip that is suddenly exposed to the warmth of the sun, and as the outer covering begins to thaw, it releases foul liquids from within. All in all, it was an agonizing yet at the same time joyous process. Viscous tears oozing from the corners of his eyes blurred his vision and created the illusion of vast numbers of Northeast Gaomi Township citizens kneeling in front of him, their upturned faces imbued with affecting expressions of gratitude. From their mouths emerged simple yet mov-

ing mutterings: Our great and upright Laoye . . . Our great and upright Laoye
. . .

The woman placed three large black bowls in front of them, each with a black spoon. Then she dumped pieces of flatbread into each bowl, followed by shreds of coriander and some spiced salt. Her movements quick and deft, she did not bother to ask what they would like, as if they were regular customers and she knew exactly what they wanted. As he looked into her fair, round face, a reservoir of warm feelings opened up deep down inside the Magistrate, who was struck by what seemed like an intimate connection between this woman and the one who sold dog meat back in Gaomi County. Having finished with the preparations, she stuck her ladle into the pot and stirred the bovine hearts livers intestines stomachs lungs in the bubbling mixture, beguiling the Magistrate with the mouth-watering aroma. Then she fished out a ladleful of the stew, dumped it into the Magistrate's bowl, and filled it up with soup, topping it off with half a spoonful of ground pepper. "The pepper takes the bite out of the cold," she said softly. He nodded, touched by her concern, and stirred the contents of his bowl with the spoon. Then he bent over until his mouth nearly touched the rim of the bowl and, with a loud slurp, sucked in a mouthful. It was so hot, it felt as if a burning mouse had been let loose in his mouth; spitting it out would have been undignified, to say the least, and holding it in his mouth would likely burn his tongue, so he swallowed it whole, and as the mixture burned its way down, a welter of feelings rose up and drove the mucus from his nose and the tears from his eyes.

After several mouthfuls of bovine stew had found their way into the men's stomachs, beads of sweat squeezed out through their pores like itchy little insects. The woman's ladle never stopped its motion in the pot, except to add increasingly rich soup to their bowls, which remained full to the brim. When they sped up, so did she; when they slowed down, she followed. Eventually the Magistrate brought his hands together in front of his chest to thank her. "Enough," he said. "You can stop now, madam."

"I'm sure you can eat more than that, Laoye," she said with a smile.

Although he was energized by the bovine stew he had just finished, the pain in his legs had not gone away; but at least he could stand unaided. He noticed a crowd of rubberneckers watching from the wall behind them. What he could not tell was whether they were just watching to see what would happen next or if they were potential customers who dared not come forward while the man in the official hat was on the scene. He told Chunsheng to pay for the meal, which the woman refused to accept. "It was a great honor to have Laoye partake of my simple fare, for which I could not possibly accept payment," she said. For a moment, he said nothing. Then he reached down and removed a jade pendant from the pouch at his waist. "Madam," he said, "I cannot adequately compensate you for your extravagant hospitality, so please take this trifle as a keepsake for your husband." As her ears reddened from embarrassment, she made as if to refuse the gift, but the Magistrate had already handed it to Chunsheng, who stuffed it into her hand. "Our Laoye wants you to have this, and courtesy demands that you accept it," he said. The woman stood there, pendant in her hand, speechless, as the Magistrate tidied up his appearance, turned, and headed off to the prefectural yamen, fully aware that many eyes observed his progress. He was aware, too, that in years to come, people might tell the story of the Gaomi County Magistrate who stopped here and had a meal of bovine stew at this outdoor stand, embellished with each telling, maybe even introduced into the repertoire of an opera, his adventure narrated in song by a Maoqiang actor for generations. If only he had paper and a brush, he mused, he would happily give a name to this little diner whose proprietor had treated him so warmly. Or he might write a poem in the finest calligraphic style to be displayed as an attraction for future customers. He raised his head and threw out his chest as he walked along the main prefectural street, exuding the prestige and dignity of an official representative of the Imperial Court. As he walked, he entertained visions of the lovely Sun Meiniang and of the fair-skinned, fine-figured woman who sold bovine stew; he did, of course, also think about his wife. Three women: one was ice, another was fire, and the third was a warm bed.

4

The County Magistrate was granted an immediate audience with the Prefect. It took place in the Prefect's study, where a scroll written by the famous artist and one-time Magistrate of Wei County, Zheng Banqiao, hung on the wall. The Magistrate had the look of a tired man, with dark circles under his eyes and red lids; he yawned constantly as he reported in detail what had led to the incident in Northeast Gaomi Township and its consequences, focusing on the massacre perpetrated by the Germans. His personal loathing for the Germans and sympathies toward the township residents were patently obvious in his report. After quietly hearing him out, the first thing the Prefect said in response was, "Gaomi County Magistrate, is Sun Bing in custody?"

The County Magistrate sighed.

"Excellency," he responded, "Sun Bing managed to escape and has not yet been brought to justice."

The Prefect's penetrating stare made the County Magistrate squirm. With a dry little laugh, he said softly:

"Elder Brother, word has it that you and Sun Bing's daughter . . . ha ha, what does the woman have that you find so bewitching?" The Magistrate was tongue-tied, his back cold with sweat.

"I expect an answer!" the Prefect demanded, his demeanor suddenly harsh.

"Your humble servant, Excellency, has had no improper relations with Sun Bing's daughter. I simply find her dog meat to my liking . . ."

"Elder Brother Qian," the Prefect, having resumed a friendly demeanor, replied in the manner of a counselor, "our lives are devoted to serving the nation, and to that end we are the beneficiaries of the Empress Dowager and the Emperor's favor. Our conscience compels us to carry out our duties to the best of our ability. If, however, we serve our own selfish interests or bend the law to help friends or relatives and are unfaithful to our calling, then that . . ."

"Your humble servant would never . . ."

"The death of a scant few stubborn and unruly subjects means nothing," the Prefect said dispassionately, "and if that will mollify the Germans and end the provocations, well, that would be a good thing, wouldn't it?"

"But twenty-seven lives were lost . . . the common folk deserve fair treatment."

"Just how do you propose to manage that?" The Prefect punctuated his question by pounding on the table. "Don't tell me you expect reparations from the Germans or expect them to pay with their lives."

"But something must be done, in the name of justice," the Magistrate complained, "or how do I face the citizens back home?"

With a chilling laugh, the Prefect said:

"I cannot give you the justice you seek. Nor, I'm afraid, will you find it from Circuit Attendant Tan or Governor Yuan, not even if you were to present yourself to the Emperor or the Empress Dowager."

"We're talking about twenty-seven lives, Excellency!"

"If you had carried out your duties and taken Sun Bing into custody immediately after the incident and turned him over to the Germans, they would not have sent in troops, and those twenty-seven individuals would be alive today!" The Prefect patted a pile of documents on his desk and, with another chilling laugh, said, "Elder Brother Qian, people are saying that you facilitated Sun Bing's escape by warning him. The last thing you want is for that sort of talk to reach the ears of Excellency Yuan."

By now the County Magistrate was sweating profusely.

"And so," the Prefect continued, "the most urgent task before my Elder Brother is not to seek some sort of justice for the people back home, but to arrest Sun Bing as soon as humanly possible and bring him to justice. Taking Sun Bing into custody will be good for all concerned—high, low, those within and those without. No one benefits from failing to do so."

"Your humble servant understands . . ."

"Elder Brother," the Prefect said with a smile, "this Sun Meiniang must be a raving beauty to have planted the seeds of desire so deeply in you." He added in a mocking tone, "She doesn't have two pairs of breasts and two points of entry, does she?"

"Your Excellency is making fun of me . . ."

"I'm told that you fell in the street a while ago, and that you lost your hat in the process. Is that true?" he said with obvious portent as he glanced up at the County Magistrate's hat. Before the Magistrate could answer, he held out his teacup and banged the lid against the lip. "Elder Brother," he said as he got to his feet, "be careful, be very careful. Losing one's hat means nothing, but losing one's head . . ."

<hr>

5

The Magistrate fell ill upon arriving home. At first his symptoms included headaches, dizziness, vomiting, and diarrhea; those in turn led to a persistent high fever and periods of delirium. The First Lady split her time between tending to her husband, including seeing that he received appropriate medications, and offering up nightly prayers at an outdoor incense altar. Whether it was the efficacy of his treatment or the intervention of the gods, no one knew, but half a bowlful of dark, rank blood abruptly spewed from the Magistrate's nose, and almost immediately his fever broke and the diarrhea stopped. It was then the middle of the second month, a time when telegrams pressing for the arrest of Sun Bing were streaming in from provincial, circuit, and prefectural offices, sending the county government clerks into a frenzy of anxious activity. Yet all the while, the Magistrate lay in the space between wakefulness and sleep, neither eating nor drinking, let alone returning to his duties; there was even concern that he might never recover from what ailed him. The First Lady personally went into the kitchen to prepare the finest food of which she was capable, but all to no avail—the Magistrate's appetite for food had vanished.

One afternoon a couple of weeks before Qingming, the First Lady summoned the Magistrate's loyal follower Chunsheng to the Eastern Parlor.

Chunsheng entered the hall nervously and was met by the First Lady, who sat in a chair, her brow deeply furrowed, a somber cast to her face, all in all looking a bit like a temple idol. Chunsheng fell to his knees and said, "I have come in response to the First Lady's summons. What is it you would have your humble servant do?"

"It's all your fault!" she said icily.

"What did I do?"

"What is going on between Laoye and the woman Sun Meiniang?" she demanded to know. "I assume that you served as a go-between, you little bastard!"

"Madam, that is untrue. I have done nothing of the sort," Chunsheng defended himself. "I am merely a loyal dog at Laoye's side, prepared to attack wherever the Magistrate points me."

"Don't you dare quibble with me!" insisted the indignant First Lady. "You little bastards have led Laoye astray!"

"I have done nothing of the sort . . ."

"Chunsheng, you dog-headed wretch, as Laoye's most trusted follower, instead of admonishing him to be pure of heart and wary of desires, as a good official must be, you have encouraged him to have illicit relations with a common woman, a loathsome deed, and one for which you deserve to have your dog legs broken. But I may be prepared to be forgiving, since you have served him diligently and well for several years, but only this one time. From today on, you are to report to me everything that involves His Eminence. If you do not, you will be punished for your crimes, old and new!"

Chunsheng nearly soiled himself as he banged his head on the floor. "I thank the First Lady for not having me beaten. You will have no further need to be upset with Chunsheng."

"I want you to go to that shop that sells dog meat and inform Sun Meiniang that I wish to see her," the First Lady said with seeming innocence. "I will have words with her."

"Madam," Chunsheng screwed up the courage to say, "Sun Meiniang is a good-natured woman . . ."

"Shut up!" The First Lady's face darkened. "Laoye is not to know about this. If I find that you have had the audacity to breathe a word of this to him . . ."

"I would not dare . . ."

6

When news of the County Magistrate's lingering illness reached Sun Meiniang, she was so upset that she could neither sleep nor eat; her distress eclipsed even that which she had suffered upon the tragic deaths of her stepmother and her siblings. She tried several times to deliver spirits and dog meat to the yamen and, she hoped, see the Magistrate, but she was stopped at the gate each time by guards with whom she had gotten friendly over time. Now they acted as if they didn't know her, almost as if there had been a regime change within. An order specifically forbidding her to enter had been handed down.

Meiniang was a woman without a soul, distracted beyond the limits of endurance. Day in and day out, she roamed the streets aimlessly, carrying a basket of dog meat and followed everywhere by malicious chatter, as if she were some sort of monster. She visited every temple in town, large and small, where she offered up prayers for the health of the County Magistrate to a host of deities and divinities. She even lit joss sticks and kowtowed in the celebrated Bala Temple, which was devoted to issues and concerns other than sickness, and when she emerged, she was surrounded by a clutch of children who sang a song that had obviously been written by adults:

> Gaomi's Magistrate has the lovesick disease, food has lost its taste, sleep can
>   no longer please.
> He spits blood up top and passes filth down past his knees.

> Gaomi's Magistrate has a beard so long, day and night one thought only, of
>   Sun Meiniang.
> One man and one woman, Mandarin ducks made famous in song.

> A pair of Mandarin ducks, yet unhappily apart, he thinks of death, she has
>   a broken heart.
> But dying and crying the First Lady will not let start.

On the children's lips, this sounded like a message from the Magistrate, and it raised towering waves of passion in Sun Meiniang's heart. Now that she had learned that his illness was more serious than she had feared, tears spurted from her eyes. Silently she repeated his name, over and over, and, relying upon her imagination, conjured up a vision of the damage the illness had done to his face. Dearest, she said to herself, you have fallen ill, all because of me, and if something should happen to you, I could not go on living! I am miserable, I must see you, no matter what. I need to enjoy one last decanter of spirits with you, share one last meal of dog meat. Though I know you do not belong to me, in my heart you are mine, for I have tied our fates together. I know, too, that you and I are different people, and that the things you and I think about are a million miles apart. I also know that what you feel for me is not true love, that I just happened to be there when you felt a powerful need for a woman.

What you love about me is my body and my passion, and when the luster fades from my body, you will simply cast me aside. Something else I know is that you were the one who plucked my dieh's beard clean, and that while you may steadfastly deny it, you ruined his life and brought about the destruction of Northeast Gaomi Township's Maoqiang opera. I am aware that you vacillated about whether or not you should arrest my dieh, but that if Governor Yuan Shikai promised you a promotion and a fancy title for taking Sun Bing into custody, you would do it. If His Imperial Majesty the Emperor ordered you to kill me, you would take a knife to me without hesitation, even though it would sadden you to do so . . . I know all these things, I know everything, especially that my infatuation will end tragically, and yet that knowledge has no effect on my obsession. The truth is, you happened to be there when I felt a powerful need for a man. What I fell in love with was your appearance and your knowledge, not what was in your heart. I do not know what is in your heart, but why should I care about that? Enjoying a passionate relationship with a man like you is enough for an ordinary woman like me. Because of you, I have neither the time nor the heart to worry about my own dieh, who has suffered the grievous loss of his family. In my heart, in my flesh, in my bones there is only you. I freely admit that I am in the grip of a sickness, one that claimed me on the day I first saw you; it is a sickness every bit as serious as the one you are suffering now. You have said that I am the remedy that can cure you. Well, you are the opium that sustains me. If you die inside your yamen, I will die out here. There are many reasons why you are dying inside your yamen, and I am but one of them; but there is only one reason why I would die out here, and that is you. If I die and you do not, you will grieve over me for three days; if you die and I do not, I will grieve over you for the rest of my life. If you die, in truth my life will be over. It is an unequal transaction, in which I am a willing partner. I am your loyal dog; you need only whistle for me to come running, wagging my tail, rolling in the dirt, nipping at your heels, whatever you desire. I know that you love me the way a greedy cat loves a nice fat fish; I love you the way a bird loves a tree. My love for you knows no shame. Because of you, I have forsaken my honor, my will, and my future. I cannot control my legs, and have no control over my heart. Since I would climb a mountain of knives or dive into a sea of fire for you, malicious gossip means nothing to me. From the children's song, I have learned that it is your wife who has made it impossible for me to enter the yamen and see you. I know that she comes from a respected family of high officials and that she is endowed with great learning and a talent for scheming; if she were a man, she would surely climb high in the official ranks. I readily admit that I, the daughter of an actor and wife of a butcher, cannot claim to be her peer, but I am the blind man at the door: if it is closed, I am rewarded with a bloody nose, but I gain entrance if luck is with me and it is open. I've lost all sense of the rules of decorum and taboos. If the main gate stands in my way, I will go around to the back; if the rear gate is closed, I will try a side door; and if that too does not admit entry, I will climb a tree and jump over the wall. So all the rest of that day I paced the area around the wall, trying to find a way into the yamen.

A half moon illuminated the rear wall and the flower garden behind it, where he and his wife strolled on most days. The limb of a tall elm tree reached out across the wall, its moonlit bark shining like dragon scales—a living, glittering creature. She stood on her tiptoes to reach the limb, which, cold to the touch, reminded her of snakes. Into her mind flashed the recollection of a time, several years before, when she had been in the field, obsessed by the desire to find a pair of snakes, and that thought produced feelings of desolation and humiliation.

Dearest Magistrate, my love for you is torture, agony you cannot possibly comprehend. And your wife, descendant of a famous official, member of an illustrious family, how can she understand what is in my heart? Madam, I have no desire to take your husband from you. In truth, I am but a sacrificial object willingly offered up for the pleasure of a temple god. Madam, can you possibly not have noticed how your husband has become a thirsty stalk of grain finally getting the spring rain it needs, all because of me? Madam, if you are the open-minded, charitable person you are reputed to be, then you must support my relationship with your husband. If you are a woman of reason and good sense, then you should not bar my entry into the yamen. Trying to keep me out, madam, will prove to be futile. You may be able to bar the way to Tripitaka, the monk who went to India to fetch scriptures, and to his disciples, the Celestial Horse and Sun Wukong, but you will fail to keep me, Meiniang, from being with Qian Ding. Qian Ding's glory Qian Ding's status and Qian Ding's property all belong to you, but Qian Ding's body Qian Ding's smell and Qian Ding's sweat are mine. Madam, I, Meiniang, followed my father onto the opera stage to sing and dance from an early age. My body may not be as weightless as a swallow, but I am light on my feet; I cannot fly onto eaves or walk on walls, but I know how to climb a tree. They say that when a dog is frightened it jumps over a wall, and when a cat is frightened it climbs a tree. Meiniang is neither a dog nor a cat, but I am going to climb a tree and jump over a wall. I am not afraid to demean myself, and I am perfectly capable of reversing the yin and the yang. You will not find me waiting for the moon in the Western Chamber, like Cui Yingying. No, I prefer to leap across the wall at night, like Zhang Junrui, who scaled a wall to be with Yingying; Meiniang will leap across the wall to be with her lover. Eight or ten years from now, someone may act out this *Western Chamber* drama in reverse.

She took two steps backward, cinched the sash around her waist, adjusted her clothes, limbered her joints, and then, after taking a deep breath, leaped into the air and grabbed hold of the limb with both hands. It bent from the weight, so frightening a perched owl that it shrieked, spread its wings, and glided silently into the yamen. Owls were among the Magistrate's favorite birds. Ten or more of them often perched on a large scholar tree in the grain-storage compound, and he was given to referring to them as its guardian spirits, the bane of rodents. He would sometimes walk by, stroking his beard and intoning: "Rodents in the storehouse, big as a large jar; if someone comes in, they stay where they are . . ." Dearest Magistrate, you of great learning, filled with classical wisdom, my lover. She pulled herself up until she was sitting on the limb.

The third watch had just been sounded, the sole interruption of silence in the yamen. From her perch she saw the silvery glass ball atop the pavilion in the center of the flower garden and the shiny ripples on the little pond beside it. Patches of light emerged from the Western Parlor, apparently the Magistrate's sickroom. My dear Magistrate, I know you are craning your neck, hoping to see me; your mind must be as unsettled as boiling water. Do not be worried, my dear, for your Meiniang, daughter of the Sun family, is about to leap over this wall. I am determined to see you, even if your wife is sitting at your side, like a lioness keeping watch over her kill, even if she lashes me across the back!

After edging her way along the limb, she jumped down onto the wall, but what happened next was something she would not forget as long as she lived. Her foot slipped when it landed on the wall, and she came crashing down on the other side, decapitating stalks of green bamboo, with the accompanying noise. Her backside ached, her arms suffered painful scrapes, and her insides were badly jumbled. With difficulty she managed to stand by holding on to a bamboo stalk, and, overcome by resentment over having to go through this to see him, she focused on the lamplight emerging from the Western Parlor. She reached down to rub her backside and felt something sticky. What *is* that? Her first thought was that she was bleeding from the fall, but when she brought her hand up to her nose, the foul-smelling, sticky dark substance could only be dog filth. My god, what black-hearted, unscrupulous wretch thought up this sinister plan to turn Sun Meiniang into such a sorry figure? Does this mean I am reduced to seeing Magistrate Qian with dog filth on my behind? Could I even want to see him after the way he has disgraced and humiliated me? Utterly dispirited, she felt rage build up inside her alongside feelings of low self-esteem. Go on, Qian Ding, be sick and die, and leave your respectable wife to her widowhood. If she chooses not to remain a widow, she can take poison or hang herself in defense of her wifely virtue and become a martyr; the citizens of Gaomi will then contribute to the purchase of a commemorative stone arch dedicated to her chastity.

She walked up to the elm tree, wrapped her arms around the trunk, and started to climb. Where the nimble, springy, squirrel-like energy of only a few moments before had gone, she could not explain, but she barely made it half-way up before she slid back down, once, twice, several times, until her arms and legs were coated with a dark, smelly substance—more dog filth, which had been smeared all over the tree trunk. Meiniang wiped her hands on the ground, tears of indignation slipping from her eyes, when she heard the sound of mocking laughter from behind the rockery. Then two black-clad, veiled figures emerged, preceded by a lantern that cast a muted red glow, reminiscent of the lantern the legendary Fox Fairy used to lead people to safety. The two figures, who could have been men and could have been women, gave no signs of their true appearance.

Terror-stricken, Sun Meiniang raised her hands to cover her face, but stopped when she recalled that they were smeared with dog droppings. So she lowered her head and instinctively shrank back all the way to the base of the wall. The taller of the two figures held the lantern up close to Meiniang's face, as if to illuminate it for the benefit of the shorter person, who raised a thin stick used to frighten snakes hidden in the grass, stuck it under Meiniang's chin, and lifted up her face. Utterly mortified and ashamed, she was powerless to resist. So she squeezed her eyes shut and let the tears run freely down her cheeks. She heard the person holding the stick heave a long sigh, and could tell that it was a woman's voice. It was only a guess, but she assumed that it must be Magistrate Qian's wife, and in that split second, the anguish she had felt turned to defiance; she was energized. Holding her head high, she smiled and searched for the words that would inflict the most pain on her foe. Her initial instinct was to ask the First Lady if she was covering her face with a black veil to hide her pockmarks. But before she could get the words out, the person stepped up, thrust her hand down inside Meiniang's collar, and yanked away a bright, shiny object. It was the jade Buddha the Magistrate had given her in exchange for the jadeite thumb guard, not exactly a pledge of love, more a protective amu-let. She sprang frantically forward to retrieve the object, but a kick behind her knee from the taller person sent her down on all fours. She saw the First Lady's black veil flutter and her body shift slightly. It's too late to worry about saving face, since I am already soiled by dog filth, she was thinking, so now I need to find the most hurtful words possible as payback for how she has violated me. "I know who you are," she said, "and I know all about your pockmarks. The love of my life tells me you have a terrible body odor, that your mouth smells like maggots, and that he hasn't slept with you for three years. If I were you, I'd hang myself out of humiliation. Any woman who outlives a man's desire is no different than a coffin anyway."

Meiniang's gratifying outburst was interrupted by a stern retort from the short black-clad individual: "You little slut, how dare you come whoring around the yamen. Beat her, give her fifty lashes, then kick her out through the dog door!"

The taller person took a whip out from under his black clothes, kicked Meiniang to the ground, and, before she could utter another curse, laid the whip across her buttocks. She shrieked in pain just before the second lash connected with her buttocks; she looked up in time to see the other figure, the Magistrate's stinking wife, turn and wobble off. The third lash landed as hard as the first two, but the next one did not hurt as much, and those that followed got lighter and lighter, until the person was hitting the wall, not her. Meiniang knew that her assailant was a decent person at heart, although her exaggerated screams continued for their dramatic effect, to their mutual benefit. When he was done, the man dragged her over to the side gate of the Western Parlor, opened it, and shoved her outside, where she lay in a heap on the cobblestone lane east of the yamen.

7

Sun Meiniang lay on the kang, gnashing her teeth one minute and heartbroken the next. She gnashed her teeth out of hatred toward that savage, cold-hearted woman, while she was heartbroken that the Magistrate was confined to a sick-bed, and cursed herself for a lack of willpower; even when she bit her own arm till it bled, she could not drive the image of the wonderful Qian Ding out of her mind. Chunsheng came to see her when her torment had reached a fever pitch, just the familiar face she needed to see. She grabbed him by the arms and said tearfully:

"Chunsheng, dear Chunsheng, tell me, how is Laoye?"

Her anxiety moved him deeply. After glancing into the yard, where Xiaojia was skinning a dog, he said softly, "He's improving physically, but mentally he is in bad shape; he gets agitated easily. He's wasting away, and if he doesn't start eating soon, I'm afraid he'll starve to death."

"My dear Magistrate!" Sun Meiniang cried out mournfully, accompanied by a cascade of tears.

"The First Lady has sent me to ask you to take some millet spirits and dog meat to the yamen, both to make Laoye feel better and," he said with a little laugh, "to get his appetite back."

"The First Lady? Don't mention her to me," she said with a gnashing of her teeth. "Your First Lady is worse than a sadistic scorpion spirit."

"Mistress Sun, our First Lady is kind and honest, and always reasonable. How can you curse her like that?"

"What do you know?" Meiniang replied angrily. "Kind and honest, you say? Well, I say that her heart must have steeped in a vat of black dye for twenty years, and that one drop of her blood would be enough to kill a horse!"

"What did the First Lady ever do to you?" Chunsheng said with a little laugh. "This is like a mugger getting angry instead of his victim, or a lack of tears from a child that has lost its mother but wails from one whose mother is still alive."

"Get out of my sight!" Meiniang demanded. "I'll have nothing more to do with anyone in that yamen."

"Mistress Sun, does this mean that your concern for Laoye no longer exists?" Chunsheng said with a supercilious grin. "If you no longer care about Laoye, does that mean you no longer care about his queue? And if you no longer care about his queue, does that mean you no longer care about his beard? And if you no longer care about his beard, does that really mean you no longer care about Laoye himself?"

"I said get out of my sight! Laoye, Shaoye, what difference does it make? What could his death possibly mean to a commoner?" Despite her tone of voice, tears continued to flow.

"Mistress Sun," Chunsheng said, "you might fool others, but not me. You and the Magistrate are so close you might as well be one person. Break the bone, and there's still meat attached; tug on the ear, and the cheek twitches. But enough of that. Don't pull back on the reins now. Get ready and come with me."

"I will not step foot in that place as long as your First Lady is there."

"But, Mistress Sun, she has ordered me to come for you."

"Chunsheng, don't treat me like a circus monkey. How could I face someone who did what she did to me?"

"Apparently, Mistress Sun, someone has done something terrible."

"Do you really not know, or are you just pretending?" Meiniang asked in anger. "They used a whip on me in that yamen of yours!"

"What are you saying, Mistress Sun?" Chunsheng was clearly shocked. "Who would dare use a whip on you in the yamen? We who work there see you as the

Second Lady. We try our best to get on your good side. Who in his right mind would dare to even threaten you with a whip, let alone use it?"

"That First Lady of yours, that's who. She had someone give me fifty lashes!"

"I'm afraid I'll have to ask for proof," Chunsheng said as he moved to look under her clothes.

Sun Meiniang knocked his hand away. "Don't get fresh with me," she said. "Aren't you worried the Magistrate would chop off your grubby paw?"

"You see what I mean, Mistress Sun, you do have feelings for him. All I did was stick out my hand, and you stopped me by bringing up his name. The truth is, the Magistrate is seriously ill this time, and the First Lady has no choice but to invite you, our Living Bodhisattva, to work your magic. Think for a minute—would she be doing this if there were any other path open to her? Even if she did order someone to use a whip on you, why is this so surprising? Sending me for you is an admission of defeat. This hill is the excuse you need to ride the donkey, so what are you waiting for? If your ministrations speed up the Magistrate's recovery and set him on the road to health, even the First Lady will praise you for having performed a great service. What was once hidden will be out in the open; the private will be made public. That, Mistress Sun, will usher in good times for you. But it is your decision. Are you coming or aren't you?"

8

Dog meat basket in hand, Sun Meiniang pushed open the door to the Western Parlor and spotted a slightly pock-scarred woman with dark skin and a down-turned mouth seated in an armchair. Meiniang's heated body abruptly turned icy cold, and the elation with which she had arrived was suddenly coated with frost. Dimly she sensed that she had fallen into another trap, one also engineered by the Magistrate's wife. She was, however, the daughter of an actor, well acquainted with all sorts of poses; and she was, after all, the wife of a butcher, equally well acquainted with the glint of a knife and the sight of blood; and she was, in the end, the Magistrate's lover, and thus familiar with the ways of officials. All that made it possible for her to bring her tangled emotions under control, brace herself, and match stratagems with the Magistrate's wife. Two women, two pairs of eyes meeting, neither about to back down. As their gazes fought for supremacy, their hearts carried on a resounding dialogue.

Magistrate's wife: Are you aware that I come from an old and distinguished family?

Sun Meiniang: It is clear to anyone with eyes that I am a great beauty.

Magistrate's wife: I am his legal and formal wife.

Sun Meiniang: I am his most intimate soul mate.

Magistrate's wife: You are nothing but a remedy for my sick husband, no different than a canine gallstone or bezoars of ox.

Sun Meiniang: You are, in fact, the Magistrate's backroom ornament, a marionette, a clay sculpture.

Magistrate's wife: All your bewitching talents and seductive airs can have little effect on my position here.

Sun Meiniang: What good is being the revered First Lady if you are denied the Magistrate's love? He has told me that he fulfills his conjugal duties with you only once a month, but with me . . .

Thoughts of lovemaking with the Magistrate sent shivers through Meiniang's heart, and as vivid scenes of romance flooded her mind, radiant lights, moist and bright, glowed in her eyes. The somber First Lady had become a blurred outline.

The Magistrate's wife noticed that the face of the woman across from her, fresh and tender as a freshly picked honey peach, had flushed, that she was breathing fast, and that her eyes were suddenly unfocused, all signs that her emotions were heating up. She had, she felt, achieved a moral victory, and her face, taut and unyielding up till then, softened slowly as her ivory white teeth poked out between purplish-red lips. Tossing a jade bodhisattva on a red cord at Meiniang's feet, she said arrogantly:

"I had worn that since childhood, until some dog stole it and covered it with ugly canine smells. Since dogs are butchered at your house every day, you should not find it objectionable. You may have it."

Sun Meiniang blushed. The sight of the jade bodhisattva sent stabbing pains into her backside and brought back the memory of what had happened that night. Rage boiled inside her, and she'd have rushed up and scratched the woman's pock-scarred face if her legs would have done her bidding. For the Magistrate, all for the Magistrate, you may have your little victory. She knew that more than just a piece of jewelry, the First Lady had tossed over her status, her position, her challenge, and her grievance. Meiniang wavered. Bending down to pick it up would feed the First Lady's vanity; by refusing the offer, Meiniang could retain her dignity. Picking it up would satisfy the First Lady; not picking it up would outrage her. Satisfying the First Lady would establish a covenant for the love between Meiniang and the Magistrate; outraging the First Lady would erect a barrier between them. She had detected in the Magistrate's comments about his old-fashioned wife that he revered her. Her illustrious family may well have been a factor in that. For despite its recent decline, the Zeng family retained some of its influence. If the Magistrate could kneel before his wife, why should simply bending over bother Meiniang? And so she bent down and picked up the jade bodhisattva, all for the love of Magistrate Qian. And she did not stop there. One does not build a wall without digging up mud, so it was time to let the curtain fall on this drama. She went down on one knee, as if to show her gratitude for an unexpected favor.

"This common woman thanks the First Lady for her grace."

The First Lady exhaled loudly.

"Go," she said. "The Magistrate is in the document room."

Meiniang got to her feet, picked up the basket of dog meat and millet spirits she'd brought with her, and started to walk off. But the First Lady called her to a halt. With her dark eyes focused on the window, not on Meiniang, she said:

"He's getting on in years, while you are young . . ."

The First Lady's hint was not lost on Sun Meiniang. Her face was burning, and she did not know what to say to that. The First Lady walked out of the Western Parlor and headed to the rear of the compound. A welter of emotions fought for primacy in her mind—loathing, love, the pride of winning, and the humiliation of losing.

9

The Magistrate's appetite gradually returned under Meiniang's ministrations, and he grew stronger each day. Clouds of melancholy creased his brow as he read the documents that had piled up during his illness.

"Meiniang," he said as he stroked her nicely rounded backside, "dear Meiniang, if I refuse to arrest your dieh, Excellency Yuan will arrest me."

Meiniang rolled over and sat up.

"Magistrate, my dieh had good reason to attack the German. Yet they responded by killing my stepmother and siblings, and what's more, they slaughtered twenty-four innocent civilians. Isn't that enough? Why do they want my dieh arrested? Is this what people call justice?"

With a bitter smile, the Magistrate said:

"What does a woman know about such things?"

Meiniang grabbed his beard and said coquettishly:

"I may not know much about such things, but I know that my dieh is guilty of nothing."

The Magistrate sighed.

"I never said he was. But I cannot disobey an order from my superior."

"Be a good man and let him off the hook," Meiniang said as she moved seductively on his lap. "Is a County Magistrate powerless to protect an innocent member of the community?"

"How can I make you understand, my precious?"

Meiniang wrapped her arms around his neck and began rubbing her silken body against him enticingly.

"Even by taking care of you the way I do, can I still not save my dieh?"

"Enough," the Magistrate said, "that is enough. A carriage cannot reach the mountain without a road, but a boat can sail even against the wind. Qingming is nearly here, Meiniang, and, as in the past, I am going to have a set of swings put up in the parade ground for your enjoyment. I will also plant peach trees as a gift to the people. I am doing these things this year, Meiniang, because I cannot say where I will be next year."

"By this time next year, you will have been promoted to Prefect, no, even higher!"

10

When he learned that Sun Bing had led an attack on the railroad shed on Qingming, the County Magistrate suffered a momentary lapse in his ability to function. He threw down the tool he was using to plant a peach tree and, without a word to anyone, crawled into his palanquin. He did not need to be told that his official career was about to end.

Back at the yamen, he summoned his clerks and secretaries.

"You must all know that today has signaled the end of this Magistrate's official career," he told them. "You are welcome to continue in your present positions and await the appointment of my replacement. If, however, you prefer to leave, I advise you to do so without delay."

They exchanged looks, but said nothing.

With a bitter laugh, the Magistrate turned and went into his document room, slamming the door behind him.

The loud noise stunned them all. Deflated, they were at a loss for what to do. The revenue clerk went up to the window and said, "There is a popular adage, Laoye, that goes, 'Confront soldiers with generals, and dam water with earth.' What that means in essence is that heaven never seals off all the exits. We urge you to take a broad view." His plea was met with silence from inside.

So he whispered to Chunsheng:

"Hurry out to the rear compound and tell the First Lady what has happened. Be quick, before something terrible happens."

Meanwhile, the Magistrate had taken off his official garb and dropped it on the floor. Then he took off his hat and threw it into the corner.

"Happy is the man relieved of his duties," he said to himself, "and lacking a head means no more worries. Your Imperial Majesty, Empress Dowager, I am unable to carry out my vow of fealty; Excellency Yuan, Excellency Fan, Excellency Cao, I am unable to complete the duties entrusted to me; dear wife, I am unable to fulfill my conjugal responsibilities; my dearest Meiniang, I am unable to stay with you. Sun Bing, you no-account son of a bitch, I have done well by you."

The County Magistrate stood on a stool, untied the satin sash around his waist, and looped it over a crossbeam. Then he made a noose and inserted his head, carefully placing his beard outside the noose so that it fell neatly across his chest. He was able to see bits of the hazy sky and fine threads of rainwater through a hole poked in the paper covering of the latticed window, put there by a passing sparrow; he also saw his chief assistant, his clerks, his personal attendant, and his constables, all standing in the rain, as well as a pair of swallows that had made their nest under the eaves. Amid the hiss of falling rain and the twitter of swallows, the rich smell of life caressed his face. A light spring chill raised gooseflesh on his arms, in contrast to the sentimental longing for Sun Meiniang's warm body that filled him up, body and soul. Every cell in his body thirsted for her. Woman, ah, woman, you are a miracle, a true wonder. I know that the destruction of my future occurred on your body, and yet I am still madly in love with you . . . The County Magistrate knew that if he let his thoughts go on like that, his courage to say good-bye to the world would slip away. So he clenched his teeth and kicked the stool out from under him. Vaguely he heard a scream, a woman's voice. Was his wife coming to him? Or could it be Meiniang? Regret was already setting in, and he strained to reach up and free himself. But his arms were useless . . .

CHAPTER THIRTEEN

A City Destroyed

1

The County Magistrate set out in his four-man palanquin for Masang Township. In order to project a commanding aura, he took twenty county troopers—ten archers and ten musketeers—along with him. Two hundred forty German soldiers were going through their paces when the procession passed the Tongde Academy parade ground. Outfitted in colorful military attire, the tall, muscular soldiers displayed an impressive battle formation, rocking the area with their cadenced shouts. The Magistrate was shocked by what he saw, but did not show it. More than the tight formation and the Mauser weapons the soldiers carried, what truly impressed him was the row of twelve Krupp cannons crouching on the edge of the parade ground. Looking like enormous tortoises with bright shells and short, thick necks raised skyward, they rested on iron wheels that sat heavily on the ground. When Yuan Shikai had assumed office as Governor of Shandong, the County Magistrate and dozens of other County Magistrates had traveled to Jinan to observe a new force of five thousand soldiers that Yuan had brought from Jinan; it was an eye-opening experience for men who believed that the country now had an army that could stand up to the Great Powers. But compared to the German troops on the parade ground, it was a second-rate military force, even after receiving German weapons and training by German officers, who would not likely put their most powerful weapons in the hands of people whose country they had invaded. Excellency Yuan, what a fool you are.

Truth is, Yuan was not the fool, the County Magistrate was. And that was because Yuan had no intention of confronting the Great Powers with his newly created force.

Back on the Jinan parade ground, Yuan had ordered his artillery unit to fire three volleys. The shells flew over a river and a mountain and landed on a gravelly sandbar. In the company of his fellow officials and led by the artillery unit commander, the County Magistrate had ridden to the spot where the shells had created deep triangular craters in the sandbar, shattering the stones and sending their sharp-edged shards flying in all directions. Several young trees in the nearby wooded area had been truncated, with beads of sap dotting the new stumps. All the County Magistrates had gasped in admiration. But the cannons fired that day might as well have been the sons of the twelve cannons crouching at the edge of the Tongde Academy parade ground. The County Magistrate now understood why Yuan always acquiesced to the Germans' unreasonable demands, and why, in regard to the Sun Bing incident, he acted like a feckless father who slaps his own son in a cowardly display to ingratiate himself with a powerful man whose son has bullied his. No wonder he warned the people of Gaomi in his proclamation: "Let it be known that the German forces are invincible. Stir up more trouble, and you will come to even greater grief. Only a fool would ignore this advice. Have you not heard the adage 'Obedience is the path to survival, stubbornness leads only to trouble'? I trust you will keep this wise adage in mind."

The musketeers and archers under the Magistrate's once-proud command were a pathetic contrast to the German troops. Qian could barely hold up his head in the face of such disparity. And his embarrassment was shared by the men, who felt like adulterers being paraded naked past the Academy grounds. The Magistrate, a representative of the mighty Imperial Court, had come to the negotiations with an armed escort as a show of strength for the Germans, but now realized that this was as foolish a gesture as facing a mirror with his eyes covered. No wonder his men grimaced when he ordered them to dress in full battle attire. They had seen the military hardware and the disciplined troops at the Tongde Academy back when he lay ill in the yamen. He recalled being informed by subordinates that German troops had entered the county's capital without formal approval and had turned the Tongde Academy into a military camp, their excuse being that the Academy's name—Tongde—could be interpreted as meaning "for De-guo, or Germany." Having decided to end his life, he had turned a deaf ear to the shocking news. But once his death wish had passed, he realized that the Germans' arrogant entry into town and forcible occupation of the Tongde Academy grounds was nothing less than a piratical act in defiance of the sanctity of Gaomi County as well as that of the Great Qing Empire. He wrote a stern diplomatic note to the German commander, von Ketteler, which was hand delivered by Chunsheng and Liu Pu, demanding an apology and an immediate return to the base site stipulated in the 1898 Sino-German Jiao-Ao Treaty. His messengers returned with von Ketteler's response that Yuan Shikai and the Imperial Court in Peking had approved the establishment of a camp in Gaomi's capital. As he contemplated the report— unsure whether or not he should believe it—a messenger from Laizhou arrived on horseback with a telegram from Excellency Yuan, sanctioned by Prefect Cao. Yuan had ordered the County Magistrate to extend every courtesy to the

Germans as they established a camp in Gaomi and to gain the release of the German hostages taken by the criminal Sun Bing. Brooking no nonsense, Yuan wrote:

"In a recent incident involving foreign missionaries in Juye, Shandong Province suffered a significant loss of sovereignty, and if any of the captives are killed this time, it is hard to imagine what the cost to us will be. Not only will the nation be forced to cede precious land to the foreigners, but our lives will be in jeopardy. In difficult times such as we face today, you must think only of the national well being; you must work unstintingly, and you must successfully resolve issues. People who act out of personal considerations or pervert the law, and those who shirk their responsibilities and hamper the implementation of their duties will be severely punished. As soon as I have dealt with the Boxer rebels here in Northern Shandong, I will come to survey the situation in Gaomi County . . . in the wake of the February 2nd Incident, I sent a telegram ordering Magistrate Qian to arrest and imprison the rebel leader Sun Bing to ensure that no further incidents occurred, only to receive a return telegram asking that the rebel bandit be absolved of his crimes. I have rarely seen a more muddleheaded request. Such attempts at shifting responsibility and equivocation will inevitably lead to chaos and instability. For this dereliction of duty, Magistrate Qian, you deserve to be removed from office, but the nation is in need of competent officials, and you have ties to a former high official of the current dynasty, so I am prepared to show leniency. Now that you have committed a serious error, I expect you to redeem yourself with devoted service. Devise a plan, without delay, to free the hostages and appease the Germans . . ."

When he finished reading the telegram, he turned to his wife, who wore a clouded look, and heaved a long sigh.

"Dear wife," he said, "why did you not let me die?"

"Do you honestly believe that what you are facing now is worse than what my grandfather faced after his defeat at the hands of the Taiping rebels at Jinggang?" The First Lady's eyes blazed as she looked at her husband.

"But your grandfather jumped into a river to kill himself!"

"You're right, he did," she said. "But he was pulled from the river by subordinates, and drew a lesson from the experience. Spurred into rallying his forces, he staged a comeback, refusing to yield and enduring every imaginable hardship as he fought his way into Nanking, where he wiped out the Taiping 'Long Hairs,' an exploit that earned him a reputation as an official of great renown, a pillar of the state. His wife received honorary titles, and his children were given hereditary ranks along with considerable wealth. Memorial temples were erected in his honor so that his good name would live for all time. That is the essence of a man worthy of the name."

"In the two centuries and more since the beginning of this dynasty, there has been only one Zeng Guofan." The Magistrate looked up at the photograph of the posthumously named Lord Wenzheng hanging on the wall—even in his dotage he had lost none of his dignity. "I have little talent and insubstantial learning," he said feebly, "and I am weak-willed. You saved my life, but not my reputation. How sad, dear wife, that you, the daughter of an illustrious family, should be married to someone who is little more than a walking corpse."

"Why, my husband, must you belittle yourself?" she asked gravely. "You are possessed of great learning, are well versed in military strategy, enjoy good health, and have exceptional physical skills. You have had to submit to others not because you are inferior to them, but because your time had not yet come."

"What about now?" he asked, the hint of a mocking smile on his lips. "Has my time finally come?"

"Of course it has," the First Lady said. "The Boxers are inciting the masses to rebel, the Great Powers are like tigers eyeing their prey, and the Germans are enraged over Sun Bing's rebellious actions. All this has put the nation in a precarious position. If you can develop a plan to rescue the hostages and take Sun Bing into custody at the same time, you will gain favor with Excellency Yuan. Not only will your punishment be expunged, but you will be rewarded with a high-level position. Can you deny that it is time for you to accomplish great things?"

"What you have just said has caused me to look at everything with new eyes," the Magistrate said with a hint of sarcasm. "But the unpleasant Sun Bing business has its roots."

"Yes, my husband. Sun Bing could be pardoned for avenging his wife's humiliation by beating the German transgressor. But the Germans can also be pardoned for avenging their countryman. Following the incident, Sun Bing should have accepted his punishment instead of joining the outlawed Boxer movement and, after taking it upon himself to set up a sacred altar, leading an attack by his followers on the railway shed. Most inexcusable of all, he took hostages. If that is not a rebellious act, I do not know what is," the First Lady said sternly. "Your livelihood is guaranteed by the Great Qing Court, and as its official representative, instead of single-mindedly coming to the defense of the nation in its hour of peril, you sought to absolve Sun Bing of his crimes. Your apparent sympathy was actually an act of harboring the guilty; what you considered benevolence was in truth collusion with the enemy. How could anyone as well read and sensible as you do something so foolish? And all because of a woman who peddles dog meat!"

The shamefaced Magistrate bowed his head under the penetrating gaze of his wife.

"I know that being barren is one of the seven causes for divorce, and I am grateful to you, my husband, for choosing not to abandon me," she remarked delicately. "That is something I shall not forget . . . once things have settled down, I will find a woman of virtue for you, someone who will bear your off-spring to carry on the Qian name. But if your infatuation with the Sun woman endures, we can arrange a divorce from her butcher husband so you can install her as your concubine. You have my word that I will treat her as family. But this cannot happen now. If you fail to free the foreign hostages and arrest Sun Bing, you and I are fated to come to a bad end, and you will be denied the pleasure of her charms."

As sweat soaked the Magistrate's back, he tried but failed to stammer a response.

2

As he sat in his palanquin, the Magistrate's mood oscillated between righteous indignation and utter dejection. Rays of sunlight filtering in through gaps in the bamboo curtain landed first on his hands and then on his legs. He saw the sweat-soaked necks of the bearers up front through those same gaps. His body shifted with each rise and fall of the shafts, a reflection of his drifting thoughts. The dark, sedate face of the First Lady and the bewitchingly fair image of Mei-niang entered his mind, one after the other. The First Lady represented reason, his official career, and the dignity that went with it. Meiniang was emotion, life, romance. He would not willingly give up either one, but if he had to choose, then . . . then . . . it would have to be his wife. The granddaughter of Lord Wenzheng was, without question, the proper choice. If he failed to rescue the hostages and take Sun Bing into custody, all would come to naught anyway. Meiniang, oh, Meiniang, your dieh may be your dieh, but you are you, and for you I must take him into custody. It is for you that I must arrest your dieh.

The palanquin crossed the Masang River stone bridge and headed toward Masang Township's western gate along a badly pitted dirt road. It was the middle of the day, but the gate was tightly shut. Broken bricks and shards of roof tiles had been piled atop a rammed-earth wall, behind which men with knives and spears and clubs were on the move. Flapping high above the gateway was an apricot banner embroidered with the large single word YUE, representing the Song Dynasty hero Yue Fei. Young men in red kerchiefs and sashes, their faces smeared with a red substance, kept guard over the banner.

The Magistrate's palanquin was lowered to the ground in front of the gate. He stepped out, bent slightly at the waist. A voice from high up on the gateway demanded:

"Who comes calling?"

"Magistrate Qian of Gaomi County."

"What is the purpose of your visit?"

"To see Sun Bing."

"Our Supreme Commander is practicing martial skills and is unavailable."

With a sardonic little laugh, the Magistrate said:

"Yu Xiaoqi, you can stop putting on airs for my benefit. When you held a gambling party last year, I spared you from the obligatory forty lashes for the sake of your seventy-year-old mother. You haven't forgotten that, have you?"

With a smirk, Yu Xiaoqi replied:

"I have taken the place of the Song general Yang Zaixing."

"I don't care if you've taken the place of the Jade Emperor, you are still Yu Xiaoqi. Summon Sun Bing, and be quick about it. Otherwise, the next time I see you will be in the yamen when you are getting the lashes you deserve."

"Wait here," Yu Xiaoqi said. "I'll take a message in for you."

Wearing an inscrutable smile, the Magistrate glanced at his attendants. They are nothing but simple farm boys, he was thinking.

Sun Bing, wearing a long white gown and a silver helmet adorned with a pair of stage-prop plumes, appeared in the gateway. He was still carrying his date-wood club.

"Visitor at our city wall, state your name!"

"Sun Bing, oh, Sun Bing," the Magistrate said sarcastically, "you still know how to put on a show."

"The Supreme Commander does not converse with the unidentified. I repeat, state your name!"

"Sun Bing, you are truly lawless. Hear me out. I am a representative of the Great Qing Empire, Gaomi County Magistrate Qian Ding, with the style name Yuanjia."

"So, it is the trifling Magistrate of Gaomi County," Sun Bing remarked. "Why have you come here instead of functioning as a good official in your yamen?"

"Will you let me be a good official, Sun Bing?"

"As Supreme Commander, my only concern is to exterminate the foreigners. I have neither the time nor the interest to bother with an insignificant County Magistrate."

"Exterminating the foreigners is what I have come to see you about. Open the gate and let me in. We will both be losers if their army decides to come."

"Whatever you have to say, you can say it from out there. I can hear you."

"What I have to say is extremely confidential. I must talk to you privately."

After a thoughtful pause, Sun Bing said:

"All right, but just you."

The Magistrate stepped back into his palanquin.

"Raise the chair!" he ordered.

"The chair stays outside!"

The Magistrate parted the curtain.

"As a representative of the Imperial Court," he said, "I am expected to be carried in."

"All right, but only the chair."

The Magistrate turned to the head of his military escort. "Wait for me out here."

"Excellency," Chunsheng and Liu Pu said as they held on to the shafts, "you must not go in there alone."

The Magistrate smiled.

"Don't worry," he said, "Supreme Commander Yue is a sensible man. He will not do injury to this official."

With a series of loud creaks, the gate opened inward to permit the Magistrate's palanquin to enter, swaying from side to side. The musketeers and archers of the escort attempted to storm their way in after him, only to be pelted by rubble raining down from atop the wall. When they took aim at their attackers, the Magistrate ordered them to lower their weapons.

The palanquin passed through the newly reinforced wooden gate and was quickly enveloped in the heavy fragrance of pine oil. Through gaps in the bamboo screen, he spotted half a dozen furnaces that had been set up on either side of the street, the fires kept red-hot by large bellows. Local blacksmiths were hard at work forging swords, their clanging hammers sending sparks flying. Women and children walked up and down the street with flatbreads and leeks stripped of their hard skins; lights flashed in the eyes of the glum-looking women. A little boy with tufted hair and an exposed belly who was carrying a steaming black clay pot cocked his head to gape at the Magistrate's palanquin, then suddenly raised his juvenile voice in a rhythmic Maoqiang aria: *"A cold, cold day and heavy snow~~northwest winds up my sleeves do blow~~"* The boy's high-pitched voice made the Magistrate laugh, but what came next was a dose of bone-chilling sorrow. Reminded of the German soldiers who drilled alongside cannons lined up on the Tongde Academy grounds, the Magistrate took a hard look at the ignorant Masang Township residents, who had been whipped into a state of fanaticism by the bewitching black arts of Sun Bing, and he was struck by feelings of obligation to rescue them from their plight. The sonorous inflections of a pledge rang out in his mind—what the First Lady had said made perfect sense: at this critical, perilous juncture, he must reject all thoughts of dying, whether in the name of the nation or of the people. To seek death at this moment would be shameful and cowardly. A world in turmoil gives rise to great men, and it is incumbent upon me to take a lesson from Lord Wenzheng, who defied difficulties and laughed at danger, who fought to save desperate situations and liberate the masses from peril. Sun Bing, you bastard, you have led thousands of Masang residents into the jaws of death, all to satisfy your thirst for personal vengeance, and I am morally and legally bound to see that you are punished.

Sun Bing rode ahead of the Magistrate's palanquin on a dejected-looking chestnut horse. Its harness had rubbed the hair off the starving animal's forelegs, exposing the green-tinted skin. Bits of watery excrement hung on the bony hindquarters of what the Magistrate easily identified as a plow horse, a pitiful animal taken from the fields to become Supreme Commander Yue's personal mount. A young man with a red-painted face led the way, hopping and bouncing down the street with a shiny club that looked like a hoe handle, while a more somber young man, whose face was painted black, walked behind the horse carrying his own shiny club, also, apparently, a hoe handle. The Magistrate assumed that they had fashioned themselves after combatants in the novel *The Story of Yue Fei*, with Zhang Bao leading the way and Wang Heng bringing up the rear. Sun Bing sat tall in the saddle, reins in one hand and date-wood club in the other, his every stylized move and affected gesture the sort that a man might make astride a great galloping charger as he guarded a frontier pass under a chilly moon or while crossing vast open plains—What a shame, the Magistrate was thinking, that all the man had was an old nag with loose bowels, and that he was riding down a dusty, narrow street on which hens pecked at food and spindly dogs ran loose. The palanquin followed Sun Bing and his guards up to the bend in a dried-out river in the heart of the township, where the Magistrate was treated to the sight of hundreds of men in red kerchiefs and sashes sitting quietly on the dry riverbed, like an array of clay figurines. Other men in bright garb sat on a platform made of piled-up bricks in front of the seated men, intoning funereal strains of Maoqiang opera at the top of their lungs, the meaning virtually incomprehensible to the Magistrate, a celebrated graduate of the metropolitan examination: *A black tornado blows in from the south~~a white cat spirit set free by Grand Commander Hong in camp~~white cat spirits, oh, white cat spirits~~white coats and red eyes~~intent on sucking our blood dry~~most exalted Laozi, appear in our midst~~train the magic fists as protectors of the Great Qing~~slaughter the white cat spirits~~skin them, gouge out their eyes, and light the heavenly lamp~~* Sun Bing dismounted in front of a makeshift mat shed. The horse shook its dirty, ratty mane and began to wheeze as it bent its hind legs and released a burst of watery excrement. Zhang Bao stepped back and tied the horse's reins to a dried-up old willow tree; Wang Heng took the club from Sun Bing, who glanced back at the palanquin with an expression that seemed to the Magistrate to be a cross between arrogance and doltishness. The carriers laid down their shafts and pulled back the curtain for the Magistrate, who scooped up the hem of his official robe and stepped out. Head high and chest thrust out, Sun Bing entered the shed, followed by the Magistrate.

The tent was illuminated by a pair of candles, whose light fell on the image of an idol on one of the walls. Pheasant tail feathers rose above the head of the figure, which was clad in a ministerial python robe and sported a magnificent beard, looking a little like Sun Bing and a lot like the Magistrate. Thanks to his relationship with Sun Meiniang, the Magistrate knew quite a bit about the history of Maoqiang opera, and he immediately recognized the image as that of Chang Mao, the school's founder, who had somehow been appropriated as the revered Taoist protector of Sun Bing's Boxers of Righteous Harmony. Upon entering the tent, the Magistrate was greeted by intimidating sounds and the sight of eight wild-looking youths, four on each side of the image. Half had black faces, half had red; half were dressed in black, half in red. Their clothing rustled in the stirred-up air, as if made of paper, and when he took a closer look, he saw that that's exactly what it was. Each was holding a club, the shiny surfaces indicative of hoe handles. They served to further diminish the Magistrate's respect for Sun Bing. Can't you manage something new, something fresh, Sun Bing? After all this time and energy, the best you can come up with is some tired old rural opera tricks. And yet he knew that the Germans did not share his disdain; nor did the Imperial Court or Excellency Yuan. Nor, for that matter, did the three thousand residents of Masang Township, the youthful attendants in the tent, or their leader, Sun Bing.

Following a ragged series of shouts announcing the discussion of military matters by Supreme Commander Yue, Sun Bing strutted over to a rosewood chair and swayed his way into it. With a dramatic flair, he intoned hoarsely:

"State your name, visitor!"

With a sarcastic laugh, the Magistrate said:

"Sun Bing, that's enough of your insatiable play-acting. I have come neither to listen to you sing opera nor to share the stage with you. I have come to tell you that either the cinders are hot or the fire is."

"Who do you think you are, speaking to the Supreme Commander like that?" Zhang Bao, the horse preceder, said, pointing his club at the Magistrate. "Our Supreme Commander leads an army of tens of thousands, men and horses, unimaginably greater than anything you can boast of!"

"I trust you haven't forgotten, Sun Bing," the Magistrate said as he stroked his beard and stared at Sun Bing's scarred and scabby chin, "how you lost your beard."

"I always knew that it was you, you double-dealer," Sun Bing raged. "I also know that prior to our battle of the beards, you—crafty, petty tyrant that you are—treated your beard with a mixture of ashes and a glue-like substance, which is the only way you could have beaten me. Losing is one thing, but you had no right to pluck out my beard after pardoning me."

"Would you like to know who really did it?" the Magistrate asked with a smile.

"It had to be you."

"Right," the Magistrate replied calmly. "Without doubt, you had the better beard, and if I hadn't taken precautions, you would surely have won. I pardoned you to show the people that I am a generous, forgiving man. Then I covered my face that night and ripped the beard off your face in order to quell your arrogance and turn you into an obedient member of society."

"You dog!" Sun Bing pounded his fist on the table and jumped to his feet enraged. "Grab this lousy dog of an official, men, and pluck out his beard! My chin has become barren thanks to you, and I am going to turn yours into the Gobi Desert!"

Zhang Bao and Wang Heng raised their clubs threateningly and bore down upon the Magistrate, aided by shouts from the wild youngsters.

"I am an official representative of the Imperial Court," the Magistrate warned them, "dignified and properly assigned. Don't you dare so much as touch a single hair on my body!"

"*I curse the merciless, insignificant little Qian Ding~~In your role you are a moth that has flown into the fire, fallen into a trap, landed in my hand~~a blood debt will be paid on this day~~*" With the Maoqiang aria on his lips, Sun Bing charged, raised his club high over his head, yelled "You rat . . . !" took aim at the Magistrate's head, and swung mightily.

Calmly, the Magistrate moved backward, easily sidestepping the blow, and grabbed hold of the offending club, pushing it ahead of him and forcing Sun Bing down on all fours. Zhang Bao and Wang Heng raised their clubs and swung in the direction of the Magistrate's head; he dodged their blows with a cat-like leap backward and then sprang forward like a leopard, causing the two heads to bang together with a loud thud. Somehow both of their clubs landed in his hands. With his left he hit Zhang Bao, and with his right Wang Heng. "You damned freaks," he cursed, "get out of my sight!" The two men shrieked and scampered out of the shed, holding their heads in their hands. With them out of the way, the Magistrate tossed one of the clubs away, but held on to the other. "And you little freaks," he cursed, "are you waiting for me to do the same to you, or will you clear out on your own?" Seeing how fast the tide had turned, the eight wild youngsters took the latter course, some throwing down their clubs, others dragging theirs out the door with them.

The Magistrate grabbed Sun Bing by the neck and lifted him off the ground. "Sun Bing," he said, "where are the three German hostages?"

"Qian," Sun Bing said with a teeth-grinding snarl, "go ahead, kill me, if that's what you want. Everyone else in my family is dead, so it makes no difference to me if I live or die."

"Tell me where the Germans are."

"Them?" With a sarcastic grin, he began to sing: *"When you ask where all the German dogs are~~that makes this Supreme Commander's spirits fly far~~they are sleeping in heaven~~they are hidden deep in the ground~~they exist in latrines~~they line the stomachs of dogs, that is where they are~~"*

"Have you killed them?"

"They are alive and well, and it is up to you to go find them."

"Sun Bing," the Magistrate said as he let go of the neck and adopted a friendlier tone, "I have to tell you that Meiniang is now in the hands of the Germans, and if you do not release their people, they will hang her from the city gate."

"That is up to them," Sun Bing replied. "Marrying off a daughter is like spilling a pail of water. She is no longer my concern."

"But she is your only daughter, and you owe her a lifetime of debts. If you refuse to free your German hostages, then I have no choice but to take you back with me today." The Magistrate took Sun Bing by the arm and walked him out of the shed, where they were met by a burst of crowd noise. There on the dry riverbed, hundreds of men in their red kerchiefs, red sashes, and painted faces, under the leadership of several other men in stage costume, were heading their way, a bawling, raucous wave of black heads closing in and surrounding the Magistrate and Sun Bing before they could react. One of them, a general in a tiger-skin apron, his face painted like a monkey, leaped into the center, pointed his iron cudgel at the Magistrate's head, and, affecting an accent from somewhere, said:

"Alien evildoer, how dare you cause our Supreme Commander to suffer such an outrage!"

"I, Gaomi County Magistrate, have come to negotiate the release of hostages and to take Sun Bing into custody!"

"County Magistrate, you shall do nothing of the sort! You are an evil spirit in human form. Destroy his evil powers, my children!"

Before he knew it, the people behind the Magistrate had dumped a pail of dog's blood over his head, followed by a coating of manure. This was more filth than had ever degraded and soiled the fastidious Magistrate's body. As his stomach lurched and nausea began to claim him, he bent over to vomit and, in the process, let go of Sun Bing's arm.

"Sun Bing, bring the hostages to the north gate of the county seat tomorrow at noon, or your daughter will suffer grievously." The Magistrate wiped his face with his hand, revealing a pair of eyes clouded with manure and blood; he presented a sad sight, and yet spoke with firm self-assurance: "Do not let what I say drift past your ears on the wind!"

"Kill him! Kill this dog-shit official!" many in the crowd shouted.

"I am doing this for your own good, fellow townsmen." The Magistrate spoke from his heart. "After you deliver the hostages tomorrow, you may do whatever you please. Do not make the mistake of following Sun Bing." He turned to the pair of Righteous Harmony Boxers and said in a mocking tone, "Then there's you two. His Excellency Yuan, Governor of the Province, has sent an edict that Boxers are to be killed, down to the last man. None are to be spared. But since you have come from far away, that makes you guests of a sort, and I am willing to send you on your way in peace. Leave now, before provincial troops arrive, for by then it will be too late."

His words had a stupefying effect on the men in the roles of Sun Wukong and Zhu Bajie, so he quickly took advantage of the changed mood. "Sun Bing," he called out loudly, "your daughter's life is at stake, and you must meet your responsibility. At noon tomorrow I will be waiting for you at the San Li River Bridge outside the north gate." With that, he parted the crowd and strode purposefully down the street. His carriers rushed to pick up the palanquin and trot after him. He was also followed by the slightly off-tune strains of a Maoqiang opera, intoned by Sun Wukong:

"*Righteous Harmony, we sacred Boxers~~slaughter the foreigners to preserve our land! Boxers of Righteous Harmony~~our power is great~~indestructible ~~together we band . . .*"

Once he was on the outskirts of town, the Magistrate began to run, faster and faster, his carriers and attendants straining to keep up, like a flock of sheep. The stink of the man's body easily reached them, and the sight he presented, a mixture of red and brown, so completely flummoxed them that they dared not laugh, they dared not cry, and they dared not ask what had happened; so they just kept running. When they reached the Masang River Bridge, the Magistrate jumped in, spraying water in all directions.

"Eminence!" Chunsheng and Liu Pu shouted together.

Suicide was what they were thinking. They ran down to the riverbank, prepared to jump in and save their Magistrate, until they saw his head break the surface. Though it was by then the fourth lunar month, a bit of wintry weather lingered on, and a chill rose from the clear blue water. Still in the middle of the river, the Magistrate shed his official clothing and rinsed it out in the river. He repeated the action, this time with his hat.

With his clothing now clean, he waded unsteadily up to the riverbank, aided by his attendants. He seemed shrunken, thanks to the cold water, and had trouble straightening up, but after draping Chunsheng's jacket over his shoulders and stepping into Liu Pu's pants, he crawled into his palanquin. Then, once Chunsheng spread his official garments over top of the palanquin and Liu Pu hung his hat from one of the shafts, the carriers picked up the chair and hurried home, followed by the Magistrate's troops and attendants.

"Damn!" he was thinking as he was carried along, "I look like one of those opera-stage adulterers!"

3

The story that the Germans had taken Sun Meiniang hostage was a complete fabrication, either something the Magistrate had made up on the spot or what he had assumed the Germans would do if Sun Bing refused to repatriate their countrymen. Now he led his personal attendants to meet the German Plenipotentiary, von Ketteler, and his entourage at the prearranged site on the San Li River bridgehead near the city's north gate, where they awaited the arrival of Sun Bing. The Magistrate had not mentioned a hostage swap to the German official, telling him only that a repentant Sun Bing had agreed to release the hostages. The Plenipotentiary, inordinately pleased by the news, told the Magistrate through his interpreter that if his countrymen were returned unharmed, he would praise the Magistrate's efforts to Excellency Yuan himself. This did little to ease the Magistrate's misgivings, and he responded with a bitter smile as he recalled the dreadful premonition that Sun Bing's ambiguous comments had left him with the day before, a fear that the three German captives had already come to grief. He prepared for the meeting trusting to luck that all would end well, and with that in mind, he mentioned Sun Meiniang to no one, including Chunsheng and Liu Pu. He merely told them to ready a two-man palanquin, in which he had them place a large rock.

The Plenipotentiary, who was growing impatient as the sun rose high in the sky, kept looking at his pocket watch and telling his interpreter to ask whether Sun Bing was playing them for fools. The Magistrate equivocated as much as possible, avoiding a direct response to the man's questions and his growing suspicions. Though he was churning with anxiety, he put on a brave, jovial face.

"Please ask the Plenipotentiary for me," he said to the rat-faced interpreter, "why his eyes are blue."

The befuddled interpreter could only sputter in response. The Magistrate had a big laugh over his little joke.

A pair of magpies were chattering loudly in a nearby willow tree, their black and white feathers making a lively show around branches that were just turning yellow. The scene was a work of art. Across the river, men with handcarts or carrying poles were making their way up the levee; before they reached the bridgehead, they spotted the foreign Plenipotentiary, who had remained in the saddle of his mighty steed, and the County Magistrate, who was standing in front of his palanquin; they turned tail and ran back down the levee.

When the sun was directly overhead, the sound of horns and drums signaled the arrival of a delegation from the north. The Plenipotentiary hastily lifted his field glasses to his eyes; the Magistrate shaded his eyes with his hand and strained to see who was coming, and heard the Plenipotentiary shout out to him:

"Qian, where are the hostages?"

The Magistrate took the field glasses the official held out to him. The still-distant contingent of men leaped into his line of vision. He saw that Sun Bing was still wearing his tattered stage costume, still holding his date-wood club, and still riding the same old nag. It was hard to tell whether the smile on his face was that of a dull-witted man or a crafty one. In front of his horse, as always, was Zhang Bao the monkey, while the silly-looking Wang Heng was walking behind him, followed by Sun Bing's senior attendants, Sun Wukong and Zhu Bajie, who were both on horseback. They were followed by four musicians—two playing the suona and two on horns—who preceded a slow-moving mule-drawn wagon with wooden wheels on which a tent had been set up. Next in the procession were a dozen red-kerchiefed young men carrying swords and spears. Only the Germans were missing. The Magistrate's heart turned to ice, and his vision blurred. Even though this was what he had anticipated, he held out a ray of hope that the three German captives were there in the tent on the slow-moving mule-drawn wagon. He handed the field glasses back to the foreigner and avoided the German's anxious eyes. In his mind's eye he gauged whether or not the tent could accommodate three good-sized Germans. Two scenarios played out in his head: One was that Sun Bing was according his German hostages the courtesy of riding to their salvation in a mule-drawn wagon. The other was that three bloody corpses were piled inside that tent. Neither superstitious nor much of a believer in ghosts and spirits, the Magistrate surprised even himself by offering up a silent prayer: All you spirits and demons in heaven and on earth, I beg you to let those three German soldiers step unharmed from that wagon. If they cannot walk, being carried off is acceptable. As long as there is still breath in their bodies, all is not lost. If three bloody corpses were carried out of the tent, the Magistrate could not bear to think of what that would lead to. A bloody, full-scale war was a distinct possibility, or a massacre. One thing was certain: his career would be over.

While thoughts thronged the Magistrate's mind, Sun Bing's procession approached the bridgehead, making field glasses unnecessary to see all the men, their animals, and the mysterious mule-drawn wagon; the Magistrate's attention was focused on the wagon, which bounced and bumped its way along, appearing to have plenty of heft without being overly heavy. The iron-rimmed wooden wheels turned slowly, creaking noisily with each revolution. As soon as it reached the bridgehead, the procession halted, and the musicians put down their instruments. Sun Bing spurred his horse up the levee, and when he reached the top he shouted, "You are in the presence of the great Song general Yue Fei. I demand to know the name of the general I face!"

The Magistrate responded loudly:

"Sun Bing, release your captives at once!"

"First tell that dog beside you to let my daughter go!" Sun Bing replied.

"The truth is, Sun Bing, they never did take your daughter," the Magistrate said as he pulled back the curtain of his palanquin." There is nothing but a large rock in here."

"I knew it was a lie," Sun Bing said with a smile. "This Supreme Commander has eyes and ears everywhere in the city. You cannot make a move there without my learning of it."

"If you do not free the hostages, I cannot guarantee Meiniang's safety," the Magistrate warned him.

"This commander's emotional attachment to his daughter no longer exists. You decide whether she lives or dies," Sun Bing replied. "But in the spirit of magnanimity, and despite the alien dog's lack of humanity, this commander must retain his righteousness, and so I have brought the three alien dogs with me and herewith hand them over."

With a casual wave, Sun Bing signaled the Boxer troops behind him to remove three burlap sacks from the mule-drawn wagon, which they dragged up to the bridgehead. The Magistrate saw signs of struggle inside the sacks and heard strange muffled sounds. The Boxers stood in the middle of the road waiting for Sun Bing's command:

"Let them out!"

They opened the three bags, picked them up from the bottom, and dumped out the contents: a pair of pigs dressed in German uniforms and a white dog wearing a German soldier's cap. With squeals and frantic barks, the animals scrambled across the ground, heading straight for the Plenipotentiary, like children rushing into the arms of family.

"They turned themselves into pigs and dogs!" Sun Bing announced earnestly.

His troops echoed his words:

"They turned themselves into pigs and dogs!"

Magistrate Qian did not know whether to laugh or cry at the scene playing out in front of him. The Plenipotentiary, on the other hand, drew his pistol and fired at Sun Bing, hitting the club in his hand and producing an unusual sound. But to look at Sun Bing, one would have thought that his club had hit the bullet rather than the other way around. At the very instant when the foreigner fired his pistol, one of the young musketeers behind Sun Bing took aim at the German and fired a spray of buckshot, some of which struck the man's horse, which reared up in pain and threw its rider; his foot was caught in the stirrup, and he was dragged by the blinded animal toward the river. The Magistrate flew to the rescue, like a panther pouncing on its prey; he wrapped his arms around the horse's neck and slowed it enough for the foreign attendants to rush up and free the Plenipotentiary, who had been hit in the ear by a buckshot pellet, from the stirrup. He reached up to feel his ear, and when he saw the blood on his hand, he screamed something unintelligible.

"What did His Excellency shout just now?" the Magistrate asked the interpreter.

"He sa . . . said he . . . he's reporting you to Excellency Yuan!" the man stammered.

4

After marching all night from Jinan, German troops, in a joint operation with a battalion of Imperial Right Guardsmen, surrounded Masang Township and attacked, Chinese troops in front, Germans bringing up the rear. The County Magistrate and Infantry Regiment Commander Ma Longbiao stood on opposite sides of the Plenipotentiary, whose wounded ear was bandaged, as if they were his personal bodyguards. In the woods behind them, German cannons were in place and ready to commence firing, with four soldiers standing at attention behind each piece, like wooden posts. The Magistrate did not know whether von Ketteler had already telegraphed a complaint to Yuan Shikai, since Ma Longbiao and his infantry troops had arrived, travel-worn and weary, on the afternoon of the hostage-exchange farce.

After arranging board and lodging for the regiment, the Magistrate held a welcoming dinner for Commander Ma, a modest man who, throughout the meal, proclaimed his enormous respect for Lord Wenzheng and made a point of saying that he had long admired the Magistrate as a learned man. When the meal was nearly over, Ma whispered to him that Qian Xiongfei, who had suffered the slicing death in Tianjin, had been a close friend, a revelation that convinced Qian that he and his guest had a special relationship, as if they had been fast friends for years, someone from whom there were no secrets.

To help ensure Commander Ma's success in his mission, Magistrate Qian lent him fifty of the county militiamen, who were assigned as scouts for the government troops and foreign soldiers, deploying them around the township in the darkness just before daybreak. The Magistrate himself made a personal appearance to help compensate for the ridiculous travesty the day before, when the anticipated hostage swap had blown up in his face. Sun Bing had made fools out of him and the German; his proclamation and the shouts of his followers rang in the County Magistrate's ears: "They turned themselves into pigs and dogs! They turned themselves into pigs and dogs!" I should have known they would not let those three German soldiers live, he was thinking. As a matter of fact, he had heard that Sun Bing and his followers had tied the captives to trees and taken turns urinating in their faces. After that, he was sure, they would have offered the men's hearts and livers in sacrifice to the souls of their twenty-seven dead. I should have followed my instincts instead of blithely believing that the German soldiers were still alive. Even more laughable was my thought that if I rescued the hostages, Excellency Yuan would take note of my achievement and view me with favor. My mistake was listening to my wife and letting what she said convince me to do something incredibly stupid. Von Ketteler's luck was hardly better than mine. By taking a shot at Sun Bing, he had set in motion the creation of a legend that Sun's martial skills were so advanced he could redirect bullets in midair, while his followers could fire a fowling piece without aiming and not only bring down a powerful horse but put a hole in its rider's ear. The Magistrate assumed that von Ketteler had already sent his telegram, but even if he hadn't, it was only a matter of time. For all he knew, Yuan had already left Jinan for Gaomi, and his only hope of keeping his head attached to his shoulders was to capture or kill Sun Bing before His Excellency arrived.

The County Magistrate watched as his militiamen, under the command of Liu Pu, approached the fortified town at a crouch from a position in front of the Imperial Right Guard troops, who treated ordinary citizens with the ferocity of wolves or tigers, but as soon as fighting broke out, they were as gutless as mice. They started out in a loose formation, but each step nearer to the fortified wall drew them closer together, like chickens huddling for warmth. Though he had no battle experience, the Magistrate had read everything Lord Wenzheng had written many times, and he knew that a tight formation was an invitation to be wiped out by fortress defenders. He wished he'd given them a bit of basic training before heading into battle, but it was too late now. They pressed forward, drawing closer and closer to the wall, which appeared unmanned; but he knew by the puffs of smoke rising every few yards above the wall and the smell of porridge cooking that there were people on the other side. He had learned from Lord Wenzheng's military writings that defenders of walls did not prepare pots of boiling porridge to satisfy their appetite; the real purpose was something he knew only too well, yet tried not to think about. His militiamen stopped when they were but a few yards from the protective wall, and began the attack—musketeers shooting their fowling pieces, archers letting their arrows fly. The anemic sound of gunfire—some twenty or so shots altogether—was no demonstration of military might. Then the guns fell silent. Some of the archers' arrows had sailed over the wall; others were lucky to have made it *to* the wall, a showing that failed to match even that of the musketeers. It was more like a children's game than anything. After firing their fowling pieces, the men knelt in place and reached for the powder horns hanging from their belts. The horns were actually bottle gourds coated with tung oil, which made them glossy and strikingly attractive. In earlier days, when the Magistrate had led his musketeers out searching for bandits and highwaymen, those twenty gleaming powder horns had been a source of pride. Now, seen alongside the Imperial Right Guard and German battle formations, they looked like toys. The kneeling men finished loading their fowling pieces with powder, fired off a second scattered volley, and stormed the fortified wall, filling the air with battle cries. Last year's straw on the ten-foot gently sloped wall quivered under the onslaught of running feet. Or was it the County Magistrate's quivering heart? A pair of palanquin bearers ran up carrying a ladder. Years of carrying a palanquin had left them with a prancing gait that was in evidence even now; they no longer knew how to actually run. Despite the fact that this was an assault against an enemy fortification, they moved as if they were carrying the County Magistrate's chair through the countryside. As soon as they reached the wall, they leaned the ladder up against it, and still there was no sign of defenders; the Magistrate was prepared to thank his lucky stars. Now that the ladder was ready, the bearers steadied it for their comrades, who began climbing with their fowling pieces and their bows and arrows. Three men were on the ladder, the first having just about reached the top of the wall, when the heads of Boxers in red kerchiefs appeared on the other side; they dumped full pots of steaming porridge onto the county militiamen. The screams were like stakes driven into the Magistrate's heart. At any minute, he felt, the accumulated filth in his colon would empty into his trousers, and he had to bite down on his lower lip to hold it in. He watched as his men fell backward into their comrades, who had already begun beating a chaotic, panicky retreat to the raucous delight of the Boxers on the wall. But then a regimental bugler gave a signal to the better-trained Imperial Right Guards, who shouldered their rifles and opened fire on the fortified wall.

After watching the defenders repel the first assault on their fortification by the Imperial Right Guard with boiling water, hot porridge, homemade bombs, bricks, roof tiles, and rocks, even a couple of powerful and enormous local cannons, the Magistrate began to wonder if he had underestimated Sun Bing. Up till then, Sun had impressed him merely as a self-styled mystic; he had never entertained the thought that the man might actually be a military genius. Performing onstage had given him the same knowledge the Magistrate had acquired through extensive reading, and not just in military theories, but in practical applications that produced results. The Magistrate was comforted to see the mighty Imperial Right Guard suffer the same setback as his own rag-tag militia; it was the sort of outcome he could almost revel in. As his anxieties vanished, they were replaced by resurgent courage and self-confidence. But now it was time for the Germans. He glanced at von Ketteler, who was training his field glasses on the fortified wall, blocking a view of his face, except for his cheeks, which were twitching. Not only had his soldiers, who had taken up positions behind the Imperial Right Guard, not mounted an assault, they had actually moved far back to the rear. Something was in the works. Von Ketteler lowered his field glasses and faced the scene with a smile of contempt before turning to his artillerymen and shouting a command. The stick figures leaped into action, and in a matter of seconds a dozen cannon shells screamed overhead on their way to the fortification, like a formation of crows, sending geysers of white smoke into the air on both sides of the wall, followed by deafening explosions. The Magistrate saw shells make direct hits on the wall itself, shattering bricks and tiles and flinging the shards high into the air, mixed here and there with human body parts. Another volley pounded eardrums, and this time many more body parts flew through the air. Howls of pain and anguish rose from behind the wall, whose pine gateway had been reduced to rubble. At this point, von Ketteler waved a red flag handed to him by his adjutant, a sign to his foot soldiers to begin the assault on the gateway's yawning gap, rifles at the ready, battle cries on their lips, long legs striding forward. The Imperial Right Guard, having regrouped, launched their assault from a different direction, leaving behind the Magistrate's wounded militiamen, who lay in a depression in the ground and wept piteously. The Magistrate's mind was in a state of shock; this time, he knew, Masang Township was doomed, and a bloodbath awaited its thousands of residents. The most prosperous township in all of Gaomi County would simply cease to exist. In the face of German swagger, the Magistrate's love for the common man was reborn, although he knew that the situation had deteriorated to the point where he was helpless to alter the outcome. Even if the Emperor himself made an appearance, He would be unable to halt the Germans, for whom total victory was assured. Symbolically, he now stood with the citizens behind the fortification, and he fervently hoped that they might escape with their lives, heading south before the enemy soldiers entered town. They would, of course, be forced to cross the Masang River, but villagers who live near water know how to swim. There was, he knew, a squad of Imperial Right Guardsmen lying in ambush on the southern bank of the river, but he was confident that many of the villagers would be taken to safety downriver. The Guardsmen would not fire on women and children as they crossed the river, he assumed; they were, after all, Chinese.

But events did not unfold as the Magistrate expected. The German soldiers disappeared from sight after passing through the gateway opening. A cloud of smoke and dust was followed by howls in German, and the Magistrate knew at once that the clever and resourceful Sun Bing had set a trap by digging a deep pit just inside the gate. The look on von Ketteler's face said it all as he frantically waved his flag as a signal for his men to fall back. The German soldiers' lives were what counted, and von Ketteler's plan, which had called for victory without the loss of a single man, had failed. He was certain to order a second bombardment by his artillerymen, who had been given enough shells to turn the town into a wasteland. The Magistrate would be fooling himself if he believed that this battle would result in anything but a German victory. As expected, von Ketteler turned to the commander of his artillery unit and shouted a command, just as the outline of an idea in the Magistrate's mind was suddenly transformed into a bold plan of action. He turned to von Ketteler's interpreter.

"Ask von Ketteler to hold off. I have something important to say to him."

The interpreter did as he was told, and von Ketteler honored the request. Suddenly two pairs of eyes were fixed on the County Magistrate: the Plenipotentiary's deep green eyes and those of Ma Longbiao, whose expression was one of dejection.

"There is a popular adage, sir, that goes, 'If you want to defeat an enemy, first go after his king.' The commoners in town are under a spell woven by Sun Bing. That is the only thing that would have led them to do battle with your honorable soldiers. Sun Bing is the sole culprit in this episode. As long as we capture him and punish him severely—in effect, execute him as a warning to the masses—there will be no more vandalism against the railroad, and you will have carried out your assignment. It is my understanding that you have come to China in search of riches, not to subject the people of either nation to bloodshed. If what I say strikes you as reasonable, I offer my services to enter the town and convince Sun Bing to give himself up."

"Are you sure you don't plan to go in there for the purpose of cooking up a new strategy with Sun Bing?" The interpreter was kept busy interpreting for both men.

"I am an official representative of the Great Qing Court. My family is still in the county yamen," the Magistrate replied. "The reason I am willing to put my life on the line is to spare your men from injury or worse. They have crossed a vast ocean to be here, and each of their lives is of great value. If large numbers of them were to be killed or wounded, the Kaiser would not reward you for a job well done, I believe."

"I will agree if Ma Longbiao stays behind as your guarantor," the interpreter said.

"Elder Brother Qian," Ma said, his heavy-hearted tone unmistakable, "I know what you have in mind. But if unruly people inside . . ."

"Commander Ma," the Magistrate said, "I am fifty percent sure of success. I cannot stand by and watch one of the county's most flourishing towns be leveled by these foreigners and, even worse, see my people cut down for no good reason."

"If you manage to enter town and convince Sun Bing to surrender," Ma Longbiao said earnestly, "keeping our Imperial forces from harm while also protecting the lives of countless civilians, I will personally testify to your achievement to Excellency Yuan himself."

"We have reached the point where I can lay no claim to any achievements," the Magistrate replied. "I only hope that I do not make matters worse. Please get an assurance from von Ketteler that once I bring Sun Bing out, he will withdraw his forces."

"You can trust me on that," Ma Longbiao said as he took out a new pistol he was carrying and handed it to the Magistrate. "Elder Brother Qian," he said, "keep this with you, just in case."

The Magistrate waved the gesture off. "In the name of all the inhabitants of the town, I ask Elder Brother Ma to see that von Ketteler does not fire his cannons." With that, he mounted his horse and headed for the open gateway.

"I am the Magistrate of Gaomi County," he called out. "A friend of your commander. I need to speak with him. It is of the utmost importance!"

5

The Magistrate rode unimpeded into town, where he gave the trap a wide berth, but not before looking down into the pit, where a dozen or more German soldiers were struggling and screaming in pain. The floor of the pit, which was at least ten feet deep, was lined with pointed bamboo and metal spikes; some of the trapped Germans were already dead, while others had suffered grievous wounds and lay there like frogs on a spit. The stench rising out of the pit was proof that Sun Bing, not content merely to line the bottom of his trap with sharp objects, had dumped in a layer of excrement as well. That reminded the Magistrate of the time, decades earlier, when the foreigners had first come to China, and a certain frontier ambassador had petitioned the Emperor with a plan for dealing with them: the foreigners, he said, were obsessed with cleanliness and sanitation, and anything to do with bodily waste horrified them. So, he suggested, if each imperial soldier carried a bucket of shit into battle, all he had to do was spread his filth on the ground to send the enemy fleeing in disgust, holding their noses and maybe even vomiting until they died. The Xianfeng Emperor was said to have enthusiastically approved what He considered to be an especially creative suggestion, since it not only had the potential to vanquish this new enemy, but required a minimum of expense. The Magistrate's wife had told him this, treating it as a joke, and he had had a good laugh over it. Never in his wildest imagination would he have thought that Sun Bing would employ that very method, with a bit of modification, a military tactic that had all the characteristics of a practical joke; he did not know whether to laugh or to cry. In point of fact, in the wake of the farcical hostage exchange of the previous day, the Magistrate had gained an understanding of Sun Bing's approach to military tactics. Juvenile, to be sure, the stuff of children's games, and yet, contrary to all expectations, they made people stop and think, as more often than not they proved effective. As he rode past the pit, the Magistrate also saw a good many dead and dying Boxers on both sides of the fortification, as well as smashed porridge pots whose steamy contents lay in pools of blood. The wounded were voicing their agony. Red-kerchiefed Boxers, as well as women and children, were running headlong up and down the street on which he had traveled not so long before. For all practical purposes, the town had been laid waste, the Magistrate concluded. The Germans could take it almost without a fight, and this realization underscored his sense of self-worth. By sacrificing Sun Bing, one man, he could save thousands. Sun Bing had to be delivered, at all costs. If persuasion failed, force would have to have to be employed. Even though he had refused Ma Longbiao's offer of a pistol, the Magistrate was confident that Sun Bing was no match for him. He had such a deep sense of valor and solemnity that he could all but hear drums and horns heralding his arrival. Spurring his horse into a gallop, he flew down the street, heading straight for the mat shed that stood at the bend in the river, where he would find Sun Bing.

There he saw hundreds of Boxers down in the dry riverbed ingesting Taoist charms. Using both hands, each man held a bowl in which paper ashes were mixed with water. Sun Bing, the man he sought, stood atop a pile of bricks and filled the air with a loud incantation. His primary outside help, the Caozhou Righteous Harmony Boxer Sun Wukong, was nowhere to be seen; the second-in-command, Zhu Bajie, was demonstrating martial skills with his rake to lend an impressive air to Sun's ritual. The Magistrate slid down off his horse and walked up to the brick pile, where he kicked over the incense altar in front of Sun Bing.

"Sun Bing," he said loudly, "how can you continue to beguile and bewitch your followers when rivers of your men's blood already flow across the fortification?"

When Sun Bing's bodyguards rushed up from behind, the Magistrate quickly moved around Sun, took a glistening dagger from his sleeve, and placed the point in a spot directly behind Sun's heart.

"Do not move!" he commanded.

"You dog of an official!" Sun Bing hissed. "Once again you have broken my boxing magic! I am iron head, iron waist, iron body, impervious to bullets, resistant to water and fire!"

"Fellow townsmen, go take a look at the fortification, then tell me if flesh and blood can stand up to cannon shells!" He chose this moment to make a bold assumption: "There you will even find the mangled body of your finest warrior, the mighty Sun Wukong!"

"You lie!" Sun Bing screamed.

"Sun Bing," the Magistrate said callously, "have you really mastered the art of resisting knives and spears?"

"Nothing can penetrate my body, not even shells fired by those dog soldiers!"

The Magistrate bent down, picked up a brick, and struck it against Sun Bing's forehead before he had time to react. Sun fell backward, but the Magistrate caught him by the collar and held him up.

"Now show these people your indestructible body!"

Dark blood snaked down from Sun Bing's forehead, like worms squirming across his face. Zhu Bajie swung his rake at the Magistrate, who jumped out of the way and flung his dagger; it stuck in Zhu's abdomen, sending him tumbling off the brick pile with agonizing screams.

"Have you seen enough, fellow townsmen? These are your altar master and one of his senior aides. If they have failed to withstand even the modest brick-and-dagger efforts of a local official, how are they going to repel enemy cannon fire?"

The adherents' confidence was shaken, to which the buzzing below the platform bore irrefutable witness.

"Sun Bing," the Magistrate said, "as a man of valor, you must not send these people to certain death just to satisfy a personal desire. I have secured a promise from the German Plenipotentiary that he will withdraw his troops if you surrender to him. You have already accomplished something so astonishing it has captured the attention of the whole world, and if you are willing to sacrifice yourself in order to keep your fellow townsmen from harm, your legacy will live forever!"

"Heaven's will!" Sun Bing said with a sigh. "It is heaven's will." Then he began to sing: "*Ceding territory and vanquished by the Jin~~I forsake the Central Plain and abandon the common people, a decade of exploits squandered in a single day~~Humiliated, we sue for peace, remorse follows an overturned nest~~I fear the whale will swallow our land away. Do not falsely consign me to confinement with no end, for when I am gone, the Yue army will stay~~* Fellow countrymen, disperse!"

The Magistrate led Sun Bing down from the brick pile, taking advantage of the chaos below to head to the township's main gate. He forgot that he had come on horseback.

6

As he single-handedly brought Sun Bing out of Masang Township, the Magistrate was bursting with a sense of his own valor. What happened next dealt him a crippling blow, causing anguish over the knowledge that he had made yet another imbecilic mistake, this one far worse than the humiliating hostage exchange. Instead of withdrawing his troops, as he had promised, von Ketteler ordered the artillery commander to open fire the moment the Magistrate and Sun Bing were standing before him—with a roar, twelve cannons sent deadly shells flying past the defenses. Explosions erupted all over town, sending flames and smoke into the air. The screams of dying townspeople raised a terrible cacophony as an enraged Sun Bing spun around and began throttling the Magistrate, who put up no resistance, welcoming the death he felt he deserved. But Ma Longbiao signaled his guards to pull Sun Bing away and save his colleague's life. County Magistrate Qian Ding closed his eyes as Sun Bing railed against him. Though he was lightheaded, he heard the clamor of the German attack, and he knew that Gaomi County's most prosperous township had ceased to exist. Who had caused that to happen? Sun Bing, perhaps, or the Germans. Or maybe he himself.

BOOK THREE

Tail of the Leopard

CHAPTER FOURTEEN

Zhao Jia's Soliloquy

I am Zhao Jia, preeminent executioner in the Board of Punishments for more than forty years, a period during which I lopped off more heads than I can count, a wagon or a boatload at least. In my sixtieth year, thanks to the grace of the Empress Dowager, I was permitted to return home in retirement with a grade seven official rank medallion for my cap. At first I planned to conceal my identity in a butcher's home in a humble lane in this little town, to engage in moral cultivation, conserve my nature, and live out my allotted time, from duties released. What spoiled my plan was my qinjia, Sun Bing, who beguiled the local throngs, hoisted the flag of rebellion, and, by running afoul of the nation's laws, ignited armed conflict with the alien beast. To unnerve unruly subjects and preserve discipline and the rule of law, the Shandong Governor, Excellency Yuan, invited me out of retirement to inflict the sandalwood death. A popular adage has it that "A scholar will die for a true friend, a bird will sing for an admirer." So as to repay a debt of gratitude to Excellency Yuan, I picked up the knife again, my burden increased. Truly a case of:

In the early morning my hand burned as if it held hot cinders, and I knew that heavy responsibilities awaited my shoulders. (ya-ya-wei) The self-important Magistrate of Gaomi County, Qian Ding, felt that I, Zhao Jia, was unworthy of his attention (wei-ya-ya), yet a gift from the Emperor had him groveling at my feet. (ha-ha ha-ha) As they say, People are spirited when good things happen, a triumphant general has a broad view of the world. (ya-ya-ah-wei) I lost two of my teeth, for which Qian Ding's right to an official's cap has ceased. Old Zhao Jia sits in front of his house, wind in his face, as grumbling yayi carry favored objects, item by case by basket by chest, into my yard, north, south, west, and east.

—*Maoqiang* Sandalwood Death. *Soliloquy and nonsense*

1

The chief yamen attendant, Song Three, only yesterday a browbeating toady who took advantage of his favored position, a universally feared man whom people called Third Master, today stood at my door with an ingratiating smile. A petty servant who only the day before had stood tall and proud was now bent nearly double. You young men, in more than forty years, there is nothing I did not see in the capital, men and affairs, and I tell you that shitty little functionaries are all like that. If one from this county were to be the exception, then Gaomi would be outside the Great Qing Empire's sphere of influence. He bowed deeply at my door and sputtered:

"Old . . . old . . . sir, if it please you, shall we carry in what you requested?"

I curled my lip and smiled inwardly. I knew that the "old" dripping from that dog's mouth was intended to be followed by "master," but clearly I was not his master. I think he wanted to be familiar by calling me Old Zhao, but I was sitting in a chair bestowed upon me by the Emperor Himself. Having no choice, he had to settle for "old sir." A wily son of a bitch. With an almost imperceptible wave of my hand, I said, "Bring everything in."

Mimicking a stage voice, he announced loudly:

"Bring the old gentleman's things inside!"

Like a line of black ants, the yayi entered the compound carrying everything I had requested from Excellency Yuan. Each item was presented at the door for my approval:

A purple sandalwood stake five feet long and five fen wide, like the metal spike used by the Tang general Qin Shubao. The absolutely indispensable item.

A large white rooster with a black comb, legs tied with a strip of red cloth, which lay in the arms of a fair-faced yayi like a bawling, unhappy baby boy. A rare breed, one of which they had managed to find somewhere in Gaomi County.

New leather straps that still gave off the pungent smell of tanning salt, light blue in color, as if grass-stained.

Two wooden mallets with a reddish luster that had been used in an oil mill as far back, perhaps, as the reign of the Kangxi Emperor, two centuries before. Made from date-wood knots and in constant contact with oil, they had by now drunk their fill and were heavier than their metal counterparts. But they were nonetheless wood and not metal, and thus more yielding. Hardness with a bit of give was what I had specified.

Two extra-large baskets, each filled with a hundred jin of the finest white rice. The unique fragrance and blue tinge were proof that it had come from

Tengzhou Prefecture, which produced rice of a quality unmatched anywhere in Gaomi County.

Two hundred jin of flour packed in four gunnysacks stamped with the Tonghe Refined Flour Mill trademark.

A basket of red-shelled eggs, one of which, a first egg, was stained by real blood. Just seeing it evoked the image of a little red-faced hen straining to lay her first egg.

A sizeable cut of beef on a large platter, the sinews in the meat seemingly still vibrating.

An enormous cauldron, carried by two men, big enough to cook a whole cow.

Song Three was carrying half a jin of ginseng under his clothes. He took it out and handed it to me. Even through the paper wrapper, the bitter smell of fine ginseng was strong.

"Old sir," Song Three said as his face lit up, "your humble servant personally visited the herbal shop and kept his eye on Qin Seven, that wily old fox, as he opened a catalpa cabinet with three locks and selected this ginseng from a blue and white porcelain jar. 'If it's not the real thing,' he said, 'you can twist my head right off my shoulders.' This is prized ginseng. Just by carrying it next to me this little while and smelling its fragrance, your humble servant grew light on his feet, sharp-eyed and clear-headed; I felt like I was becoming an immortal. Just think what eating it could do!"

I peeled back the paper wrapping and counted the gnarled brown roots whose necks were tied together with a red string: one, two, three . . . five . . . eight altogether, each as thick as a chopstick at the top and as thin as a bean stalk at the end, from which a beard of fine hairs fluttered in the slightest breeze. Half a jin? I don't believe it. I gave the man a cold glare. Well, the bastard bent at the waist and, with an unctuous smile, said softly:

"Nothing gets past the gentleman's eyes. These eight roots only weigh four liang, not eight, but that is all Qin Seven had in his shop. He said you could boil them in water, pour the liquid into a dead man's mouth, and he'd jump out of his coffin—do you think, sir . . ."

I waved him off without saying a word. What was I supposed to say? Chief yayi like him are craftier than demons and sneakier than a monkey. He got down on one knee to pay his respects. That, he thought, made up for the shortage. The swine was getting away with at least fifty liang of silver from the ginseng alone. But then he took a small chunk of silver out from under his clothes and said:

"This, old squire, is what your humble servant was given to buy pork, but it occurred to me that one does not fertilize another's field, and since you have someone here in your home who slaughters pigs, why go elsewhere? This should be yours."

Now, I knew that this little bit of silver was worth far less than what he had skimmed from the ginseng, but I thanked him anyway. "You put a great deal of thought into this," I said, "so take the silver and divide it among your fellow yayi as a little bonus."

"We thank the old squire!" He bowed again, as did the men who had come with him.

Money talks! A tiny bit of silver had that bastard calling me "old squire" instead of the vapid "sir." If I'd given him a gold ingot, he'd be down on all fours, banging his head on the ground and calling me Daddy! Again I waved my hand, this time for him to get up, and without a trace of emotion, as if commanding a dog, said: "Go now. You and your men take all these things to the execution site, where you are to set up a big cook stove. Dump the sesame oil into the cauldron, fill the belly of the stove with kindling, and light it. Then set up a smaller stove for stewing the beef. After that, put up a mat shed near the stoves, place a vat inside, and fill it with water—be sure it's fresh drinking water. And ready an earthen pot for herbal medicine along with a hollow horn used to medicate livestock. Carpet the ground in the shed with a thick layer of this year's dry wheat straw. Then I want you personally to carry in my chair— you know its background, I take it. That master of yours and the Provincial Governor, Excellency Yuan, both got down on their knees and performed the rite of three bows and nine kowtows in front of it, so be very careful. If you so much as knock off a chip of paint, Excellency Yuan will skin you like a dog. Everything I've told you must be ready precisely at noon. If you are missing anything, go see your laoye." The man bowed and proclaimed loudly:

"It will be as you say, Laoye."

After they left, I checked off the remaining objects in the yard again: the sandalwood stake—the single most important item—would require much painstaking work, but nothing I would let those bastards watch, not with their unclean eyes, for that would spoil the effect. Nor would I let them hold the rooster, not with their dirty hands, for that would sap its power. I shut the gate; two armed yayi were posted to keep people out. Apparently our Magistrate Qian had seen to everything. Of course, I knew it was all for Excellency Yuan's benefit. Oh, how he hated me, but my gums still bled from losing two teeth, and to teach the dog a lesson I needed to let him know who he was dealing with. I must not demean myself. I was not putting on airs or throwing my weight around, flaunting the fact that I had been favored by gifts from the Empress Dowager and the Emperor. And this assuredly was not a case of abusing public power to avenge a personal slight. It was a matter of national honor.

Since I had been chosen to end the life of a man whose shocking criminal acts had gained worldwide attention, an extravagant display was both proper and necessary. The extravagance would belong not to me, but to the Great Qing Empire. Being laughed at by foreigners could not be tolerated.

Damn you, von Ketteler, I know you Europeans have used wooden stakes on people, but that is simply nailing someone to a crossbar and leaving him to die. I am going to let you see what a real punishment is like, one that is so exquisite, so refined, that the name alone reveals its resounding elegance: *sandal—wood—death*, a term with a rough exterior but an aesthetic core, displaying the patina and aura of antiquity. It is a form of punishment beyond the imagination of any European. Out on the street, my neighbors, all hopelessly rustic and short-sighted, craned their necks to get a peek into my yard. The looks on their faces revealed envy and admiration. Attracted by wealth, they were blind to the dangers that lay behind it, and my son was no less wooly-headed than they, though his muddled mind had its endearing qualities. Hearing my shifu tell how he had dismembered the woman with skin like pure snow had brought an end to my sexual life. Not even the lascivious women of the capital's infamous Eight Lanes, who oozed lust, had the power to arouse me. At some point—when I cannot say—my beard stopped growing, and I was reminded of Grandma Yu: "My sons," he said, "people in our profession are like palace eunuchs: Their potency has been excised with a knife, but their desire lives on. Our physical maleness remains intact, but our hearts have been purged of desire." Grandma Yu said that when the day comes that the sight of a woman has no effect on you, when even the thought does not cross your mind, you are on the verge of becoming a totally accomplished executioner. Some decades ago, when I came home from an assignment and went to bed, a hint of potency remained, and I somehow sired a foolish but not totally worthless offspring, something hard to imagine, on the order of producing a stalk of sorghum from a fried seed. The reason I tried so hard to retire and return to my native home was that I had a son to return to, someone I wanted to train to become the Great Qing Empire's next preeminent executioner. The Empress Dowager Herself once said that every profession has its zhuangyuan. I was one, and my son would follow in my footsteps. My daughter-in-law was a spirited woman who kept Qian Ding's bed warm and subjected me to humiliation. But heaven has eyes, and saw to it that my qinjia fell into my hands. I laughed as I said to her: "Daughter-in-law, I must show him some favor, since we are related. All these things you see here are for him."

She glared at me, eyes wide open, mouth agape, face pale with fright, unable to say a word in response. My son, who was crouching in front of the rooster, cackled as he asked:

"Will we be able to keep this rooster, Dieh?"

"Yes, we can keep it."

"How about all this rice and flour and meat?"

"Yes, we can keep it all."

"Ha-ha . . ."

He laughed happily. That son of mine may have looked like a fool, but knowing the value of good things kept him from being one. "All this will be ours to keep, son, but we have a job to do for the nation. Tomorrow at this time will be our moment to shine."

"Are you really going to kill my dieh?" my daughter-in-law asked piteously. A face that had always been radiant and sleek seemed suddenly covered by a coat of rust.

"That is his good fortune!"

"How do you plan to kill him?"

"With a sandalwood stake."

"Swine . . ." Her shouts were eerie. "You bastard . . ."

She yanked open the gate and burst out of the compound, swaying her hips.

I sent the crazed young woman off with a resounding comment: "Dear daughter-in-law, I am going to see that your dieh's name will live forever, that his legend will become the stuff of grand opera, just you wait and see!"

2

I told my son to shut the gate as I placed the length of sandalwood on top of the flesh-and-blood-stained slaughtering rack, and had him fetch a saw, which I used to cut the wood in two lengthwise. Saw teeth biting into the wood produced the harsh, ear-piercing sound of metal on metal; sparks flew from the blade, which was too hot to touch, and a strange burning odor assailed my nose. Picking up a plane, I then painstakingly shaved the two halves into stakes with blunted tips and tapered edges, slightly rounded, like the leaves of a chive plant. Once that was done, I used sandpaper, coarse at first, then fine, turning the stakes over and over as I worked, until they shone like mirrors. True, I had never carried out a sandalwood execution, but I knew instinctively that success in this epochal event lay in the quality of the instrument. A job of this magnitude required meticulous preparation, something I had learned from Grandma Yu. The sanding alone took me half the day—a sharp ax makes the best kindling, or, as the adage goes, "The best work requires the finest tools." I had no sooner sanded the two treasures to perfection than a yayi knocked at the gate to report that Gaomi County Magistrate Qian Ding's workers had erected something called an Ascension Platform on the parade ground in front of the Tongde Academy in the center of town, one that adhered to my specifications and was sure to become the stuff of legend for a century or more. The mat shed I had requested was also in place, and sesame oil was churning in the large cauldron, while beef stewed in its smaller companion. I sniffed the air, and there it was, the heavy fragrance of sesame oil and meat carried on the autumn wind.

After running out early in the morning, my son's wife still had not returned. I could understand what was troubling her—it was, after all, her dieh who was to be executed, and she had to be experiencing emotional, even physical, pain because of it. But where could she have gone? To plead her case with her gandieh, Magistrate Qian? Maybe, but my dear daughter-in-law, your gandieh is like a clay bodhisattva who must worry about its own survival while crossing the river. I do not intend to curse him by predicting that the day your dieh breathes his last will also see his downfall.

I changed into a new set of official clothes: a black robe cinched with a red sash, a red felt cap with red tassels, and black leather boots. There is truth in the adage that "People are known by their clothes, horses by their saddles." With new clothes, I was no longer an ordinary man. With a grin, my son asked me:

"What are we going to do, Dieh, sing Maoqiang opera?"

Maoqiang? Songs from your idiotic dog opera, maybe! I cursed inwardly. Talking to him was a waste of time, so I simply told him to get out of his greasy clothes, which were stained with pig fat and dog blood. Guess what he said to me.

"Close your eyes, Dieh, don't look. That's what she tells me to do when she changes clothes."

Keeping my eyes slitted, I watched him take off his clothes. He had a coarse, ugly body, and that thing drooping above his scrotum was an obviously useless appendage.

Yet in his high-topped, soft-soled black leather boots, red waist sash, and red-tasseled cap, his size gave him a formidable, martial appearance. But then he made a face, tugged at his ear, and scratched his cheek, and he was just another monkey in human form.

With the two stakes over my shoulders, I told him to pick up the rooster and follow me out the gate on our way to the Tongde Academy. The streets were lined with would-be spectators, men and women, young and old, all standing wide-eyed and open-mouthed, like fish sucking air above water. With my head up and my chest thrown out, I appeared to be oblivious to their presence, though in fact I saw everything out of the corner of my eye. My son, on the other hand, kept looking right and left and greeting the crowds with a foolish grin, as the rooster struggled to get free, squawking frantically. The dull-witted people gaped as we passed. Xiaojia was stupid, all right, but the people were worse. The show hasn't even begun, you clods, and if that's how you look now, what are you going to be like tomorrow during the grand performance? It's your good fortune to have a man like me in your midst. The finest play ever staged cannot compete with the spectacle of an execution, and no execution on earth can begin to compare with the sandalwood death. And where in China will you find another executioner talented enough to kill a man with it? With me in your midst, you will be treated to a show the likes of which no one has ever seen, nor likely ever will again. If that is not good fortune, what is? I ask you, if that is not good fortune, what is?

Old Zhao Jia walks with his stakes and says with respect to the gathered fold, I carry the law of the nation in my arms; it is weightier than gold. I call out to my son to pick up the pace and stop gawking like a fool. Tomorrow we will show them who we are, like carp transformed into dragons so bold. Three steps instead of two, two steps outpacing one, strides faster than a shooting star—the Tongde Academy awaits.

We look up, ahead is the parade ground, flat and even, its sand white and cold. An opera stage on one side, where Pear Garden actors will come to play. Kings and princes, generals and ministers, heroes and warriors, scholars and beauties, three religions and nine schools of thought . . . all brought together like a running-horse lantern of old.

There, in front of the stage, the County Magistrate has erected an Ascension Platform, fronted by soldiers, our presence to behold. Black and red batons on the shoulders of some, broadswords in the hands of others. In front of the platform, a mat shed secured with rush rises behind a cauldron in which sesame oil churns. Fellow countrymen, the grand opera is about to begin, the story to be told!

3

I tied the rooster to a shed post. The creature cocked its head and looked up at me, its eyes the color of yellow gold, sparkling and blinding bright. I turned to my son. "Xiaojia," I said, "knead some dough with fresh water." He cocked his head to look at me, gawking like the rooster.

"What for?"

"Do as I say, and don't ask questions."

I studied the shed while he was kneading the dough. The front was open, the back closed. It stood opposite the opera stage. Perfect, just the way I wanted it. The floor was laid well enough, with a gold-colored rush mat on top of the noisy layer of wheat stalks. New wheat, new rush, both exuding a fresh aroma.

My sandalwood chair had been placed in the center of the tent, enticing my backside to sit in it. I went first to the cauldron, where I dropped the two spear-shaped stakes into the fragrant oil. They sank straight to the bottom, with only the squared-off butt ends floating to the top and breaking the surface. Ideally they should cook for three days and nights, but I did not have three days. A day and a night would work, since sandalwood this smooth would soak up little blood even without being cooked in oil. Fate has smiled on you, Qinjia, by allowing this to be the instrument of your death. I sat in my chair and looked up at the red sun setting in the west, ushering in dusk. The Ascension Platform, built of thick red pine, had a gloomy appearance in the twilight and exuded the aura of death, like a great frowning idol. I could not fault the County Magistrate's preparations; the platform, encircled in mist and hooded by somber clouds, fairly epitomized the solemnity of the occasion. Magistrate Qian, you should take your rightful place in the Board of Public Works as a supervisor of grand projects. Your talents are hopelessly stifled in piddling little Gaomi County. Sun Bing, Qinjia, you too are one of Northeast Gaomi Township's outstanding individuals, and though I do not like you, I cannot deny that you are a dragon among men, or perhaps a phoenix; it would be a crime for you not to die in spectacular fashion. Anything less than the sandalwood death, and this Ascension Platform would not be worthy of you. Sun Bing, your cultivation in a previous life has brought you the good fortune of falling into my hands, for I will immortalize your name and make you a hero for the ages.

"Dieh," my son said excitedly from behind me with a platter of dough the size of a millstone, "the dough is ready."

Believe it or not, he had used up the entire sack of flour. But no harm done, since we would expend a great deal of energy tomorrow, and would need plenty of nourishment to get through the day. I twisted off a chunk of dough, rolled it between my hands, and pulled it into a long strip, which I dropped into the oil. It rolled and twisted in the churning oil like an eel fighting to stay alive. With a clap of his hands, my son jumped up and down.

"Fried fritter!" he shouted. "It's a fried fritter!"

Together we dumped a steady stream of dough twists into the oil. They sank to the bottom, but quickly floated to the top and tumbled in the space between the sandalwood spears. I was frying them in the same oil so the essence of grain would attach to the wood. I knew that these stakes would enter Sun Bing's grain passage and travel up through his body, and that the grain coating would be beneficial. The aroma of frying fritters spread—they were done, so I fished them out with a pair of tongs. "Eat one, son." With his back to the mat shed, he started in on the lip-burning fritter; his bulging cheeks showed how happy he was. I picked one up and took a bite, slowly savoring its unique sandalwood taste and its Buddhist aura. I had stopped eating meat after receiving the string of prayer beads from the Old Buddha Herself. Kindling blazing beneath the stove crackled and spit; the oil in the cauldron bubbled and popped. After eating several of the fritters, I went to work cutting the slab of beef into fist-sized chunks and tossing them into the oil. I did that so the essence of meat would overlay that of grain and soften the wood even more. All this I was doing for Qinjia! My son moved up close and muttered:

"I want some meat, Dieh."

"Son," I said affectionately, "this is not for us. In a while you can have some from the small cauldron. Once the punishment is administered to your Mao-qiang-singing gongdieh, you can eat the meat and he'll drink the broth."

Just then the crafty chief yamen attendant, Song Three, came up and asked what I wanted him to do next, slavishly bowing and scraping as if I were a powerful official. Naturally, I had to assume the proper air, so I coughed importantly and said:

"Nothing more. Preparing the stakes is all there is to do today, and that is my job, not yours, so you may leave and do whatever you are supposed to do."

"Your humble servant may not leave." The words slithered out of his oily mouth like loaches. "We dare not leave."

"Has His Eminence your master the County Magistrate told you to stay?"

"Not His Eminence, but His Excellency Governor Yuan, who ordered us to stay for your protection. You have become a living treasure, sir."

He stuck out his paw, picked up an oil fritter, and stuffed it into his mouth. As I stared at his greasy lips, I said silently: I am not the treasure, you bastards; it is that which I carry with me. I reached under my clothes and took out the sandalwood prayer beads given to me by the wise and august Empress Dowager Cixi, and began fingering them, closing my eyes and striking the calming pose of a meditating monk to keep those bastards from knowing what was on my mind. I could have crushed them into pulp without their ever guessing what I was thinking.

———

4

———

*Old Zhao Jia sits by the shed, his state of mind a mass of tangles. (What
are you thinking, Dieh?) Images of earlier days float past his eyes from all
angles. (What images?) The benevolent Yuan Shikai had not forgotten his
old friend, and that is how father and son have reached this day. (What day
is this?)*

—Maoqiang Sandalwood Death. *A father and son duet*

After completing the slicing death on the brave Qian Xiongfei, I picked up my
tools and, along with my apprentices, planned to return overnight to Peking.
People say that one should avoid crowded, hectic places and not linger where
disputes arise. With our belongings on our backs, we were about to set out
when our way was blocked by one of Excellency Yuan's most loyal retainers, a
fierce-looking man who gazed up into the sky and said:

"Do not leave, Slay-master. Excellency Yuan wants to see you."

After getting my apprentices settled in a tiny inn, I fell in behind the retainer.
We passed through a series of sentry posts before I was kneeling in front of
Excellency Yuan. Sweat dripped from my back, and I was out of breath. I
banged my head loudly on the floor, managing between kowtows to sneak a
look at his corpulent image. Over the previous twenty-three years, as I well
knew, thousands of high officials and talented individuals had passed in front
of the great man's eyes like a running-horse lantern, so what chance was there
that he would remember someone as insignificant as me? But I remembered
him, remembered him well. Twenty-three years earlier, as a handsome young
man who could not even grow a moustache, he had spent much of his time in
the yamen with his uncle, Yuan Baoheng, Vice President of the Board of Punishments. Bristling at his enforced idleness, he had come to the Eastern Compound, where we executioners lived, and struck up a conversation with me.
Excellency, you were fascinated by our profession—putting people to death—
and said to Grandma Yu, who was still healthy and active, "Take me on as
your apprentice, Grandma!" Seized with terror at the request, Grandma Yu
said, "Young scion, are you toying with us?" With a straight face, Excellency,
you replied, "I am serious. Great men appear in chaotic times, and if the seal of
authority is beyond their reach, the knife is not!"

"You did your job well, Grandma Zhao." The great man's comment brought
my reveries to an abrupt end. His words seemed to come from the depths of a
bell, like deeply moving chimes.

I admit that I had carried out my duty in a manner that did nothing to undermine the Board of Punishment's reputation, and I was confident that I was the only person in the Great Qing Empire who could have performed the slicing death to such a high standard. But that was not the attitude I could assume in the presence of Excellency Yuan. I might be a man of little importance, but I knew that Excellency Yuan, who commanded an elite modern army, was a prominent figure in the Imperial Court. "It was not an effort I can be proud of," I said humbly, "and I can only beg forgiveness for disappointing Your Excellency."

"Grandma Zhao, you sound like an educated man."

"I respectfully confess that Excellency Yuan's humble servant can neither read nor write."

"I see," he said with a smile. Then he abruptly switched to his native Hunan dialect, as if swapping his official clothing for a jacket of homespun cloth: "If you raise a dog in an official yamen, in ten years it will speak like a classical scholar."

"A wise comment, Excellency. In the Board of Punishments I am a dog."

Excellency Yuan laughed lustily at my remark.

"Well spoken," he said once he had finished laughing. "It takes a good man to humble himself! You are a dog in the Board of Punishments, and I am a dog at the Imperial Court."

"Your humble servant does not deserve to be mentioned in the same breath as Your Excellency . . . gold-inlaid jade, while I am nothing but a cobblestone . . ."

"Zhao Jia, how shall I thank you for helping me accomplish something so important?"

"Your humble servant is a dog raised by the nation; Your Excellency is a pillar of the state, whom I am obliged to serve."

"I find nothing wrong in what you say, but I wish to reward you nonetheless." He turned to his attendant. "See Grandma Zhao off to the capital with a hundred liang of silver."

I got down on my knees and thanked him with a resounding kowtow.

"Your humble servant will never forget Excellency Yuan's generosity," I said, "but I cannot accept your gift of silver."

"Why is that?" he said coldly. "Is it too little?"

"Your humble servant has never in his life received a hundred liang of silver," I said after a second loud kowtow, "and I dare not take it now. By bestowing the honor of bringing me to Tianjin to carry out his orders, Excellency Yuan has enhanced my status in the Board of Punishments, and I fear that taking Excellency's silver could shorten my allotted time on earth.

Excellency Yuan grew pensive.

"Grandma Zhao," he said after a moment, "this was a difficult assignment."

Once again I responded first with a kowtow.

"Excellency, I was thrilled to do it. I am indeed fortunate to have had the opportunity to put my talents to work for the Imperial Court."

"What would you say if I asked you to stay on as a member of my criminal affairs unit, Zhao Jia?"

"I would not dare decline to be so favored by Your Excellency. I have worked in the Board of Punishments for more than forty years, and have put to death a total of nine hundred eighty-seven criminals, not counting those executions in which I assisted. I have been so favored by the nation that I should spare no effort to continue working until I am stopped by death or old age. But ever since the execution of Tan Sitong and his five fellow criminals, I have been bothered by a wrist that is sometimes so sore I cannot even use chopsticks. I have been hoping to return home and beg Your Excellency to seek permission from the Board of Punishments on my behalf."

He merely laughed grimly. I did not know what to make of that.

"Excellency, your humble servant deserves death. I am a low-class nobody who is unworthy of inclusion in any of the lower nine trades. I am a dog if I leave and a dog if I stay, and I have no business troubling any of my superiors. And yet I can boldly assert that while I am a man of demeaned status, the work I perform is not, and as such I am a symbol of national power. We are a nation with a thousand laws, but in the end it is I who enforce them. My apprentices and I have no annual stipend and no monthly wage, and must rely upon the sale of our victims' cured flesh as a medical restorative. I have accumulated no savings after more than forty years in the Board of Punishments. It is my hope that the Board will give me a settling-in allowance so that I will not have to wander the streets destitute. I venture to ask for fair treatment for my brethren in the profession by including executioners in the personnel ranks of the Board of Punishments with a monthly wage. I ask this not just for myself, but for all of us. As I see it, executioners will be indispensable for as long as the nation exists. This is a parlous age, with a host of criminals among official ranks and legions of robbers and bandits on the loose, the precise moment in time when skillful executioners are most in demand. With unforgivable audacity, I implore Excellency Yuan to grant this humble request."

I followed my bold statement with a series of resounding kowtows, then remained on my knees and waited with sly glimpses to see how he would react. He stroked his dark moustache, with the calm look of a man deep in thought. Suddenly he laughed.

"Grandma Zhao, there is more to you than a lethal hand. Your mouth is nearly as lethal!"

"I deserve death, but I have spoken the truth. Only because I know that Excellency is a man of great wisdom and uncommon magnanimity have I had the audacity to make the request."

"Zhao Jia," Excellency Yuan said, suddenly lowering his voice in an aura of mystery, "do you still recognize me?"

"For someone as impressive and dignified as His Excellency, a single glance can last a lifetime."

"I do not mean now; I am talking about twenty-three years ago, when my uncle was Left Vice President of the Board of Punishments and I was a frequent visitor to the yamen when I had some free time. You had not met me then, had you?"

With bad eyes and a poor memory, I truly had not known who he was. But I did know Yuan Baoheng, Excellency Yuan, who had bestowed favors on me at the time.

"Truth is, how could I not recognize such a distinguished appearance? Back then, Excellency Yuan, you were a mischievous youngster. Your uncle wanted you to take up studies and make your name as a civil service scholar. But you were not scholar material, and you never missed an opportunity to come to the Eastern Compound to spend time with us. Once you gained an understanding of our rules and traditions, you talked Grandma Yu into letting you put on a set of executioner's clothing without telling your uncle, then you smeared your smooth, round face with rooster blood and went with us to the marketplace for the execution of a criminal who had impudently hunted a rabbit near the Imperial Mausoleum and disturbed the sleep of deceased emperors. I pulled the criminal's queue to expose his neck while you raised your sword and, with no change of expression and a steady hand, needed but one chop to separate him from his head. When it was all over, your uncle learned what you had done and slapped you in front of us. We were so terrified we fell to our knees and banged our heads on the floor as if we were crushing cloves of garlic. 'You miserable wretch,' your uncle exploded, 'how dare you do something like that!' But you leaped to your own defense: 'Do not be angry, revered uncle; killing someone during a crime is a heinous offense, but killing someone who has committed a crime is an act of patriotism. Your unworthy nephew is determined to make his name on the battlefield, and the reason I assumed the appearance today was to fortify my courage for the future.' Your uncle continued to rage, but we all knew that he was looking at you with increased respect . . ."

"Old Zhao, you are too smart a man," a smiling Excellency Yuan said, "not to recognize me. You are afraid I will blame you for what happened. In truth,

I do not regard what happened as anything to be ashamed of. Back when I was studying with my uncle in the Board of Punishments, I read up on the executioner's trade and benefited greatly from it. Going with you to execute that criminal was a rare and unforgettable experience that has had a major impact on my life, and I have summoned you here today to thank you."

I responded with more kowtows and expressions of gratitude.

"Get up," Excellency Yuan said. "Go back to Peking and wait there, quite possibly for welcome news."

<hr>

5

A civil zhuangyuan, a military zhuangyuan, a civil and military zhuangyuan, for as they say, every profession has its zhuangyuan. I am the zhuangyuan of executioners. Son, the Empress Dowager Herself bestowed this designation on me, and the precious words that come out of Her mouth are not mere pleasantries.

—*Maoqiang* Sandalwood Death. *A father and son duet*

News of the Tianjin executions and the informal audience with Yuan Shikai created ripples of excitement in the Board of Punishments compound. My fellow tradesmen gave me curious looks, a mixture of envy and admiration. Even mid-level bureau officials, the various vice directors who came to work carrying their official clothing in a bundle, nodded silent greetings that told me that these graduates of the Imperial Examination had begun to see me in a different light. I would be lying if I said this displeased me, but I refused to let it go to my head. A lifetime in the yamen had taught me that the ocean is deeper than a pond and that flames are hotter than cinders. I did not have to be told that the tallest tree stands beneath the heavens, the tallest man is dwarfed by a mountain, and the brawniest slave obeys his master. On my second day back in the capital, the Board's Vice President, Excellency Tie, summoned me to his document room, where the Deputy Director of the Bureau of Detentions, Eminence Sun, was in attendance. Excellency Tie grilled me about the Tianjin executions, wanting to know even the smallest detail. I answered all his questions. He then asked about the New Army's military preparedness at Small Station, including a description of the soldiers' uniforms, even the colors. How was the weather there, what was the state of the Hai River . . . Finally, when there was nothing more to ask, he asked how Excellency Yuan looked and felt. "He is fine," I said, "a nice ruddy complexion, and a voice like a brass bell. I personally watched him eat half a dozen eggs, a large steamed bun, and a full bowl of porridge in one sitting." Excellency Tie glanced at Eminence Sun and said with a sigh: "He is in his prime; his future is assured." Eminence Sun added: "With Yuan Shikai's military background, it is natural to have a hardy appetite." Encouraged by what I saw in Excellency Tie's eyes, I decided to offer up a blatant falsehood: "His Excellency asked me to pass on his best wishes," I said. "Indeed?" Excellency Tie said excitedly. I nodded to assure him. "It is worth mentioning that Excellency Yuan and I are related. His great-uncle Yuan Jiasan's second concubine's niece is the wife of my father's younger brother!" "I seem to recall that Excellency Yuan mentioned that once." "Family connections like that are not that important!" Excellency Tie said. "Grandma Zhao, your success at the Tianjin executions has burnished the reputation of the Board of Punishments. Grand Secretary Wang has expressed his satisfaction, and I have summoned you here today to reward you. I hope that this will not lead to arrogance and rash behavior, and that you will continue to work for the nation to the best of your ability." "Excellency," I said, "ever since returning from Tianjin, I have been bothered by a sore wrist, and I . . ." Excellency Tie interrupted me: "The Court has initiated a series of reforms that may well mean the abolishment of such cruel punishments as the slicing death and cleaving a criminal in two. I am afraid that Grandma Zhao may become a hero denied a place to demonstrate his skills. Eminence Sun," he said as he stood up, "give Zhao Jia ten liang of silver from your Bureau of Detentions funds and charge it to the Board, on Grand Secretary Wang's authority." I fell to my knees and kowtowed before backing out of the hall bent at the waist; I saw a cloud spread across Tie's face, in contrast to the genial look he'd worn while bragging about his family connection to Excellency Yuan. High officials were subject to mercurial mood changes, but I was familiar enough with their temperament to not let that bother me.

The new year had barely begun, and the second lunar month was already upon us. The weeping willows lining the stream beside Board of Punishments Avenue were beginning to turn green, and the crows perching on the scholar trees in the compound were getting livelier by the day, and yet there was no sign of the welcome news Excellency Yuan had promised. The ten liang of silver from Excellency Tie could not have been what he was referring to, could it? No, of course not. Not when I had turned down his offer of a hundred liang. How could ten liang of silver be considered welcome news? I was convinced that he was not in the habit of jesting. He and I had formed an amicable relationship, and he would not string me along, like someone who teases a dog with an air-filled bladder.

On the second night of the new month, Deputy Director Sun brought word that I was to rise by the fourth watch the next morning, bathe, eat a light breakfast that included nothing that dispersed internal heat—no spicy foods such as ginger or garlic—dress in new clothes, and carry no sharp instruments. I was to appear at the Bureau of Detentions by the fifth watch and wait for him. I considered asking what this was all about, but one look at his long, somber face convinced me to hold my tongue. I had a premonition that Excellency Yuan's welcome news awaited. But never in my wildest imagination could I have anticipated that I was about to be received in a solemn audience by Her Royal Highness, the Empress Dowager Cixi—may She live forever—and His Imperial Majesty, the ageless Emperor!

The third watch had just been announced, and I was too tense to sleep, so I got out of bed, lit a lantern, smoked a pipe, and told the nephews to boil some water. Filled with excitement, they clambered out of bed bright-eyed and spoke in hushed tones. First Aunt assisted me into a large tub to bathe, Second Aunt dried me off, and Third Aunt helped me get dressed. We had rescued this youngster, with his fair complexion and nicely chiseled features, a boy who managed everything he touched with clever assurance, from the life of a beggar, and he treated me like a filial son. The joy he felt flowed from his eyes. All my apprentices enjoyed a shared sense of joy that morning. When auspicious things happened to their shifu, they reaped benefits, and I could see that their good feelings were heartfelt, with no hint of pretense.

"Don't be too quick to celebrate," I said, "for we do not know whether this news is good or bad."

"It's good," Third Aunt insisted. "I know it is!"

"Your shifu is getting on in years," I said with a sigh, "and the slightest slip could cost him his head . . ."

"That cannot happen," First Aunt said. "Old ginger is the spiciest. Besides, Grandma carried out an execution on the Palace grounds decades ago."

I had assumed that another Palace eunuch had committed a crime and that I was being summoned to carry out his execution. But I could not dismiss the feeling that something was different. Back when I was apprenticed to Grandma Yu and assigned the responsibility of putting Little Insect to death with Yama's Hoop, the Palace had spelled out our duties well ahead of time and had said nothing about bathing or eating a modest breakfast beforehand. But if this was not about plying my trade, what possible reason could there be for summoning an executioner? Could it be . . . could it be my turn to go on the chopping block? In a state of agitation, I ate half a meat-stuffed wheat cake, brushed my teeth with roasted salt, and rinsed my mouth with fresh water. I walked outside, where I saw that the constellation Orion had moved a bit to the west, though the fourth watch had not yet been announced—it was still early. So I engaged my apprentices in conversation until I heard a rooster's crow. "Better early than late," I said. "Let's go." So, escorted by my apprentices, I arrived at the entrance to the Bureau of Detentions.

Though the weather in the capital on that early day of the second month was still quite cold, I wore only a lined jacket under my official clothes in order not to appear frail. But my teeth chattered under the onslaught of the chilled early morning winds, and I instinctively tucked my neck down into my shoulders. There was a sudden change in the sky, which turned pitch-black and seemed to light up the stars. We waited an hour, until the fifth watch was announced, when the sky turned a fish-belly gray and the city and its outskirts began to stir. The city gate creaked open to welcome in water wagons that groaned under their heavy loads. Then a horse-drawn carriage rumbled quickly into the compound, preceded by a pair of servants carrying red lanterns, the shades stamped with the black character "TIE," which told us that Excellency Tie had arrived. The servants pulled back the protective curtain to allow Excellency Tie, a fur coat over his shoulders, to step down. His servants moved the carriage to the side of the road as His Excellency walked my way with faltering steps. I greeted him with a respectful salute. He coughed, spat out a mouthful of phlegm, and looked me over.

"Old Zhao," he said, "limitless blessings have been bestowed on you."

"I am unworthy and can only throw myself at Your Excellency's feet."

"Once you are inside, answer with care, saying only what is expected of you." His eyes sparkled in the dim light.

"I understand."

"You others may leave now," he said to my apprentices. "Rare good fortune has arrived for your shifu."

My apprentices departed, leaving only me and Excellency Tie standing in front of the Bureau of Detentions. His servants stayed with the carriage, lanterns now extinguished. I heard the sound of horses eating feed in the darkness; its fragrance carried all the way over to me—it was, I detected, a mix of fried soybeans and rice straw.

"Excellency, what do you want me to . . ."

"Keep your mouth shut," he said coldly. "If I were you, I would not say a word except in response to questions by the Empress Dowager or the Emperor."

Could it really be . . .

When I stepped out of the small, canopied palanquin carried by two eunuchs, a slightly hunchbacked eunuch in a loose tan robe nodded enigmatically to me. I fell in behind him and passed through a maze of gardens and corridors, finally arriving in front of a hall that seemed to reach the heavens. By then the sun had climbed into the sky, its redness sending rays of morning sunlight in all directions. I sneaked a look around me, and saw that magnificent linked buildings in resplendent golds and greens surrounded me, as if ringed by a prairie fire. The eunuch pointed to the ground at my feet; I was standing on green bricks that shone like the bottom of a scrubbed frying pan. I looked up, hoping to see in his face a sign that would tell me what he meant, but the old fellow had already turned away from me, and all I could see was his back as he stood respectfully, arms at his sides, and I realized that he wanted me to wait where I was. By then I knew precisely what awaited me—Excellency Yuan's welcome news. The next thing I saw was a progression of high officials in red caps backing out of the hall, heads down and bent at the waist. They wore somber looks and looked out of breath; oily drops of perspiration dotted some of their faces, and the sight made my heart race wildly. My legs trembled, and my palms were sweaty despite the cold. I did not know whether what awaited me was good fortune or ill, but if I'd had the chance, I'd have slunk out of there as fast as possible and taken refuge in my little room, where I could quell my fears with a decanter of fine spirits. But now that I was here, that was out of the question.

A eunuch whose face glowed beneath his red cap emerged through an enormous doorway that I dared not even glance at; he gestured to the old eunuch who had brought me there. The man's large face was as radiant as a Buddhist treasure, and though no one has ever told me who he was, I suspect it was the Chief Eunuch, Li Lianying. He and my confidant, Excellency Yuan, were sworn brothers, and it was all but certain that it was he who had arranged my audience with his benefactress, the Empress Dowager. I stood there like a fool, my mind a blank, until the hunchbacked old eunuch tugged my sleeve and said softly: "Move! They are summoning you!"

That was when I heard someone call out in a booming voice:

"Summoning Zhao Jia—"

I have no recollection of walking into the hall that morning, and recall only the scene of splendor that greeted my eyes once inside, as if a golden dragon and a red phoenix had suddenly materialized. When I was a child, my mother told me that the Emperor was the reincarnation of a golden dragon, and the Empress Dowager the reincarnation of a red phoenix. Terror-stricken, I knelt on the floor, which felt as hot as a newly heated brick bed. I kowtowed and I kowtowed and I kowtowed; it wasn't until later that I realized how badly I had injured my forehead, which was a bloody mess, like a rotten radish, which must have nauseated the Empress Dowager and Emperor. I deserved a thousand deaths. I was supposed to wish Them long, long lives, but I was so flummoxed by then that my head might as well have been filled with paste. All I could do was kowtow over and over and over.

It must have been a hand grabbing hold of my queue that brought my head banging to a halt. I struggled to keep connecting with the heated floor, but was stopped by a voice behind me:

"No more kowtows. The Old Buddha has asked you a question."

Peals of laughter erupted up ahead, and I was by then so disoriented that I looked up. And there, in front of my eyes, on a throne sat an old lady whose body radiated light. The words "I deserve death" slipped from my mouth. Seated in front of me was the wise, ageless Empress Dowager, the Old Buddha Herself. A question floated slowly down from on high:

"I asked you, Slay-master, what is your name?"

"Your servant is Zhao Jia."

"Where are you from?"

"Your servant is from Gaomi County in Shandong Province."

"How many years have you plied your trade?"

"Forty years."

"How many people have you put to death?"

"Nine hundred eighty-seven."

"Ah! You must be a death-dealing demon king!"

"Your servant deserves death."

"Why should you deserve death? Those whose heads you detached are the ones who deserved death."

"Yes."

"I say, Zhao Jia, when you kill someone, are you afraid?"

"I was at first, but no longer."

"What did you do for Yuan Shikai in Tianjin?"

"Your servant went to Tianjin to carry out a slicing death for Excellency Yuan."

"You mean carving up a living person so he will suffer before he dies?"

"Yes."

"The Emperor and I have decided to abolish the slicing death punishment. Are We not expected to initiate reforms? Well, this is one of them. Is that not right, Your Majesty?"

"Yes." It was a melancholy sound that floated over to me, and when I boldly looked up, I saw someone in a chair to the left and a bit ahead of the Empress Dowager. He was wearing a bright yellow robe, a golden dragon with glittering scales embroidered on the chest, and a tall hat whose centerpiece was a sparkling pearl the size of a hen's egg. The face beneath that hat was large and as white as fine porcelain. The August Ruler, the Son of Heaven, Emperor of the Great Qing Dynasty. Of course I knew that he had fallen out of favor with the Empress Dowager over the commotion caused by Kang Youwei and his fellow reformers, but that did nothing to alter the fact that He was the Emperor. Long live His Majesty the Emperor, may He live forever and ever! The Emperor said:

"What my august progenitor says is true."

"Yuan Shikai has said that you desire to return to your native home in retirement."

The sarcastic tone in the Empress Dowager's comment was unmistakable, and I felt two of my three souls departing in abject fear. "Your humble servant deserves to die ten thousand deaths," I said. "Your humble servant is a pig and a dog, and has no right to cause the Old Buddha any concern. But your humble servant is not thinking of himself alone. It is his thought that while an executioner may be demeaned, the work he performs is not, and as such he is a symbol of national power. We are a nation with a thousand laws, but in the end it is we who enforce them. Your humble servant ventures to propose that executioners be included in the personnel ranks of the Board of Punishments with a monthly wage, and hopes for the creation of a retirement system for executioners, who can subsist on a national pension and not be reduced to wandering the streets in poverty. Your humble servant . . . humble servant hopes as well for the creation of a hereditary system for executioners, so that this ancient profession will be viewed as an honorable one . . ."

A stately cough by the Empress Dowager sent shivers through me. I stopped talking, went back to kowtows, and said over and over:

"Your humble servant deserves death . . . humble servant deserves death . . ."

"What he says is sensible and has merit," the Empress Dowager said. "No single trade may be excluded from the list of professions. It is said that every profession has its zhuangyuan. Zhao Jia, in my view, you are the zhuangyuan of your profession."

"By investing me with the designation zhuangyuan of my profession, the Empress Dowager brought me immeasurable glory." More kowtows.

"Zhao Jia, you have put many people to death on behalf of the Great Qing Empire, which has brought you credit for hard work, if not for good work, and has earned praise from Yuan Shikai and Li Lianying. So I shall break from precedent and award you a grade seven medallion for your cap and allow you to return home in retirement." The Empress Dowager tossed a ring of sandalwood prayer beads at my feet and said, "Lay down your knife and turn at once to a life of Buddhist contemplation."

My kowtows continued.

"How about Your Majesty?" she asked. "Should you not reward him with something for all the people he has put to death for us, including those running dogs of yours whose heads he lopped off?"

I sneaked a glance at His Majesty, who, clearly flustered, got to His feet and said:

"We have nothing prepared. What do you suggest We reward him with?"

"I think, maybe," the Empress Dowager said with a distinct chill, "You should give him the chair You have just vacated!"

<hr>

6

<hr>

When I listened to my dieh-dieh relate history, my heart sang. Dieh-dieh, Dieh-dieh, you are wonderful, for the Imperial audience you had. Xiaojia wants to be an executioner, to learn the trade from his dad . . .

—Maoqiang Sandalwood Death. *A father and son duet*

Xiaojia sat on the rustling straw mat, leaning against a tent post as the night deepened. He looked like an oversized rabbit, his eyes dim with sleep. Flames in the belly of the stove flickered on his young face, and words that sometimes sounded foolish and sometimes not emerged from his grease-encrusted mouth to find their way into my recollections and my narrative—"Dieh, what does the Emperor look like?"—creating a close link between my recollections and narrative and the scene and situation we faced. "Dieh, does the Empress Dowager have breasts?"—All of a sudden, I smelled something burning in the sesame oil cauldron. With shocking clarity, I realized what was happening. My god, boiling oil is not boiling water! Water cooks something till it is soft; oil can burn it to a crisp! I jumped up off the mat and shouted:

"Come with me, son!"

I bounded over to the cauldron, reached into the oil barehanded—no time to worry about tongs—and fished out the two sandalwood spears, holding them up to a lantern to check them carefully. They had a dark, muted sheen and a powerful fragrance. I saw no singed spots. They burned my hands, so I laid them on a piece of cloth to rub them and turn them over and over, thanking my lucky stars there were no burn marks. The beef, on the other hand, was not so fortunate; I scooped out the burned pieces and threw them away, just as the chief yamen attendant sidled up and asked enigmatically:

"Something wrong, Laoye?"

"No."

"That's good."

"Old Song," my son cut in, "my dad is a grade seven official, so I am not afraid of you people anymore! If you harass me in the future, I'll see that a bullet has your name on it." My son pointed a finger at Song's head. "Pow! There go your brains!"

"Young Brother Xiaojia, when did I ever harass you?" Song Three said inscrutably. "Even if your father were not a grade seven official, I would never think of making things difficult for you. If your wife were to utter a single word against me to Magistrate Qian, I would be kicked out of the yamen."

"Don't you know he's not quite right, you foolish man?"

I could see a number of yayi standing in the shadows of the stage and the Ascension Platform. I lowered the fire under the cauldron and added oil. Then I carefully put my precious spears back into the cauldron, reminding myself, Pay attention, Old Zhao. Wild geese leave behind their cry; men leave behind a name. You need only carry out this sandalwood execution with perfection to live up to your designation as the zhuangyuan of executioners. If you fail, your name will die with you.

I draped the Empress Dowager's sandalwood prayer beads around my neck, got up out of the Emperor's chair, and looked heavenward, where a scattering of stars twinkled and the moon, like a silver platter, was rising in the east. That extraordinary brightness put me on edge, as if something monumental were about to happen, a feeling that persisted until it occurred to me that it was the fourteenth day of the eighth month and that the next day, the fifteenth, was the Mid-Autumn Festival, a day for families to come together. How lucky you are, Sun Bing, that Excellency Yuan has chosen that auspicious day for you to receive your punishment! In the light of the flames beneath the cauldron and the bright moonlight above, I watched the two sandalwood spears tumble in the oil like a pair of angry black snakes. I picked one out of the oil with a white cloth—taking care not to damage it—unimaginably sleek, it glistened with beads of oil that flowed to the tip and then formed liquid threads that fell silently back into the cauldron, where they coagulated and exuded a pleasant scorched aroma. It felt heavier in my hand now that it had absorbed so much fragrant oil; it was no longer the same piece of wood, but had taken on the characteristics of a hard, slippery, and exquisite instrument of death.

While I was taking solitary pleasure in admiring the spear, Song Three sneaked up behind me and said in a spiteful tone: "Laoye, why are you taking such pains simply to impale the man?"

I looked askance at him and snorted disdainfully. How could he understand what I was doing? He was good only for flaunting the power of his superior to oppress and extort money from the common people.

"You really ought to go home and get a good night's sleep and leave these trivial matters to us." Tailing along behind me, he added: "That son of a bitch Sun Bing is no one to take lightly. He's skillful and courageous, a man of substance who refuses to blame others for his actions. It was his misfortune to have been born in Gaomi, an insignificant little place that gave him no room to put his talents to good use." Song Three was clearly trying to ingratiate himself with me. "You have been away for many years, Laoye, and there is much about your qinjia that you do not know. He and I were friends for many years, so close that I can tell you how many moles he has on his you-know-what."

I had seen too many people like this fellow—toadies and bullies who know how to say what you want to hear, whoever you are, man or demon—but I was in no mood to expose him for what he was, not then; allowing him to carry on behind me served a purpose.

"Sun Bing is a man of extraordinary talents. Words flow from his mouth as if written by a scholar, and he is endowed with a flawless memory. If only he knew how to read and write, he could be a capped scholar ten times over. Some years back," Song Three continued, "when Old Qin's mother died, they asked Sun Bing's troupe to perform in the mourning hall. Qin and Sun were good friends—Qin's mother was Sun's ganniang—and Sun sang the funeral passages with deep emotion. But it was more than that—not only did his singing break the hearts of the filial descendants, they heard a pounding sound emerge from the coffin itself; the gathered descendants and people who had dropped by out of curiosity nearly died of fright, their faces a ghostly white. Isn't that what's called shocking the dead back to life? Well, Sun Bing walked up to his ganniang's bier, opened the lid in grand fashion, and the old lady sat up, light streaming from her eyes, like a pair of lanterns tearing through the dark curtain of night. Then Sun Bing sang these lines: *'When I call out Ganniang, listen carefully as your son sings "Chang Mao Wails at the Bier." If you have not lived enough, get up and live some more. If you have, then when my song is finished, fly to heaven, away from here.'* Sun Bing kept changing roles, from the sheng to the dan, weeping one moment and laughing the next, interspersed with all sorts of cat cries, turning the bier into a living, lively opera stage. All the filial descendants put aside their grief, while the casual spectators forgot that an old lady, just brought back from the dead, was sitting up in her coffin, listening to the performance. When Sun Bing sang the final high note, which hung in the air like the tail of a kite, Old Lady Qin slowly closed her eyes, released a contented sigh, and fell back into her coffin like a toppled wall. That is the story of how Sun Bing sang someone back from the dead. And there is more: he can also sing the living to death. Old Lady Qin is the only person he ever sang back from the dead, but the bastard has sung more living people to death than there are stars in the sky." While he was spouting his story, Song Three sidled over to the cauldron, reached in, and snatched a piece of beef. "This beef of yours," he said with an impudent smile, "has a wonderful flavor—"

Before he could finish what he was going to say, I saw the bastard straighten up as something erupted on his head and he tumbled into the cauldron of boiling oil. While my eyes were riveted on the scene in front of me, my ears pounded from the explosion of bone, and my nose was assailed by the smell of gunpowder merging with the sesame-enhanced smell of sandalwood. I knew immediately what had happened: someone had fired a shot in ambush, one meant for me. The greedy Song Three had been my unwitting stand-in.

CHAPTER FIFTEEN

Meiniang's Grievance

Dieh, oh, Dieh, Zhao Jia says he will impale you on a sandalwood stake,
and Meiniang has nearly lost her mind. She flies to the county yamen to
appeal to Qian Ding, but the gate is shut, guarded by soldiers malign.
To the left, Yuan Shikai's Imperial Guards, to the right, von Ketteler's
German troops, standing heads high, chests out, Mauser rifles aligned. I
step forward; those German devils and Chinese soldiers glare with eyes
big and round as brass bells, their ferocious snarls meant to keep me out.
My heart pounds, my legs tremble, I fall. With wings on my shoulders, I
could not enter the yamen, for these are powerful, strong-willed soldiers,
not bumbling militiamen, those friends of mine. They have enjoyed my
company, and the iron railing would come down by letting them have their
way, I opined. But the Germans are hard-hearted, the Imperial Guards an
impressive cadre, and if I break for the gate, the holes in my body would be
of their design. In the distance stand the lockup and Main Hall, both with
roofs of green. My tears fall—tin tin tine tine. I think of my dieh suffering
in his prison cell, and of our kinship. I think of how you taught me to sing
an opera feline, trained me to be an acrobat and martial artist. I followed
you from village to town, from temple to shrine, singing in roles female,
major and minor, to Little Peach, all truly divine. On mutton buns and
beef noodles, flatbreads fresh from the oven we dined. My dieh's cowardice
purged from my mind, his virtues of a heroic kind. To save his life, his
daughter to bold action is resigned. Calling up nerves of steel, I rush the
gate, leaving shouts of protest far behind.

—*Maoqiang* Sandalwood Death. *A soliloquy*

1

A crowd of people in vivid dress, faces painted all the colors of the rainbow, some tall and some short, emerged from Rouge Lane, southwest of the county yamen. The leader had powdered his face the white of a handsome young actor and painted his lips the bright red of a ghost of someone hanged. His upper body was covered in a red satin unlined robe (almost certainly appropriated from a corpse) that fell below his knees and revealed a pair of greasy black legs and bare feet. A live monkey was perched on his shoulder, enjoying its bumpy ride as the man hopped along, brass gong in hand. He was none other than Hou Xiaoqi of the beggar troupe. After three beats of the gong—*clang clang clang*—he sang a line from a Maoqiang opera:

"*Beggars celebrate a festival in their own wretched way, ah~~*"

He had the ideal voice for opera, with a unique lingering quality that made his listeners wonder whether they should laugh or cry. After he'd sung his last note, the other beggars responded with cat cries:

"*Meow~~meow~~meow~~*"

Then a few of the younger beggars imitated a cat fiddle as a prelude to a new aria:

"*Li-ge-long-ge li-ge-long-ge long~~*"

When they had finished the prelude, my throat began to itch, but this was not a day for me to sing. On the other hand, it certainly was for Hou Xiaoqi. Melancholy affects people everywhere, rulers and subjects, at least to some degree. Except for beggars. Hou Xiaoqi began anew:

"*With boots on my head and a cap on my feet, come hear my topsy-turvy song~~meow~~meow~~Mother goes into mourning when her son gets married, a Magistrate travels afoot while in a chair we are carried~~meow~~meow~~a rat chases a cat that is harried, snow falls in midsummer and a city is buried~~meow~~meow~~*"

A thought broke through the fog in my head that tomorrow was the fifteenth day of the eighth month, which meant that today, the fourteenth, was Beggars' Day, celebrated throughout Gaomi County. On this day each year, beggars from all over the county parade three times past the official yamen. They sing Maoqiang opera the first time and perform acrobatics the next. On their third pass, they untie sacks from around their waists and, first on the south side of the avenue, then on the north, they approach women, young and old, standing in their doorways, to fill their sacks from proffered gourds and bowls, some with various grains, others with uncooked rice, and others still with rice noodles. When they come to our door each year, I dump greasy brass coins from a bamboo tube into a chipped ladle in the hands of a crafty little beggar who opens his throat to let loose a cry of gratitude: "Thank you, Ganniang, for that tip!" All those greedy eyes then turn to me, and I know what they want! But I cock my head, curl my lip, and flash a smile, letting my eyes sweep the crowd, getting a rise out of all those monkeys, which turn somersaults to the screaming delight of the children behind them and the onlookers lining the street. My husband, Xiaojia, takes greater pleasure in this festive day than the beggars themselves. He gets up bright and early and, without stopping to slaughter pigs or butcher dogs, falls in behind the parading beggars, dancing for joy, singing along with them one minute and making cat cries the next. Lacking the voice to sing Maoqiang, Xiaojia has a talent for cat cries, sounding like a tomcat one minute and a tabby the next, then a tomcat calling out to a tabby and a tabby calling out to her kittens, and finally lost kittens crying for their mother, this last call bringing tears to the eyes of anyone within earshot, like an orphan who longs for her mother.

Niang! How tragic you died so young, leaving your daughter to suffer torment alone. But your early passing spared you from the paralyzing anxiety and crippling fear for which my dieh must atone . . . I watched the contingent of beggars swagger past the imposing array of soldiers. *Hou Xiaoqi's voice does not crack; the beggars' cat cries never waver.* On the fourteenth day of the eighth month, beggars rule the roost in Gaomi County, and even my gandieh's loyalists must quietly make way for their procession. *Beggars carry a rattan chair over their heads with Zhu Ba, the reprobate. He has worn a tall red-paper hat and a yellow satin dragon robe of late.* For a pauper, a commoner, or a minor bureaucrat to dress like that would have been a crime, one that would likely cost them their life. But Zhu Ba had license to overstep all authority, for the beggars had created their own kingdom, and freely did as they pleased. But this year there was a new twist: they escorted an empty chair—Zhu Ba was nowhere to be seen. Where had he gone? *Why is he not sitting imperiously in his Dragon Chair? Glory as great as an official in the top-tier range. Meiniang hears her heart skip a beat. The beggars this year, I think, are acting strange.*

I, Meiniang, born and raised in Gaomi, came to the county town as a bride in my late teens. Before that, I sang Maoqiang opera in my father's troupe, performing in all nine villages and eight hamlets. I'd come often to the county town, which seemed like a big place to me, and I have a vague recollection of my father teaching opera to the town's beggars. I was still young then and wore my hair like a boy, which is what people thought I was. Actors and beggars, my father said, are alike. Beggars are no different than actors; actors are the same as beggars. Which is why beggars and I came together naturally. And why I saw nothing unusual in a beggars' parade. But those German soldiers from Qingdao and the Imperial Guards from Jinan had never seen such a sight. They slapped the butts of their rifles, ready to confront the enemy, and then stood wide-eyed—some eyes round, some slanted—gawking at the bizarre, raucous assemblage of approaching humanity. But when the procession drew near, they loosened their grip on their weapons as odd, scrunched-up expressions crept onto their faces. Those of the Imperial Guards weren't nearly as comical as those on the faces of the German soldiers, since they at least were familiar with the tunes emerging from Hou Xiaoqi's mouth. To the Germans it was gibberish, all but the obvious cat cries mixed with lyrics. I knew they were wondering why all those people were yowling like cats. And while their attention was riveted on the parade of beggars, they forgot about the one person who wanted to storm the yamen gate—me. My brain was engaged. The moment had arrived, and I'd have been a fool to let it pass. Turn the gourd upside down, and the oil spills out. When opportunity falls into your lap, do not stand up. For me it was trying to catch fish in muddy water, frying beans in a hot skillet, adding salt to boiling oil. The chaos on the street was Meiniang's invitation to dash through the gate. *Meiniang would crash the yamen gate to free her dieh from his prison cell. Though she be smashed like an egg against steel, her tale as a martyred daughter the people would tell.* I waited for the chance, my mind made up. Hou Xiaoqi's gong rang out louder and louder; his topsy-turvy tune was getting increasingly dreary, and the cat-criers were holding out just fine, filling the air with their exaggerated yowls as they made faces at the soldiers and guards. When the procession got to where I was standing, as if on a signal, the beggars pulled cat skins out from under their clothes; large head-to-tail skins were draped over their shoulders, and smaller ones went on their heads. This unexpected, stupefying turn of events stunned the guards. I'd never get a better chance, so I stepped to the side and slipped between the German soldiers and the Imperial Guards, heading for the yamen gate. Momentarily dumbstruck, they quickly came to their senses and blocked my way with bayonets. But I would not be denied—the worst they could do was kill me—I was going into that yamen, bayonets or not. But at that critical moment, two powerful beggars pulled out of the procession, grabbed me by the arms, and dragged me back. I made a show of struggling to break free and run toward the bayonets, but a half-hearted one. Though not afraid to die, I was in no rush to do so now. I wouldn't be able to close my eyes in death without seeing Qian Ding one last time. Truth is, I was like a poor donkey trying to walk down a flight of steps. With eerie shouts, the beggars surrounded me, and before I knew it, I was sitting in the rattan chair tied to a pair of bamboo poles. I fought to get down, but four strapping, grunting beggars hoisted the poles onto their shoulders, and I was up in the air, rising and falling with the motion of the chair beneath me. I felt a sudden sadness; tears filled my eyes. But that made the beggars happier, as their leader, Hou Xiaoqi, beat a frantic tattoo on his gong and raised his voice higher than ever:

"*The street walks on people's toes, a dog flies in tail to nose. Pick up the dog and hit a brick, the brick bites the hand of a man expecting a lick~~meow meow~~*"

My beggar escort carried me southward, leaving the yamen gate behind. After slanting off the main road, we traveled another ninety paces or so until we were in front of the Temple of the Matriarch, whose roof tiles made a good bed for cattails, known locally as dogtail grass. The beggars had stopped singing and screeching once we were off the main road, for that is when they broke cadence and quickened their pace, and it was also the moment I realized that today's procession was not about stocking up on provisions, but was all about me. If not for them, by then I'd likely have been lying dead, bayoneted by a German soldier.

My rattan chair was no sooner settled on the temple's chipped and cracked stone steps than two of the beggars picked me up by the arms and bundled me into the dark confines.

"Is she with you?" a voice in the darkness asked.

"She is, Eighth Master!" said the two men who had carried me in.

There, on a tattered mat in front of the statue of the Matriarch, fumbling with something that gave off a bright green light, sat Zhu Ba.

"Light a candle!" he commanded.

His words hung in the air when a little beggar lit a piece of touch paper and with it the stubby half of a candle hidden behind the statue. Light suffused the temple's interior, including the guano-covered face of the Matriarch. Zhu Ba pointed to the ratty mat he was sitting on.

"Have a seat."

At this point, what could I say? I sat down without a whimper—I had to, since I had no feeling in my legs. My poor legs! Ever since Dieh was imprisoned, you've been running all over the place, leaping and jumping, until you've worn the soles right off your shoes . . . dear left leg, precious right leg, this has all been hard on you.

Zhu Ba stared holes in me, apparently waiting for me to say something. The green light from whatever he was fumbling with was now more muted, but thanks to the bright candlelight, I was able to discern that it was a gauzy sack that held hundreds of fireflies. For a moment I couldn't imagine why this village elder was playing with bugs. Once I was settled on the mat, all the other beggars found places to sit, except for those who sprawled on the floor. But whether seated or lying down, none of them said a word, and that included Hou Xiaoqi's sprightly little monkey, which squatted at his feet and limited itself to jerky movements of its head and clawed feet. Like Zhu Ba, they all had their eyes glued to me, and that too included the monkey. I greeted Zhu with a kowtow.

"Compassionate and merciful Master Zhu—! *Tears flow before a word she can say, the distressed young woman cannot find her way.* Please, Eighth Master, save my dieh from the Provincial Governor Yuan, the German von Ketteler, and the minor county official Qian Ding—*Three dignities a ruthless plan do make, to impale my dieh on a sandalwood stake*—the executioners will be my gongdieh, Zhao Jia, and my husband, Zhao Xiaojia. They are determined to make the process inhumanely cruel, forcing him to linger impaled between life and death for five days, until the rail line between Qingdao and Gaomi is completed. I beg Eighth Master to save him, and if that cannot be done, then to kill him with merciful speed. The foreign devils' conspiracy must be foiled, oh, Eighth Master . . .''

"*I tell you, Meiniang, worry not; eat some mutton rolls while they are hot.*" Once he had sung these two lines, Eighth Master said, "These rolls did not come to us as alms. I sent a boy to buy them at the home of Jia Si."

A young beggar dashed behind the Matriarch's statue and emerged carrying an oilpaper packet in both hands. He placed it on the mat in front of me. Zhu Ba touched it to see if it was hot, and said:

"*People are iron, food is steel, and you will starve if you miss a meal. Have one while it's still hot.*"

"My situation is too dire to have any appetite for stuffed rolls, Eighth Master."

"*Sun Meiniang, don't give in to alarm, for that ruins harvests and to the heart brings harm. It's said that earth can stop a flood and a general can block an army, so hear me out and eat your rolls while they're warm.*"

Zhu Ba stuck out his right hand, the one with the extra finger; he waved it in front of my eyes, and a glistening dagger appeared. A flick of the dagger, and the oilpaper parted to reveal four steaming stuffed rolls. Song Xihe's layered cakes, Du Kun's baked wheat buns, Sun Meiniang's stewed dog meat, and Jia Si's meat-filled rolls were Gaomi's most famous snack foods. Plenty of shops in Gaomi sold dog meat, so why had mine become one of the famous four? Because it tasted better than everyone else's. And why was it so tasty? Because I secretly stuck a pig's leg in with the dog meat, and when everything in the pot—meat, raw ginger, a bit of cinnamon, and prickly ash—was boiling, I stirred in a bowlful of strong spirits. That was my secret recipe. Master Zhu Ba, if you find a way to save my dieh, I'll bring you a cooked dog's leg and a jug every day for the rest of your life. One large roll sat atop three others on the oilpaper in the shape of a candelabrum. Their reputation was well earned. *Jia Si's rolls, steamy white as snow, tops twisted into a plum-blossom bow, a spot of red in the center~~a spun-gold date, charming and mellow.* Zhu Ba laid his dagger down in front of me, an invitation to spear one of the rolls. Either he was concerned that I might burn my fingers if I picked one up, or he was afraid that my hands were not clean. I waved off his offer, reached down, and grabbed one. It warmed my hand as the fragrance of leavened dough filled my nostrils. *With my first bite I devour that gold-spun date, and its sweetness coats my throat. The red date slides into my stomach, where it awakens juices there afloat. With my second bite I open the wheaten folds, and expose the mutton-carrot filling inside. The mutton is salty, the carrot sweet, with leeks and ginger the taste is complete. If you've not eaten Jia Four's rolls you haven't lived.* Now, I may not have been a pampered heiress, but I was a respectable woman, and should not display traits of anything less in front of all those beggars. Small, dainty bites were called for, but my mouth had a mind of its own, and before I knew it I had gobbled up half a roll that was larger than my fist. I'd been taught that a decent girl chewed slowly and swallowed with care, but my throat acted like a greedy hand, reaching up and pulling down every bite as soon as it entered my mouth. The first roll was gone before I had a chance to actually taste it, and I had to wonder if it had really found a home in my stomach. I'd heard that beggars have an uncanny ability to strike down a dog through a wall and move objects by thought alone. I could not be sure, but that roll seemed to have entered my mouth and slid down to my stomach, though in fact it had done no such thing, and now lay in the stomach of somebody else, somebody like Zhu Ba. That is the only way to explain why my stomach seemed empty and why I felt hungrier than I'd been before the roll disappeared. Then my willful hand snatched the second roll out of its wrapping, and, like its predecessor, I finished it off it in three or four bites. Now that I'd put away two of the rolls, my stomach actually felt like there was something in it. So I turned to the third roll, wolfed it down, and now there was a heaviness in my stomach. By then I was stuffed, but I reached out for the last roll anyway. In my little hand it looked bigger than ever, had greater heft, and wasn't all that appealing. The mere thought that three big, heavy, ugly things just like it were already nestled in my stomach sent an embarrassing belch up and out of my mouth. But while my stomach was sated, my mouth was not. With three large rolls having laid a foundation down there, I could eat more slowly for a change, and at the same time pay a bit of attention to my surroundings. I looked up and saw Zhu Ba staring at me, and behind him were dozens more twinkling eyes. All those beggars were watching me, and I knew that in their eyes I had gone from something approaching a goddess to a common woman with a greedy mouth. They ought to change the adage that "Man eats to live" to "Man lives to eat." Nothing makes you worry about dignity like a full belly, and nothing overcomes thoughts of shame quicker than an empty one.

"Had enough?" a smiling Zhu Ba asked after I'd polished off the last roll.

I nodded abashedly.

"Well, then," he said softly, his hands busy with the dagger and the sack of fireflies, his eyes emitting a green light, "now you can listen to what I have to say. To me, your dieh is a true hero. You probably don't recall—you were very young—but he and I were quite close at one time. He taught me twenty-four Maoqiang arias, which gave my youngsters here something they could trade for food. Why, it was your dieh who helped me devise this Beggars' Day idea. You can put aside everything else, and I am ready to rescue your dieh for his bellyful of Maoqiang arias alone. I've already come up with a foolproof plan. I've bought off the jailer, Old Fourth Master, known to you as Su Lantong, that scar-eyed old reprobate, who will help us with a scheme known as stealing beams and changing pillars—in other words, a switcheroo. I've already found someone to take your dieh's place—that's him over there." He drew my attention to a beggar fast asleep in the corner. "He says he's had a full life, and he looks enough like your dieh to get by. He'll willingly die in your dieh's place. Of course, after he's gone, we'll set up a memorial tablet and burn incense for him every day."

I fell to my knees and kowtowed in the man's direction; tears filled my eyes.

"Old Uncle," I said, my voice quaking, "righteousness such as yours reaches the clouds, for you are prepared to die for a cause. With high moral character, your name will live for all eternity. Only a hero of gigantic stature would willingly sacrifice his life for my dieh, and that burdens my heart. If his life is saved, I will see that he writes you into a Maoqiang opera, so that your courageous deed will be the stuff of song for the masses . . ."

The man opened his eyes—droopy as a drunken cat—gave me a bleary look, then rolled over and went back to sleep.

2

I awoke from a terrible nightmare just before nightfall. In the dream I'd seen a black pig standing like a gentleman on the stage erected on the Tongde Academy parade ground. My gandieh, Qian Ding, was standing behind the pig, but the space in the center was reserved for a red-headed, green-eyed, big-nosed foreigner with an injured ear. If that wasn't the man who killed my stepmother, slaughtered my stepbrother and sister, butchered all those villagers, and had the blood of our Northeast Township on his hands, Clemens von Ketteler, I don't know who it was! My eyes blazed when they spotted my mortal enemy, and it was all I could do to keep from charging and sinking my teeth into his neck. But for a defenseless young female, that would have been suicidal. Seated beside him was a red-capped, square-jawed official with a moustache, and I knew at once that he was the celebrated Governor of Shandong, Yuan Shikai, the man who had ordered the execution of the Six Gentlemen of the Hundred Days' Reform, who had murderously put down the Righteous Harmony Boxer movement in Shandong, and who had brought back my gongdieh, that horrid creature, to put my dieh to death in the cruelest manner imaginable. Stroking his moustache and narrowing his eyes, he sang:

"Sun Meiniang, Queen of Flowers in song, a cute little thing, and a face to go along. No wonder Qian Ding was smitten, for even my heart itches to you to belong."

I was secretly delighted. That seemed to be the moment for me to kneel down and beg for my dieh's life. But then Excellency Yuan's face hardened, like frost settling over a green gourd. A curt signal from him brought my gongdieh, carrying a sandalwood stake saturated with sesame oil, followed by Xiaojia, oil-soaked date-wood mallet in hand—one tall, one short, one fat, one skinny, the yin and the yang, a madman and a moron—up to the black pig. Yuan Shikai eyed Qian Ding and said, his voice dripping with contempt:

"What do you have to say, Eminence Qian?"

Qian Ding prostrated himself at the feet of Yuan Shikai and von Ketteler and said, his voice suffused with reverence:

"To ensure that nothing goes wrong at tomorrow's execution, your humble servant has invited Zhao Jia and his son to practice on this pig. With your permission, of course."

Excellency Yuan looked over at von Ketteler, who nodded his approval. Yuan Shikai nodded his, a signal for Qian Ding to get up, quick-step his way over to the black pig, reach out and grab it by the ears, and say to my gongdieh and Xiaojia:

"Commence."

My gongdieh placed the tip of the sandalwood stake, from which sesame oil still dripped, up against the pig's anus and said to Xiaojia:

"Commence, son."

With his legs spread, Xiaojia spat into his hands, made a circle in the air with his oil mallet, and gave a mighty whack to the butt end of the stake, half of which slurped its way up inside the pig. An involuntary arching of the back was followed by an ear-shattering screech. The animal lurched forward, knocking Qian Ding off the stage. The "oof!" when he hit the ground sounded as if he had landed on the head of a drum. The next thing I heard from him was a shrill:

"Heaven help me! I could have been killed!"

Now, although I was unhappy with Qian Ding, we were, after all, lovers, and it pained me to see him hurt. So despite the fact that I was pregnant, I jumped down off the stage and tried to help up the man I held in my heart. His face had a deathly pallor, his eyes were shut, and for all I knew, he could have been dead. So I bit his finger, pinched the groove between his nose and upper lip, and kept at it till I heard him sigh and saw the color return to his face. He clutched my hand and, with tears spiraling in his eyes, said:

"Ah, Meiniang, you are what makes my heart beat, so tell me, am I dead or alive, am I dreaming or am I awake, am I a man or a ghost?"

"Dearest Qian Ding, my love, though I say you are dead, you live on, though I say you are awake, you sleep on, and though I say you are a man, you look like a ghost."

All hell broke loose up on the stage, *A beaten drum, a clanging gong, a cat fiddle goes li-ge-long. A black pig, sandalwood stake up its rear, in circles runs, chased by my gongdieh and his son. The pig bites off Yuan Shikai's leg, blood everywhere, then takes off half the German commander's buttocks. How happy I am, two unlucky stars have fallen, but thunder and lightning prove me wrong. Yuan Shikai's leg returns, von Ketteler's buttocks are whole again, they sit on the stage looking fit and strong. But the black pig is no more, replaced by Sun Bing, to whom I belong. He suffers cruel torture, as the air fills with mallet sounds~~bong bong bong~~and the stake splits his body, his screams loud and long . . .*

My heart pounded in my chest, and cold sweat soaked through my clothes.

"Did you have a nice sleep?" Zhu Ba asked, his eyes smiling.

"Eighth Master," I said sheepishly, "I'm so embarrassed to have fallen asleep at such a critical moment . . ."

"That is a good sign, for people capable of accomplishing great things at critical moments are normally able to enjoy good food and a restful sleep." He placed four more rolls in front of me. "Eat these while I tell you what's happened today. This morning, your gongdieh put the finishing touches on his sandalwood stakes, and the County Magistrate erected an Ascension Platform across from the opera stage on the Tongde Academy parade ground. *By the platform stands a matted shed, a large stove in front, a small one in back, there for your gongdieh and his son. The stakes steep in sesame oil, the fragrance traveling far. Oil in the large pot, beef in the small, for father and son it is an oily treat. But tomorrow at noon, one of those stakes will be driven up your dieh's back, his life undone.* The yamen entrance is still guarded like a fortress, security is tight, and there have been no sightings of your dear Qian Ding, Yuan Shikai, or von Ketteler. I sent one of my cleverest youngsters disguised as a food delivery boy, hoping he could get in through the gate to check things out. A German bayonet abruptly ended his mission. Going in through the main gate, it seems, is out of the question . . ."

Just as Zhu Ba was getting started, a shout from outside cut him off in mid-sentence. Hou Xiaoqi's monkey startled us when it skittered in through the front entrance, with Hou himself hard on its heels. His face was lit up, as if coated with moonbeams. He ran straight to Zhu Ba.

"Eighth Master," he said, "wonderful news! My vigil by the ditch behind the yamen has paid off. Fourth Master passed on the news that we are to climb over the rear wall late at night, when the sentries are sleepy. We can pull the switch, make the exchange, right under their noses. I scouted the terrain and discovered a crooked-necked old elm tree ready-made for scaling the wall."

"Monkey," an obviously pleased Zhu Ba said excitedly, "damned if you don't have a couple of tricks up your sleeve! All of you, sleep if you can, but lie there and conserve your energy if sleep won't come. The time to act has arrived. Pulling this off will be like ramming it up von Ketteler's ass, and none of those bastards will know what hit them." Zhu Ba then turned his attention to the corner, where the good fellow who would take my dieh's place was fast asleep. "Xiao Shanzi," he said, "that's enough sleep. Time to get up. I've got a jug of fine spirits here, that and an off-the-bone roast chicken. You can share that with me as my going-away gift. If you're having second thoughts, I can find someone else, though this promises to be not only a sensation, but one in which the name of the central figure will go down in history. I know what a fine singer you are, a disciple of Sun Bing. Your voice is an exact replica of his, and there is hardly any difference in appearance between you two. Look closely, Sun Meiniang, and tell me if this fellow isn't the spitting image of your dieh."

The fellow got lazily to his feet, yawned grandly, and wiped off the slobber that had crept out of his mouth while he slept. Then, rousing himself out of his lethargy, he turned to show me his coarse, long face. His eyes and brows certainly did resemble my dieh's, and he had the same high nose. But he had a slightly different mouth. My dieh had full lips, while this fellow's were thin, but that was all that kept him from being my dieh's double. Add the right clothes, and he could fool anyone.

"Oh, I forgot one thing, Eighth Master," Hou Xiaoqi said sheepishly. "Fourth Master wanted me to be sure to tell you that when Sun Bing was being interrogated, he angered von Ketteler with such foul curses that the German hit him with the butt of his pistol and knocked out two front teeth . . ."

Every eye in the room was immediately focused on Xiao Shanzi's mouth. His lips parted to reveal two perfect rows of teeth. Most beggars have good teeth, since they survive on hard, crunchy food most of the time. Zhu Ba studied Xiao Shanzi's mouth.

"You heard what he said. Yes or no, it's up to you. I won't hold it against you if you say no."

Xiao Shanzi spread his lips wide, as if to show off his perfectly aligned, albeit yellow, teeth. Then he smiled.

"Shifu," he said, "if I'm willing to give up my life, why would I want to hold on to a couple of teeth?"

"Good for you, Shanzi," Zhu Ba said emotionally as he turned the sack of fireflies over and over in his hand. "That's what I'd expect a true disciple to say." The light from the agitated insects rose like a mist and lit up the few scraggly white hairs on Zhu Ba's chin.

"Shifu," Shanzi said, tapping his front teeth with a fingernail. "They're starting to itch, so bring on the food and drink."

Beggars swarmed the area behind Zhu Ba to be the first to bring out a jug and the cooked chicken, wrapped in clean lotus leaves. I could smell the chicken even before the leaves were peeled away, and the aged spirits before the stopper was removed. The two aromas were totally different, but came together as a potent reminder of the Mid-Autumn Festival, which was only days away, and the ambience surrounding it. A moonbeam filtered in through a crack in the temple door: a hand peeled away the oily lotus leaves in the light of the moonbeam; a golden-red cooked chicken glimmered in the light of the moonbeam; a black hand laid two shallow black glazed bowls next to the chicken in the light of the moonbeam; Zhu Ba put the sack with the fireflies into a pouch at his waist and clapped his green hands. I noticed how long, slender, and nimble his fingers were, looking like little people with something to say. He hopped forward a couple of spots, still seated on the mat, until he was right in front of Xiao Shanzi, the man who was going to take my dieh's place in his cell and die in his stead. Zhu Ba held one of the bowls out for Xiao Shanzi, who accepted it but said with what looked to be much embarrassment:

"I can't let you serve me like this, Shifu."

Zhu Ba picked up the second bowl and clinked it against Xiao Shanzi's, loud enough for all of us to hear it and hard enough to splash out some of the contents. Their eyes met, and to us sparks seemed to fly, like steel striking a flint. Their lips were quaking, and they both seemed about to speak—but they didn't. Instead, they tipped back their heads and, with audible glugs, emptied the bowls. Zhu Ba laid down his bowl and tore off a drumstick with the skin attached. He handed it to Xiao Shanzi, who took it and seemed about to say something. But still nothing. A moment later, his mouth was stuffed to capacity with roast chicken, which rotated twice before it slipped down his throat like a greased rat. I'd have loved to run home to cook a dog's leg for him, but there was no time for that, since a dog's leg had to cook all day and all night. Now that he'd eaten the meat, he gnawed on the bone to pick it clean, almost as if to show us what his teeth could do. The image was of a squirrel chewing on an acorn. Though they were undeniably yellow, they were solid teeth. As soon as the tendons were picked clean, he started in on the bone itself, which produced the most noise. Not a single thing emerged from that mouth, not even bone chips. You poor man. If I'd known earlier that you were willing to die in my dieh's stead, I'd have invited you to a sumptuous feast, making sure you got a taste of the best food anywhere. Too bad life does not allow for predictions or do-overs. As soon as Xiao Shanzi finished off one drumstick, Zhu Ba tore off the other one and held it out for him. But this time, Xiao Shanzi cupped his hands respectfully in front of him and said devotedly:

"I thank Shifu for giving me this opportunity!"

Then he reached behind him, picked up a broken brick, and smacked himself in the mouth, producing a dull thud. A front tooth fell to the ground, and blood spurted from his mouth.

Everyone froze, staring and speechless. Their gazes bounced back and forth between Xiao Shanzi's bloody mouth and the gloomy face of Zhu Ba, who moved the tooth around on the floor with his index finger, then looked up at Hou Xiaoqi.

"How many teeth did Sun Bing lose?"

"Two, according to Fourth Master."

"Are you sure that's what he said?"

"I'm sure, Eighth Master."

"After what you've done," Zhu Ba said to Xiao Shanzi, his awkwardness showing, "I don't have the heart to ask you to do it again."

"There's no reason to feel bad, Shifu. Once, twice, what's the difference?" Xiao Shanzi said, blood bubbling from his mouth. He picked the brick up again.

"Wait—" Zhu Ba cried out.

But too late—Xiao Shanzi smacked himself in the mouth a second time.

He tossed the brick away and lowered his head. Two teeth fell to the ground.

The sight of the gaping hole in Xiao Shanzi's mouth drove Zhu Ba into a frenzy.

"You dumb bastard," he cursed, "I told you to wait. Now you've knocked out too many teeth, damn it! With too few we could have figured something out, but what are we going to do now?"

"Don't get mad, Shifu, I'll keep my mouth shut the whole time," Xiao Shanzi said with a pronounced slur.

3

In the middle of the night I draped a tattered jacket over my shoulders, as instructed by Zhu Ba, added a beat-up old straw hat, and quietly exited the temple in the company of the beggars. There wasn't a sound on the deserted streets, which were suffused in the chilled green of beams sent down from a full moon, painting everything with ghostly airs. I shivered and my teeth chattered, the clicking sound striking my eardrums with such force I was afraid I might wake up the whole town.

Hou Xiaoqi led the way with his monkey, followed by Xiao Luanzi, who was carrying a spade and was the group's tunneling advance guard. Xiao Lianzi, the undisputed master of tree climbing, walked alongside Xiao Luanzi, a leather rope girding his waist. Next in line was that valiant figure Xiao Shanzi, he of great virtue—upholder of allegiance, defender of righteousness and morality, disfigurer of his own face, death-defying—a man whose name was destined for eternal glory. I watched as he walked along, never wavering, his gait firm and steady, bold and spirited, almost as if he were on his way to a fine year-ending meal. A man like that comes along once a century, if that. The beggar chief, old Zhu Ba, himself a steely, dauntless figure, followed behind Xiao Shanzi, holding me, a young, beautiful woman, by the hand. We formed a small but potent procession of ancient figures: Zhan Zhao, Judge Bao, his attendants Wang Chao to the left and Ma Han to the right, with Di Long out front and Di Hu in the rear. Zhuge Liang harnessed the east wind but angered Zhou Yu, and there was a perfect match at Dew Drop Monastery.

Hou Xiaoqi led us into Smithy Lane, and from there into the sandals market, where we followed the contours of a low wall whose shadow concealed us as we trotted along at a crouch, all the way to Lu Family Lane, and from there to the bridge over the Xiaokang River, which flowed like a band of silver. On the far side of the bridge we streamed into Oil Mill Lane, at the end of which we could see the yamen's high wall directly ahead; the rear garden was on the other side.

I was breathing hard as I crouched at the base of the wall, my heart pounding. Breathing came more easily for the beggars, whose eyes flashed, even the monkey's.

"It's time," Zhu Ba said, "get to work."

Xiao Lianzi took the rope from around his waist and looped it over a tree limb. Using both hands and feet, he climbed like a monkey—no, better than a monkey—and one-two-three, he was safely in the crotch of the tree, from which he easily dropped onto the top of the wall, and then continued down the other side, where he and his rope vanished from sight. But a moment later, he flung another rope over. Zhu Ba grabbed this one and pulled it toward him, confident that things were going smoothly. He handed the rope to Hou Xiaoqi, who plucked the monkey off his shoulder and sent it flying up into the tree, where it landed spryly on one of the branches, while he himself walked up the wall with the help of the rope, hand over fist, and then grabbed the other rope and disappeared behind the wall. Who was to be next? Zhu Ba pushed me up front. My heart was racing, cold chills ran up and down my spine, and my palms were sweaty. I grabbed hold of the rope, which was cold to the touch, like a snakeskin. I gripped it in both hands, but I'd barely taken two steps when my hands began to ache, my legs felt rubbery, and I was shaking all over. It hadn't been all that long since I'd climbed that tree without the aid of a rope, but now I couldn't make it up the wall with one. That other time I'd been nimble as a cat; now I was clumsy as a pig. This was not a case of worrying more about my lover than my dieh, nor was it the new life growing inside me. What was stopping me now were thoughts of what had happened on the other side of that wall the first time. You know the adage: "Get snakebit once, and you'll fear ropes for three years." Well, that wall and that tree brought a reminder of being covered in dog filth and going home with a sore backside. But then I heard Zhu Ba say:

"We're here to rescue *your* dieh, not ours!"

How right he was. These beggars were risking their lives to rescue my dieh. How, then, at this critical juncture, could I run like a coward? And that sparked the return of my courage, as I was reminded of Hua Mulan, who went to war in place of her father, and of the hundred-year-old She Taijun, who rallied the troops for her slain grandson, Yang Zongbao. If there's dog filth, so be it; if a whip lashes out, let it come. Suffering is the road to respectability; danger is the path to prominence onstage. In order to ensure that my name would live on, I clenched my teeth, stomped my foot, and spat in my hands: rope in hand, feet on the wall, face turned to the moon above. Propped up from behind by some of the beggars, I soared to the top of the wall in less time than it takes to tell, and found myself gazing down at rooftops in the yamen, tiles flickering in the moonlight like fish scales. Hou Xiaoqi stood ready to help me to the ground, so I grabbed hold of the rope hanging from the tree and, closing my eyes and steeling myself, sailed down into the grove of green bamboo.

My thoughts returned to boudoir frolics with Qian Ding in the Western Parlor, where by standing on the four-poster bed and looking out the window, I could see the splendor of the flower garden out back; the first thing to catch my eye was always that grove of green bamboo. Then my gaze would travel to the tree peonies, Chinese roses, herbaceous peonies, and blooming lilacs, whose perfume was nearly suffocating. The garden was also a showcase for potted mums on a little manmade hill. Prized Lake Tai rocks, all delicately shaped, lined a small pond whose lotus leaves were surpassingly lovely. I recalled seeing a pair of butterflies taking nectar from flowers around which buzzing bees flitted. A woman with a ruddy complexion strolled through the garden, the dour look on her face more severe than any seen on Judge Bao. A slim-waisted, light-on-her-feet serving girl followed close behind, and I knew that, though the older woman was not much to look at, she was the Magistrate's wife, an intelligent woman from a good family who excelled in both talents and intrigues. Feared by the yayi, she was an intimidating presence in the Magistrate's life. I had once entertained a desire to stroll through the garden, but Qian Ding insisted that I put that thought out of my mind. He kept me hidden in the Western Parlor to prevent our illicit relationship from going public. So here I was tonight, standing in the garden, not to stroll but to stage a rescue.

Once we were all together in the bamboo grove, including Hou Xiaoqi's monkey, which he'd brought down from the tree, we crouched out of sight, waiting for the night watchman to sound the third watch on his clapper before moving on. Noise came on the air from up front, most likely an exchange by one team of sentries relieving the other. Then there was silence, broken only by the forlorn dying chirps of late autumn insects. My heart was pounding; I wanted to say something, but dared not. Meanwhile, Zhu Ba and the others sat peacefully on the ground, neither moving nor speaking, like five dark stone statues. That excluded, of course, the monkey, which began to fidget; Hou Xiaoqi quickly forced it to settle down.

As the moon traveled westward, its late-night rays grew increasingly cold. Chilled dew settled on bamboo leaves and stalks, lending them an oily sheen. The dew dampened my straw hat, my tattered jacket, even my armpits. If we don't do something soon, Eighth Master, the sun will be up, I thought anxiously. But then there was more noise from up front, with shouts and bawling and the clanging of a brass gong, followed immediately by a red light that painted the compound scarlet.

A young yayi in uniform emerged from a path alongside the Western Parlor and, bent at the waist, stole over to us. He beckoned for us to follow him back onto the path, past the Western Parlor, the tariff room, the chief clerk's office, and the dispatch office all the way up to the lockup, which was in front of the Prison God Temple.

Flames shot thirty feet into the air in the square fronting the lockup. The mess hall kitchen was on fire. Clouds beget rain, fire creates wind. Thick, choking smoke made us cough. The scene was as chaotic as ants on the move, as raucous as a disturbed crows' nest. Soldiers scurried back and forth with buckets of water. We took advantage of the confusion to slip past the outer cells and the women's jail, as if our feet were oiled, spry as cats, undetected, all the way up to the condemned cells. The stench nearly made us gag. The rats there were bigger than cats; fleas and ticks were everywhere. Windowless cells were fronted by low doors, the interiors black as pitch.

As he unlocked the door, Master Four urged us to move fast fast fast! Zhu Ba tossed his firefly sack inside, abruptly flooding the cell with a green glow. I saw my dieh; his face was bruised black and blue, his mouth caked with dried blood. His front teeth had been knocked out. He no longer looked human. My shout of "Dieh!" was cut short by a hand over my mouth.

Dieh had been chained, hands and feet, to a "bandit's stone" in the center of the cell. It was immovable, no matter how much strength was employed. In the flickering firefly light, Master Four removed the padlock on the chains and set him free. Then Xiao Shanzi took off his jacket, which he'd worn over tattered clothes the same color as my dieh's, and sat down in the vacated spot, where he let Master Four put the chains on him as the others quickly dressed my dieh in the jacket Xiao Shanzi had taken off. With a disjointed stammer, my dieh sputtered:

"What are you people doing? What do you want?"

Master Four clamped his hand over his mouth.

"Dieh," I said softly, "snap out of it. It's me, Meiniang. I've come to save you."

He was still making noise, trying to talk, so Zhu Ba doubled up his fist and hit him in the temple, knocking him unconscious. Xiao Luanzi bent down, slipped his hands under my dieh's arms, and hoisted him onto his back.

"Let's get out of here," Master Four urged softly.

We squeezed out of the cell at a crouch and, as the confusion outside continued, ran all the way to the path behind the Prison God Temple, where we spotted a pack of yayi carrying water headed our way from the secondary gate. Magistrate Qian Ding was standing on the gateway steps shouting:

"Stay in line; careful with that water!"

Hidden in the shadows of the Prison God Temple, we froze in place as a line of red lanterns led the way for a high-ranking official who materialized on the pathway in front of the side gate, a cluster of bodyguards behind him. If that wasn't the Shandong Governor Yuan Shikai, I don't know who it was. We watched as Qian Ding ran up, knelt at the man's feet, and sang out:

"Your humble servant has failed to keep the mess hall from catching fire and disturbing Your Honor. I deserve to die a thousand deaths!"

We heard Yuan Shikai respond with a command:

"Send someone to the jail to see if anyone has escaped, and do it this minute!"

We watched the Magistrate scramble to his feet and run with attendants in the direction of the condemned cells.

We held our breath, wishing we could disappear into a hole in the ground as our ears filled with shouts from Master Four in the prison yard. The cell doors clanged open. We kept our eyes peeled for a chance to run, but Yuan Shikai and his bodyguards were in no hurry to vacate the path in the center of the courtyard. After what seemed like an eternity, the Magistrate puffed his way up to Yuan Shikai, fell a second time to one knee, and announced:

"Reporting to Your Excellency: I have examined the jail cells. All prisoners are present and accounted for."

"What about Sun Bing?"

"Chained to a stone."

"Sun Bing is the Imperial Court's foremost criminal. Tomorrow he is to be executed, and your heads are on the line if anything goes wrong."

Yuan Shikai turned and headed back to the Official Guesthouse, sent off by the County Magistrate with a courtly bow. We breathed a sigh of relief, but it was short-lived, for my dieh, that damned fool, chose that moment to regain consciousness, and with a vengeance. He stood up, disoriented, and blurted out:

"Where am I? Where are you taking me?"

Xiao Luanzi grabbed his leg and pulled him to the ground. But he rolled over, out of the shadows and into the moonlight. Xiao Luanzi and Xiao Lianzi pounced on him like marauding tigers, each grabbing a leg to pull him back into the shadows. He fought like a madman.

"Let me go, you bastards!" he shouted. "I'm not going anywhere with you!"

His shouts caught the attention of the soldiers, whose bayonets and brass buttons reflected the cold light of the moonbeams.

"Run, boys!" Zhu Ba said, keeping his voice low.

Xiao Luanzi and Xiao Lianzi let go of my father's legs and stood there for a moment, not knowing what to do, before running straight at the onrushing soldiers, whose shouts merged with crisp gunfire: "Assassins!" Like a hawk, Zhu Ba pounced on my dieh and, unless my eyes deceived me, began to throttle him. I knew at once that he was trying to kill my dieh to keep them from subjecting him to the sandalwood death. Hou Xiaoqi grabbed my hand and dragged me over to the path on the western edge, where we were met by a gang of yayi coming straight at us. Without missing a beat, Hou Xiaoqi flung his monkey at the men. With a screech, the animal attached itself to the neck of one of the petty officials, who voiced his agony with appropriate shrillness. Still holding me by the hand, Hou Xiaoqi ran from the dispatch office back to behind the Main Hall. Yayi were streaming from the Central Hall, and my ears rang with the sound of gunfire, the roar of flames, and men's shouts, all coming from the courtyard beyond the side gate, while my nostrils were assailed with the smell of blood and fire. The moon abruptly changed color, from silver to blood red.

We kept running, heading north, desperate to make it to the rear garden, our only chance of escape. More and more footsteps sounded behind us; bullets whizzed overhead. When we reached the side of the Eastern Parlor, Hou

Xiaoqi jerked a time or two, and the hand holding mine fell away weakly as steamy green blood, like newly pressed oil, streamed from a hole in his back. I stood there, not knowing what to do, when a hand reached out and pulled me off the path, just in time for me to see soldiers run down the path past me.

I had been saved by the County Magistrate's wife, who quickly led me into a private room in the Eastern Parlor, where she removed my straw hat and stripped the tattered jacket off me, rolling it into a ball and tossing it out a rear window. Then she shoved me down onto the four-poster bed and under the covers. Next she lowered the silk drapes on both sides of the bed, with her on one side and me on the other, in total darkness.

I heard the loud voices of soldiers, who were now in the rear garden. Raucous human noise rose everywhere—the garden's front and rear paths, the compounds fronting the two main halls, and the side courtyards. Then the moment I'd feared arrived: the pounding of footsteps had reached the Eastern Parlor courtyard. "Commander," someone said, "these are the Magistrate's private quarters." The next sound I heard was that of a whip landing on someone's back. The drape was pulled back, and a scantily clad, chilled body slipped into my bed and pressed up against me. It was, of course, the Magistrate's wife, the body my lover had once embraced. There was a knock at the door; the knock then became a pounding. We held each other tight, and though I could tell she was trembling, I knew that I was more frightened than she. The door flew open; she pushed me to the far side of the bed and covered me from head to toe before parting the drape. Her hair was a mess, I assumed; she was dressed for bed, and she must have looked like someone who has been startled out of a deep sleep.

"First Lady," a coarse voice said, "we have been ordered by Excellency Yuan to search for an assassin!"

With a sarcastic little laugh, she said:

"Back when my great-grandfather Zeng Guofan led soldiers into battle, Commander, he had one inviolable rule to maintain discipline and preserve the cardinal guides and constant virtues, and that was, no soldier was permitted to enter women's chambers. Apparently the New Army personally trained by Yuan Shikai, Excellency Yuan, has no use for that rule."

"Your humble servant would not dare offend Your Ladyship!"

"What does daring or not have to do with anything? And what do you mean, offend me? You search what you wish and see what you want. You people have already destroyed the revered Zeng family name, with no voice at the court, and you take your puffed-up courage from that fact."

"Those are harsh words, Your Ladyship. Your humble servant is only a soldier who obeys his superior's orders."

"Then go tell Yuan Shikai that I want to know if it is acceptable for soldiers to break into women's quarters in the middle of the night, humiliating their occupants and besmirching their virtuous good name. Is Yuan Shikai an official of the Great Qing Dynasty or isn't he? Does he have no womenfolk of his own? A popular adage has it that 'A warrior can be killed but not dishonored; a woman can die but not be defiled.' I shall let my death stand in opposition against Yuan Shikai!"

Just then a flurry of footsteps sounded outside the door.

"The Magistrate is here," someone whispered.

The First Lady burst into tears.

The Magistrate came through the door and, in a voice quivering with emotion, said:

"Dear wife, I am a worthless man for letting them give you such a fright!"

4

Once the commander and his troops were scolded out of the room, the door was shut, and the candle extinguished, I climbed out of the Magistrate's bed, with moonlight filtering in through the window lattice, lighting up part of the room and leaving the rest in darkness.

"I thank Your Ladyship for saving me from certain death," I said softly. "If there is another life after this one, I hope I can return to serve you, even as a beast of burden!"

I turned to leave, but she stopped me by tugging on my sleeve. I saw a glimmer in her eyes and detected the subtle fragrance of cassia on her body. That took my thoughts back to the cassia tree that stood tall in the courtyard of the Third Hall. The Mid-Autumn Festival was a time when the perfume of cassia blossoms filled the air, and the County Magistrate and his wife ought to be enjoying a shared drink and the beauty of a full moon. I knew I was not fated to share that enjoyment with my beloved, but the taste of a lovers' tryst in the yamen late at night was nearly overpowering. People said that my dieh was guilty of disturbing the peace, but in my view, it was the tyrannical behavior of the Germans that had caused all the problems. I thought about the anguish my dieh felt, as if his heart were tied up in knots. Dieh, you old fool! Your daughter nearly ran her legs off, and a gang of beggars did not rest, day or night, all in an attempt to rescue you. In order to do that, Xiao Shanzi knocked out three of his own teeth and bled all over his chest. In order to rescue you, Zhu Ba himself led the effort, which wound up costing the lives of some of his beggars. We exhausted ourselves, devising a ruse to free you from your condemned cell, but when success was nearly in our grasp, you opened your big mouth and sounded the alarm . . .

"You cannot leave, not yet," the First Lady said, a chill to her voice as she broke into my confused thoughts. I could hear that the situation outside remained unsettled, with the occasional soldier's shout.

On orders from Yuan Shikai, the Magistrate had been sent to keep watch at the Main Hall. Thoughts of the danger I had barely managed to escape when the commander burst into the women's quarters with his men would not leave me. The First Lady went over and closed the door, and in the light from the weepy red candle, I saw how red her face was, without knowing whether she was excited or angry.

"My husband," I heard her say, the chill still in her voice, "your humble wife took it upon herself to hide your lover in your bed."

The Magistrate took a look outside through the window before rushing up to the bed and pulling back the covers to reveal my face. He hurriedly covered me back up, and I heard him say softly:

"My dear, you magnanimously put aside all previous concerns. You are an extraordinary woman, and Qian Ding thanks you from the bottom of his heart!"

"The question is, should I send her away or let her stay where she is?"

"That is for you to decide."

There was a shout in the yard. Qian Ding left, obviously flustered. While he appeared to be leaving to carry out his official duties, in truth he was running from an awkward situation. It was the sort of thing that occurred often on the operatic stage, so I knew what he was doing. His wife blew out the candle and let the moon light up the room again.

Feeling awkward, I got up and sat on a stool in the corner, my tongue parched, my throat dry and raspy. As if she could read my mind, she poured a cup of cold tea and held it out to me. Hesitant at first, I took it from her and drank every drop.

"I thank Your Ladyship."

"I could never have pictured you as a brave and resourceful woman!" the Magistrate's wife said, her voice dripping with sarcasm.

How was I supposed to respond to that?

"How old are you?"

"May it please Your Ladyship, I am twenty-four this year."

"I understand that you are pregnant."

"I am young and ignorant, and I can only ask Your Ladyship's forgiveness for any offense I have given. As the popular adage has it, 'A great man overlooks the flaws of a lesser man, and a Prime Minister has a capacious nature.'"

"What a clever little mouth you have," the First Lady replied with the sobriety of her station. "Can you say with certainty that the child in your belly is Laoye's?"

"Yes, I can."

"Then," she said curtly, "do you want to stay or leave?"

"I want to leave," I said without a moment's hesitation.

5

I stood beside a gatepost in front of the yamen staring blankly inside. I'd not slept a wink, suffering through a hellish night worse than any performed onstage. This was no performance, but it would not take long for it to find its way into operatic lore. Before I left the yamen, the First Lady urged me to go somewhere far away to keep myself safe. She even handed me five liang of silver. But I was not about to leave. My mind was made up. If I was going to die, it would be in Gaomi County, nowhere else. Whatever happened, happened.

All the local people knew that I was Sun Bing's daughter, and they spared no effort to shield me, like mother hens protecting a single chick. White-haired old ladies tried to hand me still-warm eggs, and when I refused to take them, they stuffed them into my pockets.

"Eat, young lady," they said tearfully, "you must eat to stay well and strong."

Truth is, as I knew all too well, before troubles had beset my dieh, all these county women—young and old, daughters of fine families and prostitutes from local brothels—had ground their teeth when they heard my name mentioned and would have loved to take a bite out of me. They hated the fact of my relationship with the County Magistrate, they hated the fact that I lived better than they did, and they hated the fact that I had healthy, unbound feet that could run and hop and were prized by the Magistrate. Dieh, when you raised the flag of rebellion, their attitude toward me changed for the better, and better still when you were taken into custody. When the Ascension Platform was erected on the Tongde Academy parade ground and an announcement was posted in all the villages that you were to be dispatched by the sandalwood death, well, Dieh, your daughter was transformed into everyone's favorite niece, loved by all.

Dieh, last night we tried to save you, and almost won. If you'd not lost your head, the deed would now be done. Dieh, oh, Dieh, four beggars' lives were lost. Look at the winged walls beside the gate~~your heart will ache, blood from your eyes will run. On the left two heads, on the right three, one monkey and two human. On the left Zhu Ba and Xiao Luanzi, on the right Xiao Lianzi, Houqi, and his monkey, all rotting in the sun. (So vicious that even an innocent monkey was not spared!)

The sun climbed slowly into the sky, yet all was quiet inside the yamen. I imagined they would wait till noon to take my dieh out of his cell. But already, people—dignified individuals in robes and hats—were emerging slowly from Shan Family Lane, opposite the yamen gate. As the most famous lane in town, it had gained notoriety for being home to not one, but two Imperial licentiates. That glory, however, belonged to the past. Now the family's reputation was propped up by a single metropolitan licentiate, not quite so honored, but still worthy of admiration. No one in the county enjoyed higher prestige or greater respect than Shan Wen, an old man whose style name was Zhaojin. Although he had never visited our home to buy spirits or dog meat and was a virtual recluse who spent his days reading, writing, and painting, he was no stranger to me. I must have heard Qian Ding mention his name a hundred times, and when he did, his eyes glowed as he stroked his beard and studied samples of the old man's painting and calligraphy hanging on his wall. "How can a man like that suffer such neglect!" he said with a sigh, and followed that with "How can a man like that *not* suffer such neglect!" When I asked what he meant by such confusing talk, he would only lay his hand on my shoulder and say, "All the notable talent in this county of yours is concentrated in a single individual, but now the Royal Court plans to do away with the examination system, and he will never have a chance to pass the Imperial Examination, to 'win laurels in the Moon Palace,' as they say." But as I studied the scrolls, with hills and trees that looked like none I had ever seen, with dim outlines of people, and with written characters that did not conform to those I knew, I failed to see a sign of greatness. But what did I, a mere woman who could sing a few Maoqiang arias, know? Master Qian, on the other hand, was an Imperial licentiate, a man of vast knowledge who knew many things; if he said something was good, then good it was, and so in my eyes old Mr. Shan was truly a great man.

Licentiate Shan had bushy eyebrows, a prominent nose and mouth on a large face, and a beard that, while finer than most, was inferior to Qian Ding's, the most impressive beard anywhere in Gaomi after my dieh's was plucked clean; old man Shan now owned the second-finest beard in the county. He was striding at the head of the procession emerging from the lane, head held high, a man comfortable in the position of leader. His head was cocked at a slight angle, and I wondered whether that was a permanent impairment or something unique to today's circumstance. I recalled having seen him in the past, more than once, in fact, but that detail had escaped me. Cocking his head gave him sort of a wild look, more like a bandit chief than a man of learning. The crowd behind him was composed exclusively of prominent Gaomi personages. They included the corpulent pawnbroker Li Shizeng, in his red-tasseled cap; the skinny Su Ziqing, proprietor of the local fabric shop, who never stopped blinking; and pockmarked Qin Renmei, proprietor of the herbal medicine store . . . everyone who was anyone in Gaomi's county town was there. Some wore somber looks and kept their eyes straight ahead; others, clearly skittish, kept glancing around, almost as if looking for support; and still others walked with their heads down, staring at the tips of their shoes, seemingly afraid of being recognized. Their emergence from Shan Family Lane drew the immediate attention of everyone on the street, taking many by surprise. But there were those who knew exactly what this augured.

"Well, now," they said, "Licentiate Shan has made an appearance, which surely means that Sun Bing will be saved!"

"Not only Master Qian, but even Excellency Yuan will find it necessary to give Licentiate Shan a bit of face, especially since all the other Gaomi luminaries have shown up."

"Not even the Emperor himself would oppose the people's wishes. Let's go!"

And so the people fell in behind Licentiate Shan and the other distinguished gentlemen as they walked over to the square across from the county yamen and formed a sprawling crowd. Like languid dogs suddenly splashed with cold water, the German sentries and Yuan Shikai's Imperial Guard snapped out of their lethargy, turning the "canes" on which they were resting back into rifles. Green rays spurted from their eyes.

All sorts of strange revelations had floated in the air since the German devils first came ashore at Qingdao. One report had it that their legs were straight and rigid, with no kneecaps to allow them to bend. When they fell over, it was said, they could not get back up. I knew that was a ludicrous rumor because I could see the foreign soldiers' knees bulging out like little garlic hammers in their tight uniform pants. Another story about those creatures was that they screwed like horses and donkeys, shooting their wads as soon as they made it in. But a prostitute in the red light district said to me: "Shoot their wads like horses and donkeys, you say? I tell you, these self-styled gods are like oversized boars, and once they climb on top of you, they stay there for the next hour, at least." People also said that the creatures were always on the hunt for good-looking, clever, quick-witted boys, and when they found them, they pared their tongues with sharp knives so they could learn how to talk like the barbarians. When I asked Master Qian, he had a good laugh over that. "Maybe they do," he said, "but you don't have to worry because you don't have a son." Then he gently rubbed my belly and, as his eyes lit up, said, "Meiniang, oh, Meiniang,

I want you to give me a son!" I told him I didn't think that was possible. If I could have a child, I said, after all these years with Xiaojia, I'd have one by now. With a gentle squeeze, he said, "Didn't you tell me your husband is a fool who hasn't grasped the concept of intimacy?" He squeezed harder, hard enough to bring tears to my eyes. "I haven't let Xiaojia touch me since the first day I gave myself to you," I said. "Go ask him if you don't believe me." "Are you actually suggesting that I, a dignified Magistrate, the county's most respected individual, should go calling on an idiot?" "Not even the county's most respected individual's prick is carved out of stone," I said, "and when the most respected individual is soft, what's the difference between that and a puddle of snot? The most respected individual isn't above jealousy, is he?" Well, after I said that, he loosened his hand and giggled. Then he took me in his arms and said, "My little treasure, you make my chest swell and my heart soar; you are a magic potion sent down to me by the Jade Emperor . . ." Burying my face in his chest, I said coquettishly, "Why won't you find a way to take me from Xiaojia so I can spend every day of the year looking after you? I don't need a formal title; I'll be content to be your personal serving girl." He just shook his head. "Don't be ridiculous. How could I, a dignified County Magistrate, a representative of the Throne, take a citizen's wife from him? If word of that got out, being mocked would be nothing compared to the certain loss of my official hat." "Then let me go," I said. "From this day forward I will never again set foot in this yamen." Well, he kissed me and said, "But I cannot give you up." Then, in the style of a Maoqiang actor, he sang, *"This official is in dire straits~~"* "When did you learn how to sing Maoqiang? Who was your teacher, my dear man of the hour?" *"If wisdom you wish to reap, then with a teacher you must sleep,"* he said roguishly as he patted me on the buttocks as a prelude to more singing, this time in the style of my dieh, and remarkably similar: *"The sky turns yellow as the sun sinks in the west, a tiger runs into the hills, a bird returns to its nest. Only this county boss has nowhere to hide, and must sit in his hall, loneliness to abide~~"* "What sort of loneliness must you abide when you have me keeping you company in bed?" Instead of answering me, he turned my buttocks into a cat drum, pounding out a rhythmic, sonorous beat as he continued to sing: *"I have been a parched seedling sprinkled with dew, ever since the day I first met you."* "You are forever trying to sweet-talk me," I said, "me, a village woman who sells dog meat for a living. What good is someone like that?" *"Your virtues know no end~~in the heat of summer you are ice, in the depths of winter I'm warmed by the flames you send. Your greatest virtue is how you slake my thirst, till I sweat from every pore and my aging joints once again can bend. To lie in bed with the Sun mistress in my arms surpasses the immortals with their heavenly charms~~"* As his song came to an end, he laid me down and covered my face with his beard, as if it were a fanned-out horse's tail. "Gandieh, ah, the words go:

"Flowers planted will not bloom, stick a willow branch in the ground and give it room. We could not have guessed that our conjugal bliss that day would plant the precious seeds of a dragon child. I was ready to reveal glad tidings when~~Heaven help me~~you arrested my dieh to impale him on a stake defiled~~"

I watched as the country squires led by Licentiate Shan moved toward the contingent of wolfish soldiers, whose eyes widened as they held their rifles in both hands, parallel to the ground. At that point, all but the licentiate slowed down and, as if stepping on eggshells or mired in mud, stopped moving altogether. Little by little, Licentiate Shan separated himself from the crowd, like the leader of a bird formation, but one who left the flock frozen in place behind him. When he passed beneath the Education Memorial Archway, he was met by the sound of rifles being slapped into readiness. The country squires cowered behind the archway, but Licentiate Shan stood fast before it. I tore free of the crowd of women and ran to the archway, where I fell to my knees in front of the craven men and behind Licentiate Shan and howled, startling them all. As they turned to gawk at me, I appealed as if chanting on stage: "Revered elders, respected uncles, honorable shopkeepers, worthy squires, hear my plea. I, Sun Bing's daughter, Sun Meiniang, kowtow to you and beg you to come to my dieh's rescue. He was forced into rebelling by another. Everyone knows that even a rabbit will bite in defense, a truth that surely applies to a courageous, upright man who abides by the cardinal guides and constant virtues, a defender of ceremony and propriety. He fomented rebellion among the masses for the benefit of all. Good masters, good uncles, good squires, I beg you, do the merciful thing, for his life is in your hands."

In the midst of my tears and pleas, I saw Licentiate Shan, a towering man, lift up the hem of his robe, take two or three steps forward, and fall to his knees at the feet of the soldiers. I knew he was kneeling not out of respect for them, but for the county yamen and for Magistrate Qian Ding, my gandieh Qian Laoye.

Oh, Gandieh, Meiniang's belly swells, the birth of our precious son it foretells. He is the issue of your mighty seed and will carry on the family line. If not for the monk, then for the Buddha himself, come set my dieh free from the condemned cells.

Now that Licentiate Shan was kneeling, the gentlemen behind him did the same, until the street was a sea of bowed black heads. He took a rolled-up document out from under his robe, opened it with both hands, and, in a loud voice, read each of the words written there:

"Sun Bing caused an incident, but not without reason. When his wife and daughter were abused, his wrath surfaced. He led a rebellion, but on behalf of the common people. His crimes do not warrant the penalty of death, and clemency under the law is what we ask. Release Sun Bing in the name of the people . . ."

Licentiate Shan raised the petition over his head and held it there with both hands, making no move to rise, as if waiting for someone to come take it from him. But all was quiet inside the yamen, so effectively sealed by the wolfish soldiers that it took on the appearance of a rundown temple. Wisps of green smoke continued to rise from scorched beams in the mess hall kitchen that had gone up in flames the night before, and on the walls hung a row of reeking beggars' heads.

Last night heroic men rioted in the Magistrate's lair, flames lit up the sky and chaos was carried on the air. If I hadn't witnessed it with my own eyes, on pain of death I would not have believed the scene that was playing out before me. The thought alone struck fear in me. But a second thought removed that fear, for it belonged to the courageous beggars who had looked death in the eye, proclaiming that losing their heads merely produced bowl-sized scars. *I think about what occurred last night and cringe at my dieh's crazed way, a foolproof plan that quickly went astray. That you will not live costs little, that others died is a heavy price to pay. Your erstwhile saviors gave up their lives. If the First Lady had not played her hand, your daughter would not have survived this day.* Why? Why, Dieh, tell me why!

From time to time, a somber-faced yayi sped by like a cat on the prowl. Licentiate Shan stayed frozen in his kneeling position—a human statue—for as long as it takes to smoke a bowlful of tobacco. The gentlemen and commoners arrayed behind him created flesh-and-blood statuary. And still all was quiet inside. There was no change—a second bowlful up in smoke. And then a third. The soldiers stood there, wide-eyed, rifles at the ready, as if facing menacing enemies. Sweat dripped down Licentiate Shan's neck. Another bowlful, and his legs began to twitch; sweat stains spread across his back, and still there was no movement inside the yamen, which was as quiet as death.

Suddenly, from deep within the crowd, the cry "Have mercy—" from old Granny Sun broke the silence.

The cry was echoed by others in the crowd:

"Have mercy—"

"Have mercy—"

Hot tears blurred my vision, but through the watery veil I saw all the supplicants bang their heads in kowtows. Bodies behind and in front of me rose and fell; on both sides rose a cacophony of tearful shouts and thuds of bone against stone.

The crowd of local residents remained on the street until the sun was nearly overhead and the sentries had changed shifts twice, and yet no one had emerged from the compound to accept Licentiate Shan's petition. Slowly, inevitably, the old man's hands fell lower and lower, and his back began to arch forward. Then, finally, he toppled over in a faint. At that moment, I heard *drums pound, horns toot, cymbals and bells ring. Cannons fire three times as the gate makes its rumbling swing. From it emerges an honor guard. I turn away from the wolfish sentries and from the official party. My eyes are fixed on a prison van, on which two cages stand, a prisoner in each. One is my dieh, the true Sun Bing, the other Xiao Shanzi, the sham Sun Bing.*

Meow meow, meow meow, my heart was breaking . . .

CHAPTER SIXTEEN

Sun Bing's Opera Talk

Good, all right, bravo, wonderful! Now the real drama has begun~~Sun Bing stands alone in his prisoner cage, down streets turned bright by the mid-autumn sun. Looking out through the bars, his gaze falls on kin and friends one by one. Yayi sound the call in front of crazed armed troops, swords unsheathed, arrows on the string, bullets in every gun. German devils, Chinese soldiers, nerves high-strung. All because Zhu Ba's plans at the jail had come undone. Xiao Shanzi would have taken my place, but death I would not shun. Zhu Ba, oh, Zhu Ba, I, Sun Bing, was unworthy of you and your tribe, and to the yellow springs you have gone. Your heads now from the yamen wall are hung, but your names will live on in Maoqiang songs from this day begun.

—*Maoqiang* Sandalwood Death. *Sun Bing's death procession*

1

Zhu Ba clamped his vise-like hands around my throat until I saw stars, my ears rang, my eyes bulged, and my temples throbbed . . . I knew my life was ebbing fast. But no, I cannot die like this; to have the life choked out of me by Zhu Ba would be a travesty. Alive I must be heroic, and I will be defiant unto death. Brother Zhu Ba, Sun Bing knows why you are doing this, that you are afraid of my being impaled on the stake. You are afraid that I will not be able to endure the punishment and will cry for my father and mother. You are afraid that the moment will come when both a speedy death and a life worth living are denied me. And so you plan to foil the Germans' scheme by leaving them only my corpse. Take your hands away, Brother Zhu Ba, for killing me this way will ruin my good name. You should know that my resistance to the Germans has been only partially realized; if I shy from my goal now, it will be like a tiger-head start and a snake-tail finish, a cowardly abandonment. I look forward to walking proudly down the street singing a Maoqiang aria, to live like a warrior and die as a martyr. I want to stand tall and shout my militancy; I want to be the agent of a popular awakening and the cause of crippling fear among the foreign devils. Only moments before death claimed me, I suddenly knew what I had to do: I first clawed at my would-be killer's eyes with both hands and then kneed him in the groin. Something hot and wet dripped down my body as the hands fell away, freeing my neck from danger.

As bright moonlight streamed down, I saw that Zhu Ba and I were surrounded by Imperial Guards, their faces bloated like inflated pig bladders. A couple of those pig bladders came up, grabbed me by the arms, and dragged me away, and as my vision cleared, I saw my old friend, the beggar Zhu Ba, lying crumpled on the ground and twitching uncontrollably. Gobs of foul-smelling blue matter were oozing from his head, and I realized that he hadn't let go because of my struggle, but because he had been clubbed.

I was immediately bundled by a clutch of shouting men through the secondary gate, past the Exhortation Memorial Arch, and deposited on a platform in front of the Main Hall. I looked up, and was nearly blinded by the array of lanterns that lit up the interior of the hall while others, hung high from the eaves, threw the placard bearing the official title of Yuan Shikai into sharp relief. The Gaomi County formal hall lanterns had been moved to the sides. The soldiers carried me inside and flung me onto the stone kneeling bench. By propping my hands on the floor, I managed to stand up on wobbly legs, but only long enough for a soldier to kick me behind the knee and send me back to the stone bench. Again using my hands, I moved my legs out in front to use the bench as a chair. I refused to kneel.

Once I was in a comfortable sitting position, I looked up and laid eyes on the moon-shaped, oily face of Yuan Shikai and the long, gaunt face of the German von Ketteler. Magistrate Qian Ding was standing to the side, bent at the waist, his back arched, looking both pathetic and anxious.

"You, down there, villain." It was Yuan Shikai's voice. "State your name!"

"Ha-ha, ha-ha . . ." My laughter rang through the hall. "Excellency Yuan's eyesight does not serve him well," I said. "With pride I shall tell you who I am. I am the leader of the resistance against German aggression, once known as Sun Bing, but I have been anointed the great spirit Yue Fei, carrying the posthumous name of Wumu. I suffered cruelly when imprisoned in the Pavilion of Wind and Waves!"

"Bring the lanterns closer!" Yuan Shikai demanded.

Several lanterns materialized in front of my face.

"Magistrate Qian, what is going on here?" Yuan Shikai said icily.

Qian Ding rushed up, flicked his sleeves, and lifted the hem of his robe so he could get down on one knee.

"Excellency, your humble servant personally went to the condemned cells, where I found Sun Bing chained to the bandit's stone."

"Then who is this?"

The Magistrate rushed up and stood in front of me to get a closer look with the aid of the lanterns. His eyes flashed like will-o'-the-wisps. I thrust out my chin, parted my lips, and said:

"Take a good look, Eminence Qian. This is a chin you ought to recognize. There was a time when it sprouted a beard so grand that each strand stayed perfectly straight even when immersed in water. And in this mouth there were once two perfect rows of teeth so tough they could bite through bone and leave marks in iron. It was you who personally yanked out the hairs of that beard, and von Ketteler who knocked out my teeth with the butt of his pistol."

"Well, if you are Sun Bing, then who is the Sun Bing in the cell?" Qian Ding asked. "Don't tell me you can be in two places at the same time."

"I cannot be in two places at the same time. It's you who are blind."

"Guards, sentries, be on your toes. Bolt the main doors and search the grounds," Yuan Shikai commanded his men. "Bring every one of those villains to me, dead or alive." Regardless of rank or station, they swarmed out of the hall. "And you, County Magistrate, take someone with you to the condemned cells and bring that Sun Bing here to me. I want to see for myself which is the true Sun Bing and which is a fake."

Hardly any time passed before the soldiers returned with the corpses of four beggars and one monkey. Actually, four corpses is not quite accurate, for a gurgling sound rumbled in the throat of Zhu Ba and bloody drool formed in the shape of chrysanthemum blossoms around his mouth. I was no more than three feet away, close enough to see light streaming from his still-open eyes. It stabbed straight to my heart. Old Zhu Ba, we have been friends, more like brothers, for twenty years. I still recall how I brought my Maoqiang troupe to perform in town, and you invited me to drink three cups with you in the Temple of the Matriarch. You were obsessed with Maoqiang opera, and had already committed great portions of fine operas to memory. You had a voice like a gander, which imparted a unique quality to your singing. No one sang the old-man parts any better than you. Surges of emotion unsettle my heart when I recall the old days, my brother, and favorite lines of opera want to spill from within. I was about to burst into an operatic aria when I heard the commotion outside the hall.

The clanking of chains made its way into the hall, as Xiao Shanzi appeared in the custody of a clutch of yayi. He was wearing a ripped white robe and was shackled hand and foot. Dried blood stained his skin and clothing; his lips were cut and torn, and he was missing three teeth. Flames seemed to shoot from his eyes . . . his every step, his every move, his every gesture, were just like mine, though he had one more missing tooth than I. I was secretly shocked, seeing what a spectacular production Zhu Ba had put together. If not for that extra missing tooth, I'm sure my own mother could not have told us apart.

"Excellency," the Magistrate came forward to report, "your humble servant has brought the foremost criminal Sun Bing to the hall."

I watched as Yuan Shikai and von Ketteler gaped in wide-eyed amazement.

Xiao Shanzi stood straight, head up, and gave them a foolish grin.

"Insolent criminal," Yuan Shikai thundered, "why are you not on your knees?"

"I am the great Song General," Xiao Shanzi replied fervently in imitation of my voice. "I bow down before heaven and earth, I kneel at the feet of my parents, but nothing can make me fall to my knees in front of barbarians and mangy dogs."

He was a natural, an actor with an ideal voice. Back when Zhu Ba had invited me to teach opera to the beggars in the Temple of the Matriarch, few of them could boast of much talent. In fact, he alone had the necessary adaptability, able to immediately grasp the essentials. I taught him to sing *The Hongmen Banquet* and *In Pursuit of Han Xin*, which he learned well, with perfect pitch and a splendid stage appearance; it was as if he were made for them. I tried to get him to join the troupe, but Zhu Ba wanted to keep him around to take over the leadership after his death.

"Good Brother Shanzi," I said, saluting him with cupped hands, "you have been well since last we met?"

"Good Brother Shanzi," he repeated my greeting, "you have been well since last we met?" His shackles clanked when he brought his hands together to return my salute.

How absurd, utterly preposterous that was, a performance of the true and false Monkey King there in the middle of the Great Hall!

"On your knees, condemned prisoner," Yuan Shikai demanded majestically, "and answer my question!"

"I am like bamboo in the wind, which will break before it bends, like the mountain jade that will shatter before it is taken whole."

"Kneel!"

"Kill me, take my head, do as you please, but I will not kneel!"

"Put him on his knees!" Yuan ordered, by now nearly apoplectic.

The yayi pounced on Xiao Shanzi like wild beasts, grabbed him by the arms, and forced him to his knees. But the minute they took their hands away, he shifted his legs out in front, just as I had done. Now we were sitting side by side. I grimaced; so did he. I glared; he did too. I said, "Shanzi, you are a scoundrel." He said, "Shanzi, you are a scoundrel." We were like performers in a comic skit, one aping the other, with the surprising effect of taking the edge off of Yuan Shikai's anger. He actually chuckled, while von Ketteler, who was sitting right beside him, laughed like an idiot.

"In all my years as an official, I thought I had seen every type of bizarre behavior possible. But this is the first time I've watched two people vying to be a condemned prisoner. Gaomi Magistrate, you are a wise and worldly man," Yuan said sarcastically. "Explain to me what has just happened."

"Your humble servant is a man of little learning," Qian Ding said in a reverential tone, "and requires guidance from above."

"Then tell me which of the two people sitting on the floor is the true Sun Bing."

Qian Ding walked up to us and looked first at one and then at the other. The look in his eyes said he was having trouble making up his mind, but I knew that this official, cleverer than a monkey, was able to tell the real Sun Bing from the fake at first glance. So why the hesitant look? Could it be as simple as trying to protect the father of his lover? Was it possible that he would willingly let a beggar suffer the sandalwood death in my stead?

The Magistrate studied the two of us for a long moment before turning to report to Yuan Shikai:

"Excellency, my eyesight is poor, and I truly cannot tell them apart."

"Look closer."

The Magistrate put his face right up next to us. He shook his head.

"I still cannot tell, Excellency."

"Look at their mouths."

"They are both missing teeth."

"Do you see a difference?"

"One is missing three teeth, the other is missing two."

"How many teeth is Sun Bing missing?"

"Your humble servant cannot recall."

"The dog bastard von Ketteler knocked out three of my teeth with the butt of his pistol," Xiao Shanzi eagerly volunteered.

"No," I corrected him forcefully, "von Ketteler knocked out two of my teeth."

"Gaomi Magistrate, you should remember how many of Sun Bing's teeth were knocked out."

"Your humble servant truly cannot recall, Excellency."

"So you are telling me that you cannot tell the real from the fake, is that it?"

"My eyesight is poor, and I truly cannot tell them apart."

"Well, then, if even the local Magistrate cannot tell them apart, there is no need to keep trying," Yuan Shikai said with a wave of his hand. "Lock them both up in condemned cells. Tomorrow they will both have a date with a sandalwood stake. Gaomi Magistrate, tonight you will watch over them. If there is a problem with either one, it will be on your head."

"Your humble servant will do his best . . ." The Magistrate bowed deeply, and I saw that the back of his robe was wet from perspiration. Nothing remained of his erstwhile poise and proud demeanor.

"This switch could not have taken place without the assistance of someone in the yamen," Yuan Shikai said, having seen the obvious. "I want the jailer and all those assigned guard duties at the condemned cells here first thing tomorrow to answer some serious questions!"

2

Before Yuan's soldiers could carry out his order, the jailer had hanged himself in the Prison God Temple. Yayi dragged his corpse out of the compound like a dead dog and deposited it alongside those of Zhu Ba, Hou Xiaoqi, and the others. While soldiers were dragging me over to the condemned cells, I saw executioners cutting off the dead beggars' heads on someone's orders. Sick at heart, I experienced intense feelings of remorse. Maybe, I thought, I've been wrong; maybe I should have done what Zhu Ba wanted me to do, which was to quietly slip away and foil the scheming collaboration between Yuan Shikai and von Ketteler. I'd wanted to render a great service, to leave a good name for posterity, and to have been loyal, trustworthy, merciful, and benevolent, but I wound up causing the deaths of so many. Enough; no more such thoughts. I'll cast away all that has tormented me and somehow make it through the night, waiting for the light of tomorrow.

The County Magistrate had his men chain Xiao Shanzi and me to the same bandit's stone and light three candles inside the cell and a row of lanterns outside. He moved a chair up and sat just beyond the door. Through the tiny window I saw seven or eight yayi assembled behind him and an array of soldiers behind them. The fire in the mess hall kitchen had been put out, but the air was still thick with smoke, and it was getting worse.

The fourth watch was sounded.

Roosters crowed, some near, some far, and lantern light dimmed; the candles in the cell had burned down halfway. The County Magistrate was still in his chair, head slumped down on his chest, like a wheat stalk weighted down after a frost, seemingly neither dead nor alive. I knew he was in a perilous situation, that even if he didn't lose his head over what had happened, his days as an official were over. Ah, Qian Ding, what happened to that hard-drinking, poem-writing man you once were? County Magistrate, oh, County Magistrate, mortal enemies are bound to meet; my death tomorrow will erase all debts of gratitude and enmity.

Xiao Shanzi, Xiao Shanzi, whom I count as my protégé, by disfiguring your own face and taking another's place in jail, you have earned a place in the annals of history for your incorruptible loyalty. Why did you adamantly insist that you are Sun Bing? Had you told the truth, you would have lost your head, but how much easier that would be than suffering the sandalwood death!

"Worthy brother, why did you do what you did?" I asked him softly.

"Shifu," he replied in an even softer voice, "if I had taken the easy way out by letting them lop off my head, wouldn't I have lost three teeth for nothing?"

"But have you given any thought to the sandalwood death?"

"Shifu, we beggars are hard on ourselves from the moment we're born. On the day Master Zhu Ba took me on as his disciple, he made me stab myself with a knife. I have trained myself in the ruse of self-injury, and I have trained myself in taking a knife to the head. There are blessings in this world not meant for beggars, but no suffering we do not endure. I urge Shifu to disavow his claim to be Sun Bing; let them punish you with a quick death, and allow your young brother to take the punishment meant for you. By letting me suffer the sandalwood death in your place, it will be your good name that gains the credit."

"Since your mind is made up," I said, "then let us crash the Gates of Hell arm in arm. We will show them the meaning of a heroic death and give those foreign devils and treacherous officials a taste of Gaomi courage!"

"Shifu, daybreak is still a ways off," Xiao Shanzi said. "While you have the chance, won't you tell me about the origins of Maoqiang opera?"

"Yes, Shanzi, I will. My good young protégé, there is an adage that goes, 'When death looms, a person can speak only good.' As your shifu, I will relate for you the history of Maoqiang opera, from its beginnings up to the present.

3

"It is told that during the reign of the Yongzheng Emperor, in the eighteenth century, a truly remarkable man by the name of Chang Mao was born in Northeast Gaomi Township. Single and childless, he had but one companion, a black cat. A crockery mender by trade, he walked the streets and alleys from dawn to dusk carrying his tools and his cat in baskets on a shoulder pole, stopping to mend people's cracked and broken crockery. He was very good at his trade and, as a man of fine character, was well liked by all. One day, at the funeral of a friend, as he stood before the gravesite, sadness welled up inside him as he thought back to how decently this friend had treated him, and he was moved to pour out his grief in a voice with such lush qualities that the family of the deceased stopped crying and everyone within earshot fell silent. Listening with rapt concentration, they were amazed to discover that a crockery mender had such an affecting voice.

"This was a seminal moment in the history of Maoqiang opera. Chang Mao's sung recitation surpassed women's cries of anguish and men's dry-eyed wails. He brought solace to the grief-stricken and entertainment to the uninvolved, launching a revolution in traditional funeral expressions of bereavement and giving rise to a new era with fresh sights and sounds. It was like a Buddhist devotee laying eyes on the Land of Ultimate Bliss, with celestial flowers raining down, or someone covered in dirt slipping into a bath to wash away the grime, then drinking a pot of hot tea to force sweat out of every pore. And the talk began, how Chang Mao was more than a fine mender of crockery, that he had a voice that resounded like a brass bell, an unrivaled memory, and the gift of eloquence. As time went on, more and more grieving families requested his attendance at graveside ceremonies, asking him to appease the souls of the departed and lessen the sorrows of the survivors. Understandably, at first he declined the requests. Why in the world would he offer vocal laments at the gravesite of a total stranger? No, he'd say the first time, and the second. But the third invitation was always difficult to turn down—did not Liu Bei manage to get Zhuge Liang to his cottage the third time he asked? Besides, they would be fellow townsmen, tied together one way or another, people you could not help meeting from time to time, and in a hundred years or so, everyone would be related anyway. So if he could not do something for the sake of the living, he ought to do it for the departed. Seeing a dead man is like encountering a tiger; seeing a dead tiger is like meeting up with a lamb. The dead are noble, the living worthless. So he went. Once, twice, a third time . . . and he was always treated as an honored guest, warmly welcomed by all. Human waste spoils a tree's roots; spirits and good food intoxicate a man's heart. How could a lowly crockery mender not be moved by such expansive treatment? And so he put his heart into what he was asked to do. A honed knife is sharp; a practiced skill is perfected. Each funeral gave him an opportunity to whet his skills, until finally his artistry was unmatched. In order to introduce something new into his art, he called upon the wisest man in town, Ma Daguan, to whom he apprenticed himself as a student of tales, ancient and new. Then each morning he went alone to the riverbank to practice his singing voice.

"The first to ask Chang Mao to sing at funerals were humble families, but once word of his artistry began to spread, well-to-do families sought his services as well. During those days in Northeast Gaomi Township, any burial ceremony in which he participated became a grand event. People came from miles around, bringing with them the elderly and the very young. And the ceremonies in which he did not participate? However lavish the procession or plentiful the sacrificial offerings might be—banners and pendants blotting out the sun, forests of food and rivers of liquor—the turnout would be sparse. The day finally arrived when Chang Mao laid down his pole and mending tools for the last time and began life as a master bereavement singer.

"People spoke of a local family of bereavement singers in the Confucian homeland whose womenfolk had fine voices. But their specialty was to assume the roles of surviving family members of the deceased to wail and howl songs of piteous sorrow, and bore no resemblance to Chang Mao's performances. Why compare those bereavement singers to our Patriarch? Because many decades ago, a rumor spread that the founder of our tradition had set out on the path of bereavement singing inspired by Confucian singers. So I made a special trip to Qufu, the birthplace of Confucius, and found that women who sang bereavements still existed there, but that their songs had few lines, mostly "Oh, heaven! Oh, earth!" Our Patriarch's artistry went far beyond that. Comparing those women to him is like equating heaven with earth or a pheasant with a phoenix.

"Our Patriarch improvised at gravesites, weaving the life of the deceased into his lyrics. He had a quick wit and a brilliant tongue, rhyming in all the right places, colloquial and easy to understand, but soaring with literary grace. His lines of sorrow were essentially a funeral elegy. As demands to meet his listeners' expectations intensified, he no longer limited his recitations to the life and virtues of the deceased, but introduced philosophical views of life in general. And Maoqiang opera was born."

At that point in my narration, I turned to see the Magistrate, who was sitting outside the condemned cells, cocking his ear as if listening to what I was saying. Go ahead, listen. I want you to hear. If you don't have an ear for Maoqiang, you'll never truly understand Northeast Gaomi Township. Ignorance of its history means you cannot comprehend what is in the hearts of its residents. So I raised my voice even though my throat burned and my tongue ached.

"I said at the beginning that our Patriarch had a cat, a very clever cat, much like the Red Rabbit steed the Three Kingdoms hero Guan Yu rode. He loved that cat, and the cat loved him back. He never went anywhere without it. When he sang a graveside elegy, that cat would sit on the ground in front of him, listening intently, and when the sorrowful climax was reached, it joined in with a doleful howl of its own. The Patriarch's voice stood out among his peers; the cat's howls were themselves incomparable. Owing to the shared intimacy, people of the day took to calling him "Chang the Cat," since the word for cat—*mao*—sounded the same as his name.

"Even now, there is a popular ditty in Northeast Gaomi Township that goes——

"Better to hear Chang Mao screech than listen to the Master teach," Xiao Shanzi said with deep emotion.

"Well, one day the cat died; how it died is unclear. One version ascribes it to old age. Another insists that it was poisoned by an out-of town-actor who was envious of the Patriarch's talent. There is even a version in which the cat was strangled by a vengeful woman who was rebuffed by the Patriarch in her desire to become his wife. Whatever the truth, the cat did die, an event that so traumatized our Patriarch that he held the cat in his arms and cried for three days and nights, interspersing his wails with songs of bereavement, until blood leaked from his eyes.

"After overcoming the worst of his grief, the Patriarch fashioned two items of cat clothing from the skins of wild animals. The smaller of the two, made from the pelt of a feral cat, he wore on his head for daily use—ears rising from each side, tail hanging down past the nape of his neck alongside his modest queue. The larger item, made from the skins of a dozen or more cats, was a ceremonial robe, trailing a long cat's tail behind him; he wore it thereafter when he performed graveside bereavements.

"The death of his companion initiated a major change in the Patriarch's singing style. Before that, cheerful banter had been woven into his songs; now forlorn strains dominated from start to finish. There was also a change in his singing style, for now the desolate contents were dotted with dulcet or melancholy or bleak cat cries that changed constantly, like a series of interludes. The new style not only has survived to this day, but has become the central feature of Maoqiang opera."

"Meow—— Meow—" On an impulse, Xiao Shanzi interrupted my narration with a pair of cat cries pregnant with nostalgia.

"After the death of his cat, our Patriarch adopted the walking and speaking style of a cat, as if possessed by the spirit of his dead companion. He and his cat had become one. Even his eyes underwent a change: slitted during the day, they glowed in the darkness of night. Then one day the Patriarch died, and a legend was born that he turned into a large cat on his deathbed, but with wings that grew from his shoulders and carried him through the window and onto the limb of a giant tree. From there he flew straight to the moon.

"The vocation of bereavement singing died with the Patriarch, but his melodic, heartbreaking elegies never stopped swirling in the hearts of our people."

4

"Later, during the nineteenth-century reigns of the Jiaqing and Daoguang emperors, small family troupes mimicked the vocal offerings of the Patriarch in performances, usually consisting of a male singer, echoed by his wife, and complemented by their child, dressed in a cat costume, who supplied the feline cries. When the opportunity arose, they sang funeral elegies for rich families—by then, 'bereavement laments' had become 'bereavement songs'—but most of the time they put on public performances at open markets. Husband and wife sang and acted out their parts while their child moved cat-like, making a variety of feline sounds as he circled the crowd with his donations basket. Short performances were the order of the day, including such favorites as *Lan Shuilian Sells Water*, *A Widow Weeps at a Gravesite*, and *Third Sister Wang Misses Her Husband*. In reality, these performances were a form of begging. Maoqiang actors are cousins to professional beggars, and that is how you became my protégé."

"Shifu speaks the truth," Xiao Shanzi said.

"That was how things stood for several generations. Musical instruments were not used in the Maoqiang of those days, and there was no staging. It was operatic but not yet opera. Besides the small family troupes I spoke of a moment ago, there were peasants who made up musical interludes during leisure periods, accompanied by gongs used for peddling candy and clappers used by bean curd peddlers, singing them for themselves in cellars where straw sandals were made or on heated brick beds in their own homes, all to dispel loneliness and ease a life of suffering. Those gongs and clappers were the forerunners of today's Maoqiang instruments.

"I was young and clever back then—I'm not boasting—and I had the finest voice in all of Northeast Gaomi Township's eighteen villages. I began to gain a reputation when I joined my voice with others. People—locals at first, then outsiders—came to listen, and when the cellars and brick beds could no longer accommodate them all, we moved into yards and onto threshing grounds. People could be seated when they sang in those cellars and on brick beds, but not in open spaces, where movement was required. But then movement in ordinary clothing did not feel natural, so costumes were required. But then costumes and unadorned faces did not produce the right effect, so singers painted their faces. Costumes and painted faces needed something more—instruments more varied than gongs and clappers. Ragtag troupes from other counties gave performances in town, including the "Donkey Opera" specialists from Southern Shandong, who rode their animals onto the stage. There were also the southern Jiao County "Gliders," whose ending note of each sentence glided from high to low, like sledding down a mountain slope. Actors in one so-called "rooster troupe" from the Henan-Shandong border area ended each line with a sort of hiccup, the sound a rooster makes at the end of its crow. All these troupes came with instrumental accompaniment, for the most part huqin, dizi, suonas, and laba—fiddles, flutes, woodwinds, and horns. The visitors played their instruments at our performances, and the effects were more impressive than those with singing alone. But I am so competitive, I've never been satisfied with someone else's brainchild. By this time our opera was already known as Maoqiang, and I was thinking that if I wanted to create a unique opera form, it had to be all about cats. And so I invented an instrument called the mao hu—the cat fiddle. With that instrument, Maoqiang had found its place.

"My instrument was bigger than other fiddles; it had four strings and a double bow, which produced fascinating compound notes. Their fiddles were snakeskin-covered; for ours we used tanned cat skins. Their fiddles were good for ordinary tones, while ours could produce cat cries dog yelps donkey brays horse whinnies baby bawls maiden giggles rooster crows hen cackles—there wasn't a sound on earth that our fiddles could not reproduce. The cat fiddle put Maoqiang opera on the map, and ragtag troupes found no place in Northeast Gaomi Township after that.

"I followed my invention of the cat fiddle with another—the cat drum, a small drum made of cat skin. I also came up with a dozen facial designs: happy cats, angry cats, treacherous cats, loyal cats, affectionate cats, resentful cats, hateful cats, unsightly cats . . . would it be an exaggeration to say that without Sun Bing, today there would be no Maoqiang opera?"

"Again Shifu speaks the truth," Xiao Shanzi said.

"Of course I am not the opera's Patriarch. That was Chang Mao. If Maoqiang were a tree, then Chang Mao would be our roots."

5

"Worthy young brother, which operas did I teach you to sing all those years ago?"

"*The Hongmen Banquet*, Shifu," Xiao Shanzi replied softly, "and *In Pursuit of Han Xin*."

"Ah, those, both stolen—by me—from other operas. You probably are unaware that Shifu played bit roles with at least ten opera troupes in other counties in order to poach bits of their performances. My desire to learn opera took me down south, out of Shanxi, across the Yangtze, and into Guangxi and Guangdong. There isn't an opera anywhere that Shifu cannot perform, and no role that Shifu cannot act. Like a bumblebee, I have taken nectar from all the operatic flowers to create the fine honey of Maoqiang opera."

"Shifu, you are a miraculous talent!"

"Your shifu once had a grand desire to take Maoqiang opera to Peking at least one time before he died and perform for the Emperor and the Empress Dowager. I wanted it to become a national dramatic form. Once that happened, rats would disappear from the land north and south of the great river. What a shame that before I could put this grand plan into action, a treacherous individual yanked the beard right off my face. That beard was the symbol of Shifu's prestige, my courage, my talent, the very soul of Maoqiang. Shifu without a beard is like a cat without whiskers like a rooster without tail feathers like a horse with a shorn tail . . . worthy young brother, Shifu had no choice but to leave the stage and drift through life as the owner of a little teahouse, fated to die with unfulfilled aspirations, something that has bedeviled heroic figures since time immemorial."

At this point in my narration, I noted that the Gaomi County Magistrate was shuddering, and that Xiao Shanzi's eyes were filled with tears.

"My young protégé, the featured opera in our repertoire is *Chang Mao Weeps for a Departed Spirit*, my first major creation. It has always been the first performed for each new season. If it is well done, the success of our run that season is ensured; if not, there are bound to be problems down the line. You've lived your life in Northeast Gaomi Township. How many times have you seen *Chang Mao Weeps for a Departed Spirit*?"

"I'm not sure, but it must be dozens of times."

"Has it ever been the same twice, in your view?"

"No, Shifu, I always came away with something new," Xiao Shanzi said dreamily, his thoughts going back in time. "I still remember the first time I saw *Chang Mao Weeps for a Departed Spirit*. I was just a boy then and wore a cat-skin cap. You played the role of Chang Mao, and when you sang, sparrows dropped out of the trees. But what impressed me most was not your songs. No, it was the big boy who played the role of the cat. He filled the air with cat cries, no two alike, and long before the opera was finished, everyone at the foot of the stage went crazy. We boys ran around, threading our way through the crowd of adults and making cat sounds. *Meow meow meow*. Three large trees stood at the edge of the square, and we fought to climb them. As a rule, I wasn't very good at climbing trees, but that day I climbed so nimbly you'd have thought I was a cat. Well, the tree was already filled with real cats. I had no idea when they'd climbed up there, but they joined us in a chorus of loud meows, until the stage and the area around it, sky and ground, were alive with cat cries. Men women adults children real cats pretend cats, all joined together in opening up their throats to release sounds previously unknown to them and began to move in ways they'd never dreamed possible. Eventually they lay spent on the ground, bodies soaked with sweat, faces awash in tears and snot, like empty shells. We cat children fell out of the trees, one after another, like so many black stones. The cats up there floated down to the ground, as if they'd grown webbing between their paws, like flying mice. I still recall the last line of that day's opera: 'Cat oh cat oh cat oh cat oh cat, my dear, precious cat . . .' Shifu, you drew out that last 'cat,' making it tumble skyward until it was a hundred feet higher than the tallest poplar tree, taking everyone's heart into the clouds with it."

"My young protégé, you are as capable of singing *Chang Mao Weeps for a Departed Spirit* as I am."

"No, Shifu, but if I could be on the stage with you, I'd like to be the cat boy."

I took a long, emotional look at this fine Northeast Township youngster. "My boy, you and I are right now acting out the second signature Maoqiang opera, which we can call *Sandalwood Death*."

6

Tradition dictated that we be brought out to the Main Hall, where a tray with four plates of food, a pot of strong spirits, some flatbreads, and a bunch of leeks were laid out. There was braised pig's head, a plate of stewed chicken, a fish, and some spicy beef. The flatbreads were bigger than the lid of a wok, the leeks fresh and moist, the spirits steamy hot. Xiao Shanzi and I sat across from each other and smiled. Two Sun Bings, one real and one fake, clinked glasses and then emptied them noisily. Tears spurted from our eyes as the heated spirits worked their way down; we were like members of a loyal brotherhood, impassioned. On Wangxiang tai, the terrace in Hell from which we can see our homes, we will walk hand in hand, shoulder to shoulder, and fly up to the ninth heaven on a rainbow. So we feasted, swallowing the food nearly whole, since we were missing so many teeth. As we looked death calmly in the face, fearless and exuberant, a grand and solemn opera had begun. The prison van turned onto the main street, lined by jostling crowds. What actors want most is an audience bristling with feverish anticipation, and there is no more solemn, stirring moment in life than being taken to the execution ground. I, Sun Bing, had acted on the stage for thirty years, but this was going to be my finest day ever.

I saw light glinting off the tips of bayonets up front and shiny red- and blue-tasseled caps behind. My fellow townspeople's eyes flashed on both sides of the street. Many of the country squires' beards quivered, and many women's eyes were wet with tears; many children stood with their mouths agape, slobber running down their chins. Suddenly, hidden there among all those women was my daughter, Meiniang, and I experienced a sadness that nearly made me weep. A true man can spill blood but not tears; he must not sacrifice his manly virtues for the love of family.

As the van's wooden wheels rumbled down the cobblestone street, the harsh sunlight made my scalp itch. The clang of a gong leading the way was carried on an early fall breeze, and as I looked up into the azure sky, I experienced a sense of desolation. The blue sky and white clouds turned my thoughts to the puffy white clouds reflected in the crystal-clear waters of the Masang River. I had carried water from that river for customers who arrived from all corners. I thought of Little Peach, my wonderful wife, and of my two delightful children. My loathing for the Germans, whose railroad had destroyed the feng shui of our Northeast Gaomi Township, knew no bounds. Grievous thoughts made my throat itch, and I raised my voice in tribute to my fellow villagers and townspeople:

I travel amid shouting crowds, unafraid~~I wear a python-and-dragon robe, my hat of gold threads made. I swagger, my waist cinched by a belt of jade~~look at those pigs and dogs, who dares step on my heel in this parade~~

I had only managed those few lines before the teeming crowds along the street roared their delight—"Bravo!" Xiao Shanzi, my good protégé, did not miss a beat, chiming in with cat cries, each slightly different~~*Meow meow meow*~~adding a veneer of luster to my singing.

Look up at swirling winds of gold, then farther down lush trees behold~~a martyr's spirit, I raise the flag of rebellion, as commanded on high, to preserve China's rivers and mountains, and not allow a foreign railroad our land to enfold~~I have eaten the dragon's liver and the phoenix's brain, fiery spirits and ambrosia drink have made me bold~~

Meow meow meow~~

My fine young protégé filled in the gaps with his cries . . .

There were tears in my fellow villagers' eyes, but then, starting with the children, they echoed Xiao Shanzi's cat cries. It must have sounded as if all the cats in the world had come together at this place.

As my song and my fellow villagers' cries swirled in the air together, I saw that the color had left Yuan Shikai and von Ketteler's faces, and that the frightened soldiers, foreign devils included, were ashen-faced, as if confronted by mortal enemies. Sun Bing could now die with no regrets, in the wake of this spectacular operatic moment!

Good, wonderful, bravo, fellow townsmen do not fret——fret fret fret, all you traitors, be on your guard——watch watch watch, our people rise in rebellion——go go go, go tear up those tracks——die die die, die a good death——fire fire fire, flames reach into the sky——finish finish finish, finished not yet——demand demand demand, a cry for justice be met——

Meow meow meow meow~~

Mew~~

CHAPTER SEVENTEEN

Xiaojia Sings in Full Voice

Cannons draped in red create a rumbling boom, wind in a clear sky where wind and thunder loom~~meow meow meow~~I'm with Dieh-dieh on this execution day, and in my heart flowers bloom, glowing reds lucid purples glistening yellows pure whites blues, ah, soulful blues~~having a dieh is wonderful, having a dieh is wonderful~~meow meow~~when Dieh-dieh said that killing a person is better than killing a pig, I nearly jumped out of my skin~~wuliaoao, wuliao~~this morning I had plenty to eat, oil fritters that can't be beat, and from the small pot my fill of meat. Blood-soaked fritters a tasty treat, better than a dead rat with tiny feet~~wuliaoao, wuliao~~Another dead rat is the blood-soaked flesh~~Sandalwood stakes tested on a pig, Dieh-dieh training me to match his masterful skills. All to impale Sun Bing from the bottom up. Pound in the stake, ah, pound in the stake, pound in the stake~~meow meow meow~~A raucous crowd comes our way down the street, a cannon fires, bad news brings a change to my eyes. Then the tiger whisker spirit reappears, and the scene around me augurs defeat. No more people, the ground is full of pigs and dogs and horses and cows, bad people turned into savage wild animals, even a big turtle carried on an eight-man palanquin seat. It is Yuan Shikai, that bastard effete, a high official who is no match for my dieh~~meow meow meow~~mew~~

—*Maoqiang* Sandalwood Death. *A childish aria*

1

Brilliant reds greeted me when I opened my eyes—Hey! Where's the fire? Heh-heh, there's no fire. The sun had come out. The bed of wheat straw was alive with insects that bit me all over. Half-cooked oil fritters lay heavily in my stomach all night long, and I could not stop breaking wind. I could see that Dieh was no longer a panther, just my dieh, a mystical dieh who sat primly in the sandalwood Dragon Chair given to him by His Majesty the Emperor, fingering his string of sandalwood prayer beads. There were times when I wanted to sit in that chair just to see how it felt, but Dieh said no. "Not just anyone can sit in this chair," he said. "If you don't have a dragon bunghole, you'll get up with hemorrhoids." Liar! If Dieh had a dragon bunghole, how could his son not have one? If he did and his son didn't, then the dieh wouldn't be the dieh and the son wouldn't be the son. So there! I was used to hearing people say "A dragon begets a dragon, a phoenix begets a phoenix, and when a rat is born, it digs a hole." So Dieh was sitting in his chair, half his face red, the other half white, eyes barely open, lips seeming to quiver, all sort of dreamlike.

"Dieh," I said, "please let me sit in that chair just for a moment before they get here."

"No," he said, pulling a long face, "not yet."

"Then when?"

"After we've completed the important task ahead of us." The expression on his face had not changed, and I knew that was intentional. He was very, very fond of me, a boy everyone was drawn to. How could he not be? I went up behind him, wrapped my arms around his neck, and touched the back of his head with my chin. "Since you won't let me sit in the Dragon Chair," I said, "then tell me a Peking story before they get here."

"I do that every single day," he said, seemingly annoyed. "How many stories do you think there are?"

I knew his annoyance was just an act. Dieh enjoyed nothing more than telling me Peking stories. "Please, Dieh," I said. "If you don't have any new stories, tell me one of the old ones."

"What's so appealing about the old stories?" he said. "Have you never heard the adage 'Repeat something three times, and not even the dogs will listen'?"

"I'll listen even if the dogs won't," I said.

"What am I going to do with you, my boy?" He looked up at the sun. "We have a little time," he said finally. "I'll tell you a story about Guo Mao, how's that?"

2

I have not forgotten a single story my dieh told me, not one of the hundred and forty-one. Each of them is packed away in my head, which has lots of drawers, like those cabinets in herbal pharmacies. Every story has a drawer of its own, and there are still lots of drawers left over. I started pulling out drawers, and found that none of them held a story about Guo Mao. Happy? I was thrilled!

A new story! I pulled out the hundred and forty-second drawer, into which I would put the story of Guo Mao.

"During the Xianfeng reign in the mid-nineteenth century, a father and son showed up in Tianqiao. The father's name was Guo Mao, or Guo the Cat. His son's name was Xiaomao, or Kitten. Both father and son were accomplished mimics. Do you know what that is? It's someone who uses his mouth to imitate all the different sounds in the world."

"Could they imitate the cry of a cat?"

"Children mustn't interrupt when grownups are talking! Anyway, father and son quickly gained a reputation as street performers in Tianqiao. When I heard about them, I sneaked over to Tianqiao, without telling Grandma Yu, and joined the crowd milling at the square. I was pretty small back then, and skinny, and I had no trouble squeezing my way up front, where I saw a boy sitting on a stool, holding a hat. I got there just in time for the performance to begin: a rooster crows behind a dark curtain, a sound that's immediately echoed by dozens of roosters, near and far, some of them squeaky attempts by young birds still with fledgling feathers. The squawks are accompanied by the *thup-thup* of flapping wings. Then an old woman tells her husband and son that it is time to get up. The old man coughs, spits, lights his pipe, and bangs the bowl against the side of the heated bed. The boy snores on until she forces him to get out of bed, which he does, muttering and yawning noisily as he gets dressed. A door opens, and the boy goes outside to pee before fetching water to wash up. The old woman starts a fire in the stove with the help of a bellows, while the old man and the boy go out to the pigsty to catch one of the pigs, a noisy process. The pig crashes through the gate and starts running around in the yard, where it knocks over a water bucket and smashes a bedpan. Then it bursts into a henhouse, producing an uproar of squawks from the terrified chickens, several of which flap their way up onto a wall. The boy grabs the squealing pig by a hind leg and is joined by his father, who takes hold of the other hind leg and helps him pull the animal out of the henhouse. But its head is caught, which its shrill complaints vividly attest. In the end they tie its legs with a rope and carry it over to the slaughtering rack. The pig fights to get free. The boy whacks it over the head with a club. Agonizing squeals follow. Then the boy sharpens a knife on a whetstone, while his father drags over a clay basin to catch the blood. The boy buries the knife in the pig's neck. The stuck pig squeals. Blood spurts, first onto the ground, then into the basin. After this, the woman brings out a tub of hot water, and the three of them busily debristle the animal. That done, the boy opens the pig's belly and scoops out the internal organs. A dog comes up, steals a length of intestine, and runs off. The old woman curses the dog, managing a hit or two before it's out of range. The man and his son hang the butchered meat on a rack. Customers come up to buy cuts of pork. There are older women, older men, young women, and children. After selling off the meat, father and son count their money before the family of three enjoy a meal of slurpy porridge . . . all of a sudden, the dark curtain parted and all anyone saw was a scrawny old man sitting on a stool. He was rewarded with enthusiastic applause. Then the boy got down off his stool and passed the hat. Coins rained down into the cap, except for those that landed on the ground. Your dieh saw it with his own eyes and did not make up any of it. The old adage holds true: 'Every trade has its zhuangyuan.'"

3

Now that he had told his story, Dieh sat quietly with his eyes shut. But I was too enraptured to want to extract myself from the tale. It was yet another story about a boy and his father, and I could not help feeling that all his stories about a boy and his father were really about me and him. Dieh was the mimic, Guo Mao, and I was the boy who walked through the crowd, hat in hand—*Meow meow~~meow~~*

My dieh had performed countless executions in the capital to audiences of thousands, people who were drawn to his unparalleled skill, and it seemed to me that I could actually see tears in the people's eyes. Wouldn't it have been wonderful if I'd been there with Dieh at the time, hat in hand, a cat cap on my head, collecting donations from onlookers? While I was collecting money, I'd be practicing my cat cries~~*meow meow*~~and how wonderful that would be! Just think about all the money I'd get! I tell you, Dieh, why did you wait so long to come home and introduce yourself to your son? You could have taken me to the capital with you. If I'd been at your side ever since I was a boy, by now I'd be a man-slaying zhuangyuan . . .

When my dieh first showed up in town, people took me aside and whispered, "Xiaojia, your dieh isn't human." "What is he, then?" "He's a ghost that has taken over a corpse and brought it back to life. Think about it, Xiaojia, before your mother died, did she ever say you had a father? No? Of course not. So your mother said nothing about a father on her deathbed, and then he shows up, like he'd dropped out of the sky or popped up out of the ground. What could he possibly be except a ghost?"

"Go fuck yourself!" *Meow meow.* I rushed those tongue-wagging bastards with a cleaver. I went without a dieh for more than twenty years, and now, by some miracle, I suddenly have one, and you people have the nerve to say not only that is he not my dieh, but that he's a ghost. You're as brazen as rats that'll lick a cat's ass. I raised my cleaver and ran at them. *Meow meow.* With one swing of my cleaver I could chop them in two, from their heads all the way down to their heels. My dieh said that particular chop is called the "big cleave," and today I'm going to use it on any son of a bitch who has the guts to say my dieh isn't really my dieh. Well, they nearly shit their pants when they saw the look of rage on my face, and could not get out of there fast enough. *Meow meow,* watch out, you bunch of long-tailed rats. Provoke my dieh, and you're asking for trouble. The same goes for me. *Meow meow.* Come give it a try if you don't believe me, any of you. My dieh is an executioner who sits in the Emperor's chair. His Majesty gave him leave to report an execution after it had been carried out, to kill without constraints, man or dog. And when I take my place, knife in hand, at my dieh's side, I can kill a man as easily as I can butcher a pig or a dog.

I pleaded with Dieh to tell me another story. He said:

"Quit dawdling and get things ready. I don't want you rushing around when it's time to do our job."

I knew that a spectacle was planned for today—spectacles always made for happy days for Dieh and me—and that there would be plenty of time later for stories. Good food needs to be savored. Once the sandalwood death was successfully carried out, Dieh would be in a good mood, and there'd be nothing holding him back from spitting out all the stories he held inside, for my ears alone. I walked out behind the shed to relieve myself—numbers one and two—and took a look around while I was at it. The opera stage and Ascension Platform were there, and I watched a flock of wild pigeons, their wings flapping loudly, fly past in the bright sunlight. The parade ground was surrounded: soldier, wooden post, soldier, wooden post. A dozen cannons hunkered down at the field's edge. People called them turtle cannons, I called them dog cannons. Turtle cannons, dog cannons, slick and smooth, loud barks, green moss on the turtles' shells, dogs' bodies covered with fur, *meow meow.*

I retraced my steps to the front of the shed, itching for something to do. I needed a job of some sort. By this time on most days, I'd already have slaughtered the day's pigs and dogs and hung the carcasses on the a rack, letting the smell of fresh meat join the birds in the sky. Customers would be lined up in front of the shop, while I stood at the butcher block, cleaver in hand to chop off a hunk of the still-warm fatty meat, giving my customers the exact amount they asked for, not an ounce more or an ounce less. They'd give me a thumbs-up. "Xiaojia," they'd say, "you're quite the man!" I didn't need them to tell me that. But this was the first time I was to be part of a spectacle with Dieh, one that was a lot more important than butchering pigs. But what about all those customers? What do we do? Sorry, folks, I guess you'll have to be vegetarians for a day.

I was getting bored now that there were no more stories, so I went up to the stove, where the fire had gone out. There were no ripples on the surface of the glistening oil. It was no longer a cauldron of oil, but a mirror, a big bronze mirror, brighter than my wife's mirror at home, and so clear that I could count the whiskers on my face. There were dried stains in the mud in front of the stove and on the stand—Song Three's blood. And those weren't the only places his blood had landed; some had splattered into the cauldron. Was that why the oil had such a bright sheen? After this business of the sandalwood death is done with, I'm going to move this cauldron into the yard back home and let my wife see her face in it, but only if she refrains from mistreating my dieh. Last night I was half asleep when I heard a loud pop. Song Three's head was buried in the churning oil, and before they could pull it out, it was about half cooked. I got a kick out of that. *Meow meow.*

That was good shooting. Who did it? My dieh didn't know, and the government soldiers who started looking the moment they heard the shot didn't know. I'm the only one who knew. Gaomi County could boast only two marksmen that good. One was the rabbit hunter Niu Qing; the other was County Magistrate Qian Ding. Niu Qing had one eye—the left one. He'd lost his right one when his gun blew up in his face. A distinct improvement in his marksmanship followed the accident. He mastered the skill of shooting rabbits on the run. If he raised his fowling piece, a rabbit would be on its way to the netherworld. Niu Qing was a good friend of mine. My good friend. The other marksman was the venerable Qian Ding, our County Magistrate. Once, when I was in the Great Northern Wilderness hunting for herbal medicine for my wife's illness, I saw Qian Ding, with his attendants Chunsheng and Liu Pu, out hunting. Chunsheng and Liu Pu were on donkeys driving rabbits out of the bushes so the Magistrate, sitting astride his horse, could draw his pistol and, seemingly without aiming, send a rabbit flying up into the air to land with a thud—dead.

From where I hid in the brush, not daring to make a sound, I could hear Chunsheng praise the Magistrate to the skies with words like "crack shot," while Liu Pu sat in the saddle, head down, a blank look on his face that gave away nothing of what he was thinking. My wife once told me that the Magistrate's loyal follower, Liu Pu, was Qian Ding's wife's ganerzi, and the son of some big shot. He was, she said, a wise and talented man. I refused to believe her. What talented man would serve as somebody's lackey? A talented man would be like my dieh, who lifted up his sword, smeared his face with blood, and—thwack thwack thwack thwack thwack thwack, six heads rolled on the ground.

The Magistrate was no marksman, was how I saw it, just a lucky shot, like a blind cat bumping into a dead rat. He'd probably miss the next. Well, as if he knew what I was thinking, he pointed his pistol into the air and brought down a bird. A dead bird, like a black stone, plopped down right next to me. Would you believe it! A superhuman marksman, *meow meow*. The Magistrate's hunting dog came bounding over to me. I stood up with the dead bird, its body heat burning my hand. The dog leaped and jumped up and down, barking the whole time. Now, I'm not afraid of dogs; dogs are afraid of me. Every dog in Gaomi County runs away with its tail between its legs, yelping like crazy, when it sees me coming. Dogs' fear of me proves how much I take after my dieh, a panther. The Magistrate's dog looked mean, but I could tell from its bark that it was expecting to be backed up by its master to make me think it wasn't afraid. Me, Gaomi County's King of Hell for dogs! The dog's barks brought Chunsheng and Liu Pu riding up from two sides. I was a stranger to Liu Pu, but Chunsheng was a friend of mine. He'd often visited the shop, where he was treated to cut-rate food and drink. "What are you doing here, Xiaojia?" he asked. "Searching for herbal stuff," I said. "My wife is sick, and she sent me out to find some heartbreak grass with red roots and green leaves. Know where I can find any? If so, tell me, and hurry, because she's in a bad way." By then the Magistrate had ridden up and was giving me the once-over with a pitiless look in his eyes. "Who are you?" he demanded. "What is your name?" He sputtered when I didn't answer. When I was still a little boy, my mother told me to act dumb in the presence of an official. "He's Dog-Meat Xishi's husband," Chunsheng whispered, "a borderline idiot." Well, fuck you, Chunsheng! I felt like saying. I was just saying how you were a friend of mine, and that's no way for a friend to talk. Would a real friend say that his friend is a borderline idiot? *Meow meow*, fuck you! Who are you calling a borderline idiot? If that's what I am, then you're a total idiot.

When Niu Qing pulled the trigger, only buckshot came out of the barrel. But the Magistrate fired a single bullet each time he pulled the trigger. A neat little hole dotted Song Three's head, and if that doesn't prove it was the Magistrate, I don't know what does. But then why would the Magistrate want to kill Song Three? Oh, now I get it. Song Three, you must have stolen money from the Magistrate, something most people would not dare to do. Stealing from the Magistrate was signing your own death warrant. Most of the time you pranced around the yamen like a big shot and refused to even acknowledge my presence. You refused to settle up the five strings of cash you owed the shop, and I didn't have the nerve to ask you for it. Well, things worked out in the end. We're out the money, but you're out for good. Now, which was more important, your money or your life? Your life, of course, so take your unpaid debt and talk it over with the King of Hell.

4

Government troops were swarming our way even as the sound of gunfire hung in the air. They dragged the top half of Song Three's body out of the oil. His head reeked of sesame oil, which dripped along with his blood back into the cauldron. It looked like a newly fried hawthorn berry. *Meow meow.* The soldiers laid him out on the ground, where his legs, a thread of life still in them, twitched uncontrollably, evoking the image of a half-dead chicken. The soldiers stared wide-eyed at the soon-to-be corpse, not knowing what to do. One of their officers rushed up and bundled my dieh and me into the shed, then turned to look in the direction from which the bullet had come and fired his weapon. I'd never had a rifle fire that close to me, a foreign rifle, at that—I'd heard it was a German weapon whose bullets could penetrate a wall at over a thousand yards. The other soldiers took his lead and fired at the same spot. Smoke emerged from their muzzles when they stopped shooting, and the smell of gunpowder engulfed us, like New Year's, when firecrackers are set off. "Go after him!" the officer commanded. *Meow meow.* The soldiers took off running, whooping and hollering. If Dieh hadn't grabbed me by the arm, I'd have taken out after them to watch the fun! Those morons, I was thinking, what do they think they're going to find? By the time you dragged Song Three out of the boiling oil, the Magistrate was already back in the yamen, thanks to his spirited horse, a Red Rabbit thoroughbred. With its sleek red coat, it looked like a fiery red blur when it galloped at high speed, faster and faster, filling the air with a whistling sound. The animal, which had once belonged to Master Guan Yu, did not eat hay. When it was hungry, it ate a mouthful of fresh dirt, and when it was thirsty, it drank the wind. Or so Dieh told me. He also said that instead of Red Rabbit, it ought to be called an earth-eating or wind-drinking thoroughbred, because those traits described the animal's essence. It was a fine animal, a rare treasure, and I wondered whether I would ever own such a horse. If that happened one day, I'd let my dieh be its first rider. He'd probably want that privilege to be mine, but I'd insist. As a filial son, I always let him have the best. The most filial son in Gaomi County, the most filial son in Laizhou Prefecture, the most filial son in Shandong Province, the most filial son in all of the Great Qing Empire! *Meow meow.*

After searching the area, the soldiers started heading back in twos and threes.

"Grandma Zhao," the officer said, "Excellency Yuan asks you to please remain inside the shed from now on. It's for your protection."

Dieh merely grinned in response. Several dozen soldiers quickly surrounded the shed, *meow meow*, as if we were treasures to be protected. The officer blew out the candle and moved the two of us out of the moonlight. Then he asked my dieh if the sandalwood stakes in the cauldron were ready. "More or less," Dieh replied. So the officer removed the kindling under the stove and dumped it in water. I love the smell of charred wood, so I breathed in deeply. In the darkness I heard Dieh say, either to me or to himself:

"Heaven's will, it was heaven's will. A sacrifice to the sandalwood stakes!"

"What did you say, Dieh?"

"Go to sleep, son. Tomorrow is our big day."

"Would you like me to massage your back, Dieh?"

"No."

"Scratch your back?"

"Go to sleep!" he said, starting to get annoyed.

Meow meow.

"Go to sleep."

5

Once the sun was up, the cordon of government soldiers around the shed was replaced by a contingent of German soldiers that ringed the parade ground, facing out. Once they were in place, another contingent, this time of government troops, moved in and took up positions around the parade ground, but facing in. Finally, six government troops and six German soldiers marched in and took their positions: one at each corner of the shed, one at each corner of the Ascension Platform, and four in front of the opera stage. Two of the four men at our shed were foreign; the other two were Yuan's troops. They all had their backs to the shed, standing at attention, as if competing to see who could stand the straightest. *Meow meow*, straight as an arrow.

As he fingered his prayer beads, Dieh looked like a meditating old monk, Amita Buddha. Amita Buddha, my wife said that a lot. My eyes, like awls, bored into Dieh's hands. *Meow meow*, they were uncommon hands; the Great Qing Empire's hands, the nation's hands, the hands of the venerable Empress Dowager Cixi and the ageless Emperor. My dieh's were the hands They used to kill anyone They wanted dead. If the Empress Dowager said to my dieh: "Slay-master, go kill someone for Me," my dieh would say, "As you wish!" If the ageless Emperor said: "Slay-master, go kill someone for Me," my dieh would say, "As you wish!" My dieh had wonderful hands. Still, they were a pair of little birds; in motion, they were like feathers. *Meow meow.* I still remember how my wife once said to me, "Your dieh's hands are abnormally small," and as I looked at those hands, I couldn't help feeling that he was somehow not an ordinary human being. If not a ghost, he had to be an immortal. On pain of death, you would never believe that those hands were capable of killing a thousand people. Hands like his belonged to a midwife. Where I come from, we call a midwife an auspicious grandma. Auspicious Grandma, Grandma Auspicious, ah-ya-ah, and I suddenly understood why people in the capital referred to him as Grandma. He was a midwife. But then again, midwives are all women, and my dieh is a man. Or is he? Of course he is; I've seen his little pecker when I bathed him. It's like a little frozen green carrot, heh-heh . . . What are you laughing at? Heh-heh, a little carrot . . . Idiot son. *Meow meow,* can men really be midwives? Wouldn't a male midwife be a laughingstock? And wouldn't he have a clear view of a woman's privates? And wouldn't that be all her menfolk needed to beat him to death? I didn't know what to think, and the harder I tried, the more confused I became. To hell with it. Who's got time to waste on stuff like that?

My dieh's eyes snapped open; he draped his prayer beads around his neck, stood up, and went to check the cauldron of oil. I could see our upside-down reflections in the oil. The surface was brighter than a mirror, and so clear I could see every pore in our faces. Dieh lifted one of the sandalwood stakes out, breaking the smooth surface and turning my reflection into the long face of a goat. What a shock! All along, my true form has been that of a goat, with a pair of horns. *Meow meow.* What a disappointment. Dieh's true form is a black panther, the County Magistrate is a white tiger, my wife is a white snake, and me? I'm a bearded goat. A goat! What kind of animal is that! I didn't want to be a damned goat! Dieh examined the stake in the sunlight, like a master blacksmith examining a newly forged sword. Bright threads of oil dripped back into the cauldron, creating little eddies on the surface of the slightly gummy oil. He waited till the last of the oil had dripped from the stake before taking out a piece of white silk and wiping the stake dry. The silk quickly absorbed all the oil residue. Dieh laid the silk on the cauldron stand, then held the stake in two hands—one on the butt, the other on the tip—and tried to bend it. I detected a slight arch when he did that; it returned to its original shape as soon as he loosened his grip. After placing the stake on the cauldron stand, he lifted out the second stake, first letting all the oil drip off, then wiping it dry with the silk, and tried to bend it. As before, when he loosened his grip, it returned to its original shape. A look of satisfaction spread across his face. I couldn't remember the last time I'd seen him so happy, and it affected me the same way, *meow meow*. What a wonderful thing, the sandalwood death, for it made my dieh happy, *meow meow*.

Dieh carried the two sandalwood stakes into the shed and laid them on a small table. He then knelt on the straw mat and bowed down to pay his respects, as if an invisible apparition were ensconced behind the table. His obeisance completed, he got up and sat in his chair, shielding his eyes with his hand as he gazed heavenward. The sun had begun its climb in the morning sky; normally by this time I'd have sold off all that day's fresh pork, and it would be time to slaughter dogs. Having noted the sun's progress, without looking at me, Dieh said:

"You can kill the rooster, son!"

Meow meow~~mew~~

6

My heart soared when Dieh said that! *Meow meow meow*, Dieh, dear Dieh, my dear dieh! My seemingly unending wait was over, and the long-delayed moment of excitement had arrived. I selected a razor-sharp paring knife from the knife hamper and showed it to Dieh. He nodded. Then I went up to the rooster, which began flapping its wings; its tail feathers jerked up, and out came a puddle of white excrement. On most mornings at this time, it would be perched on the wall at home crowing loudly, but today it was tied to a post. With the knife held between my teeth, I reached down and grabbed it by its wings and held its legs down with my foot. Dieh had told me this rooster was for its blood, not for eating, so I placed a black bowl under its neck to catch the blood. The rooster, burning hot, was struggling to free its head from my hand. I squeezed hard. Behave yourself, damn it, how am I supposed to do this if you don't behave yourself? Pigs are stronger than you, dogs meaner, and they don't scare me, so what makes a rooster think it can scare me? Fuck you. I plucked its neck clean, stretched it taut, and made a pass with my knife. The skin parted. No blood appeared at first, which made me nervous, because Dieh had said that if you kill a rooster prior to an execution and it doesn't bleed, things will not go well that day. I made a second cut, and this time it worked: purplish blood gushed from the wound, like the stream a young boy makes when he gets up after a good night's sleep. *Splash splash, meow meow*. More blood spurted than the bowl could take, and some of it spilled over the side. "There, Dieh," I said as I tossed the limp bird to the ground, "that does it." With a broad smile, he waved me over and told me to get down on my knees. Then he plunged both hands into the blood, almost as if he expected them to drink it up. Dieh's hands come equipped with mouths, I was thinking, and can drink blood. He smiled.

"Close your eyes, son," he said.

I closed them, as he said. I am an obedient child. Wrapping my arms around his legs, I banged my forehead into his knees and sputtered: *Meow meow* . . . "Dieh Dieh Dieh Dieh . . ."

Dieh clasped my head between his knees.

"Raise your head, son," he said.

So I did, and I was looking into his impressive face. I am an obedient child. Before I had a dieh, I obeyed my wife, but after that I obeyed my dieh. That thought reminded me of my wife, whom I hadn't seen for a day and a half. Where had she gotten to? *Meow meow* . . . Dieh rubbed his blood-soaked hands all over my face, sending a stench much worse than pig's blood into my nostrils. I hated the idea of having my face smeared with rooster blood, but Dieh had the final word on that. If I didn't obey him, he'd send me into the yamen to be paddled, five ten fifteen twenty swats from a big wooden paddle that would leave me with a bloody behind. *Meow meow.* Dieh plunged his hands back into the bowl and smeared more blood over my face. Including my ears. Whether he meant to or not, he got some of it in my eyes, and—*ouch!*—that stung, *meow meow.* It also blurred my vision, veiling everything in a red haze. With a *mew mew* I complained, "Dieh, Dieh, you're blinding me." I rubbed my eyes with the heels of my hands and mewed loudly. Everything got brighter the more I rubbed, until the light itself was blinding. Oh, no, that's bad, *meow meow,* the magical tiger whisker was working again, *meow meow,* no more Dieh, in front of me now was a panther. It was standing on its hind legs and dipping its front paws in the blood bowl, staining them red with pearls of blood dripping from the black fur, making it look like the paws were injured. He reached up and smeared blood all over the coarse fur of his face, turning it red as a cockscomb. I was well aware that Dieh's true form was a panther, so that was nothing to make a fuss over. But I didn't want the power of that tiger whisker to last and last—just a little while would be plenty. But its power this time wouldn't fade away, *meow meow,* and what would it take for things to return to normal? No matter how upset I was, there was nothing I could do about it. I was torn between worries and happiness. Worries over my strange inability to see human beings, happiness over the knowledge that no one but me had the ability to see people's true forms. I took a look around, taking in all of Yuan's government troops and the German soldiers standing guard over the parade ground—long-tailed wolves, dogs with hairless tails, plus a few raccoons and other animals. There was even one that looked like a cross between a wolf and a dog; its uniform identified it as a junior officer. It was probably the offspring of a wolf-dog mating. I gave it a name: lobo-dog. It was sneakier than a wolf and meaner than a dog; anything it bit was doomed, *meow meow*.

After using up all the blood in the bowl on his face and front paws, my panther dieh focused his bright black eyes on me and treated me to a barely perceptible smile, lips parted just enough to show his yellow teeth. Even though the change in his appearance was enormous, the expressions and mannerisms were unmistakably Dieh's. I returned his smile, *meow meow*. He swaggered over to the purplish-red chair; his tail made his pants stand up in back. He sat down and narrowed his eyes, looking perfectly serene. I surveyed the area around us, yawned, mewed once, and sat on a board next to him, within view of the slanting shadow of the Ascension Platform on the ground. As I stroked Dieh's tail, he stuck out his rough tongue and began licking the hair on my head. *Mew*, I wheezed just before falling asleep.

I was awakened by raucous noise, *meow meow*, a mixture of horns and trumpets and gongs and Western drums, and all of it punctuated by the low rumble of cannon fire. I saw that the shadow cast by the Ascension Platform was much shorter than before and that blinding lights were making their way onto the parade ground from the street. At some point the green tarpaulins covering the cannons on the edge of the parade ground had been removed to reveal the weapons' blue steel. Four wolfhounds behind each of the cannons were in motion, and even though they were quite a ways away, the hair on their bodies did not escape my sharp eyes. The barrels of the cannons were like turtles' necks, recoiling back into their shells each time a shell was spat out, followed by puffs of white smoke. The wolfhounds moved like puppets behind the cannons, comical little figures. My eyes began to sting badly, and it only took a moment's thought to realize that I was sweating. I wiped my face with my sleeve; it came away red. That was nothing to worry about, but the scene in front of me had changed again. My dieh no longer wore the face of a panther, but his body was still that of a panther, and his pants rose up behind him because of the tail. Then the heads of the soldiers standing guard were once again human, sitting atop wolfhounds' bodies. It was a comforting sight, and it made me feel better, knowing I was still living in the world of humans. And yet the look on Dieh's face puzzled me, since it didn't look especially human. But he was still my dieh, and when he licked my head, I moaned with pleasure, *mew~~*

A palanquin covered in blue wool was part of the contingent emerging onto the parade ground, preceded by wild animals with human heads, all carrying banners and gongs and umbrellas and fans. The chair was carried by horses with human heads and humans with horse heads, plus a few humans with cow heads. A thoroughbred horse trailed the palanquin, a bizarre wolf-headed human in the saddle, and I knew that was the German Plenipotentiary from Qingdao, Clemens von Ketteler. I'd heard that my gongdieh had shot the man's first horse out from under him with a shotgun, so the one he was riding now he'd probably taken from one of his subordinates. More horses preceded a prison van that held a pair of cages. I thought the sandalwood death was reserved for my gongdieh alone. Why two cages? A long procession spread out behind the prison van, flanked by crowds of local residents. What I actually saw was a sea of hairy skulls, but I knew they were local residents. I was secretly thinking of someone, someone I tried to spot among all those dark heads. Do I need to say who that person was? No. I was searching for my wife. I hadn't seen her since my dieh had sent her racing fearfully out of the house yesterday morning. I had no idea if she'd eaten or drunk anything, and though she was a white snake, she was a good white snake, like Bai Suzhen, the heroine of *The Legend of the White Snake*. She was Bai Suzhen, and I was her lover, Xu Xian. But who was the Green Snake Demon and who was the sorcerer Fa Hai? Of course. Yuan Shikai was Fa Hai. My eyes lit up. I see her, I see her! She's standing with a bunch of women! Her flat white head is raised, her purple tongue flicks in and out, she's slithering this way. *Meow meow*, I felt like crying out, but my dieh's panther eyes were fixed on me.

"Son," he said, "stop looking around!"

<hr>

7

<hr>

After three bursts of cannon fire, the official in charge of the execution announced loudly to Yuan Shikai and von Ketteler, who had taken seats in the center of the stage:

"Your humble servant, Gaomi County, respectfully reports to His Excellency the Governor that the midday hour has arrived, and the Imperial prisoner Sun Bing has been identified as the condemned. The executioners are in place and await instructions from His Honor!"

Yuan Shikai, seated on the stage, stuck his turtle neck out from under his shell, which looked like a pot lid and gave his official robe the look of an oil-paper umbrella, the very umbrella that Xu Xian had given to the White and Green Snakes. But how had that umbrella wound up on Yuan Shikai's body? Oh, it's not an umbrella, it's a turtle shell. How wonderful that a turtle would be a high official, *meow meow*. Turtle Yuan stretched his neck toward the mouth of Gray Wolf von Ketteler and sputtered something in turtle-wolf talk; then he took a red command flag from one of his subordinates and swung it in a hard downward chop. This was no meaningless demonstration: like a knife cutting through a tangle of jute or slicing through a cake of bean curd, it was a deft and resolute action, proof that this turtle had reached profound Taoist attainments. This was no ordinary turtle; no, it was exceptional, for official status of this magnitude was beyond the reach of an ordinary reptile. Of course, he was still no match for my dieh. When the official in charge saw Excellency Yuan drop the little red flag, he sprang into action, growing half an inch in height; rays of light, green in color, surged from his eyes, menacing enough to frighten anybody. His tiger whiskers twitched; he bared his fangs. He looked good to me. Drawing on the power of his throat, he announced loudly:

"It is time——let the execution begin——"

His body shrank back to normal as soon as the proclamation ended, and his whiskers retreated to his cheeks. You don't have to reveal your identity. I know you're Qian Ding. That may be an official's cap resting on your tiger head and a red robe girding your body, and while you may be able to hide your tail under your clothes, I knew it was you as soon as I heard you speak. His proclamation ended, he stood beside the execution stand, bent at the waist, his back arched, as his face slowly regained its human form; drenched in perspiration, it made for a pitiful sight. Three more thunderous blasts from the dozen cannons shook the ground. Now that it was nearly time to join Dieh in our spectacle, I took one last look around. There were, I saw, throngs of people surrounding the parade ground—men and women, young and old, some in their true form, others having reverted to their human form, and others still in the midst of changing from one to the other—half human, half beast. At that distance I couldn't tell Zhang Three from Li Four, whether pigs or dogs or cows or sheep, nothing but a swarm of heads, big and small, all awash in sunlight. Feeling a surge of pride, I threw out my chest and raised my chin, *meow meow*, and then looked down at the new ritualistic clothes I was wearing: a black Buddhist robe with a vestment over my left shoulder, a wide red sash with long tassels around my waist, black trousers tied at the ankles, and high deerskin boots. I couldn't see the hat with a circular crown that rested on my head, of course, but everybody else could. My face and ears were smeared with a layer of rooster blood, which had dried and begun to crack, making my skin feel funny. But no matter how it felt, it had to be done, since it was a tradition handed down by our ancestors. My dieh often said that traditions are the essence of any endeavor. Because the dried blood on his face had begun to crack, in my eyes he was looking more and more human—now a half man–half panther dieh. His paws were becoming hands, and his face was changing, but he still had the ears of a panther: thin and nearly transparent, they stuck up in the air and were topped by bristly hairs. Dieh reached out to straighten my clothes and said softly:

"Don't be afraid, son. Just do as your dieh taught you, courageously. It is time for father and son to show what we can do!"

"I'm not afraid, Dieh!"

Dieh looked at me with tenderness in his eyes.

"You are a good son!"

Dieh Dieh Dieh Dieh, do you know that people say the County Magistrate and I are in the same pot fighting over a ladle . . .

8

I noticed right away that there were two cages on the prison van, with a Sun Bing in each of them. Two cages, two Sun Bings. At first glance they looked identical; but a closer look revealed significant differences. The true form of one was a big black bear, the other a big black pig. My wife's father was too heroic a character to be a pig, so he had to be the bear. The eighty-third story my dieh told me was about a fight between a black bear and a tiger. In the story, the bear and the tiger always fought to a draw, until finally the tiger won. The bear lost not because it was an inferior fighter, but because it was too practical an animal. After each fight, the tiger went hunting for food—pheasants, gazelles, or rabbits—and went to drink from a mountain stream. But there was no food or drink for the bear, which angrily dug up trees on the battlefield, since it never felt there was enough space. Once the tiger had eaten and drunk its fill, it returned to start the fight all over. Eventually, the bear, its strength sapped, was beaten, and the tiger was anointed king of the beasts. I could also tell which of the two was my gongdieh by the look in his eyes. Sun Bing's eyes were bright and lively, and when they settled on something, they seemed to emit sparks. The fake Sun Bing's eyes were dark, his gaze evasive, sort of fearful. The fake Sun Bing looked familiar somehow, and it didn't take much thought to figure out that he was Xiao Shanzi, a member of the beggar community, Zhu Ba's right-hand man. Each year, on the fourteenth day of the eighth month, Beggars' Day, a pair of chili peppers hung from his ears in his role as a matchmaker. Now he'd assumed the role of my gongdieh. What did the fool think he was doing?

My dieh had seen that there were two criminals even before I had, but he'd witnessed so much in his life that one more criminal, or ten for that matter, had no effect on him. I overheard him say under his breath:

"I'm glad I prepared an extra stake."

My dieh was a man of foresight, a modern-day Zhuge Liang.

Who would be first? First impale the real criminal or the imposter? I tried to find the answer in my dieh's face. But his gaze was glued to the face of the official in charge of the execution, Qian Ding, who was returning the look, though his gaze was clouded, sort of like a blind man. The look in Qian Ding's eyes told my dieh that he was seeing nothing. It was up to my dieh to choose the first to be impaled. So he turned his eyes to the two criminals in front of him. The eyes of the fake Sun Bing were unfocused. Those of the real Sun Bing emitted a strong, steady gaze. He nodded to my dieh and said loudly:

"You are well, I assume, Qinjia!"

My dieh responded with a smile and a respectful bow with his fists closed over his chest.

"A joyous day for you, Qinjia!" he replied.

"For both of us," my gongdieh said jubilantly.

"Who first, you or him?"

"Do you really need to ask?" my gongdieh replied forthrightly. "As they say, 'Relatives tend to favor each other.'"

Dieh said nothing in response; he merely smiled and nodded. But then, as if a sheet of paper had been removed, his smile gave way to a face the color of pig iron. He turned to the prisoner's escorts.

"Unlock the shackles!" he ordered.

Unsure of what to do, they looked around, as if waiting for a command from someone. My dieh repeated himself, impatiently:

"Unlock the shackles!"

One of them stepped up and, with trembling hands, unlocked my gongdieh's chains. Now freed, he moved his arms around to limber them up, eyed the instruments of execution, and, as if this was the moment he'd waited for, strode confidently up to the pine plank, which was considerably narrower than his body, and lay down on his belly.

The plank, which Dieh had commissioned from the county's finest carpenter, was as slick as glass. It had been placed across a hog-butchering rack that I'd used for more than a decade. By now the wood, saturated with pig's blood, was as heavy as a bar of iron. It had required four strapping yayi to carry it over from our yard, forced to take ten or more breaks along the way. From where he lay on the wooden plank, my gongdieh turned his head toward us and asked modestly:

"Like this, Qinjia?"

Ignoring the question, my dieh reached under the stand to retrieve the leather strap we'd readied. He handed it to me.

About time, I was thinking. I snatched the strap out of Dieh's hand and began to tie up my gongdieh just the way I'd practiced it. My gongdieh was not pleased.

"You must not think much of me, worthy son-in-law," he said.

My dieh, who was watching my every move from right beside me, reached down to retie a knot I'd bungled. My gongdieh huffed and puffed to show his displeasure at being tied down. He was overdoing it, I thought; so did my dieh, who had to remind the man sternly:

"Don't be so stubborn, Qinjia. I'm not sure you will be in control of your body when this trial of strength and will commences."

But my gongdieh's complaints kept coming, even after I'd strapped him down tightly on the wooden plank. Dieh tried to slip his finger between the strap and the man—he couldn't. That was how he wanted it, and he nodded to show he was satisfied.

"Begin," he said softly.

I went over to the knife hamper and removed the knife I'd used on the rooster a short while ago. With it I sliced open my gongdieh's pants to expose his buttocks. After laying the oil-saturated mallet next to my hand, Dieh selected the sandalwood stake that seemed the smoothest, and wiped it down with an oilcloth. Taking a position to the left of my gongdieh, he held the stake in both hands and placed the pointed end, which was as round as a calamus leaf, at a spot just below my gongdieh's tailbone, as he continued to complain, loudly and obstinately, interspersed with snippets of Maoqiang opera, as if what was about to happen was of no concern to him. But I could tell from the slight tremors in his voice and the twitching of his calf muscles that deep down he was tense and fearful. My dieh, who by then had stopped conversing with my gongdieh, held the stake tightly; I saw a serene expression on his red face as he raised his head and gave me an encouraging, expectant look. His affection toward me was plain to see, *meow meow*, and I knew there wasn't a better dieh anywhere in the world. How lucky I was to have such a wonderful dieh, *meow meow*, and that was all made possible by my mother's lifelong devotion to the Buddhist way. Dieh signaled with his chin for me to begin. So I spat in my hands, leaned to one side and took a step backward, and dug in my heels until I was anchored like a stake in the ground.

I picked up the mallet and gave the butt end of the sandalwood stake a light tap to see how it felt. *Meow meow*, not bad, no trouble at all. Now the real pounding began, neither fast nor slow, and I watched as my pounding drove the stake into my gongdieh's body, inch by inch. The sound it made wasn't heavy——*beng*——*beng*——*beng*——*meow meow*——not even loud enough to cover the sound of my gongdieh's heavy breathing.

As the stake penetrated more deeply, my gongdieh's body began to shake; despite the fact that he was strapped down so tightly he couldn't move, every muscle in his body convulsed, causing even the heavy plank under him to move violently. But I kept pounding——*beng*——*beng*——*beng*——keeping in mind my dieh's instructions: "Son, you must use only half the strength in your arm."

I saw my gongdieh's head shake uncontrollably. He seemed to be stretching his neck out of shape. If I hadn't seen it with my own eyes, I'd never have believed that a man could do that to his neck. Fiercely stretching it out—— stretch——stretch——stretch——as far as it would go, until, like a leather strap about to snap in two, his head looked like it was on the verge of separating itself from his body. Then his neck snapped back with incredible force, until it completely disappeared, as if his head were growing straight out of his shoulders.

beng——*beng*——*beng*——

Meow meow——

My gongdieh's body was heating up; his clothes were drenched with sweat. Whenever he raised his head, I saw rivulets of sweat coursing down from his damp hair, sweat that was a sticky yellow, like rice soup straight from the pot; and when he turned his head toward me, I saw how puffy his face had gotten, looking like a bronze-colored basin. His sunken eyes reminded me of those butchered pigs I puffed up before skinning them, *meow meow*, just like the hollow eyes of a puffed-up pig.

pa——*pa*——*pa*——

Meow . . .

The sandalwood stake was nearly halfway in——*meow* . . . sweet-smelling sandalwood . . . *meow* . . . Up to this point, my gongdieh had not uttered a sound. The look on Dieh's face showed his admiration toward the man. Long before we began, Dieh and I had striven to anticipate every situation that might arise during the execution. Dieh's greatest fear was that my gongdieh would fill the air with wild shrieks and howls that would unnerve me, a neophyte, at my first execution, and that I'd start doing things wrong, like driving the stake too hard and damaging the internal organs. To keep that from happening, he'd wrapped a pair of date pits in cotton, ready to stuff into my ears if his fears were borne out. But my gongdieh still hadn't made a sound, except for heavy breathing that was louder and huskier than any I'd ever heard from a buffalo pulling a plow. He did not bellow in pain, nor did he weep or beg for mercy.

pa——*pa*——*pa*——

Meow . . .

Dieh was sweating, too, something he never did, *meow*, and I noticed a slight tremor in his hands as he continued guiding the stake. He was getting anxious; the look in his eyes made that clear, and that worried me. *Meow*, Sun Bing clenching his teeth and refusing to cry out was not something we'd hoped for. We'd gotten used to shrieks of pain when we experimented on that pig, and in more than ten years of slaughtering pigs, there had only been one mute, and that animal had nearly been my undoing. For weeks I'd suffered nightmares in which the pig looked at me and sneered. Cry out, gongdieh, I beg you to cry out! *Meow meow*, but not a sound. My wrist was getting sore, my legs were weakening, my head felt swollen, my eyes were failing me and had begun to sting from invading sweat; the stench of dried rooster blood was making me nauseous. A panther's head had replaced Dieh's human head, and black fur now covered those lovely hands. Black fur also grew on my gongdieh, whose head, which kept rising and falling, was now that of a huge bear. His body had grown dramatically, as had his strength, while the leather strap holding him down was stretched thin and brittle, ready to snap. That was when my hand slipped. Carelessly, I hit Dieh's paw instead of the butt end of the stake; with an audible moan, he dropped his hand. I swung again, harder this time. The stake flew out of Dieh's hands and arched upward. The tip obviously went somewhere it wasn't supposed to, injuring something inside Sun Bing and sending a stream of blood running down the length of the stake. A shriek erupted from Sun Bing's mouth, *meow meow*, more hideous than I'd heard from any of the pigs I'd slaughtered. Sparks flew from Dieh's eyes.

"Careful!" he said under his breath.

I wiped my face with my sleeve and took several deep breaths. In the midst of howls that got louder and louder, I began to calm down. My wrist was no longer sore, my legs were strong again, my head was no longer swollen, and my vision returned, *meow*. Dieh had regained his human face, and my gongdieh no longer had the head of a bear. Pumping myself up as my strength surged back, I recommenced pounding the stake:

beng——beng——beng——

Meow meow——

There was no stopping Sun Bing's howls now, shrieks that drowned out all other sounds. The stake was back in the right position, guided by Dieh as it inched its way deeper into him, between his vital organs and his backbone . . .

Ow——oh——ahh——yeow——

Meow meow mew——

Disturbing sounds emerged from inside his body, like cats in heat. What was that? I wondered. Are my ears deceiving me? Strange strange really strange, there are cats in the stomach of my wife's father. I was on the verge of losing my concentration again, but before that happened, I received calm assurances from Dieh. The louder Sun Bing screamed, the more comforted I was by the smile on Dieh's face. Even his eyes, which had narrowed to a slit, were smiling. He looked like a man who was enjoying a leisurely smoke and listening to opera, not someone inflicting the cruelest form of punishment on a man, *meow meow* . . .

The stake finally broke through Sun Bing's skin just above his shoulders, making a small tent of his collar. My dieh's original idea was to have the stake emerge from Sun Bing's mouth, but for someone who had sung opera all his life, a stake through the mouth would have ended that possibility, so he decided to have it emerge from between his shoulder blades. I laid down the oily mallet, picked up my knife, and cut open the collar of his shirt. Dieh signaled me to keep pounding, so I picked up the mallet and swung it another ten or fifteen times, *meow meow*, until the same length of stake impaling Sun Bing was visible top and bottom. Sun Bing's howls continued without weakening. Dieh examined the points of entry and exit, in each of which a trickle of blood had stuck to the wood. A contented look spread across his face. I heard him breathe a huge sigh of relief. I did the same, I breathed a huge sigh of relief.

Meow . . .

9

Under Dieh's direction, four yayi lifted the pine plank, with my gongdieh on it, off the rack and carried it carefully up the Ascension Platform, which was taller than the rooftop of any house in town. The platform was next to the shed, connected by a long, gently sloping ramp of rough wood and some logs to make it easy to negotiate. And yet the four strong men were sweating profusely, leaving damp footprints on the wood as they climbed. Sun Bing, who was strapped tightly to the plank, was still howling, but he was losing his voice, and his energy level was dropping fast. Dieh and I followed the men up the ramp to the spacious top of the platform, whose new flooring smelled refreshingly of pinesap. A three-foot-long crossbar of white wood had been attached to a spot just below the top of a thick pine pole that had been erected in the center of the platform, creating a frame that looked like the cross I'd seen at the Seventh-day Adventist Church.

The yayi gently laid down the plank to which Sun Bing was attached and retreated to the side to await further instructions. Dieh told me to cut the leather straps holding Sun Bing to the plank. His body immediately expanded, and his limbs flailed wildly, but that was the only movement the stake would allow. So as not to completely sap what strength he had left and, at the same time, to protect against injury to his internal organs, with me looking on, Dieh had the yayi pick Sun Bing up and tie his legs to the dark pole and his hands to the crossbar. He was now standing upright in the center of the platform, but only his head enjoyed freedom of movement. Out came the curses:

"Fuck your old granny, von Ketteler——fuck your old granny, Yuan Shikai——fuck your old granny, Qian Ding——fuck your old granny, Zhao Jia——fuck your old granny——ow——!"

Black blood streamed from his mouth and ran down onto his chest.

Meow meow . . .

10

Before walking down off the platform, I took a look around, and my heart suddenly seemed to contract, so violently was I having trouble breathing, *meow* . . .

All four sides of the parade ground were packed with people, bright sunlight glinting off their heads. The only reason for that, I knew, was that all those heads were wet with sweat. Sun Bing's curses merged with the pigeons soaring above us and spread out in all directions, like waves rushing to the shore. Soldiers—foreign troops and Yuan's government troops—stood as motionless as posts amid the crush of local residents. There was someone on my mind at that moment, *meow*, know who that was? I searched among the onlookers. Found her! Two burly women were gripping my wife by the arms, and a tall woman was holding her tightly around the waist to keep her from taking even one step forward; she could only leap backward. I heard her cry out in agony, a knife-edged sound as sharp and as oily green as a bamboo leaf.

My wife's wails threw my mind into upheaval. There was no denying that my feelings toward her had decreased after Dieh came into my life, but I'd had strong feelings toward her before that. She used to let me suck on her breasts even during the daytime, a thought that got an immediate response from my little pecker. *Meow meow*, I recalled how she said: "Go on, go to your dieh, go ahead and die in your dieh's room!" When I wouldn't move, she kicked me . . . memories of my wife's virtues brought a soreness to my eyes and an ache to my nose, *meow meow*, I was nearly in tears. I started to run down the ramp, intent on going straight to my wife, so I could feel her breasts again and smell her. I'd give her the remainder of a malt candy Dieh had given to me that was still in my pocket. But a small heated hand grabbed hold of my wrist; I knew it was Dieh without having to look. He pulled me over to the pig-slaughtering rack, where another criminal awaited, along with an oil-steeped sandalwood stake that emitted a strong sesame aroma. Dieh got his message across without having to say a word; his hand said it all. Then his words pounded against my eardrums: "Son, you are doing something too important to let your thoughts run wild. You mustn't cast aside the nation and the Imperial Court over a woman. I cannot let you commit a capital offense like that. Dieh has told you many times that once our faces are smeared with the blood of a white rooster, men in our line of work are no longer people, and the suffering of the human world is none of our concern. We are tools in the employ of the Emperor, visible, corporal manifestations of the law. How could you even think of giving your wife that piece of candy under these circumstances? Even if I said it was all right, Yuan Shikai and von Ketteler would not permit it. Take a good long look at the impressive figures sitting on the stage where your wife's father once performed, and tell me if either one of them looks any less fierce than a tiger or a wolf."

I looked over at the stage, where Yuan Shikai and von Ketteler sat stony-faced, pinpoints of green light boring down on me from both pairs of eyes. Quickly lowering my head, I followed Dieh back to the stand. Wife of mine, I muttered under my breath, stop crying. After all, that father of yours isn't much of a dieh. Didn't you say he once let a donkey bite you on the head? That sandalwood stake has him pinned to a post, and that's a fact. If he'd been a good dieh, like mine, then you'd be right to cry if he was pinned by the stake. But don't cry over one like Sun Bing. You probably think he's in agony. Well, you're wrong. This is the moment of his greatest glory. He and my dieh were celebrating that a while ago, *meow meow*.

Qian Ding was rooted to the spot, staring at something, though I knew he saw nothing. For someone supposedly in charge of the execution, he hadn't done a damn thing and was worse than useless. Better to let Dieh and me do our job without waiting for him to give orders. Since the prison van had brought us two Sun Bings, we were required to inflict the sandalwood death on both of them. The real Sun Bing was already up on the Ascension Platform, thanks to us, and while I could see on Dieh's face a bit of unhappiness over minor mistakes during the process, overall he was pleased. With one success behind us, it was time to move to the next, and it would be another assured success. Two yayi carried the pine plank no longer needed for Sun Bing down from the platform and laid it across the slaughtering rack. My dieh turned to the man watching over the fake Sun Bing and said in a casual manner:

"Unlock the shackles."

The man removed the heavy chains from the fake Sun Bing's body, but unlike the real Sun Bing, who had immediately straightened up, this one slumped helplessly to the ground like a wax-softened candle. His face was ashen, his lips as pale as torn paper window covering. Only the whites of his eyes showed, a pair of tiny moth eggs. He was dragged up to the slaughtering rack, and when they let go of him, he crumpled to the ground like a pile of mud.

My dieh told them to lift him onto the plank atop the slaughtering rack, where he lay flat on his belly, twitching uncontrollably. Dieh signaled for me to strap him down, which I managed to do expertly. Then, without waiting to be told, I cut open his trousers with my paring knife; but when I pulled them back to expose his backside——Aiya! Would you believe it!——a horrible stench rose up from the bastard's crotch——he'd shit his pants!

Dieh frowned as he placed the sandalwood stake just below the fake Sun Bing's tailbone; I picked up my oily mallet and stepped forward. But before I could raise it for the first strike, an even more disgusting smell assaulted me. I threw down the mallet and backed off, holding my nose, like a dog assailed by the rotten smell of a skunk. Dieh called out in a stern, deep voice:

"Come back here, Xiaojia!"

The summons reawakened my sense of responsibility; I stopped backing up and, in a roundabout fashion, headed toward him. The fake Sun Bing's insides were probably a pile of mush by now. Normal excrement didn't smell that scary bad. Now what? Dieh was still holding the stake in place, waiting for me to start pounding, while I was wondering what would come out of his backside once the stake entered his body. Dieh had emphasized over and over the importance of what we were doing that day, and I knew I'd have to put that mallet to use even if he fired bullets out of his ass. Truth is, the smell that emerged from his asshole was worse than bullets could possibly have been. I took a tentative step forward despite the vomit rising into my throat. Show me some mercy, Dieh! If you make me follow through with this execution, I'm afraid I'll die of suffocation before the stake pokes out from between his shoulders.

Well, the heavens came to my rescue. At that crucial moment, Yuan Shikai, who looked like he was about to fall asleep up on the stage, ordered that Xiao Shanzi, originally sentenced to die by the sandalwood death, be beheaded instead. Dieh wasted no time tossing the sandalwood stake to one side; holding his breath and scowling, he unsheathed the sword at the waist of the nearest yayi, took several quick steps, looking more energetic than his years, raised the sword, and created a shining downward arc; before anyone could so much as blink, the head of the real Xiao Shanzi, the fake Sun Bing, lay on the ground beneath the slaughtering rack.

Meow——

CHAPTER EIGHTEEN

The Magistrate's Magnum Opus

Sandalwood grows deep in the hills; its blood red flowers bloom in the fall,
Champion of trees and hero of the forest, it stands the tallest of all.
People say that red lips open softly, a song of beauty their goal,
Song of the phoenix, murmurs of the swallow, cry of the oriole.
People say that maidens throw fruit at the young man with cheeks like a
  rose,
Graced with a tender visage, until his cart overflows.
People say that sandalwood clappers produce a crisp new sound,
In the performance of the Pear Garden actors peace and prosperity abound.
People say that a parade of sandalwood chariots by warhorses pulled,
Moonlight of the Qin, soldiers of the Han, by emperors ruled.
People say that Zhuge Liang's Empty City Strategy came to jell,
While playing a lute amid the lingering sandalwood smell.
People say that Tanyue befriended Buddhism in his style of living,
And escaped the karma of poverty by good deeds and giving.
But who has ever seen sandalwood used to impale a man?
In the dying days of dynasty, a wicked punishment inhumane!

—Maoqiang Sandalwood Death. *A noble air*

1

When Xiao Shanzi's head fell to the ground, the sun turned from white to red. As he picked it up, I knew that the dignified look Zhao Jia wore was false— Disgusting! Nauseating! That son of a bitch, no better than a pig or a dog, raised Xiao Shanzi's bloody head high in the air and announced to me:

"May it please Your Honor, the execution has been carried out!"

My mind was a tangle of confusing thoughts. A curtain of red fog rose before my eyes as thunderous bursts of cannon fire rang in my ears. The stench of blood was everywhere, such a foul, repulsive smell, one that has already infiltrated the doomed Qing Court. Am I abandoning you, or will I be buried with you? Not knowing what to do, I vacillate, I hesitate; everywhere I look, there is nothing but desolation. There is evidence that the Empress Dowager has fled with His Majesty to Taiyuan. Peking has become a city of wild savagery; the sacred halls of the Imperial Palace have been turned into the playground of the willful Eight-Power Allied Forces. An Imperial Court that brought the capital to its knees now exists in name only, does it not? But Yuan Shikai, Excellency Yuan, has taken from the Imperial Treasury tens of thousands of silver ingots to form and train a cohort of crack troops, not to defend the capital against invaders and protect royalty, but to join forces with the foreign demons to crush my loyal Shandong countrymen. The wolf's ambition is abundantly clear, his designs known to all, as were those of the Three Kingdoms usurper Sima Zhao. Even urchins in shantytowns sing a ditty: "The Qing is no more, swept away; Yuan has become the Cao Cao of his day." Ah, Great Qing, breeding tigers only courts disaster; ah, Yuan Shikai, you harbored treacherous thoughts. You have slaughtered my citizens to safeguard foreigners' rights of passage. You have purchased the favors of the Allies with the people's blood. Backed by a powerful army, you sit back and wait to see what will happen, confident in your ability to maneuver. The fate of the Great Qing Empire now rests in your hands. Empress Dowager, Your Majesty, have You come to Your senses? Have You? If You still see him as the defender of the people in their peril, then the three-hundred-year foundation on which the dynasty has stood will crumble in an instant. When I examine my own conscience, I find that I too am not the loyal official I thought I was. I lack the faith and the allegiance to die for a righteous cause, to pick up a knife and end the life of that treacherous official, even though I have studied the classics and the martial arts since childhood. The actor Sun Bing is braver than I, the beggar Xiao Shanzi more loyal. I am a cringing coward, a weakling given to making concessions. At times strong passion surges in my chest; at other times I am torn between opposing wills. Caution is my watchword; my appearance is but a deceptive mask. I swagger around the common people, but treat my superiors and foreigners to flattery and obsequious smiles. I am a petty, shameless toady to those above and a tyrant to those below. Hopeless coward Gaomi County Magistrate Qian Ding, though breath remains in your body, you are a walking corpse. Even Xiao Shanzi, who shit his pants from fear just before he died, was three thousand times the man you are. Since you are bereft of a heroic spirit, live on like the running dog you are. Benumb yourself, and, as a dog, carry out your duties as official in charge of the execution. By refocusing my eyes, I looked closely at the head the executioner Zhao Jia was holding as he made his boastful announcement, and understood what was expected of me at that moment. I walked quickly over to the opera stage, where I flicked my sleeves, raised the hem of my robe, and saluted by going down on one knee before reporting to that traitor and thug loudly:

"May it please Your Honors, the execution has been carried out!"

Yuan Shikai said something to von Ketteler, keeping his voice low, to which the German responded with hearty laughter. Then they stood up, walked down the steps on the side of the stage, and came up to me.

"On your feet, Gaomi County!" Yuan Shikai said coldly.

I got to my feet and followed them up to the Ascension Platform. Yuan Shikai, who was robust and stocky, and von Ketteler, who was thin as a pole, walked shoulder to shoulder like a duck and an egret, but took slow steps. I kept my head down, eyes shielded, yet still able to see their backs. Truth is, I had a dagger hidden in my boot, and if I'd had half the courage of my young brother, I could have killed them both on the spot. The calmness and unflappability I'd demonstrated when I went alone into the rebels' camp to apprehend Sun Bing had given way to crippling fear as I followed along behind them. That alone was proof that I was a tiger in my dealings with ordinary citizens and a sheep in the presence of superiors or foreigners. No, not a sheep, for a ram can butt with its horns, while I have the nerve of a frightened mouse.

I stood at the feet of the intrepid Sun Bing and looked up into his face, bloated by the mass infusion of blood, some of which trickled out of the corners of his mouth. His puffy eyes were mere slits. The absence of teeth slurred the vituperations emerging from his mouth, but not so much as to make them unintelligible. Not only was he was flinging abuse at Yuan Shikai and von Ketteler, but he was straining to spit bloody foam into their faces. He simply did not have the strength, and all he could manage was childish dribbles. His mouth resembled nothing so much as the bubbly opening of a crab's mouth. Yuan Shikai nodded his satisfaction.

"Gaomi County, reward Zhao Jia and his son with the agreed-upon amount of silver, place them into the second rank of yayi, the 'black,' and give them a land-tax waiver."

Zhao Jia, who was in line behind me, fell to his knees on the inclined plank up to the platform.

"Humble thanks for Your Excellency's boundless generosity and favor!" he intoned loudly.

"Listen carefully, Zhao Jia," Yuan said to him in a somber yet intimate tone of voice. "You must not allow him to die, not until the ceremony to commemorate the completion of the rail line on the twenty-second. Foreign photographers will be on hand to memorialize the event. If he dies before then, do not expect our friendship to save you."

"Fret not, Excellency," Zhao Jia said, confident of his plan to keep the victim alive. "I will do whatever is necessary to ensure that he will not die before the ceremony on that day."

"Gaomi County, in the name of the Empress Dowager and His Majesty, stay here with your three ranks of yayi and keep watch over the prisoner in shifts." Yuan smiled. "There is no need to return to the yamen. Once the rail line has been completed, Gaomi County will become a major hub in the Great Qing Empire. While that may not guarantee a transfer and promotion for you, riches will migrate toward you. Have you not heard the adage 'When the train whistle blows, a river of gold flows'? My friend, in point of fact, I am making it easy for you to govern your county and keep its people in line."

Yuan Shikai roared at his little joke while I hastily knelt at his feet.

"I humbly thank Your Excellency for his patronage. Your humble servant will diligently carry out his duties!" I said over the background of Sun Bing's hoarse curses.

2

Like a pair of bosom friends, Yuan Shikai and von Ketteler made their way down the platform, arm in arm. Then, within a protective ring of soldiers, Chinese and foreign, they left the premises, Yuan in his eight-man palanquin and the German on his massive horse, on their way back to the yamen. Dust flew over the Academy parade ground, accompanied by the clatter of horse hooves on the cobblestone road. The yamen had been turned temporarily into the two dignitaries' official residence; the Tongde Academy compound had been transformed into barracks and stable facilities for the foreign troops. Now that the official parties had left, local residents, who had been confined to the outer edges of the parade ground, began moving toward the center. A momentary sense of bewilderment was followed by a jolt of terror. Excellency Yuan's comment just before he departed sent an upsurge of emotion through my heart. "While that may not guarantee a transfer and promotion for you . . ." Transfer and promotion, ah, transfer and promotion; a whisper of hope threaded its way out of my heart, proof that Excellency Yuan still considered me a man of ability: Excellency Yuan bore me no malice. A close examination shows that I had handled the Sun Bing case properly. I entered the enemy stronghold alone and apprehended Sun Bing with no help from anyone, thus keeping the Imperial Guards and foreign soldiers out of harm's way. As preparations for the sandalwood death were being carried out, I took command, working day and night, managing in less time than anyone thought possible to ready the tools and site of execution for this spectacle, something no one else could have managed as well. Maybe, just maybe, Excellency Yuan isn't as sinister as people think he is; maybe he is a loyal and upright individual who happens to be prudent and farsighted. A man of great allegiance can appear disloyal; a man of great wisdom can sometimes seem slow-witted. For all I know, he could be a pillar in the resurgence of the Great Qing. Hai! I am an insignificant County Magistrate charged with carrying out his superior's orders, fulfilling duties in furtherance of remaining true to his individual calling. Great affairs of state are the province of the Empress Dowager and His Majesty, beyond the reach of minor functionaries like me.

Now that I had overcome my confusion and was no longer wavering, I was once again in control of my wits and abilities. I issued orders for the three shifts of yayi to keep watch around the clock over Sun Bing, who was bound to a crossbar on the Ascension Platform. Local spectators crowded forward, until it seemed that the entire county had turned out, faces painted blood red in the rays of the dying sun. At sunset, crows flew past on their way to their nests and their families in the golden canopies of trees east of the parade ground. "County elders, friends and villagers, go home, please, there to live your lives in humiliation in the name of this important mission. Heed your Magistrate's word that it is better to be a sacrificial lamb than to rise up in resistance against the tyrannical forces arrayed before us. Take Sun Bing, your Maoqiang Patriarch, who stands impaled upon a sandalwood stake on the Ascension Platform, as a solemn and stirring cautionary example."

But the local gawkers turned a deaf ear to my admonition and swept up to the Ascension Platform like waves crashing against the shore. Yayi drew their swords, as if to confront an enemy surge. But the people, though silent, looked on with alarmingly strange expressions, sending an upsurge of panic to my heart. The sun settled in the west in all its redness; the moon's jade rabbit climbed into the sky; warm, soft rays of golden sunlight merged with cool, refreshing silver moonbeams on the Tongde Academy parade ground, on the Ascension Platform, and on the faces of the mass of humanity.

"County elders, friends and fellow villagers, disperse and return to your homes . . ."

The people remained silent.

All of a sudden, Sun Bing, whose voice had been long stilled, broke into song. His mouth leaked air and his chest thumped in and out, very much like an old beat-up bellows. From his vantage point, he could see what was going on all around him, and for a man like him, as long as there was breath in his body, not even the sorry circumstances in which he now found himself could keep him from singing. It would not be unreasonable to say that this was the very opportunity he had sought. And I realized at that moment that the swelling crowd had no intention of freeing him from his predicament, but had drawn closer to hear him sing. See how they all raised their heads and let their mouths fall open? That was the perfect image of an opera devotee.

The fifteenth day of the eighth month, the moon is bright~~wildwood breezes sweep past the platform at night~~

Sun Bing opened with a sorrowful Maoqiang aria. He had hurled abuse for so long that his voice was hoarse and scratchy, but the combination of that hoarseness and the bloody mess his body had become merged to invest his tune with a chilling aura of solemnity and to confer upon it the power to stir hearts. I must admit that Sun Bing, a product of Gaomi, a small, out-of-the-way county, was a true genius, a heroic figure equal to those who appeared in the biographies of Sima Qian's *Records of the Historian*. His name will be spoken down through the ages, praised by the masses and memorialized in Maoqiang opera. My subordinates reported to me that in the immediate wake of his apprehension, a Maoqiang troupe formed spontaneously in Northeast Gaomi Township, and that its performances were tied to burial and funeral activities conducted during chaotic events involving the deaths of so many. Every performance began and ended with howls of grief and was tied to the tragedy of Sun Bing's resistance against the Germans.

By cruel torture my body torn~~this ancient land I tearfully mourn~~

The sobs of the people at Sun Bing's feet filling the air contained bleak strains of meow, a sign that even in their agonizing sorrow, they had not forgotten to provide the singer with a chorus.

I gaze at distant blazing fires in this ancient land~~ah, my wife, my children~~

At that moment, the people seemed to know what was expected of them. As if by prior agreement, they intoned every form of meow known to them, and into that chorus was thrust a climactic cry of desolation, like a whirling pillar of white smoke funneling into the cloudy sky:

"Dieh-dieh~~my beloved Dieh-dieh~~"

It was a cry of heartbreaking dolefulness, yet one that highlighted the sorrowful Maoqiang aria and, in concert with the hoarse, scratchy singing from the platform and the chorus of meows by the onlookers, produced a climactic moment. Pile-driving pains thudded into my heart, as if from a human fist. My lover was here, the woman who had stolen my heart, Sun Bing's daughter, Sun Meiniang. Despite the fact that I had been in the grip of terror for days, like a yellowed leaf fluttering precariously from a branch in the elements, this woman had been on my mind the whole time, and not just because she was carrying my child. I watched as she moved forward, parting the crowd like a black eel emerging from the school against the current. The people slipped away, to her left and her right, opening up a path to the Ascension Platform. Her hair was in disarray, her clothing in complete disorder, and her face grimy, looking like a demon incarnate; she had shed all signs of the flirtatious, singular woman she had been, no longer sleek nor young, but undeniably still Meiniang. Who but Meiniang would dare to come running up at a time like this? What a discomfiting moment! What was I to do now, allow her up onto the platform or not?

"I, I, I have brought forth Heavenly Warriors and Generals, an invincible force~~"

A violent coughing fit cut Sun Bing's aria short and produced a rooster-like wheeze from deep in his chest. Only a scarlet haze in the west remained from the ebbing sun, while chilled moonbeams cast their light onto his bloated face, turning it the color of polished bronze. His head rocked clumsily from side to side and made the pine crossbar creak and groan. Dark, oily blood spurted from his mouth and quickly overspread the platform with a foul odor. His head slumped weakly onto his chest.

Panic set in, as an inauspicious thought crowded everything else out of my mind. Is he dead, just like that? If he was, it was hard to imagine the reaction I could expect from Excellency Yuan, not to mention von Ketteler, who would erupt in anger. The riches promised to Zhao Jia and his son would disappear like a burst bubble, and my prospects for advancement would fade into nothing. I could only sigh. But then the thought occurred to me that his dying might not be such a bad thing, that maybe in the end it was best, since that would bankrupt von Ketteler's evil plans and cast a pall of gloom over his public celebration for the completion of the rail line. Sun Bing, you died a timely death, quick and meaningful, keeping your heroic stature and your moral character intact. You are an example for all of your fellow villagers. I cannot begin to imagine the extent of your suffering if you had lived on for four more days. Qian Ding, in this historic moment, when the nation's destruction looms, when the Imperial

Court has been hounded out of the capital, when the people have been thrown into abject misery and rivers of blood run in the street, your personal advancement is uppermost in your despicable, benighted mind. Sun Bing, it is time for you to die. You must not live on. Soar up into the Kingdom of Heaven, where you can be elevated to nobility . . .

Zhao Jia and his son emerged from their shed. The first one out held a paper-covered lantern—that was Zhao Jia; behind him, carrying a black bowl in both hands, came Xiaojia. They walked in step, easy and smooth, onto the plank leading to the platform, where they passed Meiniang shoulder to shoulder."Oh, Dieh-dieh, what have they done to you?" . . . In full lament, she fell in behind them and threw herself down on the platform floor. When I moved to one side to let them pass, my yayi turned to look at me; but I was scarcely aware of their glances, for my eyes were riveted on Zhao Jia, Xiaojia, and Meiniang. Three members of one family, all gathered around Sun Bing as he suffered the cruelest of punishments, and it seemed somehow fitting and proper. Even if Excellency Yuan had been present at that moment, he would not likely have had reason to interfere.

Zhao Jia raised the lantern overhead, throwing its golden light onto the mass of hair spread across Sun Bing's skull. With his left hand under the chin, he lifted the head up for my benefit. I'd thought that he had died, but no. His chest continued to thrust in and out, and labored breaths still emerged from his mouth and nose, all signs that his vitality remained strong. I was disappointed, but relieved. A picture began to form in my mind, hazy and unreal: Sun Bing was not a criminal suffering from a cruel punishment, but a desperately ill man, beyond all hope, and yet the people were equally desperate to prolong his life, wanting him to live on . . . I wavered between wanting Sun Bing to die or to go on living.

"Give him some ginseng tonic!" Zhao Jia ordered his son.

That command awakened me to the acrid yet sweet smell of fine ginseng wafting up out of the black bowl Xiaojia was holding. Deep down I had to admire Zhao Jia for his attention to detail. In the wake of the infliction of the punishment, when all around us was a scene of chaos, he was calmly preparing a ginseng concoction. Maybe it had already been steeping over a fire in a corner of the shed even before he began, one of many preparations for what he knew would be required.

Xiaojia stepped forward, with the bowl in one hand and a spoon in the other, scooped up a spoonful, and held it up to Sun Bing's mouth. When the spoon touched Sun's lips, his mouth opened greedily, like a newborn puppy that has found its mother's teat. Xiaojia's hand shook slightly, spilling most of the liquid onto Sun Bing's chin, where a fine beard had once grown.

"Be careful!" Zhao Jia snapped unhappily.

Obviously, Xiaojia, a man who butchered pigs and dogs, was not cut out for a job that required finesse. Most of the second spoonful ended up dripping onto Sun Bing's chest.

"What are you trying to do?" The loss of the ginseng pained Zhao Jia, who held the lantern out to his son and said, "Hold this. I'll feed him!"

But before he could take the bowl from Xiaojia, Meiniang stepped up and snatched it away.

"Dieh," she said in a comforting tone, "you are suffering so. Drink some of this ginseng tonic, it'll make you feel better . . ."

Tears filled Meiniang's eyes. Zhao Jia, lantern still in hand, raised it for Xiaojia to tilt Sun Bing's head up by the chin so Meiniang could spoon the liquid into her father's mouth, little by little, without wasting a drop.

For a moment I forgot that I was standing on the Ascension Platform, where a man was being put to death, and imagined that I was watching a family of three feeding a tonic to a sick relative.

Sun Bing started coming back to life by the time the bowl was empty. His breathing was not as labored, his neck had regained the strength to hold his head up, and he was no longer spitting up blood. Even the bloating in his face had begun to recede. Meiniang handed the bowl to Xiaojia and reached out to untie the straps binding his arms to the crossbar, muttering comfortingly:

"Don't be afraid, Dieh, you're going home . . ."

My mind went blank. How was I supposed to deal with this sudden turn of events? Zhao Jia, an old hand, sprang into action. Thrusting the lantern into his son's hands, he interposed himself between Sun Bing and Meiniang, as cold gleams of light flashed in his eyes.

"Good daughter-in-law," he said with a dry, sinister laugh, "snap out of it. This man has been condemned by the Imperial Court. If he is freed, the family of whoever lets him go will be slaughtered all the way to the ninth cousins!"

Sun Meiniang slapped Zhao Jia in the face, then turned and did the same to me. Then she got down on her knees before us both and released a gut-wrenching wail.

"Free my dieh," she sobbed. "I beg you . . . free my dieh . . ."

Aided by the bright moonlight, I saw the crowd below the platform fall heavily to their knees as a din arose from their depths, and only a single utterance:

"Free him . . . free him . . ."

Powerful emotions surged through my heart. People, I sighed, you do not know what is happening up here. You cannot know what is in Sun Bing's mind. All you see is how he suffers physically, but you do not realize that by swallowing the tonic, he has shown us that he is not ready to die. Nor is it life he seeks.

If he had wanted to live, he could have made his escape from the prison and gone to a place where no one could find him. But the way things were now, I could do nothing but wait and see what happened. Sun Bing's suffering had already transformed him into a saint, and I could not defy the will of a saint. So I signaled for several of the yayi to come up, where I quietly told them to carry Sun Meiniang down off the platform. She fought and cursed me in the vilest of language, but the result was never in doubt, not when she was up against four men who managed to drag her down off the platform. My next order was for two shifts to stand guard on the platform, while the other two rested, trading places every hour. They were to take their rest in an empty Tongde Academy room facing the street. On the platform I said, "Permit no one but Zhao Jia and his son to come up the plank. You are also to ensure that no one attempts to climb onto the platform from any side. If anything happens to Sun Bing—if he is put out of his misery or taken away, Excellency Yuan would begin by having my head lopped off. But I'd see that yours already lay on the ground before that happened."

<hr />

3

The next two days and nights passed with agonizing slowness.

After making my inspection of the Ascension Platform at dawn on the third day, I returned to the Academy room and lay down on the mat-covered brick floor, fully dressed, to rest. Yayi between shifts filled the room with their thunderous snores; some even talked in their sleep. Mosquitoes on that summer morning were a true scourge, attacking silently, drawing blood with each bite. Covering my head with my lapel to keep them away offered no help. From outside came the sounds of shifting bits and halters on German horses that were being fed under the poplars to which they were tied, that and the impatient pawing of their hooves and the desolate chirps of autumn insects in weedy spots at the bases of walls. The intermittent sound of rushing water entered my consciousness, and I entertained the thought that the Masang River was singing a melancholy song. With depressing thoughts rippling through my mind, I fell into a fitful sleep.

"Bad news, Laoye, bad news!" Startled out of my sleep by that frantic cry, I was immediately chilled by a cold sweat. There before me was the face of Xiaojia, his dull eyes harboring the threat of treachery. "Laoye, Laoye," he stammered, "bad news. Sun Bing Sun Bing is going to die!"

Without a second's hesitation, I jumped to my feet and raced out of the room. The bright early autumn sun was high in the southeastern sky, spreading its light all across the land, so intense that I was momentarily blinded. Shielding my eyes with my hand, I followed Xiaojia up to the platform, where Zhao Jia, Meiniang, and the men on duty were crowding around Sun Bing. A foul stench struck me in the face before I'd even gotten close, and I was confronted by the sight of flies swarming around Sun's head. Zhao Jia was shooing them away with a horsetail whisk, sending many of them crashing to the floor; but their places were taken by newcomers, thudding against Sun's body in suicidal waves. I did not know if they were drawn to him by a smell emanating from his body or were being spurred on by some dark, mystical force.

Meiniang cared not a bit about the filth she was encountering as she wiped away the eggs deposited on her father's body, soiling her white silk handkerchief. As feelings of disgust rose up inside me, I followed the movements of her fingers: from Sun Bing's eyes down to his mouth; from his nose over to his ears; from the open, seeping wound between his shoulders down to the scabbed wounds on his bare chest . . . the eggs had no sooner been laid than maggots began to squirm over damp spots on his body. If not for Meiniang, they would have made short work of Sun Bing. The smell of death lingered in the stench floating around me.

More than just a fetid smell emerged from Sun Bing's body—he was also emitting powerful waves of heat, like a roaring furnace; if he still had functioning organs, they were probably baked to a crisp. His lips, cracked and dry, looked like singed bark; his hair had taken on the texture of an old straw kang cover, so dry that a single spark could incinerate every strand, and so brittle that it could not withstand the slightest touch. But he was still alive, still breathing, the sound of each breath strong. His ribcage, which swelled and retreated violently, produced a deep rattle.

Zhao Jia and Meiniang stopped what they were doing when I arrived, and together they turned to stare at me hopefully. Holding my breath, I reached out to touch Sun Bing's forehead. It was as hot as blazing cinders, so hot it nearly seared my hand.

"What do we do, Laoye?" Zhao Jia implored, a look of helplessness in his eyes for the first time in memory. So, you old bastard, even you know fear, I see! "If something isn't done right away," he said weakly, subdued by anxiety, "he'll be dead by nightfall . . ."

"Laoye, save my daddy . . ." Meiniang was sobbing. "Do it for my sake, please . . ."

Though I remained silent, my heart was breaking, all because of Meiniang, that foolish woman. Zhao Jia was afraid of what Sun Bing's death meant for him;

but Meiniang was beyond reason. Oh, Meiniang, wouldn't his death release him from the abyss of misery and usher him into heaven? Why must he endure unspeakable suffering, his life hanging by a thread, all to embellish a ceremony to laud the completion of the rail line? Every hour he lives is sixty minutes of agony, and not the sort that human beings can comprehend, but struggling on the tip of a knife, tormented by boiling oil. On the other hand, each day he survives burnishes his stirring legend, creating yet another indelible impression on the people's hearts, and writing another bloody page in the history of Gaomi, and for that matter the history of the Great Qing Dynasty . . . back and forth my thoughts went, from one side to the other, over and over, until I lost my resolve. To save Sun Bing was to flow with the current; to let him be was to swim against it. No, this was no time to seem wise. "Sun Bing, how do you feel now?" With difficulty, he raised his head; fragments of sound escaped through his quivering lips, and heated black rays with red threads shot from his slitted eyes, seemingly right through my heart. His exceptional life force shook me to the core, and in that brief moment a powerful thought sprang up in my mind: Let him live. He mustn't die, for this solemn and stirring drama cannot end like this!

I ordered a pair of duty yayi to fetch the county's preeminent doctors: Cheng Buyi, our expert surgeon, from Nanguan, and Su Zhonghe, the renowned internist, from Xiguan. "Tell them to come with the most effective nostrums at their disposal as quickly as humanly possible. Say that you have come on the order of the Shandong Governor, Yuan Shikai, Excellency Yuan, who will tolerate neither disobedience nor delay. No mercy will be shown to anyone who defies his order!" They left at once.

I then told one of the yayi to summon Chen Qiaoshou, the papier-mâché craftsman, who was to bring with him all his tools and craft material. "Say that you have come on the order of the Shandong Governor, Yuan Shikai, Excellency Yuan, who will tolerate neither disobedience nor delay. No mercy will be shown to anyone who defies his order!" He left at once.

I then ordered another yayi to fetch Pockface Zhang, the tailor at the clothing store, who was to bring with him his tools and two yards of white gauze. "Say that you have come on the order of the Shandong Governor, Yuan Shikai, Excellency Yuan, who will tolerate neither disobedience nor delay. No mercy will be shown to anyone who defies his order!" He left at once.

4

Led by the two yayi, expert surgeon Cheng Buyi and renowned internist Su Zhonghe stepped onto the Ascension Platform. Cheng was a tall, lanky man with a dark, clean-shaven face; wizened and seemingly devoid of body fat, he moved with quick and nimble ease. Su, on the other hand, was short and portly; completely bald on top, he sported a lush, graying beard. Both local men of distinction, they had been ensconced in front-row seats during the battle of the beards between Sun Bing and me. Su Zhonghe had arrived with a full backpack; Cheng Buyi carried a small white cloth bag. Their nervousness showed. A gray cast underlay Cheng's dark complexion, as if he were unusually cold. Su's paler face was tinged with yellow and covered with a slick layer of sweat. They knelt at my feet, but before they could say a word, I bent down and had them rise. "This is an emergency," I said, "which requires the medical mastery of the finest physicians. You know the identity of this individual and are fully aware of why he is here in this condition. Excellency Yuan has commanded that he must remain alive until the twentieth of this month. Today is the eighteenth, which gives us two days and two nights to carry out Excellency Yuan's orders. One look at him will tell you why I have summoned you here. So now I ask you two gentlemen to come forward and put your skills to use!"

The physicians deferred to one another over and over, neither willing to step up and attend to their new patient. Two men—one tall, the other short; one fat, the other skinny—bowed back and forth, up and down, producing such a comical scene that a young and inexperienced yayi actually covered his mouth to stifle a laugh. I felt nothing but disgust over their ludicrous demonstration of superficial etiquette. "That's enough decorum," I said assertively. "If he dies before the twentieth, you"—I pointed to Cheng Buyi—"you"—I pointed to Su Zhonghe—"you"—with a sweeping motion, I pointed my finger at the people crowding around the platform—"and, of course, me—all of us will be buried with him"—I pointed to Sun Bing. You could almost cut through the tension in the air up there. The dumbstruck physicians could only stand and stare. I turned to Cheng Buyi. "You're a surgeon. You first."

Cheng stepped gingerly up to Sun Bing like a dog stealing a piece of meat off a butcher block, reached out, and gently touched the tip of the sandalwood stake between Sun's shoulders with one slender finger. Then he went behind Sun to examine the butt end of the stake. Each time the stake moved, top or bottom, colored bubbles oozed out, carrying the stifling stench of rotting flesh and sending the flies into convulsions of deafening buzzes. The physician staggered up to me and slumped to his knees on wobbly legs. His face twitched and his mouth twisted, like a man about to break down completely. His teeth chattered as he managed to say:

"Laoye . . . his internal organs have shut down . . . there is nothing I can do . . ."

"Nonsense!" Zhao Jia, his eyes wide, glared at Cheng Buyi. "Take my word for it," he said sternly, "there is nothing wrong with his internal organs!" Then his gaze shifted to me. "If they had suffered any damage," he defended himself, "he'd be dead by now. He could not have lived this long. You can see that for yourself, Laoye!"

I weighed his comment for a moment. "Zhao Jia is right," I said. "Sun Bing's injuries are just beneath the skin. The pus and blood you see are coming from infections, something a surgeon sees all the time. If you cannot deal with that, who can?"

"Laoye . . . Laoye . . ." He was nearly incoherent. "This humble . . . I . . ."

"Stop wasting time with that Laoye and humble business!" I cut him off. "Do what you're here to do. If it's a dead horse, treat it as if it were alive!"

Cheng finally summoned the courage to remove his robe and spread it on the platform floor, wind his queue atop his head, roll up his sleeves, and ask for water to wash his hands. Xiaojia ran down the plank and brought up a bucket of water, then waited on Cheng as he washed his hands. That done, Cheng laid his white cloth bag down on his robe, opened it, and removed its contents: two knives, one long and one stubby, two pairs of scissors, one big and one small, two pairs of tweezers, one thick and one thin, and two glass vials, one tall and one short. The taller vial held alcohol, the shorter one medicinal ointment. There were also cotton balls and a roll of gauze.

He picked up a pair of scissors and—snip snip—cut open Sun Bing's clothing. He then poured alcohol onto a cotton ball, with which he cleansed the open wounds, top and bottom, squeezing out quite a bit of blood and pus, not to mention all the foul odors. Sun Bing shuddered violently and moaned with such agony that it made my skin crawl and gave me the shivers.

Cheng Buyi's confidence and courage returned in force as he ministered to the injured Sun Bing; professional honor had won out over fear. At that point he stopped what he was doing and walked up to me, not bent over submissively, but standing tall and proud.

"Laoye," he said, "if you remove the stake from his body, I guarantee that not only will he survive until the day after tomorrow, but he will regain his health completely . . ."

I stopped him in mid-sentence. "If you are willing to have the stake inserted in your own body," I mocked him, "then feel free to remove it from his."

Cheng's face turned ghostly white, his back went from straight to bent, and his eyes shifted evasively. He went back to Sun Bing and continued rubbing his wounds with alcohol-soaked cotton, but this time his hands shook. Next he scooped some dark red medicinal ointment out of the small purple vial with a sliver of bamboo and daubed it on Sun Bing's injuries.

His work finished, he backed away, bent at the waist. I next summoned Su Zhonghe, who came closer, shaking from head to toe as he reached out with one long-nailed hand and laid it on Sun Bing's wrist where it was tied to the crossbar. With his hand in the air, his shoulder slumped to one side, and his head bowed in a meditative pose, he presented a comical yet pitiful sight.

His diagnostics completed, Su Zhonghe announced:

"Your Honor, the patient's eyes are red, his mouth foul; his lips are dry, his tongue charred; his face is swollen, his skin hot to the touch. All symptoms point to internal heat, but his pulse has a floating quality, hollow like a green onion from excessive blood loss, all symptoms of weakness masked as strength, a deficit in the guise of plenty. An inferior physician would be powerless to cure what ails him, and treating him with heat or prescribing the wrong medication would place him at death's door."

Su Zhonghe's reputation as a third-generation master physician was well earned. He was a man of exceptional knowledge, and I was impressed by his diagnosis. "What do you prescribe?" I demanded.

"An immediate infusion of pure ginseng tonic is required!" he said with staunch assurance. "If he is given three bowls of it each day, your humble servant believes he will survive until noon the day after tomorrow. But as an additional precaution, I will prepare three packets of a yin-nourishing concoction that will enhance the effects of the remedy."

Without leaving the platform, Su reached into his medicine bag and with three fingers extracted a mixture of weeds and tree bark without recourse to his scale, which he placed on a tiny piece of paper; after repeating the action twice more, he folded them into small packets and turned to us, not sure who to hand them to. In the end, mindful of what he was doing, he placed them in front of me.

"A half hour after he's had the ginseng tonic, boil one of these in water and give it to him," he said softly.

I dismissed the two physicians with a wave of my hand. They backed out, bent at the waist, manifestly relieved of their onerous responsibility, and fled, not caring where they were headed.

As I pointed to the mass of crazed flies, I turned to Chen Qiaoshou, the papier-mâché craftsman, and Pockface Zhang the tailor. "I don't have to tell you what I expect from you, do I?"

5

By midday, when the sun was blazing down with a vengeance, Chen Qiaoshou and Pockface Zhang had built a sort of cage around Sun Bing, with matting on the top to protect against the sun, matting on three sides, and a curtain made of sheer white gauze in front. It served both to block the scorching sunlight and to keep the voracious flies away. To further lower the temperature inside, Zhao Xiaojia spread a wetted blanket over the top; and in order to lessen the foul smells that attracted the flies, yayi washed the accumulated filth off of the platform with buckets of water. With Zhao Jia's help, Meiniang emptied a bowl of ginseng into her father's stomach, and then, half an hour later, followed that with one of Su Zhonghe's medicinal packets. Sun Bing cooperated with their ministrations, a sign that he planned to live as long as possible. If he'd longed to die, he'd have clamped his mouth shut.

The emergency treatment worked, as Sun Bing's condition slowly improved. I could not see his face through the sheer curtain, but his breathing was regular, his body odor less repellent than before. I made my way down off the platform, so tired that I could barely hold my head up and weighed down with an indescribable sadness. I had no reason to be worried. Excellency Yuan's instructions had been to keep Sun Bing from dying. Now Sun was determined to live on, while Zhao Jia was not about to let him die, and neither was Meiniang. The tonic had infused his body with the strength to go on; exhaustion was no longer his enemy. Go ahead, keep on living. That went for me, too—I was determined to keep on living until my luck ran out.

With bold confidence, I left the Tongde Academy grounds and walked out onto a street that no longer seemed so familiar, heading straight for a public house. A young waiter rushed eagerly up to me, shouting:

"We have an honored guest——"

The rotund proprietor sort of rolled up to me, a smile of manifest puffery on his oily face. I looked down to examine my official garb, which made passing as a common citizen impossible. Besides, even dressed in ordinary clothing, my face was known to everyone in town. Each year on Insect-Waking Day, the beginning of spring, I joined the peasants toiling in the field; on Grave-Sweeping Day, I helped with planting peach trees on the outskirts of town; and on the first and fifteenth of each month, I set up a table in front of the Propagation Hall to read from the classics and instruct the people on the tenets of loyalty, filial piety, benevolence, and righteousness . . . I am a good official, close to the people, and were I to leave office, I am confident that I would be rewarded with a very large umbrella from the masses . . .

"I welcome the esteemed gentleman to this humble establishment. Your presence brings me great honor . . ." The proprietor was reaching the heights of pedantry. "May I ask your pleasure, sir?"

"Two bowls of millet spirits and a dog's leg," I said.

"My apologies, Laoye," the proprietor said unhappily, "but we do not sell dog meat or millet spirits . . ."

"Why is that? Why would you not sell such fine items?"

"All I can say is . . ." The proprietor stumbled over his words, apparently trying to screw up the courage to say what was on his mind. "Laoye is probably aware that the finest millet spirits and dog's legs in town are supplied by Sun Meiniang. We cannot compete with her . . ."

Heated millet spirits, fragrant dog meat, scenes of the past in my head repeat . . .

"What do you sell?"

"To answer Laoye, we sell Baigar and Erwotou sorghum spirits, baked sesame cakes, and stewed beef."

"Then bring me two liang of Baigar, one jiao of the beef, plus two hot sesame cakes."

"Right away, Laoye," the man said as he disappeared around back.

The Gaomi Magistrate sits in a shop, his thoughts running apace, and all he can think of is Meiniang's lovely face. She possesses what it takes to create stirrings of love, like water for frolicking fish, or nectar for honeybees, weaving soft romantic lace . . .

After he placed my order in front of me, I dismissed him with a wave of the hand. "I'll pour my own today," I said as I picked up the bottle and filled a green cup to the brim. The first spicy cupful brought a pleasant sensation as it slid down my throat; the second heated cupful made me slightly woozy; and the third turbid cupful made me sigh and sent tears streaming down my cheeks. I drank and I ate, I ate and I drank, and when I'd eaten and drunk my fill, I said to the proprietor, "Make out a bill for what I've had. I'll send someone over to pay in a day or two."

"The mere presence of Laoye has brought great fortune to this establishment."

I walked out, so light on my feet that I felt as if I were strolling amid the clouds and mist.

6

A yayi roused me out of bed on the morning of the fourth day. The effects of the alcohol had abated but not gone away. I was still in a fog and suffering from a headache; I could barely recall what had happened yesterday, which seemed so long ago. I staggered over to the parade ground, blinding sunlight auguring yet another fine day. Sun Bing's steady, seemingly happy moans filtered down to me from the Ascension Platform, and I knew that he was holding up well. The duty yayi, Liu Pu, scampered down off the platform and, with a furtive look, said:

"Laoye . . ."

I followed the line he was pointing with his chin. A group of people had gathered in front of the opera stage. Dressed in colorful clothing, they presented a strange sight. Some had powdered their faces and painted their lips; others had red faces and ears. I saw some with blue faces and golden eyes, and others whose faces were shiny black. My heart lurched as I recalled the opera troupe Sun Bing had led not so long ago. Was it possible that the remnants of his troupe had come together to make their entry into town? The sweat oozing from my pores sobered me up at once. Quickly straightening my clothes and adjusting my cap, I hurried over toward them.

They had formed a ring around a large red chest on which sat a man who had painted his face with whites and yellows like a faithful and courageous "justice cat." A big black cat-skin cloak was draped over his shoulders; a cat cap, with ears that stood straight up and were tipped with patches of white fur, rested on his head. Cat cloaks covered others' shoulders as well, and some in the group wore cat caps. Quiet and solemn, they looked ready to mount the stage and perform. The top of the chest was covered with red-tasseled spears, knives, swords, and halberds, the whole range of stage props. So the Northeast Gaomi Township Maoqiang Troupe had returned. I breathed a sigh of relief. But I had to wonder if they had come to the Ascension Platform solely to put on a performance. Courage and toughness were hallmarks of Northeast Gaomi Township folkways, something of which I had a clear understanding. With its mystical, gloomy nature, Maoqiang opera had the power to drive its spectators into a frenzy, making them lose touch with reality . . . a chill settled over my heart as I envisioned a scene with glinting knives and flashing swords and thought I heard the sound of battle drums and horns.

"Laoye," Liu Pu whispered, "I feel something in my bones——"

"Tell me."

"This sandalwood death is major bait, and these Northeast Gaomi Township actors are fish who have come to take the hook."

Maintaining a calm demeanor, I smiled and walked toward the actors with measured steps, being sure to look the part of the Laoye. With Liu Pu beside me, I confronted them.

Though none of them said a word at first, the chilling looks they gave me spoke clearly of their animus toward me.

"This is His Honor the County Magistrate," Liu Pu said. "What is it you've come to say?"

They held their tongues.

"Where have you come from?" I asked them.

"From Northeast Township," Justice Cat said in a muffled stage voice from his seat on the chest.

"For what purpose?"

"To put on an opera."

"Who told you to come here to put on an opera at this time?"

"Our cat chief."

"Who is your cat chief?"

"Cat Chief is our cat chief."

"Where is he?"

Justice Cat pointed to Sun Bing up on the Ascension Platform.

"Sun Bing is a criminal condemned by the throne and is being punished appropriately. He has been on public view for three days, so how could he have summoned you here to give a performance?"

"That up there is just his body. His soul returned to Northeast Gaomi Township a long time ago," Justice Cat replied dreamily.

I heaved an emotional sigh.

"I know what you must be feeling. Even though Sun Bing committed a terrible crime, he is, after all, your second-generation Maoqiang Patriarch, and staging an opera for him before he dies is fitting and proper. But this is neither the time nor the place. You are citizens of this county, and I have always treated you as my own sons and daughters. With that in mind, I urge you to leave this dangerous spot for your own safety and that of your families. Return to your Northeast Township, where you are free to put on any performance you like, with no interference from me."

Justice Cat shook his head and in a soft but uncompromisingly firm voice said:

"No, Cat Chief has instructed us to put on our performance in front of him."

"A moment ago you said it is only your cat chief's body up there on the Ascension Platform, and that his soul returned to Northeast Gaomi Township long ago. If you put on your performance here, aren't you doing so for a soulless human form?"

"We obey Cat Chief's instructions," Justice Cat said unflinchingly.

"Are you not afraid of losing your heads?" Pointing in the direction of the yamen, I said in a threatening tone, "Excellency Yuan's crack troops are stationed in the yamen." Then I pointed to a compound in the Tongde Academy. "There is where the German cavalry troops are camped. A ceremony to celebrate the completion of the rail line is scheduled for tomorrow, and both the foreign and government soldiers are on full alert. If you stage one of your cat-and-dog operas under their noses, they will treat that as tantamount to a rebellion or a riot." Finally, I pointed up to Sun Bing. "Is that how the rest of you want to wind up?"

"We are not afraid," Justice Cat grumbled. "We came to put on a performance, and that is what we are going to do."

"I have long known that Northeast Gaomi Township residents are fond of performing onstage, and I am a fan of your Maoqiang opera. Why, I can even sing some arias. Maoqiang promotes loyalty, filial piety, benevolence, and justice. Teaching people to be reasonable and understanding corresponds exactly with my principles of instruction. I have always supported your performance activities and hold you in high esteem for your deep-seated love of the arts. But not here and not now. I order you to leave. After this is all over, if you desire, I will personally make a formal visit to Northeast County to extend you an invitation to return to stage an opera here."

"We obey Cat Chief's instructions," Justice Cat replied obstinately.

"I am the highest official in this county, and if I say you may not perform, you may not."

"Not even His Majesty the Emperor has the authority to stop people from performing an opera."

"Have you never heard the adage 'Fear not the official, just the office'? Or 'A Governor lops off a head, a County Magistrate destroys a family'?"

"You can chop our bodies to pieces, but our heads will perform an opera." Justice Cat got defiantly to his feet and commanded his disciples and followers, "Open the chest, my children."

The cats picked up weapons from atop the chest, turning their numbers into a traditional opera troupe. They then threw open the mahogany chest and dug out python-decorated robes and jade belts, phoenix caps and embroidered women's capes, masks and jewelry, gongs and drums and other props . . .

I ordered Liu Pu to hurry over to the Academy and bring back all the off-duty yayi.

"I, your Magistrate, have admonished you as earnestly as I know how, and for your own good. But you have decided to ignore your sympathetic Laoye and go your own way." I turned to my yayi and pointed to Justice Cat. "Arrest the cat leader," I said, "and drive the rest of this motley feline crew away with your clubs!"

My yayi began swinging their red-and-black batons amid threatening shouts, though it was really a show of bluff and bluster. Justice Cat dropped to his knees and rent the air with a desolate wail, then began to sing. Seeing him on his knees like that, I assumed that he wanted to plead with me; until, that is, I realized that he was kneeling before Sun Bing, up on the Ascension Platform. I also assumed that the wail was an expression of torment over seeing the Mao-qiang Patriarch endure such suffering. Once again I realized my mistake, for the mournful cry was actually a call for the musicians to prepare their instruments, an opening note. A torrent of music burst forth, as if set free by an open floodgate.

Cat Chief~~golden feathers adorn your head purple clouds swath your body you ride a long-maned lion vanquishing foes a pure gold cudgel in hand~~you are the foe of thousands of tens of thousands are the reincarnation of Yue Fei the mortal embodiment of Guan Yu you reign supreme throughout the land~~

Meow~~meow~~

As if by design, all the black-faced cats red-faced cats multihued cats big cats small cats male cats female cats embellished Justice Cat's cloud-bursting aria with cat cries inserted in all the right places, with perfect timing, all the while reaching into the storage chest to deftly extract gongs and drums and other stage props, including an oversized cat fiddle, each actor expertly adding the sound of his instrument in perfect orchestral fashion.

The first blow topples Taihang Mountain~~reclaims Jiaozhou Bay~~the second blow levels Laizhou Prefecture~~terrifying the ferocious white-headed tiger~~the third blow brings down the mainstay~~takes the Most Exalted Patriarch Lao's Eight Trigrams Furnace out of play~~

Meow~~meow~~

The performance, filled with music and passion, had an irresistible appeal. Fully half the yayi, all born and raised in the county, were from Northeast Township, and therefore were infatuated with Maoqiang opera, an inbred affinity well beyond the ability of someone like me, an outsider, to comprehend. Despite the fact that I had learned to sing a respectable number of arias, thanks to Sun Meiniang, Maoqiang opera simply did not affect me the way it did Gaomi residents, whose eyes could fill with rapturous tears. Almost immediately I sensed that this was no ordinary performance, and that Justice Cat was a singer of virtually peerless caliber. His voice had that classical raspy Mao-qiang timbre and the ability to reach a pitch beyond an aria's highest note, a quality peculiar to Maoqiang and mastered throughout the genre's history only by the progenitor, Chang Mao, and the Patriarch, Sun Bing. When Sun Bing took his leave from the stage, even Meiniang believed that he was the last in a line of actors on whom that talent had been bestowed. But then, out of nowhere, this consummate skill had been reborn in the person of the Justice Cat. I would be the first to admit that the quality of his singing was nothing less than brilliant, easily worthy of expression in the most refined surroundings. I could tell that my men, including the unusually competent and clear-headed Liu Pu, were mesmerized by what they were hearing. Their eyes shone, their lips were parted; they no longer knew where they were, and it was clear that before long they would be crying out meows along with those cat figures, and might even start rolling around on the ground, climbing walls, and shinnying up trees, until this pitiless execution site turned into a paradise for cat-calling, a menagerie of dancing. Feeling helpless, I had no idea how to bring this to a close, especially when I saw that the yayi guarding the Ascension Platform were equally distracted, frozen in place. From a spot just outside the opening of the shack, Sun Meiniang added her sobs to the singing, and Zhao Xiaojia had turned wild with joy. His dieh had to grab hold of his clothes to keep him from running over to join in. From all appearances, Zhao Jia's long absence from his hometown had insulated him from the noxious influence of Maoqiang; able to keep a cool head in the midst of all that ferment, he remained focused on his heavy responsibility. As for Sun Bing, while I could not see his face clearly through the gauzy curtain, the sound he was making—it could have been a cry, it could have been muted laughter—told me everything I needed to know about how he was holding up.

Justice Cat sang and danced, the wide sleeves of his robe swirling in the air like puffy white clouds as his meaty tail swept the ground. His effect on everyone around him as he sang and danced was profound—demonic and infectious, soul captivating and bewitching; he climbed up to the Ascension Platform, one casual step after another, and the other cats followed his lead. Thus was the curtain raised on a grand and spectacular performance.

7

Cats were at the center of the disastrous turn of events. With cat attire fluttering in the air above the platform and cat music rising from below, my thoughts carried me back to when I first laid eyes on Sun Meiniang. On a trip to one of the county villages to apprehend gamblers, my small palanquin was carried onto a stone-paved street in the county town. It was a late spring day, with a fine rain ushering in dusk earlier than usual. Shops on both sides of the street had closed for the day; puddles of water filling spaces between the stones reflected the light. The silence on the deserted street was broken only by my bearers' watery footfalls. A slight chill in the air created feelings of melancholy. Frogs croaking in a nearby pond reminded me of tadpoles I'd seen swimming in puddles among green sprouts of wheat, and that made the melancholy even worse. I wanted to have the bearers speed up to facilitate an early return to the yamen, where I could make myself a cup of hot tea and peruse some of the classics. The only thing lacking was a lovely young woman to keep me company. My wife was the daughter of an illustrious family, a woman of noble nature and high moral character. But where relations between a man and a woman were concerned, she was as cold as ice and frost. I promised her that I would not take a concubine, but I must admit that the bleak bedroom atmosphere had tested my patience. I was in a terrible mood at that moment, when the sound of a door opening onto the street drew my attention. A public-house sign hung above the open doorway, from which emerged the tantalizing odors of strong spirits and meat. A young woman all in white was standing beside the door filling the air with rude talk, though the sound of her voice was pleasantly crisp. Then a dark object came flying my way and hit my palanquin.

"You damned greedy cat, I'll kill you!"

A wild feline tore across the street and huddled under the eaves of a house, where it licked its whiskers and kept its eye trained across the way.

"How dare you!" my lead bearer fumed. "Are you blind? You actually struck Laoye's personal flag!"

The woman bowed in hasty contrition and immediately changed her tone of voice, sending sweet apologies my way. Even through the curtain I could see that she was a woman who knew how to flirt and was taken by the flash of coquettish beauty against the darkening sky. Unfamiliar feelings rose up inside me. "What is sold in that shop?" I asked the lead bearer.

"This shop's dog meat and millet spirits are the finest in town, Your Honor. The woman's name is Sun Meiniang, known locally as 'Dog-Meat Xishi.'"

"Stop here," I said. "You have here a hungry and cold Magistrate. I believe I will step inside and warm myself with a bowl of heated millet spirits."

Liu Pu leaned over and whispered:

"Laoye, there is a popular adage that 'A man of high standing does not enter a lowly establishment.' I urge you not to honor a roadside shop like this with your presence. I humbly submit that you would be better off returning to the yamen without delay, so as not to worry the First Lady."

"Even His Majesty the Emperor sometimes travels incognito to gauge the public mood," I said. "I am a mere County Magistrate, far from high standing, so what harm can there be in drinking a bowl when I'm thirsty and eating rice when I'm hungry?"

The bearers set down the chair in front of the shop; Sun Meiniang rushed up and got down on her knees as I stepped to the ground.

"I beg Laoye's forgiveness," she said. "This common woman deserves death. That greedy cat tried to steal a fish, and in my haste I flung it into Laoye's palanquin. I beg your forgiveness . . ."

I offered her my hand. "Please get up, Elder Sister, for an unwitting error does not constitute a crime. I have forgotten it already. I have left my palanquin with the intent of partaking of some food and drink in your establishment. May I follow you inside?"

Sun Meiniang stood up, bowed a second time, and said:

"I thank Laoye for such magnanimity! Magpies sang at my door this morning, but I never thought my good fortune would arrive in the person of Laoye. Come in, please. Your party is welcome as well." Sun Meiniang ran out into the street to retrieve the fish, which she flung in the direction of the wild cat without a second glance. "This is your reward, you greedy cat, for bringing an honored guest to our shop."

With speed and agility, Sun Meiniang lit lanterns and trimmed the candlewicks, then polished the tables and chairs till they shone. That done, she heated a jug of spirits and brought out a plate of dog meat, setting it down on the table in front of me. Her beauty was made even more striking in the muted light, so lovely was she that waves of carnal desire undulated in my heart. My retainers' eyes lit up like will-o'-the wisps, a reminder that I must commit no breach of moral behavior. Keeping my restless heart in check, I managed to climb back into my palanquin afterward and return to the yamen, accompanied by the image of Sun Meiniang.

The pounding of gongs and drums, the squeal of a cat fiddle, and the raised voices were like a flock of birds passing overhead. At first, local residents moved cautiously into the square in twos and threes, then in small clusters, making their way up to the opera stage on the Academy parade ground. By the looks of it, they had already forgotten that an unimaginably cruel punishment had been meted out on this spot, had forgotten that a man impaled on a sandalwood stake was at that moment suffering on the Ascension Platform across from where they stood. A risqué opera was in progress on the stage in front of them, the story of a soldier taking liberties with the lovely daughter of an innkeeper. It was a comforting sight for me, since Sun Bing's anti-German lyrics had all been sung, and if Excellency Yuan were to turn up to watch the performance, he would find nothing to object to.

What will you have to drink, honorable soldier?
I want some Daughter's Red fresh from the vat.

We have no Daughter's Red.
Elder Sister has a lovely smell.
What will you have to eat, honorable soldier?
Slice some Heavenly Phoenix for me to try.
We have no Heavenly Phoenix.
Elder Sister, you are Golden Phoenix

. . .

Up on the stage, amorous glances from the innkeeper's alluring daughter created an erotic atmosphere below. Each bit of repartee was like the shedding of clothing, one garment at a time. This was a standard opening drama in the Maoqiang repertoire, loved by the young for its lively irreverence. I was well into my middle years, graying at the temples, but was I immune to amorous thoughts? No, the steamy scene on the stage reminded me of how Sun Meiniang had sung snatches of this kind of play for me in the yamen's Western Parlor ~~*Meiniang, oh, Meiniang, how often you transported the soul of this Magistrate~~baring your jade-like form, wearing only cat clothing as you frolicked on my bed and cavorted atop my body~~by brushing your hand across your face, you presented to me the spirited face of a lovely kitten~~your body taught me that no animal in the world has more natural charm than a cat~~when you licked my skin with your scarlet tongue, I felt as if I had died and been spirited to the land of immortals, as if my heart had been butted out of my body~~oh, Meiniang, if your gandieh's mouth were big enough, he would wrap it around you, all of you~~*

The young soldier and the alluring young maiden were swept to the back of the stage, as if blown there by a strong gust of wind, and their place was taken by Justice Cat in full cat regalia, his arrival announced by a drumroll and the clang of a gong. He first made several quick rounds of the stage before sitting down in the center and launching into a cadenced narration:

"*I, Sun Bing, am Chief Cat, a Maoqiang actor who once led a troupe to perform in villages far and wide. My repertoire includes forty-eight operas that bring to life emperors and kings, generals and ministers that through history abide. In my middle years I offended the County Magistrate, who then plucked out my beard though his identity he did hide. My acting days ended, I relinquished my troupe to make a living selling tea, in my native home to reside. Little Peach, who bore me a son and a daughter, was a loving and dutiful wife, true and tried. But loathsome foreign devils invaded our land to build a railroad and savage our feng shui. A traitorous bully made off with my darling children while others made sport in the square with my wife, whose calamitous results cannot be denied. I have wept sobbed cried wailed myself sick~~from hatred loathing abhorrence repulsion my heart has died~~*"

Justice Cat intoned his tragic song with fervor, rising and falling like a stormy sea, while arrayed behind him was a cohort of armed cat actors whose outrage spilled over into the audience, triggering a reaction of meow calls and angry foot stomping, rocking the Academy grounds and raising clouds of dust. My unease rose with it, as an inauspicious cloud gradually enshrouded the site. Liu Pu insistently whispered a warning into my ear, sending chills up and down my spine. Yet I felt helpless in the face of the incendiary mood among the actors and their spellbound audience; it was like trying to rein in a runaway horse with one hand, or to put out a raging fire with a ladle. Things had reached the point where I could trust only to Providence, give the proverbial horse free rein.

I retreated to a spot in front of the shed to watch with detachment. Up on the Ascension Platform, Zhao Jia was standing to one side of the protective cage, quietly watching with a sandalwood peg in his hand. Sun Bing's moans were drowned out by the clamor below the stage, but I knew that he was still alive and as well as could be expected, that his spirit was as high as ever. A popular legend has it that if a Gaomi resident who is on the verge of dying while away from home hears the strains of Maoqiang opera outside his door, he will leap bright-eyed out of his deathbed. Sun Bing, though you have been subjected to a punishment worse than death, seeing this performance and listening to these arias—for your benefit—is surely the opportunity of a lifetime. I turned my gaze to the crowd, searching for the idiot son of the Zhao family, and I found him, saw him sitting atop one of the opera stage posts, adding his calls of meow to those of the crowd. Slowly he slid down the post, but as soon as his feet hit the ground, he shinnied back up, cat-like. I then searched for Meiniang of the Sun family, and I found her, saw her, her hair in disarray as she beat on the back of a yayi with a stick. When this revelry would end, I could not say, but as I looked into the sky to check the time, I saw that a dark cloud had blotted out the sun.

8

Twenty or more armed German soldiers emerged from the encampment on the Academy grounds. Oh, no! A silent cry escaped from my mouth. This was going to end badly. I rushed up to stop their advance, placing myself directly in front of a junior officer armed with a pistol, eager to clarify the situation to him. Worthy . . . officer, that's what I'll call you, you bastard. Well, the worthy officer, whose eyes were the color of green onions, said something I couldn't understand and shoved me out of his way.

The soldiers quick-stepped up to the Ascension Platform and stomped heavily up the wooden ramp, which bent under weight it was never intended to sustain; the platform began to sway. "Stop," I shouted to the actors on the opera stage and the viewers beneath it. "Stop—Stop—" But my voice was too weak to carry, like throwing a cotton ball at a stone wall.

The soldiers lined up in tight ranks and fixed their eyes on the opera stage, where a fierce battle was being played out. Actors in the roles of cats were trading blows with actors dressed up as tigers and wolves. Justice Cat, seated in the center of the stage, was providing the musical accompaniment to the action in a powerful voice that seemed to reach the sky. This was yet another unique characteristic of Maoqiang opera: sung arias accompanying fighting scenes, from start to finish, their contents often bearing no relevance to the action; as a result, staged fights in the context of an opera actually served as a background for the talents of a principal singer.

Ai yo, Dieh, ai yo, Niang~~ai yo my little son done wrong~~he scratched my itch with his cute little hand~~waiting to grow up big and strong~~his life cut short, now the ghosts among~~two lines of bloody tears as I sing my song~~

Meow meow~~meow meow~~

I looked up at the soldiers, pleading with my eyes; my nose began to ache. "You up there, German soldiers, I'm told that you have opera back home, a place with its own customs and mores, and I ask you to compare those with theirs, and contrast their number with yours. Do not consider the actions onstage to be a provocation, and do not confuse them with the anti-German army led by Sun Bing, even though his men also painted their faces and dressed in stage costumes. You are witnessing pure theatrics, performed by a troupe of actors, and while it may appear manic, it is a common feature of the Maoqiang repertoire, and the actors are merely following long-established traditions. They act to memorialize those who have passed on to ease them into heaven, and they act to bring peace to those about to die. This performance is for Sun Bing, the inheritor of the Maoqiang mantle of Patriarch, for it was in his hands that Maoqiang reached the magnificent level of achievement you see before you today. They are performing for Sun Bing the way a cup of the finest spirits is given to a dying distiller, as a thoughtful gesture and an expression of humanity. German soldiers, lay down your Mausers, I beg you in the name of compassion and reason. You must not kill any more of my subjects. A river of blood has already flowed in Northeast Gaomi Township, and the once-bustling Masang Township is now a wasteland. You have fathers and mothers back home and hearts that beat in your chests; they are not made of iron or steel, are they? Can it be that in your hearts we Chinese are nothing but soulless pigs and dogs? You have Chinese blood on your hands, and I believe you must be visited by terrible dreams at night. Lay down your weapons, lay them down." I ran up to the platform.

"Do not open fire!" I shouted.

Unfortunately, my shout sounded like an order to fire, which they did, seemingly ripping a dozen holes in the sky with the cracks of their rifles, whose muzzles released puffs of smoke, like white snakes that slithered upward before beginning to break up. The pungent odor of gunpowder burned the inside of my nose and struck my mind with mixed feelings of grief and joy. Why grief? I didn't know. Why joy? I didn't know that, either. By then hot tears blurred my vision, and through those tears I watched as a dozen blurry red bullets escaped from the German soldiers' rifles and spun their way forward slowly, very slowly, almost hesitantly, reluctantly, irresolutely, as if wanting to turn away or fly up into the sky or bury themselves in the ground, as if wanting to stop their momentum or to slow down time or to wait till after the actors on the stage had run for cover before completing their split-second journey, as if they were tied to the German rifles by an invisible thread that was pulling them back. Kind-hearted bullets good and decent bullets mild and gentle bullets compassionate bullets Buddhist bullets, slow down to give my people a chance to fall to the ground before you reach your targets. You don't want their blood to stain your bodies, you chaste and holy bullets! But those ignorant citizens on the stage were not only oblivious to the need to fall to the ground to avoid your arrival, they actually seemed to be waiting in welcome anticipation. When the hot, fiery red shells penetrated their bodies, some reacted by throwing their arms in the air in what looked like an attempt to pull leaves off of trees; some fell to the ground and grabbed their bellies with both hands, fresh blood seeping out between their fingers. In the center of the stage, Justice Cat was thrown backward, along with his chair, the interrupted strains of his song caught in his throat. The first volley cut down most of the actors on the stage. Zhao Xiaojia slid down his post, cast a dazed look all around until he realized what was going on, wrapped his arms around his head, and ran behind the stage, shouting:

"They're shooting people, trying to kill me—"

The Germans had no intention of shooting the post-sitter, at least I didn't think so; his executioner's attire probably saved him. He'd been an object of fascination for many people over the past several days. After the first volley, the soldiers in back stepped up to the front row and raised their rifles in perfect formation. Their movements were rapid and skillful; they had no sooner taken aim than they pulled the triggers, creating a second volley of explosions that rang in my ears, and before the sound died out, their bullets had hit their marks.

Not a single living soul was now left on the opera stage, abruptly stained by rivulets of multihued blood, while beneath the stage members of the audience were emerging from their Maoqiang trance. My poor subjects scrambled madly to get away, bumping and shoving, wailing and roaring, a chaotic mass of humanity. I saw the Germans up there lower their weapons, glum smiles on their long faces, like a red thread of sunlight poking out from behind dark clouds on a bitter cold day. The shooting had stopped, and once again I experienced mixed feelings of grief and joy. Grief over the destruction of Northeast Gaomi Township's last Maoqiang opera troupe, joy over the Germans' lack of interest in turning their guns on the fleeing commoners. Did I say joy? Gaomi County Magistrate, was there really joy in your heart? Yes, there was, great joy!

Puddles of actors' blood merged and flowed to the sides of the stage, where it streamed into wooden gutters that were intended for rainwater runoff, but now served to channel blood off the stage and onto the ground. After the initial cascades, the flow slowed to a drip, one large drop of heavy, treasured blood on top of another——drip, drip, drip, heavy, treasured . . . the Heavenly Dragon's tears, that's what they were.

The common folk made their escape, leaving behind a field littered with shoes and cat clothing crushed beyond recognition; among the litter were bodies trampled in the stampede. My eyes were riveted on the two gutter openings, which continued to send drops of blood to the ground—one drop splashing on top of another. No longer blood, but the Heavenly Dragon's tears, that's what they were.

9

As I was returning to the Academy grounds from the yamen, a half moon on the nineteenth day of the eighth month sent cold beams earthward. I stepped through the gate and spat out a mouthful of blood; a brackish, saccharine taste filled my mouth, as if I'd overindulged in honeyed sweets. Liu Pu and Chunsheng were worried.

"Laoye, are you all right?"

Brought to my senses by the sound of voices, I looked at them and asked:

"Why are you two still with me? Get lost, go away, stop following me."

"Laoye . . ."

"You heard me, I said leave me alone; get lost, the farther the better. I don't want to lay eyes on you again. If I so much as see you, I'll break you in two!"

"Laoye . . . Laoye . . . have you lost your mind?" Chunsheng could hardly get the words out through his sobs.

I unsheathed the sword at Li Pu's waist and pointed it at them, the glint of steel as cold as my tone of voice:

"Father's dead, Mother's remarried, now it's every man for himself. If you two retain any good feelings from the years we have been together, you will get out of my sight. Come back sometime after the twentieth to collect my body." I flung the sword to the ground, where it clanged loudly and sent waves of sound into the night sky. Chunsheng took a couple of steps back, then turned and ran, slowly at first, then faster and faster, until he was out of sight. Liu Pu just stood there, head down, frozen in place.

"Why aren't you leaving?" I asked him. "Go in and pack some things to take back home to Sichuan. When you get there, don't tell anyone your real name. Tend to your parents' graves and stay away from all local officials."

"Uncle . . ."

That gut-wrenching word brought on a torrent of tears.

"Go on," I said with a wave of my hand. "You have to look out for yourself; now go. There's nothing for you here."

"Uncle," Liu Pu repeated, "your unworthy nephew has been thinking about many things in recent days, and I cannot help but feel deeply ashamed. Everything that has happened to you, Uncle, is my fault." He was tormented. "I dressed up to look like you so I could yank out Sun Bing's beard, which was why he left the troupe, married Little Peach, and had two children. If he hadn't married and become a father, he would never have clubbed the German engineer to death, and none of this would ever have happened . . ."

"You foolish, worthy nephew," I cut him off. "Everything proceeded according to fate's plan, not because of anything you did. I've always known it was you who plucked Sun Bing's beard, and I know you did that on behalf of the First Lady. It was her attempt to plant the seeds of hatred toward me in Sun Meiniang and to put an end to any romantic liaison between us. I also know it was the two of you who smeared dog droppings on the wall, because you were afraid that an illicit relationship with one of my subjects could ruin my official career. What neither of you knew was that Sun Meiniang and I were fated to meet in this place because of what happened in our past three lives. I bear no grudge toward you or toward her. I bear no grudge toward anyone, for we were all acting in accordance with our fates."

"Uncle . . ." Li Pu fell to his knees and, his voice breaking with sobs, said, "please accept your unworthy nephew's obeisance!"

I went up to him and raised him off his knees.

"Now this is where we say good-bye, worthy nephew."

I turned and headed to the Tongde Academy parade ground.

Liu Pu fell in behind me.

"Uncle," he said softly.

I looked back.

"Uncle!"

I walked back to him.

"Is there something else you want to say?"

"I, your unworthy nephew, want to avenge my father; I want to avenge the Six Gentlemen and my Uncle Xiongfei. By doing this, I would also extirpate the hidden evil that imperils the Great Qing Dynasty!"

"Do you plan to assassinate him?" I stopped to think for a moment. "Is this a deed to which you are irrevocably committed?"

He nodded decisively.

"Then I can only hope that you have better luck than your Uncle Xiongfei, worthy nephew."

I turned and once again headed to the parade ground. This time I did not look back. The moon cast its light into my eyes, and I suddenly had the feeling that my heart was like a garden in which countless flowers were ready to bloom. Each of those blooming flowers was a rousing Maoqiang aria. Long and lingering, the arias swirled rhythmically in my head so that all my movements were musically cadenced:

Gaomi Magistrate leaves the yamen, heart full of sorrow~~meow meow~~autumn winds and cold moonbeams and loud drumbeats herald the morrow~~

The moon cast its light on my body, and on my heart. You moonbeams, how bright you are, brighter than I've ever seen before, and brighter than I'll ever see again! I followed the path of moonbeams with my eyes, and what I saw was my wife lying in bed, her face as white as paper. She had dressed in ceremonial attire—phoenix headdress and tasseled cape—and laid a last note on the bed beside her. "The Imperial Capital has fallen," she had written, "the nation is lost. A foreign power has invaded the country and partitioned the land. I have been graced by Imperial favor in all its majesty. I cannot live an ignoble life, on a par with the animals. A loyal minister dies for his country; a chaste wife dies for her husband. These virtues have been praised down through the ages. Your faithful wife has gone on ahead and is waiting for her mate to join her. Alas and alack, my sorrow is endless."

My beloved! Knowing the path of righteousness, you have taken poison for the sake of our land. You have set a glorious example for me~~I have chosen to take the same route, for I too cannot live ignobly~~my death has long been planned. But my work is not yet finished, and I cannot die before the end of the story is told. Wait for me at Wangxiang tai~~once I have done what I set out to do, I shall join you and the emperors of old~~

The parade ground was overlaid with a solemn stillness; the moon soundlessly spilled its beams on the ground. Owls and bats cast gliding shadows from above; the eyes of feral dogs flashed on the edges. You pilferers of putrid flesh, are you waiting to feast on the bodies of those who lie where they died? No one has come to collect my subjects' bodies, which lie in the moonlight waiting for the sun's rays. Yuan Shikai and von Ketteler are engaged in revelry, drinking good wine and enjoying fine food brought to them from sizzling woks in the yamen kitchen. Are you not worried that I will put Sun Bing out of his misery? You must know that if I want to go on living, Sun Bing will not die. What you do not know is that I have no desire to go on living. I want to follow my wife's lead and sacrifice myself for the Great Qing Nation after ending Sun Bing's life. I want it to be his dead body that is the focus of your rail line ceremony, to let your train pass by a Chinese corpse as it rumbles down the track.

I staggered up to the Ascension Platform. Sun Bing's Ascension Platform; Zhao Jia's Ascension Platform; Qian Ding's Ascension Platform. A lantern hung high above the platform, identified as belonging to the Main Hall of the county yamen. My gaze took in the listless yayi standing like marionettes at the platform's edge, red-and-black batons gripped tightly in their hands. An earthenware pot in which herbal medicine stewed sat atop a small wood-burning stove directly beneath the lantern, sending steam into the air and spraying ginseng fragrance in all directions. Zhao Jia was sitting beside the stove, his narrow, dark face lit up by the fire's light, his arms wrapped around his knees, on which he was resting his chin. He was staring intently at the flames licking out of the stove's belly, like a youngster lost in dreams. Xiaojia was leaning against a post behind his father, legs spread apart to accommodate a container of sheep's intestines, which he was stuffing into steaming cakes before cramming them into his mouth as if he were alone up there. Sun Meiniang was leaning against another post across from Xiaojia, her head lolled to the side, her face hidden behind a mass of uncombed hair. Looking more dead than alive, she had lost every vestige of her once-graceful bearing. I was able to distinguish the hazy outline of Sun Bing's face behind the gauzy curtain. His low moans told me that he was barely hanging on. The stench of his body was drawing hordes of owls to the site, where they soared in the sky directly above, the silence broken by their frequent chilling screeches. Sun Bing, you should be dead by now, *meow meow*, that Maoqiang opera of yours is a fount of myriad feelings, and now the sound that has such complex implications—that *meow*—has actually made a wild dash out of my mouth, *meow meow*. Sun Bing, it all happened because I was so muddleheaded, blessed or cursed with a soft heart, always cautious and indecisive, a mind too cluttered to see through their cunning scheme. Keeping you alive cost the lives of too many of Northeast Gaomi Township's residents and cut Maoqiang opera off from its future. *Meow meow* . . .

I woke the club-wielding yayi out of their stupor and told them to go home to sleep, that I would take care of things up on the platform. I'd just taken a heavy load from their shoulders, and they scooted down the plank, dragging their clubs behind them, as if they feared I'd change my mind; they vanished into the moonlight.

My arrival sparked no reaction from the two men up there, almost as if I were nothing but an empty shadow, or a minor accomplice. Well, they'd have been right, because that's exactly what I was, one of their accomplices. I was trying to decide which of them to stab first when Zhao Jia picked up the medicine pot by its handle and poured its contents into a black bowl.

"Son," he said with authority, "are you done eating? If not, finish later. I want you to help me pour this down his throat."

Xiaojia, ever the obedient son, got to his feet. His monkey-like clownish airs had largely receded after what had happened earlier that day. He smiled at me, then parted the gauzy curtain of the enclosure, exposing Sun Bing's body, which had shriveled considerably. His face had gotten smaller, his eyes bigger; I could count his ribs, and was reminded of a dead frog I'd seen down in the countryside, nailed to a tree by mischievous children.

Sun Bing moved his head when Xiaojia opened the curtain and began to mumble:

"Hmm . . . hmm . . . let me die . . . just let me die . . ."

It was a stirring snippet of speech, and it gave my plan even more cause and meaning, for now Sun Bing no longer wanted to live, having finally comprehended the sinful nature of trying to stay alive. Plunging my knife into his chest would grant him his wish.

Xiaojia willfully thrust an ox-horn funnel designed for medicating domestic animals into Sun Bing's mouth, then gripped his head to hold it steady and let Zhao Jia slowly pour in the ginseng. A gurgling sound emerged from that mouth, emanating from deep down in his throat, as the mixture slid into his stomach.

"What do you say, Old Zhao," I said in a mocking tone from where I stood behind him. "Think he'll live till tomorrow morning?"

Suddenly on his guard, he turned and said, a bright, piercing light in his eyes:

"I guarantee it."

"Granny Zhao is the author of a true wonder in the world of humans!"

"I could not have reached the pinnacle of my profession without the support of my betters," Zhao Jia said humbly. "I cannot lay claim to achievements made possible by others."

"Zhao Jia," I said with a chill to my voice, "don't be too quick to claim success. I do not think he will survive the night—"

"I will stake my life on it. If Your Eminence will grant me another half jin of ginseng, I can keep him alive another three days!"

I laughed out loud before reaching down and extracting a razor-tipped dagger from inside my boot. Knife in hand, I leaped forward to plunge it into Sun Bing's chest. But the chest it penetrated was not Sun Bing's. Seeing what was about to happen, Xiaojia had thrown himself between Sun and me. He slumped to the ground at Sun Bing's feet when I pulled my knife out. Blood spurting from the wound seared my hand. Zhao Jia released a plaintive cry:

"My son . . ." He was disconsolate.

He flung the bowl in his hand at my head; I too let out a plaintive cry when the hot, fragrant liquid splashed on my face. The sound still hung in the air as Zhao Jia crouched down, like a panther about to pounce, and flung himself headfirst at me. His skull struck me flush in the abdomen, sending me flying, arms flailing, to the platform floor, face-up. He wasted no time in straddling me and digging his seemingly soft, delicate hands into my throat, like the talons of a bird of prey, at the same time gnawing on my forehead. Everything went dark as I struggled, but my arms were like dead branches.

Zhao Jia's fingers loosened their grip at the very moment I saw my wife's face above Wangxiang tai, and he stopped gnawing on my forehead. I rolled him off me with my knee and struggled to my feet. He lay on the platform floor, a knife in his back, his gaunt face twitching pitifully. Sun Meiniang stood over him, a dazed look in her eyes. The muscles in her pale face were quivering, and her features had shifted; she looked less human than demonic. The moonbeams were like water, like liquid silver; they were ice, they were frost. I would not see such brilliant moonbeams ever again. Looking past them, I believed I could see the worthy nephew of the Liu family suddenly appear in front of Yuan Shikai and, in the name of his father, and of the Six Gentlemen, and of the Great Qing Nation, draw a pair of shiny golden pistols, just as my brother had done . . .

My mind reeled as I got to my feet. I reached out to her. Meiniang . . . my beloved . . .

She screamed, turned, and ran down the plank. Her body looked like a mass of moldy cotton floating through the air, as if weightless. Was there any need for me to go after her? No, my affairs were coming to an end, and we would have to wait to meet again in another world. I pulled her knife out of Zhao Jia's back and wiped the blood from the blade on my clothing. Then I walked up to Sun Bing and, with the light from the lantern and from the moon—the former was a murky yellow, the latter bright and transparent—looked closely into his tranquil face.

"Sun Bing, I have wronged you in so many ways, but it was not I who plucked out your beard." With that heartfelt comment, I drove the knife into his chest. And when I did, brilliant sparks flew from his eyes, producing a bright halo around his face, brighter than the moonlight. I watched blood flow from the corners of his mouth, along with a single brief statement:

"The opera . . . has ended . . ."

Author's Note

As this novel was taking shape, friends asked me what it was about. I had trouble coming up with an answer, though I tried. Not until a couple of days after I handed the final manuscript in to my publisher, and I could breathe a sigh of relief, did it occur to me that it is all about sound. Each chapter title in the first and third parts—"Head of the Phoenix" and "Tail of the Leopard"—is in the style of speech of that particular narrator: "Zhao Jia's Ravings," "Qian Ding's Bitter Words," "Sun Bing's Opera Talk," and so on. In Part Two, "Belly of the Pig," I employ an objective, omniscient narrator, though in fact it is in the style of a historical romance whose narration follows the oral tradition, complete with chorus—again, at bottom, sound. It was sound that planted the seed for the novel and drove its creation.

Twenty years ago, as I set out on the road to becoming a writer, two disparate sounds kept reappearing in my consciousness, ensnaring me like a pair of enchanting fox fairies and, in their persistence, often putting me on edge.

The first of those sounds—rhythmical, resonant, powerful, evoking a somber, blue-black color, weighty as iron and steel, and icy cold—was the sound of trains, specifically those on the historic Jiaozhou-Jinan line, which has linked the cities of Jinan and Qingdao for a century. For as long as I can remember, gloomy weather has been the backdrop for train whistles that sound like the mournful, drawn-out lowing of cows: hugging the ground, they pass through the village and enter our houses, where they startle us out of our dreams. They were followed by the crisp, icy sound a train makes as it crosses the majestic steel bridge over the Jiao River. Back then, the two sounds—the whistle and the wheels on the bridge—coalesced with the overcast sky and humid air to merge with my emotionally starved, lonely youth. Each time I was awakened by those two sharply contrasting sounds in the middle of the night, my head filled with vivid images from tales of trains and railroad tracks told to me by people of all kinds. They first appeared in the guise of sound, followed by visual forms as annotations of sounds. Put another way, the visual images were mental associations with sounds.

I heard, then saw the tracks of the Jiaozhou-Jinan rail line, which were laid around 1900, when my grandparents were infants, by gangs of pigtailed Chinese coolies who carried wooden stakes across fields some twenty li from my village under the direction of German civil engineers with equipment brought from home and, so I was told, inlaid with tiny mirrors. German soldiers then cut the queues off many strapping young Chinese men and buried them under railroad ties. Shorn of their queues, the men were instantly turned into useless, almost inanimate, objects. After that, other German soldiers transported Chinese boys on donkeys to a secret spot in Qingdao, where they trimmed their tongues with scissors so they could learn to speak German in preparation for becoming future managers on the completed rail line. A preposterous legend, obviously, as I learned later, when I asked the director of the Goethe Institute whether Chinese children had to have their tongues surgically trimmed to learn German. "Ja," he said with a deadpan expression, "das ist korrekt." Then he burst out laughing, proving the absurdity of my question. And yet this legend has gained staunch adherents over the years. We refer to people who can speak a foreign language as "trimmed tongues." In my mind's eye, I can see a long line of boys on donkeys walking along the muddy banks of the twisting Jiao River. Each donkey is carrying two baskets, with a little boy in each one. They have an escort of German soldiers. Slightly to the rear of this procession is a contingent of weeping mothers, their sorrowful wails reverberating in all directions. I heard that a distant relative of mine, who was one of the boys sent to Qingdao to study German, later took a position as general accountant for the Jiaozhou-Jinan Railroad at an annual salary of thirty thousand silver dollars, and that even his family's servant, Zhang Xiaoliu, went home and built a mansion with three courtyards. Here is a sound and an image that swirl around in my head: a dragon hidden deep underground moans in pain as the rail line bears down on it. When it arches its back, the rail line rises up, sending a passing train off the tracks and onto its side. If the Germans had not built that line, Northeast Gaomi Township was destined to become a capital city. But when the dragon turned, flipping the train off the tracks, the dragon's back was broken, which destroyed the feng shui of my hometown. And I heard another legend: The rail line had just been completed, and a number of local young men thought that the train was a giant beast that fed on grass and grains. So they came up with a plan to build a branch pathway out of straw and black beans to lead the train over to a nearby lake, where it would drown. The train was not fooled. They later learned the facts about the trains from the train station workers, who were third-generation Russians, and they were devastated to have wasted all the straw and black beans. But one fantastic story had no sooner ended than another followed on its heels. The Russians told them that the train's boiler had been forged from a gigantic gold ingot. Otherwise, how could it withstand the buildup of heat year in and year out? They believed every word the Russians said, because of the adage "Real gold is fireproof." In an attempt to make up for the wasted straw and beans, they removed a section of track, causing a train to flip over. But when they converged upon the locomotive with their tools, there was not an ounce of gold to be found.

Even though my small village was no more than twenty li from the Jiao-Ji line, the first time I actually stood near the tracks and witnessed one of those impressive monsters scream past was one night when I was sixteen, out with some friends. I will never forget the striking image of that scary single light in front and the awesome roar of its engine. Now, although I later rode trains regularly, none, it seemed to me, was anything like the one I saw as a youngster back in Northeast Gaomi Township, nor like any of the trains I heard about back then. Those were living creatures, while the trains I rode in later were inanimate machines.

The second sound is the opera popular all over Gaomi—Maoqiang. Its songs are sad and dreary, especially those sung by the dan, or female characters, which, simply stated, are tearful accountings of the oppression of women. Everyone in Northeast Gaomi Township, both adults and children, can sing snatches of Maoqiang opera. This talent—natural, it seems, and not taught—has long been a fact of life among Northeast Gaomi Township residents, passed down from one generation to the next. Legend has it that when an old woman who had followed her son north beyond the Great Wall was dying, a visiting relative handed the son an audio tape he had brought from home, and when the unique strains of Maoqiang arias emerged, the old woman, whose life was ebbing away, suddenly sat up, her face imbued with a healthy glow, her eyes bright and clear, and when the tape ended, she lay back and died.

As a boy, I often tagged along behind bigger kids from the village chasing will-o'-the-wisps on their way to neighboring villages to watch opera performances. Fireflies danced in the air, adding their light to the glow of the earthbound will-o'-the-wisps. In the distance, foxes barked and train whistles blew. From time to time we spotted beautiful women in red or in white sitting by the roadside crying, their sobs and wails sounding very much like Maoqiang arias. We figured they were fox fairies and gave them a wide berth, taking pains not to provoke them. I had seen so many operas, I had committed many of the arias to memory, filling in the blanks by making up my own lyrics; and when I was a bit older, I took bit parts in village stagings, playing villains. At the time, only revolutionary operas were performed, so I was either a spy or a bandit. Things loosened up a bit in the waning years of the Cultural Revolution, when folk operas were added to the revolutionary corpus. The Maoqiang opera *Sandalwood Death* was born. As a matter of fact, the story of Sun Bing's resistance against the Germans had already been performed on the operatic stage by Maoqiang actors in the last years of the Qing, and some local elders could still sing some of those arias. Using my childhood talent for writing jingles to start rumors and spread gossip, I teamed up with an illiterate old villager who played the erhu, sang opera, and was a master storyteller to write a nine-act opera we called *Tanxiang xing*. An elementary-school teacher who had been labeled a rightist, and who loved literature, gave us a lot of help. The reason I had gone with the other kids to see the train that first time was to get some real-life experience in order to enhance the opera.

Eventually I left my hometown to take a job elsewhere, and my interest in Maoqiang decreased, owing to the pressures of work and the trials of everyday life. A dramatic form that had once stirred the hearts of Northeast Gaomi Township residents went into decline, and even though one professional drama troupe remained, they performed infrequently, and that caused the younger generation to lose interest in Maoqiang.

I went home for a visit over New Year's in 1986, and the moment I emerged from the train station, my ears picked up the sadly moving strains of a Maoqiang aria coming from a diner on the edge of the station plaza. The sun had just burned its way into the sky, so the plaza was virtually deserted; the forlorn lyrics merged with the shrill whistle of the train as it pulled out of the station, and my heart was filled with mixed emotions. I had the feeling that these two sounds that had accompanied me as I grew up—trains and Maoqiang—were seeds planted in my heart, where they grew and matured to become the underpinnings of one of my important creations.

I began writing *Sandalwood Death* in 1996. After I had written some 50,000 words, all caught up with fantastic legends surrounding trains and rail lines, I set the work aside for a while. When I came back to it, the resemblance to magical realism was too obvious to miss, so I started over. Some of the best writing fell into that category, and had to be jettisoned. In the end, I decided to focus less on trains and the sound of trains, and put Maoqiang center stage, as it were, even though that may have diluted the overall richness of the novel as a whole, in favor of stronger images of the people and a purer Chinese style. It was a sacrifice I willingly made.

In the same way that Maoqiang cannot be performed in grand halls alongside Italian opera or Russian ballet, this novel of mine will likely not be a favorite of readers of Western literature, especially in highbrow circles. Just as Maoqiang is performed on open-air stages for the working masses, my novel will be appreciated only by readers who have an affinity with the common man. It may in fact be better suited to hoarse voices in a public square, surrounded by an audience of eager listeners, not readers, who participate in the tale they are hearing. With that open-air audience in mind, I have taken pains to fill the work with rhymes and dramatic narration, all in the service of a smooth, easy to understand, overblown, resplendent narrative. Popular spoken and sung dialogues are the progenitors of the Chinese novel. Nowadays, when what was once mere popular entertainment has become a refined literary offering suitable for grand temples, at a time when borrowings from Western literary trends have all but brought an end to our popular traditions, *Sandalwood Death* may be out of keeping with the times, and might be thought of as a step backward in my writing career.

Glossary of Untranslated Terms

The following terms have been left untranslated in the text
(most can be intuited from the context):

dan 旦: a female role in Chinese opera

dieh 爹: dad (father), especially popular in northern China

gandieh 干爹: a benefactor, surrogate father, "sugar daddy"

ganerzi 干儿子: the "son" of a gandieh

ganniang 干娘: a surrogate mother

gongdieh 公爹: father-in-law

jin 斤: a traditional unit of weight with sixteen liang 两

kang 炕: a brick sleeping platform, often heated by a fire beneath

laotaiye 老太爷: a respectful term of address for a man of advanced age or
high status

laoye 老爷: a more common form of laotaiye

niang 娘: mom (mother), especially popular in northern China

qinjia 亲家: related as in-laws; the parent(s) of a married couple

shaoye 少爷: a young "laoye"

sheng 生: a male role in Chinese opera

shifu 师傅: a teacher, master of a trade

yamen 衙门: an official government office and residence in dynastic China

yayi 衙役: yamen clerks, runners, minor functionaries

yuanwailang 员外郎: an official who has retired to his native home; an
official title

zhuangyuan 状元: the top scholar in the Imperial Examination; the best in a
field